The Editor

MARGOT NORRIS is Professor of English and comparative literature at the University of California, Irvine. She is the author of four books on the works of James Joyce: *The Decentered Universe of "Finnegans Wake," Joyce's Web: The Social Unraveling of Modernism, Suspicious Readings of Joyce's "Dubliners,"* and *Ulysses,* a study of the 1967 Joseph Strick film of the novel. She has two additional books on modern literature, philosophy, science, and culture: *Beasts of the Modern Imagination: Darwin, Nietzsche, Kafka, Ernst, and Lawrence* (Johns Hopkins University Press, 1985) and *Writing War in the Twentieth Century* (University of Virginia Press, 2000).

W. W. NORTON & COMPANY, INC.
Also Publishes

ENGLISH RENAISSANCE DRAMA: A NORTON ANTHOLOGY
edited by David Bevington et al.

THE NORTON ANTHOLOGY OF AFRICAN AMERICAN LITERATURE
edited by Henry Louis Gates Jr. and Nellie Y. McKay et al.

THE NORTON ANTHOLOGY OF AMERICAN LITERATURE
edited by Nina Baym et al.

THE NORTON ANTHOLOGY OF CHILDREN'S LITERATURE
edited by Jack Zipes et al.

THE NORTON ANTHOLOGY OF DRAMA
edited by J. Ellen Gainor, Stanton B. Garner Jr., and Martin Puchner

THE NORTON ANTHOLOGY OF ENGLISH LITERATURE
edited by M. H. Abrams and Stephen Greenblatt et al.

THE NORTON ANTHOLOGY OF LITERATURE BY WOMEN
edited by Sandra M. Gilbert and Susan Gubar

THE NORTON ANTHOLOGY OF MODERN AND CONTEMPORARY POETRY
edited by Jahan Ramazani, Richard Ellmann, and Robert O'Clair

THE NORTON ANTHOLOGY OF POETRY
edited by Margaret Ferguson, Mary Jo Salter, and Jon Stallworthy

THE NORTON ANTHOLOGY OF SHORT FICTION
edited by R. V. Cassill and Richard Bausch

THE NORTON ANTHOLOGY OF THEORY AND CRITICISM
edited by Vincent B. Leitch et al.

THE NORTON ANTHOLOGY OF WORLD LITERATURE
edited by Sarah Lawall et al.

THE NORTON FACSIMILE OF THE FIRST FOLIO OF SHAKESPEARE
prepared by Charlton Hinman

THE NORTON INTRODUCTION TO LITERATURE
edited by Alison Booth and Kelly J. Mays

THE NORTON READER
edited by Linda H. Peterson and John C. Brereton

THE NORTON SAMPLER
edited by Thomas Cooley

THE NORTON SHAKESPEARE, BASED ON THE OXFORD EDITION
edited by Stephen Greenblatt et al.

For a complete list of Norton Critical Editions, visit
www.wwnorton.com/college/English/nce_home.htm

A NORTON CRITICAL EDITION

James Joyce
DUBLINERS

AUTHORITATIVE TEXT
CONTEXTS
CRITICISM

Edited by
MARGOT NORRIS
UNIVERSITY OF CALIFORNIA, IRVINE

Text Edited by
HANS WALTER GABLER
WITH WALTER HETTCHE

W. W. NORTON & COMPANY • *New York* • *London*

W. W. Norton & Company has been independent since its founding in 1923, when William Warder Norton and Mary D. Herter Norton first published lectures delivered at the People's Institute, the adult education division of New York City's Cooper Union. The Nortons soon expanded their program beyond the Institute, publishing books by celebrated academics from America and abroad. By mid-century, the two major pillars of Norton's publishing program—trade books and college texts—were firmly established. In the 1950s, the Norton family transferred control of the company to its employees, and today—with a staff of four hundred and a comparable number of trade, college, and professional titles published each year—W. W. Norton & Company stands as the largest and oldest publishing house owned wholly by its employees.

The text of this book is composed in Fairfield Medium
with the display set in Bernhard Modern.
Composition by Binghamton Valley Composition, LLC.
Manufacturing by the Maple-Vail Book Group.
Production manager: Benjamin Reynolds.

Library of Congress Cataloging-in-Publication Data

Joyce, James, 1882–1941.
Dubliners: authoritative text, contexts, criticism / James Joyce; edited by Margot Norris.
p. cm. — (A Norton critical edition)
Includes bibliographical references.

ISBN 0-393-97851-6 (pbk.)

1. Dublin (Ireland)—Fiction.   2. Joyce, James, 1882–1941. Dubliners.
3. Dublin (Ireland)—In literature.   I. Norris, Margot.   II. Title.   III. Series.
PR6019.O9D8 2005
823'.912—dc22

2005053410

W. W. Norton & Company, Inc., 500 Fifth Avenue,
New York, N.Y. 10110-0017
www.wwnorton.com

W. W. Norton & Company Ltd., Castle House,
75/76 Wells Street, London W1T 3QT

Contents

Criticism

Preface

James Joyce's *Dubliners* is arguably one of the most famous collections of short stories written in English. In their own day, these stories were applauded for their "style of scrupulous meanness," as Joyce called it, and for their thematic seriousness in presenting a direct and penetrating view of the city of Dublin in the modernity of the early twentieth century. "The book is not a collection of tourist impressions but an attempt to represent certain aspects of the life of one of the European capitals," Joyce wrote to a publisher in September of 1905.[1] He elaborated this point when he wrote to another publisher, Grant Richards, a month later. "I do not think that any writer has yet presented Dublin to the world. It has been a capital of Europe for thousands of years, it is supposed to be the second city of the British Empire and it is nearly three times as big as Venice. Moreover, on account of many circumstances which I cannot detail here, the expression 'Dubliner' seems to me to have some meaning and I doubt whether the same can be said for such words as 'Londoner' and 'Parisian' both of which have been used by writers as titles."[2] As to the seriousness of the subject matter, Joyce wrote to Grant Richards in 1906, "My intention was to write a chapter of the moral history of my country and I chose Dublin for the scene because that city seemed to me the centre of paralysis."[3] The collection's first story, which presents the moral ambiguity of a boy's relationship to a priest, draws particular attention to the word "paralysis." In the same letter, Joyce announced that the sequence in which he arranged the stories was significant. "I have tried to present it to the indifferent public under four of its aspects: childhood, adolescence, maturity and public life." In spite of these urgent claims for the importance of the volume, Joyce encountered numerous objections from publishers and printers that delayed the work's publication until 1914—a complicated history that Hans Walter Gabler's "Introduction" to this edition details and discusses.

1. Letter to William Heinemann, 23 September 1905. *Letters of James Joyce, Vols. II and III.* Edited by Richard Ellmann. New York: The Viking Press, 1966. 109.
2. Letter to Grant Richards, 15 October 1905. *Letters* 122.
3. Letter to Grant Richards, 5 May 1906. *Letters* 134.

But *Dubliners* was published at last, and abetted by the acclaim of Joyce's later works—*A Portrait of the Artist as a Young Man* (1916), *Ulysses* (1922), and *Finnegans Wake* (1939)—the volume's reputation and interest has grown impressively over the years. In the last two decades, more than a half-dozen scholarly books and special issues of journals[4] have been devoted to *Dubliners*—a testament to the complexity and craft of its seemingly simple stories. This complexity has also allowed the stories to yield their interpretation to a wide range of theoretical approaches, including the Bakhtinian,[5] the Lacanian,[6] the ethical,[7] the postcolonial,[8] and more. *Dubliners* is therefore that special phenomenon of a piece of writing with equal appeal to a range of readers from the novice to the sophisticated scholar. On the one hand, the stories are easily readable and quite accessible to students and common readers. They can be read separately, and individual stories have therefore been widely anthologized. On the other hand, their narrative and thematic intricacy makes them ideal subjects for elementary literature courses—including high school English classes and "Introduction to Fiction" courses for college freshmen and sophomores. In my introduction to *Suspicious Readings of Joyce's "Dubliners"* I describe the benefits of teaching *Dubliners* in this way:

> For getting students to go beyond considerations of theme, and beyond considerations of style, even, to think about how textuality itself works, it would be difficult to find a better curriculum than *Dubliners*. The stories can be taught in a way that makes narration opaque rather than transparent to them and obliges them to interpret the narrative operation itself. The stories can help them see fiction as a text, as a bundle of dynamic meaning-producing strategies that put various possible, and often conflicting, interpretations into destabilizing and produc-

4. For important book-length studies of *Dubliners*, see Warren Beck, Garry M. Leonard, Donald T. Torchiana, Earl G. Ingersoll, Craig Hansen Werner, Bernard Benstock, R. B. Kershner, and Tanja Vesala-Varttala. Older volumes of collected essays on *Dubliners* include Peter K. Garrett's 1968 edition of *Twentieth Century Interpretations of "Dubliners,"* the 1969 *James Joyce's "Dubliners": A Critical Handbook*, edited by James R. Baker and Thomas F. Staley, and Clive Hart's *James Joyce's "Dubliners": Critical Essays*, published in 1969. More recently, Rosa M. Bollettieri Bosinelli and Harold F. Mosher Jr. expanded a special *Dubliners* issue published by the journal *Style* in 1991 into the volume *ReJoycing: New Readings of "Dubliners,"* published in 1998. The *James Joyce Quarterly* also published special issues on *Dubliners*, in 1991 and 1999/2000, as did *Studies in Short Fiction* in 1995. And in 1997, the series *European Joyce Studies* devoted volume 7 to *New Perspectives on "Dubliners,"* edited by Mary Power and Ulrich Schneider.
5. See R. B. Kershner. *Joyce, Bakhtin, and Popular Literature: Chronicles of Disorder*. Chapel Hill: University of North Carolina Press, 1989.
6. See Garry M. Leonard. *Reading "Dubliners" Again: A Lacanian Perspective*. Syracuse: Syracuse University Press, 1993.
7. See Tanja Vesala-Varttala. *Sympathy and Joyce's "Dubliners": Ethical Probing of Reading, Narrative, and Textuality*. Tampere, Finland: Tampere University Press, 1999.
8. See Vincent J. Cheng. *Joyce, Race, and Empire*. Cambridge: Cambridge University Press, 1995.

tive play. And the stories can help students to read self-reflectively, to think about how the text positions them as readers and provides them with prompts or invites their resistance. *Dubliners* can lead students into the act of reading as a meaning-producing *process* rather than as merely confrontation with a meaning-laden *product* (14).[9]

This Norton Critical Edition of *Dubliners* is intended to serve students directly, while also addressing the teachers, scholars, and common readers who comprise the work's widely ranging readership. On the one hand, it offers a recent edition published by the famous Joyce editor Hans Walter Gabler with Walter Hettche—along with Gabler's introduction to the volume's publication history and editing process, and his editorial notes to the text. This apparatus provides the serious Joyce scholar valuable information with which to assess textual emendations and changes. At the same time, I have included an array of materials intended to make the stories come to life for a first-time twenty-first-century reader unfamiliar with their setting, an Irish city of another century. The additional materials include reprints of some of the stories as they were first published, an early advertisement, and Joyce's satirical poem about his publication problems, all to illustrate this aspect of the volume's background. The notes to the stories gloss not only historical, literary, and cultural references but also Irish colloquialisms and what are increasingly becoming archaic names for all sorts of once common objects and practices. I have also included maps of the itineraries of the characters in various chapters and photographs of landmarks and sites mentioned throughout the texts. This visual component is intended to reinforce the important element of *realism* in the stories—that is, Joyce's precision in naming public buildings and actual shops and commercial products in his text. One can also think of *Dubliners* as a cultural anthology of turn-of-the-century Ireland, with its many references to both popular and serious literature, to newspapers and poetry, to opera and folk ballads, to ecclesiastical and political lore. I have therefore provided portraits, poems, and the words and music of songs sung or referred to in the stories. As the stories bring a world of a hundred years ago to life, so I hope that the additional materials will bring the stories to greater life.

Unfortunately, the constraint of space prohibited selecting a scholarly article for each story in the collection. I therefore gave some priority to essays helpful in illuminating the stories that are most frequently taught and tried in addition to select scholarly essays

---

9. Margot Norris. *Suspicious Readings of Joyce's "Dubliners."* Philadelphia: University of Pennsylvania Press, 2003.

that represented a range of critical and theoretical approaches. The criterion of critical diversity in turn dictated articles of relatively recent publication, giving readers the benefit of the latest scholarship in the field. But these essays should be considered chiefly as a sample of the rich store of scholarship that is available to students, teachers, and scholars. The selected, but large, bibliography at the end of the volume suggests the many other interpretations and treatments of the text that can further illuminate the stories. I have also tried to have the bibliography reflect the most current scholarship on *Dubliners* available at the time of the Norton Critical Edition's publication. My hope is that readers of this volume will find it exciting and packed full of useful information, interesting materials, and helpful suggestions for further study—an enhancement of the considerable pleasure that the study of Joyce's stories is certain to provide.

The success of this project has depended on the talent, skill, encouragement, and generosity of a great many people. My first thanks go to Hans Walter Gabler for his immediate and unstinting generosity in permitting us to use his 1993 edition of *Dubliners* as the text for this volume along with his valuable introduction and textual glosses. Professor Gabler's work in producing beautifully researched and documented editions of Joyce's work has provided us with irreplaceable resources for teaching and scholarship. I am grateful and honored to be able to offer one of these editions to students and readers of this volume. In researching the notes for the stories, I ran into many recalcitrant items that refused to yield meaning when I tried to track them down. I therefore brought in one of the best researchers I know to help me with the knottiest references in the stories. Jennifer Burns Levin, a doctoral student in my department at the University of California, Irvine, proved to be a genius at unearthing arcana—everything from obscure opera singers to minor moments in papal history. She made what might have been a tedious part of the process one of the most interesting and, well, fun. When it came time to gather contextual material, I encountered amazing generosity from writers and scholars in my field. Bruce Bidwell and Linda Heffer not only offered to let me use some of their original photographs: they actually entrusted me with some of the negatives. John Wyse Jackson turned out to be a fount of information and a model of supportive collegiality. Carol Kealiher, the managing editor of the *James Joyce Quarterly*, gave me yet again her perennial and efficient help in securing permissions from the journal. I also thank Sean Latham and Michael O'Shea for their generosity in providing permissions. Vincent Cheng and Morris Beja were terrific in helping me get access to their essays. Michael Groden and John Paul Riquelme offered insightful and relevant advice and support from the sidelines. And finally, I found it wonderful to work with Carol

Bemis, my editor, and Brian Baker, assistant editor, at W. W. Norton & Company. Carol patiently and promptly dealt with my numerous queries and concerns, and she and Brian helped with some of the more complicated and onerous negotiations involved in settling permissions and taking care of tricky details. Books of any kind are always collaborative projects; this one reflects the cooperation and support of many people.

Margot Norris
UNIVERSITY OF CALIFORNIA, IRVINE

Introduction

by Hans Walter Gabler

A History of Curiosities, 1904–1914†

In the first days of July 1904, probably on the 2nd or on the 4th, the Irish mystic, poet and painter, and close friend of W. B. Yeats, George Russell (otherwise "AE") wrote to James Joyce inviting him to submit a short story to *The Irish Homestead*—the weekly, self-styled "Organ of Agricultural and Industrial Development in Ireland." Russell asked for something "simple, rural?, livemaking?, pathos? . . . not to shock the readers" *Letters*, II, 43).[1] The letter was timely. Despite his poverty, the twentytwo year old Joyce was in an expansive, confident mood. His burgeoning romance with Nora Barnacle was entering its fourth buoyant week, and he had begun to circulate among his friends and admirers the (incomplete) manuscript of his autobiographical novel *Stephen Hero*, on which he continued to work energetically.[2] Russell included with his letter the current issue of the *Homestead* and advised: "Look at the story in this paper." That Joyce did so, and with important consequences for the development—then in embryo—of his *oeuvre*, has thus far slipped past the net of Joycean scholarship and biography.

That part of *The Irish Homestead* for which Russell solicited a contribution was a section entitled "Our Weekly Story." In the summer of 1904, however, there was a troubling dearth of copy. The

---

† This section, as based on fresh and original research in Dublin, was prepared in collaboration with John O'Hanlon and Danis Rose. I am most grateful for their help and advice.—For "A Curious History," as recounted by James Joyce himself, see pp. 197–200.

1. Though this letter is undated, from circumstantial evidence and from the chronology of subsequent events we can be reasonably certain that Russell must have written it on, or very shortly after, Saturday 2 July 1904.

2. His sister May lugged the bulky manuscript around to Constantine Curran (then living in Cumberland place, North Circular road, not too far from Joyce's father's house in Cabra) on June 23 (*Letters*, I, 55). After Curran had read and returned it, Joyce gave it to George Russell to read. According to Richard Ellmann (*James Joyce*, 163) and conventional wisdom, it was Russell's reading of *Stephen Hero* which inspired him to write to Joyce asking for a story for the *Homestead*. But it is surely much more likely—given the tight chronology and given the fact that on an earlier occasion Russell had responded unfavourably to the poems of *Chamber Music*—that Joyce lent him the manuscript only after Russell had approached him. Furthermore, as we shall see, Russell had a more practical reason for writing.

issues of May 21, May 28, and June 4 contained no story at all, the
section in the issues of June 11, 18, and 25 was taken up by a three-
part novelette by Louise Kenny, and the issues of July 9 and 16 again
had no story. It follows that the sole issue to which Russell could
have been referring was that of July 2, in which issue there was
indeed a story: a short piece written by Berkeley Campbell entitled
"The Old Watchman." It is a first-person narrative in which the narrator, a twelve-year old boy, recounts the circumstances of the death
of an old man he had befriended who had fallen on hard times. If
this sounds familiar, then it should; for it would appear that Joyce
not only read the story: he rewrote it. Had he called his own story
"The Old Priest," which, but for its subtler complexities of meaning
he might have done, then that would have advertised the fact. Even
so, he put into "The Sisters" clues to the source of his artifice. In
Campbell's story—which of course had the date of the issue (July 2)
just above the title—the old watchman (who it transpires is the son
of a former Dean of St Patrick's Cathedral) is sixty-five years of age;
in the *Homestead* version of "The Sisters," the card fixed to the door
of the house where the old priest died reads: "July 2nd, 189—The
Rev. James Flynn (formerly of St. Ita's Church), aged 65 years.
R.I.P."[3]

By the 15th of July, Joyce had finished writing "The Sisters" and,
indeed, having already progressed beyond the idea of one story, had
formulated an ambitious plan. In a letter to Constantine Curran he
announced: "I am writing a series of epiclets—ten—for a paper. I
have written one. I call the series *Dubliners* to betray the soul of that
hemiplegia or paralysis which many consider a city."[4] H. F. Norman,
the editor of *The Irish Homestead*, accepted "The Sisters" for publication on July 23, making one change only: "I am changing the name

3. There are other, lesser echoes. Campbell's boy usually spoke to the old watchman (he had
   pleurisy) while he was huddled over his fire-basket. Joyce's boy conversed with the old
   priest while, wrapped up in his greatcoat, he sat by his fireside. The old watchman is not
   named; though his replacement is: James. Reverberations may be felt, too, even beyond
   "The Sisters." The watchman spent his exile in Australia, which is also where the school-
   friend of Eveline's father went (see especially the *Irish Homestead* version of "Eveline,"
   lines 32–35). The watchman's earlier Dublin prodigality in drinking and gambling, albeit
   cliché, is not unlike Jimmy's in the finale of "After the Race." Lastly, the Electric Tramway
   Company's watchman at his fire-basket would seem an avatar of Gumley, the corporation's
   watchman at his brazier in "Eumaeus", the sixteenth episode of *Ulysses* (and this episode
   especially, one should recall, has its roots in the story "Ulysses" originally contemplated
   for *Dubliners*).
4. See *Letters*, I, 55, where "epiclets" is given as "epicleti." This misreading—"Greeker than
   the Greeks" (*U* 9.614)—has over the years led to deep yet, alas, misguided critical exegesis
   (see, for example, Ellmann, *op. cit.*, 163). Skeptical at what seemed to him an oblique way
   of using Greek, Wolfhard Steppe surmised that the word might simply be "epiclets" (i.e.,
   'little epics', an ordinary English diminutive). A reading of the original in University College, Dublin, has proved him right. The letter, incidentally, is rather ambiguously dated
   "The Rain, Friday." As there were showers on just about every Friday during that summer,
   the weather accounts are not terribly helpful. The cricket reports are more enlightening:
   uniquely, on the morning of Friday, July 15, there was "torrential rain" sufficient to put a
   stop to play.

of the Parish quoted in the obituary notice so as to make the details of the story more remote."⁵ He sent Joyce a sovereign in payment. By a curious, sad coincidence, the story appeared in the issue of 13 August 1904, the first anniversary of Joyce's mother's untimely death. In such humble circumstances, thus, did *Dubliners* and beyond it James Joyce's prose masterpieces see their beginning in print.

On the suggestion of Russell, Joyce adopted a pseudonym and signed the name 'Stephen Daedalus' to "The Sisters." He continued this practice with the next four or, possibly, five stories, reverting to his own name only in the summer of 1905, well into his exile. Stephen Daedalus, of course, was the name he had given to the principal character in *Stephen Hero* and the name which he had recently begun to use in signing letters to his friends (see, for example, *Letters*, I, 54–55). Apart from the first ("The Sisters") and the last ("The Dead") the *Dubliners* stories were not written in the order of their ultimate arrangement. The second, "Eveline," appeared in *The Irish Homestead* on September 10, and very likely was composed during the second half of July and/or the first weeks of August. At that time, Joyce had begun to think prospectively about his relationship with Nora, and these considerations certainly inspired, if obliquely, its theme. "After the Race" was drafted while Joyce raced about Dublin touching friends and enemies alike for the wherewithal to get away from Ireland. The story was completed on 3 October 1904⁶ and handed in to the *Homestead* office the following day, just four days prior to Joyce's departure with Nora from the North Wall docks.⁷

James Joyce always considered 8 October 1904 as the date of his "first" marriage to Nora Barnacle (the "second" being 4 July 1931). The Joyces, after brief stays in Zurich and Trieste, settled down in Pola in Austria. It was while at Zurich, however, in late October that he began his fourth story. He called it "Christmas Eve." A month later, from Pola, he reported to Stanislaus that he had written "about half" of it (*Letters*, II, 71). By this he presumably meant the fragmentary fair copy of four pages which has been preserved.⁸ Instead

---

5. Letter to James Joyce of 23 July 1904, now at Cornell.
6. Joyce wrote from St. Peter's terrace to Nora on this day: "I am in such high good humour this morning that I insist on writing to you . . . I got up early this morning to finish a story I was writing. When I had written a page I decided I would write a letter to you instead. Besides, I thought you disliked Monday and a letter from me might put you in better spirits" (*Letters*, II, 50). Ellmann has dated this letter "About 1 September 1904." This is certainly wrong. The possible contending Mondays are August 30, September 5, 12, 19 and 26, and October 3. On the first date Joyce was still at 60 Shelbourne road; on the second at his uncle's in Fairview; on the third at the Tower; on the fourth back at his uncle's; and on the fifth had a bad cold and was feeling desolate (*Letters*, II, 56). Which leaves October 3. Furthermore, he signed the letter "Jim," which he did only after his "famous interview about the letters" with Nora on September 9.
7. Jim, it turned out, was no Eveline; nor, in their tryst, was Nora.
8. All surviving manuscripts of *Dubliners* are reproduced in vol [4] of *The James Joyce Archive:*

of finishing this story he recast it as, or replaced it by, "Hallow Eve," which he sent to Dublin on 19 January 1905. "Hallow Eve," was not accepted by *The Irish Homestead,* nor is it extant today in any manuscript version. (By the end of September 1905 Joyce had retitled it "The Clay" and "slightly rewritten it" [*Letters*, II, 109]. Subsequently, this title was abbreviated to "Clay.") For the next several months, while he waited in vain for good news from Dublin and during which time he decided to dedicate the collection to Stanislaus—he subsequently changed his mind about this—Joyce did not proceed with *Dubliners* but, instead, focused his energies on *Stephen Hero.* In early May, he wrote to Stanislaus promising he would write another story if he knew the result of "Hallow Eve." Eventually he began to think seriously about finding another publisher. On 3 June he asked Stanislaus to get permission from the *Homestead* to republish the first two stories. In the next six weeks he wrote the fifth and sixth stories—"The Boarding House" and "Counterparts"—and sent them to Stanislaus in mid-July, quite possibly in the very manuscripts that still survive. The first of these, "The Boarding House," is dated 1 July 1905 in the extant manuscript and is the last physically to carry the signature "Stephen Daedalus"; yet the manuscripts of these two stories are, as documents, so clearly companion pieces that "Counterparts" too may have borne the name Daedalus on its lost final leaf. Thereafter, Joyce relinquished the pseudonymous pose and signed all subsequent *Dubliners* stories in his own name.

The summer of 1905 was for James Joyce as difficult as it was eventful. His faith in himself and in the life he had created with Nora began to falter. He suspended work on the autobiographical novel *Stephen Hero,* abandoning it in effect as a fragment of twentyfive (out of a projected sixtythree) chapters. About *Dubliners,* however, he remained sanguine, believing (incorrectly as it turned out) that he could find a publisher to bring it out sooner rather than later and that it would bring in some much needed money. The birth of his son Giorgio on 27 July spurred him on to greater efforts. The seventh story to be written was "A Painful Case." It exists both in a draft manuscript (originally entitled "A Painful Incident"), which at least in part documents the process of composition, and in a fair copy signed and dated "JAJ 15.8.05." The eighth story, "Ivy Day in the Committee Room," survives in two fair-copy manuscripts, of which the earlier is dated "29 August 1905," just two weeks later than the fair copy of "A Painful Case."[9] "An Encounter" saw com-

---

James Joyce, *Dubliners. A Facsimile of Drafts and Manuscripts,* prefaced and arranged by Hans Walter Gabler. New York and London: Garland Publishing Inc., 1978.

9. For both of these stories, and for "The Sisters" and "After the Race," Joyce requested specific information in a letter to his brother of 24 September (*Letters,* II, 109–112). Stanislaus authenticated details already present in them and in which, in the case

pletion about mid-September 1905 (within three weeks of "Ivy Day") and was sent to Stanislaus on 18 September. "A Mother," the tenth to be written, followed within a fortnight. Both of these stories are extant in fair-copy manuscripts.

Although Joyce's original plan (adumbrated in his letter to Constantine Curran of 15 July 1904 quoted above) of a suite of *ten* little epics was now complete, he had in the meantime changed his plans. Writing to William Heinemann on 23 September 1905, Joyce offered him *Dubliners*: "a collection of twelve short stories." On the following day he enumerated the sequence to Stanislaus: three stories of childhood, "The Sisters," "An Encounter," and another one (the as yet unwritten "Araby"); three stories of adolescence, "The Boarding House," "After the Race," and "Eveline"; three stories of mature life, "The Clay," "Counterparts," and "A Painful Case"; and, completing the pattern, three stories of public life, "Ivy Day in the Committee Room," "A Mother," and the last story of the book (the as yet unwritten "Grace"). (This arrangement, as we shall see, was subsequently altered at least twice.) By mid-October 1905 the eleventh story, "Araby," was completed and the twelfth, "Grace," begun. At the same time, as is indicated by the range of questions in the letter to Stanislaus of 24 September, Joyce was busy revising the existing texts. The opening story of the collection benefitted tangibly from his brother's investigations, as is evident from the few but important variants between the version represented by the *Irish Homestead* printing and the first of the two extant manuscripts for "The Sisters." The changes prove that this manuscript postdates *The Irish Homestead* and suggest late October 1905 as its date. It is significant that a first reconsideration of the opening of the book thus apparently coincided with the composition of the then concluding story, "Grace."

In the meantime, and apparently at the instigation of Stanislaus, Joyce wrote to Arthur Symons, who replied saying that he thought that Constable's might be interested in both *Chamber Music* and *Dubliners*. Joyce sent them the former but held back the latter, offering it instead to Grant Richards on 15 October, adding, foolishly perhaps, that he believed that "people might be willing to pay for the special odour of corruption which, I hope, floats over my stories" (*Letters*, II, 123). Richards asked to see the manuscript three days later.[1] Both "Grace" and the revision of the earlier stories were com-

---

of "Ivy Day in the Committee Room," both manuscripts accord. The textual changes one finds entered in the second fair copy of "Ivy Day" (as opposed to those revealed by collation with the first fair copy) are not related to the period and occasion of its composition but to its later history. It was one of several stories over which, time after time, publication difficulties arose.

1. For Grant Richards's side of the correspondence, see Robert Scholes, "Grant Richards to James Joyce," *Studies in Bibliography* XVI (1963), 139–160.

pleted by the end of November and he sent the manuscript to Richards on 3 December. He did not then know it, but the nine-year ordeal of getting his book *Dubliners* printed and published had begun.

During the following two months, while he waited for word, Joyce added a new story, "Two Gallants." Richards finally responded on 17 February 1906, making Joyce an offer which was accepted. The book was to be published in May or June or in September in a slim crown octavo volume priced at 5/–. A contract followed on 23 February. The previous day Joyce had sent Richards "Two Gallants" with the instruction that it should be inserted between "After the Race" and "The Boarding House." (This suggests that, perhaps when he sent the stories to Richards, Joyce had interchanged the positions of "The Boarding House" and "Eveline" from their order as cited in his letter to Stanislaus of 24 September.) Returning the contract signed on 28 February, Joyce wrote: "I would like the printer to follow the manuscript accurately in punctuation and arrangement. Inverted commas, for instance, to enclose dialogue always seemed to me a great eyesore" (*Letters*, II, 131). He added that he had written part of a fourteenth story ("A Little Cloud"). This was still unfinished on 13 March when he wrote to say that it was to be inserted between "A Boarding House" and "Counterparts." It was finished on 22 April. Before it could be fair-copied and sent, however, the storm clouds began to gather. Richards passed the manuscript of *Dubliners* to his printer on 12 April and instructed him to prepare sample pages. By a stroke of the worst possible luck, it seems that when Joyce had sent him the thirteenth story, "Two Gallants," Richards had not inserted it into its proper place in the sequence, but had merely placed it on top of the pile. To provide the sample pages, then, the printer chose the beginning of "Two Gallants" and had at least two pages set up (these survive and are now at Harvard). When he read his compositor's handiwork he was horrified, scrawled "We cannot print this" on the second proof, and sent it back to Richards. On 23 April Richards informed Joyce of the printer's refusal and added that he had strong objections to two passages in "Counterparts." He returned the manuscripts of the two stories and, further, asked for another word to replace "bloody" in "Grace." Joyce replied three days later, refusing to compromise. A long and protracted correspondence ensued, in which Joyce made some concessions and Richards demanded more deletions (*Letters*, I, 60–63, and II, 132–143). Finally, the parties appeared to reach agreement. On 19 June Richards sent back the entire manuscript to Joyce in order that he might make the necessary alterations. On its resubmission on 9 July Joyce stated that he had "re-arranged and renumbered the stories in the middle of the book" and that he had included "A Little Cloud" in the position that he had earlier indicated. This sequence was to remain stable. He also said that he had rewritten "The Sisters." It may be assumed that Richards received the opening story at this time in its second extant fair copy. In "Grace," by contrast, Joyce had removed only two instances of "bloody." These, however, exist undeleted in the extant fair copy, which also incorporates passages following from Joyce's research at the Biblioteca Vittorio Emanuele in Rome in November 1906 into the proceedings of the Vatican Council of 1870. Among the surviving manuscripts of the *Dubliners* stories, this fair copy of "Grace" is thus identified as postdating the original negotiations for publication with Grant Richards. Incidentally, it bypasses Richards's censorial strictures.

At the end of July 1906, Joyce moved with his family to Rome. During August he contemplated rewriting "After the Race" and he also asked Stanislaus to send him the manuscript of "A Painful Case" as he wanted to revise it.[2] On 31 August he said that he had "some loose sheets in my pocket about 5 pages" to add to "A Painful Case," but that he did not have the energy to continue working. The heat and the inhospitability of Rome oppressed him and he began to feel homesick for the British Isles, "rashers and eggs in the morning, the English variety of sunshine, a beefsteak with boiled potatoes and onions, a pier at night or a beach and cigarettes" (*Letters*, II, 157). By 25 September his nostalgia had grown stronger, "Sometimes thinking of Ireland it seems to me that I have been unnecessarily harsh. I have reproduced (in *Dubliners* at least) none of its ingenuous insularity and its hospitality" (*Letters*, II, 166). It has often been said that in these words of Joyce lies the germ of the last story of *Dubliners*, "The Dead."[3] Yet the conception and execution of "The Dead" lay still almost a year ahead. More immediately, Joyce added four days later: "I have a new story for Dubliners in my head. It deals with Mr Hunter" (*Letters*, II, 168). This story which—at least in this context—never got any further than its title, but which was centered upon a spontaneous act of hospitality, was to be called "Ulysses."

Out of the blue, Grant Richards wrote on 24 September 1906 breaking his contract and rejecting *Dubliners*. Joyce reacted by making new concessions, but to no avail. The manuscript was returned on 26 October. A barrister advised Joyce not to waste his money seeking legal redress. Wisely in this instance, he concurred. Summoning up a little energy and turning to his manuscript, he made some corrections: he added the name of the laundry where Maria worked—the "Dublin by Lamplight Laundry"—to "The Clay,"

2. *Letters*, II, 148. This would seem to indicate that, in addition to the set sent to Richards, Joyce left a spare manuscript of *Dubliners* with Stanislaus in Trieste.
3. Though in this story surely the sentiment comes under heavy irony, and the general miasma of frustration and pathos that pervades *Dubliners*, far from being dispelled, is thickened.

revised "Grace,"[4] and re-introduced "bloody" into "Ivy Day in the Committee Room." He also thought of another story, "The Last Supper," about the son of his old landlady, but though he asked Stanislaus to supply details about the incident behind the idea for this story, and also (for the projected "Ulysses") to send his reminiscences of Mr Hunter (a proto-model for Leopold Bloom), Joyce never wrote it. In early December he sent the partly revised manuscript of *Dubliners* to John Long, the publisher. For the next few months he did little else but read. He did, however, conceive of new "titles" for stories: "The Dead," "The Street," "Vengeance," and "At Bay" (*Letters,* II, 209)—to add to the already mentioned "Ulysses" and "The Last Supper." In mid-January 1907 Long replied discouragingly and followed this up with a final rejection on 21 February.

In the meantime Joyce had had a bellyfull of Rome. He felt it was time he made up his mind to become a writer. He handed in notice at the bank where he worked, packed his bags, and rearrived in Trieste (his palm out to Stanislaus) on or about 7 March. Nora was again pregnant. Joyce's first few months back in the city were spent striving to make ends meet until, in midsummer, a few days before the birth on 26 July of his daughter Lucia, he was struck down with rheumatic fever. He spent a few weeks in hospital and another couple of months recovering. During this period of ill-health he wrote the fifteenth, final story and capstone of *Dubliners,* "The Dead." It was finished on 20 September. Though only fragments of its beginning and end have survived from Joyce's 77-page holograph, the story's full text, (incompletely) corrected and amended by the author, is preserved in a scribal copy of 18 typewritten pages and an allograph of 38 pages in two hands, one of them Stanislaus Joyce's.[5] The composition of "The Dead" marked the end of Joyce's creative engagement with *Dubliners.* He returned to his abandoned autobiographical novel, now entirely reconceived, reorganised and newly styled as *A Portrait of the Artist as a Young Man.*

Even now the saga of *Dubliners* was not over. On 24 September 1907 Joyce offered the book (now for the first time comprising all fifteen stories) to Elkin Mathews, the publisher of *Chamber Music.* Mathews asked to see the manuscript on 23 October, but laid it aside until after the Christmas season, and finally rejected it on 6 February 1908. When he turned it down, Mathews suggested sending the manuscript to Maunsel and Co. of Dublin,[6] but Joyce, preferring an English publisher, demurred and asked (on 9 February) for it to be

---

4. It is probable that it was at this time that he wrote out the extant fair copy of this story.
5. Only page 29, from the fifth word onwards, is in Stanislaus's hand. The 'family likeness' of the other hand suggests that it may be that of Joyce's sister Eileen.
6. In his letter (now at Cornell) Mathews wrote that he "mentioned it to Mr. Hone (Maunsel and Co., Dublin) the other day, and he said 'Oh, send the ms. on to us, as it might suit us.' "

returned to him. He next tried Hutchinson's (they refused to look at the manuscript), Alston Rivers (ditto), Sisleys (they wanted Joyce to pay), Greening and Co. (No!), Archibald Constable (No!), and Edward Arnold (No! yet again).

By the end of the year, Joyce began to come around to the idea of having the book published in Ireland and he conceived the idea of sending Stanislaus to Dublin to push the business on. On 13 February 1909 he wrote to Mathews and asked him to arrange for a communication with Hone (Joseph Maunsel Hone, the money behind Maunsel and Co., which George Roberts ran). This was done, and at the end of July Joyce himself (and not as originally planned Stanislaus) went to Dublin to meet Hone and Roberts. The negotiations went well and a contract was duly drawn up and signed on 19 August. *Dubliners* was to appear in March of the following year in dark grey binding with dark red lettering, at a price of 3/6 (*Letters*, II, 230–38). Satisfied, and missing Nora considerably, Joyce returned to Trieste in early September.

Two months had not passed before he was back again in Dublin with a plan to set up the first cinema in Ireland. (The enterprise was not, for reasons not here entered into, a financial success.) According to his own account (*Letters*, II, 292) it was while he was in Dublin in December that George Roberts first asked him to alter the narrative passage in "Ivy Day in the Committee Room" dealing with Edward VII. He agreed, much against his will, and "altered one or two phrases."[7] He returned to Trieste at the beginning of January 1910.

On 23 March Roberts wrote promising the proofs in early April and publication in May. The proofs, however, did not turn up until June, during which month Joyce was "very busy" correcting them. On 10 June Roberts wrote again and complained that he was still not happy with "Ivy Day in the Committee Room" and asked that the entire passage referring to the late King be removed or entirely rewritten. Joyce corrected and returned both a set of galleys and a set of page proofs. Curiously, the proofs for "Ivy Day" contained the original version—and not the (presumed late 1909) autograph alternative—of the disputed passage. Publication, scheduled for July, was nevertheless postponed once again. In December Roberts set 20 January 1911 as the new publication date and he sent Joyce another set of the proofs of "Ivy Day in the Committee Room." He once again asked him to delete or radically to alter the passage concerning Edward VII. The evidence indicates that he sent Joyce a copy of the uncorrected early page proofs. Joyce proposed either (a) deletion of the passage with a prefatory note of explanation added, or (b) arbi-

---

7. It is possible that it was on this occasion that he wrote in the "alternative" passage on folio 16 of the extant (Cornell) manuscript.

tration as a solution of the matter (*Letters,* II, 289). Roberts, infu-riatingly, did not reply. On 10 June, at the end of his tether, Joyce wrote again repeating his proposal and threatening—if he failed to receive a reply forthwith—legal action. He further swore that he would communicate the whole affair to the press by way of a circular letter.

For the second time the legal advice received was that it would not be worth while to sue. Redirecting himself, Joyce next deter-mined—like Anna Livia in *Finnegans Wake*—to present the case to and to seek the opinion of the King (now George V, Edward VII's son), to whom on 1 August 1911 he accordingly sent the proofs of "Ivy Day" with the disputed passage clearly marked.[8] Understandably declining to opine, the King commanded his private secretary to return the enclosures. Not entirely displeased with this partial suc-cess, Joyce immediately set about putting into effect the next phase of his campaign. First he carefully corrected and revised the moot passage[9] and had a number of slips of it printed (in an attractive art-nouveau type-font, presumably locally in Trieste). He then wrote (on 17 August 1911) his famous 'Letter to the Editor' into which he pasted a copy of the reprinted fragment (*Letters,* II, 291–93). Copies of the letter were sent to interested parties such as Grant Richards and to nearly all of the newspapers in Ireland. It appeared in the Belfast *Northern Whig* on 26 August with the passage from "Ivy Day" omitted and—in full—in the Dublin-based *Sinn Féin* on 2 Septem-ber. To a man, the major organs refused to publish it, and, in sum, it had no effect on Maunsel and Co.

Thoroughly depressed, and living in straitened circumstances, Joyce was at a complete loss as to what to do next. Around this time, also, he (temporarily) suspended work on *A Portrait of the Artist as a Young Man.*[1] The seasons passed. In 1912 he decided to send Nora—who was anxious to see her family once more—with Lucia to Ireland. The new plan was for Nora to intercede at Maunsel's on her hus-

8. This set of proofs is now at the Beinecke Library at Yale. It is almost certainly the very set that Roberts had sent Joyce seven months earlier. The twin parallel lines in the margins of pages 193–194 marking the passage (see *Archive,* vol. [5], pp. 79–80) might be Rob-erts's, or they might be Joyce's. It is unlikely that when he sent it to the King the passage contained Joyce's autograph corrections and revisions (these would have confused His Majesty) or Joyce's smaller diagonal lines indicating the passage's beginning and end. These, as we shall argue, were added immediately *after* the King's return of the proofs to Joyce.

9. These improvements—which indicate an alteration of Mr Henchy's diction and a decision to remove some 'stage-Irish' spellings and punctuation—are of considerable textual impor-tance in that, made just one year later when his memory was still relatively fresh, they probably correspond in nature to those corrections and revisions made on the lost cor-rected copy of the early page proofs returned to Maunsel's.

1. Indeed, it may have been at this time that he threw the *Portrait* manuscript in the fire; see the "Introduction" to the critical edition of *A Portrait of the Artist as a Young Man,* New York: Garland Publishing Inc., 1993, p. 4, and to the forthcoming Norton Critical Edition.

band's behalf. She arrived in Dublin on 8 July and saw Roberts soon after, but to no avail. On another impulse, Joyce decided that he would himself travel at once to Ireland, bringing Giorgio with him. En route, while passing through London he called on Joseph Maunsel Hone. He, however, could do nothing. In Dublin he met Roberts who came up with a new proposal: Joyce could delete disputed passages in "Ivy Day" and also in "An Encounter" or, alternatively, he could buy out the book from him, printed and bound, and have it distributed by Simpkin Marshall of London. Joyce said he would think about it, and left for Galway to join Nora. Further negotiations ensued, with Roberts now suggesting that Joyce buy the sheets from him and offer them to Grant Richards. Joyce arranged for a solicitor, John G. Lidwell, to advise him and returned to Dublin. After much haggling and toing-and-froing, threats and counter-threats of legal action, the matter seemed to be settled between them: Joyce would publish the book himself; of the total costs of printing the book, named at £57, he would pay Roberts £30; £15 were due within 15 days; on receipt, Roberts would let him have 104 copies of the sheets; and, on further receipt of a second £15 within a further 15 days, he would hand over the remainder of the total of 1000 sheets (*Letters*, II, 301–316). But this plan too came to grief in the end when the printer, John Falconer, refused to hand over even one set of the sheets. According to Joyce, Falconer said he was going to break up the type and burn the sheets. According to Roberts, the sheets were in fact guillotined (*Letters*, II, 319n.). The following day, 11 September 1912, having managed to obtain from Roberts "by a ruse" a complete set of proofs, James Joyce left Dublin in utter disgust, never again to return.

    Such at any rate is the story that has come down to us. But is it true? There are several serious implausibilities in it. Take the question of the printer's hire: the £57 owed by Maunsel to Falconer for printing 1000 copies of *Dubliners*. This was by no means an inconsiderable sum in 1912. The printer's claim that he cared nothing for that money—or even just for the £30 that Joyce was to have been made to pay—is risible.[2] Hence, whether valued at £30 or £57, one wonders: was the merchandise available at all? Moreover, with 104 copies promised within two weeks, and a remaining 896 another two weeks ahead, the important question doesn't even begin to be answered of *when* and *why* 1000 copies, and copies of precisely *what* text, may be supposed to have been printed in the first place. While the events considered were those of the summer of 1912, *Dubliners* were set in galleys two years earlier. The surviving galley proofs of "A Mother" are dated 8 June 1910 and those for "The Dead" 19 June

---

2. Joyce's later paranoid suspicion that his enemies in Dublin had paid the £57 is equally incredible.

1910. Assuming an even progress of work, this times the galleys for "Ivy Day in the Committee Room," specifically, to the early days of June, which would allow just enough time for Joyce to have corrected and returned them to inspire Roberts's letter to him of 10 June expressing dissatisfaction with the state of the passage on Edward VII. We know also that Joyce was still engaged in correcting proof on 24 June—by which time he must have been working on the early page proofs—and that he completed the task (*Letters*, II, 287–88). Final page proofs—made from the corrected early page proofs—are extant for "The Dead." From the opening of the book, too, late page proofs—sheets A to K—exist up to and partly including "A Painful Case." This total of fifteen sheets of late page proofs extant was presumably pulled in June or July 1910. Six full sheets, however, are absent (i.e., sheets L-Q). So technically defined is this as a reservation of space that these sheets may in fact never have been printed. From June 1910 and yet more stubbornly from December 1910 George Roberts was not satisfied with the text as it stood. When, after his June letter, he wrote again in December, the final page proofs for "Ivy Day" (and with them, by inference, those of the remainder of "A Painful Case," and of all of "A Mother" and "Grace") seem not yet to have been prepared. Nothing happened in 1911 or in 1912 to make him change his mind about "Ivy Day" or to induce him to give the order for the printing of 1000 copies of the whole of *Dubliners*. Such an order would have been tantamount to a decision to go ahead with publication. The conclusion to be drawn from these inferences and these facts is that the one thousand copies of the sheets of *Dubliners* never existed.

The re-surfacing precisely of Joyce's spoil from the Dublin publishing disaster at the Stanislaus Joyce sale at Sotheby's in London in 2004 may confirm our distrust in the orthodox versions of the events of 1910–1912 and strengthen our alternative assumptions. In collational terms, the set begins with six gatherings—A to F—in late page proofs. Early page proofs follow for a stretch of 32 pages (or two gatherings: G and H). Though already carrying page numbers, they are easily distinguished as leaves of early page proofs because they are printed on one side of the paper only. The leaves are of uneven length; apparently, they were printed on galley-length paper, three pages to a galley, and then scissored apart. Gatherings I and K are again in late page proofs, while the stretch of 96 pages to become gatherings L to Q are once more in early page proofs. Finally, from gathering R, which begins with the half-title for "The Dead," the home stretch of the book is, as before, in late page proofs. It ends on signature X2r, with X2v blank. On page 289 by Maunsel's page numbering (that is: on the first page of gathering T), there is an entry in ink in the top margin: 'Proof Sept. 6/10.'

Altogether, the mix of late and early page proofs in the two sets of proofs that we now have differs in interesting ways. In the set earlier known, gatherings A to K are throughout in late page proofs. The newly found set, by contrast, alternates between late and early proofs through these quires. Yet on the other hand, both sets are identical in having early page proofs only for gatherings L to Q, as well as being in late page proofs from gathering R to the end, that is: for "The Dead." It is only the newly discovered set, moreover, that preserves the last of these late page-proof pages, and thus the end of the final story and of the book, in the three printed pages from gathering X.

The main discovery to be made from the set of Maunsel proofs that Joyce "obtained by a ruse," however, is that it bears marks of service as an in-house working copy at Maunsel's in Dublin. On the opening page of each gathering, be it in late or in early page proofs, there is a pencilled entry with a number over an oblique stroke, and under the stroke the initials 'J. H.', standing, most likely, for Joseph [Maunsel] Hone, "the money behind Maunsel and Co.," as we stressed above. It seems that Hone shared actively in the planning of the firm's work—and since he was the money behind it, he would also have seen to its economy. The numbering he enters numbers the gatherings; it runs from 1 to 17 through gatherings A to Q; and it begins afresh with the number '1' at gathering R (the beginning of "The Dead"). As the numbers in the first sequence rise, it is noticeable that they also get slightly, but increasingly, out of sync with the actual quire division. Why this should be so becomes clear on considering what it would mean, in economic terms, to print the book as before us in proof. Running into gathering X, it overshoots by three pages the length of twenty full gatherings (320 pages). The marking, therefore, looks like an attempt to re-impose the book sufficiently to bring it within this limit.

Yet why two number sequences beginning with '1'? Let us assume that the sequences were worked over in reverse order. This would mean that the calculations to contain the book within twenty gatherings concentrated first on "The Dead," and that the re-impositions through all gatherings from the beginning were found necessary only because the problem of overflow at the end could not be solved over the stretch of quires R to U alone. But in addition, it is also suggestive to assume that "The Dead" was in late page proofs before (some of) the rest of the book. We would conclude that the proof markings reflect the preparations for the book at a point before gatherings L to Q were put into late page proofs, and that it was precisely at this interval that the opportunity was seen and taken to prevent the text's overflow into a gathering X.

Joseph Hone, then, could be assumed to have marked the working-copy set of proofs in advance of putting gatherings L to Q into late page proof. His pencilings would thus appear to be planning notes (as it were) for the completion of the publisher's and printer's job on the book. As to their timing, they could have been made at any time between September 1910 and September 1912, when Joyce absconded with the set. The explicit date on gathering T favours the likelihood that Hone's adjustments were devised in the autumn of 1910. Thereafter, they would have been held, pending the time when Roberts's, and eventually Falconer's, objections to the text of various passages along the stretch of gatherings L to Q would be met. Yet, as we have argued above, that time never came. It is true that we cannot tell with absolute certainty from these proofs as such whether, finally, the book actually did go into full production regardless of the unresolved conflicts over it between publisher, printer and author. Yet they do not, on the whole, make us readier to accept that such was the truth of the matter. On the contrary, the material evidence of this set of proofs that we take to be the Roberts/Hone in-house working copy for their contracted edition of *Dubliners* might in actual fact be the best underpinning presently available of our contention that *Dubliners*, between 1910 and 1912, and under the hands of Maunsel and Co. in Dublin, went just so far, and no further, towards completion. As for the narratives engendered by the case, they would appear as a conflagration of Irish facts. Roberts would have bluffed with his offer of 1,000 sheets, counting on Joyce's inability to raise the money. When the pecuniary deterrent did not work, Falconer's moral objections had to smoke-screen the non-existence of the goods haggled over. The shredding or sending up in flames of the non-existent sheets could be outshone finally only by the ardent fictionalisation of James Joyce's own "Gas from a Burner."[3]

While in London in transit to Trieste, Joyce tried without success to interest Ford Madox Hueffer's *English Review* in *Dubliners*. He also took it to Mills and Boon to whom Padraic Colum had given him an introduction. On 13 September he handed over to Mr Boon the set of sheets he had wangled out of Roberts (*Letters*, II, 320). Ingenuous to the last, he included as a preface a copy (presumably a press-cutting obtained in Dublin) of his letter to *Sinn Féin*. He considered that it would act as a "selling point" for the book; whereas

3. Hugh Kenner is inimitably illuminating on "Irish Facts" in the introductory essay, "Warning," to *A Colder Eye. The Modern Irish Writers*. Harmondsworth: Penguin, 1983. Roberts's version was recounted to Richard Ellmann many years later. Falconer's version, which we know only secondhand from Joyce's letters, must have been an embellishment made in the heat of the moment. Had Joyce allowed himself to perceive what had been going on with a colder eye, he would, of course, have lost the title of the broadside which—energised with ire—he composed a few days later in the waiting-room of a railway station at Flushing in Holland.

to the publisher it acted merely as a frightener. Boon had his letter of rejection in the post in less than a week.

In the year that followed, *Dubliners* once again did the rounds. In December Joyce sent his set of Maunsel proofs to Martin Secker; in February 1913 he approached (for the second time) Elkin Mathews; in April John Long (ditto); and in July he tried Macmillan. There may well have been others. Finally, back at square one, on 23 November 1913 he wrote to Grant Richards and asked him to reconsider his 1906 rejection. Richards, who was a relatively decent chap for a publisher, had in the long interim experienced some twinges, if not pangs, of conscience over his earlier treatment of Joyce and, besides, Joyce did offer to cover part of the expenses of publication (*Letters*, II, 324). Richards wrote back at once asking to see the book again. Joyce, still intent on the inclusion of his preface, quickly brought it up to date, entitled it "A Curious History" (*Letters*, II, 324–25) and submitted it, together with the set of Maunsel proofs.[4] With "A Curious History" and the printer's copy, a title-page was also included (*Letters*, II, 330).

While Joyce waited for news from Richards, a vortex of change entered his life in the person of Ezra Pound, brass band and bandwagon. At first drawn to and by the poetry, Pound soon became an important and influential advocate for *A Portrait of the Artist as a Young Man*. But he did not lack in engagement for *Dubliners*. Joyce sent him "A Curious History" which Pound printed in his regular column in *The Egoist* on 15 January 1914. While the surviving correspondence is confusing and perhaps misleading on the subject,[5] it appears that he also sent him some stories. Writing as he did on 19 January that he was forwarding "the" three stories (one of which was "An Encounter") to the New York magazine *Smart Set*,[6] Pound must have had them in hand. Perhaps he was even temporarily in possession of the entire collection. That Joyce did assemble at some time after 1910, though more probably after 1912, a complete run of the *Dubliners* stories distinct (and textually different) from Richards's

---

4. Robert E. Scholes still argued in "Observations on the text of *Dubliners*" and "Further Observations on the text of *Dubliners*," *Studies in Bibliography* XV (1962), 191–205, and XVII (1964), 107–122, that this set was throughout a set of early page proofs. His conclusion could only be inferential, from internal collation evidence. Forty years ago, Scholes did not see Richards's printer's copy, nor was he even given to know it had survived. Yet, as discussed, it resurfaced in 2004. Footnote 9, p. xxx, surveys the traces it bears from the London printinghouse.
5. For Pound's letters to Joyce of the period, see Forrest Read, *Pound/Joyce* (New York: New Directions Paperback, 1970), pp. 24–25.
6. On 14 February he sent on the magazine's reply (delicately described by Pound as a prime "piece of bull shit"), which though lost was evidently a rejection. Forrest Read (*op. cit.* p. 24) assumes the other two were "The Boarding House" and "A Little Cloud" because, in May 1915, at the behest of B. W. Huebsch, *Smart Set* published these two stories. Read's argument is unsound, as the 1915 copy appears to have been provided by Huebsch.

printer's copy is certain, as, apart from two pages of "A Little Cloud," it has survived. It comprises: (a) the 1910/1912 final proofs (pages [i]–160) of "The Sisters" to "A Painful Case"; (b) manuscripts of "A Painful Case" and "Ivy Day in the Committee Room," (c) the galley proofs of "A Mother"; (d) a manuscript of "Grace"; (e) the (incomplete) final proofs (pages [257]–320) of "The Dead"; and (f) the final pages of the manuscript of "The Dead."[7] It is thus possible that Joyce sent Pound the whole text in this exemplar.[8]

In the meantime, on 20 January 1914, Grant Richards replied requesting further information from Joyce. This was sent on 24 January (*Letters*, II, 328–29). Joyce wrote: "The book is in the form approved by me, i.e. with one or two slight changes already made."[9] Richards finally agreed on 29 January to publish *Dubliners*, though shorn of the preface. He sent a signed agreement on 23 March.[1] Setting from printed copy, Richards's printer bypassed galley proof stage and in April sent page proofs to Joyce.[2] Joyce quickly corrected

7. At the end of (b) is written "Next Story of *Dubliners* A *Mother* in printed proofsheet"; at the end of (c) "Next Story of Dubliners *Grace* in MS"; at the end of (d) "Next Story of *Dubliners The Dead* part in book from page 160 to page 320 part in MS"; and at the beginning of (f) "End of Story *The Dead*": all in the same markedly sprawling authorial hand. The late page proofs themselves (what Joyce calls the "book," in which the unnumbered title-page of "The Dead" [257] follows page 160) are unmarked. In the *James Joyce Archive*, vol. [4], p. xxx, I essentially identified this mixed-copy assembly of the *Dubliners* text.

8. But if he gave him only a selection, it is not impossible that he sent a typescript, as Forrest Read (*op. cit.* p. 1) holds. *Dubliners* as a whole, it is true, was never typed. But this was a time when Joyce, to prepare copy for the *Egoist* serialisation of *A Portrait of the Artist as a Young Man*, for the first time in his life employed a typist. In late March or early April (the letter is undated) Pound wrote again, saying that he had sent off "Araby" to the U.S., of which again, therefore, he must have had a copy.

9. Taking 'one or two' as a considerable understatement, one would infer from this remark that Joyce was sufficiently aware that the prize set of proofs obtained "by a ruse" from Maunsel in 1912 partly contained sheets in an advanced state of revision. The autopsy made possible before the Sotheby sale in 2004 showed not only that it was indeed a mixed copy (as discussed above). It also revealed that, to serve as Richards's printer's copy, the pages carry relatively frequent pencil annotations, especially in the early gatherings. These specify questions of general lay-out, fonts, and the like; and they insist on the house-styling of Joyce's dialogue dashes into inverted (or, as Joyce called them, "perverted") commas. Off and on—possibly at change-overs of the compositorial stints—there are also indications of the page breaks for the London typesetting. Throughout, the Dublin printed page numbers are altered in pencil. This is a printinghouse requirement due to the fact that the London typesetting is less expansive that the Dublin one, and that, with the blank pages of the Dublin setting skipped (and physically already eliminated) in the copy before them, the London compositors had to be reassured that they were not missing pages of text.

1. Richards added that his printer had mislaid pages 3–4 and 13–14 of "The Sisters." Three days later (on 26 March) Joyce sent off typed copies of the "Sisters" pages in question (*Letters*, II, 392–95). These have also re-surfaced with the proofs that have now come to light. They were clearly prepared, as was easy to do, from the additional fragmentary runs of the 1910 proofs still in Joyce's possession.

2. In April 1914, the printer's copy was returned to Joyce along with two sets of the Richards page proofs (one of which, unmarked, still survives). The title-page was sent back later (*Letters*, II, 334). The Maunsel proofs remained in Joyce's possession for many years. In May 1917 he described them to John Quinn as "the only copy extant, so far as I know, of the burned first edition" (*Letters*, II, 396). In 1927 he offered the set for sale to A.S.W. Rosenbach (*Letters*, I, 252, and III, 161). Rosenbach, and after him other dealers, declined. In the event, it was Stanislaus Joyce who preserved them and prized them suf-

and returned these, expecting to see a revise. It never came. Frustrated, he prepared a list of further corrections and sent them on to Richards on 14 May. The corrections were not made, nor has the list itself survived.

Dubliners, by James Joyce, in an edition of 1250 copies, was published by Grant Richards on 15 June 1914. In 1916, B. W. Huebsch of New York bought 504 sets of sheets from Richards and issued them as the first American edition.

The Document Relationships

Of each Dubliners story, there was first—after drafts that (save for that of "A Painful Case") are all lost—an autograph fair copy. In fact, Joyce fair-copied the final draft text of most, if not all, stories more than once. The copies varied only slightly, as is witnessed by the two extant manuscripts of "Ivy Day in the Committee Room." Where only one exemplar survives, such differences as there were, are, as a rule, irrecoverable. Exceptions are "The Boarding House," where the variants in the single extant fair copy indicate that behind the printed text was another, somewhat revised manuscript; and "Eveline," which went into the book publication of Dubliners in a version—and therefore, doubtless, from a fair copy—significantly different from the text published in The Irish Homestead. For "After the Race," by contrast, also first published in The Irish Homestead, the book text, although presumably not printed from the manuscript behind the Homestead but from another exemplar, shows very little revision. The opposite is true for "The Sisters." For this story, the Homestead and the book texts are radically different versions, each represented in one surviving fair copy. Of these, the first-version manuscript, as indicated, was prepared as the original copy of the story for the book as first submitted to Grant Richards in 1905, and thus postdates the Irish Homestead publication.

Joyce's original printer's copy for the Dubliners volume was a stable set of autograph fair copies which went to Grant Richards for the first time in November 1905, then a second time in June 1906, and finally to Maunsel and Co. of Dublin in 1909. The changes and substitutions in this set were few and specific. The first submission to Grant Richards in November 1905 consisted of the twelve stories originally planned, to which the thirteenth story—"Two Gallants"—followed in February 1906, while the negotiations over the publication were ongoing. The portfolio was returned in June 1906. In July, Joyce re-submitted it with the second fair-copy version of "The

---

ficiently not to include them in the cache of Joyceana that went to Cornell in the late 1950s. This is why Robert Scholes, who catalogued the Cornell collection, did not see them, nor knew of them (see p. xxix, n. 4).

Sisters" in place of the first, a replacement leaf or two in "Ivy Day in the Committee Room," and possibly in "Counterparts," and the fourteenth story, "A Little Cloud," inserted between "The Boarding House" and "Counterparts." Thirteen of the fourteen manuscripts seen, and in the end declined, by Richards (and preliminarily even handled by his printers, as in the case of "Two Gallants"), three years later became the copy for Maunsel in Dublin, with the addition now of "The Dead," written in 1907. For "Grace," as indicated, Maunsel received a fresh manuscript. The manuscript of the story as submitted to Richards has not survived.

The Richards/Maunsel set of manuscripts is not entirely lost. The extant fair copies of "The Sisters," "An Encounter," "A Painful Case," "Ivy Day in the Committee Room" (the Cornell copy), "A Mother," "Grace" (being the post-1906 version) and "The Dead" (with two large middle sections missing) belonged to it. The fair copies preserved of "The Boarding House" and "Counterparts," on the other hand,[3] as well as the other surviving fair copy of "Ivy Day in the Committee Room" (the Yale copy), are manuscripts slightly pre-dating the assembly of the printer's copy in November 1905. While their pre-dating is suggested by minor as yet unrevised readings, collation nevertheless confirms them as sufficiently satisfactory substitutes for their lost counterparts in the Richards/Maunsel set.

The Maunsel edition, though never published, went through three stages of proof in 1910: galleys, early page proofs and late page proofs. Each stage is documented, though in the case of the galleys only by surviving fragments. Galleys exist for "Counterparts" (a fragment of one galley slip), "A Mother" (complete) and "The Dead" (with the end, to the length of probably one galley slip, missing). The alternation of early and late page proofs in the Maunsel in-house working copy, as well as the interlacing, in Joyce's own patch-up copy, of stories in autograph with runs from the 1910/1912 proofs from Dublin, have already been described above.

When Grant Richards rescinded his refusal of 1906 and offered to publish *Dubliners* in 1914, the Maunsel in-house mix of proofs, as said, became his printer's copy. Joyce received, corrected and returned page proofs in April 1914. These were the only proofs provided for the first edition. They survive in one unmarked set.[4] As indicated, the list of some 200 corrections, dispatched to Richards

3. Their present location at Cornell, as part of the Stanislaus Joyce collection of Joyceana, would seem to identify them as vestiges of the set of *Dubliners* manuscripts held by Stanislaus (see p. xxi, n.2).
4. All Maunsel and Richards proofs that in the 1970s were known to have survived are reprinted in vols. [5] and [6] of *The James Joyce Archive*: James Joyce, *Dubliners. The 1910 Proofs* and *Dubliners. The 1914 Proofs*, prefaced and arranged by Michael Groden. New York and London: Garland Publishing, 1977.

when Joyce realised that he was not receiving revises, has not been preserved (nor were the corrections themselves made). After publication of the first edition, a further autograph list entitled "Dubliners / Misprints" was assembled and still exists (see *James Joyce Archive*. vol [4], pages 51–63). It is not clear whether this is the list prepared by Joyce in 1915 for a putative second Grant Richards edition, or a revised version made in 1917 for B. W. Huebsch. The typed version of the list, however, was almost certainly made in 1917 (*Letters*, II, 392–95). Beyond it, there is no evidence that Joyce attended to the text of *Dubliners* in his lifetime.

The Transmission of the Text through the Documents

Each *Dubliners* story reached its final stage of manuscript revision in the fair-copy exemplar incorporated in the Richards/Maunsel set of manuscripts. The galleys typeset from this set show conspicuous house-styling, especially in the punctuation. In a first round of proof-reading, Joyce appears to have concentrated above all on removing hundreds of commas. He continued the process in proof-reading the early page proofs. At this stage, he also turned his attention to a restyling of compounds. The late page proofs show an extensive elimination of hyphens, and compounds now appear as either one-word or two-word formations. Exactly the same proof-reading labour was in 1915/16 exercised on *A Portrait of the Artist as a Young Man*. There, as can be demonstrated, Joyce's markings were often ambiguous, resulting in two-word divisions where he wished one word formations. The corresponding documentary evidence for *Dubliners* is missing, since we lack the early page proofs that Joyce marked up. Hence, it cannot be determined which of the individual two-word compounds in the *Dubliners* late page proofs were meant by him as one word. Along with the restitution of Joyce's light punctuation in the galleys and early page proofs, and his restyling of compounds in the early page proofs, one may note a certain amount of lowering of capitals in a manner typical later for *Portrait* and *Ulysses;* and, of course, at both proof stages much necessary correction of typos was carried out. Most importantly, both the galleys and the early page proofs received an even spread of revisions. Though not numerous, they are significant throughout. But the revisions actually made in the early page proofs are recoverable only in so far as the late page proofs survive. There, however, they do stand out as distinctly recognizable authorial changes. In truth, since Joyce's proof-reading on the Maunsel edition is traceable throughout only by its results, all proof corrections, restylings and revisions that we claim as authorial must ultimately prove themselves by their kind and quality, since

marked proofs have been preserved neither of the galley nor of the
early page proof stage. Joyce's proof-reading on the Maunsel edition
is traceable only by its results.

The circumstance that, though some proofs in the set of Maunsel
pages that served as printer's copy for Grant Richards were late,
others were early, means that the first-edition text to that extent lacks
the final round of Maunsel corrections and revisions. Altogether,
marking the 1914 proofs involved repeating much of the work done
once before on the Maunsel proofs. Again, a considerable accretion
of commas was removed; compounds, which had re-acquired
hyphens in large numbers, were again restyled without them, though
not as consistently and radically as in the two rounds of Maunsel
proofing. In so far as memory served, moreover, some of the final
Maunsel revisions were once more introduced. Yet in all, Joyce did
not gain control over the first edition to the extent he wished. He
requested in vain that dialogue be styled not with "perverted commas," but with the dialogue dash. Barred the opportunity, on which
he had counted, of proofing revises, he drew up a list of some 200
further corrections—a list which has not survived—only to find
when the book was out that they had been disregarded and that,
furthermore, not all the changes he had marked in the proofs he
read had in fact been carried out.

In sum, it is not the Grant Richards first edition text of 1914, but
the text of the Maunsel late page proofs of 1910, incomplete though
these are, which represents *Dubliners* as most closely and consistently under Joyce's control in print.

The Choice of Copy-text

In critical editing, one standard method of procedure is to select a
copy-text from the texts represented in the extant documents. This
method has been adopted in this edition, which is therefore a conventional 'copy-text edition.'[5] According to rule, the editor establishes an edited text critically from the base of the 'copy-text' chosen
(in descending order of preference, this would be the text of an autograph manuscript, of a scribal copy in manuscript or typescript, of a
set of proofs, of a published edition—and if a published edition,
preferably the first). In selecting the copy-text, the editor will be
significantly guided both by what the author wrote, and by what
shape the author and others gave the text in the course of production

---

5. In this, the present edition of *Dubliners*, as well as its companion edition of *A Portrait of the Artist as a Young Man*, differs essentially from the edition of *Ulysses*, where the textual situation is greatly more complex. (The Critical and Synoptic Edition of *Ulysses*, prepared by Hans Walter Gabler with Wolfhard Steppe and Claus Melchior, was published in 3 volumes by Garland Publishing, New York, in 1984/86; the reading text from that edition is available in paperback both in the US and the UK from Random House [Vintage and Bodley Head, respectively].)

and publication. It has thus been specifically to set out the options
for the choice of copy-text, or copy-texts, that we have described
above the nature and range of the surviving documents for *Dubliners*.
In particular, we have emphasized how Joyce shared in the proof-
reading of the aborted Maunsel edition even to the extent of exploit-
ing it for his own purposes of revision. Yet we have also shown that
he failed to gain influence over both the text and its presentation in
the course of production of the first edition. What he was prevented
from doing on the first-edition proofs was, in one respect, to restore
a styling and a layout he favoured, which was a light rhetorical punctuation, and the setting-out of speech with dialogue dashes. In this,
he insisted (though in vain) on effects and an appearance of his text
as he had written it in his autograph manuscripts. In another respect,
he attempted (though equally in vain) to do on the first-edition proofs
what he had already once before performed on the Maunsel proofs:
namely, to revise the text, that is, to re-write it in specific wordings
and phrasings.

To decide, in consequence, on what course of action to take in
the critical editing under copytext-editing auspices, it is important
to consider that the first of these proofing gestures confirms the
authority of the manuscripts. At the same time, the second does not
invalidate them wholesale: authorial revision merely supersedes the
manuscript text in specific readings. The situation as a whole is one
to which copy-text editing procedures are comfortably suited. In
their light, Joyce's autograph may be singled out as the obvious document to provide the base text for the critical editing. But no entire
manuscript in Joyce's hand exists of *Dubliners*, nor does even every
single story survive in autograph. Hence, the copy-text for each story
must be chosen individually. Where this cannot be an autograph,
the alternative is fortunately straightforward: it is in such cases the
1910 proofs that provide the readiest substitute. Printer's deviations
and errors apart—which editorial vigilance should prove capable of
isolating and eliminating—these proofs represent what one might
term a 'virtual manuscript text' beyond the text of the autograph from
which they were set up. In other words, the 1910 proofs give the
(lost) fair-copy text at a (post-faircopy) stage of further authorial revision.

In the present edition, Joyce's autograph manuscripts consequently hold the copy-text wholly for eight stories, and partly for a
ninth ("The Dead"), while the Maunsel typesetting, in the state of
the late page proofs, provides the copy-text for six stories. The eight
stories edited from manuscript are: "The Sisters," "An Encounter,"
"The Boarding House," "Counterparts," "A Painful Case," "Ivy Day
in the Committee Room," "A Mother," and "Grace." The 1910 late
page proofs have provided the copy-text for "Araby," "Eveline," "After

the Race," "Two Gallants," "A Little Cloud," and "Clay." Only "The Dead," at the end of the collection, offers a situation of somewhat greater complexity. Its autograph survives only in part, and the text from its missing sections is represented merely in two distinct derivations. These are, on the one hand, a transcript partly typed and partly written out in two scribal hands (Eileen[?] and Stanislaus Joyce's), and on the other hand the 1910 galleys. While the typist and the family amanuenses appear, on the whole, to have made good sense of Joyce's punctuation, their general accuracy is highly variable and their copying is, all things considered, an amateur performance. On the other hand, the Maunsel compositors in Dublin did a professional job on setting type directly from the very same Joycean autograph that, in combination with the typist/amanuensis transcript, has survived in fragments. Having these fragments in Joyce's hand, we did not wish to dismiss them, so far as they go, as copytext suppliers. Yet in weighing the further alternatives, we chose not the (later and amateur) transcript, but the (earlier and professional) 1910 galleys as copy-text document for the sections missing in the autograph. In the case of "The Dead," therefore, a splicing of copytext documents exceptionally occurs even within the individual story. What can be said in favour of this procedure, however, though it is arbitrary, is that it brings the copy-text basis, in this instance too, closely in line with the selection of the 1910 typesetting to provide the copy-text for those stories whose autograph manuscripts are wholly lost.

The Editing

The copy-text is a text preserved in a document of transmission. It is not the text of the critical edition. A copy-text is never *in* an edition. It is, on the contrary, always *behind* the editing. The editor transforms the copy-text into an edited text through acts of critical editing. This editorial activity is recorded in an edition's apparatus. For the critical edition of James Joyce's *Dubliners*, the apparatus divides into two main sections. These are the notes at the foot of the text pages, and the historical collation. The historical collation, placed after the work's entire text, is to be found only in the 1993 (Garland) first printing of this edition. There it can be consulted and easily related to the present printing, since, regardless of the difference in volume pagination, the text, the lines, and the line-counts are identical in both printings. The purpose of the historical collation is to record in detail the differences between the edition's critically established text and the texts in the surviving documents. In practice, this makes much of the historical collation a listing of errors in transmission (defined as such through the editing). Such errors are misreadings in and of the manuscripts, as well as misprints and other non-authentic readings in the proofs and published texts. The published texts singled out for reporting in the historical collation to this edition of *Dubliners* are two only, namely the 1914 first edition and the Viking edition of 1967, edited by Robert Scholes. This narrow selection of published editions for the historical collation record is justified by the fact that—the autograph list of "Dubliners/Misprints" of around 1917 apart—the author at no time had a hand in the numerous editions and re-issues of *Dubliners* after the first edition, and in his lifetime. Consequently, all editions and issues marketed around the world before 1967, even though they inevitably introduced their own non-authentic readings or outright errors, were ultimately derivations from the first edition of 1914. Editions after 1967, and specifically after 1992 when the copyright situation for *Dubliners* changed, have predominantly modeled their texts on that prepared by Robert Scholes. His Viking edition is best characterised as an amalgamation of selective features and readings from the manuscripts and the abortive 1910/1912 Maunsel edition to the first-edition text.

By contrast, the present edition establishes the text of *Dubliners* wholly afresh. On the surface, the two editions, Scholes's and the present one, while they do not concur in every word, are close in their readings. However, constructing its critical text newly from the early documents of the writing and transmission, this edition presents the stories in the punctuation and word forms of their first sources. This amounts to a re-patterning of *Dubliners* capable of giving a new feel for the language and the rhythms of the text, and of thus subtly altering one's appreciation of the narratives' shadings of meaning and sense. For this early Joycean work, moreover, the present edition for the first time also retrieves elements of authentic text that had been lost in the transmission since 1914. It is the second main section of the apparatus, namely the notes at the foot of the pages, that serves to record such retrievals, as well as comprehensively to detail the editing carried out to transform the copy-text into the edited text.

Considering the notes at the bottom of the text pages, what is most helpful for the user of the present edition to realize is the critical potential and interpretative usefulness they have. It is a minute authentification of the text, for instance, that Mrs Mooney, of "The Boarding House," after walking out on her violent and menacing husband, "went to the priests" ("The Boarding House," line 12)—and not 'to the priest', as according to all previous editions. Yet in terms of making interpretative sense of *Dubliners*, this one-letter restoration of what Joyce wrote in manuscript amounts to no less than a re-focussing of Mrs Mooney's character, as well as of the society in which she lives. By the evidence of Joyce's plural form, she turns for support not just to her parish priest and confessor, but as it were to the whole priesthood corporately personifying the church that dominates her world. In this, as in numerous other instances, the footnote marks a 'STET' to affirm the copy-text against the printing tradition since 1914. By strict adherence to apparatus conventions, there need be no entry, since the edited text does not alter, or emend, the copy-text. The 'STET' record, however, registers an original detail of the text considered critically significant—as similarly in that other instance in the same story, where Mrs Mooney, amusingly to our ears, sends her daughter out to be "a typewriter in a cornfactor's office" ("The Boarding House," lines 53–54). We catch a usage still possible before the language conveniently disambiguated the instrument and the agent of the new invention. (Polly Mooney the typist belongs to a new generation of office workers, while Farrington of "Counterparts" is still a clerk doing his allotted copying with pen and ink in longhand at the stand-up writing desk.)

The incidence of emendations and footnotes varies considerably between the stories. For some, as for "Araby," "A Little Cloud," or "Clay," they are scarce, and for obvious reasons: the copy-text for these stories is the text of the 1910 late page proofs. No earlier records exist, so we lack evidence of variation at the stages of composition; nor does the transmission through the 1914 proofs, the first edition, and the Viking edition register much, if any, correction or revision. By contrast, we have the situation of "Eveline" or "After the Race." The nature and extent of Joyce's revision of these stories between their appearance in *The Irish Homestead* and their inclusion among the printer's-copy manuscripts for Richards (1906) and Maunsel (1910/12) can be extrapolated from the foot-of-the-page notes and critically analysed. Similarly, the controversy between author and publishers over "Counterparts" can be followed to a considerable extent, and the notes reveal how much of the text Joyce did rework, even while he was not giving in to the censorship demands in principle. Again, for a story like "Ivy Day in the Committee Room," the notes reveal over page after page that the author changed his attitude to phoneticising the dialogue and thereby representing in print the Dublin vernacular of his characters. Abandoning such a strategy, Joyce seems implicitly also to be distancing himself from the experiments in representing spoken language that were, around the time of his writing *Dubliners*, being initiated on the stage of the Abbey Theatre by the Irish Revivalists—experiments that Joyce had already anticipated privately half a decade earlier in his (hilariously free) translation of Gerhart Hauptmann's play *Before Sunrise* (*Vor Sonnenaufgang*).

Read not so much in terms of aiding critical analysis and interpretation, but instead in terms of the critical editing, the apparatus at the bottom of the text pages furthermore takes the user through the editor's deliberations and decisions in the course of transforming the copy-text into the edited text. The case of "The Dead" with its split copy-text base proves particularly instructive to illustrate the range of the copy-text editor's problems, options, and solutions. The documents providing the copy-text, as said, are partly the surviving fragments from the autograph originally included in the Richards (1906) and Maunsel (1910/12) printer's copy, and partly the 1910 galley proofs set up from that autograph. As it happens, each of these copy-texts is also mirrored in a near-duplicate. The galley proofs, set from the once complete autograph, naturally duplicate the text for which the manuscript fragments provide the copy-text; and for the text residing as copy-text in these galleys themselves, a parallel derivation equally exists in shape of the amanuensis transcript, copied from the sections of the autograph now lost. The text closest to the source of Joyce's own writing is thus doubly attested throughout. In instances of variation within this double transmission, the text of the autograph fragments usually takes precedence where they provide the copy-text. Where the copy-text shifts to the 1910 galleys, the textual differences between the galleys and the amanuesis transcript must be critically weighed. For it may represent an error either on the part of the compositors setting up the galleys, or an inaccuracy of the typist or family scribe fabricating the amanuensis copy. Once this relationship has been editorially mapped out and the punctuation of the amanuensis copy, in particular, accepted to emend the galley-proof copy-text, the task begins of relating to the copy-text the variants in the 1910 late page proofs and in the first-edition text.

This may be illustrated by a few examples. For instance, the edited text allows Gabriel Conroy at lines 63–64 to reassure his aunts with the words "Go on up. I'll follow," according to the text in print, though against the copy-text, which lacks the two phrases. Similarly, it makes Gabriel anticipate his after-dinner speech as "an utter failure" (line 136), not as "a complete failure"; and it specifies that Gabriel's father was an employee of the "Port and Docks" (line 150), not of the "Post Office." These are examples of emendation in instances where the copy-text resides in the autograph. The collation pattern recorded in the apparatus shows that they answer to revisions performed in marking up the 1910 and the 1914 proofs respectively. For the changes at lines 63–64 and 136, the 1910 late page proofs and the 1914 proofs that derive from those 1910 late page proofs naturally agree against the manuscript and the—unmarked—1910 galleys. The revisions must have been entered in a parallel set of these galleys or, subsequently, in the early page proofs, else they could not have become incorporated in the late proofs and thence transmitted to the 1914 proofs. At line 150, on the other hand, the revised first edition stands alone against four documents: the manuscript, the 1910 typesetting in both its surviving states (galleys and late proofs), and the extant unmarked 1914 proofs. It is in the parallel (and now lost) set of the 1914 proofs, therefore, that Joyce must have marked the change.

At the line-break 406/407, the initial autograph fragment ends. The copy-text to be confirmed, or else to be emended, is now the galley-proof text. That it represents the lost autograph authentically is best attested when the galleys and the typescript-and-amanuensis transcript agree in a given reading. Conversely, it is against such agreement that those variants are to be made out as revisions which make their first appearance in later print: in the 1910 late page proofs and the 1914 proofs in conjunction, in the 1910 late page proofs alone, or in the first-edition text alone. This is the case when Miss Ivors' brooch no longer bears "an Irish device and motto," but only "an Irish device" (line 406); or when Miss Ivors uses the racier term "rag" (line 421) for "paper" to disparage the *Daily Express*. These revisions—both of them identifiable as revisions to the galleys or the early page proofs, since the 1910 late page proofs and the 1914 proofs agree against the extant unmarked galleys and the typescript—become the edition's readings. When however the galley copy-text and the typescript-and-amanuensis transcript disagree, there may be a doubt as to which represents the lost autograph. In the case of a name, "Clohissey's" at line 432, which is the typescript reading, the galleys have "O'Clohissey's." Without further textual evidence, this, being the copy-text reading, would become the edition reading. But in fact, the form attested in the typescript exists already in the 1910 late page proofs. This suggests that the typescript reading derives authentically from the autograph and supports the decision to emend the copy-text accordingly.

In yet another type of situation, one is faced with a contradictory revision. At lines 523, 525, and 528 it is clear from the galley and typescript agreement that the authentic unrevised term is "row" by which Gretta Conroy refers to the altercation between her husband and Miss Ivors; and Gabriel, defending himself, picks it up. In all three occurrences, the 1910 late page proofs change the term to "words" (and alter the agreement in the verb). It is then very puzzling that the 1914 proofs again read "row"; and just as strangely, after the 1914 proofing, the change reappears yet once more in the first edition, though only at the reading's third occurrence. Hence, compared to the 1910 late page proofs, the first edition offers a hybrid text. This may be intentional or not. Joyce's final intention could at best be surmised. But a surmise is not strong enough to support a critical text. An edited text must be constructed, rather, by a process of critically assessing the historical givens of the work's text in transmission. In the present case, consequently, the two consecutive acts of revision have been weighed against one another. The outcome of that exercise of textual criticism has privileged for the edited text Joyce's attested treble revision as evidenced in the 1910 late page proofs, over the last, or 'final,' intervention in the 1914 proofs for the first edition.

The weakness in a stance of invoking the author's intention, or 'final intention,' as the ultimate arbiter in the critical task of establishing an edited text should become further apparent from a passage characterising Gabriel Conroy's mood during his final conversation with Gretta at night in the hotel room. It contains a sentence not heretofore present in any published text of *Dubliners*. The words, according to the double evidence of the galleys and the amanuensis copy, are: "The irony of his mood changed into sarcasm." That Joyce was aware of the sentence in the text before him at the time when he revised the early page proofs for the abortive 1910 edition is attested by the fact that he made one alteration to it. "The irony of his mood soured into sarcasm" is the wording in the 1910 late page proofs. In the 1914 proofs, however, the entire sentence is missing, and we do not know how and why it disappeared. One possibility is that Joyce asked for it to be deleted. But this is undemonstrable. It is also less than probable, since the 1914 proofs neither here nor elsewhere suggest that they differ because an instruction to change the text was given outside any markings entered on their printer's copy. That printer's copy, as we can now positively say since it has recently re-surfaced, bears no such markings. Nor would a deletion of the sentence easily concur with Joyce's known habits of writing and revision. There is no evidence anywhere in *Dubliners*—except perhaps in "Counterparts" and "Ivy Day in the Committee Room," which were however beset by outside censorship pressure—that, from writing the text, and even affirming it by revision, Joyce would turn round and opt for an outright deletion.

The sentence in either of its attested wordings—"The irony of his mood changed into sarcasm" or "The irony of his mood soured into sarcasm"—has, it is true, disappeared from the 1914 text. But to attribute its absence to authorial intention would again be feeble grounds on which to establish a critical text. Therefore, privileging once more the late 1910 state of the text over its 1914 state, the critical edition incorporates the sentence in its authorially revised form (at line 1478). That the critical edition does not follow the text of the first edition, even though this as a whole can claim James Joyce's final authorisation, may again be justified with reference to the history of the text, and quite specifically to the manifest history of the authorial writing culminating in the 1910 late page proofs.

The reader and user of the edition, on his and her part, however, should be aware of the conditionality and, in terms of the editorial rationale, the systematic contingency of the editorial decision. Editorial decisions are critical decisions, and the editorial choices they lead to must always be recognised as the considered options they are. A scholarly edition offers always a critical but never a definitive text; and in the field of discourse that such an edition opens, the instrument to involve the reader and user in critical exchanges with the text, as well as with the editor's choices and decisions that lead to the construction of the edited text, is the editorial apparatus.

The text of this edition, while offered as a reading text broadly within the standards and conventions of modern professional printing and publishing, endeavours yet to maintain the character of a scholarly edited text in preserving essential features of irregularity in the recoverable authorial writing. Word forms and word divisions, spellings, capitalization, and punctuation have been neither normalised nor modernised, nor have typographical matters such as abbreviations or ellipses been standardised. The emendations undertaken,[6] or the refusals to emend, are recorded in the apparatus, with a few specific exceptions. The absence or presence of full stops after 'Mr' and 'Mrs' is not noted, nor are quotation marks (inverted commas) surrounding dialogue speech reported, except when joined with emended punctuation. Full stops lacking in the copy-text at the end of paragraphs have been supplied silently. At the end of dialogue speech they have been silently supplied only where the copy-text original is wholly unmarked, or marked by a dash only. Joyce's intermediate dialogue dashes have been explicitly emended. Taken together, this means that Joyce's manuscript habits of marking off the segments of dialogue speech by dashes have neither been followed nor fully recorded.[7] The convention adopted in this edition's main text is that of dashes at the opening of dialogue only, placed flush left. It is the typographical solution answering to Joyce's own strong views on the marking of dialogue which, in print, and at his forceful instigation, was realised in the third edition of A Portrait of the Artist as a Young Man (London: Jonathan Cape, 1924) and has now become the com-

---

6. It should be made quite clear that 'emendations' are to be understood not in terms of changes in relation to the previous, unedited or edited, editions, but as emendations of the copy-text. Emendations of the copy-text, often drawing on the transmission, may in fact result precisely in agreement with the text in earlier print.
7. Joyce's manuscript writing, and within it the patterns and effect of his manuscript mode of setting out dialogue, may be studied in the photo-reproductions of the manuscripts in the *Dubliners* volume of the *James Joyce Archive*, or in the draft and fair-copy texts from autographs included in the section "Manuscript Traces" of the 1993 (Garland) printing of this edition.

mon feature of the critically edited texts of *Ulysses, A Portrait of the Artist as a Young Man*, and *Dubliners*.

Hans Walter Gabler

Select Bibliography

Stuart Gilbert (ed.), *Letters of James Joyce*. Volume I. New York: The Viking Press, 1957, 1966. (*Letters* I)

Richard Ellmann (ed.), *Letters of James Joyce*. Volumes II and III. New York: The Viking Press, 1966. (*Letters* II AND III)

Richard Ellmann, *James Joyce*. Oxford: Oxford University Press, 1982. (JJ)

The James Joyce Archive, 63 vols., General Editor Michael Groden. New York and London: Garland Publishing, Inc., 1977–79. Vol. [4]: *Dubliners. A Facsimile of Drafts and Manuscripts*, prefaced and arranged by Hans Walter Gabler; vols. [5] and [6]: *Dubliners. The 1910 Proofs* and *Dubliners. The 1914 Proofs*, prefaced and arranged by Michael Groden.

Robert E. Scholes, "Some Observations on the Text of *Dubliners*: 'The Dead'," and "Further Observations on the Text of *Dubliners*," *Studies in Bibliography* 15 (1962), 191–205, and 17 (1964), 107–122.

Symbols and Sigla

The symbols employed in the transcription and apparatus sections of this edition describe characteristic features of the writing and indicate sequences of correction and revision within the relevant documents.

⟨ ⟩	authorial deletion in the course of writing
[ ]	editorial conjecture, e.g. in the case of manuscript defects
⌐¹TEXT NEW¹⌐	text inserted/changed at first level of document revision
⟨⌐¹⌐TEXT OLD⟩	text cancelled at first level of document revision
⌐¹⟨TEXT OLD⟩ TEXT NEW¹⌐	text replaced at first level of document revision
	The symbols ⌐ ⌐ delimit an area of change; a given number indicates the level, an additional letter identifies the agent ('A' = author; 's' = scribe)
←¹→	paragraph cancelled at first level of document revision
◇	erasure
▢	illegible character(s) or word(s)
ǀ	line division in document

The document sigla employed in the apparatus sections are: MS, TS, AM1, AM2, 10G, 10P, 10, 14P, 14, 67. The documents they refer to are reviewed in the »Introduction« (esp. pp. xxxiv–xxxvii) and identified for each story individually in the opening footnote.

Following the lemma bracket in the emendations,

e	indicates a unique emendation in this edition;
e:	indicates a unique emendation partially supported by the document identified after the colon;
a	prefixed to a document sigla (e.g., a10P) indicates an authorial correction/revision in or to the document identified by the sigla.

This critical edition introduces for each story a through line numbering independent of the pagination. In the printing, end-of-line hyphenation occurs in two modes. The sign '=' marks a division for mere typographical reasons. Words so printed should always be cited as one undivided word. The regular hyphen indicates an authentic Joycean hyphen.

The Text of
DUBLINERS

Text Edited by
HANS WALTER GABLER
WITH WALTER HETTCHE

The Sisters

There was no hope for him this time: it was the third stroke. Night after night I had passed the house (it was vacation time) and studied the lighted square of window: and night after night I had found it lighted in the same way, faintly and evenly. If he was dead, I thought, I would see the reflection of candles on the darkened blind for I knew that two candles[1] must be set at the head of a corpse. He had often said to me: *I am not long for this world,* and I had thought his words idle. Now I knew they were true. Every night as I gazed up at the window I said softly to myself the word *paralysis*.[2] It had always sounded strangely in my ears like the word *gnomon*[3] in the Euclid and the word *simony* in the catechism.[4] But now it sounded to me like the name of some maleficent and sinful being. It filled me with fear and yet I longed to be nearer to it and to look upon its deadly work.

Old Cotter was sitting at the fire, smoking, when I came downstairs to supper. While my aunt was ladling out my stirabout[5] he said as if returning to some former remark of his: —No, I wouldn't say he was exactly ...... but there was some= thing queer ..... there was something uncanny about him. I'll tell you my opinion. ...

He began to puff at his pipe, no doubt arranging his opinion in his mind. Tiresome old fool! When we knew him first he used to be rather interesting, talking of faints and worms;[6] but I soon grew tired of him and his endless stories about the distillery.

Copy-text: Manuscript Cornell 30 –1 (MS); Collated texts: 1910 late proofs (10); 1914 proofs (14P) and 1914 first edition (14) [IDENTITY IN BOTH IS REPORTED AS '14']; 1967 Viking edition in the 1969 Viking Critical Library printing (67). [MANUSCRIPT YALE 2.1, TRANSCRIBED AND FOOTNOTED WITH THE VARIANTS OF THE FIRST PUBLICATION IN *The Irish Homestead* OF AUGUST 13, 1904, IS RENDERED IN PARALLEL WITH THE COPY-TEXT IN THE SECTION »MANUSCRIPT TRACES« OF OUR EDITION OF *DUBLINERS*, NEW YORK: GARLAND PUBLISHING INC., 1993.]

9 true.] true. ⟨The⟩ MS

1. Irish wakes customarily had lit candles by the corpse.
2. Paralysis may be caused by an apoplectic seizure or other medical condition such as syphilis.
3. Euclid, a Greek scholar living in Alexandria in 300 B.C.E., set forth principles of geometry in a work called *The Elements of Geometry*. He describes a *gnomon* as a parallelogram with a corner in the shape of a similar parallelogram removed.
4. Simony, named after the sorcerer Simon Magus, is the sin of buying or selling church offices or spiritual pardons. A catechism is a manual or guide, using questions and answers, memorized and recited, for teaching children the doctrines of the Catholic religion.
5. A porridge or gruel, often made with oatmeal.
6. Terms referring to impure spirits (faints) and metal coils (worms) that play a role in distilling liquors such as whiskey.

—I have my own theory about it, he said. I think it was one of those ... peculiar cases. ... But it's hard to say. ...

He began to puff again at his pipe without giving us his theory. My uncle saw me staring and said to me:

—Well, so your old friend is gone, you'll be sorry to hear.

—Who? said I.

—Father Flynn.

—Is he dead?

—Mr Cotter here has just told us. He was passing by the house.

I knew that I was under observation so I continued eating as if the news had not interested me. My uncle explained to old Cotter:

—The youngster and he were great friends. The old chap taught him a great deal, mind you; and they say he had a great wish for him.

—God have mercy on his soul, said my aunt piously.

Old Cotter looked at me for a while. I felt that his little beady black eyes were examining me but I would not satisfy him by looking up from my plate. He returned to his pipe and finally spat rudely into the grate.

—I wouldn't like children of mine, he said, to have too much to say to a man like that.

—How do you mean, Mr Cotter? asked my aunt.

—What I mean is, said old Cotter, it's bad for children. My idea is: let a young lad run about and play with young lads of his own age and not be. ... Am I right, Jack?

—That's my principle too, said my uncle. Let him learn to box his corner.[7] That's what I'm always saying to that rosicrucian[8] there: take exercise. Why, when I was a nipper every morning of my life I had a cold bath, winter and summer. And that's what stands to me now. Education is all very fine and large. .... Mr Cotter might take a pick of that leg of mutton, he added to my aunt.

—No, no, not for me, said old Cotter.

My aunt brought the dish from the safe and laid it on the table.

—But why do you think it's not good for children, Mr Cotter? she asked.

—It's bad for children, said old Cotter, because their minds are

41 you;] you ⟨:⟩; MS   49 a] ⁻¹a⁻ MS   50 Cotter?] Cotter⟨,⟩? MS   55 rosicrucian] 10; fellow MS   56 a nipper] 10; young MS   62 laid] 10; put MS

7. To fend for himself.
8. A Rosicrucian is a member of the fraternal organization of religious mystics called the Ancient Order Rosae Crucis. They were thought to be dreamy and otherworldly.

so impressionable. When children see things like that, you
know, it has an effect. .....

I crammed my mouth with stirabout for fear I might give
utterance to my anger. Tiresome old rednosed imbecile!   70

It was late when I fell asleep. Though I was angry with old
Cotter for alluding to me as a child I puzzled my head to
extract meaning from his unfinished sentences. In the dark of
my room I imagined that I saw again the heavy grey face of the
paralytic. I drew the blankets over my head and tried to think   75
of Christmas. But the grey face still followed me. It murmured
and I understood that it desired to confess something. I felt my
soul receding into some pleasant and vicious region and there
again I found it waiting for me. It began to confess to me in a
murmuring voice and I wondered why it smiled continually and   80
why the lips were so moist with spittle. But then I remembered
that it had died of paralysis and I felt that I too was smiling
feebly as if to absolve the simoniac of his sin.[9]

The next morning after breakfast I went down to look at the
little house in Great Britain Street.[1] It was an unassuming shop, 85
registered under the vague name of *Drapery*. The drapery
consisted mainly of children's bootees and umbrellas and on
ordinary days a notice used to hang in the window, saying
Umbrellas Recovered. No notice was visible now for the
shutters were up. A crape bouquet[2] was tied to the doorknocker   90
with ribbon. Two poor women and a telegram boy[3] were
reading the card pinned on the crape. I also approached and
read:

July 1st 1895
The Rev. James Flynn (formerly of S. Catherine's   95
Church, Meath Street)[4] aged sixty-five years.
R.I.P.[5]

The reading of the card persuaded me that he was dead and
I was disturbed to find myself at check.[6] Had he not been dead I
would have gone into the little dark room behind the shop to   100

81 moist] 10; covered MS   82 I(2)] I was [was NOT DELETED] MS   87 bootees] 10; boots
MS

9. Since simony is an offense against the Church, only a bishop or other high ecclesiastical
   official could formally absolve or forgive the sin.
1. A street, now called Parnell Street, that intersected a poor quarter north of the city center
   of Dublin and was lined with little shops and tenements.
2. Crape is a thin, sometimes crinkled fabric, used in the gowns of clergymen. Black crape
   armbands were worn by mourners, and a crape bouquet may therefore have been a funer-
   ary ornament made of this cloth.
3. A courier who delivered telegrams.
4. A Roman Catholic parish church south of the river Liffey in Dublin.
5. May he rest in peace. From the Latin phrase *requiescat in pace*.
6. At a loss.

find him sitting in his armchair by the fire, nearly smothered in his greatcoat.[7] Perhaps my aunt would have given me a packet of high toast[8] for him and this present would have roused him from his stupefied doze. It was always I who emptied the packet into his black snuffbox for his hands trembled too much to allow him to do this without spilling half the snuff about the floor. Even as he raised his large trembling hand to his nose little clouds of smoke dribbled through his fingers over the front of his coat. It may have been these constant showers of snuff which gave his ancient priestly garments their green faded look for the red handkerchief, blackened as it always was with the snuffstains of a week, with which he tried to brush away the fallen grains was quite inefficacious.

I wished to go in and look at him but I had not the courage to knock. I walked away slowly along the sunny side of the street, reading all the theatrical advertisements in the shopwin= dows as I went. I found it strange that neither I nor the day seemed in a mourning mood and I felt even annoyed at discovering in myself a sensation of freedom as if I had been freed from something by his death. I wondered at this for, as my uncle had said the night before, he had taught me a great deal. He had studied in the Irish college in Rome[9] and he had taught me to pronounce Latin properly.[1] He had told me stories about the catacombs[2] and about Napoleon Bonaparte[3] and he had explained to me the meaning of the different ceremonies of the mass and of the different vestments worn by the priest.[4] Sometimes he had amused himself by putting difficult questions to me, asking me what one should do in certain circumstances or whether such and such sins were mortal or venial[5] or only imperfections. His questions showed me how complex and mysterious were certain institutions of the church which I had always regarded as the simplest acts. The duties of the priest

122 Irish] ⁷¹Irish¹ᴿ MS

7. A very warm jacket or heavy overcoat.
8. A brand of loose snuff tobacco, inhaled through the nose.
9. A theological seminary in Rome where outstanding young Irishmen could study for the priesthood.
1. Latin was the official language of Roman Catholic liturgy and ritual, recited by priests during the Mass and other religious ceremonies.
2. Subterranean cemeteries where early Christians could attend secret services during times of persecution.
3. Emperor of France, 1804–15, thought to have said that the happiest day of his life was the one on which he made his First Holy Communion.
4. Outer garments in colors that symbolized the particular liturgical feast being celebrated by the Mass—for example, white for Christmas and Easter, purple for Lent and Advent.
5. Catholic doctrine classifies sins in order of their seriousness, with mortal sins given a moral weight approximating felonies in legal systems, while venial sins approximate misdemeanors.

towards the eucharist[6] and towards the secrecy of the con=
fessional[7] seemed so grave to me that I wondered how anybody
had ever found in himself the courage to undertake them: and I   135
was not surprised when he told me that the fathers of the
church had written books as thick as the post office directory
and as closely printed as the law notices in the newspaper
elucidating all these intricate questions. Often when I thought
of this I could make no answer or only a very foolish and   140
halting one upon which he used to smile and nod his head
twice or thrice. Sometimes he used to put me through the re=
sponses of the mass[8] which he had made me learn by heart: and
as I pattered he used to smile pensively and nod his head, now
and then pushing huge pinches of snuff up each nostril alter=   145
nately. When he smiled he used to uncover his big discoloured
teeth and let his tongue lie upon his lower lip—a habit which
had made me feel uneasy in the beginning of our acquaintance
before I knew him well.

As I walked along in the sun I remembered old Cotter's   150
words and tried to remember what had happened afterwards in
the dream. I remembered that I had noticed long velvet curtains
and a swinging lamp of antique fashion. I felt that I had been
very far away, in some land where the customs were strange, in
Persia,[9] I thought. ...... But I could not remember the end of the   155
dream.

In the evening my aunt took me with her to visit the house of
mourning. It was after sunset but the window panes of the
houses that looked to the west reflected the tawny gold of a
great bank of clouds. Nannie received us in the hall and, as it   160
would have been unseemly to have shouted at her, my aunt
shook hands with her for all. The old woman pointed upwards
interrogatively and, on my aunt's nodding, proceeded to toil up
the narrow staircase before us, her bowed head being scarcely
above the level of the banister rail. At the first landing she   165
stopped and beckoned us forward encouragingly towards the
open door of the deadroom.[1] My aunt went in and the old

---

6. The eucharist is the ritual in the Roman Catholic Mass whereby the priest transforms
   bread and wine into the body and blood of Christ. The transformed wafer and wine become
   sacred objects that must be treated with utmost reverence.
7. The priest has the power to forgive sins heard in the confessional, an enclosure that
   ensures privacy. The priest is bound to absolute secrecy and may not divulge what has
   been confessed to him even to save a life.
8. The ritual of the Catholic Mass entailed Latin words or phrases spoken or sung by
   the priest and answered with other Latin words and phrases by the altar boy or by the
   congregation.
9. Persia (present-day Iran) was regarded at the time of the story as an exotic, romantic land,
   fantasized as a place that permitted the indulgence of the senses and the passions.
1. The room where the corpse of the deceased was composed and displayed for visitors who
   wished to pay their respects.

woman, seeing that I hesitated to enter, began to beckon to me again repeatedly with her hand.

I went in on tiptoe. The room through the lace end of the blind was suffused with dusky golden light amid which the candles looked like pale thin flames. He had been coffined. Nannie gave the lead and we three knelt down at the foot of the bed. I pretended to pray but I could not gather my thoughts because the old woman's mutterings distracted me. I noticed how clumsily her skirt was hooked at the back and how the heels of her cloth boots were trodden down all to one side. The fancy came to me that the old priest was smiling as he lay there in his coffin.

But no. When we rose and went up to the head of the bed I saw that he was not smiling. There he lay, solemn and copious, vested as for the altar, his large hands loosely retaining a chalice.[2] His face was very truculent, grey and massive, with black cavernous nostrils and circled by a scanty white fur. There was a heavy odour in the room, the flowers.

We blessed ourselves and came away. In the little room downstairs we found Eliza seated in his armchair in state. I groped my way towards my usual chair in the corner while Nannie went to the sideboard and brought out a decanter of sherry and some wineglasses. She set these on the table and invited us to take a little glass of wine. Then, at her sister's bidding, she poured out the sherry into the glasses and passed them to us. She pressed me to take some cream crackers also but I declined because I thought I would make too much noise eating them. She seemed to be somewhat disappointed at my refusal and went over quietly to the sofa where she sat down behind her sister. No-one spoke: we all gazed at the empty fireplace.

My aunt waited until Eliza sighed and then said:

—Ah, well, he's gone to a better world.

Eliza sighed again and bowed her head in assent. My aunt fingered the stem of her wineglass before sipping a little.

—Did he ..... peacefully? she asked.

—O, quite peacefully, ma'am, said Eliza. You couldn't tell when the breath went out of him. He had a beautiful death, God be praised.

—And everything .... ?

170 I] 10; NO PARAGRAPH MS   182 a] a ⟨cr◇⟩ MS   186 blessed] 10; crossed MS
192 poured] 10; filled MS   195 She] ⟨Then⟩ She MS   197 spoke:] 10; spoke and MS

2. The ceremonial cup that holds the wine to be transformed at the Mass into the blood of Christ.

—Father O'Rourke was in with him a-Tuesday and anointed
him[3] and prepared him and all.
—He knew then?   210
—He was quite resigned.
—He looks quite resigned, said my aunt.
—That's what the woman we had in to wash him said.[4] She
said he just looked as if he was asleep, he looked that peaceful
and resigned. No-one would think he'd make such a beautiful   215
corpse.
—Yes, indeed, said my aunt.
    She sipped a little more from her glass and said:
—Well, Miss Flynn, at any rate it must be a great comfort for
you to know that you did all you could for him. You were both   220
very kind to him, I must say.
    Eliza smoothed her dress over her knees.
—Ah, poor James! she said. God knows we done all we could
as poor as we are. We wouldn't see him want anything while he
was in it.   225
    Nannie had leaned her head against the sofa pillow and
seemed about to fall asleep.
—There's poor Nannie, said Eliza looking at her, she's wore
out. All the work we had, she and me, getting in the woman to
wash him and then laying him out and then the coffin and then   230
arranging about the mass in the chapel! Only for Father
O'Rourke I don't know what we'd have done at all. It was him
brought us all them flowers and them two candlesticks out of
the chapel and wrote out the notice for the *Freeman's General*[5]
and took charge of all the papers for the cemetery and poor   235
James's insurance.
—Wasn't that good of him? said my aunt.
    Eliza closed her eyes and shook her head slowly.
—Ah, there's no friends like the old friends, she said, when all
is said and done, no friends that a body can trust.   240
—Indeed, that's true, said my aunt. And I'm sure now that he's
gone to his eternal reward he won't forget you and all your
kindness to him.

213 in--him] 10; in, you know, MS   224 are.] e:14; were. MS–14P; are—14   228 wore]
10; worn MS   232 him] 10; he MS

3. The dying are entitled to receive a Roman Catholic sacrament called extreme unction,
   during which a priest anoints them with oil and forgives their sins that they may die in
   grace and enter heaven.
4. Newly deceased corpses would be washed and made presentable for public viewing, a work
   now performed by funeral establishments but then generally performed by women in the
   home.
5. Eliza means to say the *Freeman's Journal*, the Dublin daily newspaper in which the obituary
   notice was placed.

—Ah, poor James! said Eliza. He was no great trouble to us. You wouldn't hear him in the house any more than now. Still, I know he's gone and all that 245

—It's when it's all over that you'll miss him, said my aunt.

—I know that, said Eliza. I won't be bringing him in his cup of beeftea[6] any more nor you, ma'am, sending him his snuff. Ah, poor James! 250

She stopped, as if she were communing with the past, and then said shrewdly:

—Mind you, I noticed there was something queer coming over him latterly. Whenever I'd bring in his soup to him there I'd find him with his breviary[7] fallen on the floor, lying back in the 255 chair and his mouth open.

She laid a finger against her nose and frowned: then she continued:

—But still and all he kept on saying that before the summer was over he'd go out for a drive one fine day just to see the old 260 house again where we were all born down in Irishtown[8] and take me and Nannie with him. If we could only get one of them newfangled carriages that makes no noise that Father O'Rourke told him about—them with the rheumatic wheels[9]— for the day cheap, he said, at Johnny Rush's[1] over the way there 265 and drive out the three of us together of a Sunday evening. He had his mind set on that. ... Poor James!

—The Lord have mercy on his soul! said my aunt.

Eliza took out her handkerchief and wiped her eyes with it. Then she put it back again in her pocket and gazed into the 270 empty grate for some time without speaking.

—He was too scrupulous[2] always, she said. The duties of the priesthood was too much for him. And then his life was, you might say, crossed.

—Yes, said my aunt, he was a disappointed man. You could 275 see that.

A silence took possession of the little room and under cover of it I approached the table and tasted my sherry and then returned quietly to my chair in the corner. Eliza seemed to have

---

246 that. ....] STET MS   262 If] If ⟨h⟩ MS   263 newfangled] 10; new-fashioned MS
265 the way] 10; ABSENT MS

6. Beef broth or clear soup, so called because it has the color of tea.
7. A prayer book with prayers for each part of the day that were recited daily by priests.
8. A poor working-class slum in the south of Dublin at the time of the story.
9. Eliza means to say "pneumatic" wheels—that is, a carriage equipped with tires inflated with air to create a quieter and more comfortable ride. "Rheumatic" refers to a variety of medical disorders of the joints or heart.
1. A Dublin rental establishment for carriages and cars.
2. Overly conscientious about moral matters, to the point of being unable to act.

fallen into a deep revery. We waited respectfully for her to   280
break the silence: and after a long pause she said slowly:
—It was that chalice he broke. ... That was what was the
beginning of it. Of course, they say it was all right, that it
contained nothing,[3] I mean. But still .... They say it was the
boy's fault. But poor James was so nervous, God be merciful to   285
him!
—And was that it? said my aunt. I heard something. ....
     Eliza nodded.
—That affected his mind, she said. After that he began to
mope by himself, talking to no-one and wandering about by   290
himself. So one night he was wanted for to go on a call and
they couldn't find him anywhere. They looked high up and low
down and still they couldn't see a sight of him anywhere. So
then the clerk suggested to try the chapel. So then they got the
keys and opened the chapel and the clerk and Father O'Rourke   295
and another priest that was there brought in a light for to look
for him. .... And what do you think but there he was, sitting up
by himself in the dark in his confession box, wideawake and
laughing-like softly to himself?
     She stopped suddenly as if to listen. I too listened but there   300
was no sound in the house and I knew that the old priest was
lying still in his coffin as we had seen him, solemn and
truculent in death, an idle chalice on his breast.
     Eliza resumed:
—Wideawake and laughing-like to himself. ... So then of   305
course when they saw that that made them think that there was
something gone wrong with him. ....

An Encounter

It was Joe Dillon who introduced the wild west to us. He had
a little library made up of old numbers of *The Union Jack,*
Pluck and *The Halfpenny Marvel.*[1] Every evening after school

293 sight] 10; sign MS   294 then(2)] ⁻¹'then¹ᶠ MS

3. Had the chalice contained a consecrated wafer already transformed into the body of
   Christ, the spilling of its contents would have been an act of desecration.

Copy-text: Manuscript Yale 2.2 (MS); Collated texts: 1910 late proofs (10); 1914 proofs (14P)
and 1914 first edition (14) [IDENTITY IN BOTH IS REPORTED AS '14']; 1967 Viking edition in the
1969 Viking Critical Library printing (67).

1. Adventure magazines for boys, published by Alfred C. Harmsworth. Although they claimed
   to provide wholesome entertainment, their content was sometimes violent or otherwise
   sensational.

we met in his back garden and arranged Indian battles.[2] He and
his fat young brother Leo, the idler, held the loft of the stable
while we tried to carry it by storm; or we fought a pitched
battle on the grass. But, however well we fought, we never won
siege or battle and all our bouts ended with Joe Dillon's
wardance of victory. His parents went to eight-o'clock mass
every morning in Gardiner Street[3] and the peaceful odour of
Mrs Dillon was prevalent in the hall of the house. But he
played too fiercely for us who were younger and more timid.
He looked like some kind of an Indian when he capered round
the garden, an old teacosy[4] on his head, beating a tin with his
fist and yelling:
—Ya! Yaka, yaka, yaka![5]
Everyone was incredulous when it was reported that he had
a vocation[6] for the priesthood. Nevertheless it was true.
A spirit of unruliness diffused itself among us and, under its
influence, differences of culture and constitution were waived.
We banded ourselves together, some boldly, some in jest and
some almost in fear: and of the number of these latter, the
reluctant Indians who were afraid to seem studious or lacking
in robustness, I was one. The adventures related in the litera=
ture of the wild west were remote from my nature but, at least,
they opened doors of escape. I liked better some American
detective stories which were traversed from time to time by
unkempt fierce and beautiful girls. Though there was nothing
wrong in these stories and though their intention was some=
times literary they were circulated secretly at school. One day
when Father Butler was hearing the four pages of Roman
history clumsy Leo Dillon was discovered with a copy of *The
Halfpenny Marvel*.
—This page or this page? This page? Now, Dillon, up! *Hardly
had the day* .... Go on! What day? *Hardly had the day dawned*[7]
..... Have you studied it? What have you there in your pocket?
Everyone's heart palpitated as Leo Dillon handed up the
paper and everyone assumed an innocent face. Father Butler
turned over the pages, frowning.
—What is this rubbish? he said. *The Apache Chief!* Is this

2. Stories of battles with Native Americans (Indians) set in the "wild" West were a staple of
   boys' magazines.
3. The Dillons, attending daily mass at St. Francis Xavier Jesuit church, were clearly very
   devout.
4. A quilted covering for a teapot to retain the heat.
5. Imitation of a Native American ritual chant.
6. A spiritual calling to become a priest.
7. The opening of several accounts of military campaigns in Julius Caesar's Gallic Wars
   (*Commentarii de Bello Gallico*).

what you read instead of studying your Roman history? Let me
not find any more of this wretched stuff in this college.[8] The
man who wrote it, I suppose, was some wretched scribbler that
writes these things for a drink. I'm surprised at boys like you,
educated, reading such stuff. I could understand it if you   45
were ..... national school boys.[9] Now, Dillon, I advise you
strongly, get at your work or .....

This rebuke during the sober hours of school paled much of
the glory of the wild west for me and the confused puffy face of
Leo Dillon awakened one of my consciences. But when the   50
restraining influence of the school was at a distance I began to
hunger again for wild sensations, for the escape which those
chronicles of disorder alone seemed to offer me. The mimic
warfare of the evening became at last as wearisome to me as
the routine of school in the morning because I wanted real   55
adventures to happen to myself. But real adventures, I reflected,
do not happen to people who remain at home: they must be
sought abroad.

The summer holidays were near at hand when I made up my
mind to break out of the weariness of school life for one day at   60
least. With Leo Dillon and a boy named Mahony I planned a
day's miching.[1] Each of us saved up sixpence. We were to meet
at ten in the morning on the canal bridge.[2] Mahony's big sister
was to write an excuse for him and Leo Dillon was to tell his
brother to say he was sick. We arranged to go along the Wharf   65
Road[3] until we came to the ships, then to cross in the ferryboat
and walk out to see the Pigeon House.[4] Leo Dillon was afraid
we might meet Father Butler or someone out of the college, but
Mahony asked, very sensibly, what would Father Butler be
doing out at the Pigeon House. We were reassured: and I   70
brought the first stage of the plot to an end by collecting
sixpence from the other two, at the same time showing them
my own sixpence. When we were making the last arrangements
on the eve we were all vaguely excited. We shook hands,
laughing, and Mahony said: 75

43 scribbler] 10; fellow MS   48 paled] 10; blenched MS   65 to say] ⁷¹to say¹ʳ MS
68 might] 10; would MS

8. Presumably Belvedere College, a highly regarded Jesuit day school for boys, attended by
   James Joyce.
9. The National Schools were public schools that emphasized vocational and trade courses
   rather than an academic curriculum.
1. Truancy or playing hooky.
2. A bridge over the Royal Canal in northeast Dublin.
3. A road along a sea wall that keeps the delta of the Tolka river, and Dublin Bay into which
   it empties, from flooding the surrounding area.
4. Originally a fort, the building housed the Dublin electricity and power station.

—Till tomorrow, mates!

That night I slept badly. In the morning I was firstcomer to
the bridge as I lived nearest. I hid my books in the long grass
near the ashpit at the end of the garden where nobody ever
came and hurried along the canal bank. It was a mild sunny   80
morning in the first week of June. I sat up on the coping of the
bridge admiring my frail canvas shoes which I had diligently
pipeclayed[5] overnight and watching the docile horses pulling a
tramload of business people up the hill. All the branches of the
tall trees which lined the mall[6] were gay with little light green   85
leaves and the sunlight slanted through them on to the water.
The granite stone of the bridge was beginning to be warm and I
began to pat it with my hands in time to an air[7] in my head. I
was very happy.

When I had been sitting there for five or ten minutes I saw   90
Mahony's grey suit approaching. He came up the hill, smiling,
and clambered up beside me on the bridge. While we were
waiting he brought out the catapult[8] which bulged from his
inner pocket and explained some improvements which he had
made in it. I asked him why he had brought it and he told me   95
he had brought it to have some gas[9] with the birds. Mahony
used slang freely and spoke of Father Butler as Bunsen Burner.[1]
We waited on for a quarter of an hour more but still there was
no sign of Leo Dillon. Mahony, at last, jumped down and said:

—Come along. I knew Fatty'd funk it.[2]   100

—And his sixpence ... ? I said.

—That's forfeit, said Mahony. And so much the better for us
– a bob and a tanner[3] instead of a bob.

We walked along the North Strand Road till we came to the
vitriol works[4] and then turned to the right along the Wharf   105
Road. Mahony began to play the Indian as soon as we were out
of public sight. He chased a crowd of ragged girls, brandishing

92 we] ⟨we⟩ we MS   97 Bunsen Burner.] 10; Old Bunser. MS

5. Powder from a whitish clay was used to clean canvas shoes, forerunners of modern tennis
   shoes, or sneakers.
6. A sheltered, tree-lined walk that served as a promenade.
7. A melody.
8. A slingshot, or shooting toy, made from a forked stick and an elastic band.
9. Fun or mischief.
1. A gas burner used in chemistry laboratories.
2. Fat Leo Dillon would not have the nerve to go through with the plan.
3. A bob is slang for a shilling, and a tanner is slang for a sixpence. A shilling is worth twelve
   pence. Each boy's sixpence may have been worth a week or more of allowance. If Leo
   Dillon's sixpence is "forfeit" or lost as a penalty because he didn't show up, the two remaining boys would increase their money by a third.
4. Vitriol is a corrosive chemical, often sulfate of iron or some form of sulfuric acid. The
   Dublin Vitriol Works on Ballybough Road served as a landmark of the area, and indicates
   that the boys were wandering through industrial Dublin.

his unloaded catapult and, when two ragged boys[5] began, out of
chivalry, to fling stones at us, he proposed that we should
charge them. I objected that the boys were too small and so we
walked on, the ragged troop screaming after us *Swaddlers!*
Swaddlers!,[6] thinking that we were protestants because Ma=
hony, who was dark complexioned,[7] wore the silver badge of a
cricket club[8] in his cap. When we came to the Smoothing Iron[9]
we arranged a siege but it was a failure because you must have
at least three. We revenged ourselves on Leo Dillon by saying
what a funk he was and guessing how many he would get[1] at
three o'clock from Mr Ryan.

We came then near the river. We spent a long time walking
about the noisy streets flanked by high stone walls, watching
the working of cranes and engines and often being shouted at
for our immobility by the drivers of groaning carts. It was noon
when we reached the quays and, as all the labourers seemed to
be eating their lunches, we bought two big currant buns and sat
down to eat them on some metal piping beside the river. We
pleased ourselves with the spectacle of Dublin's commerce—
the barges signalled from far away by their curls of woolly
smoke, the brown fishing fleet beyond Ringsend,[2] the big white
sailing-vessel which was being discharged on the opposite
quay. Mahony said it would be right skit[3] to run away to sea on
one of those big ships and even I, looking at the high masts,
saw or imagined the geography which had been scantily dosed
to me at school gradually taking substance under my eyes.
School and home seemed to recede from us and their influences
upon us seemed to wane.

We crossed the Liffey in the ferryboat, paying our toll to be
transported in the company of two labourers and a little Jew
with a bag. We were serious to the point of solemnity but once
during the short voyage our eyes met and we laughed. When

108 unloaded] 10; empty MS   129 discharged] 10; unloaded MS   130 right] 10; great
MS

5. Protestant and Catholic "ragged schools" in Dublin were charitable institutions that provided free education and sometimes free food and clothing for very poor children.
6. A derisive nickname for Methodists in Ireland.
7. Possibly a reference to "the Black Irish," an American term for dark-haired—rather than
   fair or red-haired—Irish people believed to be of Spanish, indigenous, or even Phoenician
   descent.
8. Cricket is an outdoor game played with balls, bats, and wickets or small structures in the
   ground at which the ball is aimed. The game, which has remote similarities to both baseball
   and croquet, was brought to Ireland by the British.
9. A diving rock, in the shape of a pressing iron, at a bathing place near the Wharf Road.
1. How many strokes he would be given on the palm with a pandybat—a reinforced leather
   strap—as a punishment.
2. An area on the south bank of the river Liffey, near the sea.
3. Exciting or interesting.

we landed we watched the discharging of the graceful three=   140
master[4] which we had observed from the other quay. Some
bystander said that she was a Norwegian vessel. I went to the
stern and tried to decipher the legend upon it but, failing to do
so, I came back and examined the foreign sailors to see had any
of them green eyes[5] for I had some confused notion .... The   145
sailors' eyes were blue and grey and even black. The only sailor
whose eyes could have been called green was a tall man who
amused the crowd on the quay by calling out cheerfully every
time the planks fell:
—All right! All right!   150

When we were tired of this sight we wandered slowly into
Ringsend. The day had grown sultry and in the windows of the
grocers' shops musty biscuits lay bleaching. We bought some
biscuits and chocolate which we ate sedulously[6] as we wandered
through the squalid streets where the families of the fishermen   155
live. We could find no dairy and so we went into a huckster's
shop[7] and bought a bottle of raspberry lemonade each. Re=
freshed by this Mahony chased a cat down a lane but the cat
escaped into a wide field. We both felt rather tired and when
we reached the field we made at once for a sloping bank over   160
the ridge of which we could see the Dodder.[8]

It was too late and we were too tired to carry out our project
of visiting the Pigeon House. We had to be home before four
o'clock lest our adventure should be discovered. Mahony
looked regretfully at his catapult and I had to suggest going   165
home by train before he regained any cheerfulness. The sun
went in behind some clouds and left us to our jaded thoughts
and the crumbs of our provisions.

There was nobody but ourselves in the field. When we had
lain on the bank for some time without speaking I saw a man   170
approaching from the far end of the field. I watched him lazily
as I chewed one of those green stems on which girls tell
fortunes.[9] He came along by the bank slowly. He walked with
one hand upon his hip and in the other hand he held a stick
with which he tapped the turf lightly. He was shabbily dressed   175

140 discharging] 10; unloading MS   140–141 threemaster] 10; three-master MS

4. A sailing ship with three masts. Ships powered by sails were still a major vehicle for
transporting cargo at the time of the story.
5. The ellipsis makes the meaning of green eyes deliberately ambiguous. This ambiguity is
itself an important issue in the narration because it requires the reader to speculate as to
its meaning. In Joyce's day green might have been a code for homosexuality.
6. Diligently or with concentrated attention.
7. A booth or other small open space from which a retailer sells small goods.
8. A river that enters the river Liffey just south of where the Liffey flows into the sea.
9. A plant whose growth could be read as a romantic omen, like the plucking of daisy petals
to determine if "he loves me, he loves me not."

in a suit of greenish black and wore what we used to call a jerry hat[1] with a very high crown. He seemed to be fairly old for his moustache was ashen grey. When he passed at our feet he glanced up at us quickly and then continued his way. We followed him with our eyes and saw that when he had gone on for perhaps fifty paces he turned about and began to retrace his steps. He walked towards us very slowly, always tapping the ground with his stick, so slowly that I thought he was looking for something in the grass.

He stopped when he came level with us and bade us good day. We answered him and he sat down beside us on the slope slowly and with great care. He began to talk of the weather, saying that it would be a very hot summer and adding that the seasons had changed greatly since he was a boy—a long time ago. He said that the happiest time of one's life was un= doubtedly one's schoolboy days and that he would give any= thing to be young again. While he expressed these sentiments, which bored us a little, we kept silent. Then he began to talk of school and of books. He asked us whether we had read the poetry of Thomas Moore[2] or the works of Sir Walter Scott[3] and Lord Lytton.[4] I pretended that I had read every book he mentioned so that in the end he said:

—Ah, I can see you are a bookworm like myself. Now, he added, pointing to Mahony who was regarding us with open eyes, he is different. He goes in for games.

He said he had all Sir Walter Scott's works and all Lord Lytton's works at home and never tired of reading them. Of course, he said, there were some of Lord Lytton's works which boys couldn't read. Mahony asked why couldn't boys read them—a question which agitated and pained me because I was afraid the man would think I was as stupid as Mahony. The man, however, only smiled. I saw that he had great gaps in his mouth between his yellow teeth. Then he asked us which of us had the most sweethearts. Mahony mentioned lightly that he had three totties.[5] The man asked me how many had I. I answered that I had none. He did not believe me and said he was sure I must have one. I was silent.

180 him] ⌐¹him¹⌐ MS

1. A round felt hat.
2. Irish romantic poet (1779–1852) who wrote love songs and melodies.
3. Scottish novelist (1771–1832) who wrote romantic tales of adventure, often based on Scottish legends or historical events.
4. Edward Bulwer-Lytton (1803–1873) wrote romances and historical novels (e.g., *The Last Days of Pompeii*) thought by some to be sensationalistic.
5. Sweethearts, possibly of ill repute.

—Tell us, said Mahony pertly to the man, how many have you yourself?

The man smiled as before and said that when he was our age he had lots of sweethearts. Every boy, he said, has a little sweetheart.

His attitude on this point struck me as strangely liberal in a man of his age. In my heart I thought that what he said about boys and sweethearts was reasonable. But I disliked the words in his mouth and I wondered why he shivered once or twice as if he feared something or felt a sudden chill. As he proceeded I noticed that his accent was good.[6] He began to speak to us about girls, saying what nice soft hair they had and how soft their hands were and how all girls were not so good as they seemed to be if one only knew. There was nothing he liked, he said, so much as looking at a nice young girl, at her nice white hands and her beautiful soft hair. He gave me the impression that he was repeating something which he had learned by heart or that, magnetised by some words of his own speech, his mind was slowly circling round and round in the same orbit. At times he spoke as if he were simply alluding to some fact that everybody knew and at times he lowered his voice and spoke mysteriously as if he were telling us something secret which he did not wish others to overhear. He repeated his phrases over and over again, varying them and surrounding them with his monotonous voice. I continued to gaze towards the foot of the slope, listening to him.

After a long while his monologue paused. He stood up slowly, saying that he had to leave us for a minute or so, a few minutes, and, without changing the direction of my gaze, I saw him walking slowly away from us towards the near end of the field. We remained silent when he had gone. After a silence of a few minutes I heard Mahony exclaim:

—I say! Look what he's doing!

As I neither answered nor raised my eyes Mahony exclaimed again:

—I say ..... He's a queer old josser![7]

—In case he asks us for our names, I said, let you be Murphy and I'll be Smith.

We said nothing further to each other. I was still considering whether I would go away or not when the man came back and sat down beside us again. Hardly had he sat down when Ma=

---

216 Every] STET NO PARAGRAPH MS   216 has] 10; had MS   235 wish] ⁷¹wish¹ᴿ MS

6. He appeared educated and middle class, in spite of his shabby physical appearance.
7. A fellow or chap, perhaps a simpleton.

hony, catching sight of the cat which had escaped him, sprang
up and pursued her across the field. The man and I watched the   255
chase. The cat escaped once more and Mahony began to throw
stones at the wall she had escalated.[8] Desisting from this, he
began to wander about the far end of the field, aimlessly.

After an interval the man spoke to me. He said that my
friend was a very rough boy and asked did he get whipped   260
often at school. I was going to reply indignantly that we were
not national school boys to be *whipped*,[9] as he called it; but I
remained silent. He began to speak on the subject of chastising
boys. His mind, as if magnetised again by his speech, seemed to
circle slowly round and round its new centre. He said that   265
when boys were that kind they ought to be whipped and well
whipped. When a boy was rough and unruly there was nothing
would do him any good but a good sound whipping. A slap on
the hand or a box on the ear was no good: what he wanted was
to get a nice warm whipping. I was surprised at this sentiment   270
and involuntarily glanced up at his face. As I did so I met the
gaze of a pair of bottlegreen[1] eyes peering at me from under a
twitching forehead. I turned my eyes away again.

The man continued his monologue. He seemed to have
forgotten his recent liberalism. He said that if ever he found a 275
boy talking to girls or having a girl for a sweetheart he would
whip him and whip him: and that would teach him not to be
talking to girls. And if a boy had a girl for a sweetheart and
told lies about it then he would give him such a whipping as no
boy ever got in this world. He said that there was nothing in   280
this world he would like so well as that. He described to me
how he would whip such a boy as if he were unfolding some
elaborate mystery. He would love that, he said, better than
anything in this world: and his voice, as he led me monot=
onously through the mystery, grew almost affectionate and   285
seemed to plead with me that I should understand him.

I waited till his monologue paused again. Then I stood up
abruptly. Lest I should betray my agitation I delayed a few
moments pretending to fix my shoe properly and then, saying
that I was obliged to go, I bade him good day. I went up the   290

263 subject] subject(s) MS   272 bottlegreen] e:10; sage-green MS; bottle green 10
275 ever he] 10; he ever MS   279 then--give] 10; the MS [MS TORN]   284 this] 10; the
MS   284 led] le⟨a⟩d MS

8. Scaled or climbed upon.
9. The National Schools were the Irish counterpart to what are called public schools in the
   United States. By implication, discipline in these schools would have been harsher, with
   more frequent use of the cane, than in the private Jesuit school the narrator and Mahony
   attend.
1. The green color of beverage bottles such as those that hold beer.

slope calmly but my heart was beating quickly with fear that he
would seize me by the ankles. When I reached the top of the
slope I turned round and, without looking at him, called loudly
across the field:

—Murphy!   295

My voice had an accent of forced bravery in it and I was
ashamed of my paltry stratagem. I had to call the name again
before Mahony saw me and hallooed in answer. How my heart
beat as he came running across the field to me! He ran as if to
bring me aid. And I was penitent for in my heart I had always   300
despised him a little.

Araby

North Richmond Street, being blind,[1] was a quiet street ex=
cept at the hour when the Christian Brothers' School[2] set the
boys free. An uninhabited house of two storeys stood at the
blind end, detached from its neighbours in a square ground.
The other houses of the street, conscious of decent lives within   5
them, gazed at one another with brown imperturbable faces.[3]

The former tenant of our house, a priest, had died in the
back drawingroom. Air, musty from having been long en=
closed, hung in all the rooms and the waste room behind the
kitchen was littered with old useless papers. Among these I   10
found a few papercovered books, the pages of which were
curled and damp: *The Abbot* by Walter Scott,[4] *The Devout
Communicant*[5] and *The Memoirs of Vidocq*.[6] I liked the last best
because its leaves were yellow. The wild garden behind the
house contained a central apple tree and a few straggling   15
bushes under one of which I found the late tenant's rusty
bicycle pump. He had been a very charitable priest; in his will
he had left all his money to institutions and the furniture of his
house to his sister.

Copy-text: 1910 late proofs (10); Collated texts: 1914 proofs (14P) and 1914 first edition
(14) [IDENTITY IN BOTH IS REPORTED AS '14']; 1967 Viking edition in the 1969 Viking Critical
Library printing (67).

1. A dead-end street or cul-de-sac in the northeast section of Dublin, off the North Circular
   Road.
2. A day school for boys taught by the Christian Brothers, an order of Roman Catholic lay
   clergy who had taken temporary vows. Its curriculum, aimed at poor children, emphasized
   vocational rather than academic education.
3. The houses were solidly made of brown brick.
4. A heroic novel about a page serving Mary, Queen of Scots, during her imprisonment.
5. A book of pious meditations on the sacrament of Holy Communion, written by an English
   friar, Pacificus Baker, in 1813.
6. The putative autobiographical account of a criminal, informer, and detective named
   François-Jules Vidocq (1775–1857).

When the short days of winter came dusk fell before we had   20
well eaten our dinners. When we met in the street the houses
had grown sombre. The space of sky above us was the colour
of everchanging violet and towards it the lamps of the street
lifted their feeble lanterns. The cold air stung us and we played
till our bodies glowed. Our shouts echoed in the silent street.   25
The career of our play brought us through the dark muddy
lanes behind the houses where we ran the gantlet[7] of the rough
tribes from the cottages,[8] to the back doors of the dark dripping
gardens where odours arose from the ashpits,[9] to the dark
odorous stables where a coachman smoothed and combed the   30
horse or shook music from the buckled harness. When we re=
turned to the street light from the kitchen windows had filled
the areas. If my uncle was seen turning the corner we hid in the
shadow until we had seen him safely housed. Or if Mangan's
sister[1] came out on the doorstep to call her brother in to his tea   35
we watched her from our shadow peer up and down the street.
We waited to see whether she would remain or go in and if she
remained we left our shadow and walked up to Mangan's steps
resignedly. She was waiting for us, her figure defined by the
light from the half-opened door. Her brother always teased her   40
before he obeyed and I stood by the railings looking at her. Her
dress swung as she moved her body and the soft rope of her
hair tossed from side to side.

Every morning I lay on the floor in the front parlour
watching her door. The blind was pulled down to within an   45
inch of the sash so that I could not be seen. When she came out
on the doorstep my heart leaped. I ran to the hall, seized my
books and followed her. I kept her brown figure always in my
eye and when we came near the point at which our ways
diverged I quickened my pace and passed her. This happened   50
morning after morning. I had never spoken to her except for a
few casual words and yet her name was like a summons to all
my foolish blood.

Her image accompanied me even in places the most hostile
to romance. On Saturday evenings when my aunt went market=   55
ing I had to go to carry some of the parcels. We walked through
the flaring streets, jostled by drunken men and bargaining
women, amid the curses of labourers, the shrill litanies of shop

---

7. A trial consisting of two facing rows of armed men ready to strike a person forced to run
   between them (as in "running the gauntlet").
8. Richmond Cottages, off Richmond Street, housed the very poor with many children.
9. Dumping places in the garden for ashes, garbage, and other refuse.
1. The children's last name of Mangan recalls an Irish romantic poet named James Clarence
   Mangan (1803–1849). Mangan, like poets such as Byron and Shelley, was fascinated by
   the mythic quality that hung over notions of the Middle East.

boys who stood on guard by the barrels of pigs' cheeks,[2] the
nasal chanting of street singers who sang a *come-all-you*[3] about   60
O'Donovan Rossa[4] or a ballad about the troubles in our native
land.[5] These noises converged in a single sensation of life for
me: I imagined that I bore my chalice safely through a throng
of foes.[6] Her name sprang to my lips at moments in strange
prayers and praises which I myself did not understand. My eyes   65
were often full of tears (I could not tell why) and at times a
flood from my heart seemed to pour itself out into my bosom. I
thought little of the future. I did not know whether I would
ever speak to her or not or, if I spoke to her, how I could tell
her of my confused adoration. But my body was like a harp   70
and her words and gestures were like fingers running upon the
wires.

One evening I went into the back drawingroom in which the
priest had died. It was a dark rainy evening and there was no
sound in the house. Through one of the broken panes I heard   75
the rain impinge upon the earth, the fine incessant needles of
water playing in the sodden beds. Some distant lamp or lighted
window gleamed below me. I was thankful that I could see so
little. All my senses seemed to desire to veil themselves and,
feeling that I was about to slip from them, I pressed the palms   80
of my hands together until they trembled, murmuring: *O love!
O love!* many times.

At last she spoke to me. When she addressed the first words
to me I was so confused that I did not know what to answer.
She asked me was I going to *Araby*. I forget whether I answered   85
yes or no. It would be a splendid bazaar,[7] she said; she would
love to go.
—And why can't you? I asked.

While she spoke she turned a silver bracelet round and
round her wrist. She could not go, she said, because there   90

86 said;] STET 10

2. Inexpensive pieces of pork, less nutritious and less usable in cooking.
3. A traditional type of song performed in pubs and other public places that began with the
   invitation "Come all you gallant Irishmen and listen to my song" before addressing some
   topic of current interest.
4. A nickname given to the Irish rebel leader Jeremiah O'Donovan (1831–1915). Because he
   was born in a place called Ross Carberry and advocated violent political action, he was
   also known as "Dynamite Rossa."
5. Many ballads and popular songs lamented Irish suffering during centuries of British
   occupation.
6. A possible reference to the Holy Grail, the vessel used by Jesus Christ at the Last Supper
   that disappeared, according to some versions of the legend, after Joseph of Arimathea used
   it to collect Christ's blood at the cross. The legend inspired numerous romances of heroes
   incurring dangerous adventures in quest of the sacred relic.
7. A charity bazaar called a "Grand Oriental Fête" was held in Dublin in May 1894 for the
   benefit of the Jervis Street Hospital. The actual bazaar is reputed to have been much larger
   and more lavish than the story's narration suggests.

would be a retreat that week in her convent.[8] Her brother and
two other boys were fighting for their caps and I was alone at
the railings. She held one of the spikes, bowing her head to=
wards me. The light from the lamp opposite our door caught
the white curve of her neck, lit up the hair that rested there   95
and, falling, lit up the hand upon the railing. It fell over one
side of her dress and caught the white border of a petticoat, just
visible as she stood at ease.
—It's well for you, she said.[9]
—If I go, I said, I will bring you something.   100
    What innumerable follies laid waste my waking and sleeping
thoughts after that evening! I wished to annihilate the tedious
intervening days. I chafed against the work of school. At night
in my bedroom and by day in the classroom her image came
between me and the page I strove to read. The syllables of the   105
word *Araby* were called to me through the silence in which my
soul luxuriated and cast an eastern enchantment over me. I
asked for leave to go to the bazaar on Saturday night. My aunt
was surprised and hoped it was not some freemason affair.[1] I
answered few questions in class. I watched my master's face   110
pass from amiability to sternness; he hoped I was not beginning
to idle. I could not call my wandering thoughts together. I had
hardly any patience with the serious work of life which, now
that it stood between me and my desire, seemed to me child's
play, ugly monotonous child's play.   115
    On Saturday morning I reminded my uncle that I wished to
go to the bazaar in the evening. He was fussing at the hallstand,
looking for the hatbrush, and answered me curtly:
—Yes, boy, I know.
    As he was in the hall I could not go into the front parlour   120
and lie at the window. I left the house in bad humour and
walked slowly towards the school. The air was pitilessly raw
and already my heart misgave me.
    When I came home to dinner my uncle had not yet been
home. Still it was early. I sat staring at the clock for some time 125
and when its ticking began to irritate me I left the room. I
mounted the staircase and gained the upper part of the house.

95 the (2)] STET 10

8. Convent schools, like the one the girl presumably attends, held regular religious retreats
   that obliged students to turn their attention away from worldly concerns and toward spiritual matters.
9. The girl's words imply that the boy is lucky he can attend the bazaar if he wishes.
1. Freemasons were a secret brotherhood (of Free and Accepted Masons) evolved from a
   medieval guild of builders and bricklayers. Although the Freemasons also sponsored charitable bazaars like the one in the story, Roman Catholics regarded the society as heathen
   and hostile to its interests.

The high cold empty gloomy rooms liberated me and I went
from room to room singing. From the front window I saw my
companions playing below in the street. Their cries reached me   130
weakened and indistinct and, leaning my forehead against the
cool glass, I looked over at the dark house where she lived. I
may have stood there for an hour seeing nothing but the
brownclad figure cast by my imagination, touched discreetly by
the lamplight at the curved neck, at the hand upon the railings   135
and at the border below the dress.

When I came downstairs again I found Mrs Mercer sitting at
the fire. She was an old garrulous woman, a pawnbroker's[2]
widow who collected used stamps for some pious purpose.[3] I
had to endure the gossip of the teatable. The meal was   140
prolonged beyond an hour and still my uncle did not come.
Mrs Mercer stood up to go: she was sorry she couldn't wait
any longer but it was after eight o'clock and she did not like to
be out late as the night air was bad for her. When she had gone
I began to walk up and down the room, clenching my fists. My   145
aunt said:

—I'm afraid you may put off your bazaar for this night of Our
Lord.[4]

At nine o'clock I heard my uncle's latchkey in the halldoor. I
heard him talking to himself and heard the hallstand rocking   150
when it had received the weight of his overcoat. I could
interpret these signs. When he was midway through his dinner I
asked him to give me the money to go to the bazaar. He had
forgotten.

—The people are in bed and after their first sleep now, he said.   155

I did not smile. My aunt said to him energetically:

—Can't you give him the money and let him go? You've kept
him late enough as it is.

My uncle said he was very sorry he had forgotten. He said
he believed in the old saying: *All work and no play makes Jack*   160
a dull boy. He asked me where I was going and when I had told
him a second time he asked me did I know *The Arab's Farewell*
to his Steed.[5] When I left the kitchen he was about to recite the
opening lines of the piece to my aunt.

2. Someone who lends or offers money against the security of some valuable object that is
   deposited in his or her shop. If the recipient of the money cannot repay it by a certain
   time, the "pawned" object becomes the property of the pawnbroker and may be resold
   legally.
3. The Catholic Church supported some of its foreign missionary enterprises by collecting
   used stamps that could be sold to stamp-collecting outlets for cash.
4. Possibly a reference to Saturday night, the eve of the Sunday sabbath.
5. A sentimental poem by Caroline Norton (1808–1877) in which a fictional Arab bids farewell to the horse he has sold ("Fleet-limbed and beautiful, farewell!—thou'rt sold, my
   steed, thou'rt sold!") before he reverses his decision ("I fling them back their gold") and
   rides off on his steed.

I held a florin[6] tightly in my hand as I strode down Bucking= 165
ham Street[7] towards the station. The sight of the streets
thronged with buyers and glaring with gas recalled to me the
purpose of my journey. I took my seat in a third class carriage
of a deserted train. After an intolerable delay the train moved
out of the station slowly. It crept onward among ruinous 170
houses and over the twinkling river. At Westland Row Station[8] a
crowd of people pressed at the carriage doors; but the porters
moved them back, saying that it was a special train for the
bazaar. I remained alone in the bare carriage. In a few minutes
the train drew up beside an improvised wooden platform. I 175
passed out on to the road and saw by the lighted dial of a clock
that it was ten minutes to ten. In front of me was a large
building which displayed the magical name.

I could not find any sixpenny entrance and, fearing that the
bazaar would be closed, I passed in quickly through a turnstile, 180
handing a shilling[9] to a wearylooking man. I found myself in a
big hall girdled at half its height by a gallery. Nearly all the
stalls were closed and the greater part of the hall was in
darkness. I recognised a silence like that which pervades a
church after a service. I walked into the centre of the bazaar 185
timidly. A few people were gathered about the stalls which
were still open. Before a curtain over which the words *Café
Chantant*[1] were written in coloured lamps two men were count=
ing money on a salver.[2] I listened to the fall of the coins.

Remembering with difficulty why I had come I went over to 190
one of the stalls and examined porcelain vases and flowered
teasets. At the door of the stall a young lady was talking and
laughing with two young gentlemen. I remarked their English
accents[3] and listened vaguely to their conversation.

—O, I never said such a thing! 195
—O, but you did!
—O, but I didn't!

---

172 at] STET 10   182 its] STET 10

6. A two-shilling coin. The sum would represent four sixpence—that is, a sixpence more than the three boys in "An Encounter" collect for their truant expedition.
7. A street leading southward from North Richmond Street toward the Amiens Street train station the boy will use to get to the bazaar.
8. A heavily trafficked train station in downtown Dublin.
9. If the boy begins with two shillings and spends one shilling for admission to the bazaar, he has now spent over half of his money and still has his return train fare to pay.
1. A French coffeehouse at the bazaar that would also present musical and other entertainments.
2. A possible reference to the story in the New Testament (Matthew 21:12–13) that tells how Jesus drove the moneychangers out of the temple because they defiled a house of prayer.
3. The young people at the stall are British rather than Irish. The dialogue suggests that the young lady is flirting with the young gentlemen.

—Didn't she say that?

—She did. I heard her.

—O, there's a ... fib!   200

Observing me the young lady came over and asked me did I wish to buy anything. The tone of her voice was not encour= aging: she seemed to have spoken to me out of a sense of duty. I looked humbly at the great jars that stood like eastern guards at either side of the dark entrance to her stall and murmured: 205

—No, thank you.

The young lady changed the position of one of the vases and went back to the two young men. They began to talk of the same subject. Once or twice the young lady glanced at me over her shoulder.   210

I lingered before her stall, though I knew my stay was useless, to make my interest in her wares seem the more real. Then I turned away slowly and walked down the middle of the bazaar. I allowed the two pennies to fall against the sixpence[4] in my pocket. I heard a voice call from one end of the gallery that 215 the light was out. The upper part of the hall was now com= pletely dark.

Gazing up into the darkness I saw myself as a creature driven and derided by vanity: and my eyes burned with anguish and anger.   220

Eveline

She sat at the window watching the evening invade the av= enue. Her head was leaned against the window curtains and in her nostrils was the odour of dusty cretonne.[1] She was tired.

Few people passed. The man out of the last house passed on

---

199 —She did.] STET 10   205 her] STET 10

4. If the boy began with two shillings, he began with twenty-four pence, since there are twelve pence in a shilling. We know that he spent a shilling, or twelve pence, on admission. If he now has eight pence remaining, his train fare must have cost four pence. If he rides rather than walks the more than two miles home, he would have had only four pence to spend on the gift or souvenir for Mangan's sister—a very small sum.

Copy-text: 1910 late proofs (10); Collated texts: *The Irish Homestead* OF SEPTEMBER 10, 1904 (IH) [SUBSTANTIVE IH VARIANTS ONLY ARE REPORTED IN THESE FOOTNOTES; 1914 proofs (14P) and 1914 first edition (14) [IDENTITY IN BOTH IS REPORTED AS '14']; 1967 Viking edition in the 1969 Viking Critical Library printing (67).

2 window curtains] window-curtain, IH   4 Few] NO PARAGRAPH IH

1. Strong printed cotton fabric used for curtains and upholstery.

his way home; she heard his footsteps clacking along the   5
concrete pavement and afterwards crunching on the cinder
path before the new red houses. One time there used to be a
field there in which they used to play every evening with other
people's children. Then a man from Belfast[2] bought the field
and built houses in it—not like their little brown houses but   10
bright brick houses with shining roofs. The children of the
avenue used to play together in that field—the Devines, the
Waters, the Dunns, little Keogh the cripple, she and her
brothers and sisters. Ernest, however, never played: he was too
grown up. Her father used often to hunt them in out of the   15
field with his blackthorn stick[3] but usually little Keogh used to
keep nix[4] and call out when he saw her father coming. Still they
seemed to have been rather happy then. Her father was not so
bad then, and besides her mother was alive. That was a long
time ago; she and her brothers and sisters were all grown up;   20
her mother was dead. Tizzie Dunn was dead, too, and the
Waters had gone back to England. Everything changes. Now
she was going to go away like the others, to leave her home.

Home! She looked round the room reviewing all its familiar
objects which she had dusted once a week for so many years,   25
wondering where on earth all the dust came from. Perhaps she
would never see again those familiar objects from which she
had never dreamed of being divided. And yet during all those
years she had never found out the name of the priest whose
yellowing photograph hung on the wall above the broken   30
harmonium[5] beside the coloured print of the promises made to
Blessed Margaret Mary Alacoque.[6] He had been a school friend
of her father's. Whenever he showed the photograph to a
visitor her father used to pass it with a casual word:

8 every] in the IH   17 nix] STET 10   21 Tizzie] 14; Mrs. IH; Mrs 10; This 14P
23 away--others,] away, IH   24 reviewing] passing in review IH   25–28 objects--
divided.] objects. How many times she had dusted it, once a week at least. It was the "best"
room, but it seemed to secrete dust everywhere. She had known the room for ten years—
more—twelve years, and knew everything in it. Now she was going away. IH   29 priest]
Australian priest IH   30 wall] wall, just IH   31–32 harmonium--Alacoque.]harmonium.
IH   32–33 school--father's.] friend of her father's—a school friend. IH   33 Whenever]
When IH   34 visitor] friend, IH

2. Possibly a Protestant from the more prosperous north of Ireland.
3. A stout walking stick made from the stem of the blackthorn shrub.
4. A slang term used as an exclamation of warning.
5. A reed organ or keyboard instrument whose sound was produced by vibrating a reed or
   other material with currents of air.
6. St. Margaret Mary Alacoque (1647–1690) was a French nun who fostered devotion to the
   Sacred Heart of Jesus. A divine visitation had disclosed to her twelve "promises" made by
   Christ to the faithful who honored him. The first five promises were (1) I will give them
   all the grace necessary in their state of life, (2) I will establish peace in their homes, (3) I
   will comfort them in all their afflictions, (4) I will be their secure refuge in life, and above
   all in death, (5) I will bestow abundant blessings on all their undertakings. Pope Pius IX
   declared her blessed in 1864. She was canonized and made a saint in 1920.

—He is in Melbourne[7] now.   35

She had consented to go away, to leave her home. Was that wise? She tried to weigh each side of the question. In her home anyway she had shelter and food; she had those whom she had known all her life about her. Of course she had to work hard both in the house and at business. What would they say of her   40 in the stores[8] when they found out that she had run away with a fellow? Say she was a fool, perhaps; and her place would be filled up by advertisement. Miss Gavan would be glad. She had always had an edge on her, especially whenever there were people listening.   45

—Miss Hill, don't you see these ladies are waiting?

—Look lively, Miss Hill, please.

She would not cry many tears at leaving the stores.

But in her new home, in a distant unknown country, it would not be like that. Then she would be married—she,   50 Eveline. People would treat her with respect then. She would not be treated as her mother had been. Even now, though she was over nineteen, she sometimes felt herself in danger of her father's violence. She knew it was that that had given her the palpitations.[9] When they were growing up he had never gone   55 for her, like he used to go for Harry and Ernest, because she was a girl; but latterly he had begun to threaten her and say what he would do to her only for her dead mother's sake. And now she had nobody to protect her. Ernest was dead and Harry, who was in the church decorating business, was nearly   60 always down somewhere in the country. Besides, the invariable squabble for money on Saturday nights had begun to weary her unspeakably. She always gave her entire wages—seven shillings —and Harry always sent up what he could but the trouble was

35 —He--now.] "In Australia now—Melbourne." IH   36–37 Was--wise?] Was it wise— was it honourable? IH   37 question.] question in her mind. IH   37–38 home anyway] 14P; home at least IH; home, anyway, 10   39 Of--hard] She had to work of course IH   40 say] think IH   41 found out] discovered IH   41–42 run--fellow?] gone away? IH   42 Say she was] Think her IH   42–43 and--up] and fill up her place IH   43 would-- glad.] would probably be glad. She, too, would not be sorry to be out of Miss Gavan's clutches. IH   43 She] Miss Gavan IH   43–44 had--had] had IH   44 her,] her, and used her superior position mercilessly, IH   44 especially] particularly IH   46 —Miss--waiting?] It was—"Miss Hill, will you please attend to these ladies?" IH   47 —Look lively,] "A little bit smarter, IH   47 please.] if you please." IH   48 She] NO PARAGRAPH IH   49 But] NO PARAGRAPH IH   49–50 it--that.] surely she would be free from such indignities! IH   50–51 Then--then.] She would then be a married woman—she, Eveline. She would be treated with respect. IH   52 been.] been treated. IH   52–53 now,--nine=teen,] now— at her age, she was over nineteen— IH   54–57 She--latterly] Latterly IH   57 her and say] her, saying IH   58 to her] ABSENT IH   58 only] were it not IH   62 nights] night IH

7. Melbourne, Australia, was a common destination for Irish immigrants in the nineteenth century.
8. Possibly Pim's retail store on Great George's Street; it sold clothing and household goods.
9. Increased activity of the heart brought on by stress, agitation, or disease.

to get any money from her father. He said she used to squander 65
the money, that she had no head, that he wasn't going to give
her his hard earned money to throw about the streets and much
more for he was usually fairly bad[1] of a Saturday night. In the
end he would give her the money and ask her had she any
intention of buying Sunday's dinner. Then she had to rush out 70
as quickly as she could and do her marketing, holding her black
leather purse tightly in her hand as she elbowed her way
through the crowds and returning home late under her load of
provisions. She had hard work to keep the house together and
to see that the two young children who had been left to her 75
charge went to school regularly and got their meals regularly. It
was hard work—a hard life—but now that she was about to
leave it she did not find it a wholly undesirable life.

   She was about to explore another life with Frank. Frank was
very kind, manly, openhearted. She was to go away with him 80
by the night boat[2] to be his wife and to live with him in Buenos
Ayres[3] where he had a home waiting for her. How well she
remembered the first time she had seen him; he was lodging in
a house on the main road where she used to visit. It seemed a
few weeks ago. He was standing at the gate, his peaked cap 85
pushed back on his head and his hair tumbled forward over a
face of bronze. Then they had come to know each other. He
used to meet her outside the stores every evening and see her
home. He took her to see the *Bohemian Girl*[4] and she felt elated
as she sat in an unaccustomed part of the theatre with him. He 90
was awfully fond of music and sang a little. People knew that
they were courting and when he sang about the lass that loves a
sailor[5] she always felt pleasantly confused. He used to call her
Poppens[6] out of fun. First of all it had been an excitement for
her to have a fellow and then she had begun to like him. He 95
had tales of distant countries. He had started as a deck boy[7] at a

---

68 of a] on IH   84–85 It--ago.] A few weeks ago it seemed. IH   91 awfully] very IH
92 he] Frank IH   94 of all] ABSENT IH   95 fellow] young man, IH

1. Belligerently drunken.
2. A ship or ferry, possibly carrying mail and goods in addition to passengers, departing
   Dublin at night. Many such ships stopped in Liverpool, where passengers bound for over-
   seas destinations could change to other ships.
3. The capital of Argentina in South America, a destination for Irish immigrants seeking
   agricultural and other work in the nineteenth century.
4. An 1843 operetta with music by the Irish composer Michael Balfe and libretto by Alfred
   Bunn. The story concerns a girl from a noble family who is kidnapped by gypsies but
   eventually restored to her home after many intrigues.
5. Popular old song by Charles Dibdin about the toasts that drunken sailors sing to their
   sweethearts and wives. It ends with the lines: "But the standing toast that pleas'd the most,
   / Was 'The wind that blows, / The ship that goes, / And the lass that loves a sailor.'"
6. Derived from "poppet," meaning doll, darling, or dainty person.
7. An inexperienced worker hired to help the crew on a ship with menial tasks and errands.

pound a month on a ship of the Allan line[8] going out to Canada. He told her the names of the ships he had been on and the names of the different services. He had sailed through the Straits of Magellan[9] and he told her stories of the terrible Patagonians.[1] He had fallen on his feet[2] in Buenos Ayres, he said, and had come over to the old country just for a holiday. Of course, her father had found out the affair and had forbidden her to have anything to say to him:

—I know these sailor chaps, he said.

One day he had quarrelled with Frank and after that she had to meet her lover secretly.

The evening deepened in the avenue. The white of two let= ters in her lap grew indistinct. One was to Harry, the other was to her father. Ernest had been her favourite but she liked Harry too. Her father was becoming old lately, she noticed; he would miss her. Sometimes he could be very nice. Not long before, when she had been laid up for a day, he had read her out a ghost story and made toast for her at the fire. Another day, when their mother was alive, they had all gone for a picnic to the Hill of Howth.[3] She remembered her father putting on her mother's bonnet to make the children laugh.

Her time was running out but she continued to sit by the window, leaning her head against the window curtain, inhaling the odour of dusty cretonne. Down far in the avenue she could hear a street organ[4] playing. She knew the air.[5] Strange that it should come that very night to remind her of the promise to her mother, her promise to keep the home together as long as she could. She remembered the last night of her mother's illness; she was again in the close dark room at the other side of the hall and outside she heard a melancholy air of Italy. The organ player had been ordered to go away and given sixpence. She remembered her father strutting back into the sickroom saying:

104 say to] do with IH   105 —I] "I NO PARAGRAPH IH   105 chaps,] e:10, 14; fellows," IH; chaps—10; chaps,' 14   105 he] her father IH   106 One--Frank] Frank and her father had quarrelled one day, IH   108–109 letters] 14P; letters lying IH, 10   114 made] had made IH   115 their] 14; her IH, 10; the 14P   122 the] 14P; her IH, 10

8. A steamship based in Liverpool, England, that made regular trips to the Pacific coasts of North and South America.
9. Sea passage at the tip of South America allowing ships to pass from the Atlantic Ocean to the Pacific, named after the Portuguese explorer Ferdinand Magellan.
1. The name given to a number of native tribes living at the tip of Argentina, who became fabled as exceptionally tall and fearsome.
2. Landed on his feet, achieved success.
3. A point of land projecting into the sea just northeast of Dublin. The promontory over the harbor has lovely views and is therefore a favored spot for outings.
4. A portable harmonium or reed organ generally played by itinerant musicians.
5. Melody.

—Damned Italians! coming over here![6]

As she mused the pitiful vision of her mother's life laid its   130
spell on the very quick of her being—that life of commonplace
sacrifices closing in final craziness. She trembled as she heard
again her mother's voice saying constantly with foolish insist=
ence:

—Derevaun Seraun! Derevaun Seraun![7]   135

She stood up in a sudden impulse of terror. Escape! She must
escape! Frank would save her. He would give her life, perhaps
love too. But she wanted to live. Why should she be unhappy?
She had a right to happiness. Frank would take her in his arms,
fold her in his arms. He would save her.   140

◆   ◆   ◆

She stood among the swaying crowd in the station at the
North Wall.[8] He held her hand and she knew that he was speak=
ing to her, saying something about the passage over and over
again. The station was full of soldiers with brown baggages.
Through the wide doors of the sheds she caught a glimpse of   145
the black mass of the boat lying in beside the quay wall, with
illumined portholes. She answered nothing. She felt her cheek
pale and cold and out of a maze of distress she prayed to God
to direct her, to show her what was her duty. The boat blew a
long mournful whistle into the mist. If she went, tomorrow she   150
would be on the sea with Frank, steaming towards Buenos
Ayres. Their passage had been booked. Could she still draw
back after all he had done for her? Her distress awoke a nausea
in her body and she kept moving her lips in silent fervent
prayer.   155

A bell clanged upon her heart. She felt him seize her hand:

—Come!

All the seas of the world tumbled about her heart. He was
drawing her into them: he would drown her. She gripped with
both hands at the iron railing.   160

—Come!

No! No! No! It was impossible. Her hands clutched the iron
in frenzy. Amid the seas she sent a cry of anguish.

129 —Damned] NO PARAGRAPH IH   130 As] NO PARAGRAPH IH   135 —Derevaun Seraun!] NO PARAGRAPH IH   137 would(2)] could IH   138 to live.] life. IH   145 doors--
sheds] door IH   157 —Come!] NO PARAGRAPH IH   161 —Come!] NO PARAGRAPH IH

6. Although there was no significant Italian immigration into Dublin at the time of the story,
   Italians who came to Ireland frequently held itinerant jobs as traveling artisans and vendors
   or performers.
7. Meaning unknown. Speculations include suggestions that the words may be corrupt
   Gaelic for "the end of pleasure is pain" or "the end of song is madness."
8. A dock for large ships on the north side of the river Liffey near where it empties into the
   sea.

—Eveline! Evvy!

He rushed beyond the barrier and called to her to follow. He   165
was shouted at to go on but he still called to her. She set her
white face to him, passive, like a helpless animal. Her eyes gave
him no sign of love or farewell or recognition.

After the Race[1]

The cars came scudding in towards Dublin, running evenly
like pellets in the groove of the Naas Road.[2] At the crest of the
hill at Inchicore[3] sightseers had gathered in clumps to watch the
cars careering homeward and through this channel of poverty
and inaction the continent sped its wealth and industry. Now   5
and again the clumps of people raised the cheer of the grate=
fully oppressed. Their sympathy, however, was for the blue
cars—the cars of their friends, the French.

The French, moreover, were virtual victors. Their team had
finished solidly; they had been placed second and third and the   10
driver of the winning German car was reported a Belgian.[4] Each
blue car,[5] therefore, received a double round of welcome as it
topped the crest of the hill and each cheer of welcome was
acknowledged with smiles and nods by those in the car. In one
of these trimly built cars was a party of four young men whose   15
spirits seemed to be at present well above the level of successful
Gallicism:[6] in fact, these four young men were almost hilarious.

---

164   —Eveline! Evvy!] NO PARAGRAPH IH

Copy-text: 1910 late proofs (10); Collated texts: *The Irish Homestead* OF DECEMBER 17, 1904
(IH) [SUBSTANTIVE IH VARIANTS ONLY ARE REPORTED IN THESE FOOTNOTES; 1914 proofs (14P)
and 1914 first edition (14) [IDENTITY IN BOTH IS REPORTED AS '14']; 1967 Viking edition in the
1969 Viking Critical Library printing (67).

---

12   round] measure IH, 14

---

1. The race in the title refers to the Gordon-Bennett automobile race that took place in
   Ireland on July 2, 1903. The purpose of the race was to display the relative merits of
   automobiles manufactured in different countries, and cars from France, Germany, Great
   Britain, and the United States competed. The race covered over three hundred miles
   stretching over four Irish counties.
2. A road leading into the city of Dublin from the southwest.
3. A suburb west of the city of Dublin.
4. Although a German Mercedes won the race, its driver, Camille Jenatzy, was Belgian—
   that is, from a country that shares some of the language and culture of France. Since the
   second- and third-place winners were French, the French are declared "virtual victors" by
   the narrator.
5. The nationality of the cars was identified by their color.
6. Displaying the characteristics of the French.

They were Charles Ségouin, the owner of the car; André
Rivière, a young electrician of Canadian birth; a huge Hungar=
ian named Villona and a neatly groomed young man named   20
Doyle. Ségouin was in good humour because he had unex=
pectedly received some orders in advance (he was about to start
a motor establishment in Paris) and Rivière was in good hu=
mour because he was to be appointed manager of the establish=
ment; these two young men (who were cousins) were also in   25
good humour because of the success of the French cars. Villona
was in good humour because he had had a very satisfactory
luncheon, and besides he was an optimist by nature. The fourth
member of the party, however, was too excited to be genuinely
happy.   30
    He was about twenty-six years of age, with a soft, light
brown moustache and rather innocent looking grey eyes. His
father, who had begun life as an advanced nationalist,[7] had
modified his views early. He had made his money as a butcher
in Kingstown[8] and by opening shops in Dublin and in the   35
suburbs he had made his money many times over. He had also
been fortunate enough to secure some of the police contracts[9]
and in the end he had become rich enough to be alluded to in
the Dublin newspapers as a merchant prince. He had sent his
son to England to be educated in a big catholic college[1] and had   40
afterwards sent him to Dublin university[2] to study law. Jimmy
did not study very earnestly and took to bad courses for a
while. He had money and he was popular and he divided his
time curiously between musical and motoring circles. Then he
had been sent for a term to Cambridge[3] to see a little life. His   45
father, remonstrative but covertly proud of the excess, had paid
his bills and brought him home. It was at Cambridge that he
had met Ségouin. They were not much more than acquaint=
ances as yet but Jimmy found great pleasure in the society of
one who had seen so much of the world and was reputed to   50
own some of the biggest hotels in France. Such a person (as his

51 some] several IH

7. A member of the Irish Parliamentary Party that agitated for Home Rule, or Irish independence from Great Britain.
8. A large harbor town at the southeast end of Dublin.
9. Contracts to sell meat to the police barracks and jails.
1. At the time of the story, the best Catholic college or prep school in England would have
   been Stonyhurst College in Lancashire.
2. Trinity College, founded by Queen Elizabeth I in 1591, and attended chiefly by Anglo-
   Irish Protestants.
3. One of the two great British universities, the other being Oxford. Wealthy students sometimes took courses for a term at Cambridge or Oxford to acquire additional cultural sophistication and make advantageous social connections.

father agreed) was well worth knowing, even if he had not been the charming companion he was. Villona was entertaining also —a brilliant pianist—but, unfortunately, very poor.

The car ran on merrily with its cargo of hilarious youth. The two cousins sat on the front seat; Jimmy and his Hungarian friend sat behind. Decidedly Villona was in excellent spirits; he kept up a deep bass hum of melody for miles of the road. The Frenchmen flung their laughter and light words over their shoulders and often Jimmy had to strain forward to catch the quick phrase. This was not altogether pleasant for him as he had nearly always to make a deft guess at the meaning and shout back a suitable answer in the teeth of a high wind. Besides, Villona's humming would confuse anybody: the noise of the car, too.

Rapid motion through space elates one; so does notoriety; so does the possession of money. These were three good reasons for Jimmy's excitement. He had been seen by many of his friends that day in the company of these continentals. At the control Ségouin had presented him to one of the French competitors and, in answer to his confused murmur of compli= ment, the swarthy face of the driver had disclosed a line of shining white teeth. It was pleasant after that honour to return to the profane world of spectators amid nudges and significant looks. Then as to money—he really had a great sum under his control. Ségouin, perhaps, would not think it a great sum but Jimmy who, in spite of temporary errors, was at heart the inheritor of solid instincts knew well with what difficulty it had been got together. This knowledge had previously kept his bills within the limits of reasonable recklessness and, if he had been so conscious of the labour latent in money when there had been question merely of some freak of the higher intelligence,[4] how much more so now when he was about to stake the greater part of his substance! It was a serious thing for him.

Of course, the investment was a good one and Ségouin had managed to give the impression that it was by a favour of friendship the mite of Irish money was to be included in the capital of the concern. Jimmy had a respect for his father's shrewdness in business matters and in this case it had been his father who had first suggested the investment; money to be made in the motor business, pots of money. Moreover, Ségouin had the unmistakable air of wealth. Jimmy set out to translate

4. Probably a whim or capricious indulgence.

into days' work that lordly car on which he sat. How smoothly
it ran! In what style they had come careering along the country
roads! The journey laid a magical finger on the genuine pulse   95
of life and gallantly the machinery of human nerves strove to
answer the bounding courses of the swift blue animal.

They drove down Dame Street.[5] The street was busy with
unusual traffic, loud with the horns of motorists and the gongs
of impatient tramdrivers. Near the bank Ségouin drew up and   100
Jimmy and his friend alighted. A little knot of people collected
on the footpath to pay homage to the snorting motor. The
party was to dine together that evening in Ségouin's hotel and
meanwhile Jimmy and his friend, who was staying with him,
were to go home to dress. The car steered out slowly for   105
Grafton Street[6] while the two young men pushed their way
through the knot of gazers. They walked northward with a
curious feeling of disappointment in the exercise while the city
hung its pale globes of light above them in a haze of summer
evening.   110

In Jimmy's house this dinner had been pronounced an
occasion. A certain pride mingled with his parents' trepidation,
a certain eagerness, also, to play fast and loose for the names of
great foreign cities have at least this virtue. Jimmy, too, looked
very well when he was dressed and, as he stood in the hall   115
giving a last equation[7] to the bows of his dress tie, his father
may have felt even commercially satisfied at having secured for
his son qualities often unpurchasable. His father, therefore,
was unusually friendly with Villona and his manner expressed
a real respect for foreign accomplishments but this subtlety of   120
his host was probably lost upon the Hungarian who was
beginning to have a sharp desire for his dinner.

The dinner was excellent, exquisite. Ségouin, Jimmy de=
cided, had a very refined taste. The party was increased by a
young Englishman named Routh whom Jimmy had seen with   125
Ségouin at Cambridge. The young men supped in a snug room
lit by electric candle lamps.[8] They talked volubly and with little

---

93 on] in IH, 14   99 gongs] IH; group 10   101 alighted.] descended. IH   117 for] in
IH   118 qualities--unpurchasable.]   unpurchasable qualities. IH   126 at] in IH
126 young men] five young men IH   126 supped] dined IH   126 snug] small comfortable IH   127 lit--lamps.] by candlelight. IH   127 volubly] a great deal, IH

5. A major street in the south of the city center of Dublin.
6. Another major street in central Dublin that intersects with the park known as Stephen's
   Green.
7. An effort to make the sides of the bow tie symmetrical.
8. Since gas lighting was still common at the time of the story, electric lights signaled a highly
   modern and well-appointed hotel.

reserve. Jimmy, whose imagination was kindling, conceived the lively youth of the Frenchmen twined elegantly upon the firm framework of the Englishman's manner. A graceful image of his, he thought, and a just one. He admired the dexterity with which their host directed the conversation. The five young men had various tastes and their tongues had been loosened. Vil= lona, with immense respect, began to discover to the mildly surprised Englishman the beauties of the English madrigal,[9] deploring the loss of old instruments.[1] Rivière, not wholly ingenuously, undertook to explain to Jimmy the triumph of the French mechanicians. The resonant voice of the Hungarian was about to prevail in ridicule of the spurious lutes of the romantic painters when Ségouin shepherded his party into politics. Here was congenial ground for all. Jimmy, under generous influ= ences, felt the buried zeal of his father wake to life within him: he aroused the torpid Routh at last. The room grew doubly hot and Ségouin's task grew harder each moment: there was even danger of personal spite. The alert host at an opportunity lifted his glass to humanity and, when the toast had been drunk, he threw open a window significantly.

That night the city wore the mask of a capital. The five young men strolled along Stephen's Green[2] in a faint cloud of aromatic smoke. They talked loudly and gaily and their cloaks dangled from their shoulders. The people made way for them. At the corner of Grafton Street a short fat man was putting two handsome ladies on a car in charge of another fat man. The car drove off and the short fat man caught sight of the party.

—André!

—It's Farley!

A torrent of talk followed. Farley was an American. No one knew very well what the talk was about. Villona and Rivière were the noisiest but all the men were excited. They got up on a car, squeezing themselves together amid much laughter. They drove by the crowd, blended now into soft colours, to a music of merry bells. They took the train at Westland Row and in a few seconds, as it seemed to Jimmy, they were walking out of Kingstown station. The ticket collector saluted Jimmy; he was an old man.

132 host] entertainer IH   142 buried] ancient IH   142 wake to life] awake IH
145 spite.] 14P; spice. IH, 10   148 mask] air IH   155 —André!] NO PARAGRAPH IH
156 —It's Farley!] NO PARAGRAPH IH   163 seconds,] minutes, IH

9. A short lyrical poem, suitable to being sung in a contrapuntal style, that had been popular in sixteenth century England.
1. Elizabethan instruments, such as the lute, that had accompanied madrigals, were rarely available by the time of the story except as replicas.
2. A large park in a fashionable part of Dublin, south of the river Liffey.

—Fine night, sir!

It was a serene summer night; the harbour lay like a darkened mirror at their feet. They proceeded towards it with linked arms, singing *Cadet Roussel*[3] in chorus, stamping their feet at every:

    Ho! Ho! Hohé, vraiment![4]

They got into a rowboat at the slip and made out for the American's yacht. There was to be supper, music, cards. Vil= lona said with conviction:

—It is beautiful!

There was a yacht piano in the cabin. Villona played a waltz for Farley and Rivière, Farley acting as cavalier and Rivière as lady. Then an impromptu square dance, the men devising original figures. What merriment! Jimmy took his part with a will; this was seeing life, at least. Then Farley got out of breath and cried *Stop!* A man brought in a light supper and the young men sat down to it for form' sake. They drank, however: it was bohemian.[5] They drank[6] Ireland, England, France, Hungary, the United States of America. Jimmy made a speech, a long speech, Villona saying: *Hear! hear!* whenever there was a pause. There was a great clapping of hands when he sat down. It must have been a good speech. Farley clapped him on the back and laughed loudly. What jovial fellows! What good company they were!

Cards! cards! The table was cleared. Villona returned quietly to his piano and played voluntaries[7] for them. The other men played game after game, flinging themselves boldly into the adventure. They drank the health of the queen of hearts and of the queen of diamonds. Jimmy felt obscurely the lack of an audience: the wit was flashing. Play ran very high and paper began to pass.[8] Jimmy did not know exactly who was winning but he knew that he was losing. But it was his own fault for he frequently mistook his cards and the other men had to calculate

    170

    175

    180

    185

    190

    195

---

166 —Fine] NO PARAGRAPH IH   171 *Ho--vraiment!*] NO PARAGRAPH IH   172 They] NO PARAGRAPH IH   175 —It is beautiful!] "It is delightful!" NO PARAGRAPH IH   180 seeing] ABSENT IH   181 and(1)] and they IH   183 France, Hungary,] Hungary, France, IH 186 of hands] ABSENT IH   187 back] shoulder IH   191 men] young men IH 195 high and] high: IH   196–197 winning but] winning: IH

3. A French marching song of the late eighteenth century whose many verses make fun of a young cadet of the regiment for his peculiarities.
4. One alternative of the refrain of *Cadet Roussel* goes: "*Ho! Ho! Hohé, vraiment! / Cadet Rousselle est bon enfant.*" It may be translated as "Ho Ho Hoho, truly / Cadet Roussel is a good fellow."
5. A spirit of cultural freedom from convention.
6. That is, they drank toasts to each of their countries.
7. Melodies improvised by the player.
8. Notes declaring a debt in the absence of cash. Also known as I.O.U.s, from a homophone for "I owe you."

his I.O.U's for him. They were devils of fellows but he wished
they would stop: it was getting late. Someone gave the toast of   200
the yacht *The Belle of Newport*[9] and then someone proposed
one great game for a finish.

   The piano had stopped; Villona must have gone up on deck.
It was a terrible game. They stopped just before the end of it to
drink for luck. Jimmy understood that the game lay between   205
Routh and Ségouin. What excitement! Jimmy was excited too;
he would lose, of course. How much had he written away? The
men rose to their feet to play the last tricks, talking and
gesticulating. Routh won. The cabin shook with the young
men's cheering and the cards were bundled together. They be=   210
gan then to gather in what they had won. Farley and Jimmy
were the heaviest losers.

   He knew that he would regret in the morning but at present
he was glad of the rest, glad of the dark stupor that would
cover up his folly. He leaned his elbows on the table and rested   215
his head between his hands, counting the beats of his temples.
The cabin door opened and he saw the Hungarian standing in a
shaft of grey light:
—Daybreak, gentlemen!

Two Gallants

The grey warm evening of August had descended upon the
city and a mild warm air, a memory of summer, circulated in
the streets. The streets, shuttered for the repose of Sunday,
swarmed with a gaily coloured crowd. Like illumined pearls
the lamps shone from the summits of their tall poles upon the   5
living texture below which, changing shape and hue unceas=
ingly, sent up into the warm grey evening air an unchanging
unceasing murmur.

   Two young men came down the hill of Rutland Square.[1] One

201 *The*--someone] "The Belle of Newport." Someone IH   202 one] a IH   203 The] NO
PARAGRAPH IH   205 lay] was IH   211 then] ABSENT IH   213 He] STET 10   214–
215 rest,--folly.] rest. IH   216 between] on IH   216 temples.] temple. IH   219 —
Daybreak, gentlemen!] NO PARAGRAPH IH

9. The yacht's name signals its origin in Newport, Rhode Island, in the United States—an
   enclave for the newly rich entrepreneurs (or "robber barons") of late nineteenth-century
   New England.

Copy-text: 1910 late proofs (10); Collated texts: 1914 proofs (14P) and 1914 first edition
(14) [IDENTITY IN BOTH IS REPORTED AS '14']; 1967 Viking edition in the 1969 Viking Critical
Library printing (67).

1. A square in central Dublin, north of the river Liffey, now called Parnell Square.

of them was just bringing a long monologue to a close. The   10
other, who walked on the verge of the path and was at times
obliged to step on to the road owing to his companion's
rudeness, wore an amused listening face. He was squat and
ruddy. A yachting cap was shoved far back from his forehead
and the narrative to which he listened made constant waves of   15
expression break forth over his face from the corners of his
nose and eyes and mouth. Little jets of wheezing laughter
followed one another out of his convulsed body. His eyes,
twinkling with cunning enjoyment, glanced at every moment
towards his companion's face. Once or twice he rearranged the   20
light waterproof[2] which he had slung over one shoulder in
toreador fashion.[3] His breeches, his white rubber shoes and his
jauntily slung waterproof expressed youth. But his figure fell
into rotundity at the waist, his hair was scant and grey and his
face, when the waves of expression had passed over it, had a   25
ravaged look.

When he was quite sure that the narrative had ended he
laughed noiselessly for fully half a minute. Then he said:
—Well! ... That takes the biscuit![4]

His voice seemed winnowed of vigour; and to enforce his   30
words he added with humour:
—That takes the solitary, unique and, if I may so call it,
recherché[5] biscuit!

He became serious and silent when he had said this. His
tongue was tired for he had been talking all the afternoon in a   35
publichouse[6] in Dorset Street.[7] Most people considered Lenehan
a leech but in spite of this reputation his adroitness and elo=
quence had always prevented his friends from forming any
general policy against him. He had a brave manner of coming
up to a party of them in a bar and of holding himself nimbly at   40
the borders of the company until he was included in a round.[8]
He was a sporting vagrant armed with a vast stock of stories,
limericks and riddles. He was insensitive to all kinds of dis=
courtesy. No-one knew how he achieved the stern task of living
but his name was vaguely associated with racing tissues.[9]   45
—And where did you pick her up, Corley? he asked.

2. A raincoat or outer garment impervious to water.
3. The Spanish bullfighter, or toreador, was customarily depicted as wearing a cape slung
   over one shoulder.
4. A version of the expression "That takes the cake," referring to an impudence considered
   outrageous.
5. French for desirable because rare, choice.
6. A tavern or pub.
7. A main street running north from the river Liffey in the center of Dublin.
8. A quantity of liquor served to each member of a company.
9. Bulletins or articles giving information on horse races.

Corley ran his tongue swiftly along his upper lip.

—One night, man, he said, I was going along Dame Street[1] and I spotted a fine tart[2] under Waterhouse's clock[3] and said good= night, you know. So we went for a walk round by the canal and she told me she was a slavey[4] in a house in Baggot Street.[5] I put my arm round her and squeezed her a bit that night. Then next Sunday, man, I met her by appointment. We went out to Donnybrook[6] and I brought her into a field there. She told me she used to go with a dairyman. ... It was fine, man. Cigarettes every night she'd bring me and paying the tram out and back. And one night she brought me two bloody fine cigars—O, the real cheese,[7] you know, that the old fellow[8] used to smoke. ... I was afraid, man, she'd get in the family way. But she's up to the dodge.[9]

—Maybe she thinks you'll marry her, said Lenehan.

—I told her I was out of a job, said Corley. I told her I was in Pim's.[1] She doesn't know my name. I was too hairy[2] to tell her that. But she thinks I'm a bit of class,[3] you know.

Lenehan laughed again noiselessly.

—Of all the good ones ever I heard, he said, that emphatically takes the biscuit.

Corley's stride acknowledged the compliment. The swing of his burly body made his friend execute a few light skips from the path to the roadway and back again. Corley was the son of an inspector of police and he had inherited his father's frame and gait. He walked with his hands by his sides, holding him= self erect and swaying his head from side to side. His head was large, globular and oily, it sweated in all weathers and his large round hat, set upon it sideways, looked like a bulb which had grown out of another. He always stared straight before him as if he were on parade and when he wished to gaze after someone in the street it was necessary for him to move his body from the hips. At present he was about town.[4] Whenever any job was

---

1. A major street in the south of the city center of Dublin.
2. A girl or woman of dubious or loose moral character.
3. A clock advertising the shop of Waterhouse and Company, jewelers and watchmakers, on Dame Street.
4. A female domestic or servant of low status in the household.
5. A street in a very fashionable neighborhood in southeastern Dublin.
6. A suburb of southeastern Dublin that had acquired a reputation for brawling and other unseemly behavior in the early nineteenth century.
7. The real thing, a version of the American idiom "the real McCoy."
8. Presumably the young woman's employer.
9. Knows how to avoid consequences—for example, by preventing pregnancy.
1. Pim Brothers Limited was a Quaker family-owned enterprise of wholesale and retail business in clothing, furniture, and household wares.
2. Cunning, clever, or wary.
3. Classy, or, in this context, of a station above the working class.
4. Without a job.

vacant a friend was always ready to give him the hard word.[5]   80
He was often to be seen walking with policemen in plain
clothes,[6] talking earnestly. He knew the inner side of all affairs
and was fond of delivering final judgments. He spoke without
listening to the speech of his companions. His conversation was
mainly about himself: what he had said to such a person and   85
what such a person had said to him and what he had said to
settle the matter. When he reported these dialogues he aspir=
ated the first letter of his name after the manner of Florentines.[7]

Lenehan offered his friend a cigarette. As the two young men
walked on through the crowd Corley occasionally turned to   90
smile at some of the passing girls but Lenehan's gaze was fixed
on the large faint moon circled with a double halo. He watched
earnestly the passing of the grey web of twilight across its face.
At length he said:

—Well, ... tell me, Corley, I suppose you'll be able to pull it off   95
all right, eh?

Corley closed one eye expressively as an answer.

—Is she game for that? asked Lenehan dubiously. You never
can know women.

—She's all right, said Corley. I know the way to get around   100
her, man. She's a bit gone on me.[8]

—You're what I call a gay Lothario, said Lenehan. And the
proper kind of a Lothario,[9] too!

A shade of mockery relieved the servility of his manner. To
save himself he had the habit of leaving his flattery open to the   105
interpretation of raillery. But Corley had not a subtle mind.

—There's nothing to touch a good slavey, he affirmed. Take
my tip for it.

—By one who has tried them all, said Lenehan.

—First I used to go with girls, you know, said Corley un=   110
bosoming, girls off the South Circular.[1] I used to take them out,
man, on the tram somewhere and pay the tram or take them to
a band or a play at the theatre or buy them chocolate and
sweets or something that way. I used to spend money on them
right enough, he added in a convincing tone, as if he were   115
conscious of being disbelieved.

But Lenehan could well believe it; he nodded gravely.

---

5. Reliable information.
6. This implies that Corley may be a police informant.
7. Speakers in Florence, Italy, pronounce a c as an h. Corley might therefore pronounce his
   name Horley, or, as some critics have argued, Whore-ley.
8. Infatuated.
9. A young nobleman and seducer in Nicholas Rowe's 1703 play *The Fair Penitent*. The
   name has come to stand for an unscrupulous deceiver or libertine.
1. The South Circular Road at the southern border of Dublin was a popular promenade for
   young unattached girls willing to meet young men without a proper, formal introduction.

—I know that game, he said, and it's a mug's game.[2]
—And damn the thing I ever got out of it, said Corley.
—Ditto here, said Lenehan.
—Only off of one of them, said Corley.

He moistened his upper lip by running his tongue along it.
The recollection brightened his eyes. He too gazed at the pale
disc of the moon, now nearly veiled, and seemed to meditate.
—She was ... a bit of all right, he said regretfully.

He was silent again. Then he added:
—She's on the turf now.[3] I saw her driving down Earl Street[4]
one night with two fellows with her on a car.
—I suppose that's your doing, said Lenehan.
—There was others at her before me, said Corley philosophi=
cally.

This time Lenehan was inclined to disbelieve. He shook his
head to and fro and smiled.
—You know you can't kid me, Corley, he said.
—Honest to God! said Corley. Didn't she tell me herself?

Lenehan made a tragic gesture.
—Base betrayer! he said.

As they passed along by the railings of Trinity College[5]
Lenehan skipped out into the road and peered up at the clock:
—Twenty after, he said.
—Time enough, said Corley. She'll be there all right. I always
let her wait a bit.

Lenehan laughed quietly.
—Ecod,[6] Corley, you know how to take them, he said.
—I'm up to all their little tricks, Corley confessed.
—But tell me, said Lenehan again, are you sure you can bring
it off all right? You know it's a ticklish job. They're damn close
on that point. Eh? ... What?

His bright small eyes searched his companion's face for
reassurance. Corley swung his head to and fro as if to toss aside
an insistent insect, and his brows gathered.
—I'll pull it off, he said. Leave it to me, can't you?

Lenehan said no more. He did not wish to ruffle his friend's
temper, to be sent to the devil[7] and told that his advice was not
wanted. A little tact was necessary. But Corley's brow was
soon smooth again. His thoughts were running another way.

2. A mug is a dupe or a fool.
3. Working as a prostitute.
4. A street only a block or so away from the red-light district of Dublin at the time.
5. Located in the middle of Dublin, the university is bordered by a wall topped with an iron railing.
6. A mild oath, like "Egad."
7. Telling someone to go to the devil was a form of rude dismissal.

—She's a fine decent tart, he said with appreciation, that's
what she is.

They walked along Nassau Street and then turned into
Kildare Street. Not far from the porch of the club[8] a harpist   160
stood in the roadway playing to a little ring of listeners. He
plucked at the wires heedlessly, glancing quickly from time to
time at the face of each newcomer and from time to time,
wearily also, at the sky. His harp[9] too, heedless that her
coverings had fallen about her knees, seemed weary alike of the   165
eyes of strangers and of her master's hands. One hand played in
the bass the melody of *Silent, O Moyle*[1] while the other hand
careered in the treble after each group of notes. The notes of
the air throbbed deep and full.

The two young men walked up the street without speaking,   170
the mournful music following them. When they reached Ste=
phen's Green they crossed the road. Here the noise of trams,
the lights and the crowd released them from their silence.

—There she is! said Corley.

At the corner of Hume Street[2] a young woman was standing.   175
She wore a blue dress and a white sailor hat. She stood on the
curbstone swinging a sunshade[3] in one hand. Lenehan grew
lively:

—Let's have a squint at her, Corley, he said.

Corley glanced sideways at his friend and an unpleasant grin   180
appeared on his face.

—Are you trying to get inside me?[4] he asked.

—Damn it! said Lenehan boldly, I don't want an introduction.
All I want is to have a look at her. I'm not going to eat her.

—O ... A look at her? said Corley, more amiably. Well. ... I'll   185
tell you what. I'll go over and talk to her and you can pass by.

—Right! said Lenehan.

Corley had already thrown one leg over the chains[5] when
Lenehan called out:

169 throbbed] STET 10   179 squint] STET 10

8. The Kildare Street Club, an exclusive men's club whose members were chiefly upper-class
   Anglo-Irish Protestants. The club is located on the corner of Nassau and Kildare streets.
   Nassau Street runs along the south side of Trinity College, and Kildare street runs south
   from Nassau Street toward Stephen's Green.
9. A traditional symbol of Ireland, the harp is featured in Thomas Moore's *Irish Melodies.*
1. A mournful song, "Song of Fionnuala," by Thomas Moore about "Lir's lonely daughter,"
   the daughter of the Celtic sea god, who was transformed into a swan and doomed to lonely
   wandering.
2. A street near the city park of Stephen's Green.
3. A parasol or umbrella to guard against the sun rather than rain.
4. To get inside someone is to spoil his chances by intervening in his enterprise. The term
   comes from using a spin to roll a ball between an opponent's ball and the target ball in a
   lawn-bowling game called *bowls* in England and Ireland.
5. Barriers made by posts with low-slung chains between them, separating the park from the
   street.

—And after? Where will we meet?   190
—Half ten, answered Corley, bringing over his other leg.
—Where?
—Corner of Merrion Street. We'll be coming back.
—Work it all right now, said Lenehan in farewell.

Corley did not answer. He sauntered across the road sway=   195
ing his head from side to side. His bulk, his easy pace and the
solid sound of his boots had something of the conqueror in
them. He approached the young woman and, without saluting,
began at once to converse with her. She swung her sunshade
more quickly and executed half turns on her heels. Once or   200
twice when he spoke to her at close quarters she laughed and
bent her head.

Lenehan observed them for a few minutes. Then he walked
rapidly along beside the chains to some distance and crossed
the road obliquely. As he approached Hume Street corner he   205
found the air heavily scented and his eyes made a swift anxious
scrutiny of the young woman's appearance. She had her Sun=
day finery on. Her blue serge[6] skirt was held at the waist by a
belt of black leather. The great silver buckle of her belt seemed
to depress the centre of her body, catching the light stuff of her   210
white blouse like a clip. She wore a short black jacket with
mother-of-pearl buttons and a ragged black boa.[7] The ends of
her tulle collarette[8] had been carefully disordered and a big
bunch of red flowers was pinned in her bosom, stems upwards.
Lenehan's eyes noted approvingly her stout short muscular   215
body. Frank rude health glowed in her face, on her fat red
cheeks and in her unabashed blue eyes. Her features were
blunt. She had broad nostrils, a straggling[9] mouth which lay
open in a contented leer and two projecting front teeth. As he
passed Lenehan took off his cap and after about ten seconds   220
Corley returned a salute to the air. This he did by raising his
hand vaguely and pensively changing the angle of position of
his hat.

Lenehan walked as far as the Shelbourne Hotel[1] where he
halted and waited. After waiting for a little time he saw them   225
coming towards him and when they turned to the right he
followed them, stepping lightly in his white shoes, down one

199 sunshade] STET JJ CORRECTIONS 1914; umbrella 10–14   204 to] STET 10

6. A soft woolen fabric, used in clothing at the time.
7. A furry or feathery stole or coil worn around the neck.
8. A decorative collar or ruff made of silky net.
9. Irregular rather than symmetrical.
1. An elegant and expensive hotel on Kildare Street across from Stephen's Green.

side of Merrion Square. As he walked on slowly, timing his
pace to theirs, he watched Corley's head which turned at every
moment towards the young woman's face like a big ball   230
revolving on a pivot. He kept the pair in view until he had seen
them climbing the stairs of the Donnybrook tram; then he
turned about and went back the way he had come.

Now that he was alone his face looked older. His gaiety
seemed to forsake him and, as he came by the railings of the   235
Duke's Lawn,[2] he allowed his hand to run along them. The air
which the harpist had played began to control his movements.
His softly padded feet played the melody while his fingers
swept a scale of variations idly along the railings after each
group of notes.   240

He walked listlessly round Stephen's Green and then down
Grafton Street.[3] Though his eyes took note of many elements of
the crowd through which he passed they did so morosely. He
found trivial all that was meant to charm him and did not
answer the glances which invited him to be bold. He knew that   245
he would have to speak a great deal, to invent and to amuse,
and his brain and throat were too dry for such a task. The
problem of how he could pass the hours till he met Corley
again troubled him a little. He could think of no way of passing
them but to keep on walking. He turned to the left when he   250
came to the corner of Rutland Square and felt more at ease in
the dark quiet street, the sombre look of which suited his
mood. He paused at last before the window of a poorlooking
shop over which the words Refreshment Bar[4] were printed in
white letters. On the glass of the window were two flying   255
inscriptions: Ginger Beer and Ginger Ale.[5] A cut ham was
exposed on a great blue dish while near it on a plate lay a
segment of very light plumpudding.[6] He eyed this food earnestly
for some time and then, after glancing warily up and down the
street, went into the shop quickly.   260

He was hungry for, except some biscuits which he had asked
two grudging curates[7] to bring him, he had eaten nothing since

258 segment] 14; section 10–14P

2. The lawn in front of Leinster House on Merrion Square—a historic building near the
   National Museum and the National Library.
3. A busy commercial street that will take Lenehan to O'Connell Bridge, across the bridge
   up O'Connell Street and back to Rutland Square, now Parnell Square, where the story
   began. His wanderings could be thought of as aimless and circular.
4. An eatery serving quick lunches or snacks but no alcoholic beverages, similar to a contemporary fast-food restaurant.
5. Aerated or carbonated soft drinks flavored with ginger.
6. A boiled pudding containing plums and other fruits and made with suet or meat fat.
7. Term for bartenders or waiters in informal eateries.

breakfast-time. He sat down at an uncovered wooden table opposite two work girls and a mechanic. A slatternly[8] girl waited on him.

—How much is a plate of peas? he asked.

—Three halfpence,[9] sir, said the girl.

—Bring me a plate of peas, he said, and a bottle of ginger beer.

He spoke roughly in order to belie his air of gentility[1] for his entry had been followed by a pause of talk. His face was heated. To appear natural he pushed his cap back on his head and planted his elbows on the table. The mechanic and the two work girls examined him point by point before resuming their conversation in a subdued voice. The girl brought him a plate of hot grocer's peas seasoned with pepper and vinegar, a fork and his ginger beer. He ate his food greedily and found it so good that he made a note of the shop mentally. When he had eaten all the peas he sipped his ginger beer and sat for some time thinking of Corley's adventure. In his imagination he beheld the pair of lovers walking along some dark road, he heard Corley's voice in deep energetic gallantries and saw again the leer of the young woman's mouth. This vision made him feel keenly his own poverty of purse and spirit. He was tired of knocking about, of pulling the devil by the tail,[2] of shifts and intrigues. He would be thirty-one in November. Would he never get a good job? Would he never have a home of his own? He thought how pleasant it would be to have a warm fire to sit by and a good dinner to sit down to. He had walked the streets long enough with friends and with girls. He knew what those friends were worth: he knew the girls too. Experience had embittered his heart against the world. But all hope had not left him. He felt better after having eaten than he had felt before, less weary of his life, less vanquished in spirit. He might yet be able to settle down in some snug corner and live happily if he could only come across some good simpleminded girl with a little of the ready.[3]

He paid twopence halfpenny to the slatternly girl and went out of the shop to begin his wandering again. He went into Capel Street and walked along towards the City Hall.[4] Then he

---

275 hot--peas] e; hot grocer's peas, 10 67; grocer's hot peas, 14

8. Untidy and poorly groomed.
9. The price implies that the meal is cheap and filling.
1. Lenehan's dress, speech, and manner have an air of sophistication and education about them that might make him look and sound out of place in a working-class eatery.
2. Barely managing, always on the brink of bankruptcy or disaster.
3. Ready money or cash on hand.
4. The building in central Dublin south of the Liffey where the city government, known as the Dublin Corporation, conducts municipal business.

turned into Dame Street. At the corner of George's Street he met two friends of his and stopped to converse with them. He was glad that he could rest from all his walking. His friends asked him had he seen Corley and what was the latest. He replied that he had spent the day with Corley. His friends talked very little. They looked vacantly after some figures in the crowd and sometimes made a critical remark. One said that he had seen Mac an hour before in Westmoreland Street.[5] At this Lenehan said that he had been with Mac the night before in Egan's. The young man who had seen Mac in Westmoreland Street asked was it true that Mac had won a bit over a billiard match. Lenehan did not know: he said that Holohan had stood them drinks[6] in Egan's.[7]

He left his friends at a quarter to ten and went up George's Street. He turned to the left at the City Markets and walked on into Grafton Street. The crowd of girls and young men had thinned and on his way up the street he heard many groups and couples bidding one another goodnight. He went as far as the clock of the College of Surgeons:[8] it was on the stroke of ten. He set off briskly along the northern side of the Green, hurrying for fear Corley should return too soon. When he reached the corner of Merrion Street he took his stand in the shadow of a lamp and brought out one of the cigarettes which he had reserved and lit it. He leaned against the lamppost and kept his gaze fixed on the part from which he expected to see Corley and the young woman return.

His mind became active again. He wondered had Corley managed it successfully. He wondered if he had asked her yet or if he would leave it to the last. He suffered all the pangs and thrills of his friend's situation as well as those of his own. But the memory of Corley's slowly revolving head calmed him somewhat: he was sure Corley would pull it off all right. All at once the idea struck him that perhaps Corley had seen her home by another way and given him the slip.[9] His eyes searched the street: there was no sign of them. Yet it was surely half an hour since he had seen the clock of the College of Surgeons. Would Corley do a thing like that? He lit his last cigarette and began to smoke it nervously. He strained his eyes as each tram stopped at the far corner of the square. They must have gone

---

5. A street that connects Trinity College with O'Connell Street.
6. Paid for a round of drinks. Custom required anyone who came into a bit of lucky money to treat his friends to a round of drinks at a pub.
7. A pub called *The Oval*, on Abbey Street north of the Liffey, was run by a proprietor named John Egan.
8. The College is located on Stephen's Green.
9. Eluded him or avoided running into him.

home by another way. The paper of his cigarette broke and he
flung it into the road with a curse.   340

Suddenly he saw them coming towards him. He started with
delight and, keeping close to his lamppost, tried to read the
result in their walk. They were walking quickly, the young
woman taking quick short steps while Corley kept beside her
with his long stride. They did not seem to be speaking. An   345
intimation of the result pricked him like the point of a sharp
instrument. He knew Corley would fail: he knew it was no go.

They turned down Baggot Street and he followed them at
once, taking the other footpath. When they stopped he stopped
too. They talked for a few moments and then the young   350
woman went down the steps into the area of a house. Corley
remained standing at the edge of the path, a little distance from
the front steps. Some minutes passed. Then the halldoor was
opened slowly and cautiously. A woman came running down
the front steps and coughed. Corley turned and went towards   355
her. His broad figure hid hers from view for a few seconds and
then she reappeared running up the steps. The door closed on
her and Corley began to walk swiftly towards Stephen's Green.

Lenehan hurried on in the same direction. Some drops of
light rain fell. He took them as a warning and, glancing back   360
towards the house which the young woman had entered to see
that he was not observed, he ran eagerly across the road.
Anxiety and his swift run made him pant. He called out:
—Hello, Corley!

Corley turned his head to see who had called him and then   365
continued walking as before. Lenehan ran after him, settling
the waterproof on his shoulders with one hand.
—Hello, Corley! he cried again.

He came level with his friend and looked keenly in his face.
He could see nothing there.   370
—Well? he said. Did it come off?

They had reached the corner of Ely Place.[1] Still without
answering Corley swerved to the left and went up the side
street. His features were composed in stern calm. Lenehan kept
up with his friend, breathing uneasily. He was baffled and a   375
note of menace pierced through his voice.
—Can't you tell us? he said. Did you try her?

Corley halted at the first lamp and stared grimly before him.
Then with a grave gesture he extended a hand towards the light

---

1. A fashionable cul-de-sac or dead end, near Baggot Street, where the slavey presumably
works.

and, smiling, opened it slowly to the gaze of his disciple. A   380
small gold coin[2] shone in the palm.

The Boarding House

Mrs Mooney was a butcher's daughter. She was a woman
who was quite able to keep things to herself: a determined
woman. She had married her father's foreman and opened a
butcher's shop near Spring Gardens.[1] But as soon as his father-
in-law was dead Mr Mooney began to go to the devil. He   5
drank, plundered the till, ran headlong into debt. It was no use
making him take the pledge:[2] he was sure to break out again a
few days after. By fighting his wife in the presence of customers
and by buying bad meat he ruined his business. One night he
went for his wife with the cleaver[3] and she had to sleep in a   10
neighbour's house.

After that they lived apart. She went to the priests and got a
separation[4] from him with care of the children. She would give
him neither money nor food nor houseroom and so he was
obliged to enlist himself as a sheriff's man.[5] He was a shabby   15
stooped little drunkard with a white face and a white mous=
tache and white eyebrows, pencilled above his little eyes, which
were pinkveined and raw; and all day long he sat in the bailiffs'
room waiting to be put on a job. Mrs Mooney, who had taken
what remained of her money out of the butcher business and   20

---

2. A sovereign, or a pound, worth twenty shillings. If Eveline Hill earns seven shillings per
   week as a shop girl, then the slavey presumably earns considerably less. The gold coin
   could therefore represent as much as a month or two of her wages. The story, however,
   does not make clear how she acquired the coin, whether it was her own or stolen from
   her employer.

Copy-text: Manuscript Yale 2.3 (MS); Collated texts: 1910 late proofs (10); 1914 proofs (14P)
and 1914 first edition (14) [IDENTITY IN BOTH IS REPORTED AS '14']; 1967 Viking edition in the
1969 Viking Critical Library printing (67).

4 near--Gardens.] 10; in Fairview. MS   6 till,--headlong] 10; till and ran MS   7 a]
<in> a MS   10 went for] 10; attacked MS   10 the] 10; a MS   12 priests] STET MS
13 him with] 10; her husband and MS   14–15 was obliged] 10; had MS   15 enlist--as]
10; become MS   16 stooped] 10; ABSENT MS   16–17 a--moustache] 10; white moustaches MS   17–18 and--raw;] 10; ABSENT MS   18 long] 10; ABSENT MS

1. A street between the Royal Canal and the Tolka River in northeastern Dublin.
2. To make a formal, public promise to give up alcoholic drink.
3. A heavy, square butcher's knife used to chop up animal carcasses.
4. Roman Catholics were forbidden to divorce, but were able to request a formal separation
   from the Church, which allowed them to live apart from their spouses, but without permission to remarry.
5. A deputy in a bailiff's office who does various law-enforcement errands.

set up a boarding house in Hardwicke Street,[6] was a big imposing woman. Her house had a floating population[7] made up of tourists from Liverpool[8] and the Isle of Man[9] and occa= sionally *artistes* from the musichalls.[1] Its resident population was made up of clerks from the city. She governed her house   25 cunningly and firmly, knew when to give credit, when to be stern and when to let things pass. All the resident young men spoke of her as *The Madam*.[2]

Mrs Mooney's young men paid fifteen shillings a week for board and lodgings (beer or stout at dinner excluded). They   30 shared in common tastes and occupations and for this reason they were very chummy with one another. They discussed with one another the chances of favourites and outsiders.[3] Jack Mooney, the Madam's son, who was clerk to a commission agent[4] in Fleet Street,[5] had the reputation of being a hard case.[6]   35 He was fond of using soldiers' obscenities: usually he came home in the small hours.[7] When he met his friends he had always a good one to tell them and he was always sure to be on to a good thing,[8] that is to say, a likely horse or a likely *artiste*. He was also handy with the mits[9] and sang comic songs. On   40 Sunday nights there would often be a reunion[1] in Mrs Mooney's front drawingroom.[2] The musichall *artistes* would oblige; and Sheridan played waltzes and polkas and vamped[3] accompani= ments. Polly Mooney, the Madam's daughter, would also sing. She sang: 45

---

21 set up] 10; started MS   36 usually] 10; sometimes MS   40 handy--mits] 10; an amateur boxer MS

6. A street in northwestern Dublin containing both middle-class homes and tenements.
7. Boarders who stayed for short periods only, and therefore produced considerable turnover.
8. A seaport in the northwest of England, whose harbor served as a major steamship link between England and Ireland.
9. A British island in the Irish Sea, between Dublin and Scotland.
1. Actors, singers, or dancers in the entertainment business, thought to be on the fringe of respectability.
2. Presumably a term of mock respect that may hint at the name given to the female pro- prietress of a house of prostitution.
3. Racehorses with either low odds (favourites) because everyone is betting on them to win, or high odds (outsiders) because everyone thinks they are unlikely to win.
4. A representative who works for others in return for a commission or a percentage of specific transactions. For example, collecting overdue bills might be entrusted to a com- mission agent.
5. Fleet Street in London was the site of the major newspapers and general press. But the Fleet Street in Dublin was a more general business area that contained law offices and other commercial concerns.
6. A rough character.
7. After midnight—at one, two, or three in the morning, for example.
8. A likely possibility or a good chance at lucking out.
9. Slang for the hands or, by implication, the fists.
1. A social gathering for people who know one another.
2. A room reserved for the reception of company.
3. Improvised.

I'm a .... naughty girl.
You needn't sham:
You know I am.[4]

Polly was a slim girl of nineteen; she had light soft hair and
a small full mouth. Her eyes, which were grey with a shade of   50
green through them, had a habit of glancing upwards when she
spoke with anyone, which made her look like a little perverse
madonna. Mrs Mooney had first sent her daughter to be a
typewriter in a cornfactor's office[5] but, as a disreputable sher=
iff's man used to come every other day to the office asking to   55
be allowed to say a word to his daughter, she had taken her
daughter home again and set her to do housework. As Polly
was very lively the intention was to give her the run of the
young men. Besides, young men like to feel that there is a
young woman not very far away. Polly, of course, flirted with   60
the young men but Mrs Mooney, who was a shrewd judge,
knew that the young men were only passing the time away:
none of them meant business. Things went on so for a long
time and Mrs Mooney began to think of sending Polly back to
typewriting when she noticed that something was going on be=   65
tween Polly and one of the young men. She watched the pair
and kept her own counsel.

Polly knew that she was being watched but still her mother's
persistent silence could not be misunderstood. There had been
no open complicity between mother and daughter, no open   70
understanding but, though people in the house began to talk of
the affair, still Mrs Mooney did not intervene. Polly began to
grow a little strange in her manner and the young man was
evidently perturbed. At last, when she judged it to be the right
moment, Mrs Mooney intervened. She dealt with moral prob=   75
lems as a cleaver deals with meat: and in this case she had made
up her mind.

It was a bright Sunday morning of early summer, promising
heat, but with a fresh breeze blowing. All the windows of the
boarding house were open and the lace curtains ballooned   80
gently towards the street beneath the raised sashes. The belfry
of George's church[6] sent out constant peals and worshippers,

---

52 perverse] 10; hypocritical MS   54 typewriter] STET MS; CF 229, 234, 246   54 cornfactor's] e:10; corn merchant's MS; corn factor's 10   71 understanding--though] 10; understanding. MS   72 still Mrs Mooney] 10; Mrs Mooney still MS   81 the(2)] ⟨them⟩ the
MS

4. A song that begins: "I'm an imp on mischief bent, / Only feeling quite content / When
   doing wrong! / When doing wrong!"
5. A wholesale dealer in corn and cornmeal.
6. St. George's Church, a Protestant church around the corner from Hardwicke Street.

singly or in groups, traversed the little circus before the church, revealing their purpose by their self-contained demeanour no less than by the little volumes[7] in their gloved hands. Breakfast was over in the boarding house and the table of the breakfast room was covered with plates on which lay yellow streaks of eggs with morsels of bacon fat and bacon rind. Mrs Mooney sat in the straw armchair and watched the servant, Mary, remove the breakfast things. She made Mary collect the crusts and pieces of broken bread to help to make Tuesday's bread pudding. When the table was cleared, the broken bread col= lected, the sugar and butter safe under lock and key, she began to reconstruct the interview which she had had the night before with Polly. Things were as she had suspected: she had been frank in her questions and Polly had been frank in her answers. Both had been somewhat awkward, of course. She had been made awkward by her not wishing to receive the news in too cavalier a fashion or to seem to have connived and Polly had been made awkward not merely because allusions of that kind always made her awkward but also because she did not wish it to be thought that in her wise innocence she had divined the intention behind her mother's tolerance.

Mrs Mooney glanced instinctively at the little gilt clock on the mantelpiece as soon as she had become aware through her revery that the bells of George's church had stopped ringing. It was seventeen minutes past eleven: she would have lots of time to have the matter out with Mr Doran and then catch short twelve at Marlborough Street.[8] She was sure she would win. To begin with she had all the weight of social opinion on her side: she was an outraged mother. She had allowed him to live beneath her roof, assuming that he was a man of honour, and he had simply abused her hospitality. He was thirty-four or thirty-five years of age so that youth could not be pleaded as his excuse; nor could ignorance be his excuse since he was a man who had seen something of the world. He had simply taken advantage of Polly's youth and inexperience: that was evident. The question was: What reparation[9] would he make?

There must be reparation made in such cases. It is all very well for the man: he can go his ways as if nothing had happened, having had his moment of pleasure, but the girl has

85

90

95

100

105

110

115

120

---

96 frank(1)] 10; specific MS   96 questions] 10; enquiries MS   96 frank(2)] 10; decided MS   107 lots] 10; plenty MS   108–109 short twelve] 10; short twelve mass MS

7. Presumably Bibles or prayer books.
8. A Mass without the liturgical embellishments of a "High Mass" at the Roman Catholic Pro-Cathedral.
9. Compensation for an injury, part of atonement for a sin.

to bear the brunt. Some mothers would be content to patch up such an affair for a sum of money: she had known cases of it. But she would not do so. For her only one reparation could make up for the loss of her daughter's honour: marriage.   125

She counted all her cards again before sending Mary up to Mr Doran's room to say that she wished to speak with him. She felt sure she would win. He was a serious young man, not rakish or loudvoiced like the others. If it had been Mr Sheri= dan or Mr Meade or Bantam Lyons her task would have been   130 much harder. She did not think he would face publicity. All the lodgers in the house knew something of the affair; details had been invented by some. Besides, he had been em= ployed for thirteen years in a great catholic winemerchant's office and publicity would mean for him, perhaps, the loss of   135 his sit.[1] Whereas if he agreed all might be well. She knew he had a good screw[2] for one thing and she suspected he had a bit of stuff put by.

Nearly the half-hour! She stood up and surveyed herself in the pierglass.[3] The decisive expression of her great florid face   140 satisfied her and she thought of some mothers she knew who could not get their daughters off their hands.

Mr Doran was very anxious indeed this Sunday morning. He had made two attempts to shave but his hand had been so unsteady that he had been obliged to desist. Three days'   145 reddish beard fringed his jaws and every two or three minutes a mist gathered on his glasses so that he had to take them off and polish them with his pocket-handkerchief. The recollection of his confession[4] of the night before was a cause of acute pain to him: the priest had drawn out every ridiculous detail of the   150 affair and in the end had so magnified his sin that he was almost thankful at being afforded a loophole of reparation. The harm was done. What could he do now but marry her or run away? He could not brazen it out: the affair would be sure to be talked of. His employer would be certain to hear of it.   155 Dublin is such a small city—everyone knows everyone else's business. He felt his heart leap warmly in his throat as he heard in his excited imagination old Mr Leonard calling out in his rasping voice *Send Mr Doran here, please.*

---

124 could] 10; would MS   126 She] 10; NO PARAGRAPH MS   127 him.] 10; him(:); MS
130 Bantam] 10; Mr MS   136 sit.] 10; job. MS   138 stuff] 10; money MS
139 Nearly] 10; NO PARAGRAPH MS   143 Mr] 10; NO PARAGRAPH MS

1. Situation, or position.
2. Salary, or wages.
3. A tall mirror, often between two windows or over a chimneypiece.
4. The Roman Catholic sacrament or ritual whereby the sinner, or penitent, privately recounts sins to the priest in return for formal forgiveness and restitution to God's grace.

All his long years of service gone for nothing! All his   160
industry and diligence thrown away! As a young man he had
sown his wild oats, of course; he had boasted of his freethink=
ing and denied the existence of God to his companions in
publichouses. But that was all past and done with .... nearly.
He still bought a copy of *Reynolds's Newspaper*[5] every week   165
but he attended to his religious duties[6] and for nine tenths of the
year lived a regular life. He had money enough to settle down
on: it was not that. But the family would look down on her.
First of all there was her disreputable father and then her
mother's boarding house was beginning to get a certain fame.   170
He had a notion that he was being had. He could imagine his
friends talking of the affair and laughing. She *was* a little
vulgar; sometimes she said *I seen* and *If I had've known*. But
what would grammar matter if he really loved her? He could
not make up his mind whether to like her or despise her for   175
what she had done. Of course, he had done it too. His instinct
urged him to remain free, not to marry. Once you are married
you are done for, it said.

While he was sitting helplessly on the side of the bed in shirt
and trousers she tapped lightly at his door and entered. She told   180
him all, that she had made a clean breast of it to her mother
and that her mother would speak with him that morning. She
cried and threw her arms round his neck, saying:

—O Bob! Bob! What am I to do? what am I to do at all?

She would put an end to herself, she said. He comforted her   185
feebly, telling her not to cry, that it would be all right, never
fear. He felt against his shirt the agitation of her bosom.

It was not altogether his fault that it had happened. He
remembered well, with the curious patient memory of the
celibate, the first casual caresses her dress, her breath, her   190
fingers had given him. Then late one night as he was undress=
ing for bed she had tapped at his door, timidly. She wanted to
relight her candle at his for hers had been blown out by a gust.
It was her bath night. She wore a loose open combing jacket[7] of

160 All(1)] 10; NO PARAGRAPH MS   164 past] STET MS   168 But the] 10; His MS
179 the(2)] 10; his MS   185 She] 10; She said she MS   185 herself,--said.] 10; herself.
MS   185 He] STET NO PARAGRAPH MS   186 telling her] 10; saying that she was MS
188 It] 10; NO PARAGRAPH MS   191 fingers] 10; arms MS   191–198 Then--arose.] 10;
ABSENT MS

5. A London newspaper that specialized in political and social scandals.
6. To be Catholics in good standing, the Church required its members to perform certain
   religious duties including attending Mass on Sunday, making an annual confession,
   abstaining from meat on Fridays and fasting in Lent, receiving Communion during Easter
   week, and observing the laws of the Church with respect to marriage.
7. A bed jacket adorned with a border.

printed flannel. Her white instep shone in the opening of her   195
furry slippers and the blood glowed warmly behind her per=
fumed skin. From her hands and wrists too as she lit and
steadied her candle a faint perfume arose.

On nights when he came in very late it was she who warmed
up his dinner. He scarcely knew what he was eating, feeling her   200
beside him alone, at night, in the sleeping house. And her
thoughtfulness! If the night was anyway cold or wet or windy
there was sure to be a little tumbler of punch[8] ready for him.
Perhaps they could be happy together ......

They used to go upstairs together on tiptoe, each with a   205
candle, and on the third landing exchange reluctant good=
nights. They used to kiss. He remembered well her eyes, the
touch of her hand and his delirium ......

But delirium passes. He echoed her phrase, applying it to
himself: *What am I to do?* The instinct of the celibate warned   210
him to hold back. But the sin was there: even his sense of
honour told him that reparation must be made for such a sin.

While he was sitting with her on the side of the bed Mary
came to the door and said that the missus wanted to see him in
the parlour. He stood up to put on his coat and waistcoat,   215
more helpless than ever. When he was dressed he went over to
her to comfort her. It would be all right, never fear. He left her
crying on the bed and moaning softly: *O my God!*

Going down the stairs his glasses became so dimmed with
moisture that he had to take them off and polish them. He   220
longed to ascend through the roof and fly away to another
country where he would never hear again of his trouble and yet
a force pushed him downstairs step by step. The implacable
faces of his employer and of the Madam stared upon his
discomfiture. On the last flight of stairs he passed Jack Mooney   225
who was coming up from the pantry nursing two bottles of
Bass.[9] They saluted coldly and the lover's eyes rested for a
second or two on a thick bulldog face and a pair of thick short
arms. When he reached the foot of the stairs he glanced up and
saw Jack regarding him from the door of the return room.[1]   230

Suddenly he remembered the night when one of the music=

---

199 On] 10; NO PARAGRAPH MS   200 dinner.] 10; dinner for him. MS   200 scarcely
knew] 10; could scarcely tell MS   203 sure to be] 10; ABSENT MS   205 They] 10; NO
PARAGRAPH MS   219 dimmed] 10; muffed MS   226 nursing] 10; with MS   228 on]
on ⟨t⟩ MS   229 stairs] STET MS   231 Suddenly] 10; NO PARAGRAPH MS

8. A hot beverage of wine, whiskey, rum, or other liquor mixed with hot water or milk, and
   honey or spices—popular in cold or rainy weather.
9. A brand of strong, dark ale.
1. A small addition attached to the house.

hall *artistes,* a little blond Londoner, had made a rather free allusion to Polly. The reunion had been almost broken up on account of Jack's violence. Everyone tried to quieten him. The musichall *artiste,* a little paler than usual, kept smiling and saying that there was no harm meant but Jack kept shouting at him that if any fellow tried that sort of a game on with *his* sister he'd bloody well put his teeth down his throat, so he would. 235

◆   ◆   ◆

Polly sat for a little time on the side of the bed, crying. Then she dried her eyes and went over to the lookingglass. She dipped the end of the towel in the waterjug and refreshed her eyes with the cool water. She looked at herself in profile and readjusted a hairpin above her ear. Then she went back to the bed again and sat at the foot. She regarded the pillows for a long time and the sight of them awoke in her mind secret amiable memories. She rested the nape of her neck against the cool iron bedrail and fell into a revery. There was no longer any perturbation visible on her face. 240 245

She waited on patiently, almost cheerfully, without alarm, her memories gradually giving place to hopes and visions of the future. Her hopes and visions were so intricate that she no longer saw the white pillows on which her gaze was fixed or remembered that she was waiting for anything. 250

At last she heard her mother calling. She started to her feet and ran to the banisters. 255

—Polly! Polly!

—Yes, mamma?

—Come down, dear. Mr Doran wants to speak to you.

Then she remembered what she had been waiting for. 260

234 Jack's] Jack's ⟨□⟩ MS   234 quieten] STET MS   236 Jack] Jack ⟨ha⟩ MS
246 awoke] STET MS   248 revery.] 10; mood of reminiscence. MS   255 At] 10; NO PAR-
AGRAPH MS   255–256 calling.--ran] 10; calling her and she jumped up and ran out MS
260 Then--remembered] 10; She remembered now MS   260 for.] 10; for: this was
it. MS

A Little Cloud[1]

Eight years before he had seen his friend off at the North Wall[2] and wished him godspeed. Gallaher had got on. You could tell that at once by his travelled air, his well-cut tweed suit and fearless accent. Few fellows had talents like his and fewer still could remain unspoiled by such success. Gallaher's heart was in the right place and he had deserved to win. It was something to have a friend like that.

Little Chandler's thoughts ever since lunchtime had been of his meeting with Gallaher, of Gallaher's invitation and of the great city London where Gallaher lived. He was called Little Chandler because, though he was but slightly under the average stature, he gave one the idea of being a little man. His hands were white and small, his frame was fragile, his voice was quiet and his manners were refined. He took the greatest care of his fair silken hair and moustache and used perfume discreetly on his handkerchief. The half moons of his nails were perfect and when he smiled you caught a glimpse of a row of childish white teeth.

As he sat at his desk in the King's Inns[3] he thought what changes those eight years had brought. The friend whom he had known under a shabby and necessitous guise had become a brilliant figure on the London press. He turned often from his tiresome writing to gaze out of the office window. The glow of a late autumn sunset covered the grass plots and walks. It cast a shower of kindly golden dust on the untidy nurses and decrepit old men who drowsed on the benches; it flickered upon all the moving figures—on the children who ran screaming along the gravel paths and on everyone who passed through the gardens.[4] He watched the scene and thought of life; and (as always happened when he thought of life) he became sad. A gentle melancholy took possession of him. He felt how useless it was to struggle against fortune, this being the burden of wisdom which the ages had bequeathed to him.

He remembered the books of poetry upon his shelves at

Copy-text: 1910 late proofs (10); Collated texts: 1914 proofs (14P) and 1914 first edition (14) [IDENTITY IN BOTH IS REPORTED AS '14']; 1967 Viking edition in the 1969 Viking Critical Library printing (67).

1. A possible reference to I Kings 18:44 in the Bible, where the onset of rain after a long drought is announced by the prophet Elijah: "Behold there ariseth a little cloud out of the sea, like a man's hand."
2. A dock on the north side of the Liffey from which steamboats and ships departed for Liverpool and other ports.
3. Government buildings that housed legal organizations, offices, archives, and libraries.
4. The King's Inns are located in a small park on the north side of the river Liffey.

home. He had bought them in his bachelor days and many an   35
evening, as he sat in the little room off the hall, he had been
tempted to take one down from the bookshelf and read out
something to his wife. But shyness had always held him back,
and so the books had remained on their shelves. At times he
repeated lines to himself and this consoled him.   40

When his hour had struck he stood up and took leave of his
desk and of his fellow clerks[5] punctiliously. He emerged from
under the feudal arch of the King's Inns, a neat modest figure,
and walked swiftly down Henrietta Street.[6] The golden sunset
was waning and the air had grown sharp. A horde of grimy   45
children populated the street. They stood or ran in the roadway
or crawled up the steps before the gaping doors or squatted like
mice upon the thresholds. Little Chandler gave them no
thought. He picked his way deftly through all that minute
verminlike life and under the shadow of the gaunt spectral   50
mansions in which the old nobility of Dublin had roistered.[7] No
memory of the past touched him, for his mind was full of a
present joy.

He had never been in Corless's[8] but he knew the value of the
name. He knew that people went there after the theatre to eat   55
oysters and drink liqueurs; and he had heard that the waiters
there spoke French and German. Walking swiftly by at night he
had seen cabs drawn up before the door and richly dressed
ladies, escorted by cavaliers,[9] alight and enter quickly. They
wore noisy dresses and many wraps. Their faces were pow=   60
dered and they caught up their dresses, when they touched
earth, like alarmed Atalantas.[1] He had always passed without
turning his head to look. It was his habit to walk swiftly in the
street even by day and whenever he found himself in the city
late at night he hurried on his way apprehensively and ex=   65
citedly. Sometimes, however, he courted the causes of his fear.
He chose the darkest and narrowest streets and, as he walked

---

44. Street.] Street. 10 ENDS

5. Suggests that Thomas Chandler works in the King's Inns as a law clerk.
6. A street that runs out from the King's Inns, lined with shabby dwellings and tenements at the time of the story.
7. That is, mansions that had once been the homes of the lively upper-class and aristocratic society of Dublin, now stripped and crowded with poor families.
8. An elegant bar and restaurant associated with the Burlington Hotel, in central Dublin on the south side of the Liffey.
9. Courtly gentlemen.
1. Atalanta, a princess in Greek mythology, tried to avoid marriage by challenging her suitors to a footrace and then outrunning them. However, one of her suitors threw three golden apples down as he ran, and the surprised Atalanta stooped to pick them up and thereby lost the race.

boldly forward, the silence that was spread about his footsteps troubled him, the wandering silent figures troubled him, and at times a sound of low fugitive laughter made him tremble like a leaf.

He turned to the right towards Capel Street. Ignatius Galla= her on the London press! Who would have thought it possible eight years before? Still, now that he reviewed the past, Little Chandler could remember many signs of future greatness in his friend. People used to say that Ignatius Gallaher was wild. Of course, he did mix with a rakish set of fellows at that time, drank freely and borrowed money on all sides. In the end he had got mixed up in some shady affair, some money transac= tion: at least, that was one version of his flight. But nobody denied him talent. There was always a certain ... something in Ignatius Gallaher that impressed you in spite of yourself. Even when he was out at elbows[2] and at his wits' end for money he kept up a bold face. Little Chandler remembered (and the remembrance brought a slight flush of pride to his cheek) one of Ignatius Gallaher's sayings when he was in a tight corner:

—Half time[3] now, boys, he used to say lightheartedly. Where's my considering cap?[4]

That was Ignatius Gallaher all out; and, damn it, you couldn't but admire him for it.

Little Chandler quickened his pace. For the first time in his life he felt himself superior to the people he passed. For the first time his soul revolted against the dull inelegance of Capel Street.[5] There was no doubt about it: if you wanted to succeed you had to go away. You could do nothing in Dublin. As he crossed Grattan Bridge he looked down the river towards the lower quays and pitied the poor stunted houses. They seemed to him a band of tramps huddled together along the river banks, their old coats covered with dust and soot, stupefied by the panorama of sunset and waiting for the first chill of night to bid them arise, shake themselves and begone. He wondered whether he could write a poem to express his idea. Perhaps Gallaher might be able to get it into some London paper for him. Could he write something original? He was not sure what

70 of] 14; of a 14P   94 wanted] wanted 10 RESUMES

2. Ragged, or impoverished.
3. The break or rest period in sports events when teams who are trailing have an opportunity to reassess their strategy and make corrections in their course.
4. A metaphorical hat or cap to confer wisdom or sharpen concentration—also called a "thinking cap."
5. Once a fashionable residential area, Capel Street had become a busy commercial and shopping area by the time of the story.

idea he wished to express but the thought that a poetic moment 105
had touched him took life within him like an infant hope. He
stepped onward bravely.

Every step brought him nearer to London, farther from his
own sober inartistic life. A light began to tremble on the
horizon of his mind. He was not so old—thirty-two. His 110
temperament might be said to be just at the point of maturity.
There were so many different moods and impressions that he
wished to express in verse. He felt them within him. He tried to
weigh his soul to see if it was a poet's soul. Melancholy was the
dominant note of his temperament, he thought, but it was a 115
melancholy tempered by recurrences of faith and resignation
and simple joy. If he could give expression to it in a book of
poems perhaps men would listen. He would never be popular:
he saw that. He could not sway the crowd but he might appeal
to a little circle of kindred minds. The English critics perhaps 120
would recognise him as one of the Celtic school[6] by reason of
the melancholy tone of his poems; besides that, he would put in
allusions. He began to invent sentences and phrases from the
notices which his book would get. *Mr Chandler has the gift of
easy and graceful verse. ... A wistful sadness pervades these* 125
poems. ... The Celtic note. It was a pity his name was not more
Irish looking. Perhaps it would be better to insert his mother's
name before the surname: Thomas Malone Chandler, or better
still: T Malone Chandler. He would speak to Gallaher about it.

He pursued his revery so ardently that he passed his street 130
and had to turn back. As he came near Corless's his former
agitation began to overmaster him and he halted before the
door in indecision. Finally he opened the door and entered.

The light and noise of the bar held him at the doorway for a
few moments. He looked about him but his sight was confused 135
by the shining of many red and green wineglasses. The bar
seemed to him to be full of people and he felt that the people
were observing him curiously. He glanced quickly to right and
left (frowning slightly to make his errand appear serious) but
when his sight cleared a little he saw that nobody had turned to 140
look at him: and there, sure enough, was Ignatius Gallaher
leaning with his back against the counter and his feet planted
far apart.

—Hello, Tommy, old hero, here you are! What is it to be?

124 notices] STET 10, JJ CORRECTIONS 1914   134 doorway] STET 10, JJ CORRECTIONS 1914

6. English characterization of Irish poets of the late nineteenth century as producing writing
that wistfully looked back on the lost heritage of Gaelic folklore and legend with dreamy,
otherworldly sorrow.

What will you have? I'm taking whisky: better stuff than we get   145
across the water. Soda? Lithia?[7] No mineral? I'm the same.
Spoils the flavour. ... Here, *garçon*,[8] bring us two halves of malt
whisky like a good fellow. ... Well, and how have you been
pulling along ever since I saw you last? Dear God, how old
we're getting! Do you see any signs of aging in me—eh, what? A   150
little grey and thin on the top—what?

Ignatius Gallaher took off his hat and displayed a large
closely cropped head. His face was heavy, pale and clean=
shaven. His eyes, which were of bluish slate colour, relieved his
unhealthy pallor and shone out plainly above the vivid orange   155
tie[9] he wore. Between these rival features the lips appeared very
long and shapeless and colourless. He bent his head and felt
with two sympathetic fingers the thin hair at the crown. Little
Chandler shook his head as a denial. Ignatius Gallaher put on
his hat again.   160

—It pulls you down, he said, press life. Always hurry and
scurry, looking for copy and sometimes not finding it: and then
always to have something new in your stuff. Damn proofs and
printers, I say, for a few days. I'm deuced[1] glad, I can tell you, to
get back to the old country. Does a fellow good, a bit of a   165
holiday. I feel a ton better since I landed again in dear dirty
Dublin[2] ... Here you are, Tommy. Water? Say when.

Little Chandler allowed his whisky to be very much diluted.

—You don't know what's good for you, my boy, said Ignatius
Gallaher. I drink mine neat.   170

—I drink very little as a rule, said Little Chandler modestly. An
odd half one or so when I meet any of the old crowd: that's all.

—Ah well, said Ignatius Gallaher cheerfully, here's to us and
to old times and old acquaintance.

They clinked glasses and drank the toast.   175

—I met some of the old gang today, said Ignatius Gallaher.
O'Hara seems to be in a bad way. What's he doing?

—Nothing, said Little Chandler. He's gone to the dogs.[3]

—But Hogan has a good sit,[4] hasn't he?

—Yes; he's in the Land Commission.[5]   180

7. A bottled spring water used, like mineral water or soda, to dilute alcoholic drinks.
8. A French term for a waiter.
9. The color orange is pejoratively associated in Irish politics with William of Orange, the
   Protestant British monarch who as William III led the defeat of the Irish at the 1690
   Battle of the Boyne. Pro-British Irish Protestants were sometimes called "Orangemen."
1. Devilishly or emphatically.
2. An affectionate name given to Ireland by the Irish writer Lady Sydney Morgan.
3. Failed on all fronts.
4. Situation, or position.
5. The Irish Land Commission was a governmental agency that oversaw the purchase—often
   backed by British credit—of farmland by tenants from their landlords.

—I met him one night in London and he seemed to be very flush.[6] ... Poor O'Hara! Boose, I suppose?

—Other things, too, said Little Chandler shortly.

Ignatius Gallaher laughed.

—Tommy, he said, I see you haven't changed an atom. You're the very same serious person that used to lecture me on Sunday mornings when I had a sore head and a fur on my tongue.[7] You'd want to knock about a bit in the world. Have you never been anywhere, even for a trip?

—I've been to the Isle of Man,[8] said Little Chandler.

Ignatius Gallaher laughed.

—The Isle of Man! he said. Go to London or Paris: Paris, for choice. That'd do you good.

—Have you seen Paris?

—I should think I have! I've knocked about there a little.

—And is it really so beautiful as they say? asked Little Chandler.

He sipped a little of his drink while Ignatius Gallaher finished his boldly.

—Beautiful? said Ignatius Gallaher, pausing on the word and on the flavour of his drink. It's not so beautiful, you know. Of course, it is beautiful. ... But it's the life of Paris: that's the thing. Ah, there's no city like Paris for gaiety, movement, excitement. ...

Little Chandler finished his whisky and after some trouble succeeded in catching the barman's eye. He ordered the same again.

—I've been to the Moulin Rouge,[9] Ignatius Gallaher continued when the barman had removed their glasses, and I've been to all the bohemian cafés.[1] Hot stuff! Not for a pious chap like you, Tommy.

Little Chandler said nothing until the barman returned with the two glasses: then he touched his friend's glass lightly and reciprocated the former toast. He was beginning to feel some= what disillusioned. Gallaher's accent and way of expressing himself did not please him. There was something vulgar in his friend which he had not observed before. But perhaps it was only the result of living in London amid the bustle and competition of the press. The old personal charm was still there

6. Well-off financially and otherwise; highly self-confident.
7. Slurred speech caused by drunkenness.
8. Island in the Irish Sea, between Ireland and England, that served as a quick and inexpensive destination for Dublin vacationers.
9. French for the Red Mill; the Moulin Rouge was one of the great Paris music halls of the late nineteenth century, frequented by artists and bohemians, and associated with risqué performances such as the cancan.
1. Cabarets frequented by artists and freethinking intellectuals.

under this new gaudy manner. And, after all, Gallaher had 220
lived, he had seen the world. Little Chandler looked at his
friend enviously.

—Everything in Paris is gay, said Ignatius Gallaher. They
believe in enjoying life and don't you think they're right? If you
want to enjoy yourself properly you must go to Paris. And, 225
mind you, they've a great feeling for the Irish there. When they
heard I was from Ireland they were ready to eat me,[2] man.

Little Chandler took four or five sips from his glass.

—Tell me, he said, is it true that Paris is so ... immoral as they
say? 230

Ignatius Gallaher made a catholic[3] gesture with his right arm.

—Every place is immoral, he said. Of course you do find spicy
bits in Paris. Go to one of the students' balls, for instance.
That's lively, if you like, when the *cocottes*[4] begin to let them=
selves loose. You know what they are, I suppose? 235

—I've heard of them, said Little Chandler.

Ignatius Gallaher drank off his whisky and shook his head.

—Ah, he said, you may say what you like. There's no woman
like the Parisienne for style, for go.

—Then it is an immoral city, said Little Chandler with timid 240
insistence, I mean, compared with London or Dublin?

—London! said Ignatius Gallaher. It's six of one and half a
dozen of the other. You ask Hogan, my boy. I showed him a bit
about London when he was over there. He'd open your eye. ...
I say, Tommy, don't make punch of that whisky:[5] liquor up. 245

—No, really. ...

—O, come on, another one won't do you any harm. What is
it? The same again, I suppose?

—Well ... all right.

—*François*,[6] the same again. ... Will you smoke, Tommy? 250

Ignatius Gallaher produced his cigar case. The two friends
lit their cigars and puffed at them in silence until their drinks
were served.

—I'll tell you my opinion, said Ignatius Gallaher, emerging
after some time from the clouds of smoke in which he had 255
taken refuge, it's a rum world.[7] Talk of immorality! I've heard
of cases—what am I saying—I've known them: cases of ...
immorality ....

Ignatius Gallaher puffed thoughtfully at his cigar and then,

2. Consume with avid interest and excitement, as in to "eat up."
3. All-embracing.
4. French for "hens," referring to loose women or prostitutes.
5. Don't dilute the whiskey.
6. Like calling a waiter *garçon*, this is an affectation in the form of a francophonic expression.
7. Odd, strange, or queer.

in a calm historian's tone, he proceeded to sketch for his friend 260
some pictures of the corruption which was rife abroad. He
summarised the vices of many capitals and seemed inclined to
award the palm to Berlin. Some things he could not vouch for
(his friends had told him) but of others he had had personal
experience. He spared neither rank nor caste. He revealed 265
many of the secrets of religious houses on the continent[8] and
described some of the practices which were fashionable in high
society: and ended by telling, with details, a story about an
English duchess[9]—a story which he knew to be true. Little
Chandler was astonished. 270

—Ah, well, said Ignatius Gallaher, here we are in old jogalong
Dublin where nothing is known of such things.

—How dull you must find it, said Little Chandler, after all the
other places you've seen!

—Well, said Ignatius Gallaher, it's a relaxation to come over 275
here, you know. And, after all, it's the old country, as they say,
isn't it? You can't help having a certain feeling for it. That's
human nature. ... But tell me something about yourself. Hogan
told me you had ... tasted the joys of connubial bliss.[1] Two years
ago, wasn't it? 280

Little Chandler blushed and smiled.

—Yes, he said. I was married last May twelve months.

—I hope it's not too late in the day to offer my best wishes,
said Ignatius Gallaher. I didn't know your address or I'd have
done so at the time. 285

He extended his hand which Little Chandler took.

—Well, Tommy, he said, I wish you and yours every joy in life,
old chap, and tons of money and may you never die till I shoot
you.[2] And that's the wish of a sincere friend, an old friend. You
know that? 290

—I know that, said Little Chandler.

—Any youngsters? said Ignatius Gallaher.

Little Chandler blushed again.

—We have one child, he said.

—Son or daughter? 295

—A little boy.

Ignatius Gallaher slapped his friend sonorously on the back.

8. Anti-Catholic or anticlerical rumors and fantasies of sexual orgies in convents and abbeys
   in continental Europe were not uncommon in the nineteenth century.
9. Similar rumors and fantasies about depravities among members of the British aristocracy
   were also staples of stories and gossip in Victorian England.
1. Married.
2. Presumably an expression of well-wishing for a long life, since a friend would never shoot
   another friend.

—Bravo, he said, I wouldn't doubt you,[3] Tommy.

Little Chandler smiled, looked confusedly at his glass and bit his lower lip with three childishly white front teeth.

—I hope you'll spend an evening with us, he said, before you go back. My wife will be delighted to meet you. We can have a little music and ...

—Thanks awfully, old chap, said Ignatius Gallaher, I'm sorry we didn't meet earlier. But I must leave tomorrow night.

—Tonight, perhaps. ...

—I'm awfully sorry, old man. You see I'm over here with an= other fellow, clever young chap he is too, and we arranged to go to a little card party. Only for that ....

—O, in that case. ...

—But who knows? said Ignatius Gallaher considerately. Next year I may take a little skip over here now that I've broken the ice. It's only a pleasure deferred.

—Very well, said Little Chandler, the next time you come we must have an evening together. That's agreed now, isn't it?

—Yes, that's agreed, said Ignatius Gallaher. Next year if I come, *parole d'honneur*.[4]

—And to clinch the bargain, said Little Chandler, we'll just have one more now.

Ignatius Gallaher took out a large gold watch and looked at it.

—Is it to be the last? he said. Because, you know, I have an a.p.[5]

—O yes, positively, said Little Chandler.

—Very well then, said Ignatius Gallaher, let us have another one as a *deoc an doruis*[6]—that's good vernacular for a small whisky, I believe.

Little Chandler ordered the drinks. The blush which had risen to his face a few moments before was establishing itself. A trifle made him blush at any time: and now he felt warm and excited. Three small whiskies had gone to his head and Galla= her's strong cigar had confused his mind for he was a delicate and abstinent person. The adventure of meeting Gallaher after eight years, of finding himself with Gallaher in Corless's sur= rounded by lights and noise, of listening to Gallaher's stories and of sharing for a brief space Gallaher's vagrant and trium=

---

3. Possibly a backhanded compliment to Chandler's virility, implying that the speaker never doubted his ability to produce a child.
4. French for word of honor, or "promise."
5. A.p. is short for "additional premium" and could refer to Gallaher's plans for additional drinking later in the evening. Also possibly slang for "an appointment," or a reference to "author's proof," the last critical stage in the editing process.
6. Gaelic for a drink at the door, or "one for the road."

phant life, upset the equipoise[7] of his sensitive nature. He felt
acutely the contrast between his own life and his friend's and it
seemed to him unjust. Gallaher was his inferior in birth and
education. He was sure that he could do something better than
his friend had ever done, or could ever do, something higher   340
than mere tawdry journalism if only he got the chance. What
was it that stood in his way? His unfortunate timidity! He
wished to vindicate himself in some way, to assert his man=
hood. He saw behind Gallaher's refusal of his invitation. Gal=
laher was only patronising him by his friendliness just as he   345
was patronising Ireland by his visit.

The barman brought their drinks. Little Chandler pushed
one glass towards his friend and took up the other boldly.

—Who knows? he said as they lifted their glasses. When you
come next year I may have the pleasure of wishing long life and   350
happiness to Mr and Mrs Ignatius Gallaher.

Ignatius Gallaher in the act of drinking closed one eye
expressively over the rim of his glass. When he had drunk he
smacked his lips decisively, set down his glass and said:

—No blooming[8] fear of that, my boy. I'm going to have my   355
fling first and see a bit of life and the world before I put my
head in the sack—if I ever do.

—Some day you will, said Little Chandler calmly.

Ignatius Gallaher turned his orange tie and slateblue eyes
full upon his friend.   360

—You think so? he said.

—You'll put your head in the sack,[9] repeated Little Chandler
stoutly, like everyone else, if you can find the girl.

He had slightly emphasised his tone and he was aware that
he had betrayed himself; but though the colour had heightened   365
in his cheek he did not flinch from his friend's gaze. Ignatius
Gallaher watched him for a few moments and then said:

—If ever it occurs you may bet your bottom dollar there'll
be no mooning and spooning[1] about it. I mean to marry money.
She'll have a good fat account at the bank or she won't do for   370
me.

Little Chandler shook his head.

—Why, man alive, said Ignatius Gallaher vehemently, do you
know what it is? I've only to say the word and tomorrow I can

341 only he] STET 10

7. Delicate and perfect balance.
8. British slang for "damned."
9. Possible reference to the Roman or medieval punishment of forcing a person into a sack
   and then drowning him.
1. Courting in a sentimental, or moonstruck, manner.

have the woman and the cash. You don't believe it? Well, I   375
know it. There are hundreds—what am I saying?—thousands of
rich Germans and Jews, rotten with money, that'd only be too
glad. ... You wait awhile, my boy. See if I don't play my cards
properly. When I go about a thing I mean business, I tell you.
You just wait.   380

He tossed his glass to his mouth, finished his drink and
laughed loudly. Then he looked thoughtfully before him and
said in a calmer tone:
—But I'm in no hurry. They can wait. I don't fancy tying
myself up to one woman, you know.   385

He imitated with his mouth the act of tasting and made a
wry face.
—Must get a bit stale, I should think, he said.

◆   ◆   ◆

Little Chandler sat in the room off the hall, holding a child
in his arms. To save money they kept no servant but Annie's   390
young sister Monica came for an hour or so in the morning and
an hour or so in the evening to help. But Monica had gone
home long ago. It was a quarter to nine. Little Chandler had
come home late for tea[2] and, moreover, he had forgotten to
bring Annie home the parcel of coffee from Bewley's.[3] Of course   395
she was in a bad humour and gave him short answers. She said
she would do without any tea but when it came near the time
at which the shop at the corner closed she decided to go out
herself for a quarter of a pound of tea and two pounds of
sugar. She put the sleeping child deftly in his arms and said: 400
—Here. Don't waken him.

A little lamp with a white china shade stood upon the table
and its light fell over a photograph which was enclosed in a
frame of crumpled horn.[4] It was Annie's photograph. Little
Chandler looked at it, pausing at the thin tight lips. She wore   405
the pale blue summer blouse which he had brought her home as
a present one Saturday. It had cost him ten and elevenpence;[5]
but what an agony of nervousness it had cost him! How he had
suffered that day, waiting at the shopdoor until the shop was
empty, standing at the counter and trying to appear at his ease   410
while the girl piled ladies' blouses before him, paying at the

377 rotten] rotto INTENDED? [CF *Ulysses* 1.700]

2. Late for evening supper, at which tea was the usual beverage.
3. Famous tearooms in Dublin that also sold tea, coffee, and other comestibles.
4. The substance of animal horns was sometimes used to fashion ornamental objects.
5. If this means ten shillings and eleven pence, then it is indeed an extravagant gift. Eveline
   Hill in the story "Eveline" earns only seven shillings per week as a shopgirl. Even if Chandler earns considerably more as a law clerk, the sum would still seem substantial.

desk and forgetting to take up the odd penny of his change, being called back by the cashier and, finally, striving to hide his blushes as he left the shop by examining the parcel to see if it was securely tied. When he brought the blouse home Annie   415 kissed him and said it was very pretty and stylish but when she heard the price she threw the blouse on the table and said it was a regular swindle to charge ten and elevenpence for that. At first she wanted to take it back but when she tried it on she was delighted with it, especially with the make of the sleeves,   420 and kissed him and said he was very good to think of her.

Hm! ...

He looked coldly into the eyes of the photograph and they answered coldly. Certainly they were pretty and the face itself was pretty. But he found something mean in it. Why was it so   425 unconscious and ladylike? The composure of the eyes irritated him. They repelled him and defied him: there was no passion in them, no rapture. He thought of what Gallaher had said about rich Jewesses. Those dark oriental eyes, he thought, how full they are of passion, of voluptuous longing! ... Why had he   430 married the eyes in the photograph?

He caught himself up at the question and glanced nervously round the room. He found something mean in the pretty furniture which he had bought for his house on the hire system.[6] Annie had chosen it herself and it reminded him of her. It too   435 was prim and pretty. A dull resentment against his life awoke within him. Could he not escape from his little house? Was it too late for him to try to live bravely like Gallaher? Could he go to London? There was the furniture still to be paid for. If he could only write a book and get it published, that might open   440 the way for him.

A volume of Byron's poems lay before him on the table. He opened it cautiously with his left hand lest he should waken the child and began to read the first poem in the book:

> Hushed are the winds and still the evening gloom,   445
>   Not e'en a Zephyr wanders through the grove,
> Whilst I return to view my Margaret's tomb
>   And scatter flowers on the dust I love.[7]

He paused. He felt the rhythm of the verse about him in the room. How melancholy it was! Could he, too, write like that,   450 express the melancholy of his soul in verse? There were so

418 that.] STET 10

6. On a plan to pay for it in installments.
7. The first stanza of an 1802 poem by Lord Byron called "On the Death of a Young Lady, Cousin of the Author, and Very Dear to Him."

many things he wanted to describe: his sensation of a few hours
before on Grattan Bridge, for example. If he could get back
again into that mood. ...

The child awoke and began to cry. He turned from the page   455
and tried to hush it: but it would not be hushed. He began to
rock it to and fro in his arms but its wailing cry grew keener.
He rocked it faster while his eyes began to read the second
stanza:

> *Within this narrow cell reclines her clay,*   460
> *That clay where once ...* [8]

It was useless. He couldn't read. He couldn't do anything.
The wailing of the child pierced the drum of his ear. It was
useless, useless! He was a prisoner for life. His arms trembled
with anger and suddenly bending to the child's face he shouted: 465
—Stop!

The child stopped for an instant, had a spasm of fright and
began to scream. He jumped up from his chair and walked
hastily up and down the room with the child in his arms. It
began to sob piteously, losing its breath for four or five seconds   470
and then bursting out anew. The thin walls of the room echoed
the sound. He tried to soothe it but it sobbed more convul=
sively. He looked at the contracted and quivering face of the
child and began to be alarmed. He counted seven sobs without
a break between them and caught the child to his breast in   475
fright. If it died! ...

The door was burst open and a young woman ran in,
panting.
—What is it? What is it? she cried.

The child, hearing its mother's voice, broke out into a par=   480
oxysm of sobbing.[9]
—It's nothing, Annie ... it's nothing. ... He began to cry. ...

She flung her parcels on the floor and snatched the child
from him.
—What have you done to him? she cried, glaring into his face.   485

Little Chandler sustained for one moment the gaze of her
eyes and his heart closed together as he met the hatred in them.
He began to stammer:
—It's nothing. ... He ... he began to cry. ... I couldn't ... I didn't
do anything. ... What?   490

Giving no heed to him she began to walk up and down the
room, clasping the child tightly in her arms and murmuring:

---

8. The beginning of the second stanza of Byron's poem, which continues: "such animation
beam'd: / The king of terrors seiz'd her as his prey, / Not worth, nor beauty, have her life
redeem'd."
9. A violent convulsion.

—My little man! My little mannie! Was 'ou frightened, love? ...
There now, love! There now! ... Lambabaun![1] Mamma's little
lamb of the world! ... There now!   495

Little Chandler felt his cheeks suffused with shame and he
stood back out of the lamplight. He listened while the parox=
ysm of the child's sobbing grew less and less: and tears of
remorse started to his eyes.

Counterparts

The bell rang furiously and, when Miss Parker went to the
tube,[1] a furious voice called out in a piercing north of Ireland
accent:[2]
—Send Farrington here!

Miss Parker returned to her machine,[3] saying to a man who   5
was writing at a desk:
—Mr Alleyne wants you upstairs.

The man muttered *Blast him!* under his breath and pushed
back his chair to stand up. When he stood up he was tall and of
great bulk. He had a hanging face, dark winecoloured, with fair   10
eyebrows and moustache; his eyes bulged forward slightly and
the whites of them were dirty. He lifted up the counter and,
passing by the clients, went out of the office with a heavy step.

He went heavily upstairs until he came to the second landing
where a door bore a brass plate with the inscription *Mr*   15
Alleyne. Here he halted puffing with labour and vexation and
knocked. The shrill voice cried:
—Come in!

The man entered Mr Alleyne's room. Simultaneously Mr
Alleyne, a little man wearing goldrimmed glasses on a clean=   20
shaven face, shot his head up over a pile of documents. The

---

1. An Irish expression of endearment meaning "baby lamb."

Copy-text: Manuscript Yale 2.4 (MS): Collated texts: 1910 galley proofs [FRAGMENT] (10G)
and 1910 late proofs (10) [IDENTITY IN BOTH IS REPORTED AS '10']; 1914 proofs (14P) and
1914 first edition (14) [IDENTITY IN BOTH IS REPORTED AS '14']; 1967 Viking edition in the
1969 Viking Critical Library printing (67).

11 moustache;] e:MS, 10G; moustaches; MS; moustache: 10G   13 clients,] 10; people,
MS–10G   19 The PARAGRAPH] 10; and the RUN-ON SENTENCE MS; And the PARAGRAPH 10G
20 a(2)] 10; his MS   21 documents.] 10G; papers. MS

1. A device for communicating between rooms.
2. An accent that betrays the speaker's origin in the Protestant north of Ireland.
3. A typewriter.

head itself was so pink and hairless that it seemed like a large
egg reposing on the papers. Mr Alleyne did not lose a moment:
—Farrington! What is the meaning of this? Why have I always
to complain of you? May I ask you why you haven't made a   25
copy[4] of that contract between Bodley and Kirwan? I told you it
must be ready by four o'clock.
—But Mr Shelley said, sir, ...
—*Mr Shelley said, sir.* ..... Kindly attend to what I say and not
to what *Mr Shelley says, sir.* You have always some excuse or   30
another for shirking work. Let me tell you that if the contract is
not copied before this evening I'll lay the matter before Mr
Crosbie ... Do you hear me now?
—Yes, sir.
—Do you hear me now? .... Aye and another little matter! I   35
might as well be talking to the wall as talking to you. Under=
stand once for all that you get a half an hour for your lunch
and not an hour and a half. How many courses do you want,
I'd like to know? ... Do you mind me, now?
—Yes, sir.   40

Mr Alleyne bent his head again upon his pile of papers. The
man stared fixedly at the polished skull which directed the
affairs of Crosbie and Alleyne, gauging its fragility. A spasm of
rage gripped his throat for a few moments and then passed,
leaving after it a sharp sensation of thirst. The man recognised   45
the sensation and felt that he must have a good night's drink=
ing. The middle of the month was past and, if he could get the
copy done in time, Mr Alleyne might give him an order on the
cashier.[5] He stood still, gazing fixedly at the head upon the pile
of papers. Suddenly Mr Alleyne began to upset all the papers,   50
searching for something. Then, as if he had been unaware of
the man's presence till that moment, he shot up his head again,
saying:
—Eh! Are you going to stand there all the day? Upon my word,
Farrington, you take things easy!   55
—I was waiting to see. ....
—Very good, you needn't wait to see. Go downstairs and do
your work.

22 itself] 10G; ABSENT MS   31 another] 10G; other MS   33 Do--now?] 10; D'ye hear
me?—MS; D'ye hear me now? 10G, 14P   35 —Do you] 10;—D'ye MS—10G   39 Do
you] 10; D'ye MS–10G   50 Suddenly--began] 10G; Mr Alleyne suddenly began MS
51 something. Then,] 10G; something: at last, MS   55 easy!] 10; easily—MS

4. At the time of the story, certain legal documents had to be copied by hand to be considered
   legal. Farrington's work in the law offices of Crosbie and Alleyne is therefore the work of
   a professional scribe or copyist, also called a scrivener.
5. An advance on his salary.

The man walked heavily towards the door and as he went
out of the room he heard Mr Alleyne cry after him that if the   60
contract was not copied by evening Mr Crosbie would hear of
the matter.

He returned to his desk in the lower office and counted the
sheets which remained to be copied. He took up his pen and
dipped it in the ink but he continued to stare stupidly at the last   65
words he had written: *In no case shall the said Bernard Bodley
be* ...... The evening was falling and in a few minutes they
would be lighting the gas:[6] then he could write. He felt that he
must slake the thirst in his throat. He stood up from his desk
and, lifting the counter as before, passed out of the office. As   70
he was passing out the chief clerk looked at him inquiringly.
—It's all right, Mr Shelley, said the man pointing with his
finger to indicate the objective of his journey.[7]

The chief clerk glanced at the hatrack but, seeing the row
complete,[8] offered no remark. As soon as he was on the landing   75
the man pulled a shepherd's plaid cap out of his pocket, put it
on his head and ran quickly down the rickety stairs. From the
street door he walked on furtively on the inner side of the path
towards the corner and all at once dived into a doorway. He
was now safe in the dark snug of O'Neill's shop[9] and, filling up   80
the little window that looked into the bar with his inflamed
face, the colour of dark wine or dark meat, he called out:
—Here, Pat, give us a g.p.,[1] like a good fellow!

The curate[2] brought him a glass of plain porter. The man
drank it at a gulp and asked for a caraway seed.[3] He put his   85
penny on the counter and, leaving the curate to grope for it in
the gloom, retreated out of the snug as furtively as he had
entered it.

Darkness, accompanied by a thick fog, was gaining upon the
dusk of February and the lamps in Eustace Street had been lit.   90
The man went up by the houses until he reached the door of
the office, wondering whether he could finish his copy in time.

---

71 chief clerk] 10G; head-clerk MS   74 chief clerk] 10G; head-clerk MS   77 stairs.]
10G; staircase. MS   79 dived] 10G; disappeared MS   80 O'Neill's] 10; O'Reilly's
MS–10G   82 wine] 10G; meat MS   82 meat,] 10G; wine, MS   92 the] 10; his MS–
10G

6. The office was illuminated by gas lamps, which were lit manually at a specific time by
   someone assigned to the task.
7. Presumably the toilet.
8. The implication is that Farrington would not leave the building without his hat, and since
   no hat was missing from the rack, Mr. Shelley let him leave the room without further
   question.
9. A small parlor or den attached to the bar of J. J. O'Neill on Essex Street.
1. A glass filled with a half-pint of porter.
2. Waiter.
3. The herbal flavor of the seed would mask the smell of alcohol on the breath.

On the stairs a moist pungent odour of perfumes saluted his
nose: evidently Miss Delacour had come while he was out in
O'Neill's. He crammed his cap back again into his pocket and   95
reentered the office, assuming an air of absentmindedness.
—Mr Alleyne has been calling for you, said the chief clerk
severely. Where were you?
    The man glanced at the two clients who were standing at the
counter as if to intimate that their presence prevented him from   100
answering.[4] As the clients were both male the chief clerk
allowed himself a laugh:
—I know that game, he said. Five times in one day is a little
bit ..... Well, you better look sharp and get a copy of our
correspondence in the Delacour case for Mr Alleyne.   105
    This address in the presence of the public, his run upstairs
and the porter he had gulped down so hastily confused the man
and, as he sat down at his desk to get what was required, he
realised how hopeless was the task of finishing his copy of the
contract before half past five. The dark damp night was   110
coming and he longed to spend it in the bars, drinking with his
friends amid the glare of gas and the clatter of glasses. He got
out the Delacour correspondence and passed out of the office.
He hoped Mr Alleyne would not discover that the last two
letters were missing.   115
    The moist pungent perfume lay all the way up to Mr
Alleyne's room. Miss Delacour was a middleaged woman of
Jewish appearance. Mr Alleyne was said to be sweet on her or
on her money. She came to the office often and stayed a long
time when she came. She was sitting beside his desk now in an   120
aroma of perfumes, smoothing the handle of her umbrella and
nodding the great black feather in her hat. Mr Alleyne had
swivelled his chair round to face her and thrown his right foot
jauntily upon his left knee. The man put the correspondence on
the desk and bowed respectfully but neither Mr Alleyne nor   125
Miss Delacour took any notice of his bow. Mr Alleyne tapped
a finger on the correspondence and then flicked it towards him
as if to say *That's all right: you can go.*
    The man returned to the lower office and sat down again at
his desk. He stared intently at the incomplete phrase *In no case* 130

95 O'Neill's.] 10; O'Reilly's. MS–10G   97 calling] 10; looking MS–10G   97 chief
clerk] e:10G; head-clerk MS; chief clerk, 10G   98 Where--you?] 10G; where ⟨Where MS?⟩
have you been? MS   101 chief clerk] 10G; head-clerk MS   105 correspondence] GALLEY
PROOFS END   121 handle] ⌐¹⟨knob⟩ handle¹⌐ MS   123 right] ⌐¹right¹⌐ MS   124 man]
⌐¹man¹⌐ MS

4. Presumably because mention of the toilet would be vulgar or indelicate in the presence
   of clients.

shall the said Bernard Bodley be .... and thought how strange it
was that the last three words began with the same letter. The
chief clerk began to harry Miss Parker, saying she would never
have the letters typed in time for post. The man listened to the
clicking of the machine for a few minutes and then set to work   135
to finish his copy. But his head was not clear and his mind
wandered away to the glare and rattle of the publichouse. It
was a night for hot punches.[5] He struggled on with his copy but
when the clock struck five he had still fourteen pages to write.
Blast it! He couldn't finish it in time. He longed to execrate[6]   140
aloud, to bring his fist down on something violently. He was so
enraged that he wrote *Bernard Bernard* instead of *Bernard
Bodley* and had to begin again on a clean sheet.

He felt strong enough to clear out the whole office single=
handed. His body ached to do something, to rush out and revel   145
in violence. All the indignities of his life enraged him. ... Could
he ask the cashier privately for an advance? No, the cashier was
no good, no damn good: he wouldn't give an advance. ...... He
knew where he would meet the boys: Leonard and O'Halloran
and Nosey Flynn. The barometer of his emotional nature was   150
set for a spell of riot.

His imagination had so abstracted him that his name was
called twice before he answered. Mr Alleyne and Miss Dela=
cour were standing outside the counter and all the clerks had
turned round in anticipation of something. The man got up   155
from his desk. Mr Alleyne began a tirade of abuse, saying that
two letters were missing. The man answered that he knew
nothing about them, that he had made a faithful copy. The
tirade continued: it was so bitter and violent that the man
could hardly restrain his fist from descending upon the head of   160
the manikin[7] before him:

—I know nothing about any other two letters, he said stupidly.

—*You—know—nothing.* Of course you know nothing, said
Mr Alleyne. Tell me, he added, glancing first for approval to
the lady beside him, do you take me for a fool? Do you think   165
me an utter fool?

The man glanced from the lady's face to the little eggshaped

---

133 chief clerk] 10;   head-clerk MS   155 round] 10;   round on their stools MS
156 abuse,] 10; abuse at him, MS   157 The man] 10; He MS   166 me] 10; I'm MS

5. Beverages made by mixing liquor with hot water or milk and spices or other flavorings.
6. To curse.
7. A little man of stunted stature.

head and back again: and almost before he was aware of it his
tongue had found a felicitous moment:[8]
—I don't think, sir, he said, that that's a fair question to put   170
to me.

There was a pause in the very breathing of the clerks. Every=
one was astounded (the author of the witticism no less than his
neighbours) and Miss Delacour, who was a stout amiable per=
son, began to smile broadly. Mr Alleyne flushed to the hue of a   175
wild rose and his mouth twitched with a dwarf's passion. He
shook his fist in the man's face till it seemed to vibrate like the
knob of some electric machine:
—You impertinent ruffian! You impertinent ruffian! I'll make
short work of you! Wait till you see! You'll apologise to me for   180
your impertinence or you'll quit the office instanter![9] You'll quit
this, I'm telling you, or you'll apologise to me!

◆   ◆   ◆

He stood in a doorway opposite the offices watching to see
if the cashier would come out alone. All the clerks passed and
finally the cashier came out with the chief clerk. It was no use   185
trying to say a word to him when he was with the chief clerk.
The man felt that his position was bad enough. He had been
obliged to offer an abject apology to Mr Alleyne for his
impertinence but he knew what a hornet's nest the office would
be for him. He could remember the way in which Mr Alleyne   190
had hounded little Peake out of the office in order to make
room for his own nephew. He felt savage and thirsty and
revengeful, annoyed with himself and with everyone else. Mr
Alleyne would never give him an hour's rest: his life would be a
hell to him. He had made a proper fool of himself this time.   195
Could he not keep his tongue in his cheek? But they had never
pulled together from the first, he and Mr Alleyne, ever since the
day Mr Alleyne had overheard him mimicking his north of
Ireland accent to amuse Higgins and Miss Parker: that had

169 tongue] tongue ⁻¹⟨became⟩ ⟨⁻²⸢had⟩¹⸢ MS   169 had] 10; DELETED MS   169 felicitous moment:] ⁻¹⸢²felicitous²⸢ moment ⁻² ⟨of⟩:²⸢¹⸢ MS   170 that] 10; ABSENT MS
176 wild rose] 10; tea-rose MS   179 —You impertinent] 10; —Y'impertinent MS
179 You impertinent] 10; Y'impertinent MS   180 you!] 10; ye! MS   180 Wait till] 10;
Just MS   180 You'll] 10; ye'll MS   181 your] 10; y'r MS   181 you'll] 10; ye'll MS
181 the] 10; th' MS   181 You'll] 10; Ye'll MS   182 telling] 10; tellin' MS
183 offices] STET MS   184 passed] STET MS   185 chief clerk.] 10; head-clerk. MS
186 chief clerk.] 10; head-clerk: MS   187 The--that] 10; ABSENT MS   187 enough.] 10;
enough as it was. MS   190 remember] remember⟨ed⟩ MS   190 in] in ⟨M⟩ MS
194 give] 10; ABSENT MS   196 had] 10; ABSENT MS

8. A lucky opportunity.
9. Immediately, at once.

been the beginning of it. He might have tried Higgins for the 200
money but sure Higgins never had anything for himself. A man
with two establishments to keep up,[1] of course he couldn't.

He felt his great body again aching for the comfort of the
publichouse. The fog had begun to chill him and he wondered
could he touch[2] Pat in O'Neill's. He could not touch him for 205
more than a bob—and a bob[3] was no use. Yet he must get
money somewhere or other: he had spent his last penny for the
g.p. and soon it would be too late for getting money anywhere.
Suddenly, as he was fingering his watchchain, he thought of
Terry Kelly's pawnoffice in Fleet Street. That was the dart![4] 210
Why didn't he think of it sooner?

He went through the narrow alley of Temple Bar[5] quickly,
muttering to himself that they could all go to hell because he
was going to have a good night of it. The clerk in Terry Kelly's
said *A crown!*[6] but the consignor[7] held out for six shillings[8] and in 215
the end the six shillings was allowed him literally. He came out
of the pawnoffice joyfully, making a little cylinder of the coins
between his thumb and fingers. In Westmoreland Street the
footpaths were crowded with young men and women returning
from business and ragged urchins ran here and there yelling out 220
the names of the evening editions.[9] The man passed through the
crowd, looking on the spectacle generally with proud satisfac=
tion and staring masterfully at the office girls. His head was full
of the noises of tram gongs and swishing trolleys and his nose
already sniffed the curling fumes of punch. As he walked on he 225
preconsidered the terms in which he would narrate the incident
to the boys:

—So, I just looked at him—coolly, you know—and looked at

200–201 He--money] 10; If Higgins had any money he might have asked him MS
201 had anything] 10; seemed to have any money MS   201 for himself.] 10; even for
himself– MS   202 keep up,] 10; support, MS   202 couldn't.] e; couldn't MS
205 O'Neill's.] 10; O'Reilly's. MS   205 He--for] 10; Not for MS   206 and] 10; but MS
207 somewhere--other:] 10; somewhere: MS   207–208 for--g.p.] 10; ABSENT MS
208 late--anywhere.] 10; late. MS   214 clerk] 10; man MS   215 consignor] 10; mort-
gagor MS   216 literally.] ⌐literally¹⌐. MS   221 the(1)] ⟨"□⟩ the MS   221 editions.]
10; papers. MS   228 —So,] 10; "So, NO PARAGRAPH MS

1. Presumably Higgins kept a home for a mistress and their illegitimate children, in addition
   to maintaining a home for his wife and his children with her.
2. Approach for some money; borrow from.
3. A shilling.
4. Slang for a scheme or an idea.
5. A street connecting Eustace Street and Fleet Street.
6. Five shillings.
7. A person who hands something over to another. In this case, Farrington pawns his watch—
   that is, he hands it over to the pawnbroker for a certain of amount of money with the
   understanding that he can redeem the watch at a later time, if he can repay the money.
8. A sizable amount of money, considering that Eveline Hill earns seven shillings a week as
   a shop girl.
9. Newsboys earned small wages for selling newspapers on the street to passersby.

her. Then I looked back at him again—taking my time, you
know. *I don't think that that's a fair question to put to me,*   230
says I.

Nosey Flynn was sitting up in his usual corner of Davy
Byrne's[1] and when he heard the story he stood Farrington a half
one, saying it was as smart a thing as ever he heard. Farrington
stood a drink in his turn. After a while O'Halloran and Paddy   235
Leonard came in and the story was repeated to them. O'Hal=
loran stood[2] tailors of malt,[3] hot, all round and told the story of
the retort he had made to the chief clerk when he was in
Callan's of Fownes's Street; but, as the retort was after the
manner of the liberal shepherds in the eclogues,[4] he had to   240
admit that it was not so clever as Farrington's retort. At this
Farrington told the boys to polish off that and have another.

Just as they were naming their poisons[5] who should come in
but Higgins! Of course he had to join in with the others. The
men asked him to give his version of it and he did so with great   245
vivacity for the sight of five small hot whiskies was very
exhilarating. Everyone roared laughing when he showed the
way in which Mr Alleyne shook his fist in Farrington's face.
Then he imitated Farrington, saying *And here was my nabs,*[6] *as
cool as you please,* while Farrington looked at the company   250
out of his heavy dirty eyes, smiling and at times drawing forth
stray drops of liquor from his moustache with the aid of his
lower lip.

When that round was over there was a pause. O'Halloran
had money but neither of the other two seemed to have any so   255
the whole party left the shop somewhat regretfully. At the
corner of Duke Street Higgins and Nosey Flynn bevelled[7] off to
the left while the other three turned back towards the city. Rain
was drizzling down on the cold streets and when they reached

230 *that*] 10; ABSENT MS   233 Byrne's] 10; Byrne's public-house MS   233–234 half
one,] 10; drink, MS   234 as smart--heard.] 10; the best one he had heard for many a long
day. MS   237 tailors--hot,] 10; a drink MS   237 the] 10; a MS   239 but, as] 10; But
MS   239 after] 10; somewhat in MS   240 the(1)] 10; ABSENT MS   240 eclogues,] 10;
eclogues and MS   240–241 had--admit] 10; admitted MS   242 polish--that] 10; drink
up MS   242 another.] 10; another one. MS   244 Higgins! Of] ⌐¹⌐(Higgins and, of) Hig-
gins! Of|ʳ MS   245 version] 10; account MS   245 it] 10; the story MS   246 sight]
10; aspect MS   249 *my*] 10; me MS   252 liquor] liquo(u)r MS   255 neither] 10; none
MS   255 other two] 10; others MS   256 whole] ⌐¹whole¹⌐ MS   257 bevelled] 10;
went MS

1. A pub and eatery on Duke Street.
2. Treated or paid for.
3. Measures of whiskey.
4. Mild and courtly (rather than clever and witty), like the words of the shepherds in Virgil's
   classical pastoral poems written in the first century B.C.E.
5. Ordering their drinks.
6. Colloquial for "my friend."
7. Sloped or veered.

the Ballast Office[8] Farrington suggested the Scotch House.[9] The   260
bar was full of men and loud with the noise of tongues and
glasses. The three men pushed past the whining matchsellers at
the door and formed a little party at the corner of the counter.
They began to exchange stories. Leonard introduced them to a
young fellow named Weathers who was performing at the   265
Tivoli[1] as an acrobat and knockabout *artiste*. Farrington stood
a drink all round. Weathers said he would take a small Irish
and Apollinaris.[2] Farrington, who had definite notions of what
was what, asked the boys would they have an Apollinaris too:
but the boys told Tim to make theirs hot. The talk became   270
theatrical. O'Halloran stood a round and then Farrington
stood another round, Weathers protesting that the hospitality
was too Irish.[3] He promised to get them in behind the scenes
and introduce them to some nice girls. O'Halloran said that he
and Leonard would go but that Farrington wouldn't go be=   275
cause he was a married man and Farrington's heavy dirty eyes
leered at the company in token that he understood when he
was being chaffed.[4] Weathers made them all have just one little
tincture[5] at his expense and promised to meet them later on at
Mulligan's in Poolbeg Street.   280

When the Scotch House closed they went round to Mulli=
gan's. They went into the parlour at the back and O'Halloran
ordered small hot specials[6] all round. They were all beginning to
feel mellow. Farrington was just standing another round when
Weathers came back. Much to Farrington's relief he drank a   285
glass of bitter[7] this time. Funds were running low but they had
enough to keep them going. Presently two young women with

---

260 House.] 10; House. They went down the Quay together, past a few whining matchsellers and into the Scotch House. MS   261 noise] 10; traffic MS   262–263 pushed--
and] 10; ABSENT MS   262 matchsellers] e:10; match sellers 10   263–264 at--They] 10;
in the corner and MS   268 definite] 14P; his own MS, 10   268 notions] 10; idea MS
269 what,] 10; decent, MS   269 an] 14P; ABSENT MS–10   270 told--make] 10; said
they would have MS   271 stood] stood ⟨another,⟩ MS   277 when] STET MS
279 tincture] 10; drink MS   282 the(1)] the ⟨b⟩ MS   283 hot specials] 10; whiskies
⌐hot⌐ MS   284 was--standing] 10; stood MS   284 when] 10; and then MS
285 Much] 10; This time, much MS   286 bitter--time.] 10; bitter. MS   286 Funds] 10;
The funds MS   286 running] 10; getting MS   287 keep--going.] 10; go on with. MS

8. Building on the south bank of the Liffey that housed the Dublin Port and Docks Board,
   supervisor of Dublin Harbor.
9. A pub near the Ballast Office.
1. A vaudeville and music-hall theater, just east of the Scotch House, that offered variety
   shows and other entertainments.
2. A whiskey mixed with an aerated or carbonated water or soda imported from Germany.
3. Possibly referring to the custom of treating rounds of drinks, thereby encouraging excessive
   drinking.
4. Teased.
5. A medicinal liquid, here used metaphorically for liquor.
6. Hot punch.
7. Beer.

big hats and a young man in a check suit came in and sat at a table close by. Weathers saluted them and told the company that they were out of the Tivoli. Farrington's eyes wandered at 290 every moment in the direction of one of the young women. There was something striking in her appearance. An immense scarf of peacockblue muslin was wound round her hat and knotted in a great bow under her chin; and she wore bright yellow gloves reaching to the elbow. Farrington gazed admir= 295 ingly at the plump arm which she moved very often and with much grace; and, when after a little time she answered his gaze, he admired still more her large dark brown eyes. The oblique staring expression in them fascinated him. She glanced at him once or twice and, when the party was leaving the room, she 300 brushed against his chair and said *O, pardon!* in a London accent. He watched her leave the room in the hope that she would look back at him but he was disappointed. He cursed his want of money and cursed all the rounds he had stood, particularly all the whiskies and Apollinaris which he had 305 stood to Weathers. If there was one thing that he hated it was a sponge. He was so angry that he lost count of the conversation of his friends.

When Paddy Leonard called him he found that they were talking about feats of strength. Weathers was showing his 310 biceps muscle to the company and boasting so much that the other two had called on Farrington to uphold the national hon= our.[8] Farrington pulled up his sleeve accordingly and showed his biceps muscle to the company. The two arms were examined and compared and finally it was agreed to have a trial of 315 strength. The table was cleared and the two men rested their elbows on it, clasping hands. When Paddy Leonard said *Go!* each was to try to bring down the other's hand on to the table. Farrington looked very serious and determined.

---

288 hats] 10; hats came ⟨in⟩ MS   288 young man] 10; man MS   288 came in] 10; entered MS   288 at] 10; ABSENT MS   289 told] ⟨said⟩ told MS   290–300 Farrington's--room,] 10; Farrington said he wouldn't mind having the far one and began to smile at her but when Weathers offered to introduce her he said "No⟨"⟩, he was only chaffing" because he knew he had ⌐¹⟨no⟩ not¹⌐ money ⌐¹enough¹⌐. She continued to cast bold glances at him and changed the position of her legs often and when she was going out MS   301 London] 10; Cockney MS   302–303 He--disappointed.] 10; ABSENT MS   306–307 If--sponge.] 10; He hated a sponge above all things. MS   307–308 conversation--friends.] 10; conversation. MS   310 about] 10; of MS   310–311 his--company] 10; the company his biceps muscle MS   312 uphold] 10; support MS   313 Farrington] 10; So he ⟨ac⟩ MS   313 accordingly] 10; ABSENT MS   314 muscle--company.] 10; muscle. MS   314–315 The--was] 10; They MS   316 their] their ⟨⌐¹⌐elbows, each⟩ MS   317 it, clasping] 10; it and clasped MS   317–318 When--each] 10; ⌐¹Each¹⌐ MS   318 hand--table.] 10; hand. MS

8. Since Weathers is British, the Irishmen want Farrington to stand up for Ireland as an example of physical strength.

The trial began. After about thirty seconds Weathers   320
brought his opponent's hand slowly down on to the table. Far=
rington's dark winecoloured face flushed darker still with anger
and humiliation at having been defeated by such a stripling.

—You're not to put the weight of your body behind it. Play
fair, he said.   325

—Who's not playing fair? said the other.

—Come on again. The two best out of three.

The trial began again. The veins stood out on Farrington's
forehead and the pallor of Weathers' complexion changed to
peony.[9] Their hands and arms trembled under the stress. After a   330
long struggle Weathers again brought his opponent's hand
slowly on to the table. There was a murmur of applause from
the spectators. The curate, who was standing beside the table,
nodded his red head towards the victor and said with loutish
familiarity: 335

—Ah! that's the knack![1]

—What the hell do you know about it? said Farrington
fiercely, turning on the man. What do you put in your gab for?

—'Sh,'sh! said O'Halloran, observing the violent expression of
Farrington's face. Pony up,[2] boys. We'll have just one little   340
smahan[3] more and then we'll be off!

A very sullenfaced man stood at the corner of O'Connell
Bridge waiting for the little Sandymount tram[4] to take him
home. He was full of smouldering anger and revengefulness.
He felt humiliated and discontented: he did not even feel drunk   345
and he had only twopence in his pocket. He cursed everything.
He had done for himself in the office, pawned his watch, spent
all his money; and he had not even got drunk. He began to feel
thirsty again and he longed to be back again in the hot reeking
publichouse. He had lost his reputation as a strong man,   350

---

320 The] 10; NO PARAGRAPH MS   323 having--defeated] 10; being brought down MS
328 out] 10; ABSENT MS   329 changed] 10; turned MS   330 under--stress.] 10; with
the effort. MS   331 brought] 10; brought down MS   333 curate,] 10; ⟨spec⟩ curate MS
334 loutish] 10; stupid MS   338 fiercely,--man.] 10; fiercely. MS   338 What--put] 10;
What are you putting MS   340 have just] 10; just have MS   340–341 little smahan] 14;
ABSENT MS; little sma han 10   342 sullenfaced] 10; sullen, partially drunken MS
343 the--Sandymount] ⌐¹⟨his⟩ the little Sandymount⌐ MS   344 revengefulness.] 10;
revenge. MS   346 everything.] 10; himself and his luck. MS   347 done for] 10; ruined
MS   347 watch,] 10; watch and MS   348 all his] 10; his MS   348 money;] 10; money
– MS   349 he] 10; ABSENT MS   349 in] ⌐¹in¹⌐ MS

9. Dark red.
1. A clever trick.
2. Pay up.
3. A taste, or a sip.
4. Sandymount is a little village on Dublin Bay, southeast of Dublin. Farrington gets off
   before Sandymount, on Shelbourne Road, which is a street of lower-class houses and
   tenements.

having been defeated twice by a mere boy. His heart swelled
with fury and when he thought of the woman in the big hat
who had brushed against him and said *Pardon!* his fury nearly
choked him.

His tram let him down at Shelbourne Road and he steered   355
his great body along in the shadow of the wall of the barracks.[5]
He loathed returning to his home. When he went in by the
sidedoor he found the kitchen empty and the kitchen fire nearly
out. He bawled upstairs:

—Ada! Ada!   360

His wife was a little sharpfaced woman who bullied her
husband when he was sober and was bullied by him when he
was drunk. They had five children. A little boy came running
down the stairs.

—Who is that? said the man peering through the darkness.   365

—Me, pa.

—Who are you? Charlie?

—No, pa. Tom.

—Where's your mother?

—She's out at the chapel.[6]   370

—That's right .... Did she think of leaving any dinner for me?

—Yes, pa. I ...

—Light the lamp. What do you mean by having the place in
darkness? Are the other children in bed?

The man sat down heavily on one of the chairs while the   375
little boy lit the lamp. He began to mimic his son's flat accent,
saying half to himself: *At the chapel. At the chapel, if you
please!* When the lamp was lit he banged his fist on the table
and shouted:

—What's for my dinner?   380

—I'm ... going to cook it, pa, said the little boy.

The man jumped up furiously and pointed to the fire:

—On that fire! You let the fire out! By God, I'll teach you to do
that again!

He took a step to the door and seized the walking stick   385
which was standing behind it:

—I'll teach you to let the fire out! he said, rolling up his sleeve
in order to give his arm free play.

351 defeated] 10; brought down MS   351 boy.] 10; stripling. MS   351–352 swelled
with] 10; was full of MS   352 thought] thought ⟨ᵗ⟩ᵗʳof the legs⟩ MS   352 big] 10; black
MS   358 kitchen fire] 10; fire MS   358 nearly] 10; ᴀʙsᴇɴᴛ MS   361–362 bullied--
husband] 10; tyrannised him MS   362 bullied] 10; tyrannised MS   362 him] ⟨☐⟩ him
MS   375 chairs] 10; kitchen chairs MS   376 flat accent,] 10; voice MS   382 The]
10; ɴᴏ ᴘᴀʀᴀɢʀᴀᴘʜ MS   383 that] that⟨.⟩ MS   384 again!] again!—MS ᴍs ᴇɴᴅs

5. Beggar's Bush Infantry Barracks housed the British Army's south Dublin division.
6. Presumably for an evening devotional service at church.

The little boy cried O, pa! and ran whimpering round the
table but the man followed him and caught him by the coat.   390
The little boy looked about him wildly but, seeing no way of
escape, fell upon his knees.

—Now, you'll let the fire out the next time! said the man,
striking at him viciously with the stick. Take that, you little
whelp!   395

The boy uttered a squeal of pain as the stick cut his thigh.
He clasped his hands together in the air and his voice shook
with fright.

—O, pa! he cried. Don't beat me, pa! And I'll ... I'll say a *Hail
Mary*[7] for you. ... I'll say a *Hail Mary* for you, pa, if you don't   400
beat me. ... I'll say a *Hail Mary*. ...

Clay

The matron had given her leave[1] to go out as soon as the
women's tea was over and Maria looked forward to her
evening out. The kitchen was spick and span: the cook said you
could see yourself in the big copper boilers. The fire was nice
and bright and on one of the sidetables were four very big   5
barmbracks.[2] These barmbracks seemed uncut but, if you went
closer, you would see that they had been cut into long thick
even slices and were ready to be handed round at tea. Maria
had cut them herself.

Maria was a very, very small person indeed but she had a   10
very long nose and a very long chin. She talked a little through
her nose, always soothingly: *Yes, my dear*, and *No, my dear*.
She was always sent for when the women quarrelled over their
tubs and always succeeded in making peace. One day the
matron had said to her: 15

---

395   whelp!] STET 10

7. A Roman Catholic prayer often required by the priest in confession as a "penance"—that
   is, as an offering by the sinner in return for the forgiveness of sins. It begins, "Hail Mary,
   full of grace, the Lord is with thee."

Copy-text: 1910 late proofs (10); Collated texts: 1914 proofs (14P) and 1914 first edition
(14) [IDENTITY IN BOTH IS REPORTED AS '14']; 1967 Viking edition in the 1969 Viking Critical
Library printing (67).

1. Maria, a former domestic who is Catholic, works as a scullery maid in a Protestant charitable institution called *Dublin by Lamplight* laundry, which provided work and a place to
   live for former and aging prostitutes. The establishment was supervised by a "matron."
   She gives Maria permission to leave early on this particular day, Hallow Eve, the Irish
   counterpart to the American Halloween.
2. Cakes made with a yeast dough.

—Maria, you are a veritable peacemaker!

And the submatron and two of the board ladies[3] had heard the compliment. And Ginger Mooney was always saying what she wouldn't do to the dummy[4] who had charge of the irons if it wasn't for Maria. Everyone was so fond of Maria.

The women would have their tea at six o'clock and she would be able to get away before seven. From Ballsbridge[5] to the Pillar,[6] twenty minutes; from the Pillar to Drumcondra,[7] twenty minutes; and twenty minutes to buy the things. She would be there before eight. She took out her purse with the silver clasps and read again the words *A Present from Belfast*.[8] She was very fond of that purse because Joe had brought it to her five years before when he and Alphy had gone to Belfast on a Whit Monday[9] trip. In the purse were two half crowns and some coppers.[1] She would have five shillings clear after paying tram fare. What a nice evening they would have, all the children singing! Only she hoped that Joe wouldn't come in drunk. He was so different when he took any drink.

Often he had wanted her to go and live with them; but she would have felt herself in the way (though Joe's wife was ever so nice with her) and she had become accustomed to the life of the laundry. Joe was a good fellow. She had nursed him and Alphy too;[2] and Joe used often to say:

—Mamma is mamma but Maria is my proper mother.

After the breakup at home the boys had got her that position in the *Dublin by Lamplight* laundry and she liked it. She used to have such a bad opinion of protestants but now she thought they were very nice people, a little quiet and serious, but still very nice people to live with. Then she had her plants in the conservatory and she liked looking after them. She had lovely

3. Members of the Board, or governing body, for the institution that manages the laundry.
4. Possibly a mute or mentally impaired person. The irons for pressing the laundered clothes were heated on stoves. Their temperature had to be monitored to make sure the irons wouldn't scorch the cloth—a task that required attention but little communication.
5. A very fashionable suburb in southeast Dublin in the nineteenth century, Ballsbridge became the location for a number of embassies and diplomatic offices.
6. The monument known as Nelson's Pillar was a column 134 feet high, topped by a thirteen-foot stone statue of the British naval hero Horatio Lord Nelson. It was located in front of the General Post Office on O'Connell Street, and marked a hub and transfer point for a number of Dublin's tram lines.
7. A suburb two miles north of Dublin.
8. A souvenir gift from a visit to the large, largely Protestant, city in the north of Ireland.
9. A bank holiday following the seventh Sunday after Easter, called Whitsunday, that creates a long weekend. Whitsunday coincides with the liturgical feast of Pentecost, which commemorates the descent of the Holy Spirit upon the Apostles after Christ's resurrection from the dead.
1. A crown was worth five shillings. The money in Maria's purse is therefore five shillings and some pence.
2. Tended, or looked after, when they were children.

ferns and waxplants[3] and whenever anyone came to visit her she always gave the visitor one or two slips[4] from her conservatory.[5] There was one thing she didn't like and that was the tracts on the walls;[6] but the matron was such a nice person to deal with, so genteel.   50

When the cook told her everything was ready she went into the women's room and began to pull the big bell. In a few minutes the women began to come in by twos and threes, wiping their steaming hands in their petticoats and pulling down the sleeves of their blouses over their red steaming arms.[7]   55
They settled down before their huge mugs which the cook and the dummy filled up with hot tea, already mixed with milk and sugar[8] in huge tin cans. Maria superintended the distribution of the barmbrack and saw that every woman got her four slices. There was a great deal of laughing and joking during the meal.   60
Lizzie Fleming said Maria was sure to get the ring[9] and, though Fleming had said that for so many Hallow Eves,[1] Maria had to laugh and say she didn't want any ring or man either; and when she laughed her greygreen eyes sparkled with disap=
pointed shyness and the tip of her nose nearly met the tip of her   65
chin. Then Ginger Mooney lifted up her mug of tea and proposed Maria's health while all the other women clattered with their mugs on the table and said she was sorry she hadn't a sup of porter to drink it in. And Maria laughed again till the tip of her nose nearly met the tip of her chin and till her minute   70
body nearly shook itself asunder because she knew that Mooney meant well though of course she had the notions of a common woman.

But wasn't Maria glad when the women had finished their tea and the cook and the dummy had begun to clear away the   75
tea things? She went into her little bedroom and, remembering

---

75 clear away] 14; clean up 10; clear up 14P

3. Climbing or trailing plants with glossy leaves.
4. Bits of a plant's branches or stem, which can be replanted to propagate a new plant.
5. A greenhouse, often attached to a house, where tender and exotic plants could be cultivated year-round.
6. Placards with scriptural verses or exhortations from the Bible, intended for the moral
instruction of the fallen women working and living at the laundry.
7. Laundry was washed manually at the turn of the century by being stirred with paddles in
heated tubs or cauldrons, with stubborn spots scrubbed by hand on a ridged washboard.
8. The large-scale and uniform style with which the tea is made and served suggests the
laundry's institutional character.
9. A reference to traditional Hallow Eve games of divination, thought to predict the future
through symbolic objects. For example, a ring baked into a cake that was chosen by a girl
might be thought to betoken a future marriage.
1. Hallow Eve precedes the liturgical holy day honoring the saints of the Church, All Saints'
Day, November 1. It therefore falls on October 31.

that the next morning was a mass morning,[2] changed the hand
of the alarm from seven to six. Then she took off her working
skirt and her houseboots and laid her best skirt out on the bed
and her tiny dressboots beside the foot of the bed. She changed   80
her blouse too and, as she stood before the mirror, she thought
of how she used to dress for mass on Sunday morning when she
was a young girl; and she looked with quaint affection at the
diminutive body which she had so often adorned. In spite of its
years she found it a nice tidy little body.   85

When she got outside the streets were shining with rain
and she was glad of her old brown raincloak. The tram was
full and she had to sit on the little stool at the end of the car
facing all the people, with her toes barely touching the floor.
She arranged in her mind all she was going to do and   90
thought how much better it was to be independent and to have
your own money in your pocket. She hoped they would have
a nice evening. She was sure they would but she could not
help thinking what a pity it was Alphy and Joe were not speak=
ing. They were always falling out now but when they were   95
boys together they used to be the best of friends: but such was
life.

She got out of her tram at the Pillar and ferreted her way
quickly among the crowds. She went into Downes's cakeshop[3]
but the shop was so full of people that it was a long time before   100
she could get herself attended to. She bought a dozen of mixed
penny cakes and at last came out of the shop laden with a big
bag. Then she thought what else would she buy: she wanted to
buy something really nice. They would be sure to have plenty
of apples and nuts. It was hard to know what to buy and all she   105
could think of was cake. She decided to buy some plumcake[4]
but Downes's plumcake had not enough almond icing on top of
it so she went over to a shop in Henry Street.[5] Here she was a
long time in suiting herself and the stylish young lady behind
the counter, who was evidently a little annoyed by her, asked   110
her was it weddingcake she wanted to buy. That made Maria
blush and smile at the young lady but the young lady took it all
very seriously and finally cut a thick slice of plumcake, par=
celled it up and said:

87 raincloak.] STET 10

2. The day after Hallow Eve, All Saints' Day, was considered a Holy Day of Obligation in
   the Catholic calendar—that is, a day on which Catholics were obliged to attend mass.
3. A confectioner's shop located on Earl Street North, near Nelson's Pillar.
4. A cake containing raisins, currants, and other preserved fruits.
5. There were a number of shops selling confections and sweets on Henry Street, next to
   Earl Street.

—Two and four, please.[6]   115

She thought she would have to stand in the Drumcondra
tram because none of the young men seemed to notice her but
an elderly gentleman made room for her. He was a stout
gentleman and he wore a brown hard hat; he had a square red
face and a greyish moustache. Maria thought he was a co=   120
lonel-looking gentleman and she reflected how much more
polite he was than the young men who simply stared straight
before them. The gentleman began to chat with her about
Hallow Eve and the rainy weather. He supposed the bag was
full of good things for the little ones and said it was only right   125
that the youngsters should enjoy themselves while they were
young. Maria agreed with him and favoured him with demure
nods and hems. He was very nice with her and when she was
getting out at the Canal Bridge she thanked him and bowed
and he bowed to her and raised his hat and smiled agreeably;   130
and while she was going up along the terrace, bending her tiny
head under the rain, she thought how easy it was to know a
gentleman even when he has a drop taken.[7]

Everybody said: O, here's Maria! when she came to Joe's
house. Joe was there, having come home from business, and all   135
the children had their Sunday dresses on. There were two big
girls in from next door and games were going on. Maria gave
the bag of cakes to the eldest boy, Alphy, to divide and Mrs
Donnelly said it was too good of her to bring such a big bag of
cakes and made all the children say: 140
—Thanks, Maria.

But Maria said she had brought something special for papa
and mamma, something they would be sure to like, and she
began to look for her plumcake. She tried in Downes's bag and
then in the pockets of her raincloak and then on the hallstand   145
but nowhere could she find it. Then she asked all the children
had any of them eaten it—by mistake, of course—but the
children all said no and looked as if they did not like to eat
cakes if they were to be accused of stealing. Everybody had a
solution for the mystery and Mrs Donnelly said it was plain   150
that Maria had left it behind her in the tram. Maria, remem=
bering how confused the gentleman with the greyish moustache
had made her, coloured with shame and vexation and disap=
pointment. At the thought of the failure of her little surprise

145 raincloak] e; rain-cloak 10; waterproof 14

6. Two shillings fourpence—nearly half the money in Maria's purse.
7. When he is slightly tipsy, or a little drunk.

and of the two and fourpence she had thrown away for nothing 155
she nearly cried outright.

But Joe said it didn't matter and made her sit down by the
fire. He was very nice with her. He told her all that went on in
his office, repeating for her a smart answer which he had made
to the manager. Maria did not understand why Joe laughed so 160
much over the answer he had made but she said that the
manager must have been a very overbearing person to deal
with. Joe said he wasn't so bad when you knew how to take
him, that he was a decent sort so long as you didn't rub him the
wrong way. Mrs Donnelly played the piano for the children 165
and they danced and sang. Then the two nextdoor girls handed
round the nuts. Nobody could find the nutcracker and Joe was
nearly getting cross over it and asked how did they expect
Maria to crack nuts without a nutcracker. But Maria said she
didn't like nuts and that they weren't to bother about her. 170
Then Joe asked would she take a bottle of stout[8] and Mrs
Donnelly said there was port wine too in the house if she would
prefer that. Maria said she would rather they didn't ask her to
take anything: but Joe insisted.

So Maria let him have his way and they sat by the fire 175
talking over old times and Maria thought she would put in a
good word for Alphy. But Joe cried that God might strike him
stone dead if ever he spoke a word to his brother again and
Maria said she was sorry she had mentioned the matter. Mrs
Donnelly told her husband it was a great shame for him to 180
speak that way of his own flesh and blood but Joe said that
Alphy was no brother of his and there was nearly being a row[9]
on the head of it. But Joe said he would not lose his temper on
account of the night it was and asked his wife to open some
more stout. The two nextdoor girls had arranged some Hallow 185
Eve games and soon everything was merry again. Maria was
delighted to see the children so merry and Joe and his wife
in such good spirits. The nextdoor girls put some saucers[1]
on the table and then led the children up to the table, blind=
fold. One got the prayerbook[2] and the other three got the water;[3] 190
and when one of the nextdoor girls got the ring Mrs Donnelly

167 nutcracker] STET 10

8. A strong beer.
9. A dispute, or quarrel.
1. In this game of divination, or fortune-telling, symbolic objects are placed on the table, and
   each player is blindfolded and chooses a saucer containing an object. The chosen object
   is thought to foretell the player's future.
2. Presumably signifies that the player would enter a convent.
3. Presumably signifies a long life.

shook her finger at the blushing girl as much as to say: *O, I know all about it!* They insisted then on blindfolding Maria and leading her up to the table to see what she would get; and, while they were putting on the bandage, Maria laughed 195 and laughed again till the tip of her nose nearly met the tip of her chin.

They led her up to the table amid laughing and joking and she put her hand out in the air as she was told to do. She moved her hand about here and there in the air and descended 200 on one of the saucers. She felt a soft wet substance with her fingers and was surprised that nobody spoke or took off her bandage. There was a pause for a few seconds and then a great deal of scuffling and whispering. Somebody said something about the garden and at last Mrs Donnelly said something very 205 cross to one of the nextdoor girls and told her to throw it out at once: that was no play. Maria understood that it was wrong that time and so she had to do it over again: and this time she got the prayerbook.

After that Mrs Donnelly played Miss McCloud's Reel[4] for 210 the children and Joe made Maria take a glass of wine. Soon they were all quite merry again and Mrs Donnelly said Maria would enter a convent before the year was out because she had got the prayerbook. Maria had never seen Joe so nice to her as he was that night, so full of pleasant talk and reminiscences. 215 She said they were all very good to her.

At last the children grew tired and sleepy and Joe asked Maria would she not sing some little song before she went, one of the old songs. Mrs Donnelly said *Do, please, Maria!* and so Maria had to get up and stand beside the piano. Mrs Donnelly 220 bade the children be quiet and listen to Maria's song. Then she played the prelude and said *Now, Maria!* and Maria, blushing very much, began to sing in a tiny quavering voice. She sang *I dreamt that I dwelt*[5] and when she came to the second verse she sang again: 225

> *I dreamt that I dwelt in marble halls*
> *With vassals and serfs at my side*
> *And of all who assembled within those walls*
> *That I was the hope and the pride.*
> *I had riches too great to count, could boast* 230
> *Of a high ancestral name,*

4. A traditional Irish tune, suitable for a lively dance.
5. A melodic tune from the nineteenth-century operetta *The Bohemian Girl*, by the Irish composer Michael Balfe, with libretto by Alfred Bunn. In the opera, the heroine is a girl from a noble family who has been raised by gypsies, but she dreams of the life she might have had.

But I also dreamt, which pleased me most,
That you loved me still the same.

But no one tried to show her her mistake[6] and, when she had
ended her song, Joe was very much moved. He said that there   235
was no time like the long ago and no music for him like poor
old Balfe, whatever other people might say; and his eyes filled
up so much with tears that he could not find what he was
looking for and in the end he had to ask his wife to tell him
where the corkscrew was.   240

A Painful Case

Mr James Duffy lived in Chapelizod[1] because he wished to
live as far as possible from the city of which he was a citizen
and because he found all the other suburbs of Dublin mean,
modern and pretentious. He lived in an old sombre house and
from his windows he could look into the disused distillery or   5
upwards along the shallow river[2] on which Dublin is built. The
lofty walls of his uncarpeted room were free from pictures. He
had himself bought every article of furniture in the room: a
black iron bedstead, an iron washstand, four cane chairs, a
clothesrack, a coalscuttle, a fender and irons[3] and a square table   10
on which lay a double desk.[4] A bookcase had been made in an
alcove by means of shelves of white wood. The bed was
clothed with white bedclothes and a black and scarlet rug
covered the foot. A little handmirror hung above the washstand
and during the day a whiteshaded lamp stood as the sole   15

6. That she omitted the second verse: "I dreamt that suitors sought my hand, / That knights,
   upon bended knee, / And with vows no maiden heart could withstand, / They pledg'd their
   faith to me. / And I dreamt that one of that noble host, / Came forth my heart to claim, /
   But I also dreamt, which charm'd me most, / That you lov'd me still the same."

Copy-text: Manuscript Yale 2.6 (MS); Collated texts: 1910 late proofs [FRAGMENT ONLY] (10);
1914 proofs (14P) and 1914 first edition (14) [IDENTITY IN BOTH IS REPORTED AS '14']; 1967
Viking edition in the 1969 Viking Critical Library printing (67). [DRAFT MANUSCRIPT YALE 2.5
IN A GENETIC TRANSCRIPTION, AS WELL AS IN A CLEAR-TEXT EXTRACTION PARALLELED WITH THE
COPY-TEXT, IS RENDERED IN THE SECTION »MANUSCRIPT TRACES« OF OUR EDITION OF *DUBLINERS*,
NEW YORK: GARLAND PUBLISHING INC., 1993.]

4 sombre] ⌐¹⟨gawky⟩ sombre¹⌐ MS

1. A village three miles west of Dublin, near Phoenix Park—a large park in west-central
   Dublin. The name, which means "chapel of Iseult," refers to the legendary love story of
   Tristan and Iseult, believed to have taken place there.
2. The river Liffey, which runs through Chapelizod, tends to be somewhat shallow there.
3. A metal grate in front of a fireplace, to keep the embers from spilling into the room, and
   the metal supports that hold the burning logs.
4. A hinged box for holding stationery and writing implements, with a sloping front to support
   paper for writing.

ornament of the mantelpiece. The books on the white wooden
shelves were arranged from below upwards according to bulk.
A complete Wordsworth[5] stood at one end of the lowest shelf
and a copy of the Maynooth catechism,[6] sewn into the cloth
cover of a notebook, stood at one end of the top shelf. Writing   20
materials were always on the desk. In the desk lay a manuscript
translation of Hauptmann's *Michael Kramer,*[7] the stage direc=
tions of which were written in purple ink, and a little sheaf of
papers held together by a brass pin. In these sheets a sentence
was inscribed from time to time and, in an ironical moment,   25
the headline of an advertisement for bile beans[8] had been pasted
on to the first sheet. On lifting the lid of the desk a faint
fragrance escaped—the fragrance of new cedarwood pencils or
of a bottle of gum[9] or of an overripe apple which might have
been left there and forgotten.   30

Mr Duffy abhorred anything which betokened physical or
mental disorder. A medieval doctor would have called him
saturnine.[1] His face, which carried the entire tale of his years,
was of the brown tint of Dublin streets. On his long and rather
large head grew dry black hair and a tawny moustache did not   35
quite cover an unamiable mouth. His cheekbones also gave his
face a harsh character but there was no harshness in the eyes
which, looking at the world from under their tawny eyebrows,
gave the impression of a man ever alert to greet a redeeming
instinct in others but often disappointed. He lived at a little   40
distance from his body, regarding his own acts with doubtful
sideglances. He had an odd autobiographical habit which led
him to compose in his mind from time to time a short sentence
about himself containing a subject in the third person and a
predicate in the past tense. He never gave alms to beggars and   45
walked firmly, carrying a stout hazel.[2]

He had been for many years cashier of a private bank in
Baggot Street.[3] Every morning he came in from Chapelizod by

---

5. A collection of the poetry of William Wordsworth (1770–1850).
6. The standard text for Roman Catholic religious instruction in Ireland, named after a theological college in Maynooth, fifteen miles west of Dublin.
7. Gerhart Hauptmann was a German dramatist who in 1900 published a four-act play called
   Michael Kramer, about a father whose lofty dedication to art causes him to deride the less
   rigid artistic ambitions of his son and thus contribute to his son's suicide.
8. Brand name of a medicine for conditions thought to be caused by an excess of bile or liver
   secretion.
9. An adhesive or glue.
1. In medieval astrology, persons born under the influence of the planet Saturn were thought
   to be sluggish, cold, and gloomy—a temperament similar to that believed to be brought
   on by excess bile.
2. A walking stick, made of the stem of a hazel shrub, the plant that produces hazelnuts.
3. A street bordering on the park of Stephen's Green in central Dublin, site of a number of
   small banks.

tram. At midday he went to Dan Burke's[4] and took his lunch, a
bottle of lager beer and a small trayful of arrowroot biscuits.[5]   50
At four o'clock he was set free. He dined in an eatinghouse in
George's Street[6] where he felt himself safe from the society of
Dublin's gilded youth[7] and where there was a certain plain
honesty in the bill of fare. His evenings were spent either before
his landlady's piano or roaming about the outskirts of the city.   55
His liking for Mozart's music[8] brought him sometimes to an
opera or a concert: these were the only dissipations of his life.

He had neither companions nor friends, church nor creed.
He lived his spiritual life without any communion with others,
visiting his relatives at Christmas and escorting them to the   60
cemetery when they died. He performed these two social duties
for old dignity' sake but conceded nothing further to the
conventions which regulate the civic life. He allowed himself to
think that in certain circumstances he would rob his bank but
as these circumstances never arose his life rolled out evenly—   65
an adventureless tale.

One evening he found himself sitting beside two ladies in the
Rotunda.[9] The house, thinly peopled and silent, gave distressing
prophecy of failure. The lady who sat next him looked round
at the deserted house once or twice and then said: 70
—What a pity there is such a poor house tonight! It's so hard
on people to have to sing to empty benches.

He took the remark as an invitation to talk. He was sur=
prised that she seemed so little awkward. While they talked he
tried to fix her permanently in his memory. When he learned   75
that the young girl beside her was her daughter he judged her
to be a year or so younger than himself. Her face, which must
have been handsome, had remained intelligent. It was an oval
face with strongly marked features. The eyes were very dark
blue and steady. Their gaze began with a defiant note but was   80
confused by what seemed a deliberate swoon of the pupil into
the iris, revealing for an instant a temperament of great sensi=
bility. The pupil reasserted itself quickly, this half disclosed
nature fell again under the reign of prudence, and her astra=

60 Christmas] Christmas ⁿˢ,ˢʳ MS   62 sake] sake ⁿˢ,ˢʳ MS

4. A pub on Baggot Street that served light meals.
5. Biscuits, or crackers, made with the starch of the arrowroot plant, thought to be easily
   digestible.
6. Great George's Street South, an unfashionable commercial street in the direction of
   Duffy's home in Chapelizod, contained a number of modest restaurants.
7. Fashionable young men from wealthy families.
8. The classical music of the Austrian composer Wolfgang Amadeus Mozart (1756–1791).
9. A group of buildings in Rutland Square, which housed a concert hall, lecture rooms, and
   a theater—the site of many of Dublin's most elegant entertainments.

khan jacket,[1] moulding a bosom of a certain fulness, struck the   85
note of defiance more definitely.

He met her again a few weeks afterwards at a concert in
Earlsfort Terrace[2] and seized the moments when her daughter's
attention was diverted to become intimate. She alluded once or
twice to her husband but her tone was not such as to make the   90
allusion a warning. Her name was Mrs Sinico. Her husband's
great-great-grandfather had come from Leghorn.[3] Her husband
was captain of a mercantile boat plying between Dublin and
Holland: and they had one child.

Meeting her a third time by accident he found courage to   95
make an appointment. She came. This was the first of many
meetings; they met always in the evening and chose the most
quiet quarters for their walks together. Mr Duffy, however,
had a distaste for underhand ways and, finding that they were
compelled to meet stealthily, he forced her to ask him to her   100
house. Captain Sinico encouraged his visits, thinking that his
daughter's hand was in question. He had dismissed his wife so
sincerely from his gallery of pleasures that he did not suspect
anyone else would take an interest in her. As the husband was
often away and the daughter out giving music lessons Mr Duffy   105
had many opportunities of enjoying the lady's society. Neither
he nor she had had any such adventure before and neither was
conscious of any incongruity. Little by little he entangled his
thoughts with hers. He lent her books, provided her with ideas,
shared his intellectual life with her. She listened to all.   110

Sometimes in return for his theories she gave out some fact
of her own life. With almost maternal solicitude she urged him
to let his nature open to the full; she became his confessor. He
told her that for some time he had assisted at the meetings of
an Irish Socialist Party[4] where he had felt himself a unique   115
figure amid a score of sober workmen in a garret lit by an
inefficient oillamp. When the party had divided into three
sections, each under its own leader and in its own garret, he
had discontinued his attendances. The workmen's discussions,

---

92 Leghorn.] 10; Udine. MS   93 plying] 10 ENDS   97 meetings;] 14P; meetings⌐1;1⌐ MS

1. A delicate leather with a slightly furry texture, made from lambskin.
2. A set of international exhibition buildings adjacent to Stephen's Green in which concerts
   and other cultural events were offered.
3. The Italian seaport of Livorno on the Ligurian Sea. This origin may explain the Italian
   name and perhaps hereditary occupation of Mrs. Sinico's husband.
4. A political party promoting reforms in wages and working-class conditions. The party was
   eclipsed by the greater political urgencies of the Irish independence movement and pro-
   grams for land reform, and therefore tended to sponsor chiefly small meetings and discussion groups at the time of the story.

he said, were too timorous; the interest they took in the   120
question of wages was inordinate. He felt that they were
hardfeatured realists and that they resented an exactitude
which was the product of a leisure not within their reach. No
social revolution, he told her, would be likely to strike Dublin
for some centuries.   125

She asked him why did he not write out his thoughts. For
what? he asked her with careful scorn. To compete with
phrasemongers, incapable of thinking consecutively for sixty
seconds? To submit himself to the criticisms of an obtuse
middle class which entrusted its morality to policemen and its   130
fine arts to impresarios?

He went often to her little cottage outside Dublin: often they
spent their evenings alone. Little by little as their thoughts
entangled they spoke of subjects less remote. Her companion=
ship was like a warm soil about an exotic.[5] Many times she   135
allowed the dark to fall upon them, refraining from lighting the
lamp. The dark discreet room, their isolation, the music that
still vibrated in their ears united them. This union exalted him,
wore away the rough edges of his character, emotionalised his
mental life. Sometimes he caught himself listening to the sound   140
of his own voice. He thought that in her eyes he would ascend
to an angelical stature; and as he attached the fervent nature of
his companion more and more closely to him he heard the
strange impersonal voice, which he recognised as his own,
insisting on the soul's incurable loneliness. We cannot give   145
ourselves, it said: we are our own. The end of these discourses
was that one night, during which she had shown every sign of
unusual excitement, Mrs Sinico caught up his hand passion=
ately and pressed it to her cheek.

Mr Duffy was very much surprised. Her interpretation of his   150
words disillusioned him. He did not visit her for a week; then
he wrote to her asking her to meet him. As he did not wish
their last interview to be troubled by the influence of their
ruined confessional they met in a little cakeshop near the
Parkgate.[6] It was cold autumn weather but in spite of the cold   155
they wandered up and down the roads of the Park for nearly
three hours. They agreed to break off their intercourse: every
bond, he said, is a bond to sorrow. When they came out of the
Park they walked in silence towards the tram but here she

127 with--scorn.] ⌐¹with--scorn¹⌐. MS

5. A nonnative plant, such as one from a tropical climate, that requires special artificial
   conditions to acclimatize and thrive in a northern zone.
6. The main entrance to Phoenix Park, a large park not far from Duffy's home in Chapelizod.

began to tremble so violently that, fearing another collapse on 160
her part, he bade her goodbye quickly and left her. A few days
later he received a parcel containing his books and music.

Four years passed. Mr Duffy returned to his even way of life.
His room still bore witness of the orderliness of his mind. Some
new pieces of music encumbered the musicstand in the lower 165
room and on his shelves stood two volumes by Nietzsche, *Thus
Spake Zarathustra* and *The Gay Science*.[7] He wrote seldom in
the sheaf of papers which lay in his desk. One of his sentences,
written two months after his last interview with Mrs Sinico,
read: Love between man and man is impossible because there 170
must not be sexual intercourse and friendship between man
and woman is impossible because there must be sexual inter=
course. He kept away from concerts lest he should meet her.
His father died; the junior partner of the bank retired. And still
every morning he went into the city by tram and every evening 175
walked home from the city after having dined moderately in
George's Street and read the evening paper for dessert.

One evening as he was about to put a morsel of corned beef
and cabbage into his mouth his hand stopped. His eyes fixed
themselves on a paragraph in the evening paper which he had 180
propped against the watercroft.[8] He replaced the morsel of food
on his plate and read the paragraph attentively. Then he drank
a glass of water, pushed his plate to one side, doubled the paper
down before him between his elbows and read the paragraph
over and over again. The cabbage began to deposit a cold white 185
grease on his plate. The girl came over to him to ask was his
dinner not properly cooked. He said it was very good and ate a
few mouthfuls of it with difficulty. Then he paid his bill and
went out.

He walked along quickly through the November twilight, 190
his stout hazel stick striking the ground regularly, the fringe of
the buff *Mail*[9] peeping out of a sidepocket of his tight reefer[1]
overcoat. On the lonely road which leads from the Parkgate to
Chapelizod he slackened his pace. His stick struck the ground
less emphatically and his breath, issuing irregularly, almost 195

---

164 bore witness of] 14P; testified MS   171 must not] 14P; cannot MS   176 moderately] 14P; modestly MS

7. The German philosopher Friedrich Nietzsche (1844–1900) urged independent thought
that refused to be intimidated by convention or by middle-class morality. His work was
considered quite avant-garde and freethinking at the time of the story.
8. A carafe, or water pitcher, possibly without a handle.
9. The *Dublin Evening Mail* was a conservative, pro-British paper printed on light brown, or
"buff," paper.
1. A tight-fitting outer garment made of strong, heavy cloth.

with a sighing sound, condensed in the wintry air. When he reached his house he went up at once to his bedroom and, taking the paper from his pocket, read the paragraph again by the failing light of the window. He read it not aloud but moving his lips as a priest does when he reads the prayer *In* 200 *Secretis*.[2] This was the paragraph:

DEATH OF A LADY AT SYDNEY PARADE

A PAINFUL CASE

Today at the City of Dublin Hospital[3] the Deputy Coroner[4] (in the absence of Mr Leverett) held an inquest on the body of Mrs 205 Emily Sinico, aged forty-three years, who was killed at Sydney Parade Station[5] yesterday evening. The evidence showed that the deceased lady while attempting to cross the line was knocked down by the engine of the ten o'clock slow train from Kingstown,[6] thereby sustaining injuries of the head and right 210 side which led to her death.

James Lennon, driver of the engine, stated that he had been in the employment of the railway company for fifteen years. On hearing the guard's whistle he set the train in motion and a second or two afterwards brought it to rest in response to loud 215 cries. The train was going slowly.

P. Dunne, railway porter, stated that as the train was about to start he observed a woman attempting to cross the lines. He ran towards her and shouted but before he could reach her she was caught by the buffer of the engine[7] and fell to the ground. 220

A Juror—You saw the lady fall?

Witness—Yes.

Police Sergeant Croly deposed[8] that when he arrived he found the deceased lying on the platform apparently dead. He had the body taken to the waitingroom pending the arrival of the 225 ambulance.

Constable 57 E corroborated.

200–201 *In Secretis*.] STET MS   204 the--Hospital] 14P; ⌐¹⟨◇⟩ Vincent's Hospital¹⌐ MS 206 forty-three] 14P; forty-two MS   214 motion] 14; motion⌐¹,¹⌐ MS; motion, 14P 227 57 E] 14P; 57 D MS

2. In a low voice, not meant to be shared with the congregation.
3. A charitable hospital that accepted accident and emergency cases at all hours, located on Baggot Street in south-central Dublin.
4. Someone charged with conducting an inquest into accidental or violent deaths.
5. A railroad station located on Sydney Parade Avenue in the suburban village of Merrion, south of Dublin.
6. An important harbor southeast of Dublin, now known as Dun Laoghaire.
7. A fender attached to the front and back of railway carriages to soften the impact of concussion or collision.
8. Gave evidence under oath.

Dr Halpin, assistant house surgeon of the City of Dublin Hospital, stated that the deceased had two lower ribs fractured and had sustained severe contusions of the right shoulder. The right side of the head had been injured in the fall. The injuries were not sufficient to have caused death in a normal person. Death, in his opinion, had been probably due to shock and sudden failure of the heart's action.

Mr H. B. Patterson Finlay, on behalf of the railway com= pany, expressed his deep regret at the accident. The company had always taken every precaution to prevent people crossing the lines except by the bridges, both by placing notices in every station and by the use of patent spring gates at level crossings. The deceased had been in the habit of crossing the lines late at night from platform to platform and, in view of certain other circumstances of the case, he did not think the railway officials were to blame.

Captain Sinico, of Leoville,[9] Sydney Parade, husband of the deceased, also gave evidence. He stated that the deceased was his wife. He was not in Dublin at the time of the accident as he had arrived only that morning from Rotterdam.[1] They had been married for twenty-two years and had lived happily until about two years ago when his wife began to be rather intemperate in her habits.

Miss Mary Sinico said that of late her mother had been in the habit of going out at night to buy spirits. She, witness, had often tried to reason with her mother and had induced her to join a league.[2] She was not at home until an hour after the accident.

The jury returned a verdict in accordance with the medical evidence and exonerated Lennon from all blame.

The Deputy Coroner said it was a most painful case and expressed great sympathy with Captain Sinico and his daugh= ter. He urged on the railway company to take strong measures to prevent the possibility of similar accidents in the future. No blame attached to anyone.

Mr Duffy raised his eyes from the paper and gazed out of his window on the cheerless evening landscape. The river lay quiet

228 Halpin,] 14P; Cosgrave, MS   228–229 the--Hospital,] 14P; Vincent's Hospital, MS
230 of] ⁷¹⟨on⟩ of¹ʳ MS   239 level] 14; railway MS, 14P   248 and] and ⟨□⟩ MS
251 Miss Mary] 14P; Mary MS

9. Presumably the name of the Sinico house.
1. A busy commercial port city in Holland. Captain Sinico's commercial shipping business operates between Ireland and Holland.
2. A temperance league, which would have persuaded Mrs. Sinico to take an oath to abstain from alcohol.

beside the empty distillery and from time to time a light 265
appeared in some house on the Lucan road.[3] What an end! The
whole narrative of her death revolted him and it revolted him
to think that he had ever spoken to her of what he held sacred.
The threadbare phrases, the inane expressions of sympathy, the
cautious words of a reporter won over to conceal the details of 270
a commonplace vulgar death attacked his stomach. Not merely
had she degraded herself; she had degraded him. He saw the
squalid tract of her vice,[4] miserable and malodorous. His soul's
companion! He thought of the hobbling wretches whom he had
seen carrying cans and bottles to be filled by the barman.[5] Just 275
God, what an end! Evidently she had been unfit to live, without
any strength of purpose, an easy prey to habits, one of the
wrecks on which civilisation has been reared. But that she
could have sunk so low! Was it possible he had deceived him=
self so utterly about her? He remembered her outburst of that 280
night and interpreted it in a harsher sense than he had ever
done. He had no difficulty now in approving of the course he
had taken.

As the light failed and his memory began to wander he
thought her hand touched his. The shock which had first at= 285
tacked his stomach was now attacking his nerves. He put on
his overcoat and hat quickly and went out. The cold air met
him on the threshold; it crept into the sleeves of his coat. When
he came to the publichouse at Chapelizod Bridge[6] he went in
and ordered a hot punch. 290

The proprietor served him obsequiously but did not venture
to talk. There were five or six workingmen in the shop
discussing the value of a gentleman's estate in county Kildare.
They drank at intervals from their huge pint tumblers and
smoked, spitting often on the floor and sometimes dragging the 295
sawdust[7] over their spits with their heavy boots. Mr Duffy sat
on his stool and gazed at them, without seeing or hearing them.
After a while they went out and he called for another punch.
He sat a long time over it. The shop was very quiet. The
proprietor sprawled on the counter reading the *Herald*[8] and 300
yawning. Now and again a tram was heard swishing along the
lonely road outside.

---

3. A road leading from Chapelizod to the village of Lucan.
4. The word "tract" here may refer either to an expanse, or region, or to a moral treatise, or text.
5. Beer or ale on tap purchased (presumably at a reduced price) to be poured into the customer's container to be taken home.
6. A pub called The Bridge Inn at the time of the story.
7. Fine wood particles strewn over the floor of pubs to absorb spills and facilitate cleaning.
8. *The Evening Herald,* a Dublin daily newspaper.

   As he sat there, living over his life with her and evoking
alternately the two images in which he now conceived her, he
realised that she was dead, that she had ceased to exist, that she   305
had become a memory. He began to feel ill at ease. He asked
himself what else could he have done. He could not have
carried on a comedy of deception with her; he could not have
lived with her openly. He had done what seemed to him best.
How was he to blame? Now that she was gone he understood   310
how lonely her life must have been, sitting night after night
alone in that room. His life would be lonely too until he, too,
died, ceased to exist, became a memory—if anyone remembered
him.

   It was after nine o'clock when he left the shop. The night   315
was cold and gloomy. He entered the Park[9] by the first gate and
walked along under the gaunt trees. He walked through the
bleak alleys where they had walked four years before. She
seemed to be near him in the darkness. At moments he seemed
to feel her voice touch his ear, her hand touch his. He stood   320
still to listen. Why had he withheld life from her? Why had he
sentenced her to death? He felt his moral nature falling to
pieces.

   When he gained the crest of the Magazine Hill[1] he halted and
looked along the river towards Dublin, the lights of which   325
burned redly and hospitably in the cold night. He looked down
the slope and at the base, in the shadow of the wall of the Park,
he saw some human figures lying. Those venal and furtive loves
filled him with despair. He gnawed the rectitude of his life; he
felt that he had been outcast from life's feast. One human being   330
had seemed to love him and he had denied her life and
happiness: he had sentenced her to ignominy, a death of shame.
He knew that the prostrate creatures down by the wall were
watching him and wished him gone. No-one wanted him; he
was outcast from life's feast. He turned his eyes to the grey   335
gleaming river, winding along towards Dublin. Beyond the
river he saw a goods train winding out of Kingsbridge Station,[2]
like a worm with a fiery head winding through the darkness
obstinately and laboriously. It passed slowly out of sight but
still he heard in his ears the laborious drone of the engine   340
reiterating the syllables of her name.

326 redly] 14; humanly MS, 14P   341 reiterating--name.] ⌐¹⟨"Emily Sinico" "Emily Sinico" "Emily Sinico."⟩ reiterating the syllables of her name.¹⌐ MS

9. Chapelizod Gate into Phoenix Park is not far from the bridge and The Bridge Inn.
1. A hill in Phoenix Park overlooking the river Liffey, its name derived from Magazine Fort,
   which once stored arms and munitions.
2. The terminus of the Great Southern and Western Railroad serving southern and southwestern Ireland.

He turned back the way he had come, the rhythm of the engine pounding in his ears. He began to doubt the reality of what memory told him. He halted under a tree and allowed the rhythm to die away. He could not feel her near him in the 345 darkness nor her voice touch his ear. He waited for some minutes, listening. He could hear nothing: the night was per= fectly silent. He listened again: perfectly silent. He felt that he was alone.

Ivy Day in the Committee Room[1]

Old Jack raked the cinders together with a piece of card= board and spread them judiciously over the whitening dome of coals. When the dome was thinly covered his face lapsed into darkness but as he set himself to fan the fire again his crouch= ing shadow ascended the opposite wall and his face slowly 5 re-emerged into light. It was an old man's face, very bony and hairy. The moist blue eyes blinked at the fire and the moist mouth fell open at times, munching once or twice mechanically when it closed. When the cinders had caught he laid the piece of cardboard against the wall, sighed and said: 10
—That's better now, Mr O'Connor.

Mr O'Connor, a greyhaired young man, whose face was disfigured by many blotches and pimples, had just brought the tobacco for a cigarette into a shapely cylinder but, when spoken to, he undid his handiwork meditatively. Then he be= 15 gan to roll the tobacco again meditatively and, after a mo= ment's thought, decided to lick the paper.
—Did Mr Tierney say when he'd be back? he asked in a husky falsetto.[2]
—He didn't say. 20
Mr O'Connor put his cigarette into his mouth and began to

342 come, the] 14P; come with the MS

Copy-text: Manuscript Cornell (MS); Collated texts: 1910 intermediate proofs (10P); 1914 proofs (14P) and 1914 first edition (14) [IDENTITY IN BOTH IS REPORTED AS '14']; 1967 Viking edition in the 1969 Viking Critical Library printing (67). [A TRANSCRIPT OF MANUSCRIPT YALE 2.7, FOOTNOTED WITH THE VARIANTS OF THE COPY-TEXT, IS RENDERED IN THE SECTION »MANU= SCRIPT TRACES« OF OUR EDITION OF *DUBLINERS*, NEW YORK: GARLAND PUBLISHING INC., 1993.]

1. Ivy Day commemorated the anniversary of the death of the great Irish political leader Charles Stewart Parnell (1846–1891), on October 6, 1891. Each October 6, his followers remembered him by wearing an ivy leaf in their lapels. Parnell, a powerful proponent for Irish independence and land reform, was deposed when his affair with a married woman, Katharine O'Shea, became public. His ouster from his political party occurred in Com= mittee Room 15 of the House of Parliament in London on December 6, 1890.
2. A forced voice in a register above the natural voice.

search his pockets. He took out a pack of thin pasteboard[3] cards.

—I'll get you a match, said the old man.

—Never mind, this'll do, said Mr O'Connor.   25

He selected one of the cards and read what was printed on it:

Municipal Elections[4]

Royal Exchange Ward[5]

Mr Richard J Tierney P. L. G.[6] respectfully solicits   30
the favour of your vote and influence at the coming
election in the Royal Exchange Ward.

Mr O'Connor had been engaged by Mr Tierney's agent[7] to canvass[8] one part of the ward but, as the weather was inclement and his boots let in the wet, he spent a great part of the day   35 sitting by the fire in the Committee Room in Wicklow Street[9] with Jack, the old caretaker. They had been sitting thus since the short day had grown dark.[1] It was the sixth of October, dismal and cold out of doors.

Mr O'Connor tore off a strip of the card and, lighting it, lit   40 his cigarette. As he did so the flame lit up a leaf of dark glossy ivy in the lapel of his coat. The old man watched him attent= ively and then, taking up the piece of cardboard again, began to fan the fire slowly while his companion smoked.

—Ah, yes, he said, continuing, it's hard to know what way to   45 bring up children. Now who'd think he'd turn out like that. I sent him to the Christian Brothers[2] and I done what I could for him and there he goes boosing about. I tried to make him someway decent.

---

24 you] 14; ye MS–14P   36 Room] 14; Rooms MS–14P   36 in] ⟨with⟩ in MS
40 off--of] STET MS   49 decent.] 10P; dacent—MS

3. Cardboard.
4. The municipal elections in Dublin elected aldermen and councilors to serve on the Municipal Council for the City of Dublin Corporation, the governing body of the city of Dublin.
   Each of the twenty wards or electoral districts in the city had one alderman and three
   councilors on the Municipal Council, and the members of the Council would, in turn,
   elect the Mayor of Dublin.
5. Because the Royal Exchange Ward encompassed those areas south of the Liffey that
   included the City Hall and Dublin Castle, both of which housed major governmental
   offices, the elections in this ward were of major importance.
6. Poor Law Guardian. Rather than promoting policies to support the poor, Poor Law Guard-
   ians saw themselves charged with demanding work of everyone to minimize such meager
   public assistance as was available.
7. His election campaign manager.
8. To solicit votes.
9. The Nationalist Party had its headquarters on Wicklow Street, and a committee room with
   a fireplace was apparently made available as a meeting point for the canvassers.
1. Late afternoon, between 5 and 6 P.M., in October.
2. A Roman Catholic day school for boys; it charged low fees and emphasized vocational
   rather than academic training.

He replaced the cardboard wearily.   50
—Only I'm an old man now I'd change his tune for him. I'd
take the stick to his back and beat him while I could stand over
him—as I done many a time before. The mother, you know, she
cocks him up[3] with this and that ....
—That's what ruins children, said Mr O'Connor.   55
—To be sure it is, said the old man. And little thanks you get
for it, only impudence. He takes the upper hand of me when=
ever he sees I've a sup[4] taken. What's the world coming to when
sons speaks that way to their father?
—What age is he? said Mr O'Connor.   60
—Nineteen, said the old man.
—Why don't you put him to something?
—Sure, amn't I never done at the drunken bowsey[5] ever since
he left school. *I won't keep you,* I says. *You must get a job for
yourself.* But, sure, it's worse whenever he gets a job: he drinks 65
it all.
    Mr O'Connor shook his head in sympathy and the old man
fell silent, gazing into the fire. Someone opened the door of the
room and called out:
—Hello! Is this a Freemasons' meeting?[6]   70
—Who's that? said the old man.
—What are you doing in the dark? asked a voice.
—Is that you, Hynes? asked Mr O'Connor.
—Yes. What are you doing in the dark? said Mr Hynes
advancing into the light of the fire.   75
    He was a tall slender young man with a light brown mous=
tache. Imminent little drops of rain hung at the brim of his hat
and the collar of his jacket coat was turned up.
—Well, Mat, he said to Mr O'Connor, how goes it?
    Mr O'Connor shook his head. The old man left the hearth   80
and after stumbling about the room returned with two candle=
sticks which he thrust one after the other into the fire and
carried to the table. A denuded room came into view and the
fire lost all its cheerful colour. The walls of the room were bare
except for a copy of an election address. In the middle of the   85
room was a small table on which papers were heaped.

51 Only] 14; On'y MS   51 old] 14; owl' MS–14P   52 beat] 14; bate MS–14P
53 you] 14; ye MS–14P   56 you] 14; ye MS–14P   57 only] 14; on'y MS–14P   57 the
upper] e; th'upper MS–14, 67   63 drunken] 14; dhrunken MS–14P   64 You] 67; Ye
MS–14   73 asked] 10P; said MS

3. Flatters him and builds up his ego.
4. A drink of liquor.
5. A boozer, or drunkard.
6. Secret meetings of the brotherhood of Freemasons, thought by some to plot sinister
   intrigues.

Mr Hynes leaned against the mantelpiece and asked:

—Has he paid you yet?[7]

—Not yet, said Mr O'Connor. I hope to God he'll not leave us in the lurch tonight.   90

Mr Hynes laughed.

—O, he'll pay you. Never fear, he said.

—I hope he'll look smart about it if he means business, said Mr O'Connor.

—What do you think, Jack? said Mr Hynes satirically to the   95 old man.

The old man returned to his seat by the fire, saying:

—It isn't but he has it, anyway. Not like the other tinker.[8]

—What other tinker? said Mr Hynes.

—Colgan, said the old man scornfully.   100

—Is it because Colgan's a workingman[9] you say that? What's the difference between a good honest bricklayer and a publican —eh? Hasn't the workingman as good a right to be in the Corporation[1] as anyone else—aye, and a better right than those shoneens[2] that are always hat in hand before any fellow with a   105 handle to his name?[3] Isn't that so, Mat? said Mr Hynes, addressing Mr O'Connor.

—I think you're right, said Mr O'Connor.

—One man is a plain honest man with no hunkersliding[4] about him. He goes in to represent the labour classes. This fellow   110 you're working for only wants to get some job or other.

—Of course, the working classes should be represented, said the old man.

—The workingman, said Mr Hynes, gets all kicks and no halfpence.[5] But it's labour produces everything. The working=   115 man is not looking for fat jobs for his sons and nephews and cousins. The workingman is not going to drag the honour of Dublin in the mud to please a German monarch.[6]

---

115 halfpence.] 14; ha'pence. MS–14P

7. That is, has Tierney paid O'Connor for his work canvassing for votes.
8. A traveling craftsman who mends pots and kettles, but also a gypsy, beggar, or traveling performer.
9. Colgan is presumably the Labor party candidate, politically to the left of Tierney.
1. The Dublin Corporation was the governing body for the city's municipal affairs.
2. A derisive term for upstarts who curry favor with people above their station.
3. A title or other honorific designation.
4. In nineteenth-century U.S. politics, a hunker was a conservative opposed to innovation or change. Hunkersliding may therefore refer to liberals who harbor conservative tendencies.
5. Hard work and abuse for little renumeration.
6. The story takes place after the death of Queen Victoria in 1901 but before the visit of King Edward VII to Ireland at the end of July 1903. The date of the story can therefore be fixed as October 6, 1902—during the reign of King Edward VII, whose father was Prince Albert, the German consort of Queen Victoria whose own mother was the German Princess Victoria of Saxe-Coburg-Gotha.

—How's that? said the old man.

—Don't you know they want to present an address of welcome   120
to Edward Rex[7] if he comes here next year? What do we want
kowtowing to a foreign king?

—Our man won't vote for the address, said Mr O'Connor. He
goes in on the nationalist ticket.[8]

—Won't he? said Mr Hynes. Wait till you see whether he will   125
or not. I know him. Is it Tricky Dicky Tierney?

—By God! perhaps you're right, Joe, said Mr O'Connor.
Anyway I wish he'd turn up with the spondulics.[9]

The three men fell silent. The old man began to rake more
cinders together. Mr Hynes took off his hat, shook it and then   130
turned down the collar of his coat, displaying, as he did so, an
ivy leaf in the lapel.

—If this man[1] was alive, he said, pointing to the leaf, we'd have
no talk of an address of welcome.

—That's true, said Mr O'Connor.   135

—Musha,[2] God be with them times! said the old man. There
was some life in it then.

The room was silent again. Then a bustling little man with a
snuffling nose and very cold ears pushed in the door. He
walked over quickly to the fire, rubbing his hands as if he   140
intended to produce a spark from them.

—No money, boys, he said.

—Sit down here, Mr Henchy, said the old man, offering him
his chair.

—O, don't stir, Jack, don't stir, said Mr Henchy.   145

He nodded curtly to Mr Hynes and sat down on the chair
which the old man vacated.

—Did you serve Aungier Street?[3] he asked Mr O'Connor.

—Yes, said Mr O'Connor, beginning to search his pockets for
memoranda.   150

—Did you call on Grimes?

—I did.

—Well? How does he stand?

---

121 Edward Rex] ⁷¹⟨King Edward⟩ Edward Rex¹ᴿ MS   126 Tricky] 14; Thricky MS–14P
127 By] 14; Be MS–14P   127 perhaps] 14; p'raps MS–10P; p'r'aps 14P   148 Street?]
10P; St? MS

7. A formal address of welcome to the British King Edward VII would give the appearance
of Irish approval or support for Britain's rule over Ireland.
8. The Irish Parliamentary Party, or Home Rule Party, which advocated Irish independence
from Britain.
9. American slang for cash or money.
1. Charles Stewart Parnell, in whose memory the ivy leaf is worn.
2. An Irish exclamation of emphasis, similar to "By god!" Also contracted as " 'Usha."
3. Canvass for votes on Aungier Street, which is located near Dublin Castle.

—He wouldn't promise. He said: *I won't tell anyone what way I'm going to vote.* But I think he'll be all right.   155

—Why so?

—He asked me who the nominators[4] were and I told him. I mentioned Father Burke's name. I think it'll be all right.

Mr Henchy began to snuffle and to rub his hands over the fire at a terrific speed. Then he said: 160

—For the love of God, Jack, bring us in a bit of coal. There must be some left.

The old man went out of the room.

—It's no go, said Mr Henchy, shaking his head. I asked the little shoeboy[5] but he said: *O, now, Mr Henchy, when I*   165 *see the work going on properly I won't forget you, you may be sure.* Mean little tinker! 'Usha, how could he be anything else?

—What did I tell you, Mat? said Mr Hynes. Tricky Dicky Tierney.   170

—O, he's as tricky as they make 'em, said Mr Henchy. He hasn't got those little pig's eyes for nothing. Blast his soul! Couldn't he pay up like a man instead of: *O, now, Mr Henchy, I must speak to Mr Fanning[6] ... I've spent a lot of money?* Mean little shoeboy of hell! I suppose he forgets the time his little old   175 father kept the hand-me-down shop in Mary's Lane.[7]

—But is that a fact? asked Mr O'Connor.

—God, yes! said Mr Henchy. Did you never hear that? And the men used to go in on Sunday morning before the houses were open[8] to buy a waistcoat or a trousers—moya![9]—but Tricky   180 Dicky's little old father always had a tricky little black bottle[1] up in a corner. Do you mind now? That's that. That's where he first saw the light.[2]

The old man returned with a few lumps of coal which he placed here and there on the fire.   185

169 Tricky] 14; Thricky MS–14P   171 tricky] 14; thricky MS–14P   175 old] 14; owl' MS–14P   180 Tricky] 14; Thricky MS–14P   181 old] 14; owl' MS–14P   181 tricky] 14; thricky MS–14P

4. Persons who endorsed or declared their support for the candidate.
5. Slang for a toady, or someone who is insincerely servile, in the metaphorical posture of someone who shines shoes.
6. Mr. Fanning appears in the story "Grace," in which he is called "the registration agent and mayormaker of the city." His position was an influential one because he was in charge of voter registration and presided over the election in the Municipal Council that chose the mayor of Dublin.
7. A poor neighborhood, full of tenements, in north-central Dublin.
8. Publichouses, or pubs, had very strictly controlled opening and closing times in Dublin, and did not open on Sundays until after noon.
9. An Irish expression of ironic sympathy.
1. Black market whiskey or alcohol, sold illegally when the pubs are closed.
2. Tierney, who now owns the licensed *Black Eagle* pub, was ostensibly born in a secondhand clothing store on Mary Street where his father sold drinks illegally.

—That's a nice how-do-you-do, said Mr O'Connor. How does
he expect us to work for him if he won't stump up?[3]
—I can't help it, said Mr Henchy. I expect to find the bailiffs[4] in
the hall when I go home.

Mr Hynes laughed and, shoving himself away from the   190
mantelpiece with the aid of his shoulders, made ready to leave.
—It'll be all right when King Eddie comes, he said. Well, boys,
I'm off for the present. See you later. 'Bye, 'bye.

He went out of the room slowly. Neither Mr Henchy nor the
old man said anything but, just as the door was closing, Mr   195
O'Connor, who had been staring moodily into the fire, called
out suddenly:
—'Bye, Joe.

Mr Henchy waited a few moments and then nodded in the
direction of the door.   200
—Tell me, he said across the fire, what brings our friend in
here? What does he want?
—'Usha, poor Joe! said Mr O'Connor throwing the end of his
cigarette into the fire. He's hard up like the rest of us.

Mr Henchy snuffled vigorously and spat so copiously that he   205
nearly put out the fire which uttered a hissing protest.
—To tell you my private and candid opinion, he said, I think
he's a man from the other camp. He's a spy of Colgan's, if you
ask me. *Just go round and try and find out how they're getting
on. They won't suspect you.* Do you twig?[5]   210
—Ah, poor Joe is a decent skin,[6] said Mr O'Connor.
—His father was a decent respectable man, Mr Henchy ad=
mitted. Poor old Larry Hynes! Many a good turn he did in his
day! But I'm greatly afraid our friend is not nineteen carat.[7]
Damn it, I can understand a fellow being hard up but what I   215
can't understand is a fellow sponging.[8] Couldn't he have some
spark of manhood about him?
—He doesn't get a warm welcome from me when he comes,
said the old man. Let him work for his own side and not come
spying around here.   220
—I don't know, said Mr O'Connor dubiously as he took out
cigarette papers and tobacco. I think Joe Hynes is a straight

204 fire. He's] STET MS   208–209 you ask] 14; y'ask MS–14P   210 Do you] 14; D'ye
MS–14P

3. Pay what is owed.
4. Rent collectors or sheriff's assistants.
5. Understand or "get it."
6. A decent fellow. Possibly also slang for a cheat or a miser.
7. Not as worthy as he appears to be. A carat is a measure of quality used for diamonds or
   gold. Nineteen carat would be a measure of high quality for gold jewelry.
8. Borrowing money from people without repaying them. Living off people like a parasite.

man. He's a clever chap, too, with the pen. Do you remember
that thing he wrote ..... ?

—Some of these lousy hillsiders and fenians[9] are a bit too clever   225
if you ask me, said Mr Henchy. Do you know what my private
and candid opinion is about some of those little jokers? I
believe half of them are in the pay of the Castle.[1]

—There's no knowing, said the old man.

—O, but I know it for a fact, said Mr Henchy. They're Castle   230
hacks[2] ..... I don't say Hynes .... No, damn it, I think he's a
stroke above that .... But there's a certain little nobleman with
a cockeye[3]—you know the patriot I'm alluding to?

Mr O'Connor nodded.

—There's a lineal descendant of Major Sirr[4] for you if you like!   235
O, the heart's blood of a patriot! That's a fellow now that'd
sell his country for fourpence—aye!—and go down on his
bended knees and thank the Almighty Christ he had a country
to sell.

There was a knock at the door.   240

—Come in! said Mr Henchy.

A person resembling a poor clergyman or a poor actor
appeared in the doorway. His black clothes were tightly but=
toned on his short body and it was impossible to say whether
he wore a clergyman's collar or a layman's because the collar   245
of his shabby frock coat, the uncovered buttons of which
reflected the candlelight, was turned up about his neck. He
wore a round hat of hard black felt. His face, shining with
raindrops, had the appearance of damp yellow cheese save
where two rosy spots indicated the cheekbones. He opened his   250
very long mouth suddenly to express disappointment and at the
same time opened wide his very bright blue eyes to express
pleasure and surprise.

—O, Father Keon! said Mr Henchy, jumping up from his
chair. Is that you? Come in!   255

225 lousy] ⌐¹lousy¹⌐ STET MS   226 you ask] 14; y'ask MS–14P   236 the--a] ⌐¹⟨an out-
an'-out⟩ the heart's blood of a¹⌐ MS   238 Christ] 14; God MS–14P

9. Members of the Irish Republican Brotherhood, a revolutionary independence movement
   willing to resort to violence, who called themselves Fenians after legendary Irish warriors.
   Their characterization as living in the hillsides was intended to discredit them as lawless
   and uncouth.
1. Dublin Castle housed the British government officials and law-enforcement offices in
   charge of Irish affairs and was thought to use paid informers to spy on Irish nationalist
   organizations.
2. Men doing the dirty work for Dublin Castle, such as spying and informing.
3. Presumably someone who ironically gives himself self-important airs to disguise a shifty
   or crooked character.
4. Henry Charles Sirr (1764–1841), an Irish officer serving the British military in policing
   Dublin during the Rebellion of 1798, was assisted by informants in the bloody capture of
   Lord Edward Fitzgerald, an Irish patriot who died of his wounds.

—O, no, no, no! said Father Keon quickly, pursing up his lips
as if he were addressing a child.

—Won't you come in and sit down?

—No, no, no! said Father Keon, speaking in a discreet indul= 260
gent velvety voice, don't let me disturb you now! I'm just look=
ing for Mr Fanning ...

—He's round at the *Black Eagle*,[5] said Mr Henchy. But won't
you come in and sit down a minute?

—No, no, thank you. It was just a little business matter, said
Father Keon. Thank you, indeed. 265

He retreated from the doorway and Mr Henchy, seizing one
of the candlesticks, went to the door to light him downstairs.

—O, don't trouble, I beg!

—No, but the stairs is so dark.

—No, no, I can see .... Thank you, indeed. 270

—Are you right now?

—All right, thanks ... Thanks.

Mr Henchy returned with the candlestick and put it on the
table. He sat down again at the fire. There was silence for a
few moments. 275

—Tell me, John, said Mr O'Connor, lighting his cigarette with
another pasteboard card.

—Hm?

—What is he exactly?[6]

—Ask me an easier one, said Mr Henchy. 280

—Fanning and himself seem to me very thick. They're often in
Kavanagh's[7] together. Is he a priest at all?

—'Mmmyes, I believe so ... I think he's what you call a black
sheep.[8] We haven't many of them, thank God, but we have a
few ... He's an unfortunate man of some kind 285

—And how does he knock it out?[9] asked Mr O'Connor.

—That's another mystery.

—Is he attached to any chapel or church or institution or ....?

—No, said Mr Henchy, I think he's travelling on his own
account .... God forgive me, he added, I thought he was the 290
dozen of stout.[1]

—Is there any chance of a drink itself? asked Mr O'Connor.

---

260 voice,] voice, ⟨[7.1]which is not often found except with the confessor or the sodomite,⟩
MS   290 forgive] 14; forgi' MS–14P

5. Tierney's pub.
6. What is Keon's status as a priest? That is, is he a clergyman in good standing or has he
   been defrocked or otherwise demoted by the Church for some reason?
7. A pub near City Hall and Dublin Castle where politicians gathered.
8. A member who has brought disgrace on a family or group.
9. Support himself.
1. A case of strong beer or porter.

—I'm dry too, said the old man.

—I asked that little shoeboy three times, said Mr Henchy, would he send up a dozen of stout. I asked him again now but he was leaning on the counter in his shirtsleeves having a deep goster[2] with Alderman Cowley. 295

—Why didn't you remind him? said Mr O'Connor.

—Well, I couldn't go over while he was talking to Alderman Cowley. I just waited till I caught his eye and said: *About that little matter I was speaking to you about ... That'll be all right, Mr H.,* he said. Yerra,[3] sure the little hop-o'-my-thumb[4] has forgotten all about it. 300

—There's some deal on in that quarter, said Mr O'Connor thoughtfully. I saw the three of them hard at it yesterday at Suffolk Street corner.[5] 305

—I think I know the little game they're at, said Mr Henchy. You must owe the City Fathers money[6] nowadays if you want to be made Lord Mayor. Then they'll make you Lord Mayor. By God I'm thinking seriously of becoming a City Father myself. What do you think? Would I do for the job? 310

Mr O'Connor laughed.

—So far as owing money goes ....

—Driving out of the Mansion House,[7] said Mr Henchy, in all my vermin,[8] with Jack here standing up behind me in a pow= dered wig[9]—eh? 315

—And make me your private secretary, John.

—Yes. And I'll make Father Keon my private chaplain. We'll have a family party.

—Faith, Mr Henchy, said the old man, you'd keep up better style than some of them. I was talking one day to old Keegan, the porter. *And how do you like your new master, Pat?* says I to him. *You haven't much entertaining now,* says I. *Enter= taining!* says he. *He'd live on the smell of an oilrag.*[1] And do you 320

---

302 hop-o'-my-thumb] 14; hop-o'-me-thumb MS–14P   309 By] 14; Be MS–4P
315 my] 14; me MS–14P   320 you'd] 14; ye'd MS–14P   321 to old] 14; t'owl MS; t'owl'
10P–14P   322 *do you*] 14, 67; d'ye MS–14P; do you 14   323 *You*] 14, 67; "Y" MS; Y'
10P; "Y" 14P; "You 14   324 do you] 14; d'ye MS; d'yew 10P–14P

2. Irish idiom for an informal, gossipy conference or consultation.
3. Irish for "look out" or "really."
4. A dwarfish or very small person, like "Tom Thumb" in the fairy tale, hyperbolically small enough to be told to "hop on my thumb."
5. A street corner north of the committee room on Wicklow Street.
6. Henchy may be implying that the members of the Municipal Council are likely to elect as mayor of Dublin someone who owes them money, and over whom they subsequently have control.
7. The official residence of the Lord Mayor of Dublin on Dawson Street.
8. Henchy jokingly substitutes vermin for "ermine," the white fur that trimmed the robes worn by the mayor on ceremonial occasions.
9. Part of the formal livery or uniform of eighteenth-century servants.
1. Colloquial for "needs little sustenance."

know what he told me? Now, I declare to God, I didn't believe   325
him.

—What? said Mr Henchy and Mr O'Connor.

—He told me: *What do you think of a Lord Mayor of Dublin*[2]
sending out for a pound of chops[3] *for his dinner? How's that for
high living?* says he. *Wisha!*[4] *wisha,* says I. *A pound of chops,*   330
says he, *coming into the Mansion House. Wisha!* says I, *what
kind of people is going at all now?*

At this point there was a knock at the door and a boy put in
his head.

—What is it? said the old man.   335

—From the *Black Eagle,* said the boy, walking in sideways and
depositing a basket on the floor with a noise of shaken bottles.

The old man helped the boy to transfer the bottles from the
basket to the table and counted the full tally. After the transfer
the boy put his basket on his arm and asked: 340

—Any bottles?

—What bottles? said the old man.

—Won't you let us drink them first? said Mr Henchy.

—I was told to ask for bottles.[5]

—Come back tomorrow, said the old man.   345

—Here, boy! said Mr Henchy, will you run over to O'Farrell's[6]
and ask him to lend us a corkscrew—for Mr Henchy, say. Tell
him we won't keep it a minute. Leave the basket there.

The boy went out and Mr Henchy began to rub his hands
cheerfully, saying: 350

—Ah, well, he's not so bad after all. He's as good as his word,
anyhow.

—There's no tumblers, said the old man.

—O, don't let that trouble you, Jack, said Mr Henchy. Many's
the good man before now drank out of the bottle.   355

—Anyway it's better than nothing, said Mr O'Connor.

—He's not a bad sort, said Mr Henchy, only Fanning has such
a loan of him.[7] He means well, you know, in his own tinpot
way.[8]

325 told] 14; towl' MS–14P   325 declare] 14; 'clare MS–14P   328 told] 14; towl' MS–
14P   328 *do you*] 14, 67; d'ye MS–14P; do you 14   339 tally.] 14; dozen. MS–14P
343 you] 14; ye MS–14P   343 drink] 14; dhrink MS–14P   344 told--ask] 14; towl' t'ask
MS; towl't t'ask 10P–14P   346 boy!] boy⟨,⟩! MS   346 you] 14; ye MS–14P

2. Timothy Charles Harrington, a simple man from a working-class background, served as
   Lord Mayor of Dublin at the time of the story.
3. A plain, ordinary meal of lamb chops or pork chops.
4. An Irish expression of mild amazement.
5. Bottles were cleaned and reused by brewers at the time of the story and were therefore
   collected after use.
6. Presumably a nearby pub.
7. Such a hold on him, or monopoly on his attention.
8. Cheap, paltry, like a tinker's way.

The boy came back with the corkscrew. The old man   360
opened three bottles and was handing back the corkscrew
when Mr Henchy said to the boy:

—Would you like a drink, boy?

—If you please, sir, said the boy.

The old man opened another bottle grudgingly and handed   365
it to the boy.

—What age are you? he asked.

—Seventeen, said the boy.

As the old man said nothing further the boy took the bottle,
said: *Here's my best respects, sir!* to Mr Henchy, drank the   370
contents, put the bottle back on the table and wiped his mouth
with his sleeve. Then he took up the corkscrew and went out of
the door sideways, muttering some form of salutation.

—That's the way it begins, said the old man.

—The thin end of the wedge,[9] said Mr Henchy.   375

The old man distributed the three bottles which he had
opened and the men drank from them simultaneously. After
having drunk each placed his bottle on the mantelpiece within
hand's reach and drew in a long breath of satisfaction.

—Well, I did a good day's work today, said Mr Henchy after a   380
pause.

—That so, John?

—Yes. I got him one or two sure things in Dawson Street,[1]
Crofton and myself. Between ourselves, you know, Crofton
(he's a decent chap, of course), but he's not worth a damn as a   385
canvasser. He hasn't a word to throw to a dog. He stands and
looks at the people while I do the talking.

Here two men entered the room. One of them was a very fat
man, whose blue serge clothes seemed to be in danger of falling
from his sloping figure. He had a big face which resembled a   390
young ox's face in expression, staring blue eyes and a grizzled
moustache. The other man, who was much younger and frailer,
had a thin cleanshaven face. He wore a very high double collar
and a widebrimmed bowler hat.

—Hello, Crofton! said Mr Henchy to the fat man. Talk of the   395
devil .....

---

363 you] 14; ye MS–14P   364 If--please,] 14; I'ye plase, MS–14P   383 Street,]
Street(.), MS

9. An expression for a small indulgence or irregularity that opens the way for large trans-
   gressions. Refers to a wedge used to make a notch in a log that can then be split more
   easily with an axe.
1. Runs south from Trinity College to Stephen's Green—the site of the Mansion House as
   well as shops and offices.

—Where did the boose come from? asked the young man. Did the cow calve?[2]

—O, of course, Bantam spots the drink first thing! said Mr O'Connor laughing.   400

—Is that the way you chaps canvass, said Mr Lyons,[3] and Crofton and I out in the cold and rain looking for votes?

—Why, blast your soul, said Mr Henchy. I'd get more votes in five minutes than you two'd get in a week.

—Open two bottles of stout, Jack, said Mr O'Connor.   405

—How can I? said the old man, when there's no corkscrew?

—Wait now, wait now! said Mr Henchy, getting up quickly. Did you ever see this little trick?

He took two bottles from the table and, carrying them to the fire, put them on the hob. Then he sat down again by the fire   410 and took another drink from his bottle. Mr Lyons sat on the edge of the table, pushed his hat towards the nape of his neck and began to swing his legs.

—Which is my bottle? he asked.

—This lad, said Mr Henchy.   415

Mr Crofton sat down on a box and looked fixedly at the other bottle on the hob. He was silent for two reasons. The first reason, sufficient in itself, was that he had nothing to say; the second reason was that he considered his companions beneath him. He had been a canvasser for Wilkins, the con=   420 servative,[4] but, when the conservatives had withdrawn their man and, choosing the lesser of two evils, given their support to the nationalist candidate, he had been engaged to work for Mr Tierney.

In a few minutes an apologetic *Pok!* was heard as the cork   425 flew out[5] of Mr Lyons's bottle. Mr Lyons jumped off the table, went to the fire, took his bottle and carried it back to the table.

—I was just telling them, Crofton, said Mr Henchy, that we got a good few votes today.

—Who did you get? asked Mr Lyons.   430

—Well, I got Parkes for one and I got Atkinson for two and I got Ward of Dawson Street. Fine old chap he is, too—regular old toff,[6] old conservative! *But isn't your candidate a national=*

---

397 boose] 14; stout MS–14P   399 Bantam] ⁷¹<Lyons> Bantamⁱᵣ MS   399 thing!]
thing(,)! MS   408 you ever] 14; y'ever MS–14P

2. A cow begins to produce milk after giving birth to a calf.
3. Bantam Lyons was mentioned in "The Boarding House."
4. A fictional candidate for the Irish Conservative Party, which supported land reform but not Home Rule, or Irish independence from Britain.
5. The heat from the fire expands the air in the bottle, creating pressure against the cork that eventually expels it from the bottle with a small explosive ("Pok!") sound.
6. Slang for someone who dresses stylishly so as to appear like a gentleman.

ist? said he. *He's a respectable man,* said I. *He's in favour of
whatever will benefit this country. He's a big ratepayer,*[7] I said.   435
He has extensive house property in the city and three places of
business and isn't it to his own advantage to keep down the
rates?*[8] *He's a prominent and respected citizen,* said I, *and a
Poor Law Guardian and he doesn't belong to any party, good
bad or indifferent.* That's the way to talk to 'em.   440
—And what about the address to the King? said Mr Lyons,
after drinking and smacking his lips.
—Listen to me, said Mr Henchy. What we want in this
country, as I said to old Ward, is capital. The King's coming
here will mean an influx of money into this country. The   445
citizens of Dublin will benefit by it. Look at all the factories
down by the quays there, idle! Look at all the money there is in
the country if we only worked the old industries, the mills, the
shipbuilding yards and factories. It's capital we want.
—But look here, John, said Mr O'Connor. Why should we   450
welcome the King of England! Didn't Parnell himself ....
—Parnell, said Mr Henchy, is dead. Now, here's the way I
look at it. Here's this chap come to the throne after his old
mother keeping him out of it till the man was grey.[9] He's a man
of the world and he means well by us. He's a jolly fine decent   455
fellow, if you ask me, and no damn nonsense about him. He
just says to himself: *The old one never went to see these wild
Irish.*[1] *By Christ, I'll go myself and see what they're like.* And
are we going to insult the man when he comes over here on a
friendly visit? Eh? Isn't that right, Crofton?   460
    Mr Crofton nodded his head.
—But after all now, said Mr Lyons argumentatively, King
Edward's life, you know, is not the very .....
—Let bygones be bygones, said Mr Henchy. I admire the man
personally. He's just an ordinary knockabout like you and me.   465

453 old] a10P, 14; ⟨bloody⟩ owl' MS; owl' 10P–14P   455 jolly fine] ⌐|⟨jolly, fine,⟩ jolly
fine|⌐ MS   456 you ask] a10P, 14; y'ask MS–14P   457 *old*] a10P, 67; 'owl MS–14P;
old 14   458 *By*] a10P, 67; Be MS–14P; By 14   458 *myself*] a10P, 67; meself MS–14P;
myself 14   465 knockabout] a10P, 14; fellow MS–14P

7. A payer of property taxes.
8. Henchy appeals to Mr. Ward's conservative instincts by arguing that as a property owner
and Poor Law Guardian Mr. Tierney is unlikely to vote for raising property taxes for the
benefit of measures designed to assist the poor.
9. Queen Victoria had an exceptionally long reign, from 1837 to 1901. As a result, her son
Edward, who was born in 1841, did not ascend to the throne until he was sixty years old.
1. Queen Victoria actually visited Ireland several times during her reign, most recently in
1900, two years before the time of the story. It is unclear why Mr. Henchy misrepresents
this history.

He's fond of his glass of grog and he's a bit of a rake,[2] perhaps, and he's a good sportsman. Damn it, can't we Irish play fair?

—That's all very fine, said Mr Lyons. But look at the case of Parnell[3] now.

—In the name of God, said Mr Henchy, where's the analogy   470
between the two cases?

—What I mean, said Mr Lyons, is we have our ideals. Why, now, would we welcome a man like that? Do you think now after what he did Parnell was a fit man to lead us? Do you think he was a man I'd like the lady who is now Mrs Lyons to   475
know? And why, then, would we do it for Edward the Seventh?

—This is Parnell's anniversary, said Mr O'Connor, and don't let us stir up any bad blood. We all respect him now that he's dead and gone—even the conservatives, he added, turning to Mr Crofton.   480

Pok! The tardy cork flew out of Mr Crofton's bottle. Mr Crofton got up from his box and went to the fire. As he re= turned with his capture he said in a deep voice:

—Our side of the house respects him because he was a gentle= man.[4]   485

—Right you are, Crofton! said Mr Henchy fiercely. He was the only man that could keep that bag of cats in order. *Down, ye dogs! Lie down, ye curs!* That's the way he treated them. Come in, Joe! Come in! he called out, catching sight of Mr Hynes in the doorway.   490

Mr Hynes came in slowly.

—Open another bottle of stout, Jack, said Mr Henchy. O, I forgot there's no corkscrew! Here, show me one here and I'll put it at the fire.

The old man handed him another bottle and he placed it on   495
the hob.

—Sit down, Joe, said Mr O'Connor, we're just talking about the Chief.[5]

—Aye, aye! said Mr Henchy.

466–467 He's--sportsman.] JOYCE MARGINALLY NOTES THE ALTERNATIVE: He can take a glass of grog like an honest Christian and, I grant you, he may have [SC. been] a wild lad in his day and he's a good ⌐¹⟨sportsman.⟩ sport.¹⌐ MS   466 a] 10P; ABSENT MS   473 Do you] 14; D'ye MS–14P   474–476 Do--know?] ⌐¹Do--know?¹⌐ (MARGINAL ADDITION) MS 481 tardy] ⌐¹tardy¹⌐ MS

2. King Edward VII, a husband and father, was notorious for his sexual affairs.
3. In contrast to King Edward VII, who suffered no political damage from his adulterous liaisons, the Irish politician Charles Stewart Parnell was deposed from his party after his affair with the married Katharine O'Shea became a matter of public record. Her husband named Parnell as her partner in his divorce suit.
4. That is, because he was an Anglo-Irish Protestant with wealth, social rank, and property.
5. Parnell.

Mr Hynes sat on the side of the table near Mr Lyons but   500
said nothing.

—There's one of them, anyhow, said Mr Henchy, that didn't
renege him. By God, I'll say that for you, Joe! No, by God, you
stuck to him like a man!

—O, Joe! said Mr O'Connor suddenly. Give us that thing you   505
wrote—do you remember? Have you got it on you?

—O, aye! said Mr Henchy. Give us that. Did you ever hear
that, Crofton? Listen to this now: splendid thing.

—Go on, said Mr O'Connor. Fire away, Joe.

Mr Hynes did not seem to remember at once the piece to   510
which they were alluding but, after reflecting a while, he said:

—O, that thing is it .... Sure, that's old now.

—Out with it, man! said Mr O'Connor.

—'Sh 'sh, said Mr Henchy. Now, Joe!

Mr Hynes hesitated a little longer. Then amid the silence he   515
took off his hat, laid it on the table and stood up. He seemed to
be rehearsing the piece in his mind. After a rather long pause he
announced:

The Death of Parnell
6th October 1891   520

He cleared his throat once or twice and then began to recite:

> He is dead. Our Uncrowned King[6] is dead.
> O, Erin, mourn with grief and woe
> For he lies dead whom the fell gang
> Of modern hypocrites laid low.   525
>
> He lies slain by the coward hounds
> He raised to glory from the mire:
> And Erin's hopes and Erin's dreams
> Perish upon her monarch's pyre.[7]
>
> In palace, cabin or in cot   530
> The Irish heart where'er it be
> Is bowed with woe—for he is gone
> Who would have wrought her destiny.
>
> He would have had his Erin famed,
> The green flag[8] gloriously unfurled,   535

503 By] 14; Be MS–14P   503 that] e:MS1; ABSENT MS–67   503 by] 14; be MS–14P
503 you(2)] 14; ye MS–14P   506 do you] 14; d'ye MS–14P   507 you ever] 14; y'ever
MS–14P

6. A term of reverence bestowed on Parnell by his followers.
7. A funeral pile of logs or combustible material for cremating the dead.
8. Green is the national color of Ireland.

Her statesmen, bards and warriors raised
Before the nations of the world.

He dreamed (alas,'twas but a dream!)
Of Liberty: but as he strove
To clutch that idol, treachery   540
Sundered him from the thing he loved.

Shame on the coward caitiff[9] hands
That smote their Lord or with a kiss
Betrayed him[1] to the rabble-rout
Of fawning priests—no friends of his!   545

May everlasting shame consume
The memory of those who tried
To befoul and smear th' exalted name
Of one who spurned them in his pride!

He fell, as fall the mighty ones,   550
Nobly undaunted to the last,
And Death has now united him
With Erin's heroes of the past.

No sound of strife disturb his sleep!
Calmly he rests: no human pain   555
Or high ambition spurs him now
The peaks of glory to attain.

They had their way: they laid him low.
But Erin, list, his spirit may
Rise, like the Phoenix[2] from the flames,   560
When breaks the dawning of the day,

The day that brings us Freedom's reign.
And on that day may Erin well
Pledge in the cup she lifts to Joy
One grief—the memory of Parnell.   565

Mr Hynes sat down again on the table. When he had
finished his recitation there was a silence and then a burst of
clapping: even Mr Lyons clapped. The applause continued for

9. A wretch or villain.
1. In the New Testament, Christ is betrayed by Judas, one of his apostles, who kisses Jesus
and thereby identifies him to the priests and elders come to arrest him (Matthew 26:47–
49).
2. A mythical bird that, after living for centuries, burned itself to death on a funeral pyre but
was able to rise again to a new life. The phoenix therefore serves as a symbol of death and
resurrection.

a little time. When it had ceased all the auditors drank from
their bottles in silence.   570

Pok! The cork flew out of Mr Hynes's bottle but Mr Hynes
remained sitting, flushed and bareheaded on the table. He did
not seem to have heard the invitation.

—Good man, Joe! said Mr O'Connor, taking out his cigarette
papers and pouch the better to hide his emotion.   575

—What do you think of that, Crofton? cried Mr Henchy. Isn't
that fine—what?

Mr Crofton said that it was a very fine piece of writing.

A Mother

Mr Holohan, assistant secretary of the *Eire Abu*[1] Society, had
been walking up and down Dublin for nearly a month, with his
hands and pockets full of dirty pieces of paper, arranging about
the series of concerts. He had a game[2] leg and for this his friends
called him Hoppy Holohan. He walked up and down con=   5
stantly, stood by the hour at street corners arguing the point,
and made notes: but in the end it was Mrs Kearney who ar=
ranged everything.

Miss Devlin had become Mrs Kearney out of spite. She had
been educated in a high-class convent where she had learned   10
French and music. As she was naturally pale and unbending in
manner she made few friends at school. When she came to the
age of marriage she was sent out to many houses where her
playing and ivory manners were much admired. She sat amid
the chilly circle of her accomplishments, waiting for some   15
suitor to brave it and offer her a brilliant life. But the young
men whom she met were ordinary and she gave them no
encouragement, trying to console her romantic desires by eat=
ing a great deal of Turkish Delight[3] in secret. However, when
she drew near the limit and her friends began to loosen their   20

576 do you] 14; d'ye MS–14P

Copy-text: Manuscript Yale 2.8 (MS); Collated texts: 1910 galley proofs (10G); 1914 proofs
(14P) and 1914 first edition (14) [IDENTITY IN BOTH IS REPORTED AS '14']; 1967 Viking edition
in the 1969 Viking Critical Library printing (67).

4 game] 14P; short MS–10G   14 and] 14; and her MS–14P

1. Gaelic for "mature" or "ripe" Ireland, sometimes also translated as "victorious" Ireland, an
   organization devoted to the promotion of Irish culture.
2. Lame.
3. A confection or sweetmeat made of a sugar-coated jelly of tough consistency.

tongues[4] about her she silenced them by marrying Mr Kearney
who was a bootmaker on Ormond Quay.[5]

He was much older than she. His conversation, which was
serious, took place at intervals in his great brown beard. After
the first years of married life Mrs Kearney perceived that such a   25
man would wear better than a romantic person but she never
put her own romantic ideas away. He was sober, thrifty and
pious: he went to the altar every first Friday,[6] sometimes with
her, oftener by himself. But she never weakened in her religion
and was a good wife to him. At some party in a strange house   30
when she lifted her eyebrow ever so slightly he stood up to take
his leave and when his cough troubled him she put the eider=
down quilt over his feet and made a strong rum punch. For his
part he was a model father. By paying a small sum every week
into a society[7] he insured for both his daughters a dowry[8] of one   35
hundred pounds each when they came to the age of twenty-
four. He sent the elder daughter, Kathleen, to a good convent
where she learned French and music and afterwards paid her
fees at the Academy.[9] Every year in the month of July Mrs
Kearney found occasion to say to some friend: 40

—My good man is packing us off to Skerries[1] for a few weeks.

If it was not Skerries it was Howth[2] or Greystones.[3]

When the Irish Revival[4] began to be appreciable Mrs Kearney
determined to take advantage of her daughter's name[5] and
brought an Irish teacher[6] to the house. Kathleen and her sister   45
sent Irish picture postcards to their friends and these friends

27 thrifty] 14P; economical MS; economical, 10G   35 insured] STET MS   37 elder]
14P; eldest MS–10G

4. Gossip.
5. Ormond Quay is located on the north bank of the Liffey. In the days before mass production, custom bootmaking was a respected and profitable occupation.
6. Special devotional services, not required by the Church, whose attendance indicates
   exceptional piety.
7. An insurance or savings company that offered a variety of policies and annuities.
8. A financial asset or portion of money that a woman brings to a marriage, thought to make
   her a desirable match.
9. The Royal Academy of Music, located at 6 Merrion Square, noted for its excellent musical
   instruction.
1. A fashionable seaside resort eighteen miles north of Dublin.
2. A picturesque fishing village nine miles north of Dublin that was a popular holiday and
   outing destination.
3. Another pretty fishing village south of Dublin.
4. The effort by a number of cultural organizations to revive Irish language, literature, art,
   music, mythology, and folklore at the end of the nineteenth century. These elements of
   Irish culture had been suppressed or overshadowed by centuries of British rule in Ireland,
   and a deliberate program was required to restore them to prominence in Irish cultural
   life.
5. Kathleen ni Houlihan, the protagonist of a 1902 play by William Butler Yeats, was a
   venerated symbol of Ireland.
6. Presumably to give the girls lessons in the Gaelic language.

sent back other Irish picture postcards. On special Sundays when Mr Kearney went with his family to the pro-cathedral[7] a little crowd of people would assemble after mass at the corner of Cathedral Street.[8] They were all friends of the Kearneys, 50 musical friends or nationalist[9] friends: and when they had played every little counter of gossip they shook hands with one another all together, laughing at the crossing of so many hands, and said goodbye to one another in Irish. Soon the name of Miss Kathleen Kearney began to be heard often on people's 55 lips. People said that she was very clever at music and a very nice girl and, moreover, that she was a believer in the language movement.[1] Mrs Kearney was well content at this. Therefore she was not surprised when one day Mr Holohan came to her and proposed that her daughter should be the accompanist at a 60 series of four grand concerts which his Society was going to give in the Antient Concert Rooms.[2] She brought him into the drawingroom, made him sit down and brought out the de= canter[3] and the silver biscuit-barrel. She entered heart and soul into the details of the enterprise, advised and dissuaded; and 65 finally a contract was drawn up by which Kathleen was to receive eight guineas[4] for her services as accompanist at the four grand concerts.

As Mr Holohan was a novice in such delicate matters as the wording of bills and the disposing of items for a programme 70 Mrs Kearney helped him. She had tact. She knew what *artistes* should go into capitals and what *artistes* should go into small type. She knew that the first tenor would not like to come on after Mr Meade's comic turn. To keep the audience continually diverted she slipped the doubtful items in between the old 75 favourites. Mr Holohan called to see her every day to have her advice on some point. She was invariably friendly and advising: homely, in fact. She pushed the decanter towards him, saying:
—Now, help yourself, Mr Holohan!

And while he was helping himself she said: 80
—Don't be afraid! Don't be afraid of it!

Everything went on smoothly. Mrs Kearney bought some

---

74 comic turn.] 14P; funny recitation. MS–10G

7. St. Mary's on Marlborough Street was called the pro-cathedral because it was a provisional cathedral taking the place of Dublin's medieval cathedrals, St. Patrick's and Christ Church, both of which had been taken over by the Protestant Church of England.
8. The pro-cathedral was located on the corner of Marlborough and Cathedral Streets.
9. Parnellites or citizens in favor of Irish Home Rule.
1. The efforts of the Gaelic League, founded in 1893, to restore the native Irish language to usage and currency.
2. A concert and meeting hall on Brunswick (now Pearse) Street.
3. A cut-glass vessel from which wine or sherry is poured into glasses.
4. Eight pounds and eight shillings.

lovely blush-pink charmeuse[5] in Brown Thomas's[6] to let into the front of Kathleen's dress. It cost a pretty penny; but there are occasions when a little expense is justifiable. She took a dozen of two shilling tickets[7] for the final concert and sent them to those friends who could not be trusted to come otherwise. She forgot nothing and, thanks to her, everything that was to be done was done.

The concerts were to be on Wednesday, Thursday, Friday and Saturday. When Mrs Kearney arrived with her daughter at the Antient Concert Rooms on Wednesday night she did not like the look of things. A few young men, wearing bright blue badges in their coats, stood idle in the vestibule:[8] none of them wore evening dress.[9] She passed by with her daughter and a quick glance through the open door of the hall showed her the cause of the stewards'[1] idleness. At first she wondered had she mistaken the hour. No, it was twenty minutes to eight.

In the dressingroom behind the stage she was introduced to the secretary of the Society, Mr Fitzpatrick. She smiled and shook his hand. He was a little man with a white vacant face. She noticed that he wore his soft brown hat carelessly on the side of his head and that his accent was flat.[2] He held a programme in his hand and while he was talking to her he chewed one end of it into a moist pulp. He seemed to bear disappointments lightly. Mr Holohan came into the dressing= room every few minutes with reports from the boxoffice. The *artistes* talked among themselves nervously, glanced from time to time at the mirror and rolled and unrolled their music. When it was nearly half past eight the few people in the hall began to express their desire to be entertained. Mr Fitzpatrick came in, smiled vacantly at the room and said:

—Well now, ladies and gentlemen, I suppose we'd better open the ball.

Mrs Kearney rewarded his very flat final syllable with a quick stare of contempt and then said to her daughter encour= agingly:

—Are you ready, dear?

83 lovely--charmeuse] 14; beautiful white ribbon MS–14P   84 pretty] 14; good MS–14P

5. A fine, semilustrous crepe fabric in a satin weave.
6. A fashionable shop on Grafton Street, one of Dublin's main commercial streets, special- izing in fine silks, linens, laces, hats, and hatmaking materials.
7. Tickets for reasonably good seats.
8. Entrance hall.
9. Tuxedos or formal wear.
1. Persons appointed to supervise the admission, refreshments, seating, and the like at a concert.
2. A lower-class accent considered to indicate a lack of gentility or cultivation.

When she had an opportunity she called Mr Holohan aside
and asked him to tell her what it meant. Mr Holohan did not   120
know what it meant. He said that the committee had made a
mistake in arranging for four concerts: four was too many.
—And the *artistes!* said Mrs Kearney. Of course they are doing
their best but really they are no good.

Mr Holohan admitted that the *artistes* were no good but the   125
committee, he said, had decided to let the first three concerts go
as they pleased and reserve all the talent for Saturday night.
Mrs Kearney said nothing but, as the mediocre items followed
one another on the platform and the few people in the hall
grew fewer and fewer, she began to regret that she had put   130
herself to any expense for such a concert. There was something
she didn't like in the look of things and Mr Fitzpatrick's vacant
smile irritated her very much. However she said nothing and
waited to see how it would end. The concert expired shortly
before ten and everyone went home quickly.   135

The concert on Thursday night was better attended but Mrs
Kearney saw at once that the house was filled with paper.[3] The
audience behaved indecorously as if the concert were an infor=
mal dress rehearsal. Mr Fitzpatrick seemed to enjoy himself; he
was quite unconscious that Mrs Kearney was taking angry note   140
of his conduct. He stood at the edge of the screen, from time to
time jutting out his head and exchanging a laugh with two
friends in the corner of the balcony. In the course of the
evening Mrs Kearney learned that the Friday concert was to be
abandoned and that the committee was going to move heaven   145
and earth to secure a bumper house[4] on Saturday night. When
she heard this she sought out Mr Holohan. She buttonholed[5]
him as he was limping out quickly with a glass of lemonade for
a young lady and asked him was it true. Yes, it was true.
—But, of course, that doesn't alter the contract, she said. The   150
contract was for four concerts. ...

Mr Holohan seemed to be in a hurry: he advised her to
speak to Mr Fitzpatrick. Mrs Kearney was now beginning to be
alarmed. She called Mr Fitzpatrick away from his screen and
told him that her daughter had signed for four concerts and   155
that, of course, according to the terms of the contract she
should receive the sum originally stipulated for whether the
Society gave the four concerts or not. Mr Fitzpatrick, who did

146 bumper] 14P; full MS—10G

3. Attended by patrons with free tickets.
4. A crowded hall.
5. Figuratively, to detain someone in a conversation against the person's will, as though
holding him or her fast by the edge of the jacket.

not catch the point at issue very quickly, seemed unable to
resolve the difficulty and said that he would bring the matter   160
before the committee. Mrs Kearney's anger began to flutter in
her cheek and she had all she could do to keep from asking:
—And who is the *cometty*,[6] pray?

But she knew that it would not be ladylike to do that: so she
was silent.   165

Little boys were sent out into the principal streets of Dublin
early on Friday morning with bundles of handbills. Special
puffs[7] appeared in all the evening papers reminding the music=
loving public of the treat which was in store for it on the
following evening. Mrs Kearney was somewhat reassured but   170
she thought well to tell her husband part of her suspicions. He
listened carefully and said that perhaps it would be better if he
went with her on Saturday night. She agreed. She respected her
husband in the same way as she respected the General Post
Office,[8] as something large, secure and fixed; and though she   175
knew the small number of his talents she appreciated his
abstract value as a male. She was glad that he had suggested
coming with her. She thought her plans over.

The night of the grand concert came. Mrs Kearney, with her
husband and daughter, arrived at the Antient Concert Rooms   180
three quarters of an hour before the time at which the concert
was to begin. By ill luck it was a rainy evening. Mrs Kearney
placed her daughter's clothes and music in charge of her
husband and went all over the building looking for Mr Holo=
han or Mr Fitzpatrick. She could find neither. She asked the   185
stewards was any member of the committee in the hall and,
after a great deal of trouble, a steward brought out a little
woman named Miss Beirne to whom Mrs Kearney explained
that she wanted to see one of the secretaries. Miss Beirne
expected them any minute and asked could she do anything.   190
Mrs Kearney looked searchingly at the oldish face which was
screwed into an expression of trustfulness and enthusiasm and
answered:
—No, thank you!

The little woman hoped they would have a good house. She   195
looked out at the rain until the melancholy of the wet street
effaced all the trustfulness and enthusiasm from her twisted
features. Then she gave a little sigh and said:

---

168 puffs] 14P; paragraphs MS–10G   187 out] ⌐'out'⌐ MS

6. A mimicry of Mr. Fitzpatrick's flat accent.
7. Flattering advertisements.
8. An imposing building with a classical façade on O'Connell Street in central Dublin.

—Ah, well! We did our best, the dear knows.[9]

Mrs Kearney had to go back to the dressingroom.   200

The *artistes* were arriving. The bass and the second tenor
had already come. The bass, Mr Duggan, was a slender young
man with a scattered black moustache. He was the son of a hall
porter in an office in the city and, as a boy, he had sung
prolonged bass notes in the resounding hall. From this humble   205
state he had raised himself until he had become a first-rate
artiste. He had appeared in grand opera. One night, when an
operatic *artiste* had fallen ill, he had undertaken the part of the
king in the opera of *Maritana*[1] at the Queen's Theatre.[2] He sang
his music with great feeling and volume and was warmly   210
welcomed by the gallery; but, unfortunately, he marred the
good impression by wiping his nose in his gloved hand once or
twice out of thoughtlessness. He was unassuming and spoke
little. He said *yous*[3] so softly that it passed unnoticed and he
never drank anything stronger than milk for his voice' sake. Mr   215
Bell, the second tenor, was a fairhaired little man who com=
peted every year for prizes at the Feis Ceoil.[4] On his fourth trial
he had been awarded a bronze medal. He was extremely
nervous and extremely jealous of other tenors and he covered
his nervous jealousy with an ebullient friendliness. It was his   220
humour to have people know what an ordeal a concert was to
him. Therefore when he saw Mr Duggan he went over to him
and asked:

—Are you in it too?

—Yes, said Mr Duggan.   225

Mr Bell laughed at his fellow sufferer, held out his hand and
said:

—Shake!

Mrs Kearney passed by these two young men and went to
the edge of the screen to view the house. The seats were being   230
filled up rapidly and a pleasant noise circulated in the auditor=
ium. She came back and spoke to her husband privately. Their
conversation was evidently about Kathleen for they both
glanced at her often as she stood chatting to one of her nation=
alist friends, Miss Healy, the contralto. An unknown solitary   235
woman with a pale face walked through the room. The women

203–204 hall porter] 14P; ⁷¹⟨porter⟩ hall-porter¹ᴿ MS; hall-porter 1OG

9. An Irish displacement for "God knows."
1. A nineteenth-century light opera by William Vincent Wallace (1812–1865), music, and
   Edward Fitzball (1792–1873), libretto, in which one of the principal roles is that of the
   Spanish king.
2. One of the three major theaters in Dublin at the time of the story.
3. A small grammatical irregularity that could betray his humble background.
4. An annual Irish musical festival dedicated specifically to Irish music.

followed with keen eyes the faded blue dress which was
stretched upon a meagre body. Someone said that she was
Madam Glynn, the soprano.

—I wonder where did they dig her up, said Kathleen to Miss   240
Healy. I'm sure I never heard of her.

Miss Healy had to smile. Mr Holohan limped into the dress=
ingroom at that moment and the two young ladies asked him
who was the unknown woman. Mr Holohan said that she was
Madam Glynn from London. Madam Glynn took her stand in   245
a corner of the room, holding a roll of music stiffly before her
and from time to time changing the direction of her startled
gaze. The shadow took her faded dress into shelter but fell
revengefully into the little cup behind her collarbone. The noise
of the hall became more audible. The first tenor and the   250
baritone arrived together. They were both well dressed, stout
and complacent and they brought a breath of opulence among
the company.

Mrs Kearney brought her daughter over to them and talked
to them amiably. She wanted to be on good terms with them   255
but, while she strove to be polite, her eyes followed Mr Holo=
han in his limping and devious courses. As soon as she could
she excused herself and went out after him.

—Mr Holohan, I want to speak to you for a moment, she said.

They went down to a discreet part of the corridor. Mrs   260
Kearney asked him when was her daughter going to be paid.
Mr Holohan said that Mr Fitzpatrick had charge of that. Mrs
Kearney said that she didn't know anything about Mr Fitzpat=
rick. Her daughter had signed a contract for eight guineas and
she would have to be paid. Mr Holohan said that it wasn't his   265
business.

—Why isn't it your business? asked Mrs Kearney. Didn't you
yourself bring her the contract? Anyway, if it's not your
business it's my business and I mean to see to it.

—You'd better speak to Mr Fitzpatrick, said Mr Holohan   270
distantly.

—I don't know anything about Mr Fitzpatrick, repeated Mrs
Kearney. I have my contract and I intend to see that it is carried
out.

When she came back to the dressingroom her cheeks were   275
slightly suffused. The room was lively. Two men in outdoor
dress had taken possession of the fireplace and were chatting
familiarly with Miss Healy and the baritone. They were the

238 she] 14P; it MS–10G   254 Mrs] NEW PAGE, NO INDENT MS   270 You'd] 14P; You
MS–10G

Freeman man[5] and Mr O'Madden Burke. The *Freeman* man
had come in to say that he could not wait for the concert as he   280
had to report the lecture which an American priest was giving
in the Mansion House.[6] He said they were to leave the report
for him at the *Freeman* office and he would see that it went in.
He was a greyhaired man with a plausible voice and careful
manners. He held an extinguished cigar in his hand and the   285
aroma of cigar smoke floated near him. He had not intended to
stay a moment because concerts and *artistes* bored him con=
siderably but he remained leaning against the mantelpiece.
Miss Healy stood in front of him, talking and laughing. He was
old enough to suspect one reason for her politeness[7] but young   290
enough in spirit to turn the moment to account. The warmth,
fragrance and colour of her body appealed to his senses. He
was pleasantly conscious that the bosom which he saw rise and
fall slowly beneath him rose and fell at that moment for him,
that the laughter and fragrance and wilful glances were his   295
tribute. When he could stay no longer he took leave of her
regretfully.

—O'Madden Burke will write the notice, he explained to Mr
Holohan, and I'll see it in.

—Thank you very much, Mr Hendrick, said Mr Holohan.   300
You'll see it in, I know. Now, won't you have a little something
before you go?

—I don't mind, said Mr Hendrick.

The two men went along some tortuous passages and up a
dark staircase and came to a secluded room where one of the   305
stewards was uncorking bottles for a few gentlemen. One of
these gentlemen was Mr O'Madden Burke who had found out
the room by instinct. He was a suave elderly man who bal=
anced his imposing body, when at rest, upon a large silk um=
brella. His magniloquent western name[8] was the moral umbrella   310
upon which he balanced the fine problem of his finances. He
was widely respected.

While Mr Holohan was entertaining the *Freeman* man Mrs
Kearney was speaking so animatedly to her husband that he
had to ask her to lower her voice. The conversation of the   315
others in the dressingroom had become strained. Mr Bell, the
first item, stood ready with his music but the accompanist
made no sign. Evidently something was wrong. Mr Kearney

5. The reviewer for the *Freeman's Journal and National Press,* a daily morning newspaper in
   Dublin.
6. A large house on Dawson Street originally built for the Lord Mayor of Dublin, but later
   also used for events and exhibitions.
7. Presumably to befriend him into giving her performance a good review.
8. A grand-sounding Irish name, as though from the west of Ireland.

looked straight before him, stroking his beard, while Mrs
Kearney spoke into Kathleen's ear with subdued emphasis.   320
From the hall came sounds of encouragement, clapping and
stamping of feet. The first tenor and the baritone and Miss
Healy stood together, waiting tranquilly, but Mr Bell's nerves
were greatly agitated because he was afraid the audience would
think that he had come late.   325

Mr Holohan and Mr O'Madden Burke came into the room.
In a moment Mr Holohan perceived the hush. He went over to
Mrs Kearney and spoke with her earnestly. While they were
speaking the noise in the hall grew louder. Mr Holohan became
very red and excited. He spoke volubly but Mrs Kearney said   330
curtly at intervals:

—She won't go on. She must get her eight guineas.

Mr Holohan pointed desperately towards the hall where the
audience was clapping and stamping. He appealed to Mr
Kearney and to Kathleen. But Mr Kearney continued to stroke   335
his beard and Kathleen looked down, moving the point of her
new shoe: it was not her fault. Mrs Kearney repeated:

—She won't go on without her money.

After a swift struggle of tongues Mr Holohan hobbled out in
haste. The room was silent. When the strain of the silence had   340
become somewhat painful Miss Healy said to the baritone:

—Have you seen Mrs Pat Campbell this week?[9]

The baritone had not seen her but he had been told that she
was very fine. The conversation went no further. The first
tenor bent his head and began to count the links of the gold   345
chain which was extended across his waist, smiling and hum=
ming random notes to observe the effect on the frontal sinus.
From time to time everyone glanced at Mrs Kearney.

The noise in the auditorium had risen to a clamour when Mr
Fitzpatrick burst into the room, followed by Mr Holohan who   350
was panting. The clapping and stamping in the hall were
punctuated by whistling. Mr Fitzpatrick held a few bank notes
in his hand. He counted out four into Mrs Kearney's hand and
said she would get the other half at the interval. Mrs Kearney
said: 355

—This is four shillings short.[1]

---

337 shoe:] 14; boot: MS–14P

9. A well-known English actress who was good friends with the Irish playwright George
Bernard Shaw.
1. Kathleen's fee had been negotiated as eight guineas, or eight pounds plus eight shillings,
by her contract. Mr. Fitzgerald appears to give Mrs. Kearney four pounds, and promises
her "the other half" later. But Mrs. Kearney, recognizing that one half of eight pounds,
eight shillings, is four pounds, four shillings, correctly points out that she has not received
half of the eight guineas, and that the "half" she has just been paid is four shillings short.

But Kathleen gathered in her skirt and said *Now, Mr Bell,* to the first item who was shaking like an aspen.[2] The singer and the accompanist went out together. The noise in the hall died away. There was a pause of a few seconds: and then the piano was heard.

The first part of the concert was very successful except for Madam Glynn's item. The poor lady sang *Killarney*[3] in a bodiless gasping voice, with all the oldfashioned mannerisms of intonation and pronunciation which she believed lent elegance to her singing. She looked as if she had been resurrected from an old stage wardrobe and the cheaper parts of the hall made fun of her high wailing notes. The first tenor and the contralto, however, brought down the house. Kathleen played a selection of Irish airs which was generously applauded. The first part closed with a stirring patriotic recitation delivered by a young lady who arranged amateur theatricals. It was deservedly ap= plauded; and when it was ended the men went out for the interval,[4] content.

All this time the dressingroom was a hive of excitement. In one corner were Mr Holohan, Mr Fitzpatrick, Miss Beirne, two of the stewards, the baritone, the bass and Mr O'Madden Burke. Mr O'Madden Burke said it was the most scandalous exhibition he had ever witnessed. Miss Kathleen Kearney's musical career was ended in Dublin after that, he said. The baritone was asked what did he think of Mrs Kearney's conduct. He did not like to say anything. He had been paid his money[5] and wished to be at peace with men. However, he said that Mrs Kearney might have taken the *artistes* into consider= ation. The stewards and the secretaries debated hotly as to what should be done when the interval came.

—I agree with Miss Beirne, said Mr O'Madden Burke. Pay her nothing.

In another corner of the room were Mrs Kearney and her husband, Mr Bell, Miss Healy and the young lady who had recited the patriotic piece. Mrs Kearney said that the committee had treated her scandalously. She had spared neither trouble nor expense and this was how she was repaid. They thought

360

365

370

375

380

385

390

363 lady] 14P; creature MS–10G   365 lent] 14P; gave MS–10G   372 deservedly] 14P; enthusiastically MS–10G   391 recited] 67; ⌐¹to¹⌐ recite MS; to recite 10G–14   393 They] STET NO PARAGRAPH MS

2. A poplar tree whose leaves quiver and flutter with the slightest breeze.
3. A ballad from the opera *Innisfallen* by Michael William Balfe.
4. The intermission.
5. At the time of the story, professional performers or "headliners" such as the baritone were generally paid in advance, while the amateur performers were paid after the performance, proceeds permitting.

they had only a girl to deal with and that, therefore, they could
ride roughshod over her. But she would show them their   395
mistake. They wouldn't have dared to have treated her like that
if she had been a man. But she would see that her daughter got
her rights: she wouldn't be fooled. If they didn't pay her to the
last farthing she would make Dublin ring. Of course she was
sorry for the sake of the *artistes*. But what else could she do?   400
She appealed to the second tenor who said he thought she had
not been well treated. Then she appealed to Miss Healy. Miss
Healy wanted to join the other group but she did not like to do
so because she was a great friend of Kathleen's and the
Kearneys had often invited her to their house.   405

As soon as the first part was ended Mr Fitzpatrick and Mr
Holohan went over to Mrs Kearney and told her that the other
four guineas would be paid after the committee meeting on the
following Tuesday and that, in case her daughter did not play
for the second part, the committee would consider the contract   410
broken and would pay nothing.

—I haven't seen any committee, said Mrs Kearney angrily. My
daughter has her contract. She will get four pounds eight into
her hand or a foot she won't put on that platform.

—I'm surprised at you, Mrs Kearney, said Mr Holohan. I   415
never thought you would treat us this way.

—And what way did you treat me? asked Mrs Kearney.

Her face was inundated with an angry colour and she looked
as if she would attack someone with her hands.

—I'm asking for my rights, she said.   420

—You might have some sense of decency, said Mr Holohan.

—Might I indeed? ... And when I ask when my daughter is
going to be paid I can't get a civil answer.

She tossed her head and assumed a haughty voice:

—You must speak to the secretary. It's not my business. I'm a   425
great fellow fol-the-diddle-I-do.[6]

—I thought you were a lady, said Mr Holohan, walking away
from her abruptly.

After that Mrs Kearney's conduct was condemned on all
hands: everyone approved of what the committee had done.   430
She stood at the door, haggard with rage, arguing with her
husband and daughter, gesticulating with them. She waited
until it was time for the second part to begin in the hope that
the secretaries would approach her. But Miss Healy had kindly
consented to play one or two accompaniments. Mrs Kearney   435

414 put] 14; put up MS–14P   434 kindly] ⌐ikindly⌐ MS

6. An expression mocking undeserved self-importance.

had to stand aside to allow the baritone and his accompanist to
pass up to the platform. She stood still for an instant like an
angry stone image and, when the first notes of the song struck
her ear, she caught up her daughter's cloak and said to her
husband:

—Get a cab!   440

He went out at once. Mrs Kearney wrapped the cloak round
her daughter and followed him. As she passed through the
doorway she stopped and glared into Mr Holohan's face:

—I'm not done with you yet, she said.   445

—But I'm done with you, said Mr Holohan.

Kathleen followed her mother meekly. Mr Holohan began
to pace up and down the room in order to cool himself for he
felt his skin on fire:

—That's a nice lady! he said. O, she's a nice lady!   450

—You did the proper thing, Holohan, said Mr O'Madden
Burke, poised upon his umbrella in approval.

Grace

Two gentlemen who were in the lavatory at the time tried to
lift him up: but he was quite helpless. He lay curled up at the
foot of the stairs down which he had fallen. They succeeded in
turning him over. His hat had rolled a few yards away and his
clothes were smeared with the filth and ooze of the floor on   5
which he had lain, face downwards. His eyes were closed and
he breathed with a grunting noise. A thin stream of blood
trickled from the corner of his mouth.

These two gentlemen and one of the curates[1] carried him up
the stairs and laid him down again on the floor of the bar. In   10
two minutes he was surrounded by a ring of men. The manager
of the bar asked everyone who he was and who was with him.
No-one knew who he was but one of the curates said he had
served the gentleman with a small rum.

—Was he by himself? asked the manager.   15

—No, sir. There was two gentlemen with him.

438 and,] 14P; and then, MS; and then 10G

Copy-text: Manuscript Yale 2.9 (MS); Collated texts: 1914 proofs (14P) and 1914 first edition
(14) [IDENTITY IN BOTH IS REPORTED AS '14']; 1967 Viking edition in the 1969 Viking Critical
Library printing (67).

8 trickled] 14P; issued MS

1. Assistant bartenders or waiters.

—And where are they?

No-one knew; a voice said:

—Give him air. He's fainted.

The ring of onlookers distended and closed again elastically.   20
A dark medal of blood had formed itself near the man's head
on the tessellated[2] floor. The manager, alarmed by the grey
pallor of the man's face, sent for a policeman.

His collar was unfastened and his necktie undone. He
opened his eyes for an instant, sighed and closed them again.   25
One of the gentlemen who had carried him upstairs held a
dinged silk hat in his hand. The manager asked repeatedly did
no-one know who the injured man was or where had his
friends gone. The door of the bar opened and an immense
constable entered. A crowd which had followed him down the   30
laneway collected outside the door, struggling to look in
through the glass panels.

The manager at once began to narrate what he knew. The
constable, a young man with thick immobile features, listened.
He moved his head slowly to right and left and from the   35
manager to the person on the floor as if he feared to be the
victim of some delusion. Then he drew off his glove, produced
a small book from his waist, licked the lead of his pencil and
made ready to indite.[3] He asked in a suspicious provincial
accent:[4]   40

—Who is the man? What's his name and address?

A young man in a cycling suit[5] cleared his way through the
ring of bystanders. He knelt down promptly beside the injured
man and called for water. The constable knelt down also to
help. The young man washed the blood from the injured man's   45
mouth and then called for some brandy. The constable re=
peated the order in an authoritative voice until a curate came
running with the glass. The brandy was forced down[6] the man's
throat. In a few seconds he opened his eyes and looked about
him. He looked at the circle of faces and then, understanding,   50
strove to rise to his feet.

—You're all right now? asked the young man in the cycling
suit.

—'Sha, 's nothing, said the injured man, trying to stand up.

He was helped to his feet. The manager said something   55

28 man] ᒐ¹manᴵᴦ MS

2. Mosaic, or composed of small blocks of variously colored tile.
3. To set down in writing.
4. Betrays that the constable may be an unsophisticated man from the country rather than
   the city.
5. Outfit or sports uniform for bicycle riding.
6. The strong, potent taste of brandy was thought capable of reviving the unconscious.

about a hospital and some of the bystanders gave advice. The battered silk hat was placed on the man's head. The constable asked:

—Where do you live?

The man, without answering, began to twirl the ends of his 60 moustache. He made light of his accident. It was nothing, he said: only a little accident. He spoke very thickly.

—Where do you live? repeated the constable.

The man said they were to get a cab for him. While the point was being debated a tall agile gentleman of fair complexion, 65 wearing a long yellow ulster,[7] came from the far end of the bar. Seeing the spectacle he called out:

—Hallo, Tom, old man! What's the trouble?

—'Sha, 's nothing, said the man.

The newcomer surveyed the deplorable figure before him 70 and then turned to the constable, saying:

—It's all right, constable. I'll see him home.

The constable touched his helmet and answered:

—All right, Mr Power!

—Come now, Tom, said Mr Power, taking his friend by the 75 arm. No bones broken. What? Can you walk?

The young man in the cycling suit took the man by the other arm and the crowd divided.

—How did you get yourself into this mess? asked Mr Power.

—The gentleman fell down the stairs, said the young man. 80

—I' 'ery 'uch o'liged to you, sir, said the injured man.

—Not at all.

—'an't we have a little ....?

—Not now. Not now.

The three men left the bar and the crowd sifted through the 85 doors into the laneway. The manager brought the constable to the stairs to inspect the scene of the accident. They agreed that the gentleman must have missed his footing. The customers returned to the counter and a curate set about removing the traces of blood from the floor. 90

When they came out into Grafton Street[8] Mr Power whistled for an outsider.[9] The injured man said again as well as he could:

---

66 ulster,] 14P; overcoat MS   68 man!] man⟨?⟩! MS   81 I'] 14P; I'm MS   83 'an't]
e:14; Can't MS; 'ant' 14

7. A long, loose, rough overcoat, often belted.
8. A busy commercial street that runs between Trinity College and Stephen's Green on the south side of the Liffey in central Dublin.
9. A light two-wheeled carriage.

—I' 'ery 'uch o'liged to you, sir. I hope we'll 'eet again. 'y na'e
is Kernan.

The shock and the incipient pain had partly sobered him.   95
—Don't mention it, said the young man.

They shook hands. Mr Kernan was hoisted on to the car
and, while Mr Power was giving directions to the carman, he
expressed his gratitude to the young man and regretted that
they could not have a little drink together.   100
—Another time, said the young man.

The car drove off towards Westmoreland Street. As it passed
the Ballast office[1] the clock showed half past nine. A keen east
wind hit them blowing from the mouth of the river. Mr Kernan
was huddled together with cold. His friend asked him to tell   105
how the accident had happened.

—I 'an't, 'an, he answered. 'y 'ongue is hurt.
—Show.

The other leaned over the well of the car and peered into Mr
Kernan's mouth but he could not see. He struck a match and,   110
sheltering it in the shell of his hands, peered again into the
mouth which Mr Kernan opened obediently. The swaying
movement of the car brought the match to and from the open
mouth. The lower teeth and gums were covered with clotted
blood and a minute piece of the tongue seemed to have been   115
bitten off. The match was blown out.

—That's ugly, said Mr Power.
—'Sha, 's nothing, said Mr Kernan, closing his mouth and
pulling the collar of his filthy frock coat across his neck.

Mr Kernan was a commercial traveller of the old school   120
which believed in the dignity of its calling. He had never been
seen in the city without a silk hat of some decency and a pair of
gaiters.[2] By grace of these two articles of clothing, he said, a
man could always pass muster.[3] He carried on the tradition of
his Napoleon,[4] the great Blackwhite,[5] whose memory he evoked 125
at times by legend and mimicry. Modern business methods had
spared him only so far as to allow him a little office in Crowe

---

93 I'] 14P; I'm MS   93 'eet] 14P; meet MS   93 'y na'e] 14P; My name MS   107 'an,]
14P; man, MS   107 'y] 14P; My MS   113 open] STET MS   119 frock coat] STET MS
127 spared--only] 14P; only spared him MS

1. Located on Westmoreland Street on the south bank of the Liffey, the Ballast Office housed
   the Dublin Port and Docks Board charged with supervising the harbor.
2. A cloth or leather covering for the ankles.
3. Earn approval in a formal inspection, as of troops in the army.
4. Figuratively, his general or role model, like the French military genius Napoléon Bonaparte
   (1769–1821).
5. Unknown, but presumably a salesman with legendary gifts of persuasion.

Street[6] on the window blind of which was written the name of his firm[7] with the address—London, E. C.[8] On the mantelpiece of this little office a little leaden battalion of canisters was drawn up and on the table before the window stood four or five china bowls which were usually half full of a black liquid. From these bowls Mr Kernan tasted tea. He took a mouthful, drew it up, saturated his palate with it and then spat it forth into the grate. Then he paused to judge.

Mr Power, a much younger man, was employed in the Royal Irish Constabulary Office in Dublin Castle.[9] The arc of his social rise intersected the arc of his friend's decline but Mr Kernan's decline was mitigated by the fact that certain of those friends who had known him at his highest point of success still esteemed him as a character.[1] Mr Power was one of these friends. His inexplicable debts were a byword in his circle; he was a debonair young man.

The car halted before a small house on the Glasnevin road[2] and Mr Kernan was helped into the house. His wife put him to bed while Mr Power sat downstairs in the kitchen asking the children where they went to school and what book they were in. The children, two girls and a boy, conscious of their father's helplessness and of their mother's absence, began some horse=play with him. He was surprised at their manners and at their accents[3] and his brow grew thoughtful. After a while Mrs Kernan entered the kitchen, exclaiming:

—Such a sight! O, he'll do for himself[4] one day and that's the holy alls[5] of it. He's been drinking since Friday.

Mr Power was careful to explain to her that he was not responsible, that he had come on the scene by the merest accident. Mrs Kernan, remembering Mr Power's good offices during domestic quarrels as well as many small but opportune loans, said:

—O, you needn't tell me that, Mr Power. I know you're a

130

135

140

145

150

155

160

---

153 that's] 14P; that'll be MS   154 holy alls] 14P; end MS

6. Next to Dame Street in south-central Dublin.
7. Tom Kernan reappears as a character in Joyce's novel *Ulysses*, where his firm is revealed as the London tea importer of Pulbrook, Robertson and Company. See 17.2075 in the Gabler edition of *Ulysses*.
8. The postal code for the commercial district, or East Central area, of London.
9. Office housing the administration of an armed police force under the direction of the British lord lieutenant of Ireland, thought to exceed its law enforcement role by also suppressing Irish dissidents and revolutionaries.
1. A pleasantly odd or slightly eccentric person.
2. One of the roads leading to the village of Glasnevin, near the north edge of Dublin.
3. Their accents, if vulgar, would betray deficient education and cultivation—surprising, given their father's pretensions to gentility.
4. Do himself in, ruin himself.
5. An Irish expression for "that's the holy truth."

friend of his, not like some of those others he does be with.
They're all right so long as he has money in his pocket to keep
him out from his wife and family. Nice friends! Who was he
with tonight, I'd like to know?

Mr Power shook his head but said nothing.   165

—I'm so sorry, she continued, that I've nothing in the house to
offer you. But if you wait a minute I'll send round to Fogarty's[6]
at the corner.

Mr Power stood up.

—We were waiting for him to come home with the money. He   170
never seems to think he has a home at all.

—O now, Mrs Kernan, said Mr Power, we'll make him turn
over a new leaf. I'll talk to Martin.[7] He's the man. We'll come
here one of these nights and talk it over.

She saw him to the door. The carman was stamping up and   175
down the footpath and swinging his arms to warm himself.

—It's very kind of you to bring him home, she said.

—Not at all, said Mr Power.

He got up on the car. As it drove off he raised his hat to her
gaily.   180

—We'll make a new man of him, he said. Goodnight, Mrs
Kernan.

◆   ◆   ◆

Mrs Kernan's puzzled eyes watched the car till it was out of
sight. Then she withdrew them, went into the house and
emptied her husband's pockets.   185

She was an active practical woman of middle age. Not long
before she had celebrated her silver wedding[8] and renewed her
intimacy with her husband by valsing[9] with him to Mr Power's
accompaniment. In her days of courtship Mr Kernan had
seemed to her a not ungallant figure: and she still hurried to the   190
chapel door whenever a wedding was reported and, seeing the
bridal pair, recalled with vivid pleasure how she had passed out
of the Star of the Sea Church in Sandymount,[1] leaning on the
arm of a jovial wellfed man who was dressed smartly in a frock
coat and lavender trousers and carried a silk hat gracefully   195
balanced upon his other arm. After three weeks she had found

167 minute] minute<s> MS   174 one--nights] 14P; tomorrow night MS

6. A tea, wine, and spirit merchant who is later described as having a small shop on Glasnevin
   Road.
7. Martin Cunningham, who appears later in the story.
8. Celebrating twenty-five years of marriage.
9. Waltzing.
1. "Star of the Sea" is one of the titles given the Virgin Mary, mother of Christ. Sandymount
   is a village on the south edge of Dublin, by the sea.

a wife's life irksome and later on, when she was beginning to find it unbearable, she had become a mother. The part of mother presented to her no insuperable difficulties and for twenty-five years she had kept house shrewdly for her husband. 200 Her two eldest sons were launched. One was in a draper's shop in Glasgow and the other was clerk to a tea merchant in Belfast. They were good sons, wrote regularly and sometimes sent home money. The other children were still at school.

Mr Kernan sent a letter to his office next day and remained 205 in bed. She made beef tea[2] for him and scolded him roundly. She accepted his frequent intemperance as part of the climate, healed him dutifully whenever he was sick and always tried to make him eat a breakfast. There were worse husbands. He had never been violent since the boys had grown up and she knew 210 that he would walk to the end of Thomas Street[3] and back again to book even a small order.

Two nights after his friends came to see him. She brought them up to his bedroom, the air of which was impregnated with a personal odour, and gave them chairs at the fire. Mr 215 Kernan's tongue, the occasional stinging pain of which had made him somewhat irritable during the day, became more polite. He sat propped up in the bed by pillows and the little colour in his puffy cheeks made them resemble warm cinders. He apologised to his guests for the disorder of the room but at 220 the same time looked at them a little proudly, with a veteran's pride.

He was quite unconscious that he was the victim of a plot which his friends Mr Cunningham, Mr M'Coy and Mr Power had disclosed to Mrs Kernan in the parlour. The idea had been 225 Mr Power's but its development was entrusted to Mr Cunning= ham. Mr Kernan came of Protestant stock and, though he had been converted to the Catholic faith at the time of his marriage, he had not been in the pale[4] of the Church for twenty years. He was fond, moreover, of giving side thrusts at Catholicism. 230

Mr Cunningham was the very man for such a case. He was an elder colleague of Mr Power's. His own domestic life was not very happy. People had great sympathy with him for it was known that he had married an unpresentable woman who

---

202 Glasgow] 14P; Galway MS   204 school.] ⟨□⟩ school. MS   212 book] 14; get MS— 14P   213 Two--after] 14P; In the evening MS   232 Power's.] STET MS

2. Beef broth or clear soup, so called because it has the color of tea.
3. About a mile from Kernan's office, but near enough to the Guiness Brewery to possibly let him duck in for the free glass of beer offered visitors.
4. The pale, also called the English Pale, was an area of Ireland controlled by the British in the fourteenth and fifteenth centuries. By implication, areas within the pale were safeguarded while those "beyond the pale" were wild and without regulation.

was an incurable drunkard. He had set up house for her six 235
times and each time she had pawned[5] the furniture on him.

Everyone had respect for poor Martin Cunningham. He was
a thoroughly sensible man, influential and intelligent. His blade
of human knowledge, natural astuteness particularised by long
association with cases in the police courts, had been tempered 240
by brief immersions in the waters of general philosophy. He
was well informed. His friends bowed to his opinions and
considered that his face was like Shakespeare's.

When the plot had been disclosed to her Mrs Kernan had
said: 245

—I leave it all in your hands, Mr Cunningham.

After a quarter of a century of married life she had very few
illusions left. Religion for her was a habit and she suspected
that a man of her husband's age would not change greatly
before death. She was tempted to see a curious appropriateness 250
in his accident and, but that she did not wish to seem bloody-
minded, she would have told the gentleman that Mr Kernan's
tongue would not suffer by being shortened.[6] However Mr Cun=
ningham was a capable man and religion was religion. The
scheme might do good and, at least, it could do no harm. Her 255
beliefs were not extravagant. She believed steadily in the Sacred
Heart[7] as the most generally useful of all Catholic devotions and
approved of the sacraments.[8] Her faith was bounded by her
kitchen but, if she was put to it, she could believe also in the
banshee[9] and in the Holy Ghost.   260

The gentlemen began to talk of the accident. Mr Cunning=
ham said that he had once known a similar case. A man of
seventy had bitten off a piece of his tongue during an epileptic
fit and the tongue had filled in again so that no-one could see a
trace of the bite.   265

—Well, I'm not seventy, said the invalid.

—God forbid, said Mr Cunningham.

---

235 an--drunkard.] 14P; a confirmed inebriate. MS   236 furniture on him.] 14P; furniture. MS   252 gentleman] STET MS   254 man] ⁷ˡman¹ʳ MS   258–259 Her--also]
14P; Nor was she an utter materialist for she also believed (to a certain extent) MS

5. Deposited in return for a loan from a pawnbroker, to be forfeited if the loan could not be
   repaid.
6. Presumably because Mr. Kernan has a sharp tongue.
7. Devotion to the Sacred Heart of Jesus was promulgated by the French seventeenth-century
   nun Blessed (later Saint) Margaret Mary Alacoque. Devotees received communion on the
   first Friday of every month and displayed in their homes the twelve promises that were
   made, through the saint, to those who practiced this devotional rite. The promises included
   comforting assurances such as "I will establish peace in their homes."
8. The rites of the Catholic Church, such as baptism, penance, and the Eucharist, that are
   considered either necessary or conducive to salvation.
9. A supernatural being believed by the Irish and the Scots to wail before a house in which
   someone was going to die.

—It doesn't pain you now? asked Mr M'Coy.

Mr M'Coy had been at one time a tenor of some reputation. His wife, who had been a soprano, still taught young children   270 to play the piano at low terms. His line of life had not been the shortest distance between two points and for short periods he had been driven to live by his wits. He had been a clerk in the Midland Railway, a canvasser for advertisements[1] for the *Irish Times* and for the *Freeman's Journal*, a town traveller for a   275 coal firm on commission, a private enquiry agent,[2] a clerk in the office of the Sub-Sheriff[3] and he had recently become secretary to the City Coroner.[4] His new office made him professionally interested in Mr Kernan's case.

—Pain? Not much, answered Mr Kernan. But it's so sickening: 280 I feel as if I wanted to retch off.[5]

—That's the boose, said Mr Cunningham firmly.

—No, said Mr Kernan. I think I caught a cold on the car. There's something keeps coming into my throat, phlegm or   285

—Mucus, said Mr M'Coy.

—It keeps coming like from down in my throat; sickening thing.

—Yes, yes, said Mr M'Coy, that's the thorax.[6]

He looked at Mr Cunningham and Mr Power at the same   290 time with an air of challenge. Mr Cunningham nodded his head rapidly and Mr Power said:

—Ah, well, all's well that ends well.[7]

—I'm very much obliged to you, old man, said the invalid.

Mr Power waved his hand.   295

—Those other two fellows I was with .....

—Who were you with? asked Mr Cunningham.

—A chap—I don't know his name. Damn it now, what's his name? Little chap with sandy hair ...

—And who else?   300

—Harford.

—Hm, said Mr Cunningham.

---

297 with?] with⟨,⟩? MS

1. Someone who persuades businesses to buy advertising space in the Dublin daily newspapers, the *Irish Times* and the *Freeman's Journal*.
2. A private detective.
3. The office that handled evictions for failure to pay rent and repossession of property for failure to pay.
4. The city official who conducts an inquest to determine the circumstances of a death by unnatural causes.
5. Vomit.
6. The area between the neck and the abdomen, that is, the chest.
7. The title of a Shakespeare play, now a saying for a dangerous or difficult affair that has had a good outcome.

When Mr Cunningham made that remark people were
silent. It was known that the speaker had secret sources of
information.[8] In this case the monosyllable had a moral inten= 305
tion. Mr Harford sometimes formed one of a little detachment
which left the city shortly after noon on Sunday with the
purpose of arriving as soon as possible at some publichouse on
the outskirts of the city where its members duly qualified them=
selves as *bonafide* travellers.[9] But his fellow travellers had never 310
consented to overlook his origin. He had begun life as an
obscure financier by lending small sums of money to workmen
at usurious interest.[1] Later on he had become the partner of a
very fat short gentleman, Mr Goldberg,[2] in the Liffey Loan
Bank. Though he had never embraced more than the jewish 315
ethical code[3] his fellow Catholics, whenever they had smarted in
person or by proxy under his exactions,[4] spoke of him bitterly
as an Irish Jew and an illiterate and saw divine disapproval of
usury made manifest through the person of his idiot son. At
other times they remembered his good points. 320
—I wonder where did he go to, said Mr Kernan.

He wished the details of the incident to remain vague. He
wished his friends to think there had been some mistake, that
Mr Harford and he had missed each other. His friends, who
knew quite well Mr Harford's manners in drinking, were silent. 325
Mr Power said again:
—All's well that ends well.

Mr Kernan changed the subject at once.
—That was a decent young chap, that medical fellow, he said.
Only for him 330
—O, only for him, said Mr Power, it might have been a case of
seven days without the option of a fine.[5]
—Yes, yes, said Mr Kernan, trying to remember. I remember

332 without] 14P; with MS

8. Martin Cunningham is revealed in *Ulysses* to have connections with the Crown Solicitor's
   office, which is like a district attorney's office, in Dublin Castle. This would give him
   access to police and court files.
9. Certified salesmen and others who traveled on business were exempt from the laws restrict-
   ing the consumption of liquor in restaurants and taverns at certain times.
1. Exorbitant or excessive interest.
2. The name suggests that Mr. Goldberg was Jewish.
3. Presumably Mr. Harford, although Catholic, practiced an ethic of exacting what one is
   owed no matter how painful or unreasonable, an ethic associated with the Jewish character
   Shylock in Shakespeare's *The Merchant of Venice*. Shylock demanded the pound of flesh
   stipulated in his contract with the merchant Antonio, even though the bargain was inhu-
   man and unreasonable—a characterization thought to have contributed to anti-Semitic
   caricatures of Jewish bankers and financiers as greedy and inhumane.
4. By implication, Mr. Harford employs enforcers or "muscle" to intimidate or harm debtors
   who refuse, or are unable, to repay his loans with their exorbitant interest.
5. Presumably incarceration for public drunkenness.

now there was a policeman. Decent young fellow, he seemed. How did it happen at all? 335

—It happened that you were peloothered,[6] Tom, said Mr Cun= ningham gravely.

—True bill,[7] said Mr Kernan equally gravely.

—I suppose you squared[8] the constable, Jack, said Mr M'Coy.

Mr Power did not relish the use of his Christian name. He 340 was not straitlaced but he could not forget that Mr M'Coy had recently made a crusade in search of valises and portmanteaus[9] to enable Mrs M'Coy to fulfil imaginary engagements[1] in the country. More than he resented the fact that he had been victimised he resented such low playing of the game.[2] He 345 answered the question, therefore, as if Mr Kernan had asked it.

The narrative made Mr Kernan indignant. He was keenly conscious of his citizenship, wished to live with his city on terms mutually honourable and resented any affront put upon him by those whom he called country bumpkins. 350

—Is this what we pay rates for?[3] he asked. To feed and clothe these ignorant bostoons[4] ... and they're nothing else.

Mr Cunningham laughed. He was a Castle official only during office hours.

—How could they be anything else, Tom? he said. 355

He assumed a thick provincial accent and said in a tone of command:

—65, catch your cabbage!

Everyone laughed. Mr M'Coy who wanted to enter the conversation by any door pretended that he had never heard 360 the story. Mr Cunningham said:

—It is supposed—they say, you know—to take place in the depot[5] where they get these thundering big country fellows, omadhauns,[6] you know, to drill. The sergeant makes them stand in a row against the wall and hold up their plates. 365

He illustrated the story by grotesque gestures.

—At dinner, you know. Then he has a bloody[7] big bowl of

---

6. Drunken.
7. The words of endorsement by a jury judging that there is sufficient evidence to bring a matter to trial.
8. Bribed or otherwise settled with the constable to avoid an arrest.
9. Suitcases or leather carrying cases or bags.
1. Since we have been told that Mrs. M'Coy had been a soprano, these are presumably fictitious singing engagements at provincial concerts.
2. Trickery. M'Coy seems to have pretended to borrow the suitcases for his wife's travels to concerts, and then pawned them for money.
3. Property taxes that support municipal services such as the police.
4. Boors, dolts, or coarse fools.
5. The station where police or military recruits are housed, trained, and drilled.
6. Irish for fools, idiots, or simpletons.
7. An intensifier meaning "very," that is, "a very big bowl."

cabbage before him on the table and a bloody big spoon like a
shovel. He takes up a wad of cabbage on the spoon and pegs it[8]
across the room and the poor devils have to try and catch it on   370
their plates: 65, *catch your cabbage.*

Everyone laughed again: but Mr Kernan was somewhat
indignant still. He talked of writing a letter to the papers.

—These yahoos[9] coming up here, he said, think they can boss
the people. I needn't tell you, Martin, what kind of men they   375
are.

Mr Cunningham gave a qualified assent.

—It's like everything else in this world, he said. You get some
bad ones and you get some good ones.

—O yes, you get some good ones, I admit, said Mr Kernan,   380
satisfied.

—It's better to have nothing to say to them, said Mr M'Coy.
That's my opinion.

Mrs Kernan entered the room and, placing a tray on the
table, said: 385

—Help yourselves, gentlemen.

Mr Power stood up to officiate, offering her his chair. She
declined it, saying that she was ironing downstairs and, after
having exchanged a nod with Mr Cunningham behind Mr
Power's back, prepared to leave the room. Her husband called   390
out to her:

—And have you nothing for me, duckie?[1]

—O, you! The back of my hand to you! said Mrs Kernan
tartly.

Her husband called after her: 395

—Nothing for poor little hubby!

He assumed such a comical face and voice that the distribu=
tion of the bottles of stout took place amid general merriment.

The gentlemen drank from their glasses, set the glasses again
on the table and paused. Then Mr Cunningham turned to=   400
wards Mr Power and said casually:

—On Thursday night, you said, Jack?

—Thursday, yes, said Mr Power.

—Righto! said Mr Cunningham promptly.

—We can meet in M'Auley's,[2] said Mr M'Coy. That'll be the   405
most convenient place.

369 of] 14; o' MS–14P   370 devils] 14; divils MS–14P   392 duckie?] 14P; lovey? MS
399 gentlemen] gen⟨e⟩tlemen MS

8. Aims it, as though with a cricket bat.
9. A name invented by Jonathan Swift for an imaginary race of brutes in the form of men.
1. A term of endearment.
2. A pub on Dorset Street, near the Jesuit Church of Saint Francis Xavier, where the planned
   retreat will be held.

—But we mustn't be late, said Mr Power earnestly, because it is sure to be crammed to the doors.

—We can meet at half seven, said Mr M'Coy.

—Righto! said Mr Cunningham. Half seven at M'Auley's be it!   410

There was a short silence. Mr Kernan waited to see whether he would be taken into his friends' confidence. Then he asked:

—What's in the wind?

—O, it's nothing, said Mr Cunningham. It's only a little matter that we're arranging about for Thursday.   415

—The opera, is it? said Mr Kernan.

—No, no, said Mr Cunningham in an evasive tone, it's just a little .... spiritual matter.

—O, said Mr Kernan.

There was silence again. Then Mr Power said point blank: 420

—To tell you the truth, Tom, we're going to make a retreat.[3]

—Yes, that's it, said Mr Cunningham, Jack and I and M'Coy here—we're all going to wash the pot.[4]

He uttered the metaphor with a certain homely energy and, encouraged by his own voice, proceeded: 425

—You see, we may as well all admit we're a nice collection of scoundrels, one and all. I say, one and all, he added with gruff charity and turning to Mr Power. Own up now!

—I own up, said Mr Power.

—And I own up, said Mr M'Coy.   430

—So we're going to wash the pot together, said Mr Cunning= ham.

A thought seemed to strike him. He turned suddenly to the invalid and said:

—Do you know what, Tom, has just occurred to me? You   435 might join in and we'd have a fourhanded reel.[5]

—Good idea, said Mr Power. The four of us together.

Mr Kernan was silent. The proposal conveyed very little meaning to his mind but, understanding that some spiri= tual agencies were about to concern themselves on his behalf,   440 he thought he owed it to his dignity to show a stiff neck.[6] He took no part in the conversation for a long while but listened,

---

404, 410 Righto!] 14P; Right-o⟨,⟩! MS   409 half seven,] half s⟨ix⟩even, MS   416 it?] it⟨,⟩? MS   422 M'Coy] 14P; Mr Mᶜ Coy MS

3. A period of withdrawal from worldly concerns, sponsored by the Church, to concentrate on improving one's spiritual condition.
4. Come clean, undergo a cleansing.
5. A reel is a lively dance in which two couples holding hands form figures and in some cases exchange partners in the course of their movements.
6. Obstinacy.

with an air of calm enmity, while his friends discussed the
Jesuits.[7]
—I haven't such a bad opinion of the Jesuits, he said, inter=   445
vening at length. They're an educated order. I believe they
mean well too.
—They're the grandest order in the Church, Tom, said Mr
Cunningham with enthusiasm. The General of the Jesuits
stands next to the Pope.[8]   450
—There's no mistake about it, said Mr M'Coy, if you want a
thing well done and no flies about it you go to a Jesuit. They're
the boyos have influence. I'll tell you a case in point ....
—The Jesuits are a fine body of men, said Mr Power.
—It's a curious thing, said Mr Cunningham, about the Jesuit   455
Order. Every other order of the Church had to be reformed at
some time or other but the Jesuit Order was never once
reformed.[9] It never fell away.
—Is that so? asked Mr M'Coy.
—That's a fact, said Mr Cunningham. That's history.   460
—Look at their church too, said Mr Power. Look at the
congregation they have.
—The Jesuits cater for the upper classes, said Mr M'Coy.
—Of course, said Mr Power.
—Yes, said Mr Kernan. That's why I have a feeling for them.   465
It's some of those secular priests, ignorant, bumptious ......
—They're all good men, said Mr Cunningham, each in his own
way. The Irish priesthood is honoured all the world over.
—O yes, said Mr Power.
—Not like some of the other priesthoods on the continent,[1] said   470
Mr M'Coy, unworthy of the name.
—Perhaps you're right, said Mr Kernan relenting.
—Of course I'm right, said Mr Cunningham. I haven't been in
the world all this time and seen most sides of it without being a
judge of character.   475
    The gentlemen drank again, one following another's ex=
ample. Mr Kernan seemed to be weighing something in his

---

456 Order.] ⟨o⟩ Order. MS

7. A religious order or society of priests in the Roman Catholic Church, associated particularly with rigorous intellectuality and a commitment to high academic education. Formally
   called the Society of Jesus, the Jesuits were founded as a missionary order in 1534 by St.
   Ignatius Loyola.
8. The head or general of the Jesuit order is responsible directly to the pope.
9. Was never tainted with corruption or waywardness in its mission. The Jesuits were, in
   fact, suppressed by the pope in 1773 in response to increasing hostility to the order and
   not fully reestablished until more than forty years later.
1. Vices based on national stereotypes were sometimes imputed to the clergy of different
   nations.

mind. He was impressed. He had a high opinion of Mr Cun=
ningham as a judge of character and as a reader of faces. He
asked for particulars. 480

—O, it's just a retreat, you know, said Mr Cunningham. Fa=
ther Purdon[2] is giving it. It's for business men, you know.

—He won't be too hard on us, Tom, said Mr Power persua=
sively.

—Father Purdon? Father Purdon? said the invalid. 485

—O, you must know him, Tom, said Mr Cunningham stoutly.
Fine jolly fellow! He's a man of the world like ourselves.

—Ah ... yes. I think I know him. Rather red face; tall.

—That's the man.

—And tell me, Martin .... Is he a good preacher? 490

—Mmmno ..... It's not exactly a sermon, you know. It's just a
kind of a friendly talk, you know, in a commonsense way.

Mr Kernan deliberated. Mr M'Coy said:

—Father Tom Burke,[3] that was the boy!

—O, Father Tom Burke, said Mr Cunningham, that was a 495
born orator. Did you ever hear him, Tom?

—Did I ever hear him! said the invalid, nettled. Rather! I heard
him ......

—And yet they say he wasn't much of a theologian, said Mr
Cunningham. 500

—Is that so? said Mr M'Coy.

—O, of course, nothing wrong, you know. Only sometimes,
they say, he didn't preach what was quite orthodox.

—Ah! .. he was a splendid man, said Mr M'Coy.

—I heard him once, Mr Kernan continued. I forget the subject 505
of his discourse now. Crofton and I were in the back of the ....
pit,[4] you know ... the ....

—The body, said Mr Cunningham.

—Yes, in the back near the door. I forget now what ...... O yes,
it was on the Pope, the late Pope. I remember it well. Upon my 510
word it was magnificent, the style of the oratory. And his voice!
God! hadn't he a voice! *The Prisoner of the Vatican*,[5] he called
him. I remember Crofton saying to me when we came out .....

---

2. Purdon Street was a main street of Dublin's red-light district, a site of brothels and houses
   of prostitution. The priest's name may therefore have evoked unfortunate associations.
3. Thomas Nicholas Burke (1830 –1883), a popular Irish preacher of the Dominican order
   whose lectures in Ireland, England, and the United States included topics such as "English
   Misrule in Ireland" and other political subjects. He was popularly known as "Father Tom."
4. The ground floor of a theater. Kernan's imperfect grasp of Catholic terminology leads him
   to substitute the theatrical term for the nave, or body, of a church.
5. A term referring to Pope Pius IX (pope from 1846 to 1878) and Pope Leo XIII (pope from
   1878 to 1903), whose dominion was reduced to the boundaries of Vatican City after Victor
   Emmanuel II defeated the papal army and stripped the pope of all secular and civil power.

—But he's an Orangeman,[6] Crofton, isn't he? said Mr Power.

—'Course he is, said Mr Kernan, and a damned decent Or= 515
angeman too. We went into Butler's[7] in Moore Street—faith, I
was genuinely moved, tell you the God's truth—and I remem=
ber well his very words. *Kernan,* he said, *we worship at
different altars,* he said, *but our belief is the same.* Struck me as
very well put.   520

—There's a good deal in that, said Mr Power. There used
always be crowds of Protestants in the chapel when Father
Tom was preaching.

—There's not much difference between us, said Mr M'Coy.
We both believe in   525

He hesitated for a moment.

— ... in the Redeemer. Only they don't believe in the Pope and
in the mother of God.

—But, of course, said Mr Cunningham quietly and effectively,
our religion is *the* religion,[8] the old, original faith.   530

—Not a doubt of it, said Mr Kernan warmly.

Mrs Kernan came to the door of the bedroom and an=
nounced:

—Here's a visitor for you!

—Who is it?   535

—Mr Fogarty.

—O, come in! come in!

A pale oval face came forward into the light. The arch of its
fair trailing moustache was repeated in the fair eyebrows
looped above pleasantly astonished eyes. Mr Fogarty was a 540
modest grocer. He had failed in business in a licensed house[9] in
the city because his financial condition had constrained him to
tie himself to second class distillers and brewers. He had
opened a small shop on the Glasnevin road where, he flattered
himself, his manners would ingratiate him with the housewives 545
of the district. He bore himself with a certain grace, compli=
mented little children and spoke with a neat enunciation. He
was not without culture.

Mr Fogarty brought a gift with him, a half pint of special
whisky. He enquired politely for Mr Kernan, placed his gift on 550

519 *belief*] 14; religion MS; *religion* 14P   535 —Who is it?] ⌐¹—Who is it?—⌐¹ MS

6. A pejorative name for an Irish pro-British Protestant—after William of Orange, the Protestant British monarch who as William III led the defeat of the Irish at the 1690 Battle
of the Boyne. Crofton has earlier appeared in "Ivy Day in the Committee Room" and
recurs as a character in *Ulysses*.
7. A pub.
8. Roman Catholic orthodoxy maintained that it was the only true Christian faith.
9. A tavern or pub.

the table and sat down with the company on equal terms. Mr
Kernan appreciated the gift all the more since he was aware
that there was a small account for groceries unsettled between
him and Mr Fogarty. He said:

—I wouldn't doubt you, old man. Open that, Jack, will you?   555

Mr Power again officiated. Glasses were rinsed and five
small measures of whisky were poured out. This new influence
enlivened the conversation. Mr Fogarty, sitting on a small area
of the chair, was specially interested.

—Pope Leo XIII, said Mr Cunningham, was one of the lights   560
of the age. His great idea, you know, was the union of the
Latin and Greek Churches.[1] That was the aim of his life.

—I often heard he was one of the most intellectual men in
Europe,[2] said Mr Power. I mean apart from his being Pope.

—So he was, said Mr Cunningham, if not *the* most so. His   565
motto, you know, as Pope was *Lux upon Lux*—*Light upon
Light*.[3]

—No, no, said Mr Fogarty eagerly, I think you're wrong there.
It was *Lux in Tenebris*, I think—*Light in Darkness*.

—O yes, said Mr M'Coy, *Tenebrae*.   570

—Allow me, said Mr Cunningham positively, it was *Lux upon
Lux*. And Pius IX, his predecessor's motto was *Crux upon
Crux*,[4] that is, *Cross upon Cross*, to show the difference be=
tween their two pontificates.

The inference was allowed. Mr Cunningham continued: 575

—Pope Leo, you know, was a great scholar and a poet.

—He had a strong face, said Mr Kernan.

—Yes, said Mr Cunningham. He wrote Latin poetry.

—Is that so? said Mr Fogarty.

Mr M'Coy tasted his whisky contentedly and shook his head   580
with a double intention, saying:

—That's no joke, I can tell you.

—We didn't learn that, Tom, said Mr Power, following Mr

---

577 a strong] 14P; an intellectual MS   582 can] 14P; ABSENT MS

1. Pope Leo XIII (1878–1903) hoped not only for the union of the Roman Catholic and
   Greek Orthodox Churches, but also for reunification with the Anglican Church. He was
   therefore generally not supportive of Irish anti-British sentiment.
2. Pope Leo XIII supported the Vatican Observatory, opened the Vatican Archives to
   qualified scholars, and was reputed to have been of a philosophical and poetic turn of
   mind.
3. *The Prophecy of the Popes,* ostensibly by Malachi of Armagh (1094–1148) but later
   believed to be a sixteenth-century forgery, claimed revelation as to the guiding principles,
   or mottoes, of future popes. Pope Leo XIII's motto was prophesied to be *Lumen in Coelo,*
   Latin for "Light in the Sky."
4. According to *The Prophecy of the Popes,* it would actually have been *Crux de Cruce,* Latin
   for "Cross from a Cross."

M'Coy's example, when we went to the penny-a-week school.[5]

—There was many a good man went to the penny-a-week 585
school with a sod of turf under his oxter,[6] said Mr Kernan
sententiously. The old system was the best: plain honest edu=
cation. None of your modern trumpery[7] ......

—Quite right, said Mr Power.

—No superfluities, said Mr Fogarty. 590

He enunciated the word and then drank gravely.

—I remember reading, said Mr Cunningham, that one of Pope
Leo's poems was on the invention of the photograph[8]—in Latin,
of course.

—On the photograph! exclaimed Mr Kernan. 595

—Yes, said Mr Cunningham.

He also drank from his glass.

—Well, you know, said Mr M'Coy, isn't the photograph
wonderful when you come to think of it?

—O, of course, said Mr Power, great minds can see things 600

—As the poet says: *Great minds are very near to madness*,[9] said
Mr Fogarty.

Mr Kernan seemed to be troubled in mind. He made an
effort to recall the Protestant theology on some thorny points
and in the end addressed Mr Cunningham. 605

—Tell me, Martin, he said. Weren't some of the popes—of
course, not our present man or his predecessor, but some of the
old popes—not exactly .... you know .... up to the knocker?[1]

There was a silence. Mr Cunningham said:

—O, of course, there were some bad lots[2] .... But the aston= 610
ishing thing is this. Not one of them, not the biggest drunkard,
not the most ... out-and-out ruffian, not one of them ever
preached *ex cathedra*[3] a word of false doctrine. Now isn't that
an astonishing thing?

586 oxter,] 14P; arm, MS   610 lots ....] 14P; ones .... MS

5. Early nineteenth-century schools conducted by private teachers who were paid directly by
   fees brought to them by their students, before National Schools were established in the
   mid-nineteenth century. Penny-a-week schools were an outgrowth of the secret "hedge
   schools," conducted outdoors during the early eighteenth century, when the education of
   Catholic children was effectively banned by the British.
6. Decomposed bog matter used as fuel for heating, carried to school by students under the
   armpit, or "oxter," as it was called in Scottish dialect.
7. Fraud.
8. Leo XIII did indeed write a poem in 1867 titled "The Art of Photography," celebrated as
   an "art with newest marvels fraught," whose images are a "miracle of human thought."
9. The line occurs in John Dryden's *Absalom and Achitophel* (1682) and actually reads "Great
   wits are sure to madness near allied."
1. Not first-rate, or not up to the highest standards.
2. Some medieval or Renaissance popes—for example, the Borgia pope, Alexander VI—were
   thought to have exhibited greed, nepotism, depravity, and ruthlessness during their reigns.
3. Latin for "from the chair"—that is, when speaking in his official capacity as the pontiff of
   the Church.

—That is, said Mr Kernan.   615
—Yes, because when the Pope speaks *ex cathedra*, Mr Fogarty explained, he is infallible.
—Yes, said Mr Cunningham.
—O, I know about the infallibility of the Pope. I remember I was younger then ... Or was it that?   620
  Mr Fogarty interrupted. He took up the bottle and helped the others to a little more. Mr M'Coy, seeing that there was not enough to go round, pleaded that he had not finished his first measure. The others accepted under protest. The light music of whisky falling into glasses made an agreeable interlude.   625
—What's that you were saying, Tom? asked Mr M'Coy.
—Papal infallibility,[4] said Mr Cunningham, that was the great= est scene in the whole history of the Church.
—How was that, Martin? asked Mr Power.
  Mr Cunningham held up two thick fingers.   630
—In the sacred college, you know, of cardinals and arch= bishops and bishops there were two men who held out against it while the others were all for it. The whole conclave[5] except these two was unanimous. No! They wouldn't have it!
—Ha! said Mr M'Coy.   635
—And they were a German cardinal[6] by the name of Dolling ... or Dowling ... or ...
—Dowling was no German and that's a sure five,[7] said Mr Power laughing.
—Well, this great German cardinal, whatever his name was,   640
was one and the other was John MacHale.[8]
—What? cried Mr Kernan. Is it John of Tuam?
—Are you sure of that now? asked Mr Fogarty dubiously. I thought it was some Italian or American ... [9]
—John of Tuam, repeated Mr Cunningham, was the man.   645

620 younger] ˥¹⟨very young⟩ youngerˡ˥ MS   630 thick] 14P; ABSENT MS

4. The doctrine of the pope's infallibility was formally decreed by the fourth session of the Vatican Council on July 18, 1870. It holds that the pope is immune from error and can not make a mistake when he formally pronounces on theological, ecclesiastical, or moral matters.
5. The assembly of cardinals and bishops who elect the pope or decide other ecclesiastical matters.
6. A notable German theologian (but not a member of the Vatican Council) named Johann Döllinger was excommunicated (expelled) from the Church in 1871 because he actively opposed the doctrine of papal infallibility.
7. A billiard term for a "sure thing," or a shot certain to succeed.
8. The Irish archbishop of Tuam (1835–1876) opposed papal infallibility, but was not pres- ent, and did not vote, on the occasion when it was decreed. However, once it was doctrine, he accepted and supported it.
9. Two dissenting ballots were cast against the doctrine of papal infallibility: one by Bishop Riccio of Italy and the other by Bishop Fitzgerald of Arkansas. Both accepted the doctrine after the vote.

He drank and the other gentlemen followed his lead. Then
he resumed:

—There they were at it, all the cardinals and bishops and
archbishops from all the ends of the earth and these two
fighting dog and devil[1] until at last the Pope himself stood up   650
and declared infallibility a dogma of the Church *ex cathedra*.
On the very moment John MacHale, who had been arguing
and arguing against it, stood up and shouted out with the voice
of a lion: *Credo!*

—*I believe!* said Mr Fogarty.   655

—*Credo!* said Mr Cunningham. That showed the faith he had.
He submitted the moment the Pope spoke.

—And what about Dowling? asked Mr M'Coy.

—The German cardinal wouldn't submit. He left the Church.

Mr Cunningham's words had built up the vast image of the   660
Church in the minds of his hearers. His deep raucous voice had
thrilled them as it uttered the word of belief and submission.
When Mrs Kernan came into the room drying her hands she
came into a solemn company. She did not disturb the silence
but leaned over the rail at the foot of the bed.   665

—I once saw John MacHale, said Mr Kernan, and I'll never
forget it as long as I live.

He turned towards his wife to be confirmed.

—I often told you that?

Mrs Kernan nodded.   670

—It was at the unveiling of Sir John Gray's statue.[2] Edmund
Dwyer Gray[3] was speaking, blathering away, and here was this
old fellow, crabbed-looking old chap, looking at him from un=
der his bushy eyebrows.

Mr Kernan knitted his brows and, lowering his head like an   675
angry bull, glared at his wife.

—God! he exclaimed, reassuming his natural face, I never saw
such an eye in a man's head. It was as much as to say: *I have
you properly taped, my lad.*[4] He had an eye like a hawk.

—None of the Grays was any good, said Mr Power.   680

---

649 the ends] 14P; parts MS   650 and] 14P; an' MS   650 devil] 14; divil MS–14P
661 raucous] rauc⟨u⟩ous MS   671 Sir--Gray's] (Smith O'Brien's) Sir John Gray's MS
671 Edmund] (Young) Edmund MS   679 my] 14P; me MS

1. A term of inclusion; absolutely everybody.
2. Sir John Gray (1816–1875) was a Protestant Irish patriot in whose honor a statue was
   erected on O'Connell Street, one of the major thoroughfares of Dublin. Archbishop
   MacHale did attend the unveiling, even though Gray was a Protestant.
3. Sir John Gray's son, a newspaper editor and political activist, did not actually speak until
   later on the day of the unveiling.
4. Figured out or sized up.

There was a pause again. Mr Power turned to Mrs Kernan and said with abrupt joviality:

—Well, Mrs Kernan, we're going to make your man here a good holy pious and God-fearing Roman Catholic.

He swept his arm round the company inclusively.   685

—We're all going to make a retreat together and confess our sins—and God knows we want it badly.

—I don't mind, said Mr Kernan, smiling a little nervously.

Mrs Kernan thought it would be wiser to conceal her satis= faction. So she said: 690

—I pity the poor priest that has to listen to your tale.

Mr Kernan's expression changed.

—If he doesn't like it, he said bluntly, he can .... do the other thing. I'll just tell him my little tale of woe. I'm not such a bad fellow   695

Mr Cunningham intervened promptly.

—We'll all renounce the devil, he said, together, not forgetting his works and pomps.[5]

—Get behind me, Satan![6] said Mr Fogarty, laughing and look= ing at the others.   700

Mr Power said nothing. He felt completely outgeneralled. But a pleased expression flickered across his face.

—All we have to do, said Mr Cunningham, is to stand up with lighted candles in our hands and renew our baptismal vows.[7]

—O, don't forget the candle, Tom, said Mr M'Coy, whatever   705 you do.

—What? said Mr Kernan. Must I have a candle?

—O yes, said Mr Cunningham.

—No, damn it all, said Mr Kernan sensibly, I draw the line there. I'll do the job right enough. I'll do the retreat business   710 and confession and ... all that business. But ... no candles! No, damn it all, I bar the candles!

He shook his head with farcical gravity.

—Listen to that! said his wife.

—I bar the candles, said Mr Kernan, conscious of having   715

---

5. In the Catholic baptismal rite, the godparents are asked to reply to three questions on the child's behalf: "Dost thou renounce Satan? And all his works? And all his pomps?" That is, do you renounce the sins and principles of worldliness that are contrary to the teachings of the Gospels.

6. Christ chides Peter for worldliness with these words, when Peter tries to assure him that he can elude his destiny of death and resurrection. "Get behind me, Satan, thou art a scandal to me; for thou dost not mind the things of God, but those of men" (Matthew 16: 23).

7. The godparents recite a series of vows as proxy for a baptized infant. At this retreat, the men will repeat their baptismal vows.

created an effect on his audience and continuing to shake his
head to and fro. I bar the magic lantern business.[8]

Everyone laughed heartily.

—There's a nice Catholic for you! said his wife.

—No candles! repeated Mr Kernan obdurately. That's off!   720

◆ ◆ ◆

The transept[9] of the Jesuit Church in Gardiner Street[1] was
almost full; and still at every moment gentlemen entered from
the sidedoor and, directed by the lay brother,[2] walked on tiptoe
along the aisles until they found seating accommodation. The
gentlemen were all well dressed and orderly. The light of the   725
lamps of the church fell upon an assembly of black clothes and
white collars, relieved here and there by tweeds, on dark
mottled pillars of green marble and on lugubrious canvasses.
The gentlemen sat in the benches, having hitched their trousers
slightly above their knees and laid their hats in security. They 730
sat well back and gazed formally at the distant speck of red
light which was suspended before the high altar.

In one of the benches near the pulpit sat Mr Cunningham
and Mr Kernan. In the bench behind sat Mr M'Coy alone: and
in the bench behind him sat Mr Power and Mr Fogarty. Mr   735
M'Coy had tried unsuccessfully to find a place in the bench
with the others and, when the party had settled down in the
form of a quincunx,[3] he had tried unsuccessfully to make comic
remarks. As these had not been well received he had desisted.
Even he was sensible of the decorous atmosphere and even he   740
began to respond to the religious stimulus. In a whisper Mr
Cunningham drew Mr Kernan's attention to Mr Harford, the
moneylender, who sat some distance off, and to Mr Fanning,[4]
the registration agent and mayormaker of the city, who was
sitting immediately under the pulpit beside one of the newly   745
elected councillors of the ward. To the right sat old Michael
Grimes, the owner of three pawnbroker's shops, and Dan
Hogan's nephew who was up for the job in the Town Clerk's

736 the] 14P; a MS

8. A theatrical effect created by projecting a lighted image on the wall of a darkened space
   or room. Reported visions and apparitions of a spiritual character were sometimes skep-
   tically interpreted as hoaxes produced by such devices.
9. The transverse part of a church shaped like a cross.
1. The Church of St. Francis Xavier on Upper Gardiner Street.
2. An unordained man entrusted with manual work and other secular tasks in monasteries
   or in the service of religious orders.
3. Five points disposed so as to have four occupy the corners of a square with the fifth in
   the middle.
4. Mr. Fanning was a character mentioned, but not appearing, in the story "Ivy Day in the
   Committee Room."

office. Farther in front sat Mr Hendrick,[5] the chief reporter of the *Freeman's Journal,* and poor O'Carroll, an old friend of Mr   750
Kernan's, who had been at one time a considerable commercial figure. Gradually, as he recognised familiar faces, Mr Kernan began to feel more at home. His hat, which had been rehabili= tated by his wife, rested upon his knees. Once or twice he pulled down his cuffs with one hand while he held the brim of   755
his hat lightly but firmly with the other hand.

A powerful-looking figure, the upper part of which was draped with a white surplice,[6] was observed to be struggling up into the pulpit. Simultaneously the congregation unsettled, produced handkerchiefs and knelt upon them[7] with care. Mr   760
Kernan followed the general example. The priest's figure now stood upright in the pulpit, two-thirds of its bulk crowned by a massive red face appearing above the balustrade.

Father Purdon knelt down, turned towards the red speck of light[8] and, covering his face with his hands, prayed. After an   765
interval he uncovered his face and rose. The congregation rose also and settled again on its benches. Mr Kernan restored his hat to its original position on his knee and presented an attentive face to the preacher. The preacher turned back each wide sleeve of his surplice with an elaborate large gesture and   770
slowly surveyed the array of faces. Then he said:

—*For the children of this world are wiser in their generation than the children of light. Wherefore make unto yourselves friends out of the Mammon of iniquity so that when you die they may receive you into everlasting dwellings.*[9]   775

Father Purdon developed the text with resonant assurance. It was one of the most difficult texts in all the scriptures, he said, to interpret properly. It was a text which might seem to the casual observer at variance with the lofty morality elsewhere preached by Jesus Christ. But, he told his hearers, the text had   780
seemed to him specially adapted for the guidance of those whose lot it was to lead the life of the world and who yet wished to lead that life not in the manner of worldlings. It was a text for business men and professional men. Jesus Christ,

---

5. Mr. Hendrick appears in the story "A Mother."
6. A loose, long white linen smock or outergarment worn by priests over their cassocks or everyday long black dress when officiating at certain church services.
7. Catholic ritual requires the congregation to kneel during portions of the Mass and other church services.
8. A red lantern light that indicates the presence of the Blessed Sacrament, that is, the wafer that has been consecrated and transformed into the body of Christ.
9. The end of the parable of the unjust steward found in Luke 16:1–9. Christ tells of the unjust steward, who—before he was dismissed by his master for squandering—calls together his master's creditors and reduces their debts to ingratiate himself with them. Instead of being angry, the master is impressed by his steward's shrewdness and commends him because "he had acted prudently."

with His divine understanding of every cranny of our human   785
nature, understood that all men were not called to the religious
life, that by far the vast majority were forced to live in the
world and, to a certain extent, for the world: and in this
sentence He designed to give them a word of counsel, setting
before them as exemplars in the religious life those very   790
worshippers of Mammon[1] who were of all men the least
solicitous in matters religious.

He told his hearers that he was there that evening for no
terrifying, no extravagant purpose, but as a man of the world
speaking to his fellow men. He came to speak to business men   795
and he would speak to them in a businesslike way. If he might
use the metaphor, he said, he was their spiritual accountant
and he wished each and every one of his hearers to open his
books, the books of his spiritual life, and see if they tallied
accurately with conscience.   800

Jesus Christ was not a hard taskmaster. He understood our
little failings, understood the weakness of our poor fallen
nature, understood the temptations of this life. We might have
had, we all had from time to time, our temptations: we might
have, we all had, our failings. But one thing only, he said, he   805
would ask of his hearers. And that was: to be straight and
manly with God. If their accounts tallied in every point to say:
—Well, I have verified my accounts. I find all well.

But if, as might happen, there were some discrepancies, to
admit the truth, to be frank and say like a man: 810
—Well, I have looked into my accounts. I find this wrong and
this wrong. But, with God's grace, I will rectify this and this. I
will set right my accounts.

The Dead

Lily, the caretaker's daughter, was literally run off her feet.
Hardly had she brought one gentleman into the little pantry
behind the office on the groundfloor and helped him off with

---

802 the] 14P; ABSENT MS (MS TORN)

1. A pagan god considered the personification of wealth as an evil influence.

Copy-texts: Manuscript Yale 2.10 (MS) [FOR LINES 1–406, 1182–1207, 1545–1615], 1910
galley proofs (10G) [FOR LINES 406–1181, 1207–1462] and 1910 late proofs (10) [FOR LINES
1463–1544]; Collated texts: typescript-and-amanuensis copy Cornell 31 (TS, AM1, AM2);
1910 galley proofs [INCOMPLETE] (10G); 1910 late proofs [INCOMPLETE] (10); 1914 proofs
(14P) and 1914 first edition (14) [REPORTED SEPARATELY THROUGHOUT]; 1967 Viking edition
in the 1969 Viking Critical Library printing (67).

his overcoat when the wheezy halldoor bell clanged again and
she had to scamper along the bare hallway to let in another   5
guest. It was well for her[1] she had not to attend to the ladies
also. But Miss Kate and Miss Julia had thought of that and had
converted the bathroom upstairs into a ladies' dressingroom.
Miss Kate and Miss Julia were there, gossiping and laughing
and fussing, walking after each other to the head of the stairs,   10
peering down over the banisters and calling down to Lily to ask
her who had come.

It was always a great affair, the Misses Morkan's annual
dance. Everybody who knew them came to it, members of the
family, old friends of the family, the members of Julia's choir,   15
any of Kate's pupils that were grown up enough and even some
of Mary Jane's pupils too. Never once had it fallen flat. For
years and years it had gone off in splendid style as long as
anyone could remember, ever since Kate and Julia, after the
death of their brother Pat, had left the house in Stony Batter[2]   20
and taken Mary Jane, their only niece, to live with them in the
dark gaunt house on Usher's Island,[3] the upper part of which
they had rented from Mr Fullam, the corn factor[4] on the
groundfloor. That was a good thirty years ago if it was a day.
Mary Jane, who was then a little girl in short clothes, was now   25
the main prop of the household for she had the organ in
Haddington Road.[5] She had been through the academy[6] and gave
a pupils' concert every year in the upper room of the Antient
Concert Rooms.[7] Many of her pupils belonged to better class
families on the Kingstown and Dalkey line.[8] Old as they were,   30
her aunts also did their share. Julia, though she was quite grey,
was still the leading soprano in Adam and Eve's[9] and Kate,
being too feeble to go about much, gave music lessons to
beginners on the old square piano in the back room. Lily, the

---

4 when] STET MS   17 Never--it] 14P; It had never once MS–10G; Never once it had 10
20 Stony] STET MS, 10   23 Fullam,] STET MS, 10

1. Irish version of "it was a good thing."
2. A lower-class neighborhood of little shops and flats in northwest Dublin.
3. A section of the Quay or south bank of the river Liffey, west of O'Connell Street in central
   Dublin.
4. One who buys and sells corn.
5. She worked as organist for St. Mary's Church, which is located on Haddington Road on
   the southwestern edge of Dublin.
6. The Royal Academy of Music on Merrion Square, the most important center for musical
   education in Ireland.
7. A hall or auditorium on Brunswick Street that could be rented for private concerts and
   other events.
8. Kingstown and Dalkey were two fashionable harbor and resort towns a few miles south of
   Dublin, on Dublin Bay.
9. The nickname of St. Francis of Assisi Church on Merchant's Quay, just east of Usher's
   Island, where the Morkans live.

caretaker's daughter, did housemaid work for them. Though   35
their life was modest they believed in eating well, the best of
everything: diamond bone sirloins,[1] three shilling tea[2] and the
best bottled stout. But Lily seldom made a mistake in the
orders so that she got on well with her three mistresses. They
were fussy, that was all. But the only thing they would not   40
stand was back answers.

Of course they had good reason to be fussy on such a night.
And then it was long after ten o'clock and yet there was no sign
of Gabriel and his wife. Besides they were dreadfully afraid that
Freddy Malins might turn up screwed.[3] They would not wish   45
for worlds that any of Mary Jane's pupils should see him under
the influence: and when he was like that it was sometimes very
hard to manage him. Freddy Malins always came late but they
wondered what could be keeping Gabriel: and that was what
brought them every two minutes to the banisters to ask Lily   50
had Gabriel or Freddy come.

—O, Mr Conroy, said Lily to Gabriel when she opened the
door for him, Miss Kate and Miss Julia thought you were never
coming. Good night, Mrs Conroy.

—I'll engage[4] they did, said Gabriel, but they forget that my   55
wife here takes three mortal hours[5] to dress herself.

He stood on the mat, scraping the snow from his goloshes,
while Lily led his wife to the foot of the stairs and called out:

—Miss Kate, here's Mrs Conroy.

Kate and Julia came toddling down the dark stairs at once.   60
Both of them kissed Gabriel's wife, said she must be perished
alive[6] and asked was Gabriel with her.

—Here I am as right as the mail,[7] aunt Kate! Go on up. I'll
follow, called out Gabriel from the dark.

He continued scraping his feet vigorously while the three   65
women went upstairs, laughing, to the ladies' dressingroom. A
light fringe of snow lay like a cape on the shoulders of his
overcoat and like toecaps on the toes of his goloshes;[8] and, as
the buttons of his overcoat slipped with a squeaking noise
through the snowstiffened frieze,[9] a cold fragrant air from out   70
of doors escaped from crevices and folds.

63–64 Go--follow,] e:10; ABSENT MS–10G

1. Choice cuts of beef loin.
2. Tea priced four times that of ordinary tea.
3. Intoxicated.
4. An expression meaning to pledge oneself or promise, equivalent to "I bet."
5. "Mortal" is here used as a hyperbolic intensifier to suggest expanded time.
6. Suffering from cold, hunger, and other privations.
7. Ready to be depended or counted on.
8. Water-repellent overshoes pulled over regular shoes to keep them dry in bad weather.
9. A coarse woolen cloth.

—Is it snowing again, Mr Conroy? asked Lily.

She had preceded him into the pantry to help him off with
his overcoat. Gabriel smiled at the three syllables[1] she had given
his surname and glanced at her. She was a slim growing girl,   75
pale in complexion and with haycoloured hair. The gas[2] in the
pantry made her look still paler. Gabriel had known her when
she was a child and used to sit on the lowest step nursing[3] a rag
doll.

—Yes, Lily, he answered, and I think we're in for a night of it.   80

He looked up at the pantry ceiling which was shaking with
the stamping and shuffling of feet on the floor above, listened
for a moment to the piano and then glanced at the girl who was
folding his overcoat carefully at the end of a shelf.

—Tell me, Lily, he said in a friendly tone, do you still go to   85
school?

—O no, sir, she answered, I'm done schooling this year and
more.

—O then, said Gabriel gaily, I suppose we'll be going to your
wedding one of these fine days with your young man—eh?   90

The girl glanced back at him over her shoulder and said with
great bitterness:

—The men that is now is only all palaver[4] and what they can
get out of you.

Gabriel coloured as if he felt he had made a mistake and,   95
without looking at her, kicked off his goloshes and flicked
actively with his muffler at his patent leather shoes.[5]

He was a stout tallish young man. The high colour of his
cheeks pushed upwards even to his forehead where it scattered
itself in a few formless patches of pale red; and on his hairless   100
face there scintillated restlessly the polished lenses and bright
gilt rims of the glasses which screened his delicate and restless
eyes. His glossy black hair was parted in the middle and
brushed in a long curve behind his ears where it curled slightly
beneath the groove left by his hat.   105

When he had flicked lustre into his shoes he stood up and
pulled his waistcoat[6] down more tightly on his plump body.
Then he took a coin rapidly from his pocket.

72 again,] 10; outside, MS–10G

1. Lily pronounces his name "Con-ner-roy," the extra syllable betraying her speech as lower-
   class.
2. Gaslight or a lamp lit with a flame fueled by gas.
3. Tending.
4. Flattering but idle talk.
5. Shoes with a black, shiny varnished surface.
6. A garment worn under a coat or jacket, intended to be partly viewed when worn.

—O Lily, he said, thrusting it into her hand, it's Christmas
time, isn't it? Just .... here's a little   110

He walked rapidly towards the door.

—O no, sir! cried the girl, following him. Really, sir, I
wouldn't take it.

—Christmas time! Christmas time! said Gabriel, almost trot=
ting to the stairs and waving his hand to her in deprecation.[7]   115

The girl, seeing that he had gained the stairs, called out after
him:

—Well, thank you, sir.

He waited outside the drawingroom[8] door until the waltz
should finish, listening to the skirts that swept against it and to   120
the shuffling of feet. He was still discomposed by the girl's
bitter and sudden retort. It had cast a gloom over him which he
tried to dispel by arranging his cuffs and the bows of his tie.
Then he took from his waistcoat pocket a little paper and
glanced at the headings he had made for his speech. He was   125
undecided about the lines from Robert Browning[9] for he feared
they would be above the heads of his hearers. Some quotation
that they could recognise from Shakespeare or from the mel=
odies[1] would be better. The indelicate clacking of the men's
heels and the shuffling of their soles reminded him that their   130
grade of culture differed from his. He would only make himself
ridiculous by quoting poetry to them which they could not
understand. They would think that he was airing his superior
education. He would fail with them just as he had failed with
the girl in the pantry. He had taken up a wrong tone. His   135
whole speech was a mistake from first to last, an utter failure.

Just then his aunts and his wife came out of the ladies'
dressingroom. His aunts were two small plainly dressed old
women. Aunt Julia was an inch or so the taller. Her hair,
drawn low over the tops of her ears, was grey; and grey also,   140
with darker shadows, was her large flaccid face. Though she
was stout in build and stood erect her slow eyes and parted lips
gave her the appearance of a woman who did not know where
she was or where she was going. Aunt Kate was more viva=
cious. Her face, healthier than her sister's, was all puckers and   145

127 hearers.] 10; auditors. MS–10G   130 shuffling] 10; scraping MS–10G   136 an
utter] 10; a complete MS–10G

7. A gesture seeking to avert something—in this case, Lily's thanks.
8. The room reserved for the reception of company.
9. English poet (1812–1889), considered difficult to read.
1. Thomas Moore's poems, collected in *Irish Melodies*, were published between 1807 and
1834.

creases like a shrivelled red apple and her hair, braided in the same oldfashioned way, had not lost its ripe nut colour.[2]

They both kissed Gabriel frankly. He was their favourite nephew, the son of their dead elder sister Ellen who had married T J Conroy of the Port and Docks.[3]

—Gretta tells me you're not going to take a cab back to Monkstown[4] tonight, Gabriel, said Aunt Kate.

—No, said Gabriel, turning to his wife, we had quite enough of that last year, hadn't we? Don't you remember, Aunt Kate, what a cold Gretta got out of it? Cab windows rattling all the way and the east wind blowing in after we passed Merrion.[5] Very jolly it was. Gretta caught a dreadful cold.

Aunt Kate frowned severely and nodded her head at every word.

—Quite right, Gabriel, quite right, she said. You can't be too careful.

—But as for Gretta there, said Gabriel, she'd walk home in the snow if she were let.

Mrs Conroy laughed.

—Don't mind him, aunt Kate, she said. He's really an awful bother,[6] what with green shades for Tom's eyes at night and making him do the dumbbells[7] and forcing Lottie to eat the stirabout.[8] The poor child! And she simply hates the sight of it! .... O, but you'll never guess what he makes me wear now!

She broke out into a peal of laughter and glanced at her husband whose admiring and happy eyes had been wandering from her dress to her face and hair. The two aunts laughed heartily too for Gabriel's solicitude was a standing joke with them.

—Goloshes! said Mrs Conroy. That's the latest. Whenever it's wet underfoot I must put on my goloshes. Tonight even he wanted me to put them on but I wouldn't. The next thing he'll buy me will be a diving suit.

Gabriel laughed nervously and patted his tie reassuringly

150 Port and Docks.] 14; Post Office. MS–14P   157 jolly] 10; pleasant MS–10G   158–159 head--word.] 10; head. MS–10G   167 Lottie] 10; Eva MS–10G   173 a standing] 10; an old MS–10G

2. A warm, reddish-brown color.
3. The Dublin Port and Docks Board managed the harbor facilities and customs regulation of all shipping in the Port of Dublin.
4. A fashionable and picturesque village a few miles south of Dublin on Dublin Bay. Although Monkstown could be reached easily by train, the last train—shortly after 11 P.M., would have required the Conroys to leave the party early.
5. Another village between Dublin and Monkstown.
6. Someone who gives people trouble or makes a fuss.
7. Do physical exercises with weights.
8. Cooked cereal.

while aunt Kate nearly doubled herself so heartily did she enjoy   180
the joke. The smile soon faded from aunt Julia's face and her
mirthless eyes were directed towards her nephew's face. After a
pause she asked:
—And what are goloshes, Gabriel?
—Goloshes, Julia! exclaimed her sister. Goodness me, don't   185
you know what goloshes are? You wear them over your ....
over your boots, Gretta, isn't it?
—Yes, said Mrs Conroy. Guttapercha[9] things. We both have a
pair now. Gabriel says everyone wears them on the continent.
—O, on the continent,[1] murmured aunt Julia, nodding her head   190
slowly.
    Gabriel knitted his brows and said, as if he were slightly
angered:
—It's nothing very wonderful but Gretta thinks it very funny
because she says the word reminds her of christy minstrels.[2]   195
—But tell me, Gabriel, said aunt Kate with brisk tact. Of
course you've seen about the room. Gretta was saying ....
—O, the room is all right, replied Gabriel. I've taken one in the
Gresham.[3]
—To be sure, said aunt Kate, by far the best thing to do. And   200
the children, Gretta, you're not anxious about them?
—O, for one night, said Mrs Conroy. Besides Bessie will look
after them.
—To be sure, said aunt Kate again. What a comfort it is to
have a girl like that, one you can depend on! There's that Lily,   205
I'm sure I don't know what has come over her lately. She's not
the girl she was at all.
    Gabriel was about to ask his aunt some questions on this
point but she broke off suddenly to gaze after her sister who
had wandered down the stairs and was craning her neck over   210
the banisters.
—Now, I ask you, she said almost testily, where is Julia going.
Julia! Julia! Where are you going?
    Julia who had gone half way down one flight came back and
announced blandly: 215

---

212 going.] STET MS

9. A latexlike substance derived from Malaysian trees, somewhat less elastic than India
   rubber.
1. The mainland of Europe, as opposed to the British Isles.
2. The Christy Minstrels, founded in Buffalo, New York, in 1842, toured the United States
   and England during the next decade and thereby made the blackface minstrel show, in
   which whites wore dark makeup to play racially stereotyped Negro parts, a popular form
   of comic music-hall entertainment in the late nineteenth century. The word "goloshes"
   may remind Gretta of "christy minstrels" by way of the word "golliwog"—another racial
   stereotype in the form of a grotesque, animated Negro doll.
3. An elegant hotel on O'Connell Street in the center of Dublin.

—Here's Freddy!

At the same moment a clapping of hands and a final flourish of the pianist told that the waltz had ended. The drawingroom door was opened from within and some couples came out. Aunt Kate drew Gabriel aside hurriedly and whispered into his ear:

—Slip down, Gabriel, like a good fellow and see if he's all right and don't let him up if he's screwed. I'm sure he's screwed. I'm sure he is.

Gabriel went to the stairs and listened over the banisters. He could hear two persons talking in the pantry. Then he recog= nised Freddy Malins' laugh. He went down the stairs noisily.

—It's such a relief, said aunt Kate to Mrs Conroy, that Gabriel is here. I always feel easier in my mind when he's here ..... Julia, there's Miss Daly and Miss Power will take some refresh= ment. Thanks for your beautiful waltz, Miss Daly. It made lovely time.

A tall wizenfaced man with a stiff grizzled moustache and swarthy skin who was passing out with his partner said:

—And may we have some refreshment too, Miss Morkan?

—Julia, said aunt Kate summarily, and here's Mr Browne and Miss Furlong. Take them in, Julia, with Miss Daly and Miss Power.

—I'm the man for the ladies, said Mr Browne, pursing his lips until his moustache bristled and smiling in all his wrinkles. You know, Miss Morkan, the reason they are so fond of me is .....

He did not finish his sentence but, seeing that aunt Kate was out of earshot, at once led the three young ladies into the back room. The middle of the room was occupied by two square tables placed end to end and on these aunt Julia and the caretaker were straightening and smoothing a large cloth. On the sideboard were arrayed dishes and plates and glasses and bundles of knives and forks and spoons. The top of the closed square piano served also as a sideboard for viands[4] and sweets. At a smaller sideboard in one corner two young men were standing, drinking hop bitters.[5]

Mr Browne led his charges thither and invited them all, in jest, to some ladies' punch, hot, strong and sweet. As they said they never took anything strong he opened three bottles of lemonade for them. Then he asked one of the young men to move aside and, taking hold of the decanter, filled out for him=

220

225

230

235

240

245

250

255

---

234 swarthy] 10; dark yellow MS–10G

4. Varieties of food or edible provisions.
5. An alcoholic drink made bitter by the addition of hops.

self a goodly measure of whisky. The young men eyed him
respectfully while he took a trial sip.

—God help me, he said smiling, it's the doctor's orders.[6]

His wizened face broke into a broader smile and the three   260
young ladies laughed in musical echo to his pleasantry, swaying
their bodies to and fro, with nervous jerks of their shoulders.
The boldest said:

—O, now, Mr Browne, I'm sure the doctor never ordered any=
thing of the kind.   265

Mr Browne took another sip of his whisky and said, with
sidling mimicry:

—Well, you see, I'm like the famous Mrs Cassidy who is
reported to have said: *Now, Mary Grimes, if I don't take it
make me take it for I feel I want it.*[7]   270

His hot face had leaned forward a little too confidentially
and he had assumed a very low Dublin accent[8] so that the young
ladies, with one instinct, received his speech in silence. Miss
Furlong, who was one of Mary Jane's pupils, asked Miss Daly
what was the name of the pretty waltz she had played; and Mr   275
Browne, seeing that he was ignored, turned promptly to the
two young men who were more appreciative.

A redfaced young woman, dressed in pansy,[9] came into the
room, excitedly clapping her hands and crying:

—Quadrilles! Quadrilles![1]   280

Close on her heels came aunt Kate, crying:

—Two gentlemen and three ladies, Mary Jane!

—O, here's Mr Bergin and Mr Kerrigan, said Mary Jane. Mr
Kerrigan, will you take Miss Power. Miss Furlong, may I get
you a partner, Mr Bergin. O, that'll just do now.   285

—Three ladies, Mary Jane, said aunt Kate.

The two young gentlemen asked the ladies if they might
have the pleasure and Mary Jane turned to Miss Daly.

—O, Miss Daly, you're really awfully good after playing for
the last two dances but really we're so short of ladies tonight. 290

—I don't mind in the least, Miss Morkan.

—But I've a nice partner for you, Mr Bartell D'Arcy, the tenor.
I'll get him to sing later on. All Dublin is raving about him.

—Lovely voice, lovely voice! said aunt Kate.

As the piano had twice begun the prelude to the first figure   295

6. Alcohol-based tonics were sometimes prescribed for medicinal purposes at the time of the
   story.
7. Presumably a stock joke making fun of people who use medicine as an excuse for imbibing
   liquor.
8. A lower-class accent associated with vulgarity.
9. A dark, purplish-red color.
1. A French square dance, performed by four couples, that contains five sections or figures
   each of which is a complete dance of its own.

Mary Jane led her recruits quickly from the room. They had hardly gone when aunt Julia wandered slowly into the room, looking behind her at something.

—What is the matter, Julia? asked aunt Kate anxiously. Who is it?   300

Julia, who was carrying in a column of table-napkins, turned to her sister and said simply, as if the question had surprised her:

—It's only Freddy, Kate, and Gabriel with him.

In fact right behind her Gabriel could be seen piloting   305
Freddy Malins across the landing. The latter, a young man of about forty, was of Gabriel's size and build with very round shoulders. His face was fleshy and pallid, touched with colour only at the thick hanging lobes of his ears and at the wide wings of his nose. He had coarse features, a blunt nose, a   310
convex and receding brow, tumid and protruded lips. His heavylidded eyes and the disorder of his scanty hair made him look sleepy. He was laughing heartily in a high key at a story which he had been telling Gabriel on the stairs and at the same time rubbing the knuckles of his left fist backwards and   315
forwards into his left eye.

—Good evening, Freddy, said aunt Julia.

Freddy Malins bade the Misses Morkan good evening in what seemed an offhand fashion by reason of the habitual catch in his voice and then, seeing that Mr Browne was   320
grinning at him from the sideboard, crossed the room on rather shaky legs and began to repeat in an undertone the story he had just told to Gabriel.

—He's not so bad, is he? said aunt Kate to Gabriel.

Gabriel's brows were dark but he raised them quickly and   325
answered:

—O no, hardly noticeable.

—Now, isn't he a terrible fellow! she said. And his poor mother made him take the pledge[2] on New Year's Eve. But come on, Gabriel, into the drawingroom.   330

Before leaving the room with Gabriel she signalled to Mr Browne by frowning and shaking her forefinger in warning to and fro. Mr Browne nodded in answer and, when she had gone, said to Freddy Malins:

—Now then, Teddy, I'm going to fill you out a good glass of   335
lemonade just to buck you up.

Freddy Malins, who was nearing the climax of his story, waved the offer aside impatiently but Mr Browne, having first

2. An oath or promise, sometimes made as a formal New Year's resolution, to stop drinking alcohol.

called Freddy Malins' attention to a disarray in his dress,[3] filled
out and handed him a full glass of lemonade. Freddy Malins'   340
left hand accepted the glass mechanically, his right hand being
engaged in the mechanical readjustment of his dress. Mr
Browne, whose face was once more wrinkling with mirth,
poured out for himself a glass of whisky while Freddy Malins
exploded, before he had well reached the climax of his story, in   345
a kink of highpitched bronchitic laughter and, setting down his
untasted and overflowing glass, began to rub the knuckles of
his left fist backwards and forwards into his left eye, repeating
words of his last phrase as well as his fit of laughter would
allow him.   350

◆ ◆ ◆

Gabriel could not listen while Mary Jane was playing her
academy piece,[4] full of runs and difficult passages, to the hushed
drawingroom. He liked music but the piece she was playing
had no melody for him and he doubted whether it had any
melody for the other listeners though they had begged Mary   335
Jane to play something. Four young men, who had come from
the refreshment room to stand in the doorway at the sound of
the piano, had gone away quietly in couples after a few
minutes. The only persons who seemed to follow the music
were Mary Jane herself, her hands racing along the keyboard   360
or lifted from it at the pauses like those of a priestess in
momentary imprecation,[5] and aunt Kate standing at her elbow
to turn the page.

Gabriel's eyes, irritated by the floor which glittered with
beeswax under the heavy chandelier, wandered to the wall   365
above the piano. A picture of the balcony scene in *Romeo and
Juliet*[6] hung there and beside it was a picture of the two
murdered princes in the tower[7] which aunt Julia had worked in
red, blue and brown wools[8] when she was a girl. Probably in the
school they had gone to as girls that kind of work had been   370
taught, for one year his mother had worked for him as a
birthday present a waistcoat of purple tabinet[9] with little foxes'

3. Presumably an unfastened trouser opening.
4. A musical composition requiring a high degree of technical skill for performance, used in
the training of students at the Royal Academy of Music.
5. Prayer; also a curse calling down evil on someone or something.
6. In Act II, scene 2, of Shakespeare's play, Romeo courts Juliet, who is standing on a balcony
above him.
7. The twelve-year-old King Edward V and his nine-year-old brother, Arthur, were imprisoned
in the Tower of London after the clergy raised questions about the legality of their parents'
marriage and their own legitimacy as heirs to the throne. Their uncle, subsequently
crowned King Richard III, was rumored to have ordered their murder.
8. Embroidered on canvas or cloth with wool yarn.
9. A silk or wool fabric that has a wavy, lustrous, damasklike pattern.

heads upon it, lined with brown satin and having round mulberry[1] buttons. It was strange that his mother had had no musical talent though aunt Kate used to call her the brains= carrier of the Morkan family. Both she and Julia had always seemed a little proud of their serious and matronly sister. Her photograph stood before the pierglass.[2] She held an open book on her knees and was pointing out something in it to Constan= tine who, dressed in a man-o'-war suit,[3] lay at her feet. It was she who had chosen the names for her sons for she was very sensible of the dignity of family life. Thanks to her, Constan= tine[4] was now senior curate[5] in Balbriggan[6] and, thanks to her, Gabriel himself had taken his degree in the royal university.[7] A shadow passed over his face as he remembered her sullen opposition to his marriage. Some slighting phrases she had used still rankled in his memory. She had once spoken of Gretta as being country cute and that was not true of Gretta at all. It was Gretta who had nursed her all during her last long illness in their house at Monkstown.

He knew that Mary Jane must be near the end of her piece for she was playing again the opening melody with runs of scales after every bar and while he waited for the end the resentment died down in his heart. The piece ended with a trill of octaves in the treble and a final deep octave in the bass. Great applause greeted Mary Jane as, blushing and rolling up her music nervously, she escaped from the room. The most vigorous clapping came from the four young men in the doorway who had gone away to the refreshment room at the beginning of the piece but had come back when the piano had stopped.

Lancers[8] were arranged. Gabriel found himself partnered with Miss Ivors. She was a frankmannered talkative young lady with a freckled face and prominent brown eyes. She did not wear a lowcut bodice and the large brooch which was fixed in the front of her collar bore on it an Irish device.[9]

406 device.] 10; device and motto. MS [MS ENDS], TS, 10G

1. Dark purple.
2. A tall mirror that fills the space between two windows or hangs above a chimney mantel.
3. A child's outfit that mimics the uniforms worn by sailors, often navy with white trim and consisting of a middy overblouse and bell-bottom trousers.
4. The name may have been chosen in honor of the first Christian Roman emperor, Constantine the Great, who ruled from 306 to 337 C.E.
5. A Roman Catholic vicar or clerical assistant to a pastor.
6. A seaside town twenty miles north of Dublin.
7. A Dublin institution that administered examinations and set educational standards for degrees conferred by universities and schools.
8. A set of five quadrilles, each in a different meter.
9. Celtic brooches and other ornaments had become popular as a result of the cultural interests awakened by the Irish Revival.

When they had taken their places she said abruptly:

—I have a crow to pluck with you.

—With me? said Gabriel.

She nodded her head gravely.

—What is it? asked Gabriel, smiling at her solemn manner.

—Who is G. C.? answered Miss Ivors turning her eyes upon him.

Gabriel coloured and was about to knit his brows as if he did not understand when she said bluntly:

—O, innocent Amy! I have found out that you write for the *Daily Express*.[1] Now aren't you ashamed of yourself?

—Why should I be ashamed of myself? asked Gabriel blinking his eyes and trying to smile.

—Well, I'm ashamed of you, said Miss Ivors frankly. To say you'd write for a rag[2] like that. I didn't think you were a west Briton.[3]

A look of perplexity appeared on Gabriel's face. It was true that he wrote a literary column every Wednesday in the *Daily Express* for which he was paid fifteen shillings. But that did not make him a west Briton surely. The books he received for review were almost more welcome than the paltry cheque. He loved to feel the covers and turn over the pages of newly printed books. Nearly every day when his teaching in the college was ended he used to wander down the quays to the secondhand booksellers, to Hickey's on Bachelor's Walk, to Webb's or Massey's on Aston's Quay or to Clohissey's[4] in the bystreet. He did not know how to meet her charge. He wanted to say that literature was above politics. But they were friends of many years' standing and their careers had been parallel, first at the university and then as teachers: he could not risk a grandiose phrase with her. He continued blinking his eyes and trying to smile and murmured lamely that he saw nothing political in writing reviews of books.

When their turn to cross had come he was still perplexed and inattentive. Miss Ivors promptly took his hand in a warm grasp and said in a soft friendly tone:

—Of course, I was only joking. Come, we cross now.

When they were together again she spoke of the university

421 rag] 10; paper TS, 10G   432 Clohissey's] STET TS, 10; O'Clohissey's 10G   438 trying] STET TS, 10G AGAINST tried 10

1. A conservative Dublin newspaper that favored making Irish nationalist ambitions compatible with British imperial dominion.
2. A contemptuous expression for a newspaper considered worthless.
3. An Irishman, loyal to Britain, who thinks of Ireland as the western province of Britain.
4. These were actual bookselling establishments on the quays of the river Liffey at the time of the story.

question[5] and Gabriel felt more at ease. A friend of hers had 445
shown her his review of Browning's poems. That was how she
had found out the secret: but she liked the review immensely.
Then she said suddenly:

—O, Mr Conroy, will you come for an excursion to the Aran
Isles[6] this summer? We're going to stay there a whole month. It 450
will be splendid out in the Atlantic. You ought to come. Mr
Clancy is coming and Mr Kilkelly and Kathleen Kearney.[7] It
would be splendid for Gretta too if she'd come. She's from
Connacht,[8] isn't she?

—Her people are, said Gabriel shortly. 455

—But you will come, won't you? said Miss Ivors, laying her
warm hand eagerly on his arm.

—The fact is, said Gabriel, I have already arranged to go ...

—Go where? asked Miss Ivors.

—Well, you know, every year I go for a cycling tour with some 460
fellows and so ...

—But where? asked Miss Ivors.

—Well, we usually go to France or Belgium or perhaps Ger=
many, said Gabriel awkwardly.

—And why do you go to France and Belgium, said Miss Ivors, 465
instead of visiting your own land?

—Well, said Gabriel, it's partly to keep in touch with the
languages and partly for a change.

—And haven't you your own language to keep in touch with,
Irish? asked Miss Ivors. 470

—Well, said Gabriel, if it comes to that, you know, Irish is not
my language.[9]

Their neighbours had turned to listen to the crossexamin=
ation. Gabriel glanced right and left nervously and tried to keep
his good humour under the ordeal which was making a blush 475
invade his forehead.

—And haven't you your own land to visit, continued Miss

---

453 from] 10; half TS, 10G   458 already] 10; just TS, 10G

5. The problem of how to provide advanced university education, comparable to the elite
   Protestant British institutions, to young Irish Catholics. The issue was complicated by the
   question of the admission of women to universities.
6. Islands off the west coast of Ireland whose inaccessibility allowed them to preserve the
   Gaelic language, folklore, and other elements of Celtic culture.
7. A young pianist in the story "A Mother."
8. A northwestern province of Ireland that includes County Galway and the city of Galway,
   Gretta Conroy's place of origin.
9. Gaelic, the native language of Ireland, was gradually supplanted by English during the
   centuries of British rule. At the time of the story, there was a significant movement to
   restore Gaelic as Ireland's national language and to call it the "Irish" language. When
   Gabriel says that "Irish" is not his language, he presumably means that since he was born
   into an English-speaking society, English was his first and therefore "native" language.

Ivors, that you know nothing of, your own people and your
own country?

—O, to tell you the truth, retorted Gabriel suddenly, I'm sick   480
of my own country, sick of it!

—Why? asked Miss Ivors.

Gabriel did not answer for his retort had heated him.

—Why? repeated Miss Ivors.

They had to go visiting together[1] and, as he had not   485
answered her, Miss Ivors said warmly:

—Of course, you've no answer.

Gabriel tried to cover his agitation by taking part in the
dance with great energy. He avoided her eyes for he had seen a
sour expression on her face. But when they met in the long   490
chain[2] he was surprised to feel his hand firmly pressed. She
looked at him from under her brows for a moment quizzically
until he smiled. Then, just as the chain was about to start
again, she stood on tiptoe and whispered into his ear:

—West Briton!   495

When the lancers were over Gabriel went away to a remote
corner of the room where Freddy Malins' mother was sitting.
She was a stout feeble old woman with white hair. Her voice
had a catch in it like her son's and she stuttered slightly. She
had been told that Freddy had come and that he was nearly all   500
right. Gabriel asked her whether she had had a good crossing.[3]
She lived with her married daughter in Glasgow[4] and came to
Dublin on a visit once a year. She answered placidly that she
had had a beautiful crossing and that the captain had been
most attentive to her. She spoke also of the beautiful house her   505
daughter kept in Glasgow and of the nice friends they had
there. While her tongue rambled on Gabriel tried to banish
from his mind all memory of the unpleasant incident with Miss
Ivors. Of course the girl or woman or whatever she was was an
enthusiast[5] but there was a time for all things. Perhaps he ought   510
not to have answered her like that. But she had no right to call
him a west Briton before people, even in joke. She had tried to
make him ridiculous before people, heckling him and staring at
him with her rabbit's eyes.

He saw his wife making her way towards him through the   515
waltzing couples. When she reached him she said into his ear:

506 the nice] 10; all the TS, 10G

1. Progressing as a couple around the set of the square dance or quadrille.
2. A line of dancers with hands linked.
3. The voyage across the Irish Sea between Scotland and Ireland.
4. One of the major cities of Scotland.
5. Someone with passionate commitment to a cause.

—Gabriel, aunt Kate wants to know won't you carve the goose as usual. Miss Daly will carve the ham and I'll do the pudding.

—All right, said Gabriel.

—She's sending in the younger ones first as soon as this waltz   520
is over so that we'll have the table to ourselves.

—Were you dancing? asked Gabriel.

—Of course I was. Didn't you see me? What words had you with Molly Ivors?

—No words. Why! Did she say so?   525

—Something like that. I'm trying to get that Mr D'Arcy to sing. He's full of conceit, I think.

—There were no words, said Gabriel moodily, only she wanted me to go for a trip to the west of Ireland and I said I wouldn't.   530

His wife clasped her hands excitedly and gave a little jump.

—O, do go, Gabriel, she cried. I'd love to see Galway again.

—You can go if you like, said Gabriel coldly.

She looked at him for a moment, then turned to Mrs Malins and said: 535

—There's a nice husband for you, Mrs Malins.

While she was threading her way back across the room Mrs Malins, without adverting to the interruption, went on to tell Gabriel what beautiful places there were in Scotland and beau= tiful scenery. Her son-in-law brought them every year to the   540
lakes and they used to go fishing. Her son-in-law was a splendid fisher. One day he caught a fish, a beautiful big big fish: and the man in the hotel boiled it for their dinner.

Gabriel hardly heard what she said. Now that supper was coming near he began to think again about his speech and   545
about the quotation. When he saw Freddy Malins coming across the room to visit his mother Gabriel left the chair free for him and retired into the embrasure[6] of the window. The room had already cleared and from the back room came the clatter of plates and knives. Those who still remained in the   550
drawingroom seemed tired of dancing and were conversing quietly in little groups. Gabriel's warm trembling fingers tapped the cold pane of the window. How cool it must be outside! How pleasant it would be to walk out alone, first along by the river and then through the park![7] The snow would   555
be lying on the branches of the trees and forming a bright cap

523 words] 10; row TS, 10G   525 words.] 10; row. TS, 10G   528 were no words,] 10; was no row, TS, 10G   532 cried.] ⟨said⟩ cried. TS   542–543 fish,--fish:] 10; beautiful big fish TS; beautiful big fish, 10G   543 boiled] 10; cooked TS, 10G

6. The sloping recess of a window.
7. Phoenix Park, Dublin's largest park, located a half mile or so from the Morkan residence.

on the top of the Wellington monument.[8] How much more
pleasant it would be there than at the supper table!

He ran over the headings of his speech: Irish hospitality, sad
memories, the Three Graces,[9] Paris,[1] the quotation from Brown=   560
ing. He repeated to himself a phrase he had written in his
review: *One feels that one is listening to a thoughttormented
music.* Miss Ivors had praised the review. Was she sincere? Had
she really any life of her own behind all her propagandism?
There had never been any ill feeling between them until that   565
night. It unnerved him to think that she would be at the supper
table, looking up at him while he spoke with her critical
quizzing eyes. Perhaps she would not be sorry to see him fail in
his speech. An idea came into his mind and gave him courage.
He would say, alluding to aunt Kate and aunt Julia: *Ladies and*   570
gentlemen, the generation which is now on the wane among us
may have had its faults but for my part I think it had certain
qualities of hospitality, of humour, of humanity, which the new
and very serious and hypereducated generation that is growing
up around us seems to me to lack. Very good: that was one for   575
Miss Ivors. What did he care that his aunts were only two
ignorant old women?

A murmur in the room attracted his attention. Mr Browne
was advancing from the door, gallantly escorting aunt Julia
who leaned upon his arm, smiling and hanging her head. An   580
irregular musketry of applause[2] escorted her also as far as the
piano and then, as Mary Jane seated herself on the stool and
aunt Julia, no longer smiling, half turned so as to pitch her
voice fairly into the room, gradually ceased. Gabriel recognised
the prelude. It was that of an old song of aunt Julia's, *Arrayed*   585
for the Bridal.[3] Her voice strong and clear in tone attacked with

582 on--stool] e:14; at the piano TS, 10; at the piano, 10G, 14P; on the stool, 14

8. An obelisk erected inside the main entrance of Phoenix Park to commemorate the military
   career of Arthur Wellesley (1769–1852), duke of Wellington, who had defeated Napoleon
   at Waterloo and served as British prime minister from 1828 to 1830. Although Dublin-
   born, the "Iron Duke," as he was called, was a Tory politician with conservative views
   toward Irish politics.
9. Three goddesses in Greek mythology who presided over the banquet, the dance, the elegant arts, and social enjoyment. They were the daughters of Zeus and Eurynome, and
   their names were Euphrosyne, Aglaia, and Thalia.
1. A son of Priam, king of Troy, Paris inadvertently sowed the seeds of the Trojan War when
   he judged three goddesses, Athena, Aphrodite, and Hera, in a beauty contest whose prize
   was a golden apple. Aphrodite successfully bribed Paris by offering him the most beautiful
   mortal woman in the world, Helen, whose husband, Menelaus, king of Sparta, mobilized
   the Greeks against the Trojans, after her elopement with Paris.
2. Metaphorically, like the fire of infantry guns.
3. A song arranged by George Linley, based on an aria in the opera *The Puritans* (1835) by
   Vincenzo Bellini. The song is extremely difficult, full of runs and trills that require a
   coloratura soprano voice of great virtuosity to perform it well. In the opera, the widow of
   the recently executed King Charles I, Henrietta of France, is saved by a Royalist cavalier
   whose veiled bride suggests to him a disguise for the queen's escape.

great spirit the runs which embellish the air and, though she sang very rapidly, she did not miss even the smallest of the grace notes. To follow the voice, without looking at the singer's face, was to feel and share the excitement of swift and secure flight. Gabriel applauded loudly with all the others at the close of the song and loud applause was borne in from the invisible supper table. It sounded so genuine that a little colour struggled into aunt Julia's face as she bent to replace in the music stand the old leatherbound songbook that had her initials on the cover. Freddy Malins, who had listened with his head perched sideways to hear the better, was still applauding when everyone else had ceased and talking animatedly to his mother who nodded her head gravely and slowly in acquiescence. At last, when he could clap no more, he stood up suddenly and hurried across the room to aunt Julia, whose hand he seized and held in both his hands, shaking it when words failed him or the catch in his voice proved too much for him.

—I was just telling my mother, he said, I never heard you sing so well, never. No, I never heard your voice so good as it is tonight. Now! Would you believe that now? That's the truth. Upon my word and honour that's the truth. I never heard your voice sound so fresh and so ... so clear and fresh, never.

Aunt Julia smiled broadly and murmured something about compliments as she released her hand from his grasp. Mr Browne extended his open hand towards her and said to those who were near him in the manner of a showman introducing a prodigy to an audience:

—Miss Julia Morkan, my latest discovery!

He was laughing very heartily at this himself when Freddy Malins turned to him and said:

—Well, Browne, if you're serious you might make a worse discovery. All I can say is I never heard her sing half so well as long as I am coming here. And that's the honest truth.

—Neither did I, said Mr Browne. I think her voice has greatly improved.

Aunt Julia shrugged her shoulders and said with meek pride:

—Thirty years ago I hadn't a bad voice as voices go.

—I often told Julia, said aunt Kate emphatically, that she was simply thrown away in that choir. But she never would be said[4] by me.

She turned as if to appeal to the good sense of the others

590

595

600

605

610

615

620

625

597 the] TS; her 10G   604 my] ABSENT TS

4. Contradicted or opposed.

against a refractory child while aunt Julia gazed in front of her,
a vague smile of reminiscence playing on her face.

—No, continued aunt Kate, she wouldn't be said or led by   630
anyone, slaving there in that choir night and day, night and
day. Six o'clock on Christmas morning! And all for what?

—Well, isn't it for the honour of God, aunt Kate? asked Mary
Jane twisting round on the piano stool and smiling.

Aunt Kate turned fiercely on her niece and said: 635

—I know all about the honour of God, Mary Jane, but I think
it's not at all honourable for the pope to turn out the women
out of the choirs that have slaved there all their lives and put
little whippersnappers of boys over their heads.[5] I suppose it is
for the good of the church if the pope does it. But it's not just, 640
Mary Jane, and it's not right.

She had worked herself into a passion and would have con=
tinued in defence of her sister for it was a sore subject with her
but Mary Jane, seeing that all the dancers had come back,
intervened pacifically: 645

—Now, aunt Kate, you're giving scandal to Mr Browne who is
of the other persuasion.[6]

Aunt Kate turned to Mr Browne, who was grinning at this
allusion to his religion, and said hastily:

—O, I don't question the pope's being right.[7] I'm only a stupid   650
old woman and I wouldn't presume to do such a thing. But
there's such a thing as common everyday politeness and grati=
tude. And if I were in Julia's place I'd tell that Father Healy
straight up to his face ...

—And besides, aunt Kate, said Mary Jane, we really are all   655
hungry and when we are hungry we are all very quarrelsome.

—And when we are thirsty we are also quarrelsome, added Mr
Browne.

—So that we had better go to supper, said Mary Jane, and
finish the discussion afterwards.   660

On the landing outside the drawingroom Gabriel found his
wife and Mary Jane trying to persuade Miss Ivors to stay for
supper. But Miss Ivors, who had put on her hat and was

5. On November 22, 1903 (that is, less than six weeks before the time of this story, which
   is presumed to take place between January 2 and 6, 1904), Pope Pius X issued a papal
   directive, a *Motu Proprio,* that banned women from singing in church choirs. The soprano
   and alto parts were taken over by young boys.
6. Protestant.
7. After the Vatican Council in 1870 decreed the doctrine of the pope's infallibility, his
   judgment on ecclesiastical matters or matters of faith and morality could not be questioned.

buttoning her cloak, would not stay. She did not feel in the
least hungry and she had already overstayed her time.   665
—But only for ten minutes, Molly, said Mrs Conroy. That
won't delay you.
—To take a pick itself,[8] said Mary Jane, after all your dancing.
—I really couldn't, said Miss Ivors.
—I am afraid you didn't enjoy yourself at all, said Mary Jane   670
hopelessly.
—Ever so much, I assure you, said Miss Ivors, but you really
must let me run off now.
—But how can you get home? asked Mrs Conroy.
—O, it's only two steps up the quay.   675
    Gabriel hesitated a moment and said:
—If you will allow me, Miss Ivors, I'll see you home if you
really are obliged to go.
    But Miss Ivors broke away from them.
—I won't hear of it, she cried. For goodness' sake go in to your   680
suppers and don't mind me. I'm quite well able to take care of
myself.
—Well, you're the comical girl, Molly, said Mrs Conroy
frankly.
—*Beannacht libh*,[9] cried Miss Ivors with a laugh as she ran   685
down the staircase.
    Mary Jane gazed after her, a moody puzzled expression on
her face, while Mrs Conroy leaned over the banisters to listen
for the halldoor. Gabriel asked himself was he the cause of her
abrupt departure. But she did not seem to be in ill humour: she   690
had gone away laughing. He stared blankly down the staircase.
    At that moment aunt Kate came toddling out of the supper
room, almost wringing her hands in despair.
—Where is Gabriel? she cried. Where on earth is Gabriel?
There's everyone waiting in there, stage to let,[1] and nobody to   695
carve the goose!
—Here I am, aunt Kate! cried Gabriel with sudden animation,
ready to carve a flock of geese, if necessary.
    A fat brown goose lay at one end of the table and at the
other end, on a bed of creased paper strewn with sprigs of   700
parsley, lay a great ham, stripped of its outer skin and peppered
over with crust crumbs, a neat paper frill round its shin, and
beside this was a round of spiced beef. Between these rival ends
ran parallel lines of side dishes: two little minsters of jelly, red

664 did--feel] 14; wasn't TS, 10G–14P   702 frill] ⟨filled⟩ frill TS

8. Have a bite.
9. A Gaelic farewell.
1. As if to say, the theater is rented, the patrons are seated, but where are the actors?

and yellow, a shallow dish full of blocks of blancmange[2] and   705
red jam, a large green leafshaped dish with a stalkshaped
handle on which lay bunches of purple raisins and peeled
almonds, a companion dish on which lay a solid rectangle of
Smyrna figs, a dish of custard topped with grated nutmeg, a
small bowl full of chocolates and sweets wrapped in gold and   710
silver papers and a glass vase in which stood some tall celery
stalks. In the centre of the table there stood, as sentries to a
fruit stand which upheld a pyramid of oranges and American
apples, two squat oldfashioned decanters of cut glass, one
containing port and the other dark sherry. On the closed   715
square piano a pudding[3] in a huge yellow dish lay in waiting
and behind it were three squads of bottles of stout and ale and
minerals[4] drawn up according to the colours of their uniforms,
the first two black with brown and red labels, the third and
smallest squad white, with transverse green sashes.   720

Gabriel took his seat boldly at the head of the table and,
having looked to the edge of the carver, plunged his fork firmly
into the goose. He felt quite at ease now for he was an expert
carver and liked nothing better than to find himself at the head
of a well laden table.   725

—Miss Furlong, what shall I send you? he asked. A wing or a
slice of the breast?

—Just a small slice of the breast.

—Miss Higgins, what for you?

—O, anything at all, Mr Conroy.   730

While Gabriel and Miss Daly exchanged plates of goose and
plates of ham and spiced beef Lily went from guest to guest
with a dish of hot floury potatoes wrapped in a white napkin.
This was Mary Jane's idea and she had also suggested apple
sauce for the goose but aunt Kate had said that plain roast   735
goose without any apple sauce had always been good enough
for her and she hoped she might never eat worse. Mary Jane
waited on her pupils and saw that they got the best slices and
aunt Kate and aunt Julia opened and carried across from the
piano bottles of stout and ale for the gentlemen and bottles of   740
minerals for the ladies. There was a great deal of confusion and
laughter and noise, the noise of orders and counterorders, of
knives and forks, of corks and glass stoppers. Gabriel began to

709 topped] TS; tapped 10G   717 ale] ale⟨s⟩ TS   718 the] ABSENT TS   720 green]
ABSENT TS   726 what] what ⟨I⟩ TS   736 without] TS ENDS, AM1 BEGINS

2. A congealed, sweet, white jelly made with boiled milk and gelatin, and cut into cubes or
   slices after it is set.
3. Boiled or steamed plum pudding, made with flour, bread crumbs, eggs, suet, raisins, currants, and spices, was a traditional Christmas dessert at the time of the story.
4. Mineral water.

carve second helpings as soon as he had finished the first round
without serving himself. Everyone protested loudly so that he   745
compromised by taking a long draught of stout for he had
found the carving hot work. Mary Jane settled down quietly to
her supper but aunt Kate and aunt Julia were still toddling
round the table, walking on each other's heels, getting in each
other's way and giving each other unheeded orders. Mr Browne   750
begged of them to sit down and eat their supper and so did
Gabriel but they said they were time enough so that, at last,
Freddy Malins stood up and, capturing aunt Kate, plumped her
down on her chair amid general laughter.

When everyone had been well served Gabriel said smiling: 755
—Now if anyone wants a little more of what vulgar people call
stuffing[5] let him or her speak.

A chorus of voices invited him to begin his own supper and
Lily came forward with three potatoes which she had reserved
for him.   760
—Very well, said Gabriel amiably as he took another prepara=
tory draught, kindly forget my existence, ladies and gentlemen,
for a few minutes.

He set to his supper and took no part in the conversation
with which the table covered Lily's removal of the plates. The   765
subject of talk was the opera company which was then at the
Theatre Royal.[6] Mr Bartell D'Arcy, the tenor, a dark-com=
plexioned young man with a smart moustache, praised very
highly the leading contralto of the company but Miss Furlong
thought she had a rather vulgar style of production. Freddy   770
Malins said there was a negro chieftain singing in the second
part of the Gaiety pantomime[7] who had one of the finest tenor
voices he had ever heard.
—Have you heard him? he asked Mr Bartell D'Arcy across the
table.   775
—No, answered Mr Bartell D'Arcy carelessly.
—Because, Freddy Malins explained, now I'd be curious to
hear your opinion of him. I think he has a grand voice.

---

751 supper] AM1; suppers, 10G   752 they were] there was 67   761–762 preparatory]
preparat⟨ion⟩ory AM1   769 highly] ⟨lightly⟩ highly AM1

5. Also called forcemeat, as it is the mixture used to stuff fowl and other meats.
6. A theater on Hawkins Street.
7. Several African American performers sang on various stages in Dublin during the first
   week of January 1904—although none of them perfectly fit Freddy Malins's description.
   The Gaiety presented the pantomime *Babes in the Wood* with the singer G. H. Elliott,
   who was, however, a baritone and may have been a white man in blackface makeup. Billy
   Farrell, billed as a "Creole comedian," performed at the Empire Palace Theatre, and Jim
   Hegarty played at the Tivoli just after a troupe called the "Black Troubadours." Freddy
   Malins's point, that black singers or singers in black roles were relegated to the least
   prestigious venues for racial reasons, would be valid for all of these.

—It takes Teddy to find out the really good things, said Mr
Browne familiarly to the table.   780
—And why couldn't he have a voice too? asked Freddy Malins
sharply. Is it because he's only a black?

Nobody answered this question and Mary Jane led the table
back to the legitimate opera. One of her pupils had given her a
pass for *Mignon*.[8] Of course, it was very fine, she said, but it   785
made her think of poor Georgina Burns.[9] Mr Browne could go
back farther still to the old Italian companies that used to come
to Dublin, Tietjens, Trebelli, Ilma de Murzka, Campanini, the
great Giuglini, Ravelli, Aramburo.[1] Those were the days, he
said, when there was something like singing to be heard in   790
Dublin. He told too of how the top gallery of the old Royal
used to be packed night after night, of how one night an Italian
tenor had sung five encores to *Let Me Like a Soldier Fall*,[2]
introducing a high C every time, and of how the gallery boys
would sometimes in their enthusiasm unyoke the horses from   795
the carriage of some great *prima donna* and pull her themselves
through the streets to her hotel. Why did they never play the
grand old operas now, he asked. *Dinorah*,[3] *Lucrezia Borgia?*[4]
Because they could not get the voices to sing them: that was
why.   800
—O, well, said Mr Bartell D'Arcy, I presume there are as good
singers today as there were then.
—Where are they? asked Mr Browne defiantly.
—In London, Paris, Milan, said Mr Bartell D'Arcy warmly. I
suppose Caruso,[5] for example, is quite as good, if not better   805
than any of the men you have mentioned.

786 go] ⁷¹go¹ʳ AM1   788 Trebelli,] 10; Crebelli AM1; Trebell's 10G   797 her] the AM1
798 *Dinorah*,] 14; *Norma*, AM1, 10G–14P   804 Milan,] 14; Berlin, AM1, 10G–14P;
Vienna, 10; Berlin, 14P

8. Nineteenth-century French opera by Ambroise Thomas.
9. Appeared with the Carl Rosa Opera Company, where she sang in the company of stars
   such as Barton McGuckin and Minnie Hauk. Burns's husband, the Irish baritone Leslie
   Crotty, died suddenly about seven months before the time of the story.
1. Some of the singers in this list had sad ends. Therese Tietjens (1831–1877) died relatively
   young of cancer. Ilma de Murzka (1836–1889) ended her highly successful career in
   suicide. Antonio Giuglini (1827–1865) went insane. Italo Campanini's voice failed. Zelia
   Trebelli, Antonio Aramburo, and Antonio Ravelli appear to have been more fortunate.
2. Don Caesar's aria in William Vincent Wallace's *Maritana,* sung when he is given the
   opportunity to die nobly by firing squad, rather than ignobly by hanging, if he agrees to
   marry a veiled lady before his execution.
3. Popular French opera by Giacomo Meyerbeer (1791–1864), also known as *Le Pardon de
   Ploërmel,* about a peasant girl whose marriage to a goatherd is delayed and frustrated by
   natural disasters, supernatural forces, and madness.
4. Gaetano Donizetti's 1833 opera, based on Victor Hugo's play. Its high point is Lucrezia's
   announcement that coffins have been brought for the banquet guests she has just poi-
   soned.
5. Enrico Caruso (1873–1921), an Italian tenor, was just becoming famous at the time of
   the story, when his highly successful tours to Monte Carlo, London, and New York had
   begun attracting major attention.

—Maybe so, said Mr Browne. But I may tell you I doubt it
strongly.

—O, I'd give anything to hear Caruso sing, said Mary Jane.

—For me, said aunt Kate, who had been picking a bone, there   810
was only one tenor. To please me, I mean. But I suppose none
of you ever heard of him.

—Who was he, Miss Morkan? asked Mr Bartell D'Arcy pol=
itely.

—His name, said aunt Kate, was Parkinson.[6] I heard him when   815
he was in his prime and I think he had then the purest tenor
voice that was ever put into a man's throat.

—Strange, said Mr Bartell D'Arcy. I never even heard of him.

—Yes, yes, Miss Morkan is right, said Mr Browne. I remember
hearing of old Parkinson but he's too far back for me.   820

—A beautiful pure sweet mellow English tenor, said aunt Kate
with enthusiasm.

Gabriel having finished, the huge pudding was transferred to
the table. The clatter of forks and spoons began again. Gabri=
el's wife served out spoonfuls of the pudding and passed the   825
plates down the table. Midway down they were held up by
Mary Jane who replenished them with raspberry or orange jelly
or with blancmange and jam. The pudding was of aunt Julia's
making and she received praises for it from all quarters. She
herself said that it was not quite brown enough.   830

—Well, I hope, Miss Morkan, said Mr Browne, that I'm brown
enough for you because, you know, I'm all brown.

All the gentlemen, except Gabriel, ate some of the pudding
out of compliment to aunt Julia. As Gabriel never ate sweets
the celery had been left for him. Freddy Malins also took a   835
stalk of celery and ate it with his pudding. He had been told
that celery was a capital thing for the blood and he was just
then under doctor's care. Mrs Malins, who had been silent all
through the supper, said that her son was going down to
Mount Melleray[7] in a week or so. The table then spoke of   840
Mount Melleray, how bracing the air was down there, how
hospitable the monks were and how they never asked for a
penny-piece[8] from their guests.

—And do you mean to say, asked Mr Browne incredulously,
that a chap can go down there and put up there as if it were a   845

828 blancmange] ⟨⟨rasp berry⟩⟩ blanc mange AM1   843 penny-piece] 14; penny AM1,
10G–14P   845 chap] 14; fellow AM1, 10G–14P

6. Possibly an English tenor who might have performed in Dublin in the nineteenth century.
7. A Trappist monastery in County Waterford in southeast Ireland, where alcoholics could
   go for spiritual renewal and cure.
8. The monks did not charge guests, but were generally given a donation for their hospitality.

hotel and live on the fat of the land and then come away with=
out paying a farthing?

—O, most people give some donation to the monastery when
they leave, said Mary Jane.

—I wish we had an institution like that in our church, said Mr   850
Browne candidly.

He was astonished to hear that the monks never spoke, got
up at two in the morning and slept in their coffins. He asked
what they did it for.

—That's the rule of the order,[9] said aunt Kate firmly.   855

—Yes, but why? asked Mr Browne.

Aunt Kate repeated that it was the rule, that was all. Mr
Browne still seemed not to understand. Freddy Malins ex=
plained to him, as best he could, that the monks were trying to
make up for the sins committed by all the sinners in the outside   860
world. The explanation was not very clear for Mr Browne
grinned and said:

—I like that idea very much but wouldn't a comfortable spring
bed do them as well as a coffin?

—The coffin, said Mary Jane, is to remind them of their last   865
end.

As the subject had grown lugubrious it was buried in a si=
lence of the table during which Mrs Malins could be heard
saying to her neighbour in an indistinct undertone:

—They are very good men, the monks, very pious men.   870

The raisins and almonds and figs and apples and oranges
and chocolates and sweets were now passed about the table
and aunt Julia invited all the guests to have either port or
sherry. At first Mr Bartell D'Arcy refused to take either but one
of his neighbours nudged him and whispered something to   875
him upon which he allowed his glass to be filled. Gradually as
the last glasses were being filled the conversation ceased. A
pause followed, broken only by the noise of the wine and by
unsettlings of chairs. The Misses Morkan, all three, looked
down at the tablecloth. Someone coughed once or twice and   880
then a few gentlemen patted the table gently as a signal for
silence. The silence came and Gabriel pushed back his chair
and stood up.

The patting at once grew louder in encouragement and then
ceased altogether. Gabriel leaned his ten trembling fingers on   885
the tablecloth and smiled nervously at the company. Meeting a

847 a farthing?] 10; anything? AM1, 10G   849 leave,] l⟨i⟩eave, AM1

9. The Trappists were famous for their vow of silence and the austerity of their spiritual
regimen. The detail of their sleeping in their coffins may have been an apocryphal elaboration of this reputation.

row of upturned faces he raised his eyes to the chandelier. The
piano was playing a waltz tune and he could hear the skirts
sweeping against the drawingroom door. People perhaps were
standing in the snow on the quay outside, gazing up at the   890
lighted windows and listening to the waltz music. The air was
pure there. In the distance lay the park where the trees were
weighted with snow. The Wellington monument wore a gleam=
ing cap of snow that flashed westward over the white field of
Fifteen Acres.[1]   895

    He began:

—Ladies and gentlemen.

It has fallen to my lot this evening as in years past to perform a
very pleasing task, but a task for which I am afraid my poor
powers as a speaker are all too inadequate.   900

—No, no, said Mr Browne.

—But, however that may be, I can only ask you tonight to take
the will for the deed and to lend me your attention for a few
moments while I endeavour to express to you in words what
my feelings are on this occasion.   905

—Ladies and gentlemen. It is not the first time that we have
gathered together under this hospitable roof, around this hos=
pitable board. It is not the first time that we have been the
recipients—or, perhaps I had better say, the victims—of the
hospitality of certain good ladies.   910

    He made a circle in the air with his arm and paused. Every=
one laughed or smiled at aunt Kate and aunt Julia and Mary
Jane who all turned crimson with pleasure. Gabriel went on
more boldly:

—I feel more strongly with every recurring year that our   915
country has no tradition which does it so much honour and
which it should guard so jealously as that of its hospitality. It is
a tradition that is unique so far as my experience goes (and I
have visited not a few places abroad) among the modern
nations. Some would say, perhaps, that with us it is rather a   920
failing than anything to be boasted of. But granted even that, it
is, to my mind, a princely failing and one that I trust will long
be cultivated among us. Of one thing, at least, I am sure. As
long as this one roof shelters the good ladies aforesaid—and I
wish from my heart it may do so for many and many a long   925
year to come—the tradition of genuine warmhearted courteous
Irish hospitality, which our forefathers have handed down to us

---

921 anything] 14; a thing AM1, 10G–14P

1. A large, open space in a corner of Phoenix Park, used for military reviews and drills.

and which we in turn must hand down to our descendants, is
still alive among us.

A hearty murmur of assent ran round the table. It shot   930
through Gabriel's mind that Miss Ivors was not there and that
she had gone away discourteously: and he said with confidence
in himself:

—Ladies and gentlemen.

A new generation is growing up in our midst, a generation   935
actuated by new ideas and new principles. It is serious and
enthusiastic for these new ideas and its enthusiasm, even when
it is misdirected, is, I believe, in the main sincere. But we are
living in a sceptical and, if I may use the phrase, a thoughttor=
mented age: and sometimes I fear that this new generation,   940
educated or hypereducated as it is, will lack those qualities of
humanity, of hospitality, of kindly humour which belonged to
an older day. Listening tonight to the names of all those great
singers of the past it seemed to me, I must confess, that we
were living in a less spacious age.[2] Those days might without   945
exaggeration be called spacious days: and if they are gone be=
yond recall let us hope, at least, that in gatherings such as this
we shall still speak of them with pride and affection, still
cherish in our hearts the memory of those dead and gone great
ones whose fame the world will not willingly let die.[3]   950

—Hear! hear! said Mr Browne loudly.

—But yet, continued Gabriel, his voice falling into a softer
inflection, there are always in gatherings such as this sadder
thoughts that will recur to our minds: thoughts of the past, of
youth, of changes, of absent faces that we miss here tonight.   955
Our path through life is strewn with many such sad memories:
and were we to brood upon them always we could not find the
heart to go on bravely with our work among the living. We
have all of us living duties and living affections which claim,
and rightly claim, our strenuous endeavours.   960

Therefore I will not linger on the past. I will not let any
gloomy moralising intrude upon us here tonight. Here we are
gathered together for a brief moment from the bustle and rush
of our everyday routine. We are met here as friends, in the
spirit of good fellowship, as colleagues also, to a certain extent,   965
in the true spirit of *camaraderie*, and as the guests of—what

947 gatherings] gathering AM1   951 —Hear!]—Hear⟨,⟩! AM1   966 the(1)] AM1 ENDS,
AM2 BEGINS   966 true] time AM2

2. A time of great expansiveness, when people had a wide and generous outlook.
3. From John Milton's introduction to *The Reason of Church Government*, expressing his
hope that his words will not be forgotten.

shall I call them?—the three Graces of the Dublin musical world.

The table burst into applause and laughter at this sally. Aunt Julia vainly asked each of her neighbours in turn to tell her what Gabriel had said.

—He says we are the three Graces, aunt Julia, said Mary Jane.

Aunt Julia did not understand but she looked up, smiling, at Gabriel who continued in the same vein:

—Ladies and gentlemen.

I will not attempt to play tonight the part that Paris played on another occasion. I will not attempt to choose between them. The task would be an invidious one and one beyond my poor powers. For when I view them in turn, whether it be our chief hostess herself, whose good heart, whose too good heart, has become a byword with all who know her, or her sister, who seems to be gifted with perennial youth and whose singing must have been a surprise and a revelation to us all tonight, or, last but not least, when I consider our youngest hostess, talented, cheerful, hard-working and the best of nieces, I confess, ladies and gentlemen, that I do not know to which of them I should award the prize.

Gabriel glanced down at his aunts and, seeing the large smile on aunt Julia's face and the tears which had risen to aunt Kate's eyes, hastened to his close. He raised his glass of port gallantly while every member of the company fingered a glass expectantly and said loudly:

—Let us toast them all three together. Let us drink to their health, wealth, long life, happiness and prosperity and may they long continue to hold the proud and selfwon position which they hold in their profession and the position of honour and affection which they hold in our hearts.

All the guests stood up, glass in hand and, turning towards the three seated ladies, sang in unison with Mr Browne as leader:

> —For they are jolly gay fellows,[4]
> For they are jolly gay fellows,
> For they are jolly gay fellows
> Which nobody can deny.

Aunt Kate was making frank use of her handkerchief and even aunt Julia seemed moved. Freddy Malins beat time with

970

975

980

985

990

995

1000

1005

---

969 sally.] 10; allusion. AM2, 10G   977 another] 14; a similar AM2, 10G–14P
980 whose too--heart,] ABSENT AM2   987 prize.] price. AM2   988 seeing] AM2 ENDS,
AM1 RESUMES

4. Traditional song of congratulations, possibly originating in the Crusades but popularized by the French military. It generally follows a toast or other commendation.

his pudding fork and the singers turned towards one another as
if in melodious conference, while they sang with emphasis:

> —Unless he tells a lie,
> Unless he tells a lie.   1010

Then turning once more towards their hostesses they sang:

> —For they are jolly gay fellows,
> For they are jolly gay fellows,
> For they are jolly gay fellows
> Which nobody can deny.   1015

The acclamation which followed was taken up beyond the
door of the supper room by many of the other guests and
renewed time after time, Freddy Malins acting as officer with
his fork on high.

◆   ◆   ◆

The piercing morning air came into the hall where they   1020
were standing so that aunt Kate said:
—Close the door, somebody. Mrs Malins will get her death of
cold.
—Browne is out there, aunt Kate, said Mary Jane.
—Browne is everywhere, said aunt Kate lowering her voice.   1025
Mary Jane laughed at her tone.
—Really, she said archly, he is very attentive.
—He has been laid on here like the gas,[5] said aunt Kate in the
same tone, all during the Christmas.
She laughed herself this time good-humouredly and then   1030
added quickly:
—But tell him to come in, Mary Jane, and close the door. I
hope to goodness he didn't hear me.
At that moment the halldoor was opened and Mr Browne
came in from the doorstep, laughing as if his heart would   1035
break. He was dressed in a long green overcoat with mock
astrakhan[6] cuffs and collar and wore on his head an oval fur
cap. He pointed down the snowcovered quay whence the sound
of shrill prolonged whistling was borne in.
—Teddy will have all the cabs in Dublin out, he said.   1040
Gabriel advanced from the little pantry behind the office,
struggling into his overcoat and, looking round the hall, said:

1032 in,] here, AM1   1038 whence] 10; from where AM1, 10G

5. Ubiquitous and inescapable, like gaslight in a house, as opposed to a candle, which one
can move about at will.
6. A fabric made to look like lamb's fur.

—Gretta not down yet?

—She's getting on her things, Gabriel, said aunt Kate.

—Who's playing up there? asked Gabriel.   1045

—Nobody. They're all gone.

—O no, aunt Kate, said Mary Jane. Bartell D'Arcy and Miss O'Callaghan aren't gone yet.

—Someone is strumming at the piano, anyhow, said Gabriel.

Mary Jane glanced at Gabriel and Mr Browne and said with   1050
a shiver:

—It makes me feel cold to look at you two gentlemen muffled up like that. I wouldn't like to face your journey home at this hour.

—I'd like nothing better this minute, said Mr Browne stoutly,   1055
than a rattling fine walk in the country or a fast drive with a good spanking goer[7] between the shafts.

—We used to have a very good horse and trap at home, said aunt Julia sadly.

—The never-to-be-forgotten Johnny, said Mary Jane laughing.   1060
Aunt Kate and Gabriel laughed too.

—Why, what was wonderful about Johnny? asked Mr Browne.

—The late lamented Patrick Morkan, our grandfather that is, explained Gabriel, commonly known in his later years as the   1065
old gentleman, was a glue boiler.[8]

—O now, Gabriel, said aunt Kate laughing, he had a starch mill.

—Well, glue or starch, said Gabriel, the old gentleman had a horse by the name of Johnny. And Johnny used to work in the   1070
old gentleman's mill walking round and round in order to drive the mill. That was all very well; but now comes the tragic part about Johnny. One fine day the old gentleman thought he'd like to drive out with the quality[9] to a military review[1] in the park.   1075

—The Lord have mercy on his soul, said aunt Kate com=
passionately.

—Amen, said Gabriel. So the old gentleman, as I said, har=
nessed Johnny and put on his very best tall hat and his very best stock collar[2] and drove out in grand style from his ancestral   1080
mansion somewhere near Back Lane,[3] I think.

1049 strumming] 10; fooling AM1, 10G   1052 two] t⟨oo⟩wo AM1

7. A horse with a smart and vigorous pace.
8. Glue was made by boiling the hides and hoofs of animals to a jelly.
9. Persons of nobility, high rank, or important social position.
1. Soldiers in uniform performing marching and other drills.
2. A stiff, close-fitting neck cloth worn by men in the nineteenth century.
3. A street in a poor neighborhood south of the Liffey in central Dublin.

Everyone laughed, even Mrs Malins, at Gabriel's manner
and aunt Kate said:

—O now, Gabriel, he didn't live in Back Lane really. Only the
mill was there.   1085

—Out from the mansion of his forefathers, continued Gabriel,
he drove with Johnny. And everything went on beautifully until
Johnny came in sight of King Billy's statue:[4] and whether he fell
in love with the horse King Billy sits on or whether he thought
he was back again in the mill, anyhow he began to walk round   1090
the statue.

Gabriel paced in a circle round the hall in his goloshes amid
the laughter of the others.

—Round and round he went, said Gabriel, and the old gentle=
man, who was a very pompous old gentleman, was highly   1095
indignant. *Go on, sir! What do you mean, sir? Johnny! Johnny!*
Most extraordinary conduct! Can't understand the horse!

The peals of laughter which followed Gabriel's imitation of
the incident were interrupted by a resounding knock at the
halldoor. Mary Jane ran to open it and let in Freddy Malins.   1100
Freddy Malins, with his hat well back on his head and his
shoulders humped with cold, was puffing and steaming after
his exertions.

—I could only get one cab, he said.

—O, we'll find another along the quay, said Gabriel.   1015

—Yes, said aunt Kate. Better not keep Mrs Malins standing in
the draught.

Mrs Malins was helped down the front steps by her son and
Mr Browne and, after many manoeuvres, hoisted into the cab.
Freddy Malins clambered in after her and spent a long time   1110
settling her on the seat, Mr Browne helping him with advice. At
last she was settled comfortably and Freddy Malins invited Mr
Browne into the cab. There was a good deal of confused talk,
then Mr Browne got into the cab. The cabman settled his rug
over his knees and bent down for the address. The confusion   1115
grew greater and the cabman was directed differently by
Freddy Malins and Mr Browne, each of whom had his head out
through a window of the cab. The difficulty was to know
where to drop Mr Browne along the route and aunt Kate, aunt
Julia and Mary Jane helped the discussion from the doorstep   1120

1113–14 There--cab.] ⌐∧There--cab.∧⌐ AM1   1117 Mr] Mr(s). AM1   1120 doorstep]
doorsteps AM1

4. Erected in honor of the Protestant William of Orange, who conquered the Irish at the
   Battle of the Boyne in 1690 and virtually turned Ireland into a penal colony during his
   reign as King William III. His equestrian statue near Trinity College was apparently much
   vandalized.

with cross-directions and contradictions and abundance of laughter. As for Freddy Malins he was speechless with laugh= ter. He popped his head in and out of the window every mo= ment, to the great danger of his hat, and told his mother how the discussion was progressing till at last Mr Browne 1125 shouted to the bewildered cabman above the din of everybody's laughter:

—Do you know Trinity College?⁵

—Yes, sir, said the cabman.

—Well, drive bang up against Trinity College gates, said Mr 1130 Browne, and then we'll tell you where to go. You understand now?

—Yes, sir, said the cabman.

—Make like a bird for Trinity College.

—Right, sir, cried the cabman.   1135

The horse was whipped up and the cab rattled off along the quay amid a chorus of laughter and adieus.

Gabriel had not gone to the door with the others. He was in a dark part of the hall gazing up the staircase. A woman was standing near the top of the first flight in the shadow also. He 1140 could not see her face but he could see the terracotta and salmonpink panels of her skirt which the shadow made appear black and white. It was his wife. She was leaning on the banisters listening to something. Gabriel was surprised at her stillness and strained his ear to listen also. But he could hear 1145 little save the noise of laughter and dispute on the front steps, a few chords struck on the piano and a few notes of a man's voice singing.

He stood still in the gloom of the hall, trying to catch the air that the voice was singing and gazing up at his wife. There was 1150 grace and mystery in her attitude as if she were a symbol of something. He asked himself what is a woman standing on the stairs in the shadow, listening to distant music, a symbol of. If he were a painter he would paint her in that attitude. Her blue felt hat would show off the bronze of her hair against the 1155 darkness and the dark panels of her skirt would show off the light ones. *Distant Music*⁶ he would call the picture if he were a painter.

1124 his] his ⟨head in and out⟩ AM1   1135 cried] 10; said AM1, 10G   1147 man's] 14; male AM1, 10G–14P

5. The prestigious Anglo-Protestant university whose large campus is located in the heart of Dublin on the south side of the Liffey.
6. A possible allusion to Charles Dickens's novel *David Copperfield*, in which the metaphor of distant music describes feeling stirred up in the protagonist by talk of his dead wife.

The halldoor was closed and aunt Kate, aunt Julia and Mary
Jane came down the hall, still laughing.   1160
—Well, isn't Freddy terrible? said Mary Jane. He's really ter=
rible.
Gabriel said nothing but pointed up the stairs towards
where his wife was standing. Now that the halldoor was closed
the voice and the piano could be heard more clearly. Gabriel   1165
held up his hand for them to be silent. The song seemed to be
in the old Irish tonality[7] and the singer seemed uncertain both of
his words and of his voice. The voice made plaintive by the
distance and by the singer's hoarseness faintly illuminated the
cadence of the air with words expressing grief: 1170

> —O, *the rain falls on my heavy locks*
> *And the dew wets my skin,*
> *My babe lies cold* ... [8]

—O, exclaimed Mary Jane. It's Bartell D'Arcy singing and he
wouldn't sing all the night. O, I'll get him to sing a song before   1175
he goes.
—O do, Mary Jane, said aunt Kate.
Mary Jane brushed past the others and ran to the staircase
but before she reached it the singing stopped and the piano was
closed abruptly.   1180
—O, what a pity! she cried. Is he coming down, Gretta?
Gabriel heard his wife answer yes and saw her come down
towards them. A few steps behind her were Mr Bartell D'Arcy
and Miss O'Callaghan.
—O, Mr D'Arcy, cried Mary Jane, it's downright mean of you   1185
to break off like that when we were all in raptures listening to
you.
—I have been at him all the evening, said Miss O'Callaghan,
and Mrs Conroy too, and he told us he had a dreadful cold and
couldn't sing.   1190
—O, Mr D'Arcy, said aunt Kate, now that was a great fib to
tell.
—Can't you see that I'm as hoarse as a crow? said Mr D'Arcy
roughly.

1159 Kate,] Kate ⟨and⟩, AM1   1171 *heavy*] yellow AM1   1172 *wets*] heats AM1
1173 *My--cold* ...] But if you are .... AM1   1182 Gabriel] MS RESUMES

7. Early Irish music based on a five-, six-, or seven-tone scale.
8. From a ballad variously called *The Lass of Aughrim* or "Lord Gregory," probably of Scottish
   origin. Aughrim is a small village in the west of Ireland, and Joyce appears to have learned
   the song from his wife, Nora, who came from Galway. The ballad concerns a young girl
   who has been seduced and abandoned by a lord, and who, with baby in arms, seeks
   admission to his manor.

He went into the pantry hastily and put on his overcoat. The 1195
others, taken aback by his rude speech, could find nothing to
say. Aunt Kate wrinkled her brows and made signs to the
others to drop the subject. Mr D'Arcy stood swathing his neck
carefully and frowning.

—It's the weather, said aunt Julia after a pause.   1200
—Yes, everybody has colds, said aunt Kate readily, everybody.
—They say, said Mary Jane, we haven't had snow like it for
thirty years:[9] and I read this morning in the newspaper that the
snow is general all over Ireland.
—I love the look of snow, said aunt Julia sadly.   1205
—So do I, said Miss O'Callaghan. I think Christmas is never
really Christmas unless we have the snow on the ground.
—But poor Mr D'Arcy doesn't like the snow, said aunt Kate
smiling.

Mr D'Arcy came from the pantry, fully swathed and but=   1210
toned, and in a repentant tone told them the history of his cold.
Everyone gave him advice and said it was a great pity and
urged him to be very careful of his throat in the night air.
Gabriel watched his wife who did not join in the conversation.
She was standing right under the dusty fanlight[1] and the flame 1215
of the gas lit up the rich bronze of her hair which he had seen
her drying at the fire a few days before. She was in the same
attitude and seemed unaware of the talk about her. At last she
turned towards them and Gabriel saw that there was colour on
her cheeks and that her eyes were shining. A sudden tide of joy 1220
went leaping out of his heart.

—Mr D'Arcy, she said, what is the name of that song you were
singing?
—It's called *The Lass of Aughrim*, said Mr D'Arcy, but I
couldn't remember it properly. Why? Do you know it?   1225
—*The Lass of Aughrim*, she repeated. I couldn't think of the
name.
—It's a very nice air, said Mary Jane. I'm sorry you were not
in voice tonight.
—Now, Mary Jane, said aunt Kate, don't annoy Mr D'Arcy. I 1230
won't have him annoyed.

Seeing that all were ready to start she shepherded them to
the door where goodnight was said:
—Well, goodnight aunt Kate, and thanks for the pleasant
evening.   1235

1207 Christmas] MS ENDS

9. Snow is relatively infrequent in Ireland, which is an island warmed by the Gulf Stream.
1. A semicircular window with radiating sash bars like the ribs of a fan.

—Goodnight, Gabriel. Goodnight, Gretta!
—Goodnight, aunt Kate, and thanks ever so much. Goodnight,
aunt Julia.
—O, goodnight, Gretta, I didn't see you.
—Goodnight, Mr D'Arcy. Goodnight, Miss O'Callaghan.   1240
—Goodnight, Miss Morkan.
—Goodnight again.
—Goodnight all. Safe home.
—Goodnight. Goodnight.

The morning was still dark. A dull yellow light brooded   1245
over the houses and the river and the sky seemed to be
descending. It was slushy underfoot and only streaks and
patches of snow lay on the roofs, on the parapets of the quay[2]
and on the area railings. The lamps were still burning redly in
the murky air and, across the river, the palace of the Four   1250
Courts[3] stood out menacingly against the heavy sky.

She was walking on before him with Mr Bartell D'Arcy, her
shoes in a brown parcel tucked under one arm and her hands
holding her skirt up from the slush. She had no longer any
grace of attitude but Gabriel's eyes were still bright with   1255
happiness. The blood went bounding along his veins and the
thoughts went rioting through his brain, proud, joyful, tender,
valorous.

She was walking on before him so lightly and so erect that
he longed to run after her noiselessly, catch her by the shoul=   1260
ders and say something foolish and affectionate into her ear.
She seemed to him so frail that he longed to defend her against
something and then to be alone with her. Moments of their
secret life together burst like stars upon his memory. A helio=
trope[4] envelope was lying beside his breakfast cup and he was   1265
caressing it with his hand. Birds were twittering in the ivy and
the sunny web of the curtain was shimmering along the floor:
he could not eat for happiness. They were standing on the
crowded platform and he was placing a ticket inside the warm
palm of her glove. He was standing with her in the cold, look=   1270
ing in through a grated window at a man making bottles in a
roaring furnace.[5] It was very cold. Her face, fragrant in the cold

1246 over] 14P; above AM1, 10G-10   1254 skirt] 14; skirts AM1, 10G-14P
1266 twittering] twistening AM1

2. Low walls to keep people from falling into the river.
3. A complex of eighteenth-century buildings, on the north side of the Liffey, that houses
   the Dublin law courts and library.
4. A shade of purple.
5. Handblown glass is made by heating a sand and mineral mixture to a molten state in a
   furnace, and then inflating it by blowing into a tube.

air, was quite close to his and suddenly she called out to the
man at the furnace:

—Is the fire hot, sir?   1275

But the man could not hear her with the noise of the furnace.
It was just as well. He might have answered rudely.

A wave of yet more tender joy escaped from his heart and
went coursing in warm flood along his arteries. Like the tender
fire of stars moments of their life together, that no one knew of   1280
or would ever know of, broke upon and illumined his memory.
He longed to recall to her those moments, to make her forget
the years of their dull existence together and remember only
their moments of ecstasy. For the years, he felt, had not
quenched his soul or hers. Their children, his writing, her   1285
household cares had not quenched all their souls' tender fire. In
one letter that he had written to her then he had said: *Why is it
that words like these seem to me so dull and cold? Is it because
there is no word tender enough to be your name?*

Like distant music these words that he had written years   1290
before were borne towards him from the past. He longed to be
alone with her. When the others had gone away, when he and
she were in their room in the hotel, then they would be alone
together. He would call her softly:

—Gretta!   1295

Perhaps she would not hear at once: she would be undress=
ing. Then something in his voice would strike her. She would
turn and look at him ....

At the corner of Winetavern Street[6] they met a cab. He was
glad of its rattling noise as it saved him from conversation. She   1300
was looking out of the window and seemed tired. The others
spoke only a few words, pointing out some building or street.
The horse galloped along wearily under the murky morning
sky, dragging his old rattling box after his heels, and Gabriel
was again in a cab with her galloping to catch the boat,   1305
galloping to their honeymoon.

As the cab drove across O'Connell bridge[7] Miss O'Callaghan
said:

—They say you never cross O'Connell bridge without seeing a
white horse.[8]   1310

1299 Winetavern] 10; Bridgefoot AM1, 10G

6. A street that runs into the south quay of the Liffey, along which the group is walking on
   their way from Usher's Island to O'Connell Street.
7. The most central and major of the Dublin bridges over the river Liffey.
8. A traditional symbol of power and authority, the white horse may also have been particularly associated with King William III.

—I see a white man this time, said Gabriel.

—Where? asked Mr Bartell D'Arcy.

Gabriel pointed to the statue[9] on which lay patches of snow.
Then he nodded familiarly to it and waved his hand.

—Goodnight, Dan, he said gaily.   1315

When the cab drew up before the hotel Gabriel jumped out
and, in spite of Mr Bartell D'Arcy's protest, paid the driver. He
gave the man a shilling over his fare.[1] The man saluted and said:

—A prosperous new year to you, sir.

—The same to you, said Gabriel cordially.   1320

She leaned for a moment on his arm in getting out of the cab
and while standing at the kerbstone bidding the others good=
night. She leaned lightly on his arm, as lightly as when she had
danced with him a few hours before. He had felt proud and
happy then, happy that she was his, proud of her grace and   1325
wifely carriage. But now after the kindling again of so many
memories, the first touch of her body, musical and strange and
perfumed, sent through him a keen pang of lust. Under cover of
her silence he pressed her arm closely to his side: and, as they
stood at the hotel door, he felt that they had escaped from their 1330
lives and duties, escaped from home and friends and run away
together with wild and radiant hearts to a new adventure.

An old man was dozing in a great hooded chair[2] in the hall.
He lit a candle in the office and went before them to the stairs.
They followed him in silence, their feet falling in soft thuds on   1335
the thickly carpeted stairs. She mounted the stairs behind the
porter, her head bowed in the ascent, her frail shoulders curved
as with a burden, her skirt girt tightly about her. He could have
flung his arms about her hips and held her still for his arms
were trembling with desire to seize her and only the stress of   1340
his nails against the palms of his hands held the wild impulse of
his body in check. The porter halted on the stairs to settle his
guttering candle. They halted too on the steps below him. In
the silence Gabriel could hear the falling of the molten wax
into the tray and the thumping of his own heart against his   1345
ribs.

1314 waved] ⟨moved⟩ waved AM1   1338 skirt] 14; skirts AM1, 10G–14P

9. The statue of Irish politician Daniel O'Connell (1775–1847), known as "The Liberator"
   because he successfully opposed and secured the repeal of laws that had penalized Catholics in a variety of ways.
1. If one assumes that Eveline Hill in the story "Eveline" earns seven shillings a week (or
   even a day) as a shop girl, then the shilling tip to the cabdriver is extremely generous.
2. Chairs with an arched projection or hood attached to the sides and back were used in
   hotel lobbies and other open public interiors to protect their occupants from drafts.

The porter led them along a corridor and opened a door. Then he set his unstable candle down on a toilet table[3] and asked at what hour they were to be called in the morning.

—Eight, said Gabriel.   1350

The porter pointed to the tap of the electric light[4] and began a muttered apology but Gabriel cut him short.

—We don't want any light. We have light enough from the street. And, I say, he added pointing to the candle, you might remove that handsome article, like a good man.   1355

The porter took up his candle again, but slowly, for he was surprised by such a novel idea. Then he mumbled goodnight and went out. Gabriel shot the lock to.

A ghostly light from the street lamp lay in a long shaft from one window to the door. Gabriel threw his overcoat and hat on 1360 a couch and crossed the room towards the window. He looked down into the street in order that his emotion might calm a little. Then he turned and leaned against a chest of drawers with his back to the light. She had taken off her hat and cloak and was standing before a large swinging mirror, unhooking 1365 her waist. Gabriel paused for a few moments, watching her, and then said:

—Gretta!

She turned away from the mirror slowly and walked along the shaft of light towards him. Her face looked so serious and 1370 weary that the words would not pass Gabriel's lips. No, it was not the moment yet.

—You look tired, he said.

—I am a little, she answered.

—You don't feel ill or weak?   1375

—No, tired: that's all.

She went on to the window and stood there, looking out. Gabriel waited again and then, fearing that diffidence was about to conquer him, he said abruptly:

—By the way, Gretta!   1380

—What is it?

—You know that poor fellow Malins? he said quickly.

—Yes, what about him?

—Well, poor fellow, he's a decent sort of chap after all, con= tinued Gabriel in a false voice. He gave me back that sovereign[5] 1385 I lent him and I didn't expect it really. It's a pity he wouldn't

---

1347 a(1)] ⟨the⟩ a AM1   1370 so] ⟨as⟩ so AM1

3. A dressing table.
4. The availability of electricity is a mark of the Gresham's elegance at the turn of the century, when most residences (like the Morkans') were still lit by gas lamps.
5. A gold coin representing a pound, or twenty shillings.

keep away from that Browne because he's not a bad fellow at
heart.

He was trembling now with annoyance. Why did she seem
so abstracted? He did not know how he could begin. Was she   1390
annoyed too about something? If she would only turn to him or
come to him of her own accord! To take her as she was would
be brutal. No, he must see some ardour in her eyes first. He
longed to be master of her strange mood.

—When did you lend him the pound? she asked after a pause.   1395

Gabriel strove to restrain himself from breaking out into
brutal language about the sottish Malins and his pound. He
longed to cry to her from his soul, to crush her body against
his, to overmaster her. But he said:

—O, at Christmas, when he opened that little Christmas card   1400
shop in Henry Street.[6]

He was in such a fever of rage and desire that he did not
hear her come from the window. She stood before him for an
instant looking at him strangely. Then, suddenly raising herself
on tiptoe and resting her hands lightly on his shoulders, she   1405
kissed him.

—You are a very generous person, Gabriel, she said.

Gabriel, trembling with delight at her sudden kiss and at the
quaintness of her phrase, put his hands on her hair and began
smoothing it back, scarcely touching it with his fingers. The   1410
washing had made it fine and brilliant. His heart was brimming
over with happiness. Just when he was wishing for it she had
come to him of her own accord. Perhaps her thoughts had been
running with his. Perhaps she had felt the impetuous desire that
was in him and then the yielding mood had come upon her.   1415
Now that she had fallen to him so easily he wondered why he
had been so diffident.

He stood, holding her head between his hands. Then, slip=
ping one arm swiftly about her body and drawing her towards
him, he said softly: 1420

—Gretta dear, what are you thinking about?

She did not answer nor yield wholly to his arm. He said
again softly:

—Tell me what it is, Gretta. I think I know what is the matter.
Do I know?   1425

She did not answer at once. Then she said in an outburst of
tears:

1387–88 at heart.] 10; really— AM1; really.— 10G

6. Possibly a temporary shop opened only during the holiday season, on a busy shopping
   street in central Dublin.

—O, I am thinking about that song, *The Lass of Aughrim*.

She broke loose from him and ran to the bed and, throwing her arms across the bedrail, hid her face. Gabriel stood stock= 1430 still for a moment in astonishment and then followed her. As he passed in the way of the cheval glass[7] he caught sight of himself in full length, his broad, wellfilled shirtfront, the face whose expression always puzzled him when he saw it in a mirror and his glimmering giltrimmed eyeglasses. He halted a 1435 few paces from her and said:

—What about the song? Why does that make you cry?

She raised her head from her arms and dried her eyes with the back of her hand like a child. A kinder note than he had intended went into his voice. 1440

—Why, Gretta? he asked.

—I am thinking about a person long ago who used to sing that song.

—And who was the person long ago? asked Gabriel smiling.

—It was a person I used to know in Galway when I was living 1445 with my grandmother, she said.

The smile passed away from Gabriel's face. A dull anger began to gather again at the back of his mind and the dull fires of his lust began to glow angrily in his veins.

—Someone you were in love with? he asked ironically. 1450

—It was a young boy I used to know, she answered, named Michael Furey. He used to sing that song, *The Lass of Augh=rim*. He was very delicate.

Gabriel was silent. He did not wish her to think that he was interested in this delicate boy. 1455

—I can see him so plainly, she said after a moment. Such eyes as he had, big dark eyes! And such an expression in them—an expression! ...

—O, then you were in love with him? said Gabriel.

—I used to go out walking with him,[8] she said, when I was in 1460 Galway.

A thought flew across Gabriel's mind.

—Perhaps that was why you wanted to go to Galway with that Ivors girl? he said coldly.

She looked at him and asked in surprise: 1465

—What for?

Her eyes made Gabriel feel awkward. He shrugged his shoulders and said:

1435 eyeglasses.] eyeglass. AM1   1462 mind.] GALLEY PROOFS 10G END

7. A mirror swung on a frame, large enough to reflect the whole figure.
8. Keeping company in a romantic way, implying a public courtship.

—How do I know? To see him, perhaps.

She looked away from him along the shaft of light towards 1470
the window in silence.

—He is dead, she said at length. He died when he was only
seventeen. Isn't it a terrible thing to die so young as that?

—What was he? asked Gabriel, still ironically.

—He was in the gasworks,[9] she said.   1475

Gabriel felt humiliated by the failure of his irony and by the
evocation of this figure from the dead, a boy in the gasworks.
The irony of his mood soured into sarcasm. While he had been
full of memories of their secret life together, full of tenderness
and joy and desire, she had been comparing him in her mind 1480
with another. A shameful consciousness of his own person
assailed him. He saw himself as a ludicrous figure, acting as a
pennyboy[1] for his aunts, a nervous wellmeaning sentimentalist,
orating to vulgarians and idealising his own clownish lusts, the
pitiable fatuous fellow he had caught a glimpse of in the 1485
mirror. Instinctively he turned his back more to the light lest
she might see the shame that burned upon his forehead.

He tried to keep up his tone of cold interrogation but his
voice when he spoke was humble and indifferent.

—I suppose you were in love with this Michael Furey, Gretta, 1490
he said.

—I was great with him[2] at that time, she said.

Her voice was veiled and sad. Gabriel, feeling now how vain
it would be to try to lead her whither he had purposed,
caressed one of her hands and said also sadly: 1495

—And what did he die of so young, Gretta? Consumption,
was it?

—I think he died for me, she answered.

A vague terror seized Gabriel at this answer as if, at that
hour when he had hoped to triumph, some impalpable and 1500
vindictive being was coming against him, gathering forces
against him in its vague world. But he shook himself free of it
with an effort of reason and continued to caress her hand. He
did not question her again for he felt that she would tell him of
herself. Her hand was warm and moist: it did not respond to 1505

1473 seventeen.] nineteen. AM1   1473 that?] that—nineteen?— AM1   1477 the(2)]
a AM1   1478 soured] changed AM1   1492 great with] very fond of AM1

9. A utility company producing gas for light and heating from coal. The work would have
   been dirty and the environment full of pollution, dangerous to someone with vulnerable
   lungs.
1. Presumably a boy set to small tasks and errands in return for a penny; someone at another's
   beck and call for small odd jobs.
2. Intimate, but more in a sense of intense emotional friendship than passion.

his touch but he continued to caress it just as he had caressed her first letter to him that spring morning.

—It was in the winter, she said, about the beginning of the winter when I was going to leave my grandmother's and come up here to the convent. And he was ill at the time in his 1510 lodgings in Galway and wouldn't be let out and his people in Oughterard[3] were written to. He was in decline,[4] they said, or something like that. I never knew rightly.

She paused for a moment and sighed.

—Poor fellow, she said, he was very fond of me and he was 1515 such a gentle boy. We used to go out together walking, you know, Gabriel, like the way they do in the country. He was going to study singing only for his health.[5] He had a very good voice, poor Michael Furey.

—Well, and then? asked Gabriel. 1520

—And then when it came to the time for me to leave Galway and come up to the convent he was much worse and I wouldn't be let see him so I wrote him a letter saying I was going up to Dublin and would be back in the summer and hoping he would be better then. 1525

She paused for a moment to get her voice under control and then went on:

—Then the night before I left I was in my grandmother's house in Nun's Island,[6] packing up, and I heard gravel thrown up against the window. The window was so wet I couldn't see so I 1530 ran downstairs as I was and slipped out the back into the garden and there was the poor fellow at the end of the garden shivering.

—And did you not tell him to go back? asked Gabriel.

—I implored of him to go home at once and told him he would 1535 get his death in the rain. But he said he did not want to live. I can see his eyes as well as well! He was standing at the end of the wall where there was a tree.

—And did he go home? asked Gabriel.

—Yes, he went home. And when I was only a week in the 1540 convent he died and he was buried in Oughterard where his people came from. O, the day I heard that, that he was dead! ....

1512 was--decline,] had consumption, AM1   1515–16 was--boy.] had such a gentle manner. AM1   1529 Nun's Island,] Bowling Green, AM1

3. A small village about seventeen miles north of Galway, in western Ireland.
4. Suffering from a wasting disease, commonly tuberculosis.
5. But was prevented by his poor health.
6. A semi-island in the Galway River in the city of Galway, named after a convent located there.

She stopped, choking with sobs and, overcome by emotion, flung herself face downward on the bed, sobbing in the quilt. 1545 Gabriel held her hand for a moment longer, irresolutely, and then, shy of intruding on her grief, let it fall gently and walked quietly to the window.

She was fast asleep.

Gabriel, leaning on his elbow, looked for a few moments 1550 unresentfully at her tangled hair and half open mouth, listening to her deep drawn breath. So she had had that romance in her life: a man had died for her sake. It hardly pained him now to think how poor a part he, her husband, had played in her life. He watched her while she slept as though he and she had never 1555 lived together as man and wife. His curious eyes rested long upon her face and on her hair: and as he thought of what she must have been then, in that time of her first girlish beauty, a strange friendly pity for her entered his soul. He did not like to say even to himself that her face was no longer beautiful but he 1560 knew that it was no longer the face for which Michael Furey had braved death.

Perhaps she had not told him all the story. His eyes moved to the chair over which she had thrown some of her clothes. A petticoat string dangled to the floor. One boot stood upright, 1565 its limp upper fallen down: the fellow of it lay upon its side. He wondered at his riot of emotions of an hour before. From what had it proceeded? From his aunts' supper, from his own foolish speech, from the wine and dancing, the merrymaking when saying goodnight in the hall, the pleasure of the walk along the 1570 river in the snow. Poor aunt Julia! She too would soon be a shade with the shade of Patrick Morkan and his horse. He had caught that haggard look upon her face for a moment when she was singing *Arrayed for the Bridal*. Soon perhaps he would be sitting in that same drawingroom, dressed in black, his silk hat 1575 on his knees. The blinds would be drawn down and aunt Kate would be sitting beside him, crying and blowing her nose and telling him how Julia had died. He would cast about in his mind for some words that might console her and would find only lame and useless ones. Yes, yes: that would happen very 1580 soon.[7]

The air of the room chilled his shoulders. He stretched him=

1544 emotion,] emotion AM1   1545 flung] MS RESUMES   1561 Furey] ⟨Fury⟩ Furey MS

7. In Joyce's novel *Ulysses*, set on June 16, 1904, Leopold Bloom thinks of Julia Morkan in a way that suggests that she has died by then—less than six months after the events of "The Dead."

self cautiously along under the sheets and lay down beside his wife. One by one they were all becoming shades. Better pass boldly into that other world, in the full glory of some passion, 1585 than fade and wither dismally with age. He thought of how she who lay beside him had locked in her heart for so many years that image of her lover's eyes when he had told her that he did not wish to live.

Generous tears filled Gabriel's eyes. He had never felt like 1590 that himself towards any woman but he knew that such a feeling must be love. The tears gathered more thickly in his eyes and in the partial darkness he imagined he saw the form of a young man standing under a dripping tree. Other forms were near. His soul had approached that region where dwell the vast 1595 hosts of the dead. He was conscious of, but could not appre= hend, their wayward and flickering existence. His own identity was fading out into a grey impalpable world: the solid world itself which these dead had one time reared and lived in was dissolving and dwindling. 1600

A few light taps upon the pane made him turn to the win= dow. It had begun to snow again. He watched sleepily the flakes, silver and dark, falling obliquely against the lamplight. The time had come for him to set out on his journey westward.[8] Yes, the newspapers were right: snow was general all over 1605 Ireland. It was falling on every part of the dark central plain, on the treeless hills, falling softly upon the Bog of Allen[9] and, farther westward, softly falling into the dark mutinous Shan= non[1] waves. It was falling, too, upon every part of the lonely churchyard on the hill where Michael Furey lay buried. It lay 1610 thickly drifted on the crooked crosses and headstones, on the spears of the little gate, on the barren thorns. His soul swooned slowly as he heard the snow falling faintly through the universe and faintly falling, like the descent of their last end, upon all the living and the dead. 1615

1610 Furey] ⟨Fury⟩ Furey MS

8. "To go west" is a figurative expression meaning to die, perish, or disappear.
9. An extensive area of soggy ground, some twenty-five miles south of Dublin.
1. A great river that traverses western Ireland from the north to the southwest.

CONTEXTS

A Curious History

[In 1911, enraged at the imminent failure of his second attempt to get *Dubliners* published, James Joyce wrote an open letter to the British and the Irish press. Two papers printed it. In late 1913, he refashioned the letter into a preface for the first edition of *Dubliners*. No doubt—and rightly—anticipating that Grant Richards would be less than enthusiastic about it, he simultaneously sent it to Ezra Pound, who printed it in his weekly column in *The Egoist* under the title *"A Curious History."* The present text is reprinted diplomatically from *The Egoist* of 15 January 1914, pp. 26–27, though augmented by the excerpt from *"Ivy Day in the Committee Room"* there omitted. As a text, *"A Curious History"* is strangely structured. At its center, it conjoins a letter from Buckingham Palace and a lacuna for the *"Ivy Day"* passage. (This has an exceptional publication status of its own. *The James Joyce Archive*, vol. [4], p. 269, reproduces an exemplar of the excerpt slips of the passage that Joyce had specially printed to illustrate his grievance, and from which we take the text for the present inclusion.) Letter and lacuna are boxed in Joyce's 1911 letter to the press as modified for the 1913/1914 occasion. This in turn is framed in and to its intended preface purpose, and the whole is framed finally in Pound's column commentary.—Hans Walter Gabler]

A *Curious History.*

The following statement having been received by me from an author of known and notable talents, and the state of the case being now, so far as I know, precisely what it was at the date of his last letter (November 30th), I have thought it more appropriate to print his communication entire than to indulge in my usual biweekly comment upon books published during the fortnight.

Mr. Joyce's statement is as follows:—

The following letter, which gives the history of a book of stories, was sent by me to the Press of the United Kingdom two years ago. It was published by two newspapers so far as I know: "Sinn Fein" (Dublin) and the "Northern Whig" (Belfast).

> Via della Barriera Vecchia 32 III.,
> Trieste,
> Austria.

SIR,

May I ask you to publish this letter, which throws some light on the present conditions of authorship in England and Ireland?

Nearly six years ago Mr. Grant Richards, publisher, of London, signed a contract with me for the publication of a book of stories written by me, entitled "Dubliners." Some ten months later he wrote asking me to omit one of the stories and passages in others which,

197

as he said, his printer refused to set up. I declined to do either, and a correspondence began between Mr. Grant Richards and myself which lasted more than three months. I went to an international jurist in Rome (where I lived then) and was advised to omit. I declined to do so, and the MS. was returned to me, the publisher refusing to publish, notwithstanding his pledged printed word, the contract remaining in my possession.

Six months afterwards a Mr. Hone wrote to me from Marseilles to ask me to submit the MS. to Messrs. Maunsel, publishers, of Dublin. I did so; and after about a year, in July, 1909, Messrs. Maunsel signed a contract with me for the publication of the book on or before 1st September, 1910. In December, 1909, Messrs. Maunsel's manager begged me to alter a passage in one of the stories, "Ivy Day in the Committee Room," wherein some reference was made to Edward VII. I agreed to do so, much against my will, and altered one or two phrases. Messrs. Maunsel continually postponed the date of publication and in the end wrote, asking me to omit the passage or to change it radically. I declined to do either, pointing out that Mr. Grant Richards, of London, had raised no objection to the passage when Edward VII. was alive, and that I could not see why an Irish publisher should raise an objection to it when Edward VII. had passed into history. I suggested arbitration or a deletion of the passage with a prefatory note of explanation by me, but Messrs. Maunsel would agree to neither. As Mr. Hone (who had written to me in the first instance) disclaimed all responsibility in the matter and any connection with the firm I took the opinion of a solicitor in Dublin, who advised me to omit the passage, informing me that as I had no domicile in the United Kingdom I could not sue Messrs. Maunsel for breach of contract unless I paid £100 into court, and that even if I paid £100 into court and sued them, I should have no chance of getting a verdict in my favour from a Dublin jury if the passage in dispute could be taken as offensive in any way to the late King. I wrote then to the present King, George V., enclosing a printed proof of the story, with the passage therein marked, and begging him to inform me whether in his view the passage (certain allusions made by a person of the story in the idiom of his social class) should be withheld from publication as offensive to the memory of his father. His Majesty's private secretary sent me this reply:—

                                            Buckingham Palace.
The private secretary is commanded to acknowledge the receipt of Mr. James Joyce's letter of the 1st instant, and to inform him that it is inconsistent with rule for his Majesty to express his opinion in such cases. The enclosures are returned herewith.
    11th August, 1911.

Here is the passage in dispute:

>—But look here, John,—said Mr O'Connor.—Why should we welcome the king of England? Didn't Parnell himself . . . ?—
>
>—Parnell,—said Mr Henchy,—is dead. Now, here's the way I look at it. Here's this chap come to the throne after his old mother keeping him out of it till the man was grey. He's a man of the world and he means well by us. He's a jolly fine decent fellow, if you ask me, and no damn nonsense about him. He just says to himself:—*The old one never went to see these wild Irish. By Christ, I'll go myself and see what they're like.*—And are we going to insult the man when he comes over here on a friendly visit? Eh? Isn't that right, Crofton?—
>
>—Mr Crofton nodded his head.
>
>—But after all now,—said Mr Lyons, argumentatively,—King Edward's life, you know, is not the very . . . —
>
>—Let bygones be bygones,—said Mr Henchy—I admire the man personally. He's just an ordinary knockabout like you and me. He's fond of his glass of grog and he's a bit of a rake, perhaps, and he's a good sportsman. Damn it, can't we Irish play fair?—

I wrote this book seven years ago and hold two contracts for its publication. I am not even allowed to explain my case in a prefatory note: wherefore, as I cannot see in any quarter a chance that my rights will be protected, I hereby give Messrs. Maunsel publicly permission to publish this story with what changes or deletions they may please to make, and shall hope that what they may publish may resemble that to the writing of which I gave thought and time. Their attitude as an Irish publishing firm may be judged by Irish public opinion. I, as a writer, protest against the systems (legal, social, and ceremonious) which have brought me to this pass.

Thanking you for your courtesy,
I am, Sir,
Your obedient servant,
JAMES JOYCE.

18th August, 1911.

I waited nine months after the publication of this letter. Then I went to Ireland and entered into negotiations with Messrs. Maunsel. They asked me to omit from the collection the story, "An Encounter," passages in "Two Gallants," the "Boarding House," "A Painful Case," and to change everywhere through the book the names of restaurants, cake-shops, railway stations, public-houses, laundries, bars, and other places of business. After having argued against their point of view day after day for six weeks and after having laid the matter before two solicitors (who, while they informed me that the publishing firm had made a breach of contract, refused to take up my case or to allow their names to be associated with it in any way), I consented in despair to all these changes on condition that the book were brought out without delay and the original text were restored in future editions, if such were called for. Then Messrs. Maunsel asked me to pay into their bank as security £1,000 or to find two sureties of £500 each. I declined to do either; and they then wrote to me, informing me that they would not publish the book, altered or unaltered, and that if I did not make them an offer to cover their losses on printing it they would sue me to recover same. I offered to pay sixty per cent. of the cost of printing the first edition of one thousand copies if the edition were made over to my order. This offer was accepted, and I arranged with my brother in Dublin to publish and sell the book for me. On the morning when the draft and agreement were to be signed the publishers informed me that the matter was at an end because the printer refused to hand over the copies. I took legal advice upon this, and was informed that the printer could not claim the money due to him by the publisher until he had handed over the copies. I then went to the printer. His foreman told me that the printer had decided to forego all claim to the money due to him. I asked whether the printer would hand over the complete edition to a London or Continental firm or to my brother or to me if he were fully indemnified. He said that the copies would never leave his printing-house, and added that the type had been broken up, and that the entire edition of one thousand copies would be burnt the next day. I left Ireland the next day, bringing with me a printed copy of the book which I had obtained from the publisher.

JAMES JOYCE.

Via Donato Bramante 4, II.,
Trieste,
30th November, 1913.

Gas from a Burner

[James Joyce had enormous difficulties with his Dublin publisher, Maunsel & Co., whose manager, George Roberts, demanded a large number of changes in the *Dubliners* stories to which Joyce would not agree. The publisher's complaints included the questionable subject matter of "An Encounter," coarse language (notably the adjective "bloody"), indelicate references to the British king Edward VII's personal life, and the naming of actual Dublin businesses, whose owners might

have grounds to sue for libel. Matters reached an impasse in 1912, and
Joyce agreed to purchase the sheets that the printer, John Falconer, had
already printed. But before the transaction was completed, Falconer
destroyed the sheets, possibly because under current law he was liable
for any actions brought against the book if Joyce succeeded in publishing
it elsewhere. Joyce was distraught over this destruction of his work and
left Dublin the next day, stopping briefly in London before returning to
his home in Trieste with his family. On the journey from London to Trieste, he wrote a bitter broadside called "Gas from a Burner," in which
George Roberts seems to satirically confess his cowardly hypocrisies as a
publisher.—Margot Norris]

From *Gas from a Burner*.

Ladies and gents, you are here assembled
To hear why earth and heaven trembled
Because of the black and sinister arts
Of an Irish writer in foreign parts.
He sent me a book ten years ago
I read it a hundred times or so,
Backwards and forwards, down and up,
Through both the ends of a telescope.
I printed it all to the very last word
But by the mercy of the Lord
The darkness of my mind was rent
And I saw the writer's foul intent.
But I owe a duty to Ireland:
I hold her honour in my hand,
This lovely land that always sent
Her writers and artists to banishment
And in a spirit of Irish fun
Betrayed her own leaders, one by one.
'Twas Irish humour, wet and dry,
Flung quicklime into Parnell's eye;
'Tis Irish brains that save from doom
The leaky barge of the Bishop of Rome
For everyone knows the Pope can't belch
Without the consent of Billy Walsh.
O Ireland my first and only love
Where Christ and Caesar are hand and glove!
O lovely land where the shamrock grows!
(Allow me, ladies, to blow my nose)
To show you for strictures I don't care a button
I printed the poems of Mountainy Mutton
And a play he wrote (you've read it, I'm sure)
Where they talk of *"bastard"* *"bugger"* and *"whore"*

And a play on the Word and Holy Paul
And some woman's legs that I can't recall
Written by Moore, a genuine gent
That lives on his property's ten per cent:

*   *   *

I printed folklore from North and South
By Gregory of the Golden Mouth:
I printed poets, sad, silly and solemn:
I printed Patrick What-do-you-Colm:
I printed the great John Milicent Synge
Who soars above on an angel's wing
In the playboy shift that he pinched as swag
From Maunsel's manager's travelling-bag.
But I draw the line at that bloody fellow,
That was over here dressed in Austrian yellow,
Spouting Italian by the hour
To O' Leary Curtis and John Wyse Power
And writing of Dublin, dirty and dear,
In a manner no blackamoor printer could bear.
Shite and onions! Do you think I'll print
The name of the Wellington Monument,
Sydney Parade and the Sandymount tram,
Downes's cakeshop and Williams's jam?
I'm damned if I do—I'm damned to blazes!
Talk about *Irish Names of Places!*
Its a wonder to me, upon my soul,
He forgot to mention Curly's Hole.
No, ladies, my press shall have no share in
So gross a libel on Stepmother Erin.
I pity the poor—that's why I took
A red-headed Scotchman to keep my book.
Poor sister Scotland! Her doom is fell;
She cannot find any more Stuarts to sell.
My conscience is fine as Chinese silk:
My heart is as soft as buttermilk.
Colm can tell you I made a rebate
Of one hundred pounds on the estimate
I gave him for his Irish Review.
I love my country—by herrings I do!
I wish you could see what tears I weep
When I think of the emigrant train and ship.
That's why I publish far and wide
My quite illegible railway guide.

In the porch of my printing institute
The poor and deserving prostitute
Plays every night at catch-as-catch-can
With her tight-breeched British artilleryman
And the foreigner learns the gift of the gab
From the drunken draggletail Dublin drab.
Who was it said: Resist not evil?
I'll burn that book, so help me devil.
I'll sing a psalm as I watch it burn
And the ashes I'll keep in a one-handled urn.
I'll penance do with farts and groans
Kneeling upon my marrowbones.
This very next lent I will unbare
My penitent buttocks to the air
And sobbing beside my printing press
My awful sin I will confess.
My Irish foreman from Bannockburn
Shall dip his right hand in the urn
And sign crisscross with reverent thumb
Memento homo upon my bum.

COURTESY OF THE NATIONAL LIBRARY OF IRELAND.

"The Sisters"

In July 1904, George Russell, the editor of *The Irish Homestead,* wrote to Joyce and asked, "Could you write anything simple, rural?, livemaking?, pathos?, which could be inserted so as not to shock the readers. . . . You can sign it any name you like as a pseudonym." Joyce's response was to write this version of "The Sisters," which was published in *The Irish Homestead* on August 13, 1904. Taking Russell's prompt, he signed the story "Stephen Dædalus," the name he had given to the protagonist of his work in progress, a novel called *Stephen Hero.*

OUR WEEKLY STORY.

The Sisters.

BY STEPHEN DÆDALUS.

Three nights in succession I had found myself in Great Britain-street at that hour, as if by Providence. Three nights also I had raised my eyes to that lighted square of window and speculated. I seemed to understand that it would occur at night. But in spite of the Providence that had led my feet, and in spite of the reverent curiosity of my eyes, I had discovered nothing. Each night the square was lighted in the same way, faintly and evenly. It was not the light of candles, so far as I could see. Therefore, it had not yet occurred.

On the fourth night at that hour I was in another part of the city. It may have been the same Providence that led me there—a whimsical kind of Providence to take me at a disadvantage. As I went home I wondered was that square of window lighted as before, or did it reveal the ceremonious candles in whose light the Christian must take his last sleep. I was not surprised, then, when at supper I found myself a prophet. Old Cotter and my uncle were talking at the fire, smoking. Old Cotter is the old distiller who owns the batch of prize setters. He used to be very interesting when I knew him first, talking about "faints" and "worms." Now I find him tedious.

While I was eating my stirabout I heard him saying to my uncle:

"Without a doubt. Upper storey—(he tapped an unnecessary hand at his forehead)—gone."

"So they said. I never could see much of it. I thought he was sane enough."

"So he was, at times," said old Cotter.

I sniffed the "was" apprehensively, and gulped down some stirabout.

"Is he better, Uncle John?"

"He's dead."

"O . . . he's dead?"

"Died a few hours ago."

"Who told you?"

"Mr. Cotter here brought us the news. He was passing there."

"Yes, I just happened to be passing, and I noticed the window . . . you know."

"Do you think they will bring him to the chapel?" asked my aunt.

"Oh, no, ma'am. I wouldn't say so."

"Very unlikely," my uncle agreed.

So old Cotter had got the better of me for all my vigilance of three nights. It is often annoying the way people will blunder on what you have elaborately planned for. I was sure he would die at night.

The following morning after breakfast I went down to look at the little house in Great Britain-street. It was an unassuming shop registered under the vague name of "Drapery." The drapery was principally children's boots and umbrellas, and on ordinary days there used to be a notice hanging in the window, which said "Umbrellas recovered." There was no notice visible now, for the shop blinds were drawn down and a crape bouquet was tied to the knocker with white ribbons. Three women of the people and a telegram boy were reading the card pinned on the crape. I also went over and read:—"July 2nd, 189— The Rev. James Flynn (formerly of St. Ita's Church), aged 65 years. R.I.P."

Only sixty-five! He looked much older than that. I often saw him sitting at the fire in the close dark room behind the shop, nearly smothered in his great coat. He seemed to have almost stupefied himself with heat, and the gesture of his large trembling hand to his nostrils had grown automatic. My aunt, who is what they call good-hearted, never went into the shop without bringing him some High Toast, and he used to take the packet of snuff from her hands, gravely inclining his head for sign of thanks. He used to sit in that stuffy room for the greater part of the day from early morning while Nannie (who is almost stone deaf) read out the newspaper to him. His other sister, Eliza, used to mind the shop. These two old women used to look after him, feed him, and clothe him. The clothing was not difficult, for his ancient, priestly clothes were quite green with age, and his dogskin slippers were everlasting. When he was tired of hearing the news he used to rattle his snuff-box on the arm of his chair to avoid shouting at her, and then he used to make believe to read his Prayer Book. Make believe, because, when Eliza brought his a cup of soup from the kitchen, she had always to waken him.

As I stood looking up at the crape and the card that bore his name I could not realise that he was dead. He seemed like one who could go on living for ever if he only wanted to; his life was so methodical and uneventful. I think he said more to me than to anyone else. He

had an egoistic contempt for all women-folk, and suffered all their
services to him in polite silence. Of course, neither of his sisters were
very intelligent. Nannie, for instance, had been reading out the newspaper to him every day for years, and could read tolerably well, and
yet she always spoke of it as the *Freeman's General*. Perhaps he found
me more intelligent, and honoured me with words for that reason.
Nothing, practically nothing, ever occurred to remind him of his
former life (I mean friends or visitors), and still he could remember
every detail of it in his own fashion. He had studied at the college
in Rome, and he taught me to speak Latin in the Italian way. He
often put me through the responses of the Mass, he smiling often
and pushing huge pinches of snuff up each nostril alternately. When
he smiled he used to uncover his big, discoloured teeth, and let his
tongue lie on his lower lip. At first this habit of his used to make me
feel uneasy. Then I grew used to it.

That evening my aunt visited the house of mourning and took me
with her. It was an oppressive summer evening of faded gold. Nannie
received us in the hall, and, as it was no use saying anything to her,
my aunt shook hands with her for all. We followed the old woman
upstairs and into the dead-room. The room, through the lace end of
the blind, was suffused with dusky golden light, amid which the candles looked like pale, thin flames. He had been coffined. Nannie gave
the lead, and we three knelt down at the foot of the bed. There was
no sound in the room for some minutes except the sound of Nannie's
mutterings—for she prays noisily. The fancy came to me that the old
priest was smiling as he lay there in his coffin.

But, no. When we rose and went up to the head of the bed I
saw that he was not smiling. There he lay solemn and copious in
his brown habit, his large hands loosely retaining his rosary. His
face was very grey and massive, with distended nostrils and circled
with scanty white fur. There was a heavy odour in the room—the
flowers.

We sat downstairs in the little room behind the shop, my aunt and
I and the two sisters. Nannie sat in a corner and said nothing, but
her lips moved from speaker to speaker with a painfully intelligent
motion. I said nothing either, being too young, but my aunt spoke a
good deal, for she is a bit of a gossip—harmless.

"Ah, well, he's gone!"

"To enjoy his eternal reward, Miss Flynn, I'm sure. He was a good
and holy man."

"He was a good man, but, you see . . . he was a disappointed man
. . . You see, his life was, you might say, crossed."

"Ah, yes! I know what you mean."

"Not that he was anyway mad, as you know yourself, but he was
always a little queer. Even when we were all growing up together he

was queer. One time he didn't speak hardly for a month. You know, he was that kind always."

"Perhaps he read too much, Miss Flynn?"

"O, he read a good deal, but not latterly. But it was his scrupulousness, I think, affected his mind. The duties of the priesthood were too much for him."

"Did he . . . peacefully?"

"O, quite peacefully, ma'am. You couldn't tell when the breath went out of him. He had a beautiful death, God be praised."

"And everything . . . ?"

"Father O'Rourke was in with him yesterday and gave him the Last Sacrament."

"He knew then?"

"Yes; he was quite resigned."

Nannie gave a sleepy nod and looked ashamed.

"Poor Nannie," said her sister, "she's worn out. All the work we had, getting in a woman, and laying him out; and then the coffin and arranging about the funeral. God knows we did all we could, as poor as we are. We wouldn't see him want anything at the last."

"Indeed you were both very kind to him while he lived."

"Ah, poor James; he was no great trouble to us. You wouldn't hear him in the house no more than now. Still I know he's gone and all that. . . . I won't be bringing him in his soup any more, nor Nannie reading him the paper, nor you, ma'am, bringing him his snuff. How he liked that snuff! Poor James!"

"O, yes, you'll miss him in a day or two more than you do now."

Silence invaded the room until memory reawakened it, Eliza speaking slowly—

"It was that chalice he broke. . . . Of course, it was all right. I mean it contained nothing. But still . . . They say it was the boy's fault. But poor James was so nervous, God be merciful to him."

"Yes, Miss Flynn, I heard that . . . about the chalice . . . He . . . his mind was a bit affected by that."

"He began to mope by himself, talking to no one, and wandering about. Often he couldn't be found. One night he was wanted, and they looked high up and low down and couldn't find him. Then the clerk suggested the chapel. So they opened the chapel (it was late at night), and brought in a light to look for him . . . And there, sure enough, he was, sitting in his confession-box in the dark, wide awake, and laughing like softly to himself. Then they knew something was wrong."

"God rest his soul!"

"An Encounter"

The map below shows the boys' wandering in "An Encounter."

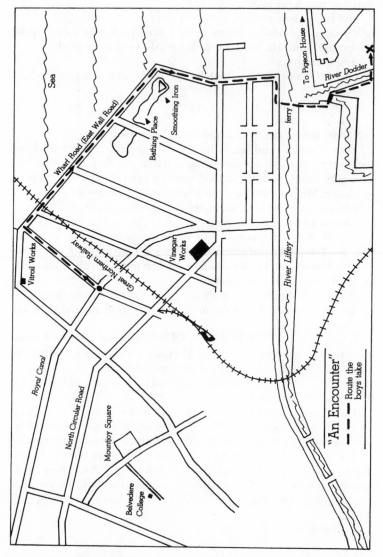

In the story "An Encounter," the boys plan to take off school for a day to seek adventure. "We arranged to go along the Wharf Road until we came to the ships, then to cross in the ferryboat and walk out to see the Pigeon House." The boys probably wished to explore the ruins of the Pigeon House Fort, located near the Dublin electric power station on Pigeon House Road. PHOTOGRAPH COURTESY OF BRUCE BIDWELL AND LINDA HEFFER BIDWELL.

"An Encounter" begins: "It was Joe Dillon who introduced the wild west to us. He had a little library made up of old numbers of *The Union Jack, Pluck* and *The Halfpenny Marvel*." The images below represent an advertisement for *Union Jack* and a typical cover of *Pluck*.

IMAGES COURTESY OF JOHN WYSE JACKSON.

"Araby"

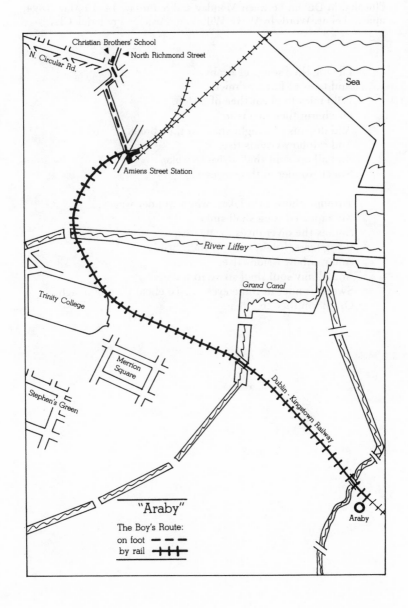

Christian Brothers' School

North Richmond Street

N. Circular Rd.

Sea

Amiens Street Station

River Liffey

Grand Canal

Trinity College

Merrion Square

Stephen's Green

Dublin-Kingstown Railway

Araby

"Araby"

The Boy's Route:

on foot – – –

by rail ┼┼┼

The words to the song that might have served as the motif of the Araby
Bazaar, the "Grand Oriental Fête" staged as a benefit for the Jervis Street
Hospital in Dublin between Monday and Saturday, 14–19 May, 1894,
appear below. Words by W. G. Wills and music by Frederick Clay.

> I'll sing thee songs of Araby,
> And tales of fair Cashmere,
> Wild tales to cheat thee of a sigh,
> Or charm thee to a tear.
> And dreams of delight shall on thee break,
> And rainbow visions rise,
> And all my soul shall strive to wake
> Sweet wonder in thine eyes . . .
>
> Through those twin lakes, when wonder wages,
> My raptured song shall sink,
> And as the diver dives for pearls,
> Bring tears, bright tears to their brink,
> And rainbow visions rise,
> And all my soul shall strive to wake,
> Sweet wonder in thine eyes . . . To cheat thee of a sigh,
> Or charm thee to a tear!

Below is the back of the "Araby" catalogue.

Magnificent Representation

OF

AN ORIENTAL CITY.
CAIRO DONKEYS & DONKEY BOYS
AN ARAB ENCAMPMENT.

INTERNATIONAL TUG-OF-WAR

DANCES BY 250 TRAINED CHILDREN.

Eastern Magic from the Egyptian Hall, London.

CAFE CHANTANT WITH ALL THE LATEST PARISIAN SUCCESSES.

SKIRT DANCING up to Date.

TABLEAUX. THEATRICALS. CHRISTY MINSTRELS.

GRAND THEATRE OF VARIETIES.

"THE ALHAMBRA," An Orchestra of 50 Performers.

Switchback Railways and Roundabouts.

"MENOTTI," The King of the Air,

THE GREAT STOCKHOLM WONDER.

BICYCLE POLO.   RIFLE & CLAY PIGEON SHOOTING.

DANCING.

THE EUTERPEAN LADIES' ORCHESTRA.

EIGHT MILITARY BANDS,

Magnificent Displays of Fireworks,

BY BROCK, OF THE CRYSTAL PALACE, LONDON.

ADMISSION   ·   ·   ONE SHILLING

The narrator of "Araby" reports that as he was about to leave for the bazaar, he had the following conversation with his uncle. "He asked me where I was going and when I had told him a second time he asked me did I know *The Arab's Farewell to his Steed*. When I left the kitchen he was about to recite the opening lines of the piece to my aunt." See pp. 214–15 for Caroline Norton's text.

Arab's Farewell to his Steed

CAROLINE NORTON[1]

My beautiful! my beautiful! that standest meekly by.
With thy proudly arch'd and glossy neck, and dark and fiery eye,
Fret not to roam the desert now with all thy winged speed,
I may not mount on thee again—thou'rt sold, my Arab steed.
Fret not with that impatient hoof, snuff not the breezy wind,
The further that thou fliest now, so far am I behind.
The stranger hath thy bridle rein—thy master hath his gold—
Fleet limbed and beautiful, farewell, thou'rt sold, my steed, thou'rt
    sold.
Farewell, these free untired limbs full many a mile must roam,
To reach the chill and wintry sky which clouds the stranger's home.
Some other hand, less fond, must now thy corn and bed prepare—
The silky mane I braided once must be another's care.
The morning sun shall dawn again, but never more with thee
Shall I gallop through the desert paths where we were wont to be.
Evening shall darken on the earth, and o'er the sandy plain,
Some other steed, with slower step, shall bear me home again.
Yes, thou must go, the wild, free breeze, the brilliant sun and sky,
Thy master's home, from all of these my exiled one must fly.
Thy proud dark eye will grow less proud, thy step become less fleet,
And vainly shalt thou arch thy neck thy master's hand to meet.
Only in sleep shall I behold that dark eye glancing bright;
Only in sleep shall hear again that step so firm and light;
And when I raise my dreaming arm to check and cheer thy speed,
Then must I startling wake to feel thou'rt sold, my Arab steed.
Ah! rudely then, unseen by me, some cruel hand may chide,
Till foam-wreathes lie, like crested waves, along thy panting side,
And the rich blood that is in thee swell in thy indignant pain,
Till careless eyes, which rest on thee, may count each started vein.
Will they ill-use thee? If I thought—but no it cannot be—
Thou art so swift yet easy curbed, so gentle yet so free.
And yet, if haply when thou'rt gone, my lonely heart should yearn,
Can the hand which casts thee from it now command thee to return?
Return, alas! my Arab steed, what shall thy master do,
When thou who wert his all of joy hath vanished from his view;
When the dim distance cheats mine eye, and, through the gathering
    tears,
Thy bright form, for a moment, like the false mirage appears?
Slow and unmounted will I roam, with weary foot, alone,

1. English writer (1808–1877).

Where with fleet step and joyous bound thou oft has borne me on.
And sitting down by that green well I'll pause and sadly think,
It was here he bowed his glossy neck when last I saw him drink.
When last I saw thee drink? Away! the fevered dream is o'er,
I could not live a day and know that we should meet no more.
They tempted me, my beautiful! for hunger's power is strong,
They tempted me, my beautiful! but I have loved too long.
Who said that I'd giv'n thee up, who said that thou wert sold?
'Tis false, 'tis false, my Arab steed, I fling them back their gold;
Thus, thus, I leap upon thy back and scour the distant plains,
Away! who overtakes us now shall claim thee for his pains.

"Eveline"

OUR WEEKLY STORY.

Eveline.†

BY STEPHEN DÆDALUS.

She sat at the window watching the evening invade the avenue.
Her head was leaned against the window-curtain, and in her nostrils
was the odour of dusty cretonne. She was tired. Few people passed.
The man out of the last house passed on his way home; she heard
his footsteps clacking along the concrete pavement, and afterwards
crunching on the cinder path before the new red houses. One time
there used to be a field there, in which they used to play in the
evening with other people's children. Then a man from Belfast
bought the field and built houses in it—not like their little brown
houses, but bright brick houses, with shining roofs. The children of
the avenue used to play together in that field—the Devines, the
Waters, the Dunns, little Keogh, the cripple, she and her brothers
and sisters. Ernest, however, never played; he was too grown-up. Her
father used often to hunt them in out of the field with his blackthorn
stick, but usually little Keogh used to keep "nix," and call out when
he saw her father coming. Still they seemed to have been rather
happy then. Her father was not so bad then, and besides her mother
was alive. That was a long time ago; she and her brothers and sisters
were all grown up; her mother was dead; Mrs. Dunn was dead, too,
and the Waters had gone back to England. Everything changes; now
she was going to go away, to leave her home.

† From *The Irish Homestead*, September 10, 1904.

Home! She looked round the room, passing in review all its familiar objects. How many times she had dusted it, once a week at least.
It was the "best" room, but it seemed to secrete dust everywhere.
She had known the room for ten years—more—twelve years, and
knew everything in it. Now she was going away. And yet during all
those years she had never found out the name of the Australian priest
whose yellowing photograph hung on the wall, just above the broken
harmonium. He had been a friend of her father's—a school friend.
When he showed the photograph to a friend, her father used to pass
it with a casual word, "In Australia now—Melbourne."

She had consented to go away—to leave her home. Was it wise—
was it honourable? She tried to weigh each side of the question in
her mind. In her home at least she had shelter and food; she had
those whom she had known all her life about her. She had to work
of course both in the house and at business. What would they think
of her in the Stores when they discovered she had gone away? Think
her a fool, perhaps, and fill up her place by advertisement. Miss
Gavan would probably be glad. She, too, would not be sorry to be
out of Miss Gavan's clutches. Miss Gavan had an "edge" on her, and
used her superior position mercilessly, particularly whenever there
were people listening. It was—"Miss Hill, will you please attend to
these ladies?" "A little bit smarter, Miss Hill, if you please." She
would not cry many tears at leaving the Stores. In her new home in
a distant, unknown country, surely she would be free from such
indignities! She would then be a married woman—she, Eveline. She
would be treated with respect. She would not be treated as her
mother had been treated. Even now—at her age, she was over nineteen—she sometimes felt herself in danger of her father's violence.
Latterly he had begun to threaten her, saying what he would do were
it not for her dead mother's sake. And now she had nobody to protect
her. Ernest was dead, and Harry, who was in the church-decorating
business, was nearly always down somewhere in the country.
Besides, the invariable squabble for money on Saturday night had
begun to weary her unspeakably. She always gave her entire wages—
seven shillings—and Harry always sent up what he could, but the
trouble was to get any money from her father. He said she used to
squander the money, that she had no head, that he wasn't going to
give her his hard-earned money to throw about the streets, and much
more, for he was usually fairly bad on Saturday night. In the end he
would give her the money, and ask her had she any intention of
buying Sunday's dinner. Then she had to rush out as quickly as she
could and do her marketing, holding her black leather purse tightly
in her hand as she elbowed her way through the crowds and returning home late under her load of provisions. She had hard work to

keep the house together, and to see that the two young children who had been left to her charge went to school regularly and got their meals regularly. It was hard work—a hard life—but now that she was about to leave it she did not find it a wholly undesirable life.

She was about to explore another life with Frank. Frank was very kind, manly, open-hearted. She was to go away with him by the night boat to be his wife, and to live with him in Buenos Ayres, where he had a home waiting for her. How well she remembered the first time she had seen him (he was lodging in a house on the main road where she used to visit). A few weeks ago it seemed. He was standing at the gate, his peaked cap pushed back on his head, and his hair tumbled forward over a face of bronze. Then they had come to know each other. He used to meet her outside the Stores every evening, and see her home. He took her to see the "Bohemian Girl," and she felt elated as she sat in an unaccustomed part of the theatre with him. He was very fond of music, and sang a little. People knew that they were courting, and when Frank sang about the lass that loves a sailor she always felt pleasantly confused. He used to call her "Poppens" out of fun. First it had been an excitement for her to have a young man, and then she had begun to like him. He had tales of distant countries. He had started as a deck boy at a pound a month on a ship of the Allan line going out to Canada. He told her the names of the ships he had been on, and the names of the different services. He had sailed through the Straits of Magellan, and he told her stories of the terrible Patagonians. He had fallen on his feet in Buenos Ayres, he said, and had come over to the old country just for a holiday. Of course, her father had found out the affair, and had forbidden her to have anything to do with him. "I know these sailor fellows," her father said. Frank and her father had quarrelled one day, and after that she had to meet her lover secretly.

The evening deepened in the avenue. The white of two letters lying in her lap grew indistinct. One was to Harry, the other was to her father. Ernest had been her favourite, but she liked Harry, too. Her father was becoming old lately, she noticed; he would miss her. Sometimes he could be very nice. Not long before, when she had been laid up for a day, he had read her out a ghost-story, and had made toast for her at the fire. Another day, when her mother was alive, they had all gone for a picnic to the Hill of Howth. She remembered her father putting on her mother's bonnet to make the children laugh.

Her time was running out, but she continued to sit by the window, leaning her head against the window-curtain, inhaling the odour of dusty cretonne. Down far in the avenue she could hear a street organ playing. She knew the air. Strange that it should come that very night to remind her of her promise to her mother, her promise to keep the home together as long as she could. She remembered the last night of her mother's illness; she was again in the close, dark room at the other side of the hall, and outside she heard a melancholy air of Italy. The organ-player had been ordered to go away, and given sixpence. She remembered her father strutting back into the sick room, saying: "Damned Italians! coming over here." As she mused, the pitiful vision of her mother's life laid its spell on the very quick of her being—that life of commonplace sacrifices closing in final craziness. She trembled as she heard again her mother's voice saying constantly with foolish insistence: "Derevaun Seraun," "Derevaun Seraun."

She stood up in a sudden impulse of terror. Escape? She must escape! Frank would save her. He could give her life, perhaps love, too. But she wanted life. Why should she be unhappy? She had a right to happiness. Frank would take her in his arms, fold her in his arms. He would save her.

She stood among the swaying crowd in the station at the North Wall. He held her hand and she knew that he was speaking to her, saying something about the passage over and over again. The station was full of soldiers with brown baggages. Through the wide door she caught a glimpse of the black mass of the boat lying in beside the quay wall, with illumined portholes. She answered nothing. She felt her cheek pale and cold, and out of a maze of distress she prayed to God to direct her, to show her what was her duty. The boat blew a long, mournful whistle into the mist. If she went to-morrow she would be on the sea with Frank, steaming towards Buenos Ayres. Their passage had been booked. Could she still draw back, after all he had done for her? Her distress awoke a nausea in her body, and she kept moving her lips in silent, fervent prayer.

A bell clanged upon her heart. She felt him seize her hand.

"Come!"

All the seas of the world tumbled about her heart. He was drawing her into them; he would drown her. She gripped with both hands at the iron railing.

"Come!"

No! No! No! It was impossible. Her hands clutched the iron in frenzy. Amid the seas she sent a cry of anguish.

"Eveline! Evvy!"

He rushed beyond the barrier and called to her to follow. He was shouted at to go on but he still called to her. She set her white face to him, passive, like a helpless animal. Her eyes gave him no sign of love, or farewell or recognition.

Twelve Promises of Jesus to Blessed Margaret Mary Alacoque

The walls of the home of Eveline Hill in the story "Eveline" contain a yellowed photograph of a priest "above the broken harmonium beside the coloured print of the promises made to Blessed Margaret Mary Alacoque." Margaret Mary Alacoque (1647–1690) was a French nun in the Visitation Order who founded the devotion to the Sacred Heart of Jesus. She was declared blessed by Pope Pius IX in 1864 and canonized by Benedict XV in 1920. Following are the Twelve Promises of Jesus to Saint Margaret Mary for those devoted to His Sacred Heart:

1. I will give them all the graces necessary for their state of life.
2. I will establish peace in their families.
3. I will console them in all their troubles.
4. They shall find in My Heart an assured refuge during life and especially at the hour of their death.
5. I will pour abundant blessings on all their undertakings.
6. Sinners shall find in My Heart the source of an infinite ocean of mercy.
7. Tepid souls shall become fervent.
8. Fervent souls shall speedily rise to great perfection.
9. I will bless the homes where an image of My Heart shall be exposed and honored.
10. I will give to priests the power of touching the most hardened hearts.
11. Those who propagate this devotion shall have their names written in My Heart, never to be effaced.
12. The all-powerful love of My Heart will grant to all those who shall receive Communion on the First Friday of nine consecutive months the grace of final repentance; they shall not die under my displeasure, nor without receiving their Sacraments; My heart shall be their assured refuge at that last hour.

The Lass that loves a Sailor

The narrator of "Eveline" tells of Frank, the sailor with whom Eveline plans to elope: "He was awfully fond of music and sang a little. People knew that they were courting and when he sang about the lass that loves a sailor she always felt pleasantly confused." Following are the words and music of Frank's song, "The Lass that loves a Sailor," by the English songwriter Charles Dibdin (1745–1814):

The Lass that loves a Sailor.

1. The moon on the o - cean was dimm'd by a rip - ple, Af - ford - ing a che - quer'd de - light; The gay jol - ly tars pass'd the word for the tip - ple, And the toast, for 'twas Sa - tur - day night. Some sweet - heart or wife, he

2.

Some drank "The Queen," and some her
    brave ships,
  And some "The Constitution;"
Some "May our foes, and all such rips,
  Yield to English resolution;"
That fate might bless some Poll or Bess,
  And that they soon might hail her;
    But the standing toast,
    That pleas'd the most,
    Was "The wind that blows,
    The ship that goes,
  And the lass that loves a sailor."

3.

Some drank "The Prince," and some
    "Our Land,"
  This glorious land of freedom;
Some "That our tars may never want
  Heroes brave to lead them;"
"That she who's in distress may find
  Such friends as ne'er will fail her;"
    But the standing toast
    That pleas'd the most,
    Was "The wind that blows
    The ship that goes,
  And the lass that loves a sailor."

"After the Race"

In April 1903, James Joyce was studying medicine in Paris, when he interviewed a French race-car driver named Henri Fournier for *The Irish Times*. Fournier was expected to be a contender in the James Gordon Bennett cup race that summer—the same automobile race celebrated at the beginning of the story "After the Race."

THE MOTOR DERBY

Interview with the French Champion†

(FROM A CORRESPONDENT.)

PARIS, SUNDAY.

In the Rue d'Anjou, not far from the Church of the Madeleine, is M. Henri Fournier's place of business. "Paris-Automobile"—a company of which M. Fournier is the manager—has its headquarters there. Inside the gateway is a big square court, roofed over, and on the floor of the court and on great shelves extending from the floor to the roof are ranged motor-cars of all sizes, shapes, and colours. In the afternoon this court is full of noises—the voices of workmen, the voices of buyers talking in half-a-dozen languages, the ringing of telephone bells, the horns sounded by the "chauffeurs" as the cars come in and go out—and it is almost impossible to see M. Fournier unless one is prepared to wait two or three hours for one's turn. But the buyers of "autos" are, in one sense, people of leisure. The morning, however, is more favourable, and yesterday morning, after two failures, I succeeded in seeing M. Fournier.

M. Fournier is a slim, active-looking young man, with dark reddish hair. Early as the hour was our interview was now and again broken in upon by the importunate telephone.

"You are one of the competitors for the Gordon-Bennett Cup, M. Fournier?"

"Yes, I am one of three selected to represent France."

"And you are also a competitor, are you not, for the Madrid Prize?"

"Yes."

"Which of the races comes first—the Irish race or the Madrid race?"

"The Madrid race. It takes place early in May, while the race for the International Cup does not take place till July."

"I suppose you are preparing actively for your races?"

"Well, I have just returned from a tour to Monte Carlo and Nice."

"On your racing machine?"

"No, on a machine of smaller power."

† From *The Irish Times*, Tuesday, April 7, 1903.

"Have you determined what machine you will ride in the Irish race?"

"Practically."

"May I ask the name of it—is it a Mercédes?"

"No, a Mors."

"And its horse-power?"

"Eighty."

"And on this machine you can travel at a rate of——?"

"You mean its highest speed?"

"Yes."

"Its highest speed would be a hundred and forty kilometres an hour."

"But you will not go at that rate all the time during the race?"

"Oh, no. Of course its average speed for the race would be lower than that."

"An average speed of how much?"

"Its average speed would be a hundred kilometres an hour, perhaps a little more than that, something between a hundred and a hundred and ten kilometres an hour."

"A kilometre is about a half-mile, is it not?"

"More than that, I should think. There are how many yards in your mile?"

"Seventeen hundred and sixty, if I am right."

"Then your half-mile has eight hundred and eighty yards. Our kilometre is just equal to eleven hundred yards."

"Let me see. Then your top speed is nearly eighty-six miles an hour, and your average speed is sixty-one miles an hour?"

"I suppose so, if we calculate properly."

"It is an appalling pace! It is enough to burn our roads. I suppose you have seen the roads you are to travel?"

"No."

"No? You don't know the course, then?"

"I know it slightly. I know it, that is, from some sketches that were given of it in the Paris newspapers."

"But, surely, you will want a better knowledge than that?"

"Oh, certainly. In fact, before the month is over. I intend to go to Ireland to inspect the course. Perhaps I shall go in three weeks' time."

"Will you remain any time in Ireland?"

"After the race?"

"Yes."

"I am afraid not. I should like to, but I don't think I can."

"I suppose you would not like to be asked your opinion of the result?"

"Hardly."

"Yet, which nation do you fear most?"

"I fear them all—Germans, Americans, and English. They are all to be feared."

"And how about Mr. Edge?"

No answer.

"He won the prize the last time, did he not?"

"O, yes."

"Then he should be your most formidable opponent?"

"O, yes . . . But, you see, Mr. Edge won, of course, but . . . a man who was last of all, and had no chance of winning might win if the other machines broke."

Whatever way one looks at this statement it appears difficult to challenge its truth.

[The photograph above (from *The Car*, 8 July 1903) shows a scene at the Gordon Bennett race that year. Fournier did not participate after all but Joyce made the occasion the background for his short story 'After the Race,' published in December that year in the *Irish Homestead* and afterwards included in the collection *Dubliners*.—National Library of Ireland Historical Documents, Document 7]

"Two Gallants"

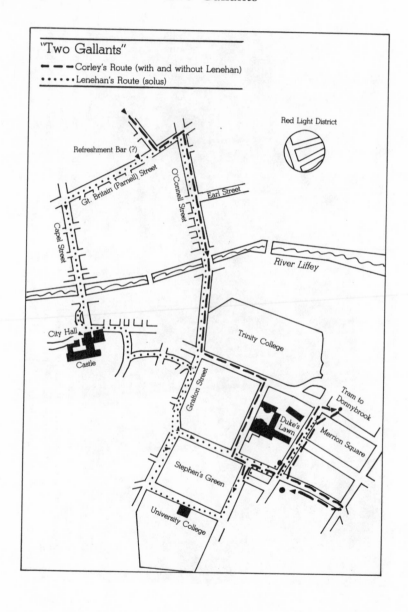

"The Boarding House"

The narrator of "The Boarding House" tells that on Sunday nights the boarders would often gather in Mrs. Mooney's front drawing room and entertain themselves. "The musichall *artistes* would oblige; and Sheridan played waltzes and polkas and vamped accompaniments. Polly Mooney, the Madam's daughter, would also sing." Below is the little song sung by Polly Mooney.[1]

Stanza I:

I'm an imp on mischief bent,
Only feeling quite content
When doing wrong!
When doing wrong!
Sometimes when I've *had* the fun
I repent of what I've done,
But not for long!
But not for long!
On my mistress tricks I play,
Telling her what love should say,
Whispering what love should do;
She believes and does it too!
I'm a naughty girl
You needn't sham;
You know, I am!
Rome is in a whirl,
Because they're all afraid
Of this naughty little maid!

Chorus:

She's a naughty girl!
We know it well
And mean to tell!
She's a bad one
If we ever had one:
Oh, she's a very very naughty little girl!

Stanza II:

At the Roman Clubs, no doubt,
Funny tales you hear about
My goings on!
Your goings on!

1. Thanks to Zack Bowen for recovering this song.

If I like to sit and chat,
What can be the harm in that
Though daylight's gone?
Though daylight's gone!
If some youth with manners free
Dares to snatch a kiss from me,
Do I ask him to explain?
No I kiss him back again!

I'm a naughty girl, etc.

"A Little Cloud"

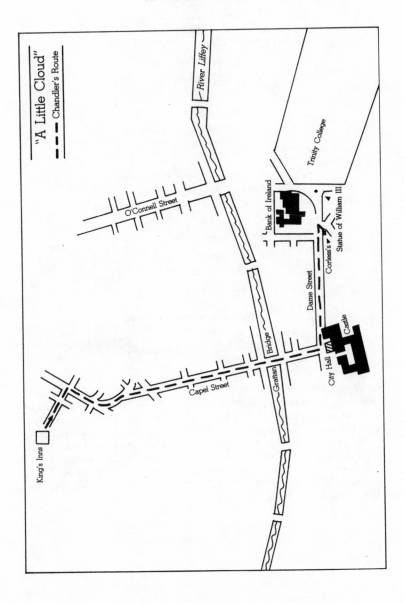

Below is an advertisement for Corless's Restaurant.

Later in the evening, after he has parted from his friend Gallaher at
Corless's, Thomas Chandler returns to his home. His wife, reproachful
that he has forgotten to bring home the coffee she requested, decides to
go to the corner grocery, and places their sleeping infant in her husband's
arms. "A volume of Byron's poems lay before him on the table. He
opened it cautiously with his left hand lest he should waken the child
and began to read the first poem in the book." The poem was Lord
Byron's "On the Death of a Young Lady: Cousin to the Author, and very
dear to him," and here is the text:

On the Death of a Young Lady
Cousin to the Author, and very dear to Him

LORD BYRON

HUSH'D are the winds, and still the evening gloom,
  Not e'en a zephyr wanders through the grove,
 Whilst I return to view my Margaret's tomb,
   And scatter flowers on the dust I love.

2.

Within this narrow cell reclines her clay,
That clay where once such animation beam'd;
  The King of Terrors seiz'd her as his prey;
Not worth, nor beauty, have her life redeem'd.

3.

Oh! could that King of Terrors pity feel,
Or Heaven reverse the dread decree of fate,
Not here the mourner would his grief reveal,
Not here the Muse her virtues would relate.

4.

But wherefore weep? Her matchless spirit soars,
  Beyond where splendid shines the orb of day,
  And weeping angels lead her to those bowers,
Where endless pleasures virtuous deeds repay.

5.

And shall presumptuous mortals Heaven arraign!
  And madly God-like Providence accuse!
  Ah! no, far fly from me attemps so vain;—
I'll ne'er submission to my God refuse.

6.

Yet is remembrance of those virtues dear,
Yet fresh the memory of that beauteous face;
Still they call forth my warm affection's tear,
Still in my heart retain their wonted place.

"Counterparts"

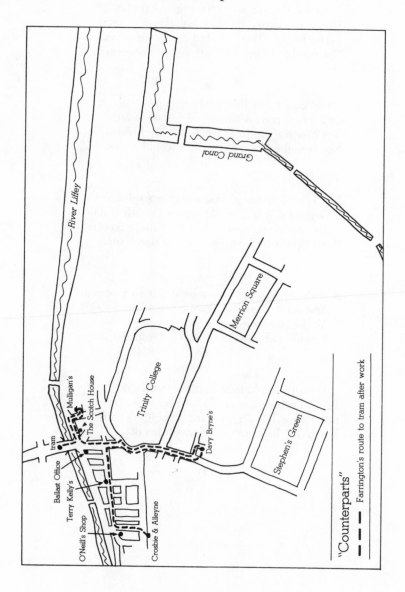

"Counterparts"

■ ■ ■ Farrington's route to tram after work

"Counterparts" describes Farrington's movement from one pub to another. "Rain was drizzling down on the cold streets and when they reached the Ballast Office Farrington suggested the Scotch House." The Scotch House, shown below, was located at 6–7 Burgh Quay, just east of the Ballast Office.

PHOTOGRAPH COURTESY OF BRUCE BIDWELL AND LINDA HEFFER BIDWELL.

"Clay"

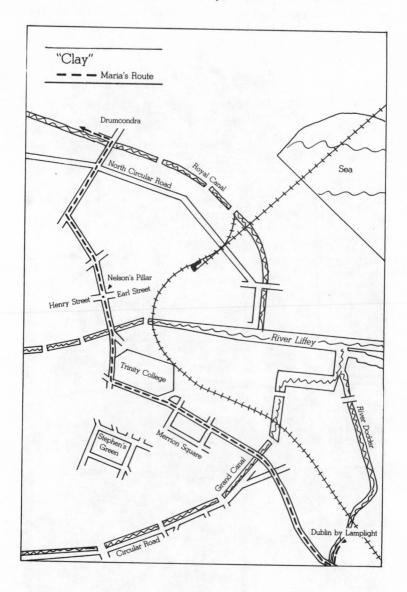

"Clay"
— — — Maria's Route

Drumcondra

North Circular Road

Royal Canal

Sea

Nelson's Pillar

Henry Street · Earl Street

Trinity College

River Liffey

River Dodder

Stephen's Green

Merrion Square

Grand Canal

Circular Road

Dublin by Lamplight

"Clay" describes the tram journey Maria plans to make to the Donnelly family from her laundry in Ballsbridge in southeast Dublin to Drumcondra in north Dublin. "From Ballsbridge to the Pillar, twenty minutes; from the Pillar to Drumcondra, twenty minutes; and twenty minutes to buy the things." The Pillar was Nelson's Pillar, shown here, a monument 134 feet tall located in the middle of Dublin, a few feet from the General Post Office, and dedicated to Lord Nelson, the famous British naval hero. Because of its central location, Nelson's Pillar served as the hub and transfer point for many of the Dublin tramlines at the turn of the century. PHOTOGRAPH COURTESY OF THE NATIONAL LIBRARY OF IRELAND.

As the evening comes to a close in "Clay," Mrs. Donnelly asks Maria if she would sing one of the old songs before she goes. "Mrs Donnelly bade the children be quiet and listen to Maria's song. Then she played the prelude and said *Now, Maria!* and Maria, blushing very much, began to sing in a tiny quavering voice. She sang *I dreamt that I dwelt* and when she came to the second verse she sang it again." Following is *I dreamt that I dwelt in Marble Halls*, with music by Michael Balfe and words by Alfred Bunn.

I dreamt that I dwelt in Marble Halls.

Words by ALFRED BUNN.

Music by M. W. BALFE.

I had rich - es too great to count— could boast Of a high an -
And I dreamt that one of that no - ble host Came forth my

ces - tral name;.............. But I al - - so dreamt, which pleas'd me
hand to claim;.............. But I al - - so dreamt, which charm'd me

most, That you lov'd me still the same, that you lov'd me, you lov'd me
most, That you lov'd me still the same, that you lov'd me, you lov'd me

still the same, That you lov'd me, you lov'd me still the same.
still the same, That you lov'd me, you lov'd me still the same.

Last verse.

"A Painful Case"

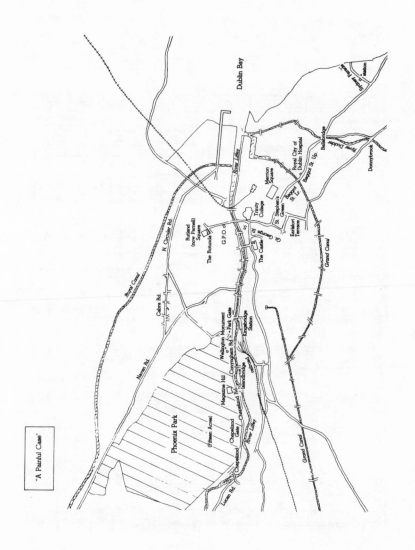

"A Painful Case"

Four years after breaking off his relationship with Mrs. Sinico, James Duffy is shocked to read in the newspaper of "an inquest on the body of Mrs Emily Sinico, aged forty-three years, who was killed at Sydney Parade Station." The article explains that the railway company "had always taken every precaution to prevent people crossing the lines except by the bridges, both by placing notices in every station and by the use of patent spring gates at level crossings." This photo shows the railroad crossing at Sydney Parade Station. PHOTOGRAPH COURTESY OF BRUCE BIDWELL AND LINDA HEFFER BIDWELL.

"Ivy Day in the Committee Room"

This portrait, by Sydney Prior Hall, is of the great Irish statesman Charles Stewart Parnell (1846–1891). Parnell's followers observed the anniversary of his death by wearing ivy sprigs in the lapels of their coats and jackets every October 6. This custom lends its name to Joyce's story.

PHOTOGRAPH COURTESY OF THE NATIONAL GALLERY OF IRELAND.

"A Mother"

The concert series reported in "A Mother" may have been inspired by James Joyce's own concert experience as a tenor. In August 1904, the young Joyce appeared on stage with two of early twentieth-century Ireland's greatest singers: J. C. Doyle, a baritone, and John MacCormack, a tenor. A private journal entry by a member of the audience, published on p. 168 of Richard Ellmann's biography of Joyce, notes that the accompanist left the concert early—though no reason for her early departure is given. Following is an announcement of that concert and the *Freeman's Journal* review, which praises Joyce for his "sweet tenor voice."

ANTIENT CONCERT ROOMS.
EXHIBITION OF IRISH
INDUSTRIES
AND
GRAND IRISH CONCERT,
THIS (SATURDAY) EVENING,
At 8 o'clock.

Artistes :—
Miss AGNES TREACY,
Miss OLIVE BARRY,
Madame HALL
Miss WALKER (Marie Nic Shiubhlaigh),
Mr. J. C. DOYLE,
Mr. JAMES A. JOYCE, and
Mr. J. F. M'CORMACK.
Orchestra conducted by
Miss EILEEN REIDY, A.L.C.M., R.I.A.M.
Prices—3s, 2s, and 1s.   80198

SATURDAY NIGHT'S CONCERT.

A concert was given in the large hall of the Antient Concert Rooms on Saturday night, and attracted a full house. The programme was a first-rate one. The Exhibition String Band played selections of Irish melodies and of operatic music of Irish composers. Mr. J. C. Doyle sang a number of songs in first-rate style. His voice is full, sweet, of considerable range, and with uncommon capability of expression. His singing is characterised by remarkable intelligence and whether in the light playful mood of the peasant ballad, the sentimental ditty, or the strength and passion of the war song, he was fully equal to the occasion. He was encored at every song. Miss Agnes Treacy sang charmingly a number of Irish airs in Gaelic and English, and was rewarded with hearty applause and imperative encores. Mr. James A. Joyce, the possessor of a sweet tenor voice, sang charmingly "The Sally Gardens," and gave a pathetic rendering of "The Croppy Boy." Madame Halle gave a

Miss Maire Nic Shiubhlaigh is a lady of considerable histrionic talent, and her selection for recitation gave an opportunity for the display of her powers in narrative, the pathetic and the impassioned, all of which she realised fully. She was not so successful in a recitative rendering of one of Mr. Yeats' poems, whether due to nervousness at the novelty of the form, or that this style is not so well within her gifts, as the natural delivery in which she excelled. She was vociferously applauded. Mr. J. F. M'Cormack was the hero of the evening. It was announced as his last public appearance in Ireland, and the evident feeling of the audience at the parting, seemed to unnerve him a good deal. His voice is one of great resonance, as well as of high range, and his powerful notes were heard in a varied selection of Irish melodies. The audience seemed as if it would never hear and see enough of him, and twice he had to respond to triple encores, while he was recalled times almost without number.

"Grace"

As they sit around Mr. Kernan's sickbed, the men discuss the merits of Pope Leo XIII. "—I remember reading, said Mr Cunningham, that one of Pope Leo's poems was on the invention of the photograph—in Latin, of course." Mr. Cunningham was correct: Pope Leo XIII did indeed write a Latin poem on the photograph called *"Ars Photographica,"* which is here reprinted with a translation by H. T. Henry.

Ars Photographica (1867)

LEO XIII

Expressa solis spiculo
Nitens imago, quam bene
Frontis decus, vim luminum
Refers, et oris gratiam.
O mira virtus ingeni
Novumque monstrum! Imaginem
Naturae Apelles aemulus
Non pulchriorem pingeret.

On Photography (1902)

H. T. HENRY, TRANS.

Sun-wrought with magic of the skies
The image fair before me lies:
Deep-vaulted brain and sparkling eyes
And lip's fine chiselling.
O miracle of human thought,
O art with newest marvels fraught—
Apelles, Nature's rival, wrought
No fairer imaging!

The image below shows Pope Leo XIII being photographed. COURTESY OF THE AMERICAN MUTOSCOPE AND BIOGRAPH CO., © 1898–2005.

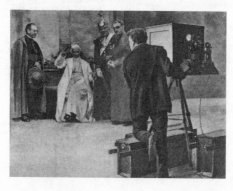

The men in "Grace" make their religious retreat at the Jesuit Church of St. Francis Xavier in Gardiner Street Upper. "The transept of the Jesuit Church in Gardiner Street was almost full; and still at every moment gentlemen entered from the sidedoor and, directed by the lay brother, walked on tiptoe along the aisles until they found seating accommodation. The gentlemen were all well dressed and orderly. The light of the lamps of the church fell upon an assembly of black clothes and white collars, relieved here and there by tweeds, on dark mottled pillars of green marble and on lugubrious canvasses." Below is a photo of the interior of the church. COURTESY OF THE NATIONAL LIBRARY OF IRELAND.

The sermon Father Purdon delivers in "Grace" is based on Jesus' "Parable of the Unjust Steward," cited in Luke 16:1–10. The narrator tells us that "Father Purdon developed the text with resonant assurance. It is one of the most difficult texts in all the scriptures, he said, to interpret properly."

The Parable of the Unjust Steward

There was a certain rich man who had a steward, who was reported to him as squandering his possessions. And he called him and said to him, "What is this that I hear of thee? Make an accounting of thy stewardship, for thou canst be steward no longer."

And the steward said within himself, "What shall I do, seeing that my master is taking away the stewardship from me? To dig I am not able; to beg I am ashamed. I know what I shall do, that when I am removed from my stewardship they may receive me into their houses." And he summoned each of his master's debtors and said to the first, "How much dost thou owe my master?" And he said, "A hundred jars of oil." He said to him, "Take thy bond and sit down at once and write fifty." Then he said to another, "How much dost thou owe?" He said. "A hundred kors of wheat." He said to him, "Take thy bond and write eighty."

And the master commended the unjust steward, in that he had acted prudently; for the children of this world, in their relation to their own generation, are more prudent than the children of the light. And I say to you, make friends for yourselves with the mammon of wickedness, so that when you fail they may receive you into the everlasting dwellings.

"The Dead"

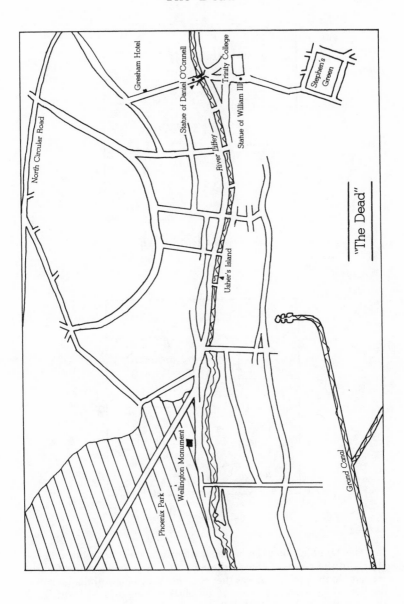

"The Dead"

Below are the floor plans for the Misses Morkan's home, 15 Usher's Island.

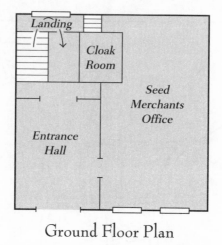

Ground Floor Plan

First Floor Plan

In "The Dead," a number of musical performances take place in the course of the evening. One of these is sung by Julia Morkan. "Gabriel recognised the prelude. It was that of an old song of aunt Julia's, *Arrayed for the Bridal*. Her voice strong and clear in tone attacked with great spirit the runs which embellish the air and, though she sang very rapidly, she did not miss even the smallest of the grace notes. To follow the voice, without looking at the singer's face, was to feel and share the excitement of swift and secure flight." *Arrayed for the Bridal* is a song adapted by George Linley from the melody "Son vergin vezzosa" ("I am a merry maiden") in the opera *I Puritani* (*The Puritans*) by Vincenzo Bellini (1801–1835).

Arrayed for the Bridal

Arrayed for the bridal, in beauty behold her,
A white wreath entwineth a forehead more fair;
I envy the zephyrs that softly enfold her, enfold her,
And play with the locks of her beautiful hair.
May life to her prove full of sunshine and love, full
      of love, yes! yes! yes!

Who would not love her?
Sweet star of the morning! shining so bright,
Earth's circle adorning, fair creature of light!

As the guests begin to leave the Morkan party, Gabriel Conroy notices his wife, Gretta, standing on the stair, listening to the music of a voice and a piano. "The song seemed to be in the old Irish tonality and the singer seemed uncertain both of his words and of his voice. The voice made plaintive by the distance and by the singer's hoarseness faintly illuminated the cadence of the air with words expressing grief." "The Lass of Aughrim" takes place in the western part of Ireland and has many versions. Most versions reproduce a dialogue between Lord Gregory and the young woman whom he has seduced and abandoned with a child.

The Lass of Aughrim

If you'll be the lass of Aughrim
      As I am taking you mean to be
Tell me the first token
      That passed between you and me.

Oh Gregory, don't you remember
      One night on the hill,
When we swapped rings off each other's hands,
      Sorely against my will?
Mine was of the beaten gold
      Yours was but black tin.

Oh if you be the lass of Aughrim,
      As I suppose you not to be,
Come tell me the last token
      Between you and me.

Oh Gregory don't you remember,
  One night on the hill,
When we swapped smocks off each other's backs,
  Sorely against my will?
Mine was of the holland fine,
  Yours was but Scotch cloth.

Oh if you be the lass of Aughrim,
  As I suppose you not to be,
Come tell me the last token
  Between you and me.

Oh Gregory, don't you remember,
  In my father's hall.
When you had your will of me?
  And that was the worst of all.

Refrain
The rain falls on my yellow locks
  And the dew it wets my skin;
My babe lies cold within my arms;
  Lord Gregory let me in.

"The Dead" ends with a scene between Gabriel and Gretta Conroy that takes place in the Gresham Hotel. The Gresham, located on O'Connell Street, Dublin's central thoroughfare, was a very fashionable hotel; its electric lighting was a rarity at the time of the story. COURTESY OF THE NATIONAL LIBRARY OF IRELAND.

CRITICISM

DAVID G. WRIGHT

Interactive Stories in *Dubliners*†

In "The Boarding House" Bob Doran, fearing that his affair with Polly will become known, reflects that "Dublin is such a small city—everyone knows everyone else's business" (*Dubliners* 66) [53.156–57]. Most readers probably skip past this comment cheerfully enough, finding it commonplace; yet it seems on reflection quite false as an account of the community depicted in *Dubliners*. It's often striking how *little* the characters know of each other's business.

The tone and meaning of *Dubliners* owe much to the gap between what the characters know and what we know (or can discover). This discrepancy in turn depends on the hermetic confinement of the major characters to a single story each and on our access to literary contexts. Such contexts continue to shape our reading, sometimes in unexpected ways.

Apart from drafting *Dubliners*, Joyce's chief literary preoccupation in 1906 was a voluminous correspondence with the publisher Grant Richards. In the course of this correspondence Joyce declares, on 5 May 1906, that he has been writing his stories

> in a style of scrupulous meanness and with the conviction that he is a very bold man who dares to alter in the presentment, still more to deform, whatever he has seen and heard. (*Letters* 2: 134)

Those of course are famous phrases. But we may not have been sufficiently skeptical in reading them. Joyce was carefully manipulating the manner in which Richards regarded the stories, and goading him into thinking out and clarifying his own standards of judgment. In the course of this correspondence, Joyce also cultivated an ability to mimic Richards's typical manner of expression, to write to him in publisher-speak. As Joyce refined this mimetic strategy he became increasingly capable of guiding the publisher's responses; and he perfected modes of address which he then deployed in the stories, notably "Counterparts," where the fussy office language closely echoes the tone of the letters.

The correspondence, in fact, became a text parallel to that of *Dubliners* itself, serving several analogous purposes. In a letter to Richards of 23 June 1906, Joyce declares

† From *Studies in Short Fiction* 32 (1995): 285–93. Copyright © 1995 by *Studies in Short Fiction*, Inc. Reprinted by permission of the publisher. Page and line references in brackets refer to this Norton Critical Edition.

> I seriously believe that you will retard the course of civilisation
> in Ireland by preventing the Irish people from having one good
> look at themselves in my nicely polished looking-glass. (*Letters*
> 1: 64)

The "looking-glass," of course, is the text of *Dubliners*. But Joyce
had been doing much the same thing in his letters to Richards:
prompting him to have a good look at himself, in a looking-glass of
Joyce's own fabrication. And Joyce was quite aware that the *Dubliners* typescript and the Richards correspondence had become inter-
related texts, each in a sense operating as a reflection or parody of
the other; he even remarks to Richards, in the course of his "scrupulous meanness" letter, "I see . . . that my letter is becoming nearly
as long as my book" (*Letters* 2: 135).

Let's return to that particular piece for a moment. Joyce's phrase
"scrupulous meanness" reflects a little harshly on his tone in the
stories but may seem broadly congruent with them. Yet the primary
meaning of "scrupulous," according to the *OED* (one of Joyce's favorite books), is "troubled with doubts or scruples of conscience."
Where Joyce deploys the word in his creative writing he normally
uses it in that sense, or else, and more often, in a parody of that
sense. Eliza Flynn tells us that Father Flynn "was too scrupulous
always. . . . The duties of the priesthood was too much for him"
(*Dubliners* 17) [10.272–73]. Being overly scrupulous, that is, helps
to kill a character in the collection's very first story.

The word "meanness" might seem in Joyce's letter to carry a more
apparent tinge of self-directed irony, as evoking noble austerity
rather than reprehensible stinginess. Yet dictionary definitions of the
word "mean" equate it to "common, base, or sordid," and it typically
appears in Joyce's fiction with a heavy critical loading. As Little
Chandler contemplates his wife's face in a photograph, "he found
something mean in it. . . . A dull resentment against his life awoke
within him" (*Dubliners* 83) [68.425; 436–37].

In the letter to Richards, Joyce ostensibly aligns himself *with* the
"scrupulous" and the "mean," by contrast with the "very bold man"
who dares to judge, "alter" or "deform" things. Yet surely, and especially in the *Dubliners* years, he would normally think of himself
precisely as one of those "bold" writers who seek to reflect their
society by judiciously depicting its follies; who may do so, indeed, by
selectively emphasizing its own scrupulousness and meanness, and
perhaps its mediocrity ("mean" as "average" may also have been in
Joyce's mind).

Joyce also came to enjoy generating meaning through the parodic
interactions he set up among his various published texts. He succeeded in his attempt to recast *Stephen Hero* as the *Portrait* partly

because he conceived the idea of basing his text on the notion of parody and, especially, of self-parody. Among other things, it incorporated a parody of *Dubliners*.

The conclusion of the *Portrait* echoes the conclusion of *Dubliners*, which Joyce was writing at precisely the time he decided to convert *Stephen Hero* into the *Portrait*; he may have conceived the two conclusions at the outset to complement and offset one another. "The Dead" ends rather sadly, with Gabriel's somber recognition of mortality, and a dissolution of individual identity in the recognition that death is a shared destiny. The *Portrait* ends exuberantly with Stephen's declaration "Welcome, O life!" (*Portrait* 252), and an assertion of individuality as he plans to elude the nets and fly beyond the world of his family and forebears: "Old father, old artificer, stand me now and ever in good stead" (*Portrait* 252–53). The final word in the text of the *Portrait*, "stead," chimes with the final word in *Dubliners*, "dead," and in a sense reverses its meaning by demanding a place to stand rather than marking a capitulation. (Incidentally, the word "stead" is also faintly echoed in the opening clause of *Ulysses*, "Stately, plump Buck Mulligan came from the stairh*ead*.")

At the end of *Dubliners*, "European" values seem for the moment routed, displaced by Gaelic ones, and Gabriel contemplates a journey to the west of Ireland. At the end of the *Portrait*, by contrast, Stephen plans to escape from Ireland for a journey eastward to the Continent. Gabriel's reflection "Better pass boldly into that other world, in the full glory of some passion, than fade and wither dismally with age" (*Dubliners* 223) [194.1584–86] seems to apply to Stephen's situation more closely than to his own, especially if we take "that other world" to denote not death but a new area of life. Stephen appears preoccupied with the future, Gabriel with the past; and while Stephen's journey no doubt will occur in reality, Gabriel's travel plans are not very convincing.

None of which suggests that the *Portrait* merely supplies a positive ending to supplant the negative ending of *Dubliners*; rather, each conclusion qualifies the other. Gabriel subordinates his ego almost completely in the face of the world, while Stephen subordinates the world to his ego. Stephen's escape to Europe will prove in many respects a failure, as *Ulysses* demonstrates. *Dubliners*, in anticipation, might well have warned him of such risks, since several characters who have ventured boldly to Europe, like Ignatius Gallaher in "A Little Cloud," seem to have gained little from the experience. (Gabriel's European excursions may seem harmless enough, but perhaps also evasive; we may sympathize with Molly Ivors's claim that he's been neglecting his own country.)

The ending of *Dubliners* underpins the endings of all Joyce's subsequent prose texts, though subtle variations are played on its details.

The final scene of "The Dead" involves the two partners in a relationship, who have a rather one-sided conversation, involving a confession; one partner then lies awake thinking after the other falls asleep. *Ulysses, Exiles,* and *Finnegans Wake* all end by depicting essentially the same situation.

In each case, there's a further reminder that the confessional narratives just ended may, in fact, have been incomplete. Overt reference is made to the interpolated text, presented by one character to another, but by implication the completeness of the larger text containing those characters may also be challenged. Gabriel, for example, reflects about Gretta's account of her encounter with Michael Furey that "perhaps she had not told him all the story" (*Dubliners* 222) [193.1563]. In every such case, by the time the auditor queries a narrative's completeness, the original narrator is asleep and cannot respond. Even the first *Dubliners* story, "The Sisters," had reminded us emphatically of the problematic and sometimes "incomplete" nature of texts, narratives and, indeed, words. We may notice, too, that throughout *Dubliners,* characters who deliberately set off in quest of the truth tend to be met by verbal confusion and inertia.

It seems apparent, nevertheless, that the individual stories in *Dubliners* do furnish contexts for each other.

In discussing "The Dead" in letters Joyce said that in the earlier stories he had slighted certain positive aspects of Dublin: "I have not [so far] reproduced its . . . hospitality" (*Letters* 2: 166). The new story might, he implies, attempt to redress the balance. The last line in "Grace"—the line that immediately precedes "The Dead"—is "I will set right my accounts" (*Dubliners* 174) [151.812–13], and the new story might seem to be Joyce's own attempt to "set right [his] accounts." This redressing nevertheless appears much more equivocal in the text than Joyce's letters imply: Gabriel's speech in praise of hospitality is itself an ambivalent performance at best (serving as a parody of Joyce's own letters on the subject of Irish hospitality, but also incorporating an inhospitable swipe at Molly Ivors); and the story abounds in depictions of social awkwardness and uncertainty. Some of the maladroitness depicted in "Grace" may have been allowed to taint the later story.

Joyce's attempt to "redress the balance" of *Dubliners* by adding "The Dead" hinged partly on his increasing fondness for self-parody. Whereas in the earlier stories he had mostly "rewritten" and probed the discourses of his fellow Dubliners, from "The Dead" onward the primary targets of such investigative rewriting became his own earlier texts. In part, then, "The Dead" operates as a kind of parody of the earlier stories in the collection.

"The Dead" begins by informing us that Lily is "literally run off her feet" (*Dubliners* 175) [151.1]. The idiom here seems more

Gabriel's than Lily's: we have no access to Lily's mind, only to Gabriel's assumptions about her thoughts. We should also notice that while Lily is in fact *figuratively* run off her feet, the expression applies much more "literally" to Tom Kernan's plight at the beginning of the previous story, "Grace," in which after Kernan falls downstairs, the pub manager and the constable "agreed that the gentleman must have missed his footing" (*Dubliners* 153) [130.87–88]. Also in "Grace," Tom's wife assumes, rightly we imagine, that a man like her husband "would not change greatly before death" (*Dubliners* 157) [135.249–50], which could mean, among other things, "when confronting the fact of death." The question remains whether Gabriel can change in this situation, surely the one that he encounters at the end of his own story.

"The Dead" also restates surreptitiously several propositions first introduced in "Araby." That earlier title reflects a yearning for exotic eastern things rather than for authentic Irish experience, something of which Gabriel will also be accused; and the boy who narrates "Araby," like Gabriel, makes a journey eastward, to a scene of disillusionment, in the course of the story. Both stories depict their protagonists in a series of encounters with women, encounters which produce sometimes bitter self-knowledge. As Gabriel learns to see himself as "a ludicrous figure," so the boy in "Araby" comes to see himself as "a creature driven and derided by vanity" (*Dubliners* 35) [26.218–19]. The links between the two stories are further reinforced by insistently repeated imagery of money, horses, darkness and winter. We could interpret this association in various ways, but in any case, it discloses implications to us which are concealed from the characters within the stories.

While we could no doubt find clear allusions in "The Dead" to all fourteen of the earlier stories, the links with the very first story, "The Sisters," are especially numerous. Eliza Flynn inadvertently refers to the newspaper, the *Freeman's Journal*, as the *Freeman's General* (*Dubliners* 16) [9.234]. This phrase anticipates a collocation used twice in "The Dead," as in Gabriel's reflection "Yes, the *newspapers* were right: snow was *general* all over Ireland" (*Dubliners* 223; emphasis added) [194.1605–06]. The snow falling in this "general" way, on everybody alike, may quietly qualify Gabriel's "generous" side (the words, of course, are cognate). His generosity needs to become more general. Analogously, Gabriel has earlier clung to the distinction of writing his specialized, esoteric literary column for one newspaper; at the end of the story he perhaps needs to acknowledge, by contrast, the wider importance of a weather report, shared generally by all the newspapers and, presumably, having some bearing on the lives of most readers of those papers. The echo of "The Sisters" makes the point about breadth all the more emphatically—at least to us.

The two story titles, "The Sisters" and "The Dead," are in effect interchangeable. The two sisters in the first story anticipate Gabriel's aunts Julia and Kate, who of course are also sisters. The story "The Sisters," likewise, concerns the world of the dead. It begins with a boy standing in the street, looking in through a dimly lighted window and imagining the death of the man inside, while "The Dead" ends with a man looking out through a window toward the dim light from the street, reflecting on human mortality in general and on the account of a particular dead boy which his wife has just related to him. These are the only two stories whose protagonists are told of a death during the narration (though James Duffy does *read* of Emily Sinico's death in "A Painful Case"). They are also the only two stories that include images of people lying in coffins and of blinds drawn down for a death. Gabriel imagines being informed by the sister of a recently deceased person about the circumstances of the death, a situation that has already been depicted for us in the earlier story. Geographically, too, *Dubliners* begins and ends in virtually the same spot. The priest's house in Great Britain Street is just around the corner from the Gresham Hotel in Sackville Street (the two streets, in fact, intersect); so you could have walked from the main location of "The Sisters" to the final location of "The Dead" in a couple of minutes.

The primary reason for all these associations is to tie the ending of *Dubliners* closely to the beginning. That tends to shape the whole collection into the circular configuration that, throughout the individual stories, has served as a symbol for Dublin paralysis and entrapment. The more associations with "The Sisters" we find in "The Dead," the more we're likely to feel that the last story assesses Dublin paralysis from a new angle but doesn't, finally, achieve a way out of it; rather, it sends us back to the beginning. (We should notice that Gabriel forces his daughter to eat stirabout, which she hates; the boy narrator of "The Sisters" might empathize with her, reflecting of Old Cotter "I crammed my mouth with stirabout for fear I might give utterance to my anger. Tiresome old rednosed imbecile!" [*Dubliners* 11] [5.70]. Stirabout is porridge, but the *word* also seems apt in the *Dubliners* context of largely purposeless circular movement.)

A text that operates in richly ironic contextual ways *within* a story is "The Lass of Aughrim." This is of course the ballad that Bartell D'Arcy sings late in "The Dead," at a moment when most of the guests have left the party and the others are preparing to leave. Gretta overhears him singing, and later she tells Gabriel that the song has reminded her of Michael Furey, who once seemingly loved her and who used to sing the same song.

Only three lines from "The Lass of Aughrim" are actually quoted in "The Dead." The ballad is a problematic work: several variant texts exist, many of them incomplete. We notice that Gretta has forgotten the name of the ballad and Bartell D'Arcy has forgotten some of the words. So the ballad as a text seems to have a fragmentary, unfinished or vulnerable quality that might recall Michael Furey, but that also evokes again the difficulty of completing narratives. In all versions the ballad records a sad case of lost or misunderstood love. In most versions the male figure seems to reject his former lover, who appears on the doorstep with her baby and begs to be let in. Believing that she has been rejected, the woman, along with her baby, soon dies. When Michael sang the song to Gretta, he might have identified himself with the female speaker, and shown an ability to empathize with female experience, a capacity that often eludes Gabriel. Michael's shy, courtly approach to Gretta in the past also contrasts, of course, with Lily's bitterness about "the men that is now" [154.93]; it's Lily, of all the characters in the story, who seems to have had an experience of seduction and betrayal. But we might reflect too that the man in the ballad would seem, for all the courtly-love context, to be capable of seducing and abandoning women, so no simple antithesis of noble past and debased present can be intuited: the men that was then may *also* have been all palaver and what they could get out of you. Incidentally, the early exchange between Gabriel and Lily, where he imagines her forthcoming wedding and she responds with a lament about sexual exploitation, is echoed quite precisely in the two contrasting songs performed later in the story: Aunt Julia's rendition of "Arrayed for the Bridal," and then "The Lass of Aughrim."

The ironies of "The Lass of Aughrim" go further, though. If we're to believe Gretta, the sequence of events at the hotel, hence the whole ending of the story and collection, follows from her reaction to hearing the ballad. But we should also scrutinize the circumstances in which Bartell D'Arcy chooses to sing it. He has refused to sing all evening, because of his cold, and he doesn't know this song well. This brings up the whole question of Miss O'Callaghan.

The coach that takes Gabriel and Gretta to the hotel also carries the only two other guests who have stayed till the end of the party, Bartell D'Arcy and Miss O'Callaghan. Gabriel and Gretta, both absorbed in their own thoughts and feelings, pay them little attention. But they also seem to leave the coach at the hotel, since at that point Gabriel insists on paying the full cab fare rather than sharing it with D'Arcy. Where do they go next?

We might deduce that they go to a hotel themselves—or back to his place. Their remaining alone together at the end of the story seems quite compromising, a significant clue in itself. But there's also the matter of "The Lass of Aughrim." Clearly, D'Arcy performs it for Miss O'Callaghan's benefit. He doesn't know that Gretta or anyone else is listening; in fact, he and Miss O'Callaghan seem to be off in a world of their own at this stage. Miss O'Callaghan is new to us, unmentioned until the story's closing sequence. We hear her speak only three times in the text, and when she does so, she seems a fraction obtuse but affable and lively. (Her three quoted speeches also refer in turn to three central motifs of the story—horses, music and snow.) She reports earlier attempts to make D'Arcy perform: "I have been at him all the evening, . . . and he told us he had a dreadful cold and couldn't sing" (*Dubliners* 211) [183.1188–90]. It's partly circumstantial, but it seems likely that, once they're alone together, D'Arcy sings for her as part of a process of seduction. She may even offer to spend the night with him if he sings for her. We might think of the conflation of singing and seduction in *Ulysses*, where Bartell D'Arcy's amorous disposition is also further illustrated. Tenors, we remember, supposedly "get women by the score."

If this scenario is valid, D'Arcy's choice of "The Lass of Aughrim" becomes especially intriguing. It's a ballad about a man who seduces a woman and then casts her off. If D'Arcy does take Miss O'Callaghan home with him after the party, all she'll get from him, we imagine, is a one-night stand (and, possibly, a cold). Is the ballad chosen as a warning? Or chosen to imply that D'Arcy is sensitive to the position of women? In either case, it would give him the opportunity later to seize the moral high ground if Miss O'Callaghan takes exception to anything he does, such as refusing (as at some point he will) to see her again. But nothing else we see or hear about D'Arcy suggests that he *is* sensitive to the position of women, or that he is self-effacing; in fact he seems to be the antithesis of Michael Furey. (This is to assume that D'Arcy chooses the ballad. It may seem conceivable that Miss O'Callaghan suggested the title. But that appears much less likely: the ballad is not well known; we get the impression that she'd be grateful if he sang anything at all; D'Arcy rather than Miss O'Callaghan must be playing the piano while he sings, to judge from its being "closed abruptly" afterward, a D'Arcyesque gesture; and if D'Arcy sings either reluctantly *or* pragmatically it seems improbable that he'd accept a suggested title with which he was less than familiar. More likely he chose the ballad himself.)

If we read "The Dead" in an orthodox manner, without reflecting on what D'Arcy and Miss O'Callaghan are probably up to, we might be struck by the remarkable social isolation and loneliness of almost all the characters, other than the Conroys. Although the story depicts quite a large party, possibly up to 40 people, there's no hint at all that anybody but Gabriel and Gretta is married or has a partner. It would appear that the guests, like the Morkans, all go off to solitary beds after the party ends. Against this backdrop, the poignancy of Gabriel and Gretta's estrangement seems all the more emphatic: the one viable sexual partnership depicted, yet they end the story desolate and at odds with one another. But the picture is richly complicated, and

Gabriel's complacency perhaps undermined all the more intricately, if this reading of D'Arcy and Miss O'Callaghan is accepted. There is, at least temporarily, one viable couple at the end of "The Dead"; but it's *not* Gabriel and Gretta. D'Arcy and Miss O'Callaghan may go off for a fulfilling night together just as Gabriel and Gretta are experiencing trauma occasioned partly by Gretta's hearing D'Arcy's song. The song was never meant for her and, for all the pathos and the courtly-love implications of its content, it has a harsher side. We needn't doubt D'Arcy's (or Miss O'Callaghan's) probable awareness of the beauty of the song, and after Gabriel hears Gretta's moving account of Michael Furey, he might well come to find the ballad haunting as well, something else to learn to be sensitive about. D'Arcy and Miss O'Callaghan may, nonetheless, have been using the song as a kind of counter in the course of arranging an essentially sexual transaction. The most poignant and resonant parallel text evoked in "The Dead," that is, may have entered the story partly as a piece of merchandise. And let's remember, too, that Gabriel and Gretta seem oblivious to the D'Arcy/Miss O'Callaghan possibility; which may be a further sign that, despite the fears of Bob Doran, the citizens of Dublin often *don't* know one another's business at all.

Works Cited

Joyce, James. Dubliners: *Text, Criticism, and Notes*. Ed. Robert Scholes and A. Walton Litz. New York: Viking, 1969.

———. *Letters of James Joyce*. Vol. 1, corrected ed., ed. Stuart Gilbert. New York: Viking, 1965. Vol. 2 and 3, ed. Richard Ellmann. New York: Viking, 1966.

———. A Portrait of the Artist as a Young Man: *Text, Criticism, and Notes*. Ed. Chester G. Anderson. New York: Viking, 1968.

HEYWARD EHRLICH

"Araby" in Context: The "Splendid Bazaar," Irish Orientalism, and James Clarence Mangan†

The story based on an actual incident in Joyce's life, "Araby," is often read on a single internal plane for its quest symbolism, its allegory of creativity, or its richness of style. But "Araby" also draws significantly upon three external contexts, namely the historical, the literary, and the biographical. Although it may seem a work of

† From *James Joyce Quarterly* 35.2–3 (Winter and Spring 1998): 309–31. Reprinted by permission of the publisher. Page and line references in brackets refer to this Norton Critical Edition.

independent invention, "Araby" refers directly to an actual bazaar
that visited Dublin in 1894, which was not only a memorable local
entertainment event but also one of a series of major local annual
events. "Araby" also evokes the distinctive version of Irish Orientalism that looked to the East for the highest sources of national identity and the very origins of the Irish language, alphabet, and people.
Writing both within and against the moment of the Celtic revival,
Joyce defined his place within the tradition of Irish Orientalism by
writing two biographical essays on the Irish poet and Orientalist
James Clarence Mangan in 1902 and 1907, the composition of
which closely bracketed and heavily shaped the writing of "Araby,"
as Joyce acknowledges by naming an essential character in the story
after Mangan. The local Dublin reader, to whom Joyce largely
directed "Araby" when he wrote it in 1905, already knew a great deal
about the several contexts of the story, the annual bazaars and fairs
such as Araby, the long literary and even musical tradition of Irish
Orientalism, and perhaps even something of the place of Mangan in
the Celtic Revival. These external and social contexts of "Araby"
come into dynamic opposition to the internal and private culture of
the boy's narrative in the voice of the first person narrator, a more
mature version of the young protagonist, who repeatedly warns the
reader against the boy's characteristic confusion and follies.

Joyce used a sense of exact historical referentiality in his early
fiction significantly to affect readers and critics, though he was fully
aware that some might take his stories as "a caricature of Dublin
life" (*LettersII* 99) or as a satire in his "nicely polished looking-glass"
(*LettersI* 64); only a few months before writing "Araby," he hoped to
extend his work into a second series to be called "Provincials"
(*LettersII* 92). The historical details in *Dubliners* mattered so much
to him that, when the publisher Maunsel and Company threatened
in 1913 to change "the name of restaurants, cake-shops, railway stations, public houses, laundries, bars and other places of business,"
Joyce hired two solicitors to support him in firmly preserving these
detailed Dublin references (*LettersII* 325). "Araby" is the only story
in *Dubliners* to be based on a famous public event; yet as historical
details come to light about the immense, sprawling, noisy Araby
bazaar that actually visited Dublin in 1894, they seem paradoxically to
contrast with the small, dark, quiet charity sale that the boy depicts in
the story. When Joyce wrote "Araby" in 1905, and even when he published it in 1914, a sizable fraction of the Dublin audience had
attended and could still remember the Araby bazaar of 1894 and similar bazaars that took place each year after 1892. Thus, the narrator's
warnings about the boy's "foolish blood," "confused adoration," and
"innumerable follies" (*D* 30, 31, 32) [21.53; 22.70; 23.101] refer

not only to the boy's youthful infatuation in the story but also to the effects of that infatuation in the distortion of the immediate historical context already familiar to the knowledgeable Dublin reader. Joyce scholars have already offered several explanations of the problem in "Araby" of the narrator's apparent distance in "looking back at the boy, detachedly and judicially,"[1] in his introduction of the element of "dissonant self-narration,"[2] and in his role as a Lacanian "Other."[3] The new historical evidence suggests, moreover, that the narratological issue in the story rests on the deeper question of why Joyce's representational methodology in depicting the bazaar stands opposed to the shared social knowledge of his original Dublin readers.

Although Joyce is known to have visited the Araby bazaar of 1894, it is no longer possible to regard "Araby" merely as a faithful rendering of his experience. Stanislaus Joyce warned us long ago that most of *Dubliners* was "pure fiction" and that "Araby," for example, takes from Joyce's personal experiences only the North Richmond Street house and the juvenile gangs: "The rest of the story of 'Araby' is purely imaginary."[4] Although Richard Ellmann shows in his biography of Joyce that there was an actual Araby bazaar that visited Dublin in May 1894, Ellmann accepts everything recounted in the story as though it were a direct and accurate account of an episode in Joyce's life, asking us to believe that it was "perhaps described much as it happened"; Ellmann conflates the boy's uncle and Joyce's father when he speaks of "his uncle's (his father's?) consent" and goes so far as to read the text of the story as though it were taking place in real time: "the boy went anyway, and by the time he arrived, the bazaar was virtually over; the lights were going out, the merriment had ceased" (*JJII* 40n). Finally, "Araby" becomes for Ellmann both signifier and signified, the emblem and the substance of Joyce's growth as an artist: "The writing of *Stephen Hero* enabled Joyce, like the little boy in 'Araby,' to carry his chalice among a crowd of foes" (*JJII* 149). Although "Araby" can be viewed as the "autobiographical nexus" from which all of Joyce's subsequent writings flow, leading to the interpretation of "Araby" as "a portrait of the artist as a young boy,"[5] recent biographical research has moved away from construing the story simply as a mirror of Joyce's life.

1. Cleanth Brooks and Robert Penn Warren, *Understanding Fiction* (1943; New York: G. S. Crofts, 1947), p. 423.
2. John Paul Riquelme, *Teller and Tale in Joyce's Fiction: Oscillating Perspectives* (Baltimore: Johns Hopkins Univ. Press, 1983), pp. 106–08.
3. See Sheldon Brivic, *The Veil of Signs: Joyce, Lacan, and Perception* (Urbana: Univ. of Illinois Press, 1991), p. 12, and Garry M. Leonard, *Reading "Dubliners" Again: A Lacanian Perspective* (Syracuse Univ. Press, 1993), pp. 73–94.
4. Stanislaus Joyce, *My Brother's Keeper* (New York: Viking Press, 1958), pp. 62, 61.
5. Harry Stone, " 'Araby' and the Writings of James Joyce," *Antioch Review*, 25 (Fall 1965), 376.

Joyce's classmate William Fallon recalled seeing Joyce at the Araby
bazaar not as the solitary figure in the text but rather as someone
amidst the jam at the rail station:

> I had just got off the train at Lansdowne Road when I spied
> him. The train used to draw in on the main line and then go
> into a siding to let off visitors to the bazaar. It was a Saturday
> night. When we reached the bazaar it was just clearing up. It
> was very late. I lost Joyce in the crowd, but I could see that he
> was disheartened over something. I recall, too, that Joyce had
> had some difficulty for a week or so previously in extracting the
> money for the bazaar from his parent.[6]

In the tale, the boy arrives by himself on a deserted train at closing
time, but Fallon sees "Joyce in the crowd" near the station on a
platform filled with many people less concerned by the late hour.

Peter Costello, in his biography, goes even further in arguing that
Joyce transformed a different event into fictional form in "Araby."[7]
For Costello, the actual Araby bazaar was more a "gala fund-raising
event" than the modest charity bazaar in the story, and other details
of Joyce's life were "largely changed from his own experience" when
he used them in the text (129). Costello connects the boy's conflict
at the Araby bazaar to Joyce's private disappointment at failing to get
a part in the annual Belvedere Whitsun week school play of 12 May
1894, performed just two days before the opening of the bazaar: "The
turmoil of his story, though largely changed from his own experience,
was real enough. But who 'Mangan's sister' was—in whom the young
boy had such an interest—no record now exists to suggest" (129).
Although Costello could not identify "Mangan's sister" in contemporary sources, he remains understandably curious as to why Joyce
should have used the significant name of Mangan.

We can better understand Joyce's curious representation of the
historical bazaar of 1894 by reconstructing it in some detail from the
Araby in Dublin Official Catalogue[8] and contemporary Dublin newspaper advertisements and reports. First, we discover that the actual
1894 Araby bazaar was not at all like the one-building charity affair
described in "Araby." Although Ellmann reproduced the artwork
from the front cover of the Araby catalog (*JJII* Plate III) and referred
to its "merriment" (*JJII* 40), he gave no supporting details. The front
cover of the official catalogue refers to Araby not as a bazaar but as

6. "William G. Fallon," in *The Joyce We Knew*, ed. Ulick O'Connor (Cork: Mercier Press,
1967), pp. 47–48.
7. Peter Costello, *James Joyce: The Years of Growth, 1882–1915* (West Cork: Roberts Rinehart, 1992). Further references will be cited parenthetically in the text.
8. *Araby in Dublin Official Catalogue* (Dublin: Browne & Nolan, 1894). Further references
will be cited parenthetically in the text.

a "Grand Oriental Fête," and the back cover lists these entertainments and amusements:

"Araby" 1894
Magnificent Representation
Of
An Oriental City.
Cairo Donkeys & Donkey Boys.
An Arab Encampment.
INTERNATIONAL TUG-OF-WAR.
Dances by 250 Trained Children.
Eastern Magic from the Egyptian Hall, London.
CAFÉ CHANTANT, WITH ALL THE LATEST PARISIAN
SUCCESSES.
Skirt Dancing Up to Date.
Tableaux, Theatricals, Christy Minstrels.
Grand Theatre of Varieties.
"The Alhambra," an Orchestra of 50 Performers.
Switchback Railways and Roundabouts.
"MENOTTI," *The King of the Air*,
The Great Stockholm Wonder.
Bicycle Polo. Rifle & Clay Pigeon Shooting.
Dancing.
The Euterpean Ladies' Orchestra.
Eight Military Bands.
MAGNIFICENT DISPLAYS OF FIREWORKS,
By Brock, of the Crystal Palace, London
Admission One Shilling.[9]

It is worth noting that Mangan's sister had in mind just such an
entertainment as this in looking forward to the "splendid bazaar"
[22.86]: "She asked me was I going to *Araby*. I forget whether I
answered yes or no. It would be a splendid bazaar, she said; she
would love to go" (*D* 31) [22.85–87]. Although she cannot attend,
Mangan's sister correctly understands that the Araby bazaar will be
a festival of music, dancing, and amusements. But the slightly
younger boy can only think of trying to please her with a fairing, a
token or keepsake traditionally brought back from a fair: "—If I go,
I said, I will bring you something" (*D* 32) [23.100].[1]

Joyce builds the story on the boy's juvenile misconception of the

---

9. See Heyward Ehrlich, "Joyce's 'Araby' and the 'Splendid Bazaar' of 1894," *James Joyce
Literary Supplement*, 7 (Spring 1993), 18–20, and John Wyse Jackson and Bernard
McGinley, *James Joyce's "Dubliners": An Illustrated Edition* (New York: St. Martin's Griffin,
1995), p. 26.
1. Interestingly, the Irish vernacular for "fairing," *faireen*, suggests, in particular, a present
bought at a fair for a child. See Richard Wall, *A Dictionary and Glossary for the Irish
Literary Revival* (Gerrards Cross; Colin Smythe, 1995), p. 67.

Araby bazaar as primarily a place where keepsakes are sold. By contrast, the historical Araby bazaar was a major public event, a huge
international commercial enterprise with attractions from as far
away as Galway, London, Stockholm, and Chicago. It also served a
local charitable purpose in raising funds to lower the debt for the
reconstruction of the Jarvis Street Hospital, which had helped
33,784 accident victims in 1893.[2] Most of the entertainments and
amusements for Araby were arranged in England, and evidently the
lion's share of the production costs were fees for the English entrepreneurs: "The builders of Araby, Messrs. Womersley and Company,
of Leeds, receive a few hundred pounds, and the contractors Messrs.
Goodfellow, receive a fair amount of money."[3] The planning for the
Araby bazaar began a year in advance and entailed the placement of
1,200 "Araby in Dublin" posters in every railway station in Ireland,
England, and Scotland as well as in Cook's travel offices, supple-
mented with placards in Dublin shops and streets, announcements
similar to the one advertising the Mirus bazaar that Bloom encounters in Ulysses (U 8.1162).[4]

The Araby bazaar further promoted itself throughout the United
Kingdom with a raffle of donated merchandise, including a diamond
tiara, a Chippendale sideboard, a polo cart, and a grand piano, a
contest echoed in Bloom's purchase of bazaar lottery tickets in Ulysses (U 12.776–77, 17.1790–91).[5] Advertisements started well in
advance in several newspapers so as to promote the special railroad
fares to Dublin for Araby: "CHEAP EXCURSIONS/DURING THE
WEEK FROM/ALL PARTS OF IRELAND." The gross revenue for
the entire event was probably between £13,000 and £18,000, and
possibly a good deal more, since production costs were said to be
between £5,000 and £6,000 and the net available after expenses for
charity was announced as £8,000 to £12,000. The local Dublin committee, uncertain as to the economic success of the event, had sold
unlimited rights to collect their own special admissions to the visiting
sideshow operators. Thus, the operators of Brock's fireworks and of
Toogood's amusement rides each paid £200 for rights for the first
week (Toogood's paid £75 more for two additional days of the second
week), and several other star performers made similar undisclosed
arrangements, all proving to be remarkably profitable investments
for the foreign operators.[6] The bazaar stalls were also profitable for

2. Irish Times, 14 May 1894, 4.
3. Irish Times, 23 May 1894, 6.
4. Irish Times, 13 May 1894, 6.
5. Irish Times, 4 May 1894, 4.
6. Freeman's Journal, 23 May 1894, 6; Irish Times, 23 May 1894, 6. In 1894, £1 was equal
   to $5, but a century later the spending power of that money has been estimated as equal
   to $20 to $50. If we calculate the average of these two estimates at $35, the gross bazaar
   revenues estimated here at £13,000 to £18,000 would be worth approximately $455,000
   to $630,000 today.

the Dublin businessmen who used them not only to promote charity through the donated items to be raffled off but also to display and sell their own merchandise. The volunteer workers at the stalls, all women and children, dressed themselves as far as possible in costumes matching an Araby motif. In all, Araby embraced thirty-seven charity stalls and forty-three entertainments, requiring a combined staff of 1,760 stallholders and performers.[7] The *Irish Times* printed an estimated attendance total of 92,000 for the entire Araby bazaar, but the *Freeman's Journal* made a slightly bolder claim, supporting it with daily paid admissions counts (said to exclude exhibitors and workers) as follows: Monday, 10,874, Tuesday, 7,933, Wednesday, 8,852, Thursday, 15,214, Friday, 21,500, Saturday 18,000, Monday, 9,000, and Tuesday, 9,500—"Thus more than 100,000 persons, or nearly one-third of the population of Dublin, visited the *fête*."[8] Indeed, the press claimed with some justification that the annual Dublin charity bazaars had become the largest of their kind in the United-Kingdom.[9]

The central feature of the Araby bazaar, its large construction of a "[r]ealistic representation of an Oriental city,"[1] was a theatrical microcosm in the tradition of nineteenth-century panoramas and dioramas. Joyce refers throughout *Ulysses* to the similar Mirus bazaar, mentioning, in particular, the opening of it by the viceroy (*U* 10.1268–70); in the actual Araby fair, seventy-five dignitaries and titled members of the nobility, including the Lord Lieutenant of Ireland and the Lord Mayor of Dublin, had lent their names as official patrons of the fair. Unlike the bazaar in "Araby," a small, one-day affair, the historical Araby bazaar lasted for more than a week and drew audiences that ranked second only to the annual Dublin Horse Show, which also used the same Royal Dublin Society grounds in Ballsbridge, a ten-minute trip by rail from central Dublin. Initially, all the regular Araby events were to take place from Tuesday, 15 May, to Saturday, 19 May, during the Whitsuntide holiday, with some preliminary athletic events on the previous Saturday, 12 May, and a twelve-hour special preliminary "Gala Fête" on Whit Monday, 14 May, a bank holiday. The regular fair hours were from 2:00 to 10:30 p.m. daily, and admission was one shilling, plus extra charges for many of the sideshows and special attractions. The charity stalls were located in the Central Hall, but there were nine additional buildings or outdoor areas of Araby devoted to entertainments, amusements, and refreshments: the South Hall featured flower gardens, tea gardens, and orchestras, with traditional amusements such as palmistry; the East Hall was noted for its dining

7. *Irish Times*, 18 May 1894, 6.
8. *Irish Times*, 23 May 1894, 6; *Freeman's Journal*, 23 May 1894, 6.
9. *Irish Times*, 11 May 1894, 6.
1. *Irish Times*, 16 May 1894, 6.

area, refreshments, and cafés; the West Hall featured the Egyptian Hall of Mystery and the Telephone Concert; the Paddock Hall was home to the traditional amusements of dancing, theatricals, and music hall; the Anglesea Hall contained several larger amusements, including a concert hall, ballroom, theater, and shooting gallery; the Grounds featured the outdoor attractions of the Café Chantant (mentioned in the story—D 34–35) [25.187–88], merry-go-rounds, roundabouts, and swing boats; the Veterinary Paddock housed the daily clay-pigeon shooting competitions; and finally, the Jumping Enclosure provided space for the larger entertainments, including Menotti's high wire act, Brock's fireworks, the Eiffel searchlight tower, and cycling and bicycle-polo events. Two of these locations, the Veterinary Paddock and the Jumping Enclosure, were named for their equestrian functions. There were performances by a total of eight military bands.

There is some confusion in the use of the words "bazaar," "fair," and "fête." The official Araby catalogue refers to the entire entertainment event as a "Grand Oriental Fête," as indicated, and to the charity stalls alone as the "Grand Oriental Fair." Although *Thom's Official Directory of the United Kingdom* for 1904 lists four businesses as bazaars,[2] in his writings, Joyce almost always uses bazaar to mean a place of entertainment rather than a market. In *A Portrait*, young Stephen Dedalus is called a "model youth" for avoiding three temptations: "He doesn't smoke and he doesn't go to bazaars and he doesn't flirt" (P 76); in *Ulysses*, while Stephen vividly remembers the sexual entertainments of Paris, Molly and Boylan first meet at a bazaar dance (U 4.525–30, 15.2826–28). Indeed, the Dublin bazaars had a very old reputation for sexual immorality. The first medieval Irish fair was established in 1204 in Donnybrook, the Dublin suburb directly adjoining Ballsbridge, the site of Araby, eventually not only lending its very name to violence and mayhem but also becoming notorious for widespread female drinking and sexual misconduct. Even the regular importation of English entertainments and amusements at Donnybrook after 1819 did not quell the mounting waves of moral protest, which eventually led to its suppression after 1855.[3] These annual Donnybrook fairs were soon replaced by a series of industrial and commercial Dublin shows, as recorded in the Dublin annals of *Thom's* for 1904: the Dublin International Exhi-

---

2. *Thom's Official Directory of the United Kingdom of Great Britain and Ireland for the Year 1904* (Dublin: A. Thorn, 1904), p. 2052. A microfiche edition was issued in Dublin by the Irish University Press in 1973.

3. Séamus ó Maitú, *The Humours of Donnybrook: Dublin's Famous Fair and Its Suppression* (Dublin: Irish Academic Press, 1995), p. 45; concerned about the fair's reputation for the ruin of women, one observer is quoted in this work as estimating that, of 40,000 women present, some 30,000 were drunk by 5:00 P.M.

bition of 1865, from 9 May to 9 November, which had drawn
900,000 people; the Dublin Exhibition of Arts, Industries, and Man-
ufacturers of 1872, which opened 1 June and ran for 154 days and
58 evenings, attracting 420,000 people; and the Masonic Centenary
Exhibition and Bazaar for the Masonic Female Orphan's School,
which opened 17 May 1892, the first of the series of annual Dublin
charity bazaars that was to include Araby two years later. This 1892
fair is confusedly remembered by the boy's aunt in the story as "some
Freemason affair," and the name of Mrs. Mercer, the pawnbroker's
widow who collects used stamps for "some pious purpose" (D 32,
33) [23.109; 24.139], alludes to the May 1904 Mirus Bazaar for
Mercer Hospital, which Joyce immortalized in Ulysses, moving it to
16 June 1904 (U 8.1162–63, 10.1268–69, 13.1166–67).

As a syndicated international fête of traveling entertainments and
amusements, the Araby bazaar reflected both its English origins and
the local sharing of Anglo-Irish culture in subtle ways, celebrating
British rule in a theater called the "Empire" and in a *tableau vivant*
representing a scene called "Britain and her Colonies," according to
the *Araby in Dublin Official Catalogue* (61). Tickets for merchandise
to be raffled off were called "ballots," a conflation of commercialism
and enfranchisement. There was an imperial British attitude, simultaneously arrogant and naïve, in claiming, as the *Official Catalogue*
does, that each attendant for the garden seats of the Arab Encampment "speaks a foreign language" and that the Cairo Donkeys and
Donkey Boys had an "Oriental" in attendance, as though all foreign
languages were the same or all "Orientals" were alike (53, 73). The
press linked Dublin to London as the other major British city
included in the itinerary of the current traveling bazaar, taking pride
in the fact that "Araby in Dublin" was scheduled before rather than
after its sister bazaar, "Constantinople in London."[4] Araby made a
show of scientific and technological progress (which Joyce satirized
at length in the "Circe" episode of Ulysses) in the displays that featured recent inventions such as the Telephone Concerts from Belfast, the electric searchlight display, and the use of electric lanterns
at night on a scale then unprecedented in Dublin.[5] But some attractions were more pseudoscientific than scientific, such as the claim,
in the *Araby in Dublin Official Catalogue*, of the "Eiffel Search-Light
Tower," said to be "80 FEET HIGH, Imported for ARABY directly
from Chicago": "This powerful light will turn night into day, and
when flashed on the Moon at 9 p.m. at night, the Man will be distinctly visible to the naked eye" (73).

Many of the amusements, such as séances, tableaux, and mirror

4. *Irish Times*, 23 May 1894, 6.
5. *Freeman's Journal*, 23 May 1894, 6.

and lighting effects were typical components of the traveling fairs and fêtes of the precinematic era.[6] In the smaller Irish county fairs, safely removed from the watchful eye of Dublin authorities, a strong undercurrent of Irish nationalism could be found in the only entertainment available, the ballad singer whose songs contained covert political messages.[7] But in "Araby," these nationalist ballads are performed far outside the Araby bazaar by "street singers, who sang a *come-all-you* about O'Donovan Rossa or a ballad about the troubles in our native land" (*D* 31) [22.60–62], allusions to the notorious harshness of the British towards imprisoned Irish nationalists and indifference to Irish suffering during the famine.[8] Moreover, the mass scale of Araby and the impersonal, commercial quality of its physical entertainment and material amusements seem to have eclipsed any political meanings that might have been found in ethnically designated performances, such as the Irish songs, Irish dances, or even Irish fireworks. Instead, the volunteer workers in the stalls expressed themselves through their own costumes, many representing Arabian, Ottoman, Egyptian, Moorish, Spanish, Gypsy, Mediterranean, Deccan, Hindu, and even Japanese expressions of the Araby theme or its Middle Eastern or Oriental variations.

Although "Constantinople in London" might reflect the view of sophisticated British and European travelers who, since 1883, could take the Orient Express train twice a week directly from Paris to Constantinople, by contrast "Araby in Dublin" was associated with more distant Moorish and Spanish cultures, the press likening its large constructed Oriental replica to "a city like Algeria [*sic*] or Granada."[9] The Irish-Spanish-Moorish link became explicit in the theme of the Galway stall, "Algeciras" (31), the Andalusian port opposite Gibraltar. Joyce reminds us that Galway, often known as the "Spanish city" of Ireland, was reputedly settled by "Spanish stock" and was still famed for the "Spanish type" in its population, anticipating the Galway-Gibraltar-Semitic association that he made in connecting Nora and Molly Bloom (*CW* 229).[1] Joyce elsewhere used some of the same geographical landmarks to define the linguistic domination of Latin at its height as extending "from Gibraltar to Arabia, and to

6. See Christiane Py and Cécile Ferenczi, *La Fête forain d'autrefois: Les années 1900* (Lyons: Manufacture, 1987).

7. Patrick Logan, *Fair Day: The Story of Irish Fairs and Markets* (Belfast: Appleton Press, 1986), pp. 127–28.

8. See *D* 467–69; Don Gifford, *Joyce Annotated: Notes for "Dubliners" and "A Portrait of the Artist as Young Man,"* 2nd ed. (Berkeley: Univ. of California Press, 1982), pp. 45–46; Donald Torchiana, *Backgrounds for Joyce's "Dubliners"* (Boston: Allen & Unwin, 1986), pp. 56–62; R. B. Kershner, *Joyce, Bakhtin, and Popular Culture* (Chapel Hill: Univ. of North Carolina Press, 1989), pp. 46–60; and Jackson and McGinley (p. 22).

9. *Irish Times*, 16 May 1894, 6.

1. For further discussion, see Suzette Henke, "James Joyce East and Middle East: Literary Resonances of Judaism, Egyptology, and Indian Myth," *Journal of Modern Literature*, 13 (July 1986), 307–19.

the stranger-hating Briton" (*CW* 30). The range of the Dublin costumes defined the domain of Araby in the popular mind as the zone
of the ancient Near East and the Phoenician Mediterranean associated with the old Irish myths, but the politically astute could see
Araby also as the community of exclusion just outside the main
perimeter of Anglo-Saxon political domination and western European hegemony. Joyce, already very sensitive to how language, literature, and culture defined nationality, may have felt a kinship with
the East in reporting from Austria shortly before writing "Araby" the
fact that Berlitz, his multinational employer, operated from its
Vienna office all its outposts in "Austria-Hungary, Italy, Switzerland,
Turkey, Greece, Egypt" (*LettersII* 84).

Had Mangan's sister in the story come to the actual Araby bazaar,
she would have discovered the extent to which popular entertainments and amusements were associated with eastern and Oriental
exoticism. In the West Hall, she would have encountered the Egyptian Hall of Mystery, featuring James Stuart, from the Egyptian Hall,
Piccadilly, London, in his "Marvelous Séance Mystique" (57); the
tableaux vivants of Androeikonismata, including such oriental or
exotic motifs as the "Graces Decorating a Statue," "Night Attack by
Matabele," "Espanita: A Spanish Restaurant on a Fête Day," and
finally the previously mentioned number, "Britain and her Colonies"
(31, 57). In addition, she would also have found in the Paddock Hall
the "Empire" theater, with skirt and serpentine dancing, Spanish
lady guitarists, and the Princess Nala Damajante, the "Hindoo Ser-
pent Charmer with Her Boa Constrictors and Pythons," and in
Anglesey Hall, the Alhambra Theater offering "musical, histrionic,
terpsichorean, and acrobatic entertainment" (61, 63, 65). The Café
Chantant was actually located in the Grounds, where it featured
French, German, Italian, Spanish, English, and Irish songs, piano
and violin solos, recitations, dances, and many other attractions. The
Grounds also had Toogood's "Merry-Go-Rounds, Ships in Full Sail,
American Swing Boats, And all the latest novelties in Locomotion,"
anticipating the hobbyhorse rides that Joyce included in "Circe" (*U*
15.2719, 4109). It is hard to know what to make of the presence at
Araby of Mrs. Cohen, a gypsy queen at the Arab Encampment, and
Master Cohen, a violin prodigy of eight at the Café Chantant, who
may have been mother and son, suggesting some possible familial
tradition in these traveling entertainments that Joyce later incorporated into "Circe" by giving Bella Cohen, whoremistress, a son she
supposedly supports at Oxford (*U* 15.1289).[2]

The two attractions that dominated Araby were the fireworks and
the high-wire act. Brock's Fireworks, specializing in narratives of "a

2. *Irish Times*, 16 May 1894, 6; 21 May 1894, 6.

magnitude and brilliancy never before seen in Ireland," featured
eastern motifs for the occasion in the form of the "Grand Naval
Spectacular Device, The Battle of the Nile (first time in Ireland),"
the "Marvelous Transformation Device, Araby (new)," and the "Triple Device, The Oriental Mystic Fountains (first time)" (77, 78), the
additional admission charge being 6 d. (2s 6d. for reserved seats).
Brock's shaped and narrative fireworks anticipate the fantasy in
"Circe," where the *"Mirus bazaar fireworks go up from all sides with
symbolical phallopyrotechnic designs"* (U 15.1494), and fireworks
elsewhere in *Ulysses* (U 13.680–86, 1166–68). Nearby, the crowds
wondered at "Menotti, the King of the Air: The Great Stockholm
Wonder," who performed in the Jumping Enclosure at 4:30 and
9:30 P.M. each day with his "Marvelous and Sensational Performance on the High Wire" (75), which was illuminated in the evening
by the electric searchlight in the background.[3] Thanks to its dazzling
electric amusements and pyrotechnic entertainments, Araby seemed
unusually attractive at night; after dark on Friday, for example, attendance was estimated at 12,000 and 15,000, about two-thirds the
daily total of 21,500.[4]

Friday night was intended to be the climax of the bazaar, according
to the official catalogue, and the attractions were to taper off gradually on Saturday until closing time at 10:30 P.M. Therefore, in
Joyce's story, by the time of the boy's arrival on Saturday at 9:50
P.M., he would have had only a few minutes in which to complete
his mission before closing time on the last night of the Araby bazaar.
But, in reality, the schedule was altered after it rained earlier in the
week. The new fair hours were extended until 11:30 P.M. on Friday
and Saturday nights, and direct trains (the boy in the story arrives
on just such a train) were provided to and from the Araby site in
Ballsbridge between 7:00 and 11:30 P.M. In fact, these special trains
were so successful in bringing immense crowds to Araby on Friday
night that a two-hour "crush at the turnstiles" developed, requiring
the intervention of the police.[5] Extra Saturday night events were
added, including performances every thirty minutes at the Café
Chantant until 10:30 P.M., an additional night session of Brock's
fireworks, and a final high-wire performance by Menotti at 9:15 or
9:30 P.M.[6] Thus, Saturday night rivaled Friday night at the Araby
fair, and the momentum carried over to the added evening sessions
on Monday and Tuesday of the following week. Perhaps the extended
late Saturday night entertainments may explain why the gate atten-

3. Perhaps Stockholm had some special significance for these traveling shows: the sailor in
   the "Eumaeus" episode of *Ulysses* claims to have seen Hengler's Royal Circus there (U
   16.411–13).
4. *Freeman's Journal,* 21 May 1894, 4.
5. *Freeman's Journal,* 19 May 1894, 5.
6. *Freeman's Journal,* 19 May 1894, 5.

dant in the story accepts the boy's admission fee at 9:50 P.M. even though the charity portion of the bazaar is closing. At 9:50 P.M., the actual Café Chantant was still in operation, with two more lively shows, said always to be full, still to come at 10:00 and 10:30 P.M.[7] If the charity stalls were empty or closed in the Central Hall after 9:50 P.M. on Saturday night, it was because the main events of the evening, the spectacular fireworks and the high-wire acts, had drawn the crowds to the Grounds and the Jumping Enclosure only a few minutes before.

The knowledgeable Dublin reader who knew the minutiae of the historical 1894 Dublin bazaar might well wonder why so few significant details survive in Joyce's text. Perhaps 6,000 people were still actively enjoying themselves in several brightly lighted sites of the actual Araby bazaar at 9:50 P.M. on Saturday evening, 19 May 1894, at the very moment that Joyce's story describes only six persons in one closing building. The actual Café Chantant had several packed performances still to come at that hour in the bustling Grounds, but its counterpart in the story is shown as already closed amidst darkening charity stalls. Even the detail in the text of the "great jars that stood like eastern guards" (D 35) [26.204] at the charity stall seems to echo an Arabian Nights tale more than the actual Araby bazaar.

But the strongest social reality that the knowledgeable Dubliner could bring to bear on the event was the awareness of the sheer magnitude and scale of the Araby bazaar, attended by some 100,000 people, requiring 1,760 workers, and grossing £18,000 or more. These circumstances focus critical attention not only on the matter of the boy's money but also on corresponding business details in the background of the story. For example, in the final scene, the boy's thoughts are diverted by the significant iteration of three triads involving money: "two men were counting money on a salver," two men talk to the girl in the sales stall, and the boy lets "two pennies . . . fall against the sixpence" in his pocket (D 35) [25.188–89; 26.214]. The boy's hope to find an affordable and appropriate gift for Mangan's sister vanishes as he sees at the stall only an array of "porcelain vases and flowered teasets" (D 35) [25.191–92]. Even though the boy is running out of time and money, these domestic ornaments for an aspiring Victorian household are utterly inappropriate for him as a personal keepsake because porcelain and tea, as commodities of the Far East trade, which the Dublin reader would immediately realize, were obvious emblems of British economic colonialism. Sadly, any of the boy's well-intentioned attempts to win the girl's esteem with a gift rather than with his deeds would degrade his chivalry into simony, the theme of the poem mentioned in the text, "The Arab's Farewell to his Steed" (D 34) [24.162–63].

7. *Freeman's Journal*, 21 May 1894, 4.

The sophisticated Dublin reader may have had further suspicions about the scene where the two young English gentlemen flirt with the young working girl. The gentlemen seem curiously out of place, being neither regular patrons nor working staff, their accents signifying not only their social superiority but also some identification with their compatriots, the English entrepreneurs behind the fair. Perhaps they wish in all sincerity to invite her to join them in the fun of the entertainments continuing elsewhere at the fair; yet if the old sexual notoriety of the Dublin Donnybrook fair was perhaps on the minds of the parents of Mangan's sister when they sent her on a retreat during the very week of the Araby bazaar, then that same reputation might have figured in the plans of the two English gentlemen who strategically engage a solitary girl in flirtatious conversation just at closing time on a Saturday night.

Of course, the boy's imagination is primed from the start to escape from all adversity seen in the external social world into his private realm of sexual and literary images. As a fictional character, he belongs to the same type as the younger boy in "The Sisters," remembering a dream, perhaps, of Persia (D 14) [7.155], the older boy in A Portrait, who is seen "praying in an ecstasy of Oriental posture" (P 258), and several characters in Ulysses who share thoughts of Turko the Terrible and Haroun al Raschid.[8] Such dreams of the East had long flourished in western literature, beginning with sometimes fabulous medieval travelers' accounts of wealth, power, and spices, inventing Araby as a place where "reality and dream become one," outside the ordinary boundaries of geographical, historical, and political Europe.[9] In English literature, images of Araby can be traced back to John Milton's "Araby the blessed" and John Skelton's phoenix as the "bird of Araby," as well as to fragrant Araby in English romantic poetry and even "Araby's gay Haram" in Thomas Moore's popular Lalla Rookh.[1] In English and French writers of the nineteenth century, Araby became an exotic, sensual, or utopian alternative to the West, an epitome of difference. But Irish writers looked to the Orient to represent their rising cultural nationalism and their rejection of British influence. For several centuries, Irish thinkers had claimed a special cultural relation to the ancient East, believing that the Irish language derived not from Celtic or other European tongues but directly from Phoenician or Hebrew and that, therefore, the Irish people were also of ancient Middle Eastern descent (if not one of

8. Such popular entertainment is deeply embedded in Ulysses as a "text of the culture"—see Cheryl Herr, Joyce's Anatomy of Culture (Urbana: Univ. of Illinois Press, 1986), p. 8 and passim.
9. Dorothee Metlitski, The Matter of Araby in Medieval England (New Haven: Yale Univ. Press, 1977), p. 240.
1. Thomas Moore, Lalla Rookh (London: Longman, 1849), p. 151.

the lost tribes of Israel).[2] Just as Aeneas had come from Troy via
Carthage to found Rome, so the ancient Milesians were said to have
made the epic voyage from Phoenicia via Scythia and Spain to Ireland. These Hebraeo-Hibernian and Phoenician myths of origin were
supported in early modern scholarly manuscripts, such as Richard
Creagh's *De Lingua Hibernica* and Geoffrey Keating's *History of Ireland,* and even in efforts published as late as the nineteenth century,
such as Francis Crawford's learned papers on "Hebraeo-Celtic Affin-
ities" and Standish James O'Grady's highly influential *History of Ireland.*[3] Significantly, by the early eighteenth century, these Oriental
myths of Irish origins had been incorporated into a distinctively Irish
literary form, the *aisling,* the dream-vision poem of love or nationality, in which the poet encounters the beautiful, noble sky-maiden,
the persona of Ireland, typically of Milesian ancestry, in an intense,
myth-laden, virtuoso-style interview.[4]

Celtic antiquarianism, already spurred by the vogue of Ossian,[5]
contributed, in the next generation, to the full flowering of popular
Irish Orientalism in the widely admired poetry and parlor songs of
Moore, who had tactfully attempted to raise English consciousness
of the problems of Ireland through such works as *Irish Melodies.*[6]
Moore subsequently exploited what has been called "the parallel
fashion for Orientalism and Celticism"[7] in his sensationally successful verse tale *Lalla Rookh,* in which he embedded a political plea for
tolerance for Irish Catholics: "*the cause of tolerance was again my
inspiring theme;* and the spirit that had spoken in the melodies of
Ireland soon found itself at home in the East."[8] The popular song
"Araby's Daughter," from *Lalla Rookh* and set to music by George

2. See Norman Vance, "Celts, Carthaginians, and constitutions: Anglo-Irish literary relations,
   1780–1820," *Irish Historical Studies,* 22 (March 1981), 226–27; Joseph T. Leerssen, "On
   the Edge of Europe: Ireland in search of oriental roots, 1680–1850," *Comparative Criticism: An Annual Journal,* 8 (1986), 94–101; and Ira B. Nadel, *Joyce and the Jews* (Iowa
   City: Univ. of Iowa Press, 1989), pp. 156–62.
3. See Norman Vance, *Irish Literature: A Social History* (Oxford: Basil Blackwell, 1990),
   pp. 21–22, 27–28.
4. Declan Kiberd, *Inventing Ireland* (Cambridge: Harvard Univ. Press, 1996), p. 318; see
   also Robert Welch, ed., *The Oxford Companion to Irish Literature* (Oxford: Clarenden
   Press, 1996).
5. James Macpherson stimulated preromantic enthusiasm for old and primitive works with
   his sensationally successful *Fingal: An Ancient Epic Poem in Six Books, Together with
   Several Other Poems* (London: T. Becket and P. A. DeHondt, 1762) and related works,
   supposedly translations of the writings of the third century bard and warrior, Ossian.
   Widely read and imitated, the writings enjoyed prolonged attention, and even after their
   exposure as Macpherson's inventions, they continued to have an influence on Romanti-
   cism and the Celtic Revival.
6. *Moore, Irish Melodies,* 10 vols. (1808–1835; Dublin: Gill and Son, 1963).
7. See David Lloyd, "James Clarence Mangan's Oriental Translation and the Question of
   Origins," *Comparative Literature,* 38 (Spring 1986), 33.
8. After twenty editions of *Lalla Rookh,* Moore added a preface in 1841 that revealed his
   covert didacticism. The italics are added to make the point in Mohammed Sharafuddin,
   Islam and Romantic Orientalism: Literary Encounters with the Orient (London: I. B. Tauris,
   1994), p. 172.

Kiallmark, went through many editions both as a separate number and in song collections.[9] Moore's *Lalla Rookh* was still so well liked in the 1870s that it could be adapted by Frederick Clay into a musical cantata with lyrics by William Gorman Wills, from which came the separate number, "I'll Sing Thee Songs of Araby," often cited as a possible direct source of the name of the 1894 Dublin bazaar.[1] The sustained vogue of *Lalla Rookh* in various incarnations served to define a distinctive genre of popular Irish poetry and music as the "songs of Araby,"[2] a fresh epidemic of which was touched off by the Dublin Araby bazaar:

> There must be something in the name of Araby that causes the divine afflatus to descend upon those who study its manners and customs. Moore's "Lallah Rookh," with its resplendent and vivid imagery and perfect poetry, was the wonder of the age, for the Irish songster's experience of the East was confined to his reading of the Arabian Nights and Oriental literature generally. With the advent of Araby in Dublin there has been a passion for producing Arabian poetry and music.[3]

Honoring this tradition, the uncle in the story associated the mention of Araby with Caroline Norton's sentimental poem, *"The Arab's Farewell to his Steed,"* which he is still reciting as the boy departs (*D* 34) [24.162–63].[4] Joyce often acknowledges the public fascination with Moore, referring or alluding to him in *Dubliners* as a favorite author of the "josser" in "An Encounter" (*D* 25, 26) [17.195; 18.248], the author of the song performed by the harpist in "Two Gallants" (*D* 54) [42.166–67], and the writer of the *Irish Melodies* that Gabriel thinks of in "The Dead" (*D* 179) [155.127–29], the title of which story echoes Moore's song, "O Ye Dead!" (*JJII* 244).

Joyce also ridiculed Moore's musical strain of Irish Orientalism as "the moore the melodest" (*FW* 468.27–28), pretending to be sick of

9. *Lalla Rookh* achieved prominence through frequent reprints, and the widespread adaptations of various portions of the work into such forms as parlor song, musical review, pantomime, opera-comique, ballet, oratorio, and Oriental extravaganza kept it before the public in England, France, Germany, Italy, and elsewhere for fully seventy years. Three well-known composers who wrote extended musical settings of *Lalla Rookh* were Robert Schumann, Jacques Offenbach, and Anton Rubenstein.

1. The Frederick Clay-William Gorman Wills version of *Lalla Rookh* was first produced as a cantata in London around 1877, and its popular signature song, "I'll Sing Thee Songs of Araby," survived well into the twentieth century in the repertory of one of Joyce's favorite Irish tenors, John McCormack, who recorded it on the Victrola label. "I'll Sing Thee Songs of Araby" may have helped to suggest the theme of the 1894 bazaar, but I find no evidence that it was ever adopted as its "theme song," as has been claimed.

2. See the *Irish Times*, 16 May 1894, 6.

3. *Irish Times*, 18 May 1894, 6

4. As Stone has pointed out (*D* 357–58), the theme of simony in the poem was echoed in a famous lawsuit brought by Norton against his wife, a well-known beauty, which publicized his exploitation of her to gain political preferment. Norton's poem was also printed in a musical setting. "Araby" was a standard nickname for a horse; an Arabian horseman was pictured on the Araby store-window posters.

the cloying popularity of Moore's *Irish Melodies* and *Lalla Rookh* in "tummy moor's maladies" (*FW* 492.34) and making Rudyard Kipling's popular *Mandalay* one too many in "Inglo-Andean Medoleys from Tommany Moohr" (*FW* 106.08), in each instance playing with the Irish pronunciation of Moore as "moor." But in complete seriousness, when it suited him, Joyce also subscribed to many of the same Irish myths, including the belief that both the Irish language and alphabet were "oriental in origin": "The Irish language, although of the Indo-European family, differs from English almost as much as the language spoken in Rome differs from that spoken in Teheran. It has an alphabet of special characters, and a history almost three thousand years old" (*CW* 155). Citing Charles Vallancey, Joyce believed that Irish folk speech still resembled the ancient Phoenician language (*CW* 156). In the late eighteenth century, Vallancey had made the extravagant claim that Irish was the source of most ancient languages by interpreting the name Iran, the place where Indo-European languages were said to have originated, as a variant spelling of Eiran, an old name for Ireland.[5] In *Ulysses*, Stephen and Bloom illustrate a variation on this idea when they compare the Irish and Hebrew alphabets (*U* 17.24–73). Joyce's schematic geography for *Ulysses*, as Michael Seidel has shown, links the Hungarian Virags to the Gibraltar-born Molly by building on the Irish myths that traced the original rulers of Ireland to Milesius, a king who could claim both ancient Phoenician and Hebrew ancestors, then to descendants who had roamed in Scythia, the region north and east of ancient Greece, later migrating via Spain to settle finally in Ireland.[6] Joyce was so passionate in stressing the literary affinity of Ireland and the Orient that he began his list of modern Irish authors with the names of two distinguished nineteenth-century translators of Oriental literature, Edward Fitzgerald and Richard Burton, confusing the actual translator of *The Rubaiyat of Omar Khayyam* with his namesake, the Irish rebel whose biography had been written by Tom Moore (*CW* 171). For Joyce, Irish literature could not be based on European literature any more than it could be on English literature: "For the Irish, the dates of Luther's Reformation and the French Revolution mean nothing" (*CW* 167).

By 1902, three years before undertaking the writing of "Araby" and while he was still an undergraduate of twenty, Joyce found in writing the essay "James Clarence Mangan" the alternative version of Irish Orientalism upon which to build his own. Eventually, Joyce

5. See Leerssen (pp. 102–08, 111–12), and Lloyd (p. 33). Perhaps Irish was technically classified as an Oriental language because the phonetic values in the Irish alphabet could not be directly transposed to the Roman alphabet.
6. See Stuart Gilbert, *James Joyce's "Ulysses,"* rev. ed. (New York: Knopf Publishers, 1952), pp. 65–66, and Michael Seidel, *Epic Geography: James Joyce's "Ulysses"* (Princeton: Princeton Univ. Press, 1976), p. 17. Joyce frequently refers to Milesius and the Milesians (*CW* 159, 166; *P* 100; *U* 12.1310, 14.372; *FW* 253.35, 347.09, 518.07).

was to rank Mangan with Dante and Henrik Ibsen, acknowledging him among those writers he especially admired by writing a musical accompaniment for Mangan's "Dark Rosaleen" and reciting Mangan from memory.[7] Joyce would have joined William Hazlitt in condemning Moore for turning the "wild harp of Erin into a musical snuffbox,"[8] and for just this reason in his essay Joyce took Mangan's isolated life as the necessary antithesis of the social success of Moore's career, embracing Mangan's primitive, compelling, and forbidding poetry as the perfect antidote to Moore's well-polished, easily accessible, and universally praised verse. Joyce paid homage to Mangan as the last of "the old Celtic bards" (CW 174), the one intense nationalist among the Irish Orientalists, the leading Byronic poseur in Dublin who flagrantly puzzled readers in his translations as to "whether learning or imposture lies behind such phrases as 'from the ottoman' or 'from the Coptic' " (CW 76). It is possible to see young Joyce being instinctively drawn to what Robert Welch has called the final images in Mangan's poetry of "freezing, dumbness, inarticulateness" in his exploration of his favorite themes of "darkness, paralysis, and the abyss."[9]

In his 1902 essay, Joyce also announced his discovery in Mangan of what were to be the main underlying themes of "Araby," the noble twin identity of "Ireland" and "Istambol" and its merger with chivalric love in its highest manifestation in Michelangelo, Dante, and Petrarch:

> East and West meet in that personality (we know how); images interweave there like soft, luminous scarves and words ring like brilliant mail, and whether the song is of Ireland or of Istambol it has the same refrain. . . . Vittoria Colonna and Laura and Beatrice—even she upon whose face many lives have cast that shadowy delicacy, as of one who broods upon distant terrors and riotous dreams, and that strange stillness before which love is silent, Mona Lisa—embody one chivalrous idea. (CW 78–79)[1]

Moreover, Joyce evidently found in Mangan's fictionalized autobiographical sketches a source for the character type of the boy in "Araby," particularly in Mangan's claim to have suffered a childhood

---

7. See Robert Scholes and Richard M. Kain, The Workshop of Daedalus (Evanston: Northwestern Univ. Press, 1965), pp. 178, 191–92, 215. Joyce planned a deluxe edition of the Mangan essay in 1930 to compete with its unauthorized issue by Jacob Schwartz (LettersIII 209 and n3). For further evidence of Joyce's interest in Mangan, see Marvin Magalaner and Richard M. Kain, Joyce: The Man, the Work, the Reputation (New York: New York Univ. Press, 1956), pp. 27–30, 67, 318n.
8. William Hazlitt is quoted in Vance (p. 232).
9. Robert Welch, Irish Poetry from Moore to Yeats (Gerrards Cross: Colin Smythe, 1980), pp. 77, 84.
1. The passage is quoted and amplified in Gilbert (p. 86), and see Mary T. Reynolds, Joyce and Dante: The Shaping Imagination (Princeton: Princeton Univ. Press), pp. 164–65, 238–40.

so wretched that he took "refuge in books and solitude," preferring to shut himself up in a "close room" in a state of high bliss: "I loved to indulge in solitary rhapsodies, and if intruded upon on these occasions, I was made very unhappy."[2] Joyce further seems to have encountered in the famous "ballad episode" of Mangan's biographers an anticipation of the basic plot situation of "Araby."[3] After his adored older sister died in childhood from a scalding incident (in another autobiographical fragment, he writes that her father's impudence drives her from the house), the child Mangan immortalizes her as a "blue-eyed cherub, her image haunting him in his dreams," and in this juvenile variation on the *aisling*, she is immediately replaced in Mangan's affections by the surrogate sister who lives next door, the "little girl of curling sunny locks, a couple of Summers his senior."[4] In this "full blown childhood romance," as Lloyd puts it (*Nationalism* 44), the beloved girl sends the quiveringly incapable child Mangan out into the streets in quest of a ballad, whereupon the rain damages his eyes.[5] Several distinctive elements of the conclusion of "Araby" are anticipated here: the beloved slightly older neighbor girl, the identification of the girl as Mangan's surrogate sister, the juvenile quest as a version of the chivalric mission, the ballads in the streets, the inadequacy of the child fully to accomplish the courtly deeds that he has undertaken, and the final damage to his eyes.

The ultimate appeal of Mangan for Joyce, as David Lloyd suggests, is in his having made his life, or at least his own fictional accounts

2. Mangan is quoted in D. J. O'Donoghue, *The Life and Writings of James Clarence Mangan* (Edinburgh: Patrick Geddes, 1897; Dublin: M. H. Gill, 1897), pp. 6–7, 9. Joyce had heard of Mangan at meetings of Irish literary societies (*CW* 76) and was also personally acquainted with O'Donoghue (*LettersII* 77). In *Nationalism and Minor Literature: James Clarence Mangan and the Emergence of Irish Cultural Nationalism* (Berkeley: Univ. of California Press, 1987), pp. 32–34, 49–77, Lloyd sorts out the chronology of Mangan's several fictional autobiographies: Mangan's earliest sketch, prepared for Father Meehan, appeared more than three decades later in *Poets and Poetry of Munster: A Selection of Irish Songs by the Poets of the Eighteenth Century* (1884; Dublin: James Duffy, 1925); the next self-sketch to be composed was the first to be published, appearing in *The Irishman*, 1 (August 1850). The John Mitchel political biography in James Clarence Mangan, *Poems with Biographical Introduction by John Mitchel* (New York: P. M. Haverty, 1859), seems to have set the tone that Joyce himself followed. In the absence of supporting documents for Mangan's fictitious autobiographical sketches, his later biographers took liberties in merging or embellishing on whatever he had published. Further references to the Lloyd text will be cited parenthetically in the text as *Nationalism*.
3. See Lloyd, in *Nationalism* (p. 33). The most recent biographer of Mangan agrees in reading "Araby" as essentially "repeating the formula of Mangan's own story"—see Ellen Shannon-Mangan, *James Clarence Mangan: A Biography* (Dublin: Irish Academic Press, 1996), p. 439 n11. This volume became available only after my article was completed.
4. John McCall, *The Life of James Clarence Mangan* (1882; Dublin: Carraig Books, 1975), pp. 4–5.
5. "Araby" particularly echoes the episode in Mangan's fictional autobiography that *McCall's Life* had mythologized into a parable of the child "knight-errant" on a dedicated "mission" (p. 5) to please his slightly older beloved. In this episode, Mangan attempts an act of gallantry far beyond his years, and the ill-advised quest results disastrously in eight years of near blindness, an anticipation of the concluding image in "Araby": "my eyes burned with anguish and anger" (*D* 35).

of his life, into the first authentically Irish version of the myth of the romantic hero, the Byronic self-inventing self, the wanderer and outcast from society who savors memories of his sinful and gloomy past (*Nationalism* 44). Joyce reports the lengths to which Mangan had gone in pursuing his self-definition: when faced with the charge that his autobiographic sketch was "wildly exaggerated and partly false, Mangan answered, 'Maybe I dreamed it' " (*CW* 181). The harshest possible external conditions of deprivation and alienation were essential elements in Mangan to produce their opposite, intense visions in the tradition of the Irish *aisling*. Following Mangan, Joyce stipulated that the highest form of poetry required a double denial, first, the negation of the usual sense of social and historical reality, and second, the rejection of whatever seemed merely literary tradition: poetry was therefore "always a revolt against artifice, a revolt, in a sense, against actuality" (*CW* 81). In a note, Mangan reported that, while translating the *aisling*, "A Vision of Connaught in the Thirteenth Century," he replaced the Irish *ceann* with its homonym, the Arabian *khan*: "Identical with Irish *Ceann*, head or chief; but I the rather gave him the Oriental title, as really fancying myself in one of the regions of Araby the blest."[6]

But in both these largely biographical essays on Mangan, Joyce had no choice but to follow the views of John Mitchel, Mangan's first biographer-editor, a political exile, who made Mangan into the Irish hero who opposed the imperialism of British criticism by his own duality between his inner and outer lives, "one well known to the Muses, the other to the police"; in tracing Mitchel's influence, Lloyd has characterized his goal in presenting Mangan as "explicitly the image of an Ireland outwardly oppressed but secretly, spiritually alive" (*Nationalism* 28–29, 32). For Joyce, the stories in *Dubliners*, similarly intended as "the first step towards the spiritual liberation of my country" (*LettersI* 63), drew on Mangan as a significant ally by depicting him, as Mitchel had done, like one of those rare poets who believe that "their artistic life should be nothing more than a true and continual revelation of their spiritual life," and who, furthermore, had rejected all ancestries and dependencies in the tenet "that the poet is sufficient in himself" and the maker of his own patrimony (*CW* 184). The boy in "Araby" knows very well that he lives in the realm of images and the imagination when he reacts to the political songs of the nationalistic street-singers: "These noises converged in a single sensation of life for me: I imagined that I bore my chalice safely through a throng of foes" (*D* 31) [22.62–64]. Although he knows both chalice and foes are unreal, the boy uses their unreality to launch his own fictional identity. In denying the

6. Jacques Chuto et al., eds., *The Collected Writings of James Clarence Mangan: Poems, 1845–1847* (Dublin: Irish Academic Press, 1997), p. 455n.

reality of both the historical Araby fair and the popular tradition of
Irish Orientalism in "Araby," Joyce seems to embrace the duality of
the Mangan-Mitchel principle as his own representational methodology. In this light, "Araby" may be an ironic satire on the boy's
follies, but it also confronts the reader with the rejection of their
binary opposite, the representation of English and Anglo-Irish material culture and literary tradition.[7]

Mangan had openly admitted the extent to which he had transformed Moore, and when confronted with the accusation that he
had exaggerated his knowledge of Oriental languages, he replied that
his translations were if not Moorish, then Tom-Moorish.[8] Nor was
Mangan troubled by the discovery that his command of Irish was so
weak that he had to rely entirely on prose paraphrases: the final result
was so effective that he could describe himself, as Joyce would have
been delighted to learn, not so much "a singular man" as "a plural
one—a Proteus."[9] Joyce, in turn, seems to be participating in Mangan's struggle, which "mangled Moore's melodies" (FW 439.09–10).
Joyce's texts also sometimes "mangled" both Moore and Mangan:
although there are far too many echoes and parodies of both Moore
and Mangan in Joyce's corpus to trace in full here, it is worth noticing that in Ulysses, young Paddy Dignam visits Mangan's pork store
(U 10.534), and the name Dignam almost becomes Mangan when
his deceased father's name is spelled in reverse as "mangiD" by
Bloom, who watches a typesetter redistribute the letters while he
thinks of Hebrew (U 7.206). More significantly, perhaps, Joyce creates a fictional historical identity for Mangan as "the most significant
poet of the modern Celtic world," a title that in reality belonged to
W. B. Yeats,[1] further projecting an image of Mangan's "hysterical
nationalism" (CW 186) into future Irish politics: "Mangan will be
accepted by the Irish as their national poet on the day when the
conflict will be decided between my native land and the foreign powers—Anglo-Saxon and Roman Catholic, and a new civilization will
arise, either indigenous or completely foreign" (CW 179). In this
passage, such a future civilization could be both "indigenous" and
"completely "foreign" for Joyce by evoking the imagination with the

7. In referring to several contexts that do not support it, "Araby" follows a curious tradition
   in Irish Orientalism of the self-contradicting text. Moore's Lalla Rookh mixes genres as a
   long prose narrative with extensive verse interludes, at times heavily supported (or is it
   undermined?) by running footnotes; Mangan followed in the same spirit in the ironic notes
   to his supposed translations from languages that he did not know in his "Literae Orien-
   tales" series.
8. An ironic joining of Moore and Mangan took place when one collector had Mangan's Irish
   and Other Poems (Dublin: M. H. Gill, 1887) bound with Moore's Lalla Rookh in a volume
   now housed in the Brigham Young University Library.
9. Mangan is quoted in Robert Welch, A History of Verse Translation from the Irish (Gerrards
   Cross: Colin Smythe, 1988), p. 111.
1. W. B. Yeats had done a good deal to promote Mangan, who was much better known in
   the time of the Celtic revival than it would appear from Joyce's essays.

appropriate "magical name" for Irish Orientalism: "The syllables of the word *Araby* were called to me through the silence in which my soul luxuriated and cast an eastern enchantment over me" (*D* 32) [23.105–07].

But the magic in "Araby" is not limited to words. One little puzzle in the story is why Joyce fixes the time of the boy's arrival at the bazaar at exactly 9:50 P.M., even though other events in the story are only given approximate times. It is simply "after eight o'clock" when Mrs. Mercer leaves and about "nine o'clock" when the uncle returns, but it is precisely "ten minutes to ten" when the boy arrives at the bazaar, emphasized by "the lighted dial of a clock" on the large building displaying "the magical name" (*D* 33, 34) [24.143, 149; 25.177, 176, 178]. And why is Joyce's expression "ten minutes to ten" used here rather than 9:50 P.M.? Apparently "Araby" evokes magical numbers in the tradition of Arabic ciphers, which use letters of the alphabet and individual numbers as substitutes for each other, as in the systems of cabala and Pythagoras. If we regard "ten" as a cipher in the Latin alphabet, we obtain the letter "J," and for two tens we get "JJ," Joyce's initials. Furthermore, if we visualize the position of the hour and minute hands at exactly "ten minutes to ten" on a large outdoor clock, we find them perfectly superimposed. At this moment, the two tens as words, the two tens as numbers, the two clock hands as visual indicators, and the two "J" 's as letters are all ciphers for the doubled, mirrored signature of Joyce.

The vectors of "Araby" take into account three dynamic contexts, the historical Araby bazaar of 1894, the popular literary tradition of Irish Orientalism dominated by Moore's *Lalla Rookh,* and the intense life of Mangan reflected in his *aisling* poems and fictional autobiographies. The boy is given no relative, teacher, or confidant close enough to tell his story to, and even the first-person narrator has a slightly different identity as the man the boy will become looking back at the boy he was. Perhaps Mangan's sister has never really mattered to the boy as a discrete individual, since the narrator never shares with the reader the particular name that the boy utters in his private adoration of her (*D* 30) [21.34–36]. If there is a use of the *aisling* in "Araby," it is less in the boy's fragmented images of the girl than in his gazing deeply into his own imagination, ultimately descending from the sublimity of his literary voyagings to what seems a final moral and emotional perception of his vanity and pain: "Gazing up into the darkness I saw myself as a creature driven and derided by vanity: and my eyes burned with anguish and anger" (*D* 35) [26.218–220]. The understandings of the boy and the narrator finally seem to be one, the several external and internal planes of context seem to coincide, and the Dublin reader can concur in the boy's admission that vanity has been the cause of his youthful infatuation, his folly of undertaking the mission of attempting to impress the girl by buying her a keepsake, and his consequent denial of reality through flights of imagination. But the boy's final vision leads to no feelings of humility and remorse, as a true Bunyanesque allegory of vanity at the fair should. On the contrary, in the inflated rhetoric of the transformation scene at the end, we find the boy playing the Manganian hero one more time, alternately inventing, effacing, and enlarging himself, now in the Araby of his own memory. At this mythopoetic level, "Araby" seems another fictional biography of Mangan, the Irish Orientalist, or perhaps an early fictional autobiography of Joyce in the process of reinventing himself.

Abbreviations

CW	Joyce, James. *The Critical Writings of James Joyce*, ed. Ellsworth Mason and Richard Ellmann. New York: Viking Press, 1959.
D	Joyce, James. *Dubliners*, ed. Robert Scholes in consultation with Richard Ellmann. New York: Viking Press, 1967.
FW	Joyce, James. *Finnegans Wake*. New York: Viking Press, 1939; London: Faber and Faber, 1939. These two editions have identical pagination.
JJII	Ellmann, Richard. *James Joyce*. New York: Oxford UP, 1959.
Letters II, III	Joyce, James. *Letters of James Joyce*. Vols. II and III, ed. Richard Ellmann. New York: Viking Press, 1966.
U	Joyce, James. *Ulysses*, ed. Hans Walter Gabler et al. New York and London: Garland, 1984, 1986.

MARGOT NORRIS

The Perils of "Eveline"†

With a small aside tucked into his brilliant 1972 essay called "Molly's Masterstroke," Hugh Kenner turned the *Dubliners* story "Eveline" upside down by listening to a couple of commas. Kenner quotes the narration—" 'He had fallen on his feet in Buenos Ayres [comma] he said [comma] and had come over to the old country just for a holiday' " (20). Kenner goes on to say, "Great issues may be said to hang on those commas, which stipulate not only that Eveline is quoting Frank, but that Frank has been quoting also: quoting from the kind of fiction Eveline will believe, the fiction in which ready lads 'fall on

---

† From *Suspicious Readings of Joyce's* Dubliners (Philadelphia: U of Pennsylvania P, 2003), pp. 55–67. Reprinted by permission of the University of Pennsylvania Press. Parenthetical page references are to James Joyce, *Dubliners: Text and Criticism*, ed. Robert Scholes and A. Walton Litz (New York: Penguin Books, 1996). Page and line references in brackets refer to this Norton Critical Edition.

their feet' " (20). The upshot of listening carefully for the literary in
these repeated and reported conversational snatches is that Kenner
is able to speculate a different end to Eveline's adventure than the
one she had fantasized. It is a different ending, too, from what the
reader is likely to imagine: "The hidden story of 'Eveline' is the story
of Frank, a bounder with a glib line, who tried to pick himself up a
piece of skirt. She will spend her life regretting the great refusal. But
what she refused was just what her father would have said it was,
the patter of an experienced seducer" (21). Kenner's reading turned
the story away from its more conventional and superficial reading as
an exemplar of Dublin paralysis, and brought it into the more sophisticated tradition of Continental "logocentric" writing. In this species
of intertextual fiction (of which Flaubert's *Madame Bovary* is an
excellent example) both the sentimental and melodramatic novel are
refigured by showing impressionable young women seduced and
abandoned first by the romance novels they take as models for their
own choices. R. B. Kershner agrees with Hugh Kenner, when he
writes that "As Kenner recognizes, she really has no choice but to
fictionalize her choices" (62). In a more recent essay published in
Semicolonial Joyce, Katherine Mullin further argues that in addition
to romance novels, Eveline would also have been vulnerable to a
different sort of textual influence: the competing and conflicting
emigration propaganda current in Ireland at the turn of the century.[1]

The elegance of Kenner's reading has survived even the convincing
challenges posed to it by Sidney Feshbach, and although Feshbach
makes a strong case that Frank's conviction as a bounder can be disputed with historical and other evidence, he cannot rule it out altogether. I hope to take up this challenge in a different vein, by asking
the question that Kenner doesn't ask until later, in *Joyce's Voices.* Why
does the story of Eveline's close shave with disgrace and ruin remain
"a hidden story," as Kenner calls it, and why doesn't the third person
narrator simply tell us what is going on? My own readings of the *Dubliners* stories repeatedly produce many such "hidden stories" concealed by the narrative voice, including another hidden seduction and
swindle in the story that immediately follows "Eveline": "After the
Race." This narrative complicity with seduction and betrayal intrigues
me. What is at stake in keeping the reader in the dark about what is
going on, and obliging the reader to draw inferences, to speculate, to
take risks in creating scenarios from uncertain and partial information? Hugh Kenner seems to suggest that Joyce delights in seducing

1. Katherine Mullin historically identifies three types of emigration propaganda a young,
single, literate female in turn-of-the-century Ireland might have had to adjudicate. The
first promised successful pioneering in Argentina, the second exposed the plight of misled
Irish immigrants, and the third conjured the prostitution in the white slave trade as the
lurid fate of the single, unprotected female émigré. "Eveline is the propagandist's sitting
target," Mullin writes (197).

and betraying the reader in order to expose reader fatuousness—
"Penny romances are the liturgy of the innocent. The reader believes
such stuff" (81). But I will suggest that the narrative stance may have
a different and more benign purpose in "Eveline." The reader obliged
to make dubious inferences, to be suspicious, to speculate with fragmented and incomplete information, to create scenarios that are
unverified and unverifiable occupies a position very similar to Eveline's own. By withholding knowledge about Frank and his motives in
courting Eveline, the narration obliges the reader to participate emo-
tionally in Eveline's dilemma in making an agonizing and difficult life
decision whose outcome risks disaster for her whatever and however
she chooses. The story may therefore have a large and serious objective when it forces readers into Eveline's own interpretive crisis. Its
aim may be to recreate in the reading experience the epistemological
anguish faced by immense numbers of Irish persons in the course of
that country's history when confronting the decision of whether or not
to emigrate. Written before Ireland's great economic recovery in the
late 1990s, Brenda Maddox writes on the first page of her 1988 biography Nora:—"In every young Irish mind, the question of emigration
is as inescapable as it has been since the Great Famine of the 1840s"
(3). Katherine Mullin has further explored how prospective emigrants
from Ireland were historically belabored with varieties of propaganda
both to stimulate and allure migrants to New Worlds, or to serve
nationalist efforts to stem the tide of emigration with frightening
warnings and exposés.

The story itself makes only a few references to emigration, but they
are sufficient to indicate that Eveline has at least a subliminal awareness of the social mobility and population movement that is going on
around her—"Everything changes" (37) [27.22], she thinks. The
childhood friends with whom she played in the field built over by the
Belfast developer have dispersed—"Tizzie Dunn was dead, too, and
the Waters had gone back to England" (37) [27.21–22]. Her father,
she learns, also saw schoolmates emigrate to such faraway places as
Australia. "He is in Melbourne now" (37) [28.35], Mr. Hill tells of the
priest in the yellowed photograph on the wall. Indeed, Eveline's father
has an insular sense of Irish emigration and southern European immigration—" 'Damned Italians! coming over here!' " (40) [31.129] he
complains—while Don Gifford maintains that "There is no evidence
of a significant Italian immigration to Ireland during this period" (51).
Rather, Gifford suggests, the Italians in Ireland at that time might
have been failed immigrants—like Frank McCourt's luckless family
in Angela's Ashes—on their way back to the old country after unsuc-
cessful efforts to get established in America. "Frank" himself—whatever his real name—would have been one of thousands who left the
Ireland of his day to seek a better life elsewhere. Brenda Maddox

reports that in 1904, 37,413 Irishmen and women left Ireland for better lives elsewhere, including, of course, James Joyce and Nora Barnacle (46). Whatever the temptation to join Eveline's father and Hugh Kenner in stereotyping sailors as "experienced seducer[s]" (Kenner 21), "Frank" deserves to be counted as an émigré in the larger social context of the story. Indeed, Sidney Feshbach historically supports Frank's story by citing the huge immigration that made turn-of-the-century Buenos Aires a city whose adult population was three-quarters European-born, including not only Italians and French immigrants, but also Irish, Welsh, and Scotch (224). However, Katherine Mullin's statistical table of Irish emigration to Argentina shows zero movement for 1902 and 1903—and she argues that at the time the story was written, the "stereotype" of the successful Irish pioneer in Argentina "had become obsolete" (176). Nonetheless, Eveline, in contemplating her escape, explicitly counts herself as part of an Irish diaspora—"Now she was going to go away like the others, to leave her home" (37) [27.22–23].

Inserted into this context of Irish emigration in the story is the focus on the erosion of Eveline's decision by indecision. The brooding of this young store clerk and involuntary homemaker and surrogate mother takes form as an attempt to sift and evaluate her alternatives through a series of memories,[2] fantasies, images, echoes, and fictions. Together these constitute a welter of what Jean-François Lyotard would call "phrases in dispute"—conflicting and competing discourses that are difficult to adjudicate because they convey different criteria and because their genres and objects are incommensurate. The discourses rioting through Eveline's mind are highly heterogeneous, a cacophony of voices in a jumble of emotional registers—fear, anxiety, desire, longing. Some are unpleasant and threatening: little Keogh warning of the approach of her father and his blackthorn stick, Miss Gavan's reproving "Miss Hill, don't you see these ladies are waiting. . . . Look lively, Miss Hill, please" (37) [28.46–47], and her father's sarcasm ("had she any intention of buying Sunday's dinner" [38] [29.69–70]) and threats ("what he would do to her only for her dead mother's sake" [38] [28.58]). Comfort, stimulation, and hope come to Eveline through fiction and art, as both Kenner and Kershner have argued. She fondly remembers the ghost story her father tells her when she is ill,[3] and enjoys the Freudian family romance of abduction and restoration to noble estate in Balfe's opera *The Bohemian Girl* [29.89]. And she listens to the "tales of distant countries" and "stories of the terrible Patagonians" (39) [29.96; 30.101] with which Frank,

2. Benoît Tadié has a particularly interesting analysis of the locutions of Eveline's memory in the story (379).
3. Brenda Maddox reports that Nora Joyce's father, Tom Barnacle, was a drunkard, like Mr. Hill, who could also be very nice with the children at times. Like Eveline, Nora and her sisters "remember how he told them ghost stories before the fire" (14).

like a modern Othello, seduces her.[4] And finally, of course, there is
the siren song Frank sings to her, and tacitly prompts her to emulate,
about "the lass that loves a sailor" (39) [29.92–93].

Eveline's indecision arises from her inability to adjudicate between
the unpleasant realities of a "Home!" (39) [27.24] that she knows,
and an abroad ("Escape!") [31.136] that is unknowable and that
presents itself to her as patently fabulous. But dichotomizing the safe
if dreary knowability of Eveline's "home" with the dangerous but
exciting unknowability of "abroad" reductively polarizes and simpli-
fies choices that are far more inscrutable and complex. Nineteen-
year-old Eveline counts at least two deaths among her
contemporaries—those of her favorite brother Ernest and her
playmate Tizzie Dunn. The Ireland of home, the narrative implies,
may not necessarily be safer than emigration abroad—the moral of
Frank McCourt's memoir of a disastrous Irish repatriation.[5] The ultimate moment of terror that convinces Eveline that she must leave
is her recognition that if physical escape from the horrors of home
is impossible, if—like Eveline's mother—one can't run away or emigrate, then the foreign and the fabulous will "invade" and colonize
the domestic, the home, the mind, until one speaks a terrible,
untranslatable language ("Derevaun Seraun! Derevaun Seraun!"
[40] [31.135]) to the tune of an Italian organ grinder. Eveline's
mother had transmogrified before her daughter's stricken eyes into
an alien, a foreign creature, a domestic Patagonian, and Eveline's
choice is therefore much more complex and desperate than choosing
between level-headed reality and a flight into fantasy. The betrayal
Eveline risks in running away with Frank is not necessarily more
egregious than the broken promises Eveline's mother suffered. These
promises, literally sacred, had been codified under the aegis of the
Sacred Heart of Jesus and Blessed Margaret Mary Alacoque, and
displayed on the parlor wall. "I will establish peace in their homes,"
they promised Mrs. Hill, "I will comfort them in all their afflictions,"
"I will be their secure refuge during life, and above all in death"
(Gifford 49). Eveline's mother clearly found neither peace, nor comfort, nor security in her Irish home—either in life or in dying. And
Garry Leonard intriguingly suggests that in her discordant linguistic

---

4. Darwin's voyage to Tierra del Fuego on the *Beagle* had stimulated general European interest in Patagonians. Sidney Feshbach writes, "In 1830, three aborigines 'were abducted'
from Patagonia or Tierra del Fuego 'and brought to England' for exhibition and education"
(224). Katherine Mullin, however, points out that "Frank's tales of the terrible Patagonians
are tall because the Patagonians became extinct many years before his birth" (176).
5. The Pulitzer Prize–winning 1996 chronicle tells of the McCourt family returning to the
slums of Limerick after failing to make a go of it in Brooklyn in the Depression, and
enduring extreme poverty, near-starvation, typhoid, and the death of several of the children. The memoir begins with the sentence, "My father and mother should have stayed
in New York where they had met and married, and where I was born. Instead, they returned
to Ireland" (11).

registers, Eveline's mother gives her daughter contradictory and impossible mandates: to hold the home together *and* to save herself from a "life of commonplace sacrifices closing in final craziness" (40) [31.131–32].

The difficulty with Kenner's melodramatic scenario of a seduced and abandoned Eveline, is that it offers a glib and easy answer to her dilemma. His reading reduces the story to a single tragic irony: that Eveline would spend the rest of her life regretting a choice that was unwittingly the right one. But was it the correct choice? While Katherine Mullin concurs with Kenner when she characterizes Frank's enticements as "misleading and exploitative emigration propaganda" (177), she also exposes the seduction and betrayal narratives of "social purity campaigners" as a "white slave trade scare" (183).[6] Garry Leonard convincingly challenges the easy assumption that remaining home was the safe choice when he refers to Eveline's twilight meditation as "this frightening lull in her life, a lull that almost certainly precedes the occasion of being beaten for the first time by her father" (96). Both Garry Leonard and Suzette Henke see the menacing and abusive father as a potentially greater threat to Eveline's safety and welfare[7] than the risk of possible seduction and abandonment by a lying sailor. But the point of the story may be less the adjudication of the correct choice than to have the reader experience the interpretive difficulty and desperate uncertainty of making such a life-altering choice. The Kenner theory sets aside as irrelevant the most interesting movement in the story, which is the difficulty of adjudicating alternatives with incommensurate risks—what Suzette Henke, in a psychoanalytic and religious gloss, calls a "trial of the soul" (22). "Eveline serves both as prosecutor and defendant, analyst and spiritual analyst and" in weighing "emotion and romantic fantasy against the judgmental voice of conscience," Henke writes. Robert Scholes's theoretically groundbreaking "Semiotic Approaches to a Fictional Text: Joyce's 'Eveline'," adumbrates the internal complexity of Eveline's "brooding" most precisely—especially with respect to her necessary negotiations of past and future. Scholes places stress on what he calls "focus"—"aspects of the events in any story maybe clarified by the narrative focus, while others may be hidden or obscured, temporarily or permanently" (74). The story's "focus" prods him into scrutinizing not only the narrative rhetoric,

---

6. Mullin notes that Joyce bought and owned a copy of Olive Mac Kirdy's *The White Slave Market*, which was published in 1912. But while Joyce wrote "Eveline" many years prior to acquiring this book, Mullen points out that "By 1904 the city [Buenos Ayres] was perceived to be the international capital of the White Slave Trade" (189).

7. Luke Gibbons fills in the broader historical and social conditions that are thought to have contributed to the dysfunctionality in post-Famine colonial Ireland (168). These include, in addition to the absence of an urban manufacturing base, the absence of a social reform agenda on the part of the Catholic Church and lack of legal protection afforded to women against domestic violence.

as Kenner does, but also the temporal rhythms (duration and fre-
quency) of Eveline's deliberative process. "She had consented to go
away, to leave her home. Was that wise? She tried to weigh each side
of the question" (37) [28.36–37], the narrator tells us. Like any
momentous decision, Eveline's decision to emigrate appears incapable of escaping provisionality and iterability even after it has ostensibly been "made." She seems to have conveyed her decision to Frank
for implementation before she has made her peace with it, and in
the hours before departure she again rehearses the pros and cons
while passage is being booked and arrangements are being made.
"The white of two letters in her lap grew indistinct. One was to Harry,
the other was to her father" (39) [30.108–10]. The letters defer the
announcement of her decision to her family in a maneuver that
simultaneously prevents obstruction of her escape and allows her to
defer burning her bridges until the last possible moment. The *time*
at issue in her realization that "Her time was running out" (39)
[30.118] is not only her time in her Dublin home, but also her time
for continued deliberation.[8] Eveline's panic attack at the dock may
reflect less her cowardice or passivity than her distress that her endless, judicious weighing of pros and cons has come to an end before
it has produced a reliable resolution to her dilemma.

Is Eveline as fatuous as Kenner supposes her to be? Is she what
Robert Scholes calls "a central intelligence who is not very intelligent"
(75)? Or is Eveline Hill far more realistic and circumspect in her considerations than, say, a Gerty MacDowell, dreaming of Reggy Wylie
and a dark stranger with burning eyes on Sandymount Strand? Curiously, what follows after the narrative tells us that "She . . . consented
to go away, to leave her home" (37) [28.36] is not a rush of romantic
thoughts of Frank, the anticipated sea voyage, the upcoming marriage, and fantasies of a home in exotic South America. Instead, her
first thought is an absolutely prosaic acknowledgment that in her present circumstance she is assured the fundamentals for survival ("In her
home anyway she had shelter and food" [37] [28.37–38])—an admission that implies her awareness that these necessities cannot be taken
for granted once she leaves home. We quickly learn what that Dublin
shelter and food costs her. Not only does she work at the Stores under
an edgy and deprecating supervisor all day. She then returns to the
house of her menacing and deprecating father ("she sometimes felt
herself in danger of her father's violence" [38] [28.53–54]) who makes
her beg for her own wages back so she can feed his younger children
and clean his dusty house. Nor does she imagine that news of her
elopement will incite jealousy in her female coworkers, speculating

8. Benoît Tadié describes Eveline's dilemma as better appreciated in terms of verbal tense,
than of time, and calls it a "verbal deadlock which can account for the aphasic collapse
of the central character at the end of the story" (379).

rather that they will "Say she was a fool, perhaps" (37) [28.42]. If anything is remarkable in these early passages, it is how resolutely Eveline refuses to cast herself as a romantic heroine. Eveline's description of her anticipated life with Frank may lack naturalistic specificity—"She was to go away with him by the night boat to be his wife and to live with him in Buenos Ayres where he had a home waiting for her" (38) [29.80–82]. But neither does it indulge in the sort of aesthetic domestic fantasy we find in Gerty MacDowell's dreams of "a beautifully appointed drawingroom with pictures and engravings . . . and chintz covers for the chairs and that silver toastrack in Clery's summer jumble sales" (13.231). Perhaps it is Hugh Kenner who may be embroidering the simple description we get of Eveline's plan. He describes Frank's improbable success—"a Dublin sailor-boy has grown affluent in South America, and bought a house and sailed all the way back to Ireland to find him a bride to fill it" ("Molly's Masterstroke" 20). *Joyce's Voices* repeats this characterization, of Frank as "a sailor who has 'fallen on his feet in Buenos Ayres'," who "has bought a house there and is spending a holiday in a rented room in Ireland." Frank's proposal is again described as a willingness to "take her back as his bride to that South American house, though for some reason not gone into they can't get married till they've gotten there" (81). But the text says nothing of Frank's buying a house in Buenos Aires—only that "he had a home waiting for her" (38) [29.82].[9] And Sidney Feshbach may be on to something when he writes, "As for the question about why Eveline doesn't think about the house she is going to, the answer may be that she is avoiding thinking about still another house to dust" (224). In other words, Eveline's allusion to the home Frank has waiting for her may be no more than a reassurance to herself that in Buenos Aires she will still have "shelter and food" (37) [28.38], as she does in her father's house. Perhaps knowing what she does about houses and their care, Eveline simply cannot imagine domestic settings as sites of marital bliss. As for Kenner's question about why Frank won't marry Eveline until they get to Buenos Aires, there are several possibilities. The most cogent is that the Catholic Church's requirement of published banns announcing upcoming marriages would have made a secret marriage impossible in Dublin. And Eveline's father, having forbidden her to see Frank, could be expected to interfere with any publicized plan for the marriage of his nineteen year-old daughter. Brenda Mad-

---

9. The discrepancy between the "house" of Kenner's account, and the "home" of the 1967 and 1996 Penguin editions—edited by Scholes and Litz—that I have been using, may be an editorial one. In his original "Molly's Masterstroke" article in the Fall 1972 *James Joyce Quarterly*, Hugh Kenner explicitly "quotes" *house* as the word used in the text of "Eveline." Kenner writes, "And he had come to Dublin, it seems, to obtain a bride, and take her back to Buenos Aires, where (to quote again) 'he had a house waiting for her.'" (20). But the article has no footnote, and it is unclear which edition Kenner might have been using. Kenner's 1978 *Joyce's Voices*, which again mentions Frank's "house," has no bibliography so that the edition of *Dubliners* to which he refers is once again indeterminate.

dox reminds us that, when Nora Barnacle eloped with Joyce at the age of twenty, "she was still a minor" (4).

Frank lends himself to easy typology as the predatory and faithless sailor because of the extent to which he appears deracinated both within and by the narrative: given no clear origin, no "people" identified by class, geography, or business. The business that seems to have finally grounded him in Buenos Aires, allowing him to leave off sailing and to settle in one place, does indeed lack the specificity of Harry Hill's work in "the church decorating business" (38) [28.60]. But Hugh Kenner's famous commas ("He had fallen on his feet in Buenos Ayres, he said, and had come over to the old country just for a holiday" [39] [30.101–02]) offer a different interpretation as well. Eveline may realize full well that she has only Frank's word for his South American condition, and she may therefore recognize how perilous it is to trust a visiting stranger in the face of her father's ominous warning, "I know these sailor chaps" (39) [30.105]. Perhaps it is precisely to disrupt that stereotype that Frank gives Eveline an extremely specific employment history—"He had started as a deck boy at a pound a month on a ship of the Allan line going out to Canada. He told her the names of the ships he had been on and the names of the different services" (39) [29–30.96–99]—one that a suspicious father would be capable of checking out if he was concerned about his daughter's welfare. Sidney Feshbach does what Eveline's father does not: he checks up on Frank's story. He determines that the Allen line did indeed conduct travelers between England and North America, and that (according to James Skobie's *Revolution on the Pampas*) Irish manual laborers in South America earned excellent wages. A rural migrant worker living in Argentina in the 1890s could apparently pay for a round trip passage between the U.S. and Europe with two weeks worth of wages (224), and therefore afford to return home on holiday. "On point after point, Frank's story checks out," Feshbach writes (225). Tales and yarns constitute the time-honored social and cultural capital of sailors, as Joseph Conrad demonstrates in his fictions. But telling stories of "the terrible Patagonians" to Eveline does not, in and of itself, turn Frank into a D. B. Murphy.

Part of the difficulty in forming a just assessment of Frank's character may be attributed to the uncertain sequence through which the narrative gives us certain information about him. One particularly illogical sequence has the information that Eveline's "father had found out the affair and had forbidden her to have anything to say to him," [30.103–04] followed by the information that "One day he had quarrelled with Frank and after that she had to meet her lover secretly" (39) [30.106–07]. The first statement suggests that Hill learns that his daughter is seeing a sailor, and forbids her to see him again, without ever having laid eyes on the young man. The second statement suggests that father and suitor have met on more than one occasion, and that the father's ban of his daughter's trysts was the result of a specific disagreement with Frank. If so, what did they quarrel about? Did Hill try to pry into Frank's financial condition and meet a rebuff? Did he insult Frank by calling him a bounder? Did the quarrel ensue on a Saturday night when Frank watched Eveline try to wrest some of her wages back from her father in order to shop for Sunday's dinner? Did Frank remonstrate with Hill about his drunkenness, or defend Eveline against her father's abuse in some other way? Was the quarrel about something inconsequential that merely symptomatized Hill's jealousy of his daughter's sexual maturation and independence? Eveline, after all, appeared to have had no expectations of ever leaving the parental home—"Perhaps she would never see again those familiar objects from which she had never dreamed of being divided" (37) [27.26–28]. Besides the ellipsis marking Eveline's standing up in terror in her room and her paralysis on the dock, there are other ellipses in this story whose content informs her decision-making process without our ability to adjudicate it.

If Eveline is remarkably restrained in imagining the *material* details of her future life with Frank in South America, she is also relatively restrained in the rhetoric imputed to her imaginings of her *emotional* life with him. For a girl ostensibly bedazzled by a handsome sailor, her feelings for him are repeatedly expressed in language that points to her concerns for safety and security, rather than to infatuation. Before we receive any description of Frank, he is mediated as the invisible vehicle for bestowing respectful treatment on her, giving her the kind of Hegelian recognition that would constitute her as a person, a subject in her own eyes: "Then she would be married—she, Eveline. People would treat her with respect then. She would not be treated as her mother had been" (37) [28.50–52]. Garry Leonard points out the fallacy of this line of reasoning, that it was precisely marriage that visited poor treatment on Eveline's mother (102). And he astutely suggests that Eveline's desire throughout the story is consistently pointed toward an indefinable "elsewhere" that may be equated with unrepresentable female desire, or *jouissance*. Clearly, the notion of *difference* between her present known life and her future unknown life, is what Eveline's ruminations attempt to dilate—expressed by the narrative in the open-ended trope of exploration, "She was about to *explore* another life with Frank" (38, my emphasis) [29.79]. The narrative description given of Frank is indeed flattering. Eveline thinks him "very kind, manly, openhearted" [29.80], handsome ("his hair tumbled forward over a face of bronze") [29.86–87], and solicitous ("He used to meet her outside the stores every evening and see her home") [29.87–89]. The evidence of his actions does nothing to undermine this judgment. He generously takes her to good seats at the opera, sings for her, gives her playful nicknames ("Poppens," "Evvy"), and, of course, tells her about both himself and his tales of distant countries (38–39) [29.94; 32.164]. Eveline's responses to this highly conventional but flawless courtship is surprisingly measured and cautious, "First of all it had been an excitement for her to have a fellow and then she had begun to like him" (39) [29.94–95]. Rather than fatuity, the most consistent note that runs throughout Eveline's meditation appears one of thoughtful calculation and consideration. She proceeds as though the explicit warnings of her father, and the tacit proleptic denunciations of her coworkers who would think her a fool for running away with a sailor, were not without effect on her deliberations. After all, Eveline knows from her father that occasional charm and kindness can coexist with relentless oppression and exploitation in the same masculine personality. And although she has no grounds for expecting ill from Frank, neither does she have guarantees that his courtship generosity and affection will perdure. When her final image of her demented mother seems to snap her decision into place— "Escape! She must escape! Frank would save her. He would give her life, perhaps love, too. But she wanted to live. Why should she be unhappy? She had a right to happiness. Frank would take her in his arms, fold her in his arms. He would save her" (40) [31.136–40]—the tropes all point to safety, security, and freedom from abuse and abasement, rather than toward romantic or sexual fulfillment. "He would give her life, perhaps love, too" is a curiously qualified locution for the thoughts of a bedazzled girl—and, indeed, nowhere does the story tell us that Eveline is in love with Frank, or loves Frank, or that he has told her he loves her. Eveline's fantasy of Frank enfolding her in his arms has an emotional cast that differs markedly from Gerty Mac-Dowell's dream of a "manly man," who would "take her in his sheltering arms, strain her to him in all the strength of his deep passionate nature and comfort her with a long long kiss. It would be like heaven" (13.210).

The hidden story of "Eveline" has many possibilities, including one that corresponds to the overt narrative. Frank could have been a seducer transformed into a savior:[1] moved by the plight of a girl he began by playfully seducing, he determines to take her away from a stultifying and dangerous home, for example. The nature of the promises that have passed between the couple are left sketchy and undetailed. Eveline has "consented" to go away with Frank to Buenos Aires; he has promised to marry her and give her a home there. The registers of emotional intimacy and commitment that may or may not inform such pledges are highly variable and incalculable in any

---

1. Torchiana writes of Frank, "I shall even be bold enough to liken him to the Christ who revealed Himself to Margaret Mary" (73).

union, and they remind us that marriage is itself an act of emotional emigration, a commitment to traverse to a different emotional, domestic, and social sphere. The vow that seems to count most in Eveline's deliberations is that Frank has promised to take care of her. Having made and fulfilled such a promise herself—to her dying mother—Eveline can both understand it and believe in the possibility that it can be honored. She can even understand its costs and rewards: "It was hard work—a hard life—but now that she was about to leave it she did not find it a wholly undesirable life" (38) [29.76–78]. Hugh Kenner concedes Eveline's concession, that in some ways her Dublin home life "is not a bad life." "But," he goes on, "it does not compare in glamour with the life Frank seems to be offering her" (20). Yet there is so little evocation of exotic glamour in Eveline's musings that some critics have imagined a gender role reversal in which it is Eveline who is the betrayer, and Frank who is betrayed. Sondra Melzer asks, "Is the innocent Eveline capable of using Frank as a passport from her present life, even with the implication that their mutual love (or at least hers) was uncertain?" (482). This suggestion opens the possibility of speculating an utterly prosaic basis to the elopement of the lass and her sailor: that of a bargained arrangement between the pair. Its fulcrum, for both the man and the woman, may have been a measure of emotional containment within security rather than romance, passion, or adventure—"He would give her life, perhaps love too" (40) [31.137–38]. Such arrangements entail risks for both partners, and although the reader's sense of Eveline's physical and emotional perils is much greater, she clearly feels that Frank has also made a material and emotional investment in their elopement. Her most painful regret on the dock is not the loss of the love of her life but a crippling sense of her own ingratitude: "Could she still draw back after all he had done for her? Her distress awoke a nausea in her body and she kept moving her lips in silent fervent prayer" (41) [31.152–55].

The "hidden story" that Hugh Kenner imputes to "Eveline" is produced by holes and ellipses in the story. Robert Scholes names these "paralipse," a discursive strategy identified by Gérard Genette. Scholes writes, "He points to the tendency of fictions to employ strategies he calls 'paralipse' or 'paralepse': that is, the withholding from the reader of information which he 'ought—according to the prevailing focus—to receive; and the presenting to the reader of information which the prevailing level of focalization 'ought' to render inaccessible. Joyce, it seems to me, is a highly paraleptic writer, in 'Eveline' and in other works as well" (75). The most significant ellipsis in the story is, of course, what happens in Eveline's mind between her two extreme and opposite terrors: her memory of her mother's dementia spurring her to escape and her paralysis on the dock when she cannot go. The interval is blank: we learn neither how she gets from her home to the North Wall, nor what, if any thoughts, have shaken her shaky resolve to go through with their plan.[2] The scene Eveline encounters at the dock reminds us of the first sentence of Brenda Maddox's 1988 biography of *Nora*: "To this day departures by sea from Ireland are noisy, anxious affairs" (3). Maddox is merely describing the modern overnight ferry crossing from Ireland to Euston Station in London. But her evocation of chaos, fatigue, and worry can be multiplied to imagine Eveline's confusion and distress on the dock, full of soldiers and brown baggage, with the whistles and bells of the steamer announcing its imminent departure. After the stillness and solitude of her twilight reverie, the sense of congested motion and human engulfment Eveline experiences on her way toward the ship conjures up in powerful figurative tropes the phenomenology of emigration. Joyce's description particularly evokes the disorientation and estrangement of joining a large aggregation of strangers in a simultaneous yet noncollective movement away from their homelands. And in another ellipsis, neither Eveline nor the reader hears what Frank is telling her "over and over again" about the passage. Is it something to do with where the ship is going, to Buenos Aires or Liverpool, as Hugh Kenner surmises (*The Pound Era* 37)? Or is he telling her that instead of steaming toward Buenos Aires in one of the staterooms with their "illumined portholes," they will be in steerage with the other immigrants? Not yet on board, is Eveline already experiencing the sensations of the seaborne immigrant—not dancing merrily like the lively crowd below deck in the film *Titanic*—but uncomfortable, ill, and frightened? Eveline's last-minute sensation of nausea and fear of drowning—"All the seas of the world tumbled about her heart. He was drawing her into them: he would drown her" (41) [31.158–59]—scarcely seems an unrealistic prolepsis of the immigration voyage.

This negative scenario of a failure to emigrate, of fear of emigration, throws into positive relief the courage required to do so, by the thousands of Irish poor who over the years made their escapes to difficult but different lives abroad.[3] By recovering the biographical

2. David Weir points out that the story elides all of the actions Eveline takes to prepare for her journey—"packing her baggage, writing a farewell note to her father, catching a tram, walking briskly to the North Wall" (345). The effect of this elision, he argues, is to have the narrative replace "passage" with representations of the "passive" (345).

3. J. C. Beckett argues that the Great Famine of 1846 altered the emigration practices of the Irish. "Emigration, formerly a last desperate remedy, was now the first thing thought of; and there was an almost hysterical rush to leave the country, to escape, at all costs, from 'the doomed and starving island,' and find safety elsewhere," he writes. He goes on to say that "In earlier years, emigrant sailings had been confined to spring and summer; and intending emigrants had made their preparations carefully. But, from the latter half of 1846 onwards, the panic-stricken crowds were clamorous to be off without delay; the traffic continued throughout the year; and thousands of helpless refugees put to sea with only the scantiest supply of provisions for the voyage, and without either means of subsistence or prospect of employment on their arrival" (344).

moment in which this story was written, one can speculatively give Eveline's moment of panic and fear of peril an informative context and illuminating range. As we all know, James Joyce met Nora Barnacle on June 10, 1904 and eloped with the unmarried twenty-year-old on the night of October 8, 1904—not quite four months later. During this interval Joyce wrote the first two *Dubliners* stories for the *Irish Homestead*—"The Sisters" and "Eveline," which was published on September 10, 1904 (Werner 35). The coincidence between Nora's situation during this interval and the donnée of "Eveline" is, as has often been noted, no coincidence at all. Joyce imported dozens of narrative similarities between his own and Nora's domestic situations into the story, to give its dispiriting home scenes their plausible textures. Eveline's fear of her father's blackthorn stick reflects the violence of Nora's uncle Tom Healy, who beat her with a stick for going out with Willie Mulvagh, according to Brenda Maddox (22). Like Eveline, Nora was then forced to date her young man secretly. Like Eveline, Joyce experienced the death of a beloved brother, George, and, of course, the death of an overworked, exhausted, and abused mother. After the death of their mother, Joyce's sisters were left with the care of the younger children with virtually no provision from a drunken father—a plight dramatized both in Stanislaus Joyce's diary and in "Wandering Rocks" in *Ulysses*. Although Joyce was not a sailor like Frank, Richard Ellmann reported that he looked like one to Nora—"She took him, with his yachting cap, for a sailor" (*JJII* 156). And Hugh Kenner points to the Constantine P. Curran photo of Joyce to note that "Frank" is Joyce's first "Portrait of the Artist" (*The Pound Era* 35). Joyce himself was more improvident than any sailor, making Nora's elopement at least as great a risk as Eveline's. "Nora appreciated the enormity of her decision, even though Joyce feared she did not," Brenda Maddox wrote. "By running away unmarried, she too was breaking with the social order and committing an open act of rebellion. She was burning her bridges and she had no way of supporting herself abroad if Joyce left her. In a non-English speaking country she was unlikely to find work even as a domestic servant" (45). Furthermore, Joyce's friends expected the worst from him—"George Russell said he pitied the poor girl, whom Joyce would certainly abandon" (45).

"Eveline" was written as Joyce was preparing to elope with a twenty-year-old woman who barely knew him, and to whom he had little to offer, except—like Frank—a love of music and a promise to enfold her in his arms. It is intriguing to remember that when the story was published in the *Irish Homestead* on September 10, 1904, Joyce did not yet know the outcome of his and Nora's own plan. What, then, did it mean for Joyce to write a predictive ending to his own elopement scenario in which the beloved refuses to go through with it? Sondra Melzer speculates that the story enacts Joyce's ambivalences about taking Nora Barnacle into his artist's exile with him. She writes, "It must have occurred to Joyce that his own simple country girl, Nora, might see him as a means of escape from the conventionality of her life, just as Eveline saw in Frank an opportunity to escape. On the other hand, did Joyce fear that Nora, upon whom he had come to depend, in some way had cheated or would cheat him of the freedom and independence he sought as artist and rebel?" (482). Melzer's point reminds us of a dramatic gender difference in portraying male and female emigration decisions in Joyce's fiction. Stephen Dedalus's diary entries at the end of *Portrait* mythologize the emigration decision as heroic—"I go to encounter for the millionth time the reality of experience and to forge in the smithy of my soul the uncreated conscience of my race" (276). This rhetoric stands in marked contrast to Eveline's "She had consented to go away, to leave her home. Was that wise?" (37) [28.36–37]. My own alternative to Sondra Melzer's biographical reading of Eveline's decision is to see the story as a dramatized projection of the perilous emotional and rational process entailed by a decision like Nora's to emigrate by way of an elopement. By making Eveline's South American destination much more foreign and remote than Nora's expatriation to the Continent, the risks she faces are intensified, and the perils of her decision are vastly multiplied. Katherine Mullin's account of the pressures of Irish anti-emigration propaganda in 1904, and particularly the scary warnings to single women to beware of white slave trade predators, would have further increased the trauma of a decision like Eveline's. By displacing the proposed elopement to Argentina, Joyce's story usefully reflects the more common emigration scenario that did not land poor Irish women and men in Paris, Zurich, or even Trieste, but rather on the uncertain shores of the Americas or Australia. Joyce writing of "Eveline" in the interval when his own young woman was making her decision could therefore be construed as either a proleptic exoneration or a proleptic homage to Nora. The story functions both as a gesture of understanding the feeling of peril that might make a young woman unable to go through with an elopement or, conversely, a reversed tribute to the courage required by one who did. The twenty-two-year-old Joyce, having already failed once as an émigré, had no illusions about the lives Irishmen lived abroad, nor about the adventure upon which he embarked his young woman. Brenda Maddox extends homage to both of them—"As they turned their backs on Ireland, at twenty-two and twenty, Joyce and Nora had enormous courage" (46).

Works Cited

Beckett, J. C. *The Making of Modern Ireland 1603–1923*. London: Faber and Faber, 1981.

Ellmann, Richard. *James Joyce*. Revised Edition. Oxford: Oxford UP, 1982.

Feshbach, Sidney. " 'Fallen on His Feet in Buenos Ayres' (D 30): Frank in 'Eveline.' " *James Joyce Quarterly*. 202. Winter 1983. 223–26.

Gifford, Don. *Notes for "Dubliners" and "A Portrait of the Artist as a Young Man."* Second Edition. Berkeley: U of California P, 1982.

Gibbons, Luke. " 'Have You No Homes to Go To?': James Joyce and the Politics of Paralysis." *Semicolonial Joyce*. Ed. Derek Attridge and Marjorie Howes. Cambridge: Cambridge UP, 2000. 150–71.

Henke, Suzette A. *James Joyce and the Politics of Desire*. New York: Routledge, 1990.

Kenner, Hugh. "Molly's Masterstroke." *James Joyce Quarterly* 10.1. Fall 1972. 19–28.

———. *Joyce's Voices*. Berkeley: U of California P, 1978.

———. *The Pound Era*. Berkeley: U of California P, 1971.

Kershner, R. B. *Joyce, Bakhtin, and Popular Literature: Chronicles of Disorder*. Chapel Hill: U of North Carolina P, 1989.

Leonard, Garry M. *Reading "Dubliners" Again: A Lacanian Perspective*. Syracuse: Syracuse UP, 1993.

Lyotard, Jean-Francois. *The Differend: Phrases in Dispute*. Trans. Georges Van Den Abbeele. Minneapolis: U of Minnesota P, 1988.

Maddox, Brenda. *Nora*. Boston: Houghton Mifflin, 1988.

McCourt, Frank. *Angela's Ashes: A Memoir*. New York: Scribner, 1996.

Melzer. Sondra. "In the Beginning There Was 'Eveline.' " *James Joyce Quarterly*. 16.4. Summer 1979. 479–85.

Mullin, Katherine. "Don't Cry for Me, Argentina: 'Eveline' and the Seductions of Emigration Propaganda." *Semicolonial Joyce*. Ed. Derek Attridge and Marjorie Howes. Cambridge: Cambridge UP, 2000. 172–200.

Scholes, Robert. "Semiotic Approaches to a Fictional Text: Joyce's 'Eveline.' " *James Joyce Quarterly*. 16.12. Fall 1978/Winter 1979. 65–80.

Tadié, Benoît. "Memory and and Narrative Deadlock in 'Dubliners.' " *Classic Joyce. Studies in Italy 6*. Ed. Franca Ruggieri. Roma: Bulzone Editore, 1999. 373–80.

Torchiana, Donald T. *Backgrounds for Joyce's "Dubliners."* Boston: Allen & Unwin, 1986.

Weir, David. "Gnomon Is an Island: Euclid and Bruno in Joyce's Narrative Practice." *James Joyce Quarterly*. 28.2. Winter 1991. 343–60.

Werner, Craig Hansen. *"Dubliners": A Pluralistic World*. Boston: Twayne, 1988.

JAMES FAIRHALL

Big-Power Politics and Colonial Economics: The Gordon Bennett Cup Race and "After the Race"†

While researching another Joycean matter recently, I stumbled on two articles in the *Irish Times* dealing with what the paper considered the highly desirable prospect of Ireland's playing host to its first major automobile race. This prospect, of course, became a reality ironically recorded in "After the Race." The pieces in the *Irish Times*, which a couple of months later printed Joyce's interview with one of the anticipated drivers in the race (*CW* 106–08), stress the race's potential monetary benefits to Ireland and its glamour as a contest among men and machines representing the world's most technologically advanced nations. They do not lead to a startling new interpretation of the story, which already has been explicated by a number of critics,¹ yet do reveal a contemporary national and international context to which Joyce was reacting as both a socialist and an Irish nationalist.

Joyce may not have read the two articles in question, which are dated January 17 and 20, 1903.² He left Ireland on the day the first one appeared and did not return until April 11 (*JJII* 119, 128). On the other hand, since he expected to become the French correspondent to the *Irish Times*, he very likely knew of its plugging of the Bennett Cup race; and in any case, the newspaper was advancing a popular view among Irishmen who had opinions on the race, which they saw as a source of money and prestige for Ireland.

On Saturday the 17th, the *Irish Times* reported the likely forthcoming approval of the proposed racecourse in the suburbs and countryside outside Dublin. The correspondent noted some "ugly corners on the route" and suggested that, since "the race . . . will bring many thousand of pound [*sic*] into the country," it would be worthwhile if the County Councils invested money in banking or

---

† From *James Joyce Quarterly* 28.2 (Winter 1991): 387–97. Reprinted by permission of the publisher. Page and line references in brackets refer to this Norton Critical Edition.

1. For example, see Zack Bowen, " 'After the Race,' " in *James Joyce's "Dubliners": Critical Essays*, ed. Clive Hart (New York: Viking, 1969), pp. 53–61; Zack Bowen, "Hungarian Politics in 'After the Race,' " *JJQ*, 7 (Winter 1970), 138–39; Donald T. Torchiana, "Joyce's 'After the Race,' the Races of Castlebar, and Dun Laoghaire," *Éire-Ireland*, 6 (1971), 119–28; Jane Somerville, "Money in *Dubliners*," *Studies in Short Fiction*, 12 (1975), 109–11; and C. H. Peake, *James Joyce: The Citizen and the Artist* (Stanford: Stanford Univ. Press, 1977), pp. 23–25. For historical background, see David F. Ward, "The Race Before the Story," *Éire-Ireland*, 2 (Summer 1967), 27–35.

2. See the *Irish Times*, "Gordon-Bennett Motor Race," January 17, 1903, p. 7, and an untitled editorial, January 20, 1903, p. 4. Further references will be cited parenthetically in the text.

widening such points in the road and touching up the course in general. The race also "would give a considerable amount of employment" in the form of jobs for officials to monitor the race and men to keep the course clear. Finally—and especially if it were held under Edward VII's patronage during his proposed visit—

> the race would attract people from every part of Europe, and Dublin, for a week or so, would become quite a motor city, its streets thronged with the latest specimen of English, French, German, and American motors. Huge sums of money would be laid out by all these people. (*IT* 7)

In addition to adducing its potential material benefits, the correspondent puffed the race as an exciting spectacle of international competition. After discussing in dramatic terms ("dangerous rival," "strive every nerve to beat," "dangerous dark horse") the cars of the different countries, he predicted:

> The race, therefore, promises to be a Titanic struggle. . . . These speeding monsters, swallowing up the miles at fifty, sixty, and seventy to the hour, will make up a thrilling spectacle as they race through the palls of dust with the best motorists of the leading nations of the earth sitting grimly behind the steering wheels, fiercely intent on winning the coveted trophy. (*IT* 7)

An editorial on January 20 offered more of the same. The writer expressed his gladness "that the suggestion to hold the race in Ireland has so far met . . . with no opposition," and, to whip up enthusiasm, extolled the race in effervescent terms as

> a magnificent advertisement for Ireland. The motor is still a luxury, and . . . may be said to concern the wealthy classes alone. Such a race, therefore, would attract . . . a great number of people of means. . . . Even if we take the competitors alone— and we may not unfairly conclude that they would . . . represent great manufacturing agencies—the money which they would expend would necessarily be very considerable. . . . May we add another consideration? Would it not be of immense educational value to our people to see these marvels flying over the highways, and demonstrating how man is advancing in the annihilation of space and time? Might not many bright Irish boys, who would see such an extraordinary sight as would be presented by the GORDON BENNETT race, be brought to apply their minds and devote their energies to scientific pursuits to the unmeasurable advantage of the country at large? (*IT* 4)

Since an English driver won the 1902 Bennett Cup, England, according to the terms of the competition, was supposed to host the next race. But English law and the relative density of population led the combined British and Irish Automobile Club to sponsor the race in Ireland, a part of the United Kingdom where law and population posed no problems.[3] Referring to this situation, the *Irish Times* editorial writer used a variation of a saying which must rarely if ever have been cited approvingly before in the pages of his conservative journal: "England's difficulty may very well prove Ireland's opportunity." In his final paragraph he quoted another enthusiast who felt that the race would bring Ireland not only "a vast sum of money" but "the beginning of a new era of prosperity" (*IT* 4).

Needless to say, most of the *Irish Times*'s golden promises did not come true. The race took place on July 2, two and a half weeks prior to the visit of Edward VII, who was more interested in fast horses than fast autos. Ireland bore much of the cost of the thousands of constables, soldiers, and officials who guarded the track and monitored the race,[4] as well as the cost of disrupting ordinary traffic on 91 miles of roads. Whatever money entered the country with the car-racing capitalists failed to trickle down into the pockets of the Irish poor or to inspire a scientific or industrial renaissance. Not until 1919 would the internal combustion engine bring a measure of local prosperity to Ireland. It was then that Henry Ford, son of a Corkman who fled to America during the great famine of the 1840s, completed a tractor factory in Cork. European tariffs caused him to convert the factory into a foundry that supplied vehicle components such as engine blocks to Ford assembly plants in other countries, but by the mid-1920s it employed 1,800 Irishmen and was Ford's third most valuable property outside North America.[5] For better or worse, though, petroleum-powered vehicles failed to spark an industrial or economic revolution in Ireland between the world wars, nor did they do so afterwards when Irish plants assembled cars for Ford, Chrysler, Fiat, Toyota, and other foreign companies. Officials of the Republic luckily resisted the blandishments of John DeLorean, a glamorous American auto maker, somewhat reminiscent of Joyce's Ségouin, who was looking for Irish investment money in the late 1970s; DeLorean's short-lived sports car factory in Belfast cost his investors far more than they received in return.[6]

"After the Race" could be Joyce's reply to the *Irish Times* and other

---

3. Ward, pp. 28–29.
4. Ward quotes the *New York Times,* July 2, 1903, p. 6: there were more police patrolling the course "than have been seen in any district of Ireland since the days of the Phoenix Park murders" (p. 29).
5. Henry Ford, in collaboration with Samuel Crowther, *Today and Tomorrow* (Garden City, N.Y.: Doubleday, Page, 1926), pp. 257–59; George Maxcy, *The Multinational Automobile Industry* (New York: St. Martin's, 1981), p. 71.
6. Prior to locating in Belfast, DeLorean had entered into negotiations with the Republic to set up a factory in Limerick; his last-minute demands prompted Irish officials to pull out in spite of their interest in the project. See William Haddad, *Hard Driving* (New York: Random House, 1985), p. 40.

boosters, both unionist and nationalist, of the Bennett Cup race. The story differs from the rest of *Dubliners* in featuring a wealthy protagonist and an international set of characters. But it has in common with the other stories (especially those of childhood and adolescence) several themes: infatuation with appearances, the desire to escape from humdrum Dublin, and paralysis as reflected in the protagonist's inability to make good this escape and to live or act meaningfully. In spite of Jimmy Doyle's money, a feeling of poverty—spiritual rather than material—pervades the story. And this poverty is directly related to what Jimmy does and does not do with the money and long dormant nationalism he has inherited from his father. Joyce already had a strong interest in socialism when he composed this early story,[7] and he was as always a nationalist in the sense of an advocate of Irish independence, even though he gave short shrift to existing nationalist groups.[8] This double orientation, together with his experience as a correspondent for the *Irish Times*, explains in large part why he used a showcase of multinational capitalism as the backdrop for the sole departure in *Dubliners* from his scrutiny of life among Dublin's middle and lower-middle classes.

I would like to look first at the national and international implications of the Bennett Cup race. Both *Irish Times* articles, perhaps unconsciously, suggested the race's aspect as a microcosm of competition among the leading capitalist and imperialist powers. The correspondent described it as "a Titanic struggle . . . with the best motorists of the leading nations of the earth . . . fiercely intent on winning" (*IT* 7). The editorialist enlisted Ireland in the contest under the Union Jack:

> After years of struggle a native of the United Kingdom on a British auto car, won it [the 1902 Bennett Cup] in the Paris Vienna struggle, and we are entitled to call upon the challengers who have had the pluck to come forward in numbers from Germany, France, and the United States to come on to the soil of the British Isles, and to take it from us if they can. (*IT* 4)

Both pieces are flanked by articles dealing with more serious aspects of international rivalry. Readers would have learned, for instance, of British Colonial Secretary Chamberlain's tour of recently pacified South Africa; of a British expedition against a mullah in North Africa; of China's protest to the United States and European coun-

---

7. In 1903, according to Ellmann, he "attended occasional meetings of a socialist group" (*JJII* 142). His brother Stanislaus recalled accompanying him to such meetings and observed in his diary a few months before Joyce wrote "After the Race": "He calls himself a socialist but attaches himself to no school of socialism." *The Complete Dublin Diary of Stanislaus Joyce*, ed. George H. Healey (Ithaca: Cornell Univ. Press, 1971), p. 54.

8. Soon he would give qualified approval to Sinn Féin (*CW* 191; *Letters II* 167, 187). He supported in particular Sinn Féin's program of economic independence.

tries over the indemnity it owed as a result of the Boxer Rebellion treaty; and of the disturbing effect on other powers of the German warship *Panther*'s attack on a Venezuelan fort. Identifying with England and Empire, the *Irish Times* sounded an aggressive note in a column abutting its challenge to rival countries to take the Bennett Cup from Britain:

> we do not agree with Mr. CHURCHILL that the regular Army at home should only be a very small one—"an Army big enough to send to fight the MAHDI of the MAD MULLAH"—but not an Army big enough "to fight the Russians, or the Germans, or the French." (*IT* 4)

Joyce hardly had to read the *Irish Times* to find out about the international situation. It was news; it was generally in the air, so to speak. Joyce's sojourns in Paris undoubtedly sharpened his awareness of big-power politics, and in August 1903 he even wrote a letter to a newspaper (presumably the *Irish Times—JJII* 138) protesting the mistreatment in North Africa of some French sailors, victims of a comic opera attempt at empire building (*CW* 113–15). In any event, car-racing rivalries among national teams naturally suggested political rivalries, especially given the economic and military implications of the technology which produced these powerful machines. (Think about tanks and armored cars and trucks—the last two soon to be used against Irish rebels.) The question was: how did Ireland fit into this perilous competition among the great powers?

The *Irish Times* saw Ireland firmly hitched to England's star as a part of the United Kingdom; it was this status that made Ireland a possible site for the Bennett Cup race in the first place. Nationalists desiring full independence traditionally had looked to France and America for support, especially in the event of English involvement in a major European war. But Joyce, judging from the evidence of his story, did not view England's difficulty as being Ireland's opportunity in either the traditional sense or the *Irish Times*'s sense. The race as he presents it seems unlikely to enrich or liberate the Irish in any way. Though Jimmy prizes his friendship with Ségouin, he may well, we suspect, lose his money in the Frenchman's business. And though the spectators' "sympathy . . . was for . . . the cars of their friends, the French"—who "were virtual victors" (*D* 42) [32.7–8, 9]—they will gain nothing from either the friendship or the victory. There undoubtedly is an echo, as Donald Torchiana perceives, of the "races of Castlebar" in 1798 when French and Irish forces routed the British, causing them to race from the field, at the beginning of a campaign which ended in honorable defeat and deportation for the French, but in massacre and tragedy for the Irish.[9] The card

9. See Torchiana, p. 81

game at the end of the story loosely suggests this outcome: the game lies between his French friend and Routh, the Englishman, his recent verbal adversary on the subject of Anglo-Irish politics; Jimmy knows that "he would lose, of course" (D 48) [38.207]; and he does in fact lose heavily, the loss at cards foreshadowing the greater potential loss of his investment. Irish involvement on any side in conflicts among the great powers, Joyce seems to be hinting, is "folly" (D 48) [38.215].[1]

Though the political aspects of the Bennett Cup race were largely implicit, its economic side was obvious. As the *Irish Times* argued blatantly, an influx of money—that of "the wealthy classes" and of the competitors who would "represent great manufacturing agencies"—was the key reason for holding the race in Ireland. Further, Joyce's interview with a French racing car driver, Henri Fournier, clearly impressed him with the capitalistic nature of the motor business, as we can see in his sketch of the headquarters of Fournier's company, "Paris-Automobile":

> Inside the gateway is a big square court, roofed over, and on the floor of the court and on great shelves extending from the floor to the roof are ranged motor-cars of all sizes, shapes, and colours. In the afternoon this court is full of noises—the voices of workmen, the voices of buyers talking in half-a-dozen languages, the ringing of telephone bells, the horns sounded by the 'chauffeurs' as the cars come in and go out. (CW 106–07)

Not surprisingly, then, "After the Race" focuses on money as a generator of status and meaning more than does any other story in *Dubliners*. "Joyce makes the reader feel this pulse of money-money-money," Jane Somerville remarks, "by pounding the word into his narrative nine times in about two pages [D 43–45] [33.34, 36, 43; 34.67, 75, 81, 87, 90, 91], and by drowning his material in other economic references."[2] The story illustrates capitalism's tendency to turn everything into a commodity. Having amassed a fortune, the elder Doyle shows it off through his son's expensive education, being "covertly proud" (D 43) [33.46] of Jimmy's conspicuous consumption at Cambridge. Even Jimmy's presentability carries an economic valence: on seeing him dressed up, his father "may have felt even commercially satisfied at having secured for his son qualities often unpurchasable" (D 45) [35.117–18].

The prime material icons, of course, are the racing cars, especially Ségouin's. This "lordly" (D 45) [35.93] machine combines in one package glamour, prestige, and physical and financial power—qual-

1. Apart from his somewhat anarchistic brand of socialism, Joyce's life-long pacifism certainly contributed to his aversion to Ireland's involvement in military conflicts either on England's side or against England.
2. Somerville, p. 110. See also Bowen, " 'After the Race,' " pp. 57–58.

ities normally absent from public scenes in Ireland, as the *Irish Times* correspondent recognized in picturing Dublin's "streets thronged with the latest specimens of English, French, German, and American motors" and with "thousands of people who, in the ordinary run of events, would have no inducement to come here" (*IT* 7). The subject and first noun of the story's opening sentence is "cars" (*D* 42) [32.1]. Images of sexual potency, the cars run "like pellets in the groove of the Naas Road . . . and through this channel of poverty and inaction"—a synecdoche for Ireland—"the Continent sped its wealth and industry" (*D* 42) [32.2–5]. Both Jimmy's attitude and that of his fellow countrymen seems to reflect the *Irish Times*'s infatuation with the racers—those "speeding monsters," those "marvellous machines," those "marvels flying over the highways" (*IT* 7). The "gratefully oppressed" Irish spectators are described as cheering not the cars' occupants but the machines themselves: "Their sympathy . . . was for the blue cars. . . . Each blue car . . . received a double round of welcome" (*D* 42) [32.7–12]. Though the *Irish Times* cited the "immense educational value" of seeing the cars demonstrate "how man is advancing in the annihilation of space and time" (*IT* 4), Jimmy is elated rather than educated by his own "Rapid motion through space" (*D* 44) [34.66]. He thinks of the Frenchman's auto:

> How smoothly it ran! In what style they had come careering along the country roads! The journey laid a magical finger on the genuine pulse of life and gallantly the machinery of human nerves strove to answer the bounding courses of the swift blue animal. (*D* 45) [35.93–97][3]

Extending this metaphor, which endows the car with more life and power than the people responding to it, a small crowd gathers later on Dame Street "to pay homage to the snorting motor" [35.102]. Then, as though without human agency, the auto "steered out slowly for Grafton Street" (*D* 45) [35.105–06].

Being "conscious of the labour latent in money" (*D* 44) [34.81], Jimmy "set out to translate [Ségouin's car] into days' work" (*D* 45) [34–35.92–93]. But Jimmy's awareness of the value of labor does not extend to the laborers themselves, nor does he intend to do any productive labor himself. Not exactly one of those "bright Irish boys" imagined by the *Irish Times* who would be inspired by the race to "devote their energies to scientific pursuits to the unmeasurable advantage of the country at large" (*IT* 4), he is a lackadaisical student

3. Regarding such passages as this, Zack Bowen comments: "Bernard Huppé has suggested to me that Joyce might in 'After the Race' be attempting a stylistic parody of a turn-of-the-century gentlemen's magazine, in anticipation of such future stylistic parodies as the one in the 'Nausicaä' chapter of *Ulysses*" (" 'After the Race,' " p. 56). A good point, but Joyce did not need to look further for a model than journalistic prose: compare the *Irish Times*'s evocations of the racing cars and its anticipatory picture of the race itself.

who wishes to acquire wealth and prestige through investing hard-earned local capital in a foreign venture. Further, as noted above, there are hints that he may lose this investment. Though he is "about to stake the greater part of his substance" (D 44) [34.83–84], Ségouin's enterprise has not been launched yet, and moreover he and the Frenchman are "not much more than acquaintances" (D 43) [33.48–49]. Jimmy's opinion of him (and even more so his father's) is based on appearances—on the racing car, on his being "reputed to own some of the biggest hotels in France" (D 43) [33.50–51], on his "unmistakable air of wealth" (D 45) [34.92], and on a general feeling of there being "money to be made in the motor business, pots of money" (D 45) [34.90–91]. A tip-off as to Ségouin's probable disingenuousness comes when the narrator, going beyond Jimmy's knowledge, reports that the Frenchman had "managed to give the impression that it was by a favour of friendship the mite of Irish money was to be included in the capital of the concern" (D 45) [34.86–88]. We need not infer fraud, but it does seem likely that the Doyles are being enticed into a highly uncertain investment,[4] their ingrained financial caution abandoning them under the influence of foreign glamour. Thus, although the Irish Times surmised that the competitors, as representatives of "great manufacturing agencies," would expend "considerable" (IT 4) sums in Ireland, the story implies that the flow of money will go in the opposite direction.

"After the Race" catapults us from the predominantly petit-bourgeois milieu of the rest of Dubliners into the circles of the newly rich. Nevertheless, it derives part of its meaning from its relationship to the other stories, much as the lives of the well-to-do in a given society are defined in part by those of the less fortunate majority. Through the efforts of his father, a "merchant prince" (D 43) [33.39], Jimmy has been freed from the capitalistic competition in which most of his fellow citizens (Eveline Hill, Mrs. Mooney, Mrs. Kearney, Farrington, Duffy, Kernan, et al.) must engage with varying degrees of modest or ill success. The time, for him, is "after the race," and he is one of the few winners. Yet what does he do with his dearly won prizes—his wealth, education, and leisure? He throws them away in pursuit of status and a vague desire to see life. Both he and his father display not a trace of civic-mindedness or social concern. Plainly, they belong to that class addressed by George Russell (AE) in an open letter written during the Dublin strike of 1913:

> You are bad citizens, for we rarely, if ever, hear of the wealthy among you endowing your city with the munificent gifts which it is the pride of merchant princes in other cities to offer. . . .

4. Cf. Bowen, " 'After the Race,' " p. 58. Even granting the Frenchman's good faith, there were "pots of money" to be lost as well as made in the motor trade, especially during the shaking-out period of the industry's infancy.

Those who have economic power have civic power also, yet you have not used the power that was yours to right what was wrong in the evil administration of this city. You have allowed the poor to be herded together so that one thinks of certain places in Dublin as of a pestilence.[5]

It is the moral failure of this class of Dubliner—nominally nationalist Catholics who have acquired wealth through business—that Joyce addresses in "After the Race." Members of Dublin's commercial aristocracy, the Doyles do nothing to benefit the city politically, socially, or economically. Their inert nationalism is one of the reasons why Dublin wears only "the mask of a capital" (D 46) [36.148], a phrase that Joyce chose carefully in order to emphasize the loss of even the limited legislative independence enjoyed by Ireland under Grattan's parliament from 1782 until the passage in 1800 of the Act of Union.[6] Mr. Doyle, "who had begun life as an advanced nationalist, had modified his views early" (D 43) [33.33–34], and has sent his son first to an English preparatory school and then to Dublin University (i.e., Trinity College, a stronghold of the Anglo-Irish establishment) and Cambridge. As to Jimmy himself, we note that it requires the stimulus of drink and excited table talk to arouse any patriotic zeal in him, and that this upsurge dissipates easily with the drinking of a toast. Socially, the Doyles' indifference to the masses of poor people who share their city is reflected in the absence of these people from the story; they certainly would have been visible in 1903 but simply do not register as significant objects on Jimmy's consciousness, through which most of the story is filtered. Especially ironic is the Doyles' intention to invest abroad rather than at home, for their money is Irish money, scraped together from the pockets of their fellow countrymen, and they themselves, unlike most of the wealthy in Ireland, are native Irish Catholics. Ignoring their heritage, however, they show their "respect for foreign accomplishments" (D 46) [35.120] by being almost pathetically eager to contribute their own "mite" [34.87][7] to the historic outward flow of capital from Ireland.[8] They are indeed "bad citizens."

We can see why Joyce chose the Gordon Bennett Cup auto race

5. George Russell, "An Open Letter to the Employers," in 1000 Years of Irish Prose, ed. Vivian Mercier and David H. Greene (1952; rpt. New York: Grosset and Dunlap, 1961), p. 228.

6. As one of his few known revisions to the story, Joyce changed "air of a capital" to the more pointed "mask of a capital." See Robert Scholes, "Further Observations on the Text of Dubliners," in Studies in Bibliography, ed. Fredson Bowers (Charlottesville: Univ. Press of Virginia, 1964), XVII, 113.

7. This term carries an ironic appropriateness, suggesting the parable (Mark 12:41–44) of the widow's mite. The Doyles' "mite of Irish money" (D 45) [34.87] represents a far greater proportionate contribution out of Ireland's general want than any capital that might be invested out of England's or the continent's general abundance.

8. Note Henchy's remark in "Ivy Day": "What we want in this country . . . is capital" (D 131) [112.443–44]. Henchy, at least, looks for English capital to follow on the heels of Edward VII's visit, whereas the Doyles plan to send Irish capital out of the country to the continent.

as the backdrop for this glimpse into the lives of Dublin's *nouveaux riches*. It provided an opportunity to show Ireland as the victim not just of England, but of the international imperialist and capitalist order, and a somewhat willing victim at that. The desire of the *Irish Times* and a broad sector of Irish public opinion to host the race is paralleled by the Doyles' desire to be associated socially and financially with Ségouin. In reality and in Joyce's story, the center of attention was that multivalent consumer fetish, the automobile. This fetish went on to triumph throughout the world, but the aftermath of the 1903 Bennett Cup race, though it was colorful and well attended, inevitably proved, after all the ballyhoo, a disappointment. Nothing changed, and as the *New York Times* reported: "General opinion in Ireland discountenances a holding of further motor races in this country as they are too great a dislocation of the regular order of things."[9] The Doyles, too, undoubtedly will suffer disappointment. Their loss, however, will not be just a personal one. It will be Ireland's, for they represent a class that has the means to do something for its country but that focuses instead on private gain and takes for its model the capitalistic competition of the great powers.

As Zack Bowen has pointed out, the ending of "After the Race," with the Hungarian Villona announcing daybreak, very likely alludes to Arthur Griffith's long essay, *The Resurrection of Hungary*.[1] Griffith offered Ireland what he saw as the promising example of Hungary's road to independence through nonviolent resistance. The need for Irish independence—political, economic, cultural—is the main theme of "After the Race," a story written by a young Irish socialist and nationalist who would soon be expressing admiration for Griffith's Sinn Féin. When Ireland gets involved as an unequal partner in a "race" or competition dominated by the great powers, the story implies, she will not be among the winners.

Abbreviations

CW   Joyce, James. *The Critical Writings of James Joyce*, ed. Ellsworth Mason and Richard Ellmann. New York: Viking Press, 1959.
D   Joyce, James. *Dubliners*, ed. Robert Scholes in consultation with Richard Ellmann. New York: Viking Press, 1967.
JJ II, III   Joyce, James. *Letters of James Joyce*. Vols. II and III, ed. Richard Ellmann. New York: Viking Press, 1966.

9. Quoted in Ward (p. 30) from the *New York Times*, July 4, 1903, p. 3.
1. Bowen, "Hungarian Politics," pp. 138–39.

FRITZ SENN

"The Boarding House" Seen as a
Tale of Misdirection†

The following views are offered as supplementary angles from which
we might profitably talk about Joyce's "The Boarding House." Some
of its features are those of a love story; we find all the conventional
trappings: a young girl and a not so young man; they are brought
together by circumstance and opportunity; there is the promise of a
marriage in the near future, except that things are not quite as they
ought to be; things are out of place. The ruling passion is practically
absent, and what is present seems to be awry. The couple, it takes
little imagination to discern, is mismatched, united by direct and
implicit forces and by scheming. What is in evidence is the trapping.
"The Boarding House" gains much of its poignancy by being set off
against a backdrop of sweet, comforting fiction of the "Matcham's
Masterstroke" type. It is a love story of wrong turnings.

Its misdirection involves readers by leaving them largely out of the
main events. We realize how we are cut off from the crucial events,
both of them; we are detained by moments in between; the actions are
off stage. We are never informed what actually happened between Mr.
Doran and Polly Mooney. We learn about the enticing beginning of
the affair but not its completion. We may guess, of course, and we
may think we know enough. Still, the overall narrative agency and all
three main characters are in harmonious collusion in withholding the
facts from us. We are not even told anything concrete about the interview between mother and daughter of the night before in which, we
read, "a clean breast" had been made "of it" (D 66) [54.181]; nor about
Mr. Doran's confession. Nothing specific is passed on to us. Whenever we come close to that recent "sin" as the cause of it all, the narrative drifts into vagueness, generalities, "his delirium . . ." (D 67)
[55.208] or "secret amiable memories . . . a revery" (D 68) [56.246–
48]; we are not let into the secret of "every ridiculous detail" (D 65)
[53.150]. The ellipsis after "delirium," Joyce's, needs to be filled, and
filled it will be, by a few readers with more certainty than the facts may
warrant. The sin is one for which "only one reparation" (D 65)
[53.124] can be made (there is tacit agreement on this between Mrs.
Mooney and Mr. Doran's priest, who both use the word independ-
ently, which in turn tells us that the case is a standard one, not
unique), but still small enough to allow of being "magnified" by a priest
(D 65) [53.151]. The one chief witness and victim remembers an

† From *James Joyce Quarterly* 23.4 (Summer 1986): 405–13. Reprinted by permission of the
publisher. Page and line references in brackets refer to this Norton Critical Edition.

exchange of "reluctant good-nights" on the third landing (*D* 67) [55.206–07]. All things known considered, Mr. Doran might have to pay for much less than what we almost automatically charge him with: this would make the reparation more cruel, less contingent on deed than on mere social attitudes, "honour" (*D* 64, 65) [52.112; 53.125], or reputation, hearsay and gossip. Anyway, we were not there, and this gap is paralleled by the one in the present, the decisive interview when Mrs. Mooney will be "hav[ing] the matter out with Mr Doran" (*D* 64) [52.108]. There is no need for us to be on the spot (nor is Polly's presence required). The issue has been predetermined by a determined woman in full charge, and by Mr. Doran's known "discomfiture" (*D* 68) [55.225]. Like a general before a battle, Mrs. Mooney has marshalled her forces, her arguments, even their phrasing. We may well stay with Polly and the vaguest of her memories, waiting, alone. We can fill *this* narrative vacuum easily, though we were somewhere else, apart.[1]

The story's technique is one of "elsewhereness."[2] There is a synoptic exposition, and then the story splits up into three distinct parts and two locations; each of the three characters is seen mainly in isolation. Separation is indeed a theme. Mrs. Mooney married her father's foreman and, when things went wrong, "got a separation"; "they lived apart" (*D* 61) [49.12–13]. Mr. Mooney, in the process, is cut off from family, occupation and even identity. When he—"a disreputable sheriff's man"—turns up, plaintively, in his daughter's office, he is not even given a name (*D* 63) [51.54–55]. Mrs. Mooney, for the rest of the story, is seen engaged in compensatory matchmaking, a venture which takes a good deal of manipulation. Joining together and putting asunder are correlated activities. Mrs. Mooney is "able to keep things to herself" (*D* 61) [49.2]; she knows when to intervene. She removes her daughter from home to an office, or back home from the office. The height of social life in the boarding house on Sunday nights is "a reunion" (and the rise of social tone is matched in that choice word, "reunion") in Mrs. Mooney's "front drawing-room" (*D* 62) [50.41]. Even language seems to put on its Sunday dress and to "oblige," as do the "*artistes*" (*D* 62) [50.42]. (Note what difference the French spelling and the French aura

---

1. Some readers, more adept at filling narrative vacuums, know that Polly Mooney is pregnant, as of course she may be. It is a pregnancy, then, that comes about more by critical than by textual annunciation. If the marriage was indeed forced by such a pregnancy, it is odd that the well-cued narrator of "Cyclops" later on fails to take up the fact for rhetorical embroidery.

2. This look at a short story is an outgrowth of an extensive investigaton into Joyce's techniques of simultaneity. Of these "elsewhereness" is one aspect, to be termed "allotopy" in its further manifestations and applied to all of Joyce's works. In the "Sirens" chapter of *Ulysses*, for example, we are consciously aware of events in several places going on at the same time, and we bear in mind, along with Leopold Bloom in the Ormond hotel, what may be happening at his home from which we are excluded for a long while. Allotopic diversion and misdirection constitute a wide area.

make: *"artiste,"* not to be confused with "artists," come from some-where else, and not the most reputable place, which shows in other contexts—"a likely *artiste"* [50.39], a few lines before.) If a misplaced "free allusion" is made, "the reunion" can be "almost broken up" (*D* 68) [56.232–33]. A more lasting reunion is now being engineered for the two lovers, but we also learn that this is a scheme for achiev-ing what "some mothers she knew" could not do—"get their daugh-ters off their hands" (*D* 65) [53.141–42]. Minuscule separation ("pieces of broken bread" [52.91]) and joinings ("the broken bread collected" [52.92–93]) can be aligned coincidentally, almost in the same breath; the same sentence has Mrs. Mooney beginning "to reconstruct" the interview of last night (*D* 64) [52.93–94]—taking apart and putting together.

Mrs. Mooney is successful in her strategies of keeping "her own counsel" (*D* 63) [51.67], watching, or throwing people together, or separating them. For this latter activity her emblematic tool is well chosen. A butcher's daughter and once a butcher's wife, "she dealt with moral problems as a cleaver deals with meat" (*D* 63) [51.75–76]. It was a cleaver also that her husband used when "he went for" her (*D* 61) [49.9–10]. It was after that that she "got a separation" [49.12–13]. It is odd and may be superfluous to reflect that the first woman ever created was made out of the first man's flesh—"bone of my bone, flesh of my flesh"—and the injunction was that he "shall cleave unto his wife" (Gen. 2.23–4): but that is a wholly different "cleaving"; fol-lowing a misdirected association, we are in the wrong shop.

There are other, related, contrasts. A sense of fixation, being stuck, enclosed, is pitted against the freedom of movement. Once the action gets under way, we are confined within the boarding house. People may move from room to room, but nobody is ever described as leaving. Mrs. Mooney reflects that a man "can go his ways" (*D* 64) [52.120], but she takes good care that Mr. Doran cannot. For him to "run away" is an inconceivable alternative (*D* 65) [53.154]. Instinct urges him to "remain free" and "not to marry" (*D* 66) [54.177]. As he follows Mrs. Mooney's summons downstairs, he longs "to ascend through the roof and fly away to another country" (*D* 67–68) [55.221–22], his own impracticable variant of a general inept desire for escape in *Dubliners*. It is then that he passes Jack Mooney coming up from the pantry, and it happens "on the last *flight* of stairs" (*D* 68; italics throughout are part of the comment, not the quotation) [55.225]. At precisely the moment when no turning away is possible, no reversal towards freedom, bulldog-faced and thick-armed Jack Mooney regards the lover "from the door of the *return* room" (*D* 68) [55.230]. Everybody seems to be static in a room for most of the time. Among the trumps in Mrs. Mooney's hand is the threat that publicity would mean for Mr. Doran "the loss of his *sit"*

(*D* 65) [53.135–36]. So we find him sitting "helplessly" in his room (*D* 66) [54.179]. When he leaves it, it is not to get away from Mrs. Mooney; he will have to walk straight into her parlor.

There is plenty of movement in the story, but it tends to go the wrong direction. Mr. Mooney "began to go to the devil"—not an ideal destination; he "ran"—but "headlong into debt"; "he went for his wife" (*D* 61) [49.5, 6, 10]. Then, relegated, he is "obliged to enlist" (*D* 61) [49.15] in an office, where he sits "waiting to be put on a job" (*D* 62) [49.19]. When he shows up at Polly's place, things go wrong again, and she has to be ordered home, out of harm's way, there to be given "the run of the young men" (*D* 63) [51.58–59]. A *run* might be a free, unhampered moving about; but the playground is narrowly defined. In fact Polly's "run" is resumed, in different words, in an echoing phrase: "Polly, of course, flirted with the young men" (*D* 63) [51.60–61], where unobtrusively, "run" has become part of a trite idiom for the naturally expected: "of course" implies that the run, course (*cursus*), of events is foreseeable, can be taken into cunning account. To "flirt" once designated a movement (of jerking and darting); it is now limited to the arena of courting with its own tacit rules. "Polly, *of course*, flirted" is in gentle tune with the governing determinism, a reliable fatality that Mrs. Mooney knows how to work to her own advantage. Her husband once was "sure to break out" (*D* 61—from the pledge into renewed drinking) [49.7]; her son is "sure to be on to a good thing" (*D* 62—and to lend some threat or muscular help, when necessary) [50.38–39]. In this world a likely lodger can be expected to toe the line; "a force" pushes him "downstairs step by step" (*D* 68) [55.223]. The combined forces may include "the weight of social opinion" (*D* 64) [52.110] or publicity, which "would mean for him, perhaps, the loss of his sit" [53.135–36]. So Mrs. Mooney can be sure "she would win" (*D* 64 and repeated at *D* 65) [52.109; 53.128]. Running the whole show, "a determined woman" (as the second sentence in the story states emphatically—*D* 61) [49.2–3], she is resolute, active, but in turn also determined by her nature and her environment, perpetuating her own failures. Things take their course, occasionally with some skillful prompting, and the run may turn out to be a dead end, without a "loophole" (*D* 65) [53.152].

Most of the running, then, is in an undesired direction. There was a hitch in Mrs. Mooney's married life; her plans miscarried, so she now masterminds her daughter's fate. Mr. Doran would rather turn somewhere else, fly through the roof, than face his prospective mother-in-law, but he obeys. It is a short step from whatever he actually "had done" to being "done for" (*D* 66) [54.176, 178] . Even his smallest actions go amiss; he has a hard time doing anything right. He is fumbling, passive, conative: "He had made two attempts to shave but his hand had been so unsteady that he had been obliged to desist"

(D 65) [53.143–45]. We notice how the men in Mrs. Mooney's environment generally "oblige" or "are obliged." Mr. Doran can hardly see and could never "brazen it out" (D 65) [53.154]. He is being sent for, summoned as to court: "she wished to speak with him" is a command that will be phrased, "the missus wanted to see him" (D 65, 67) [53.127; 55.214]. In yet another, almost deadly mechanical, near-repetition towards the end, Mrs. Mooney speaks for him and calls her daughter: "Mr Doran wants to speak to you" (D 69) [56.259]. Language allows for this usage; "wanted" is circumstantially appropriate. We know and she knows what Mr. Doran really wants; her public voicing of the intention that silent Mr. Doran cannot utter himself is a supreme example of muted, ironic misdirection.

It is misguided and unwise for a butcher to buy bad meat or to fight his wife "in the presence of customers" (D 61) [49.8]; for a young girl to go to "relight her candle" (D 67) [54.193] in a boarder's room; for a boarder to abuse the "hospitality" (D 64) [52.113] or to take advantage of a girl. It may also be unwise to force two people into lifelong cohabitation.

Even trivial matters are not quite right, somehow displaced. Sunday worshippers are on their way to George's Church, right outside the window. It is the wrong church (Protestant), the wrong time. Mrs. Mooney will "catch short twelve at Marlborough Street" (D 64) [52.108–09]. This one is the Catholic and prestigious Pro-Cathedral. (If we are not familiar with Dublin usage and envisage, for a puzzled moment, a train in some railway station, then the wording has misdirected us.) One may pick the wrong social key, the unsuitable expression, making a "free allusion" (D 68) [56.232–33]. Polly's brother, who resents such breaches of decorum, may himself deviate into "soldiers' obscenities" (D 62) [50.36]: it is all a question of when and where and who. Polly's song (through which she is introduced to the reader), with its rhymes of "sham" with "am," takes us two different ways, towards appearance or towards a reality beneath it. She appears both as a "naughty girl" (D 62) [51.46] in a music-hall sort of role, and then again as someone of "youth and inexperience" (D 64) [52.117]. And what are we to make of a paradoxical joining like "in her wise innocence" (D 64) [52.102]? Polly "had a habit of glancing upwards when she spoke with anyone"—she is looking somewhere else—that "made her look like a little perverse madonna" (D 62–63) [51.51–52, 52–53]. A "perverse" madonna is one who is turned the wrong way. Etymologically, but not culturally, "madonna" is the same as "Madam." The Italian and the French variants both go back to a Latin (mea) domina, which perfectly suits Mrs. Mooney who rules on high and knows how to put a religious front on a meretricious calculation, combining both roles with ease.

The perverse madonna with her candle in search of light guides

Mr. Doran ultimately into a "delirium" (D 67) [55.208]. A *delirium* originally meant a going out of one's furrow (Latin *lira*); or to draw a furrow awry, a going off the rail, another wrong turning, one that has serious results.

Reading "The Boarding House" amounts to a process of *redirection* (or, if you prefer, an interpretative "reparation"). We interpret—let us hope, not all in the same direction—what we are told. We translate such matter-of-fact assertions as "she was an outraged mother" (D 64) [52.111] from a truthful lament to a strategic social weapon. As it happens, "outrage" derives from *ultra*: beyond; it suggests going far in a certain direction, going beyond bounds. In the redirection of reading we may take up Mrs. Mooney's "He had simply taken advantage of Polly's youth and inexperience" (D 64) [52.116–17] and match it—and in particular the beautifully comprehensive *"simply"*— with the complex ritual of allurement that fills more than half a page (D 67) in Mr. Doran's reminiscences, with candle, perfume, caresses, slippers, timidity, and opportunity. ("Advantage" has to do with "advance," going forward, taking decisive steps; and for all we are told the advances were not Mr. Doran's.) He himself, in worried contemplation of the affair, translates the allegations Mrs. Mooney will no doubt repeat to him into his own, equally subjective, parallactic, terse version: "he was being had" (D 66—passive, of course) [54.171]. In some sense, "The Boarding House" puts several discordant, incomplete presentations of the affair against each other (including Polly's own dreaming version). The affair itself, in the center, remains unverbalized.

Misdirection may affect the wording, the syntax, especially when uncomfortable issues are at stake: "There had been no open complicity between mother and daughter, no open understanding *but*" (D 63) [51.69–71]. Pause a moment and wonder what, after "no open complicity . . . no open understanding," this *but* might lead to. A few lines before, a similar construction was linked by the same conjunction: "Polly, of course, flirted with the young men but Mrs Mooney . . . knew that the young men were only passing the time" (D 63) [51.60–62]. So we continue: "but, though people in the house began to talk of the affair, still Mrs Mooney did not intervene" (D 63) [51.71–72]. The sentence takes an unexpected, vacuous, turn, leaving us dangling, as though the sentence, and Mrs. Mooney's meditations behind it, had not dared to face whatever development, or "complicity," was to follow.

It is worthwhile inspecting the meaning of a notion like frankness: "she had been frank in her questions and Polly had been frank in her answers" (D 64) [52.95–96], as frank and symmetrical a statement as one could wish to see. The frankness has been duplicated, but it is contradicted when we stumble across four "awkwards" in close succession. The most elaborate sentence in the whole story, hurriedly unpunctuated, as though to get it over as painlessly as possible, turns awkwardness into a psychological and syntactical actuality:

> Both had been somewhat awkward, of course. She had been made awkward by her not wishing to receive the news in too cavalier a fashion or to seem to have connived and Polly had been made awkward not merely because allusions of that kind always made her awkward but also because she did not wish it to be thought that in her wise innocence she had divined the intention behind her mother's tolerance. (D 64) [52.97–103]

These are the circling movements of evasion. Embarrassment has become paraphrase (a cautious "speaking beside" the point). For once even Mrs. Mooney is caught in a passive construction: "she had been made awkward." The frankness alleged earlier surfaces now as "allusions of that kind"; allusions, by definition, are not "frank." Latin *co-nivere* meant to close one's eyes so as not to have to notice; the whole long-winded sentence connives in this. We can also reinterpret what is claimed to be "tolerance": a strategic ambush. To be "awkward" could now apply to an inelegance like "by her not wishing to receive," but it once meant to go in the direction of "awk," and "awk" was the wrong way, or back foremost. That is what the sentence windingly seems to do, turn on its heels, as though to act out its original as well as its present meanings. The fourfold "awkward" is right: "The Boarding House" is a story of awkwardness.

Apart from that one interview, however, Mrs. Mooney is quite self-assured, knows which way to turn. She is in command, sure of victory. "She governed her house cunningly and firmly" (D 62) [50.25–26]. She dispatches her husband, her daughter, the maid where she wants them. Hers are the transitive, active verbs: "she had married her father's foreman," "opened a butcher's shop," "got a separation" (D 61) [49.3, 3–4, 12]; "had taken what remained of her money" (D 62) [49.19–20]; "made Mary collect the crusts" (D 64) [52.90]; "counted all her cards" (D 65) [53.126]. She turned her husband out of the house, leaving him uprooted. She sent "her daughter to be a typewriter" (D 63) [51.53–54]; but there her displaced father intervened and made a nuisance of himself. The husband's removal somehow interfered with her daughter's positioning, and the two maneuvers backfired: so things, for all her crafty management of affairs, *were* awkward after all. The present enterprise too is a success that we see as highly qualified and costly, and we naturally tend to extrapolate.

Joyce has in fact provided extratextual continuation into another book. In *Ulysses* the misdirection is carried further, in hyperbolic exaggeration. The boarding house has become a "kip" (*Finnegans Wake* takes it as far as "boardelhouse," *FW* 186.31); Polly a down-

and-out exhibitionist "without a stitch on her, exposing her person, open to all comers" or a "sleepwalking bitch" (*U* 303). In the retelling Jack Mooney's silent glare has become an articulated threat: "Told him if he didn't patch up the pot, Jesus, he'd kick the shite out of him" (*U* 314). Dublin gossip has been at work on the "details . . . invented by some" (*D* 65) [53.133] and magnified them out of hand. Predictably, however, Mr. Doran has been progressing in the direction we imagined; he has followed in the traces of Mr. Mooney: on his annual bend, he is already drunk in mid-afternoon, unpopular among his companions, and saying the wrong things in the wrong place (*U* 302), further discomfited.

His "discomfiture" (*D* 68) [55.225] that we witness is both a perplexity and a defeat, but also what the term contains: a making up (Latin *conficere*), yet one that has gone in an unwanted direction: *dis*; a falling apart, a joining and a separation. It is like the engineering of a match and, at the same time, "going to the devil," rolled into one.

The general displacement extends to tiny touches. "The Boarding House" displays most of the ingredients of the happy-ending tale, including "caresses . . . blood glowed warmly . . . perfumed skin . . . kiss . . . the touch of her hand" (*D* 67) [54–55.190, 196, 196–97, 207, 207–08], physical prerequisites of love. It also features a heart, just one, and a heart that seems to behave according to romantic precedent: "He felt his heart leap warmly." This sounds comforting: a heart leaps (remember Wordsworth), and does so "warmly," until: "He felt his heart leap warmly in his throat" (*D* 66) [53.157]. This is not where we expect a heart to leap; it has been transferred incongruously and subjectively.[3] This dislocation can be matched with a

---

3. The slow, linear unfolding exercised here of what must be an instant of sensation is a falsification of reality. Naturally Doran does not, first, pass through a short phase of affectionate warmth and, then, abruptly feel that he does not have his heart in the right place. But it is what happens *in the telling*, since language can never be in two places at the identical moment. Different tellings show different scenarios, as translations may show. They change the process in which we readers experience the physical location of an imaginary shock. It can be glossed over in summary paraphrase, without anatomical anchoring:

Nella sua immaginazione eccitata sentiva (*Gente di Dublino,* trans. Franca Cancogni, Milano: Mondadori, 1963, p. 99).

There may be a colloquialism right in front, without a surprise:

Aveva il cuore in gola, e nella sua immaginazione (*Gente di Dublino,* trans. Marco Papi, Milano: Garzanti, 1976, p. 59).

Or else the heart can be shown, as it were, in transit:

Dans une bouffée de chaleur, il sentit le cœur lui monter aux lèvres (*Dublinois,* trans. Jacques Aubert, in *Joyce: Oeuvres I,* Paris: Gallimard, 1982, p. 162);

Sintió que su agitado corazón se le ponia de un salto en la boca (*Dublineses,* trans. G. Cabrera Infante, Barcelona: Editorial Lumen, 1972, p. 68).

Such comparisons demonstrate how Joyce has extended an idiom like "his heart in his mouth" into a delayed, dramatic misdirection.

later passage in which Mr. Doran remembers Jack Mooney shouting at a music-hall *artiste* who had referred "freely" to Polly at one of the reunions, that "he'd bloody well put his teeth down his throat, so he would" (*D* 68) [56.238–39]. The throat may be a suitable, characteristic part of Mr. Doran's anatomy at this turning point in his life, a telling synecdoche, but in the multiple misdirection and general discomfiture of "The Boarding House," the throat has become a place where one's heart might encounter one's teeth. Only a butcher with determination, and a cleaver, could make this happen.

Abbreviations

D Joyce, James. *Dubliners,* ed. Robert Scholes in consultation with Richard Ellmann. New York: Viking Press, 1967.

FW Joyce, James. *Finnegans Wake.* New York: Viking Press, 1939; London: Faber and Faber, 1939. These two editions have identical pagination.

U Joyce, James. *Ulysses.* New York: Random House, 1934, reset and corrected 1961.

MORRIS BEJA

Farrington the Scrivener: A Story of Dame Street†

> I might as well be talking to the wall as talking to you.
>   —Mr. Alleyne, in James Joyce, "Counterparts"

At the start of Herman Melville's short story "Bartleby the Scrivener: A Story of Wall Street," originally published in 1853, the narrator, an elderly lawyer, speaks of a "singular set of men" of whom, as far as he knows, "nothing" has "ever been written— . . . the law-copyists, or scriveners" (92). Since then, at least one other major writer—James Joyce—has written a story centering on such a scrivener: "Counterparts." Melville's lawyer says of his scrivener that he was "the strangest I ever saw, or heard of" (92). Nothing that we shall discover in this essay about Joyce's scrivener, Farrington, will match Bartleby for strangeness. Nor, I should stress at the outset, is my bringing the two scriveners together meant to discuss or even suggest any sort of possible "influence." I am confident that Joyce would not have known what was at that time an obscure tale by a largely neglected writer when he wrote his own story in 1905. I am not in any case interested in the question of influence; for my pur-

† From *Coping with Joyce: Essays in the Copenhagen Symposium,* ed. Morris Beja and Shari Benstock (Columbus: Ohio State University Press, 1989), pp. 11–22. Reprinted by permission of the author. Page and line references in brackets refer to this Norton Critical Edition.

poses, the fact that there was surely no awareness on Joyce's part of Melville's story makes it all the more intriguing to compare and contrast the two works, and above all the two men: Joyce's brutal bully and Melville's passive victim.

So different are the two characters, actually, that at first it would seem that only the contrasts between them and their tales are worth mentioning, and that their one genuine point of convergence is their mode of employment. On the evidence of both stories, the job of the scrivener—that is, of copying legal documents in those pre-Xerox days when typewriters were also either nonexistent (as in Bartleby's time) or not yet widely accepted for legal purposes (as in Farrington's)—would seem to have been tedious, mechanical, and alienating: a daily grind demanding no thought and yielding little self-respect.

Such characteristics seem especially emphasized in Melville's story. It is narrated by Bartleby's employer, a New York lawyer who tells about his office and its two scriveners, Turkey and Nippers, and the errand-boy, Ginger Nut; the lawyer had determined that there was too much work for his current staff and so advertised for another scrivener. In response, one day "a motionless young man" (99) stands upon his threshold: Bartleby. The lawyer hires him, and for a time the young scrivener's work is exemplary, and Bartleby does "an extraordinary quantity of writing" (100). So it is all the more surprising when the lawyer, having asked him to help examine some previously copied work, hears from Bartleby the reply, "I would prefer not to" (101). The lawyer feels at that moment too busy to pursue his anger, but he does so a few days later upon again hearing the scrivener use that enigmatic phrase: "I would prefer not to." The other members of his staff agree with him that Bartleby's behavior is reprehensible and even outrageous, but in view of the young man's excellent work otherwise, and his quiet demeanor, the lawyer does not turn him out, even when, as the days go by, the same response is forthcoming when any request is made of Bartleby—and indeed when he eventually stops copying altogether. At around that time, as well, the lawyer discovers that Bartleby apparently never leaves the office premises, before or after work hours, subsisting on "nothing but ginger-nuts" (104). Attempting to be sympathetic, the lawyer pleads with the young man to provide information about his background, but Bartleby replies only that he would prefer not to reply. The lawyer at last fires him, but to no avail: Bartleby simply remains in his little corner, behind his screen and facing a wall opposite the office window.

The lawyer comes to feel that he is no longer in control of his own offices, and in a kind of panic he resolves that if Bartleby will not leave, he will; so he changes his premises. Even after the move takes place, Bartleby continues to haunt the old offices—and then, when turned out by the new tenant, the building. Returning there on the plea of the landlord, the lawyer is so touched by Bartleby's plight that he offers to take him with him—not to the new offices but to the lawyer's own home; but Bartleby replies that he would prefer not to. Days later, the lawyer hears that the police have removed Bartleby and taken him to the Tombs, the prison in the Halls of Justice. The lawyer visits him there, where Bartleby says, "I know you . . . and I want nothing to say to you" (128). The lawyer arranges for the young man to be treated and fed well, but when he returns a few days later he finds Bartleby huddled at the base of the wall, dead. In a post-script of sorts, the lawyer informs us that some months later he heard a rumor that Bartleby had once worked at the Dead Letter Office. "Ah, Bartleby!" he ends his narrative, "Ah, humanity!" (131).

"Bartleby the Scrivener" is a complex, packed work, perhaps over-done in parts and not always in full control of its ambition; but for all that it is a genuine masterpiece, an obsessively haunting tale. Joyce's "Counterparts" is finally less ambitious, but on its own it is also masterful, perhaps even flawless. It succinctly recounts the events of a single day in the life of a man who would seem to be not so much a Bartleby as an anti-Bartleby.

Farrington, already regarded by his employer—the lawyer Mr. Alleyne—as a shirker, has failed to complete some copies when they are needed, and when asked to provide them he tries to pretend he knows nothing about them. In front of the entire staff, his furious employer asks him, "do you take me for a fool? Do you think me an utter fool?" Before he realizes it, Farrington replies, "I don't think, sir . . . that that's a fair question to put to me" (91) [74.165–66; 75.170–71].

Threatened with the loss of his position, Farrington must apolo-gize abjectly for his witticism. At the end of the day, he is still thirsty—despite his having sneaked off to a pub during working hours—and in need of a night out with his friends, so he pawns his watch. His story of the incident at the office is a success with his chums, but as the pub crawl continues the evening is disappointing. He spends too much money, is frustrated when he feels unable to respond to an apparently flirtatious woman in one pub, and then loses an arm-wrestling contest to Weathers, a younger man. On his way home, he feels "humiliated and discontented: he did not even feel drunk and he had only twopence in his pocket. He cursed every-thing. He had done for himself in the office, pawned his watch, spent all his money; and he had not even got drunk" (96–97) [80.345–48]. His wife not at home, he asks his son Tom about his dinner. The young boy says he is going to cook it; but Farrington sees that the fire has been allowed to go out and, furious, viciously beats him with a walking-stick. Terrified, the boy squeals, "Don't beat me, pa! And I'll . . . I'll say a *Hail Mary* for you . . . I'll say a *Hail Mary* for you, pa, if you don't beat me. . . . I'll say a *Hail Mary* . . ." (98) [82.399–401].

Obviously, there is a marked difference in the reader's degree of sympathy or, certainly, identification with the protagonist of each story.[1] Joyce forces us to understand a brute like Farrington, and— I shall attempt to show—to realize our own kinship with him, but most of us are readier to identify with his son, or even with Bartleby. Many readers who seem to have no qualms about identifying themselves with a catatonic and schizophrenic like Bartleby—as the existential victim—would recoil with repugnance at any attempt to associate them with Farrington, or indeed with either of the employers in the stories. Such readers are ready enough to sentimentalize Bartleby's plight by turning him into a prophet, wiser in his "irrational" existence than the rest of humanity in its desperate "sanity." Yet it does not take so romanticized a view of Bartleby to feel that there is an integrity in his self-destructive and futile mode of behavior that is lacking in Farrington's self-deceptive and futile modes of rebellion.

Not to put too fine a point on it, Farrington is after all a "ruffian" [75.179]. The term is Mr. Alleyne's—hardly a totally sympathetic or unbiased judge of Farrington's character—but the narrative voice of the story uses not dissimilar terms, as we hear that Farrington feels "savage and thirsty and revengeful" (92) [75.192–93], or that he is "full of smouldering anger and revengefulness" (96) [80.344]. Bartleby, in contrast, is said to be a "poor, pale, passive mortal . . . a helpless creature" (123). Each character is given the sort of physique that would be expected, given their roles: Bartleby the victim is described as "lean," and as "thin and pale" (109, 111), while Farrington the bully is "tall and of great bulk," and he walks "with a heavy step" (86).

They contrast with one another in additional physical ways as well. Bartleby is constantly in stasis. He seems never to move: "I like to be stationary," he remarks in his exasperating mode of understatement (126). Farrington is constantly hyperkinetic: "his body ached to do something, to rush out and revel in violence" (90) [74.145–46]. He leaves the office whenever he gets the chance (Mr. Alleyne accuses him of taking extra-long lunches, and of never being there when he is wanted; and we see him pretend to go to the men's room when he is actually going out to a pub)—in contrast to Bartleby, who

---

1. I have argued elsewhere against the frequent assertion that it is the lawyer, rather than Bartleby, who is for most readers the central interest in Melville's story. In that same essay, I pursue the relevance of "schizophrenia" as a clinical term in attempting to comprehend Bartleby, his state, and his behavior. See "Bartleby and Schizophrenia."

is at first praised by the lawyer for the fact that he is always *there*: "I observed that he never went to dinner; indeed, that he never went anywhere. As yet I had never, of my personal knowledge, known him to be outside of my office" (104). In time the lawyer becomes less sanguine about this clinging, static quality in his scrivener, who finally refuses to quit the lawyer's office altogether.

As all that suggests, the relationships between employee and employer in the two stories are also studies in antithesis, as are the employers themselves. Mr. Alleyne is impatient and short-tempered. While there has been some critical disagreement about the efficacy of the lawyer's good intentions in "Bartleby the Scrivener," and some critics have attacked, for example, his "exploitative" role as a representative of "Wall Street," few of us mere mortals (as distinct I gather from literary critics) could claim to be as patient, as generous, or as long-suffering as Melville's lawyer, who tries—truly sincerely, it seems quite clear, however ineffectively or hopelessly—to deal with and confront Bartleby's painful case. It is true that he is the one to tell us, but there seems little reason to disbelieve the lawyer's assertions that, for example, "I seldom lose my temper; much more seldom indulge in dangerous indignation at wrongs and outrages" (93); and it is clearly accurate for him to claim, as he does, that (unlike Mr. Alleyne, certainly) he resorts to "no vulgar bullying, no bravado of any sort, no choleric hectoring" (117). In contrast, we see no reason to doubt Farrington's fear that from now on "Mr Alleyne would never give him an hour's rest: his life would be a hell to him" (92) [75.193–95]. To give Mr. Alleyne his due, he does not have a model employee in Farrington, who surely would be an exasperating person to have in one's office.

So would Bartleby, no doubt. Yet in the end it is the psychological and spiritual differences between the two scriveners that seem, at least at first, to control our views when we look at them together. Both men are self-defeating; but Farrington's mode of self-destruction follows what is, unfortunately, probably the more usual pattern. For he strikes out, bitterly and openly, at other people as well, even resorting to—seeking out, and ready to "revel in"—violence: "he longed to execrate aloud, to bring his fist down on something violently" (90) [74.140–41]. In some ways, he seems closer to the other scriveners in the office of Melville's lawyer than to Bartleby himself: to Nippers, for one, who, "if he wanted anything, it was to be rid of a scrivener's table altogether" (96). Nippers, however, is "at least, a temperate man" (98), so Farrington—with his determination "that he must have a good night's drinking" (87) [71.46]—seems even more like Turkey, as they both practice a profession that Joyce's scrivener would agree is, in Melville's lawyer's words, "a dry, husky sort of business" (98). Turkey is notorious in the office for becoming less agreeable and more irascible and cantankerous after his lunch, when he has had some beer, which leads him to be (like Farrington, after his glass of porter) "rash with his tongue—in fact, insolent" (95). The alcohol also makes both men prone to violence: in the morning, Turkey seems the soul of patience with respect to Bartleby's odd conduct; after experiencing the "effects of beer," however, he displays "combativeness," throwing "his arms into a pugilistic position" and offering to "go and black his eyes" (105, 106). In contrast, Bartleby, whose "pale face clearly indicated that he never drank beer like Turkey" (111)—or Farrington—displays "freedom from all dissipation," and "great stillness" and "unalterableness of demeanor under all circumstances" (107). He is a completely nonviolent person, whose stance takes the form of totally passive resistance—a "poor, pale, passive mortal" (123). Fascinatingly, his rebellion is ultimately no less real than Farrington's, and much more effective in many essential ways: "nothing," as Melville's lawyer points out, "so aggravates an earnest person as a passive resistance" (104). Yet, after all, Bartleby's rebellion is also self-defeating, and hardly a model for others to emulate.

In that and in other key ways as well, despite all these contrasts between the protagonists of the two stories, the similarities between the two men, and between their plights, are much more revealing and suggestive, if subtle and surprising. The comparison may suggest that similar forces are present in their lives—however ultimately difficult it may be to pin down those forces—which make them both not merely unwilling but unable to get down to work, to copy their papers: to get along in their worlds. Bartleby's inability (or unwillingness) to copy is all too obvious as his story proceeds. Farrington's inability is less extreme, but it seems acute from the start, as he has for some reason been unable to finish his copy of an important contract for Mr. Alleyne, who accuses him right off of having "always some excuse or another for shirking work" (87) [71.30–31]. Farrington too would prefer not to; and he doesn't, sort of. He may not have the absolute courage of his convictions we see all too present in Bartleby, but in this pivotal matter he is his counterpart.

And indeed they are genuine "counterparts." Above all they are so to each other, but they are also counterparts to secondary figures in their respective stories. If we had any doubts about that in Joyce's story, the title makes it clear enough, with a near explicitness in which Joyce rarely indulges, except—as here—in some of his titles (A Portrait of the Artist as a Young Man, Exiles, Ulysses, Finnegans Wake). Farrington is played off against Mr. Alleyne; against Weathers, the young man who beats him at arm wrestling (and who has apparently slipped out from work in order to join them at the pub); and most compellingly against his young son, Tom. The counterpointing is so close and so effective that even in the short space of this brief tale we come to understand that, at least in respect to Mr. Alleyne and Tom, it is not a question of their merely being "foils" for Farrington: they are in fact his *counterparts*, his doubles or "doppelgangers."

As a number of critics have shown, "Bartleby the Scrivener" is also a tale of doubles,[2] with its major and minor characters serving as "counterparts" to one another: above all, the lawyer and Bartleby; but also the other two scriveners, Nippers and Turkey (mirroring one another like the morning and afternoon personalities of a single character—the nip and tuck, as it were); and the lawyer and each of those two characters (especially the elder, Turkey); as well as those scriveners (and, perhaps, Ginger Nut) and Bartleby. It is one thing to recognize that all these characters are doubles, however, and quite another to perceive the full significance of their doubling in this mysterious tale. An especially crucial area of exploration is the relationship each scrivener has with his employer/double.

Joyce's Mr. Alleyne, as we have seen, is petulant and in general apparently a hard, irritable man to work for. In the first sentence of the story he rings the bell "furiously," and speaks through the tube in "a furious voice" and in "a piercing" accent (86) [70.1–2]. In contrast, Melville's lawyer is apparently justified in claiming at the start that "I seldom lose my temper" (93). Yet he finds Bartleby's behavior so provoking that he responds at times in ways that, by his standards in any case, come quite close to the mode of response of Mr. Alleyne: at first he merely reports his "rising in high excitement," but he soon enough finds himself speaking "in a louder tone"—indeed " 'Bartleby,' I roared"; and "sometimes, to be sure, I could not, for the very soul of me, avoid falling into sudden spasmodic passions with him" (101, 106, 107).

The two employees, however, are portrayed as powerless—impotent—in their respective spheres. Bartleby manifests impotence through passivity (although through passive resistance), Farrington through impotent rage. But in each their sense of powerlessness and alienation seems exacerbated by the contrasts between themselves and their employers—and their employers' positions in the world. Bartleby shares the traits his employer ascribes to himself: he too wants a "snug retreat" and acts—with a vengeance—as though he has a "profound conviction that the easiest way of life is best" (92–93). But within the social world of the story—given, that is the sociopolitical and economic forces at work—the lawyer can convert these traits into success, authority, and power, while for Bartleby they are self-destructive.

Both Bartleby and Farrington live and work in a system in which

2. See for example the works cited for Marcus, Widmer, Rogers, Keppler, and Beja.

they cannot succeed. Bartleby's "passive resistance" occurs in a society far removed from Thoreau's; or, more accurately, given his class, his social status, and the economic realities of his situation—all of them more comparable to Farrington's than Thoreau's—there is no possibility of Bartleby attaining some genuine mode of triumph or success through such passive resistance.

Farrington clearly envies his employer's potent, active rage and energy, manifested in an ability to fire Farrington or to see that "his life would be a hell to him" (92) [75.194–95]. Mr. Alleyne's forcefulness has an outlet that society sanctions; Farrington's only outlets—or so it would seem to him—are through drink and abusing his son. But, as with Bartleby, his mode of behavior is self-destructive.

In Melville's story, all that does not make us lose sight of how the lawyer takes on a positively fatherly role in regard to his young employee—just as, perhaps, it is a similar recognition of their paternal relationship that leads Bartleby in his turn to choose the lawyer for his own needs. Those needs, as much of what I have said would suggest, seem at least twofold: for one thing, to involve a young man's need for a father, but for another to include a son's presumably inevitable need to rebel against that father. Moreover, the lawyer seems more or less to recognize his role in such a pattern, and the necessity for it. At one point, he even suggests that his own needs are thereby being met, when he says in regard to Bartleby's actions that "I burned to be rebelled against again" (106). In the end, he goes so far as to offer to bring Bartleby into his own home—to adopt him, in effect. But Bartleby would prefer not to.

Paternal benevolence is not enough, nor is mere kindness. Bartleby's employer is much more humane than Farrington's (or, as I have argued, than most employers would ever be), but that does not save Bartleby, and it would not save Farrington either.

The paternity theme in "Counterparts" is illuminated if complicated by the fact that in portraying and naming Mr. Alleyne, Joyce is—as a loyal son—paying off one of "his father's scores," as Richard Ellmann puts it (16); for a Henry Alleyn was a dishonest businessman and supervisor of a firm with which the older Joyce had worked, and he had run off with the firm's funds. But Farrington himself, unlike Bartleby (we can only assume), is also a father, not merely a son: in that context, the biographical associations are complicated by the fact that Farrington seems at least partially based on Joyce's father, John Joyce, as well as on Joyce's uncle, William Murray. According to Stanislaus Joyce in an entry in his diary during 1904, "the manner in which Uncle Willie tyrannizes his children is to me an intolerable and stupid cowardice," and Stanislaus goes on to report that "on one occasion Bertie, then an infant of six or seven, begged Uncle William not to beat him and promised to say a 'Hail

Mary' for him if he didn't" (37). Stanislaus' attitude toward such brutality is commendable, but it is one of my arguments that James Joyce's presentation, while no less damning, also brings us closer to a genuine understanding, even a degree of compassion, for Uncle William's counterpart. As Joyce once wrote in a letter to Stanislaus, "if many husbands are brutal the atmosphere in which they live (vide Counterparts) is brutal . . ." (*Letters II* 192).

Intriguingly, the authors of both stories use similar imagery in evoking the anguish and situations of their scriveners. Bartleby's story is a "Story of Wall Street," and he is constantly associated with walls, particularly "the dead brick wall" upon which his office window looks (111); at the Tombs he at last dies "strangely huddled at the base of the wall" (130). Farrington is "tall and of great bulk," and Mr. Alleyne claims that "I might as well be talking to the wall as talking to you" (86, 87) [70.9–10; 71.35–36]. And Farrington (we are told several times) has "heavy dirty eyes" (94; cf. 86) [77.251; 70.11–12], while Bartleby, at death, has "dim eyes" (130).

In a well-known letter of 1904 to Constantine P. Curran, Joyce said that he was calling his book "*Dubliners* to betray the soul of that hemiplegia or paralysis which many consider a city" (*Letters I* 55); two years later he reiterated, to Grant Richards, that "I chose Dublin for the scene because that city seemed to me the centre of paralysis" (*Letters II* 134). If anything, the sense of paralysis is even greater in Bartleby's tale than in Farrington's, for Bartleby is for all practical purposes quite literally paralyzed and static—even to the degree of seeming at last catatonic. He displays "great stillness," and "long-continued motionlessness" (107, 111); the mildness and stasis with which he utters his "I would prefer not to" portray not action but inaction, and a preference for it; he goes nowhere—"I like to be stationary"—and finally the lawyer is the one who is forced to move, since Bartleby does not and will not.

Farrington would seem to be constantly active, yet the effect is often curiously similar. Confronted with Mr. Alleyne's anger at his not yet having done his copying at the start of the story, Farrington remains in front of his employer's desk, immobile, until at last Mr. Alleyne bursts out, "Are you going to stand there all the day?" [71.54]. Returning to his desk, and despite the urgency of his need to get down to work, or because of it, Farrington is paralyzed with an inability to copy even a single word: "he continued to stare stupidly at the last words he had written" (88) [72.65–66]. At the end of his evening's pub crawl, this clerk who has longed to leave his office "loathed returning to his home" (97) [81.357], so that Bernard Benstock's phrasing is right on the mark when he observes that Farrington "moves from pub to pub until time and money run out and he is fixed in a catatonic moment of entrapment" (35).

The social context of each story brings out the stasis and paralysis on the communal level; both men are paralyzed by the worlds in which they live. Their resulting immobility and inertia are personally ruinous and seemingly irrational, as are, in context, the comments each makes to his employer which bring on the respective crises. Bartleby's "I would prefer not to" makes no ordinary "sense" at all. And for his part Farrington's reply to Mr. Alleyne's demand that he answer the question about whether he takes him for a fool—that, in effect, he would prefer not to ("I don't think, sir, he said, that that's a fair question to put to me" [91] [75.171–72])—is similarly disastrous. It is precisely equivalent to Bartleby's answer at one point in *his* story: " 'At present I prefer to give no answer,' he said . . ." (113).

It is essential to understand the significance of the closeness of their responses, which are in substance interchangeable. For in each case the behavior of the given scrivener is to himself not as outrageous, as incomprehensible or as irrational, as it will necessarily seem to the rest of the world. *It is a mode of coping.* Even perhaps a strategy, a tactic. Their action and inaction seem to them the only means they have to handle what they regard as an unlivable situation. Bartleby's behavior is clearly ludicrous, absurd, even sick, if you are not Bartleby; Farrington's behavior is clearly crude, brutal, even cruel, certainly indefensible, if you are anyone else in the world except Farrington. "At present I would prefer not to be a little reasonable," says Bartleby for both of them (113).

The ultimate point of the comparisons I have discussed, after all, is to attempt to illuminate what happens in both stories, and why—or out of what forces. I feel especially that the comparisons help us to comprehend "Counterparts" more fully. Bartleby certainly remains a mysterious figure, and any attempt to explain completely—or to explain away—his motivation, or the sources in his psyche for what he does, is doomed to failure. There are ambiguities enough in Joyce's story, but for once another writer seems even more indeterminate than he. Yet however uncertain we remain about the true sources of Bartleby's behavior and his plight, we must—given the comparisons I have pointed out—feel that at least some may well be shared with Farrington: and among those their frustration and alienation and social plight are surely central. And for my present purposes, it is Farrington's character which is particularly illuminated in this light, for the comparison enables us to see him from a perspective that grants us a greater receptivity to compassion for this fierce and ill-natured man with a wasted life. We become his as well as Bartleby's counterparts.

Ah, Farrington! Ah, humanity!

Works Cited

Beja, Morris. "Bartleby and Schizophrenia." *Massachusetts Review* 19 (Autumn 1978): 558–68.

Benstock, Bernard. *James Joyce*. New York: Ungar, 1985.

Joyce, James. "Counterparts." In *Dubliners*, 86–98, edited by Robert Scholes. New York: Viking Press, 1967.

———. *Letters of James Joyce*. Vol. I, ed. Stuart Gilbert. New York: Viking Press, 1957; reissued with corrections 1966. Vols. II and III, ed. Richard Ellmann. New York: Viking Press, 1966.

Joyce, Stanislaus. *The Complete Dublin Diary*, edited by George H. Healey. Ithaca: Cornell University Press, 1971.

Keppler, C.F. *The Literature of the Second Self*. Tucson: University of Arizona Press, 1972.

Marcus, Mordecai. "Melville's Bartleby as a Psychological Double." *College English* 23 (February 1962): 365–68.

Melville, Herman. "Bartleby the Scrivener: A Story of Wall Street." In *Selected Tales and Poems*, 92–131, edited by Richard Chase. New York: Holt, Rinehart & Winston, 1950.

Rogers, Robert. *A Psychoanalytic Study of the Double in Literature*. Detroit: Wayne State University Press, 1970.

Widmer, Kingsley. *The Ways of Nihilism: A Study of Herman Melville's Short Novels*. Los Angeles: California State Colleges, 1970.

ROBERTA JACKSON

The Open Closet in *Dubliners*:
James Duffy's Painful Case†

In *Epistemology of the Closet*, Eve Kosofsky Sedgwick appends a speculative footnote to "The Beast in the Closet," her reading of male homosexual panic in Henry James's "The Beast in the Jungle" and J. M. Barrie's *Tommy and Grizel*.[1] She notes that James's 1902 story makes "a strong implicit claim of 'universal applicability' through heterosexual symmetries, but that is most movingly subject to a change of gestalt and of visible saliencies as soon as an assumed heterosexual male norm is at all interrogated" (*Epistemology* 195). Sedgwick's analysis is grounded in what is known and not known in James's biography; however, the footnote argues that the panic

---

† From *James Joyce Journal* 37.1/2 (Fall 1999/Winter 2000): 83–97. Reprinted by permission of the publisher. Page and line references in brackets refer to this Norton Critical Edition.

1. Eve Kosofsky Sedgwick, *Epistemology of the Closet* (Berkeley: Univ. of California Press, 1990). Further references will be cited parenthetically in the text as *Epistemology*. See also Henry James, "The Beast in the Jungle," *Selected Tales of Henry James* (London: John Baker, 1947), and J. M. Barrie, *Tommy and Grizel* (London: Cassell, 1900).

emerging from "The Beast in the Jungle" and *Tommy and Grizel*
when the heterosexual norm is interrogated

> is proportioned not to the homosexual but to the nonhomo-
> sexual-identified elements of these men's characters. Thus, if
> Barrie and James are obvious authors with whom to begin an
> analysis of male homosexual panic, the analysis I am offering
> here must be inadequate to the degree that it does not eventu-
> ally work just as well—even better—for Joyce, Faulkner,
> Lawrence, Yeats, etc. (*Epistemology* 195n).

Sedgwick's definition of homosexual panic as "the most private, psy-
chologized form in which many twentieth-century Western men
experience their vulnerability to the social pressure of homophobic
blackmail" is consistent with contemporary medical definitions in
locating the condition within an overarching continuum of homosocial regulation (*Epistemology* 21). Sedgwick's explorations of panic
describe mechanisms of control that manipulate heterosexual men
into homophobic positions, but, as Eric Savoy has noted, in Sedgwick's analysis, "homosexual experience itself remains an unopened
site; . . . surely the gay man's panic over what *is* proscribed and the
heterosexual man's fear about what might *potentially* be miscon-
strued are fundamentally different kinds of anxiety."[2] The differences
between "A Painful Case" and "The Beast in the Jungle" emerge from
these two different kinds of anxieties. The stories are nearly contem-
poraneous, and although they share the same plot—a man's rejection
of a woman's love and his belated discovery of what he has lost—the
differences in their treatment of the "beast" are determined by their
individual relation to the overarching patriarchy and its attendant
homophobia.

Sedgwick's analysis of homosexual panic in "The Beast in the
Jungle" historicizes it, referring to late Victorian homosocial ten-
sions and recontextualizing it within James's own biography. She
argues that John Marcher's secret is really two secrets. The first is
his conviction that some special destiny awaits him—his "beast." He
tells this secret to May Bartram. The second secret is the nature of
his special destiny. Thus, Sedgwick believes, Marcher's "outer
secret, the secret of having a secret, functions, in Marcher's life,
precisely as *the closet*. It is not a closet in which there is a homosexual man, for Marcher is not a homosexual man. Instead, it is the
closet of, simply, the homosexual secret—the closet of imagining *a*
homosexual secret" (*Epistemology* 205). James's masking of the
nature of the "beast" results from the anxiety that Savoy notes in

---

2. Eric Savoy, "*Hypocrite Lecteur:* Walter Pater, Henry James and Homotextual Politics,"
   Dalhousie Review, 72 (Spring 1992), 15. Further references will be cited parenthetically
   in the text.

homosexual writers: "to survive within patriarchal culture, the marginalized writer attempts to purchase belletristic respectability by policing his text, removing traces . . . of homoerotic desire" (14). Joyce did not need to be so vigilant. His battles with publishers and printers over *Dubliners* testify to his willingness to offend hypocritical mores, yet as Joseph Valente observes, he was circumspect in his letters and essays on the subject of homosexual activity in English public schools.[3] Valente points out that Joyce's construction of homosexuality is consistent with what Jonathan Dollimore calls "the proximate" and this "proximate-ness of homo- and heterosexuality" leads to a very specific anxiety identified as "homosexual panic" by Sedgwick (48):[4]

> Being socially adjacent to the self, the proximate is that which can be most effectively dissociated from the self. Because it is right *here*, I can see or grasp it, and so it cannot be *right* here; the near-me can only be the not-me. . . . [H]omo- and heterosexual affect are at once constituted symbiotically and defined disjunctively, the perfect ideological condition for the concept of "proximate-ness" to emerge. (48).

In "A Painful Case," Joyce has chosen his brother Stanislaus as the person socially adjacent to him who could most easily be disowned.

Hélène Cixous and many others note that Joyce used Stanislaus as the model for Mr. Duffy.[5] Stannie is the source for Duffy's appearance, personality traits, and many of his habits, including his habit of keeping a diary. Joyce often read his brother's diary, mining it for descriptions, anecdotes, and ideas, appropriating whole sections that he found useful.[6] In his *Dublin Diary*, Stannie admits that his brother uses him "as a butcher uses his steel to sharpen his knife."[7] The image feminizes Stanislaus, but he seems not to have minded his role as his brother's whetstone. In an entry from January 1905, he tells of his regret at burning two years of entries. "Jim said he was very sorry I burnt it, as it would have been of great use to him in writing his novel, and if it would have been of use, I am sorry too" (148). The title of Duffy's diary, *Bile Beans*, is taken from Stannie's own diary, as is the

3. Joseph Valente, "Thrilled by His Touch: The Aestheticizing of Homosexual Panic in *A Portrait of the Artist as a Young Man*," *Quare Joyce*, ed. Valente (Ann Arbor: Univ. of Michigan Press, 1998), p. 47. Further references will be cited parenthetically in the text.
4. See Jonathan Dollimore, *Sexual Dissidence* (New York: Oxford Univ. Press, 1991), pp. 14–17.
5. See, for instance, Hélène Cixous, *The Exile of James Joyce*, trans. Sally A. J. Purcell (New York: David Lewis, 1972), p. 149. Further references will be cited parenthetically in the text.
6. See Robert Scholes and Richard M. Kain, eds., *The Workshop of Daedalus: James Joyce and the Raw Materials for "A Portrait of the Artist as a Young Man"* (Evanston: Northwestern Univ. Press, 1965), p. 75.
7. Stanislaus Joyce, *The Complete Dublin Diary of Stanislaus Joyce,* ed. George H. Healey (Ithaca: Cornell Univ. Press, 1962), p. 20. Further references will be cited parenthetically in the text.

incident in which he meets an older woman in a concert hall.[8] More telling is Joyce's verbatim appropriation from Stannie of Duffy's aphorism that expresses regret over the necessity to repress erotic desire between men.[9] "Love between man and man is impossible because there must not be sexual intercourse and friendship between man and woman is impossible because there must be sexual intercourse" (*D* 112) [94.170–73]. Stannie's and Duffy's explicit delineation of the constraints dictated by contemporary homophobic sexual repression indicates that the possibility of homoerotic sexuality must have occurred to them as a desirable possibility, while still allowing Joyce to keep it at arm's length from himself.

For Joyce, Stannie was also a "beast" of a species familiar to Marcher; in the *Dublin Diary*, Stannie notes his brother "has written an epiphany of a sluggish polar bear on me" (20):

> A white mist is falling in slow flakes. The path leads me down to an obscure pool. Something is moving in the pool; it is an arctic beast with a rough yellow coat. I thrust in my stick and as he rises out of the water I see that his back slopes towards the croup and that he is very sluggish. I am not afraid but, thrusting at him often with my stick drive him before me. He moves his paws heavily and mutters words of some language which I do not understand.[1]

The creature is male but feminized by Joyce's habit of referring to women as warm animals, as Stannie notes in his *Diary* (15). The bear's "arctic" sluggishness displaces the social climate of Edwardian repression to a literal climate. Joyce is not afraid of the creature; the stick that he thrusts at him marks him as emphatically male, but he does want to be free of him and so repulses him with his masculinity. Since Stannie has been identified as the beast and since he also served as the model for Duffy and is the source for his admission of homoerotic desire, Duffy also becomes a beast that Joyce must drive before him. Joyce must repel the beast. He must claim that the beast speaks a language he does not understand, because knowledge would implicate him in ways that his homophobia cannot permit. As Colleen Lamos observes, to "know about homosexuality is to be its accomplice."[2]

Joyce's writings about Oscar Wilde reveal his about-face on *The*

---

8. Stanislaus Joyce, *My Brother's Keeper: James Joyce's Early Years*, ed. Richard Ellmann (New York: Viking Press, 1958), p. 159.
9. See John Wyse Jackson and Bernard McGinley, eds., *James Joyce's "Dubliners": An Annotated Edition* (London: Sinclair-Stevenson, 1993), p. 99.
1. James Joyce, *Epiphanies*, intro. O. A. Silverman (Buffalo: Univ. of Buffalo, 1956), p. 7.
2. Colleen Lamos, "Signatures of the Invisible: Homosexual Secrecy and Knowledge in *Ulysses*," *JJQ*, 31 (Spring 1994), 338.

Picture of Dorian Gray.[3] Jean-Michel Rabaté points out that in 1906 Joyce was critical of Wilde for obscuring his subject matter:[4] "If [Wilde] had had the courage to develop the allusions in the book, it might have been better" (*LettersII* 105). Yet three years later, Joyce wrote about the necessity for distance from Wilde's work: "Everyone, he wrote, sees his own sin in Dorian Gray. . . . What Dorian Gray's sin was no one says and no one knows. Anyone who recognizes it has committed it" (*CW* 204). Joyce must assert his heterosexual identity through ignorance of its opposite.

Sedgwick's observations on the limitations and rigidities of Jamesian criticism also apply to nearly all the criticism of "A Painful Case." She begins her discussion of "The Beast in the Jungle" by noting that the

> easy assumption (by James, the society, and the critics) that sexuality and heterosexuality are always exactly translatable into one another is, obviously, homophobic. Importantly, too, it is deeply heterophobic: it denies the very possibility of *difference* in desires, in objects. One is no longer surprised, of course, at the repressive blankness most literacy criticism shows on these issues. . . . With strikingly few exceptions, however, the criticism has actively repelled any inquiry into the asymmetries of gendered desire. (*Epistemology* 196–97)

For Charles H. Peake, Duffy is simply an "unhuman egoist," a "voluntary celibate," an "upright and incorruptible man" who freely chooses the "cold, dark, silent world of his isolation."[5] Florence L. Walzl's account of Joyce's work is sometimes more explicit about complexities and ambiguities of desire.[6] For example, she comments on the presence of what were called "ould Mary Annes" in *Dubliners*: the pederast of "An Encounter" and the men in "After the Race" who dance with one another during a party to which no women have been invited (45). Joyce's depiction of this aspect of Irish society was echoed in the 1950s when Maura Laverty estimated that the male population of Ireland "consists of 10 per cent full-blooded warm-hearted men, 10 per cent libertines (most of them owing a duty to wife and children), 20 per cent soaks, and 60 per cent a mixed collection of what in various countries are known by various names. Here in Ire-

---

3. See Oscar Wilde, *"The Picture of Dorian Gray": Authoritative Texts, Backgrounds, Reviews and Reactions, Criticism,* ed. Donald L. Lawler (New York: W. W. Norton, 1988).
4. Jean-Michel Rabaté, "On Joycean and Wildean Sodomy," *JJQ*, 31 (Spring 1994), 162.
5. Charles H. Peake, *James Joyce: The Citizen and Artist* (London: Edward Arnold, 1977), pp. 34–35. Further references will be cited parenthetically in the text.
6. Florence L. Walzl, *"Dubliners:* Women in Irish Society," *Women in Joyce,* ed. Suzette Henke and Elaine Unkeless (Urbana: Univ. of Illinois Press, 1982). Further references will be cited parenthetically in the text.

land, we call them 'ould Mary Annes.' "[7] However, although Walzl concurs with this view of men in Irish society, her reading of Duffy fails to identify him as one of the "Mary Annes." She sees his rejection of romantic love with Emily Sinico as evidence of his adherence to conventional morality (50). For Cixous, Duffy is a man who "died long ago without noticing the fact. . . . Mr. Duffy only exists in the third person and the past tense" (152).

In spite of the proliferation of research and theory since the early 1980s on the history and politics of sex and gender, most recent critical studies of the story do not vary from these earlier ones. James Fairhall's 1993 study *James Joyce and the Question of History* sets out to investigate Joyce's handling of Irish history and to historicize him in turn-of-the-century Dublin.[8] Fairhall connects the stick-carrying Duffy to Eveline's father, an alcoholic bully whose walking stick becomes a symbol of sexual oppression. Instead of marking Duffy as one of those oppressed by the moral codes of the day, as I will argue he is, Fairhall ranks him with the many other heterosexual "self-important male characters who dominate or use women" (81). Suzette Henke's *James Joyce and the Politics of Desire* notes Duffy's narcissism, his "bachelor reserve," and his desire for a motherly muse rather than a lover.[9] However, as with earlier criticism, Henke's reading is marked by her assumption that sexuality always translates into heterosexuality; Duffy is once again a heterosexual man who represses the "amorous dimensions of [his] simmering liaison" with Mrs. Sinico (35). In Bernard Benstock's *Narrative Con/Texts in "Dubliners,"* Duffy is still the repressed ascetic who rejected Mrs. Sinico because his "middle-class propriety had insisted upon it," and in Susan Stanford Friedman's *Joyce: The Return of the Repressed,* Duffy's homosexual desire remains repressed.[1]

Just two articles note that Joyce's story is about homosexuality—a 1963 psychoanalytic study by Stephen Reid and David Norris's 1994 survey, "The 'unhappy mania' and Mr. Bloom's Cigar: Homosexuality in the Works of James Joyce."[2] Reid's analysis, " 'The Beast in the Jungle' and 'A Painful Case': Two Different Sufferings," sees the differences between Marcher's and Duffy's torments as arising

7. Maura Laverty, "Woman-Shy Irishmen," *The Vanishing Irish: The Enigma of the Modern World*, ed. John A. O'Brien (New York: McGraw-Hill, 1953), p. 55.
8. James Fairhall, *James Joyce and the Question of History* (Cambridge: Cambridge Univ. Press, 1993). Further references will be cited parenthetically in the text.
9. Suzette Henke, *James Joyce and the Politics of Desire* (New York: Routledge Publishers, 1990), p. 35. Further references will be cited parenthetically in the text.
1. Bernard Benstock, *Narrative Con/Texts in "Dubliners"* (London: Macmillan Publishers, 1994), p. 190, and Susan Stanford Friedman, *Joyce: The Return of the Repressed* (Ithaca: Cornell Univ. Press, 1993).
2. Stephen Reid, " 'The Beast in the Jungle' and 'A Painful Case': Two Different Sufferings," *American Imago*, 20 (1963), 221–39, and David Norris, "The 'unhappy mania' and Mr. Bloom's Cigar: Homosexuality in the Works of James Joyce," *JJQ*, 31 (Spring 1994), 357–73. Further references to both articles will be cited parenthetically in the text.

from dissimilar neurotic character structures: Marcher is phobic, and Duffy is compulsive. Reid argues that Duffy's homoerotic desire is derived from his neurotic symptoms and that the story shows "no overt homosexual concern apart from Duffy's single sentence in his notebook. . . . Duffy's homosexual impulses are at least as dangerous to him as his heterosexual tendencies" (231). Without the advantage of Sedgwick's theorizing and the gay historiography of Jeffrey Weeks and others,[3] Reid's analysis errs in its failure to consider the risk of exposure for Duffy. He seems unaware that should Duffy be exposed acting on his desire for men, he could receive two years hard labor as Wilde did. Reid's interpretation is a variant on the canonical reading: Duffy is still neurotic, and his attraction to Mrs. Sinico is still sexual.

Norris's brief discussion of the story acknowledges the homoerotic potential in the sentence from Duffy's notebook, but he argues that the "suggestion of homosexuality is introduced from outside the central events, this time to indicate the stifling impact of conventionally programmed restrictions on human sexuality" (364–65). Norris does not consider that Duffy may be recording the source of his own pain.

In spite of Reid's article, Duffy's expression of homoerotic desire has been virtually ignored by subsequent critics.[4] This critical consensus is unusual and striking; however, it is even more remarkable when we consider the Dublin that Joyce set out to document with these stories and the climate of sexual repression in Edwardian Britain in which he set out to do it. Joyce's intent is well known. In a letter to the publisher Grant Richards in May 1906, he said, "My intention was to write a chapter of the moral history of my country and I chose Dublin for the scene because that city seemed to me the centre of paralysis" (*LettersII* 134). Joyce associated paralysis with syphilis, also known as general paralysis of the insane. In his diary, Stannie notes that his brother "talks much of the syphilitic contagion in Europe, [and] is at present writing a series of studies in it in Dublin, tracing practically everything to it" (51). However, in spite of their recognition of the centrality of paralysis and its connection to Irish moral history noted by Joyce, until recently critics have consistently disregarded the homophobic climate that existed in late-

3. See, for instance, Jeffrey Weeks, *Coming Out: Homosexual Politics in Britain, from the Nineteenth Century to the Present* (London: Quartet Books, 1977); "Inverts, Perverts, and Mary-Annes: Male Prostitution and the Regulation of Homosexuality in England in the Nineteenth and Early Twentieth Centuries," *Hidden From History: Reclaiming the Gay and Lesbian Past*, ed. Martin Duberman, Martha Vicinus, and George Chauncey Jr. (New York: Meridien Publishers, 1990), pp. 195–211; and *Sex, Politics and Society: The Regulation of Sexuality Since 1800* (London: Longman Press, 1981). Further references to the first work will be cited parenthetically in the text as *Out* and to the last one as *Sex*.
4. But see Margot Norris's "Shocking the Reader in James Joyce's 'A Painful Case,' " where she examines the possibility that James Duffy is unable to love Mrs. Sinico because he is only attracted to men.

Victorian and Edwardian Britain following a number of sensational
and well-publicized homosexual scandals in the late nineteenth century, which resulted in the passage of the Labouchère Amendment
to the Criminal Law Amendment Act of 1885.[5]

The stories in *Dubliners* were virtually complete by 1905, within
ten years of Oscar Wilde's trials. Wilde's conviction for gross indecency marked "the more or less definitive loss of innocence on a
broad scale concerning the existence of homosexuals in Euro-
American culture."[6] The Wilde trials had been preceded by other
public scandals: one in 1870 involving suspected transvestite prostitutes in London, which Weeks writes about (*Sex* 101), and another
in 1884 implicating high officials in Dublin Castle in an openly
homosexual affair. Five years later, the London press reported the
involvement of aristocrats with post-office messenger boys in a
homosexual brothel; according to Weeks, Prince Albert Victor, son
of the Prince of Wales, was implicated (*Out* 19).

The scandals are one index of the climate of virulent repression
fostered by the Labouchère Amendment, under which Wilde was
convicted. This piece of legislation was so broad that it criminalized
very nearly all male homoerotic activity and speech, thereby sanc-
tioning homophobia as a legal measure of social control after 1885.
The Act encouraged the homosexual panic that Sedgwick notes in
the works of George Du Maurier, J. M. Barrie, and Henry James
(*Epistemology* 188); however, the repression codified by the Act and
enacted on the public stage by the scandals had the paradoxical
effect of making many homosexual men aware of their identity, perhaps for the first time. The scandals were a kind of wedge, driving
the cautious like Duffy further into the closet but emboldening the
more courageous and unconventional.

As well as ignoring the repressive homophobic sexual politics of
the day, the standard reading of Duffy as an egocentric, upright, and
moral man also ignores historically specific implications of the title.
The criminalization of male homosexual acts in private depended on
the new public "medical model" of homosexuality as a disease, which
provided a rationale for individualizing the crime, as Weeks notes
(*Sex* 104). Liberal sex researchers like Havelock Ellis adopted an
essentialist stance on sexual orientation as constituting identity,
thereby shifting the focus from the presumed act—sodomy—to the
person now constituted as "the homosexual."[7] Richard Dellamora

---

5. The Labouchère Amendment was used to convict Oscar Wilde and other men after it was
tacked onto the Criminal Law Amendment Act in 1885 and rushed into law. It provided
for a term of imprisonment not exceeding two years, with or without hard labor, for any
male guilty of an act of gross indecency with another male in public or in private. The law
extended an aura of criminality over British homosexual life until its repeal in 1967.
6. James Creech, *Closet Writing/Gay Reading: The Case of Melville's "Pierre"* (Chicago: Univ.
of Chicago Press, 1993), p. 64.
7. See, for instance, Havelock Ellis, *Man and Woman; A Study of Secondary and Tertiary*

points out that their naturalizing definitions brought homosexuals under medical control.[8]

"A Painful Case" is the title of the newspaper account of Mrs. Sinico's death, but, because it is also the title of the story, its reference also includes Duffy, whose rejection of her drives her to the death reported in the account. "A Painful Case" invokes the medicalization of male same-sex desire in the late nineteenth century, which saw a shift in public conceptions of male homosexuality from a notion of sin to one of sickness. In his petition to reduce his sentence, as reported by Weeks, Wilde claimed to have "been led astray by 'erotomania' and extravagant sexual appetite which indicated temporary mental collapse" (*Sex* 105). Duffy's explanation for his solitary ways is only slightly less explicit. In the midst of an intimate conversation with Emily Sinico shortly before he rejects her, Duffy confesses his "soul's *incurable* loneliness" to her, adding "[w]e cannot give ourselves . . . we are our own" (*D* 111, my emphasis) [93.145–46]. Duffy's loneliness is a disease that cannot be cured but that paradoxically both unites him with and separates him from others who are similarly afflicted. The explanation offered by the medical model contributed to the individualization of homosexuality—the concept of the homosexual as a person distinct from heterosexuals—and fostered a notion of sexuality as constituting identity, in Weeks's terms (*Sex* 105).

However, in spite of the popularity of the medical model, older notions of sin did not die out, Weeks observes, but became entangled with contemporary scientific theories (*Sex* 104). Joyce employs the discourses of both models to characterize Duffy: "He had neither companions nor friends, church nor creed. He lived his spiritual life without any communion with others, visiting his relatives at Christmas and escorting them to the cemetery when they died" (*D* 109) [91.58–61]. During the time of his emotional intimacy with Mrs. Sinico, she takes the place of a priest for this man who has rejected religion but not his belief in sin: "With almost maternal solicitude she urged him to let his nature open to the full; she became his confessor" (*D* 110) [92.112–13].

During his intimate conversations with Mrs. Sinico, Duffy comes to an awareness of his desire for men. Joyce appropriated one of Stannie's bile beans for Duffy's journal entry that expresses his pain at the prohibition against love between men, according to Jackson (99): "Love between man and man is impossible because there must not be sexual intercourse and friendship between man and woman

---

Sexual Characteristics (London: W. Scott, 1911); *Sexual Inversion in Men* (n.p., 1903); and *The Mechanism of Sexual Deviation* (n.p., 1919).
8. Richard Dellamora, *Masculine Desire: The Sexual Politics of Victorian Aestheticism* (Chapel Hill: Univ. of North Carolina Press, 1990), p. 195.

is impossible because there must be sexual intercourse" (D 112) [94.170–73]. Duffy's straightforward articulation of the double-bind created for gay men by the Labouchère Amendment indicates his awareness that his homoerotic desire separates him from other men who, Sedgwick argues, must be kept in a state of ignorance about the true nature of their own desires; they must never be certain they are not homosexual (Epistemology 185).

Duffy's isolation is more than a neurotic symptom in a man unable to give or receive love. Neurotic behavior arises from prior conflicts within an individual's psyche and is a maladaptive response to normal situations. Duffy is trapped. If he represses his desires, he becomes hopelessly isolated and neurotic, since he will not compromise his ideal of honesty and live with Mrs. Sinico openly, as if he were a heterosexual man. If he acts on his desire for men, then he risks the fate of Wilde and the others whose exploits had been so thoroughly reported in the popular press. Duffy's social isolation is not fundamentally due to his neuroticism (the standard critical reading), but rather his neuroticism arises from his necessary isolation and his need to distance himself from the homophobia of the patriarchy.

Sedgwick further argues that because "the paths of male entitlement, especially in the nineteenth century, required certain intense male bonds that were not readily distinguishable from the most reprobated bonds, an endemic and ineradicable state of what I am calling male homosexual panic became the normal condition of male heterosexual entitlement" (Epistemology 185). That is, legal persecution of given homosexual men, combined with the power of the patriarchy to enforce bonds between men as part of the normal functioning of society, prescribes the homosocial relations that Duffy so carefully avoids. I am following Sedgwick, who uses Heidi Hartmann's definition of "patriarchy itself as 'relations between men, which have a material base, and which, though hierarchical, establish or create interdependence and solidarity among men that enable them to dominate women'" (Epistemology 184).[9] Each of the ties with other men that Mr. Duffy so warily circumvents is a tie into the patriarchy: his fellow bank employees, who would be his equals; the "gilded youth" who are of the class of men who prey on women both sexually and financially (D 109) [91.53]; his family, who might wonder at his lack of interest in women; and representatives of religious life. Authority of all kinds earns his contempt. He has no wish to associate himself with the very institutions that foster and enforce

9. See Heidi Hartmann, "The Unhappy Marriage of Marxism and Feminism: Towards a More Progressive Union," Women and Revolution: A Discussion of the Unhappy Marriage of Marxism and Feminism, ed. Lydia Sargent (Boston: South End Press, 1981), p. 14.

both the homosocial cohesiveness between men and the homophobia supporting it.

Duffy remains in the closet, but the patterns of his behavior articulate his desire to resist the power of the patriarchy. Duffy's residence is located in Chapelizod, "as far as possible from the city of which he was a citizen" (D 107) [89.2]. Duffy's daily habits have the numbed, wary regularity of someone always under surveillance; every midday he dines alone in a pub on what must surely be one of the meanest meals in literature: "a bottle of lager beer and a small trayful of arrowroot biscuits" (D 108) [91.49–50]. Every evening, he eats alone in an "eatinghouse in George's Street where he felt himself safe from the society of Dublin's gilded youth" (D 109) [91.51–53], avoiding the areas of Dublin frequented by the likes of Corley and Lenehan in "Two Gallants." Duffy's isolation does not quite encompass his whole existence, however. For a time, he attends meetings of an Irish Socialist Party but ends this association because he rejects the workingmen's goals; they are too interested in wages for him and not interested enough in a revolution that might change society (D 111) [93.120–21].

Duffy's painful position as a closeted gay man might have aligned him with radicals like Ellis and Wilde, had he been willing or foolhardy enough to take the risks that Wilde did. During his last meeting with Mrs. Sinico, he tells her that no "social revolution . . . would be likely to strike Dublin for some centuries" (D 111) [93.124–25] and that "every bond . . . is a bond to sorrow" (D 112) [93.157–58]. There is no hope for the radical change he needs that would make other bonds possible. She encourages him to write out his thoughts. "For what? he asked her with careful scorn. To compete with phrasemongers, incapable of thinking consecutively for sixty seconds? To submit himself to the criticisms of an obtuse middle class which entrusted its morality to policemen and its fine arts to impresarios?" (D 111) [93.126–31]. His response echoes Wilde, making Duffy sound like a bitter Lord Henry Wotton; in the figure of Dorian Gray, Lord Henry is able to experience vicariously the life he has not the courage to live himself. Duffy has no such release. Perhaps recalling Wilde's difficulties with *The Picture of Dorian Gray,* Joyce deleted the final sentence from the paragraph that explicitly names Duffy's fear: "I, he said, will receive with disdain every *advance* on the part of this civilization which is unworthy of me, but which seeks to *entrap me.*"[1] The Labouchère Amendment was called the blackmailers' charter because it encouraged the unscrupulous to prey upon those whose sexuality made them vulnerable to its proscriptions.

1. Joyce, *"Dubliners": A Facsimile of Proofs for the 1910 Edition* (New York: Garland Publishers, 1910), p. 107, my emphases.

Since the rupturing of his bond with Mrs. Sinico marks the moment of his conscious awareness that love between men is impossible due to the proscription of homosexuality and that friendship between men and women is also impossible because of the prescription of heterosexuality, then Duffy must have hoped their friendship would lead to an alternative to this compulsory heterosexuality, hence his discussion of the social revolution with her. His hopes must have been for a society where desire between men and friendship between men and women could be realized. Their relationship ends when Duffy is convinced that she has misinterpreted him: "[O]ne night during which she had shown every sign of unusual excitement, Mrs Sinico caught up his hand passionately and pressed it to her cheek. Mr Duffy was very much surprised. Her interpretation of his words disillusioned him" (*D* 111) [93.147–51]. The unspoken and perhaps unspeakable content of Duffy's words to her may contain references to what Sedgwick has elsewhere called "occluded gay possibilities . . . (in the homophobic speech prohibition dating back to St. Paul) *non nominandum*, not to be named,"[2] " 'that sin which should be neither named or committed,' the 'detestable and abominable sin, amongst Christians not to be named' " (*Epistemology* 202). In her misreading of the nature of Duffy's interest in her, Mrs. Sinico stands in for the canonical critics who do not consider other possibilities for his behavior.

More generally, the repression of voice throughout this story is another indication of the presence of the closet. Like "The Beast in the Jungle," "A Painful Case" presents a "very particular, historicized thematics of absence, and specifically of the absence of speech" (*Epistemology* 201). Although, as Wayne Koestenbaum reminds us, poststructuralism has made us wary of the privileging of the oral over the written, the ideology of voice in this story (and in contemporary gay culture) as "original" and "identity-bestowing" carries "the values that come with uncloseting: self-knowledge, self-portrayal, presence."[3] The intimacy with Mrs. Sinico that will eventually embolden Duffy to articulate his own erotic desires to himself in his journal begins with their shared passion for vocal music and is nurtured with long, intimate conversations during which his full nature as an "exotic" can become known to him. The older religious discourse of sin and the newer medical discourse of disease intersect in Emily Sinico's darkened cottage where their meetings take place. In the discreet shadows of what will become "their ruined confessional,"

2. Sedgwick, "Tales of the Avunculate," *Tendencies* (Durham: Duke Univ. Press, 1993), p. 54. Further references will be cited parenthetically in the text as "Tales."
3. Wayne Koestenbaum, "The Queen's Throat: (Homo)sexuality and the Art of Singing," *inside/out: Lesbian Theories, Gay Theories*, ed. Diana Fuss (New York: Routledge Publishers, 1991), p. 205.

Duffy hears "the strange impersonal voice which he recognise[s] as his own, insisting on the soul's incurable loneliness" (*D* 111) [93.153–54; 143–45]. Duffy's voice and the presence it bestows lead him to a truth about the cause of his isolation. Joyce must have had voice in mind when he chose Emily Sinico's name: he appropriated it from his Triestine singing teacher, Guiseppe Sinico, an operatic composer and author of a vocal method (*LettersII* 91n).

Duffy's love of the music of Wolfgang Mozart and his association with Richard Wagner through his residence in Chapelizod (the Chapel of Isolde) connect him to German culture, as does his translation of Gerhard Hauptmann's *Michael Kramer*, his Nietszche, and his love of lager beer, which was considered a woman's drink in Britain. As Sedgwick observes,

> virtually all of the competing, conflicting figures for understanding same-sex desire—archaic ones and modern ones, medicalized and politicizing, those emphasizing pederastic relations, gender inversions, or "homo-" homosexuality—were coined and circulated in this period in the first place in German, and through German culture, medicine, and politics. ("Tales" 66)

Duffy's associations with Wagner's *Tristan and Isolde* mark him as the failed lover of a woman, but Wagner also, in Sedgwick's words, "crystallized a hyper-saturated solution of what were and were becoming homosexual signifiers" ("Tales" 66). Sedgwick cites an 1899 questionnaire by the gay sexologist Magnus Hirschfeld that was designed to reveal to those completing it whether or not they were "At All An Uranian" (that is, an invert). One question was "[a]re you particularly fond of Wagner?" ("Tales" 66).

A particular detail that seems out of character with Duffy's meticulous personality is the apple that the narrator comments "might have been left there and forgotten" inside his desk (*D* 108) [90.29–30]. The rotting apple alludes to an anecdote concerning Friedrich von Schiller, the German romantic dramatist. Johann Wolfgang von Goethe once visited Schiller in his study, and a foul smell nauseated him. He searched for the source and found it in a desk drawer filled with rotting apples. Frau Schiller explained that her husband could not write without the odor.[4] Duffy's characteristic restraint limits him to one apple, but the allusion to Goethe and Schiller is another veiled reference to emotional bonds between men. A famous statue in Weimar depicts Goethe and Schiller holding hands, celebrating their romantic friendship. A cartoon contemporary with Joyce's story commemorates the new consciousness of homosexuality and the new homophobia: Schiller asks Goethe to let go of his hand because

4. R. B. Kershner, "Mr. Duffy's Apple," *JJQ*, 29 (Winter 1992), 406.

he can see Magnus Hirschfeld coming.[5] Duffy's conversations with Mrs. Sinico integrate his emotional and intellectual life. Under her careful nurturing, his explorations of contemporary German culture enable awareness of his homoerotic desires to surface into consciousness.

Repression of voice and of Duffy's presence is also evident in the story's avoidance of direct speech. There are only two exceptions: the occasion of Duffy's meeting Mrs. Sinico at the concert and a short exchange between a juror and a witness recorded in the newspaper account of her death; the latter account is silent—Duffy does not hear it but reads it. Since Duffy habitually composes short autobiographical sentences "containing a subject in the third person and a predicate in the past tense" (D 108) [90.44–45], critics like Peake link the "inward-turned, self-regarding style" to Duffy's egocentricity (35). But once the heterosexual norm is questioned, this emerges as yet another manifestation of the requirements of the closet. Duffy must remain at some distance from his voice since he cannot risk the consequences of its full, uncloseted presence without being vulnerable to detection. His vigilance is as necessary for his voice as for his body, whose desires force him to police his existence: "He lived at a little distance from his body, regarding his own acts with doubtful sideglances" (D 108) [90.40–42]. "A Painful Case" is the last story of private life in *Dubliners* and is followed by "Ivy Day in the Committee Room," the first story of public life. Duffy is a man who has carefully avoided all the sins of the other Dubliners who precede him, according to Peake (36), yet he cannot avoid the closeting that his society requires of him. In keeping with the ideology of voice as presence, the first story of public life is told in direct speech, pointing to Duffy's exclusion from public life, such as it is in Joyce's Dublin, and to those who exclude him. Duffy inhabits what Valente has identified as an "open closet" (69). He constructs the open closet in contrast to D. A. Miller's well-known concept of the open secret.[6] Valente continues his discussion, saying that an open secret is something that is known but that we persist in guarding as if it were not known; in doing so, we do not simply hide a piece of information but hide the fact that we have hidden it, which paradoxically allows it to pass into public consciousness (68). Valente goes on to argue that, in *A Portrait of the Artist*, Joyce creates an open closet:

> Instead of a rhetorical form, the open secret, which establishes the subject's essential truths in the act of pretending to disguise them, Joyce fashions a rhetorical form, the open closet, which

5. Louis Crompton, *Byron and Greek Love: A Study of Homophobia in Nineteenth-Century England* (Berkeley: Univ. of California Press, 1985), p. 73.
6. See D. A. Miller, *The Novel and the Police* (Berkeley: Univ. of California Press, 1988), p. 207.

suspends or undermines such truths in the act of pretending to divulge them. . . . In the first case, the subject harbors a profound mystery to be exposed; in the second, the subject instances a radical uncertainty that remains flush with the text of its exposition—hidden, if you will, in plain sight. (69)

The figure of James Duffy hides Joyce's anxiety while exposing it and is undermined by Joyce with doubts and uncertainty. Duffy moves from an isolated loneliness to a conscious awareness of homoerotic desire under the influence of Mrs. Sinico's friendship. Her death precipitates a retreat from knowledge for Joyce and for Duffy: "Why had he withheld life from her? Why had he sentenced her to death?" (*D* 117) [98.321–22]. Joyce's only response is found in the image of the goods train Duffy sees, moving "like a worm with a fiery head winding through the darkness . . . reiterating the syllables of [Mrs. Sinico's] name" (*D* 117) [98.338–41]. This clichéd phallic image conflates her death with the diminishing possibility of love between men for Duffy, laying both at the feet of the patriarchy.

As Sedgwick predicted, her analysis works "even better" for Joyce than for James. Joyce's use of material drawn from his brother's diaries and his own dreams allows him to embody his own experience of homosexual panic and subject it to analysis. Joyce's homophobia constructs an open closet for Duffy, as Valente argues he did for Stephen Dedalus; he "orchestrates . . . a sexuality that defeats the categories of identity on which it continues to depend or, to turn things around, a sexuality that is framed by categories that cannot finally contain it" (69). Joyce may have veiled Duffy in uncertainty at the end, but the accumulated allusions leave no doubt as to Duffy's sexuality and to the destructiveness of a homophobia that reaches far beyond its intended target.

Abbreviations

CW   Joyce, James. *The Critical Writings of James Joyce*, ed. Ellsworth Mason and Richard Ellmann. New York: Viking Press, 1959.

D   Joyce, James. *Dubliners*, ed. Robert Scholes in consultation with Richard Ellmann. New York: Viking Press, 1967.

Letters Joyce, James. *Letters of James Joyce*. Vols. II and III, ed. Richard
II, III Ellmann. New York: Viking Press, 1966.

VINCENT J. CHENG

Empire and Patriarchy in "The Dead"†

Preface: Joyce, Politics, and the Canon

This chapter on "The Dead" attempts to reclaim the power of this justly celebrated text as engagedly political and ideological—from a canonization process that has, in large measure, managed to defang and neutralize that power within Joyce's texts by constructing "Joyce" as an apolitical, stylistic innovator. "The Dead" provides an especially suggestive case study of the clash between the Academy's institutional, canonizing practices / powers and an ideological reclamation of Joyce's works, for surely "The Dead" is a model text in the Modernist canon, a familiar favorite and staple of every collection of "great" modern short fiction, one of the most frequently taught works in introductory college literature classes, perhaps the only Joycean text widely familiar to a general reading audience.

I first tested an early version of this chapter as a paper at the 1991 Joyce Conference (June 11–16, 1991, in Vancouver, Canada). Admittedly the essay was a risky venture involving some real ideological dangers (on which I wished to elicit constructive discussion and advice). To my surprise, I learned from the controversial response to this paper more about the nature of the risks one takes in trying to repoliticize a highly canonical work: while the younger scholars and graduate students found my reading exciting and attractive, the quite vocal response from a few of the more established scholars was troubled. "Very interesting and imaginative, but I'm afraid you are doing serious violence to the story" was the vexed response of one very senior scholar, whose work I admire very much. What, I wondered, was this thing being referred to, "*the* story" that I was supposedly doing violence to? Does not "*the* story" really mean "the way *I* have always been taught to read it, the way I have invested years of my own effort in teaching it"? If so, no wonder the graduate students and younger faculty weren't troubled: they had no major investment yet in *one* particular and exclusive way of reading the story, the "Authorized Version" of "The Dead." This traditional reading of the story focuses on the Morkans' Christmas party as a display of seasonal warmth and goodwill, Irish hospitality, high spirits, and the Irish gift of gab (all qualities of the essentialized stage-Irishman;

---

† From *Joyce, Race, and Empire* (New York: Cambridge University Press, 1995), pp. 128–47. Reprinted with the permission of Cambridge University Press. Page and line references in brackets refer to this Norton Critical Edition.

the recent and popular John Huston movie followed suit). Gabriel
Conroy, the main character, is portrayed in this standard reading as
very sympathetic, as kind and sensitive—a bit of a wimp, perhaps, a
bit overly self-reflective and overly hung up on being "civilized" and
on the latest fashions from the Continent (such as goloshes), and so
on—but who nevertheless in the end arrives at a deeply moving and
universal, humanizing epiphany, a growth of personal self-awareness
by his highly-refined individual (and unified) subjectivity occasioned
by learning for the first time about an incident from his wife's past.
Such is the aesthetically pleasing curve of this reassuringly sanitized
and humanistic, canonized version of "The Dead." What I learned
from delivering this paper was that years of personal investment in
such readings can create within excellent and otherwise open-
minded Joyce scholars a monolithic reification of such a reading as
"*the* story," and a consequent resistance to radically different, especially overtly political, readings.

But Joyce was hardly an apolitical creature while he was living in
Italy and composing *Dubliners*. He wrote to his brother Stanislaus
in 1905 that "my political opinions . . . are those of a socialistic artist" (*Letters II*, 89); repeatedly he asked his brother to send him articles and editorials on the Irish/English situation, so as to keep up
with the politics at home. As early as 1903, Stannie had reported
that "[Jim] is interesting himself in politics—in which he says [he
has] original ideas . . . He calls himself a socialist but attaches himself to no school of socialism" (Manganiello, *Joyce's Politics*, 42). Nor
was Joyce's socialistic interest a purely nominal posturing: as Richard
Ellmann first noted (in 1977), "Joyce's political awareness was based
on considerable reading. His library in Trieste included especially
books by socialists and anarchists. He had, for example, the first 173
Fabian tracts bound in one volume. Among other writers who interested him were notably the two anarchists, Kropotkin and Bakunin,
and the social reformer, Proudhon" (Ellmann, *Consciousness*, 82).
In fact, among the numerous political texts in Joyce's personal library
in Trieste (see Ellmann, *Consciousness*, 97) were, notably, works by
Michael Bakunin (*God and the State*), Henri Bergson (*The Meaning
of the War*), John F. Boyle (*The Irish Rebellion of 1916*), the Irish
patriot/martyr Roger Casement (*Britisches gegen Deutsches Imperium*), Joseph Conrad (*The Secret Agent*), Fenian revolutionary
Michael Davitt (*The Fall of Feudalism in Ireland*), Paul Eltzbacher
(*Anarchism*), the first 173 Fabian Tracts, Maxim Gorky (several volumes, including *I fasti della rivoluzione russa*), Arthur Griffith (*The
Finance of the Home Rule Bill* and *The Home Rule Examined*), several books by Kropotkin, Mikhail Lermontov, Machiavelli, Marinetti,
John Stuart Mill, Nietzsche, Sydney Olivier (*White Capital and Col-*

oured Labour), Charles Stewart Parnell, P. J. Proudhon, Bertrand Russell (*Principles of Social Reconstruction*), George Bernard Shaw (including *Socialism and Superior Brains*), Irish revolutionary James Stephens, Benjamin Tucker, Sidney Webb (*Socialism and Individualism*), and H. G. Wells (including *A Modern Utopia*). Manganiello further documents that Joyce's knowledge of socialist and anarchist literature was extensive, and that he was influenced by, among others, Malatesta, Stirner, Bakunin, Kropotkin, Elisee Reclus, Spencer, Tucker, Proudhon, Tolstoy, and Conrad (*Joyce's Politics*, 72).

The Trieste Joyce lived in while writing *Dubliners* was a colonized city, a largely Italian population under Austro-Hungarian imperial rule. The two political situations confronting Joyce were strikingly analogous: both Trieste and Dublin were occupied cities, the Austrians having ruled Trieste for almost as long as the British had Dublin; both peoples claimed a language different from that forced on them by their conquerors; both were Catholic cities ruled by a foreign empire. In fact, Joyce wrote essays for Trieste's major newspaper (*Il Piccolo della sera*) arguing the similarity between Italian irredentism and the Irish independence movement.

While one could cite from a number of different critical and journalistic essays Joyce wrote while in Trieste, I will focus on a single one for illustration, on what, for my purposes, is perhaps the most interesting of Joyce's Triestine writings: his lecture on Ireland, delivered in Italian to an Italian audience in 1907 at the Università Popolare—particularly since it was written at the same time he was beginning to conceive "The Dead." The forty-six page manuscript of *"Irlanda, Isola dei Santi e dei Savi"*, translated into English under the title of "Ireland, Island of Saints and Sages" (*CW* 153–74), is a particularly interesting work to read in tandem with *Dubliners*, especially "The Dead," since it illuminates some of the issues and concerns which form the backdrop to the fictional story Joyce was in process of composing.

"Nations have their ego, just like individuals," Joyce begins—anticipating Freud's later argument (in *The Future of an Illusion* and *Civilization and its Discontents*) that civilizations and nations function (and can usefully be analyzed) like individual psychologies. It is also significant that Joyce begins by analogizing different forms of politics, here personal and international politics. He had already argued the analogy between Triestine and Dublin politics in *Il Piccolo della sera*, and was very much taken by the Italian socialist Guglielmo Ferrero, a Dreyfusard journalist for the newspaper who included Ireland in his discussion of European affairs. Ferrero's book *L'Europa giovane* (1897)—a title which echoed Mazzini's "Young Europe" movement intending "to link the various European nations together in a common crusade" (Manganiello, *Joyce's Politics*, 48)—was mentioned often by Joyce in his letters to Stannie.[1] Ferrero's view on the relationship between militarism and sexual politics—that is, that the male tradition of militarism and bellicose chauvinism results in sexual relationships being dominated by the brutality of the male rather than by the gentility and gallantry desired by the female—influenced Joyce's depiction of sexual relationships in *Dubliners*, especially (as has been well documented) in "Two Gallants" but also (as I will argue) in "The Dead." Significantly, both Joyce and Ferrero make direct analogies between sexual and international politics; between imperial politics, war, and sexual relationships.

In his lecture Joyce goes on to correlate different manifestations of international imperialism: "for so many centuries the Englishman has done in Ireland only what the Belgian is doing today in the Congo Free State," and what, he goes on to note prophetically, the Japanese "will do tomorrow in other lands" (*CW* 166). Most notably, Joyce's view of British rule in Ireland is uncompromisingly clear in this public address, hardly neutral, detached, or apolitical:

> [England] enkindled [Ireland's] factions and took over its treasury. By the introduction of a new system of agriculture, she reduced the power of the native leaders and gave great estates to her soldiers. She persecuted the Roman church when it was rebellious and stopped when it became an effective instrument of subjugation. Her principal preoccupation was to keep the country divided . . .
>
> She was as cruel as she was cunning. Her weapons were, and still are, the battering-ram, the club, and the rope; and if Parnell was a thorn in the English side, it was primarily because when he was a boy in Wicklow he heard stories of the English ferocity from his nurse . . .
>
> The English now disparage the Irish because they are Catholic, poor, and ignorant; however, it will not be so easy to justify such disparagement to some people. Ireland is poor because English laws ruined the country's industries, especially the wool industry, because the neglect of the English government in the years of the potato famine allowed the best of the population to die from hunger, and because under the present administration, while Ireland is losing its population and crimes are almost nonexistent, the judges receive the salary of a king, and governing officials and those in public service receive huge sums for doing little or nothing.
>
> (*CW* 166–67)

1. See also Robert Scholes's excellent essay on "Joyce and Modernist Ideology." Scholes argues the intriguing possibility (among other points) that both "scrupulous meanness" and the "conscience of my race" were terms Joyce picked up and translated from Ferrero's *L'Europa giovane*.

Joyce argues that, under such subjugation, a colonized people is faced with some inevitable choices, in words that bring to mind Frantz Fanon's arguments in *Wretched of the Earth:*

> When a victorious country tyrannizes over another, it cannot logically be considered wrong for that other to rebel. Men are made this way, and no one who is not deceived by self-interest or ingenuousness will believe, in this day and age, that a colonial country is motivated by purely Christian motives. These are forgotten when foreign shores are invaded, even if the missionary and the pocket Bible precede, by a few months, as a routine matter, the arrival of the soldiers and the uplifters . . .
>
> Nor is it any harder to understand why the Irish citizen is a reactionary and a Catholic, and why he mingles the names of Cromwell and Satan when he curses. For him, the great Protector of civil rights is a savage beast who came to Ireland to propagate his faith by fire and sword. He does not forget the sack of Drogheda and Waterford, nor the bands of men and women hunted down in the furthermost islands by the Puritan, who said that they would go "into the ocean or into hell," nor the false oath that the English swore on the broken stone of Limerick. How could he forget? Can the back of a slave forget the rod?
>
> (CW 163, 168)

While Joyce chafes against the racialized English stereotype of the Irish as "Catholic, poor, and ignorant" and as "the unbalanced, helpless idiots about whom we read in the lead articles of the *Standard* and the *Morning Post*" (CW 171), he is aware that neither is there any pure racial/ethnic Irish essence (or past) to posit as an alternative (whether real or nostalgic) to British influence—for a country with a longstanding history of invasions, subjugations and colonizations is irremediably now a *bricolage* of ethnically mixed diversities and shared cultures, exhibiting the multicultural characteristics of Mary Pratt's "contact zone" (33) or of Gloria Anzaldúa's "Borderlands":

> Our [Irish] civilization is a vast fabric, in which the most diverse elements are mingled, in which nordic aggressiveness and Roman law, the new bourgeois conventions and the remnant of a Syriac religion [i.e., Christianity] are reconciled. In such a fabric, it is useless to look for a thread that may have remained pure and virgin without having undergone the influence of a neighbouring thread. What race, or what language (if we except the few whom a playful will seems to have preserved in ice, like the people of Iceland) can boast of being pure today? And no race has less right to utter such a boast than the race now living in Ireland.
>
> (CW 165–66)

Joyce, however, does not entirely despair of the possibility of a non-nostalgic Irish revival ("that the Irish dream of a revival is not entirely an illusion"), engaging in a vision of a successful overthrow of imperial power and achievement of self-sufficient nationhood:

> It would be interesting . . . to see what might be the effects on our civilization of a revival of this race. The economic effects of the appearance of a rival island near England, a bilingual, republican, self-centered, and enterprising island with its own commercial fleet, and its own consuls in every port of the world. And the moral effects of the appearance in old Europe of the Irish artist and thinker . . .

As Joyce points out: "If the Irishmen at home have not been able to do what their brothers have done in America, it does not mean that they never will" (CW 163).

These were Joyce's thoughts on Ireland and England around the time he began to write "The Dead."

Manganiello reminds us that "The first work Joyce ever wrote was political. This was the poem . . . 'Et Tu, Healy,' which was composed at the age of nine shortly after Parnell's death" (Joyce's Politics, 3), lamenting Charles Stewart Parnell's betrayal by one of his own lieutenants, Timothy Healy. But one might well even refer to Joyce as a political writer if one takes on the meaning of the word "political," as I have been doing above, in the broader sense: "the whole of human relations in their real, social structure, in their power of making the world" as Roland Barthes defines the word (Ellmann, Consciousness, 73); or, in Robert Dahl's standard definition, "any pattern of human relationships that involves, to a significant extent, power, rule, or authority" (Modern, 6; Manganiello, Joyce's Politics, 8). Joyce himself, as we have already seen, exhibits a tendency to correlate and analogize similar forms of particular "politics" and the exercises of power.[2]

"The Dead" is, in this broader sense, profoundly political. For, as we shall see, it is a text that tries to analogize a number of forms of political and power relationships, suggesting and exploring their intersectionalities: imperial, racial, cultural, familial, and sexual pol-

2. In August 1904 Joyce wrote to Nora the memorable lines: "My mind rejects the whole present social order and Christianity—home, the recognised virtues, classes of life, and religious doctrines . . . When I looked on [my mother's] face as she lay in the coffin—a face grey and wasted with cancer—I understood that I was looking at the face of a victim and I cursed the system which had made her a victim . . . I cannot enter the social order except as a vagabond" (Letters II, 48). As early as 1904, Joyce recognized all the marginalized (including himself) as confederated members of victimization by a social system that encompassed colonial politics, sexual politics, familial politics, class politics, and religious hierarchies. As he wrote further to Nora, "It seemed to me that I was fighting a battle with every religious and social force in Ireland" (see Manganiello, Joyce's Politics, 218).

itics. How is one to analogize or theorize similarities and differences of particular minority discourses, of particular marginalized voices? This is a question and a project that Joyce's texts take on, from the early *Dubliners* stories (as we have seen) to the later *Ulysses* and *Finnegans Wake* (with their much more complex and highly textured versions of sameness-within-difference). "The Dead"'s attempt to analogize different forms of oppression and of responses to such oppressions plays out (in a fictional field of play) some of the problems facing any study of "minority discourses": what issues do different minority discourses have in common, and how do they impinge on, intersect with, reinforce, or even cause, each other? How can we depict and theorize a potentially enabling harmony (or collectivity) of culturally-specific differences and experiences without obliterating, occluding, or homogenizing the specificity and particularity of individual difference and experience (in what Deane calls "the harmony of indifference" [*Heroic*, 16])? How can such an insistence on pluralistic difference, local specificity, and heterology be observed without resulting in fragmentation, quiescence, and loss of collective agency—thus ultimately reaffirming the hegemony of the dominant discourse? In these respects, this story can, at one level, be usefully examined in terms of Abdul R. Jan-Mohamed and David Lloyd's vision of "the task of minority discourse, in the singular: to describe and define the common denominators that link various minority cultures," for these cultures "have certain shared experiences by virtue of their similar antagonistic relationship to the dominant culture, which seeks to marginalize them all" ("Minority Discourse," 1)—in an exploration of what might constitute "minority discourse."

Empire and Patriarchy in "The Dead"

James Joyce's "The Dead" has elicited a great deal of fine criticism which illuminates our understandings of that story. This chapter does not aim at a comprehensive and coherently balanced interpretation of the story, but at a specialized reading from a particular angle of analysis, as a study of the conjoined dynamics of empire and sexual colonization, what Gayatri Spivak has referred to as "the masculist-imperialist ideological formation" ("Subaltern," 296).[3] This is a reading of Gabriel Conroy as a well-meaning patriarch who is *almost* a

---

3. I share with critics like Spivak and Homi Bhabha the assumption that "imperialism was not only a territorial and economic but inevitably also a subject-constituting project" (Young, *White Mythologies,* 159). Spivak has argued that Europe has been constituted and consolidated as "sovereign subject, indeed sovereign and subject," while constructing the colonized in its own self-image, "consolidated itself as sovereign subject by defining its colonies as 'Others,' even as it constituted them, for purposes of administration and the expansion of markets, into programmed near-images of that very sovereign self" ("Rani," 128).

domestic tyrant (the "almost" here is an important qualification), a qualified representation by Joyce of a potentially oppressive patriarch in symbolic collaboration with the ruling masters of the English colonial empire—what Stephen Dedalus calls the "brutish empire" (U 15.4569–70). My intention is to draw parallel lines of mastery and colonization, of authority and marginalization, in terms of various and related forms of politics: imperial, racial, cultural, familial, and sexual.[4]

I would not wish to dispute that Gabriel Conroy is a quite sympathetic character, especially in contrast to all the other male rogues, drunkards, and failures who populate Joyce's gallery of Dubliners.[5] But he is no less sympathetic in spite of, or (as I would argue) because of, Joyce's scrupulously searing and unflattering portrayal of him. The very first direct impression we get of Gabriel is his voice, as he and Gretta arrive at the Morkans' annual dance, responding to Lily's relief at their arrival ("Miss Kate and Miss Julia thought you were never coming") by putting down his wife: "—I'll engage they did, said Gabriel, but they forget that my wife here takes three mortal hours to dress herself" (D 177) [153.53–54, 55–56].[6] This seemingly good-humored comment suggests, however, an essentializing of the female in a form of infantilization, similar to the affectionate attitude of the British Empire towards its colonies as incorrigible children (always unruly, always late) who can thus only be properly ruled by the parent empire. As Edward Said has thoroughly documented, English imperialist policies regarded their subjects (often their "little brown children") as "what is already evident: that they are a subject race, dominated by a race that knows them and what is good for them better than they could possibly know themselves" (Orientalism, 35).[7] The connection between imperial and sexual domination is per-

4. Such correspondences by Joyce thus anticipate not only a broader sense of the word "politics" (as I am using it), but also our correspondingly broader sense of the terms "imperialism" and "empire"—in the sense, as Fredric Jameson puts it, "which is now very precisely what the word 'imperialism' means for us— . . . one of necessary subordination or dependency . . . it now designates the relationship between a generalized imperial subject . . . and its various others or objects" ("Modernism," 48). Imperialism, in other words, is tied into—as are all these forms of "politics"—subject-object dynamics.

5. Nor do I intend to undermine the validity of the persuasive characterizations of Gabriel which previous critics have presented us—but rather to explore some of the further subtleties and dynamics of such characterizations as Joyce has encoded them.

6. Gabriel tries to speak in what Kimberle Crenshaw calls "the authoritative universal voice": "The authoritative universal voice—usually white male subjectivity masquerading as nonracial, nongendered objectivity—is merely transferred to those who, but for gender, share many of the same cultural, economic, and social characteristics" ("Black," 204). I am suggesting that this story cumulatively evinces an encoded transferral of that authoritative voice from the British imperium to the Irish male, who in turn imposes it on the Irish female—in an act (on Gabriel's part) of consensual (if unconscious) servitude and submission to an imposed hegemonic system.

7. As Frantz Fanon puts it, the imperial power is "a mother who unceasingly restrains her fundamentally perverse offspring from managing to commit suicide and from giving free

haps unintentionally but appropriately (however speculatively on my part) suggested by Gabriel's very next words, "—Here I am as right as the mail, Aunt Kate!" [153.63]—for the Royal Mail ("His Majesty's vermillion mailcars" [*U* 7.16]) was a notoriously imperial institution (often vandalized by colonial insurrectionists);[8] both the empire and the male ego are employed in the activity ("the masculist-imperialist ideological formation") of making judgments and hierarchical distinctions between what is central ("as *right* as the mail/male") and what is marginal, for domination involves the imposition of dominant order, structure, and distinctions—of gender, race, class, hierarchy, margins, and so on.[9] What Gabriel will learn tonight is how spurious and unstable those distinctions and marginalizations, the activities of the authorized Ego, are.

Gretta's own natural instinct and spirits are limited and controlled by the disapproving authority of a paterfamilias who infantilizes those instincts: "—But as for Gretta there, said Gabriel, she'd walk home in the snow if she were let" (*D* 180) [156.162–63]. Gabriel's rule and mastery extends also to the children, as Gretta reports to Aunt Kate: "He's really an awful bother, what with green shades for Tom's eyes at night and making him do the dumbbells, and forcing Lottie to eat the stirabout. The poor child! And she simply hates the sight of it!" (*D* 180) [156.165–69]. While the two aunts may laugh ("for Gabriel's solicitude was a standing joke with them") [156.173–74], the image drawn of Gabriel here is of a well-meaning domestic tyrant imposing the Law of the Father. Gretta's own resentment is only partially disguised (unlike Eva's) by her humorous banter: "O, but you'll never guess what he makes me wear now! . . . Goloshes! . . . Whenever it's wet underfoot I must put on my goloshes. To-night even he wanted me to put them on, but I wouldn't. The next thing he'll buy me will be a diving suit" (*D* 180) [156.169; 175–78].

To an uncomprehending Aunt Julia who has never heard of goloshes, Gretta explains that they are "Guttapercha things . . . Gabriel says everyone wears them on the continent" (*D* 181) [157.188–89]. Julia's response ("—O, on the continent, murmured aunt Julia, nodding her head slowly") [157.190–91] suggests her

---

rein to its evil instincts. The colonial mother protects her child from itself" (*Wretched*, 211).

8. In the "Aeolus" section of *Ulysses,* Joyce describes mailcars under the appropriately royal headline (and metonymy) "THE WEARER OF THE CROWN": "Under the porch of the general post office shoeblacks called and polished. Parked in North Prince's street His Majesty's vermilion mailcars, bearing on their sides the royal initials, E. R. [Edward Rex] . . ." (*U* 7.14–18).

9. Said notes: "it is the first principle of imperialism that there is a clearcut and absolute hierarchical distinction between ruler and ruled" ("Yeats and Decolonization," 82).

As Robert Young writes: "The creation of man as centre was effected by defining him against other, now marginalized groups, such as women, the mad, or, we would add, the allegedly sub-human 'native' " (*White Mythologies,* 74).

sotto voce resentment of Gabriel's presumably continual attempts to impose a more "civilized," continental culture on their own (by implication) wild and backward colonial Irish mentalities. "Guttapercha," a rubbery material from Malaya, and "goloshes" ("Made of India rubber or the less elastic gutta-percha" [Gifford, *Joyce Annotated*, 114]) together suggest the role (in a product economy) which India, Malaya (like India, an English colony), and other imperial colonies played in the service and material comfort of the European masters: their highly refined and "civilized" European culture of goloshes and pianos (as highly "finished" end-products) depends on the gutta-percha and the ivory ripped out of colonial nations by the labor and sweat of the colonized natives.[1] No wonder, then, that the word goloshes "reminds [Gretta] of christy minstrels" (*D* 181) [157.195], of blackface "Negro" minstrels out to entertain white audiences. Thus the wearing of goloshes becomes a correlative for a more "civilized" dominant European culture, whose very cultural superiority and refinement depended on the exploitation of its colonies—in contrast to the more primitive, unrestrained, and still uncolonized Irish free spirit allied symbolically to the West of Ireland and Gretta's roots in Galway.[2]

Similar dynamics seem to me at work in Gabriel's exchange, as he is removing his goloshes, with Lily the caretaker's daughter. Margot Norris suggests that Lily's retort—"The men that is now is only all palaver and what they can get out of you" [154.93–94]—may be a response to a Gabriel who is flirting with her ("Stifled," 495). I would suggest, rather, that the sexual dynamics here are again a case of sexual infantilization, of Gabriel's insensitivity to the fact that Lily is no longer a child, but a woman with her own voice:

—Tell me, Lily, he said in a friendly tone, do you still go to school?

1. Writes Fanon: "This European opulence is literally scandalous, for it has been founded on slavery"; "For in a very concrete way Europe has stuffed herself inordinately with the gold and raw materials of the colonial countries . . . Europe is literally the creation of the Third World" (*Wretched*, 96, 102).

   In *Ulysses* the Dubliners would likewise discuss the recent international uproar about "those Belgians in the Congo Free State . . . raping the women and girls and flogging the natives on the belly to squeeze all the red rubber they can out of them" [*U* 12. 1542–47].) The report was filed by Roger Casement. As Gifford (366) notes: "In February 1904, while serving as a consul in the Congo, Casement filed a report on the forced labor in rubber plantations and other cruelties to natives under the Belgian administration there. The report was published, and the public reaction led in January to a reconvening of the Conference of Powers that had originally established Belgian control of the Congo; the conference resulted in a measure of reform." Casement, of course, was hanged in 1916 for treason as a Sinn Feiner. Joyce owned a book of his in his Trieste library.

   In *A Portrait* Stephen Dedalus thinks of India and ivory: "ivory sawn from the mottled tusks of elephants. *Ivory, ivoire, avorio, ebur . . . India mittit ebur*" (India sends ivory; *P* 179).

2. Robert Spoo has also suggested that the word "goloshes" may remind Gretta of black or blackface figures through the missing verbal link of "golliwog," "the popular term for a grotesque black doll inspired by a series of children's books" ("Uncanny," 107); in *Ulysses*, Cissy Caffrey has "golliwog curls" (*U* 13.270).

   —O no, sir, she answered. I'm done schooling this year and
more.
   —O, then, said Gabriel gaily, I suppose we'll be going to your
wedding one of these fine days with your young man—eh?
                                          (D 178) [154.85–90]

Such patronization and infantilization elicit from Lily an assertion
("with great bitterness") [154.91–92] of her own, adult female voice:
"The men that is now is only all palaver and what they can get out
of you" [154.93–94].
   Her retort touches on one of the story's central concerns, the question of what is the proper male (or as Shaun asks about Shem in
Finnegans Wake, "when is a man not a man?" [*FW* 170.05]). Gabriel
is himself (as per Lily's accusation) a man of "all palaver," for he is,
as a writer of book reviews and after-dinner speeches, a man of
"words"—perhaps in contrast to his as-yet undiscovered counterpart,
Michael Furey, the man of romantic "fury" from whom Gabriel will
feel a challenge to his maleness.[3] Which of the two is "right as the
male"? Man of action, man of words: this is a masculine dualism/
distinction that would continue to engage Joyce, for the Royal Mail
as a phallogocentric imperial institution is behind the creation of
Shaun the Post as the macho and patriarchal twin ("right as the
mail"), himself an active carrier of words ("letters"), in constant
opposition and rivalry to his wordsmith brother Shem the Pen, like
Gabriel a shaper of words ("*write* as the male").
   Lily has rendered this moment awkward by challenging Gabriel's
masculinity and his mastery, refusing to act as the child he expects
of her.[4] Gabriel's flustered response is to thrust a coin into her hands,
in spite of her protest that "I wouldn't take it" [155.112–13] (he
allows her no choice and walks off); in other words, he buys her off
by imposing his dominance in a different field of mastery in which
he can still hold sovereignty, that of relative wealth and power.[5] In
the attempts by Gabriel's ego to gain a sense of control and mastery
during the evening, we increasingly are provided with the dynamics
of the imposition of *mastery*: of the mail/male, of wealth, power,
class, empire, and continent—over the colonized but still unruly
Irish spirit, identity, femininity, and homerule/autonomy.

3. I am invoking here a Joycean critical history that has frequently contrasted Gabriel and
   Michael Furey along the qualities suggested by the gentility of the archangel Gabriel in
   contrast to the fiery power and "fury" of the archangel Michael.
4. Jameson notes: "When the other speaks, he or she becomes another subject, which must
   be consciously registered as a problem by the imperial or metropolitan subject" ("Modernism," 49).
5. One recalls the symbolic significances of the gold sovereign in "Two Gallants," another
   story in which brutal sexual conquest is presented by Joyce as analogous to England's
   equally brutal conquest of Ireland. As Manganiello notes, commenting on the influence
   of Guglielmo Ferrero on "Two Gallants": "For Joyce [as for Ferrero] . . . the brutalism of
   love and politics were interconnected" (52).

Later in the party Gabriel has another unpleasant run-in with yet another Irish woman, his colleagues Miss Ivors, the outspoken Irish Nationalist. By this point it may seem to us apt that Miss Ivors especially should so discomfit Gabriel, since she openly stands for something he fears and has repressed, denied, or sold out: his "Irishness", that unruly, romantic, wilder, less cultured, less civilized, and uncolonizable self which the authorized Ego wishes to deny and which seems to be represented here by Gretta and Michael Furey and the West of Ireland (and Joyce's own Galway-born wife Nora). This seems a fear and repression instilled in Gabriel in part by the class snobbery of his mother, who we learn had disapproved of Gretta's "country cute"-ness (D 187) [162.388]. Appropriately, "Gabriel himself had taken his degree in the royal university" (D 187) [162.384]. This latter was a "degree-granting institution" which (according to Gifford, *Joyce Annotated*, 116) "reflected English (Protestant) academic standards and effectively determined the curricula of its member institutions (including Catholic University College, Dublin)"— in other words, a "shoneen" institution imposing the cultural values of the English masters (culture and education *à la* Matthew Arnold, whose *Culture and Anarchy* was in Joyce's personal library in Trieste).[6] And now we learn that Gabriel writes for *The Daily Express*, a conservative paper with royalist leanings, suggesting his own unconscious collusion with the Empire ("He wanted to say that literature was above politics" [D 188] [163.433–34]), a discovery by Miss Ivors that leads to her teasing charge that he should be "ashamed of [him]self" for being a "West Briton" (D 187–88) [163.417, 421; 165.495]—that is, a sellout and collaborator with the imperial masters.[7]

But Miss Ivors good-naturedly admits that she liked his review of Browning's poems in *The Daily Express,* and now invites him and Gretta to a group vacation in the West. Once again, Gabriel's snobbery is barely disguised, as he admits that his preference is to vacation "to France or Belgium or perhaps Germany" (D 189) [164.463]; all three were, we might note, powerful countries with imperial holdings and aspirations; like England, France and Belgium had extensive empires around the globe. Miss Ivors's unrelenting probing ("And why do you go to France and Belgium . . . instead of visiting your own land? . . . And haven't you got your own language to keep in touch with, Irish?" [164.465–70]) finally draws from Gabriel an exasperated response that "—O, to tell you the truth, . . . I'm sick of my own country, sick of it!" (D 189) [165.480–81].[8]

6. As we are told in the narrative of *Stephen Hero* (181), "About this time there was some agitation in the political world concerning the working of the Royal University."
7. See Manganiello, 24, on the derogatory designations of "shoneen" and "West Briton."
8. Certainly such a view would ally Gabriel closely with Joyce himself, who it is supposed similarly wanted nothing to do with Irish Nationalism, who had moved abroad into exile

When a few moments later Gretta learns about the proposal for a vacation in the West and pleads with him, "—O, do go, Gabriel, she cried. I'd love to see Galway again", Gabriel's response once again is to assert his patriarchal mastery by closing off further discussion: "—You can go if you like, said Gabriel coldly" (Gretta can only complain in frustration to Mrs. Malins, "—There's a nice husband for you, Mrs Malins" [D 191] [166.532, 533, 536]).

Stung by Miss Ivors's accusation that he is a West Briton, Gabriel twice fantasizes escaping to the snow outside (D 192 and D 202) [166.554, 555; 176.890]: in both cases, his mental picture of escape appropriately revolves around the Wellington Monument dominating the snow in Phoenix Park, that phallic obelisk symbolizing British imperial and patriarchal rule. He now decides to get back at Miss Ivors by inserting into his speech an intentional jab at her:

> Ladies and gentlemen, the generation which is now on the wane among us may have had its faults but for my part I think it had certain qualities of hospitality, of humour, of humanity, which the new and very serious and hypereducated generation that is growing up around us seems to me to lack. Very good: that was one for Miss Ivors. What did he care that his aunts were only two ignorant old women?
>
> (D 191) [167.570–77]

Only two ignorant old women?! The hypocrisy of Gabriel's speech and value judgments becomes apparent in his more pressing desire to attack Miss Ivors. This hypocrisy reveals a level of cultural snobbery already hinted at in his preference for things continental, such

---

on the continent, and who also wrote paid reviews for The Daily Express. On the other hand, Joyce knew quite well that literature was certainly not above politics, and his exploration of Gabriel here strikes me as, in part, a very complex exorcism of some of his own guilt and feelings of anti-Irish complicity. After all, Joyce was writing this story in exile but at a time when he felt that his judgments of Ireland had been too harsh and was thus having second thoughts about his homeland; "The Dead" was itself expressly conceived with the intent to recuperate some of the attractions of Ireland in the wake of the other Dubliners stories—thus he was trying not to forget his distinctly Irish heritage. As Joyce wrote to Stanislaus: "it seems to me that I have been unnecessarily harsh. I have reproduced (in Dubliners at least) none of the attraction of the city . . . I have not reproduced its ingenuous insularity and its hospitality. The latter 'virtue' so far as I can see does not exist elsewhere in Europe. I have not been just to its beauty: for it is more beautiful naturally in my opinion than what I have seen of England, Switzerland, France, Austria or Italy." Letter to Stanislaus Joyce, September 25, 1906, Letters II, 164.

Furthermore, it is interesting to note that in 1902 Joyce had reviewed for The Daily Express William Rooney's patriotic poems, published by Arthur Griffith, founder of Sinn Fein. In The Consciousness of Joyce, Richard Ellmann argues convincingly that by 1906 (at the time when Joyce was conceiving "The Dead") Joyce had been won over by Griffith's non-extremist brand of nationalism and "approved Griffith's moderate programme" (86–88). Stanislaus claimed that Joyce read Griffith's newspaper United Irishman every week and Joyce himself wrote that it was the only policy of any benefit to Ireland (Letters II, 158; Manganiello, 118). Both Ellmann and Manganiello further document not only Joyce's own Irish Nationalist leanings at this time, but his intense interest and readings in socialism and his identification of himself as a "socialist."

as goloshes and cycling in France or Belgium. Earlier he had wondered whether in his speech he should quote some lines from Browning: "for he feared they would be above the heads of his hearers. Some quotation that they could recognise from Shakespeare or from the melodies would be better. The indelicate clacking of the men's heels and the shuffling of their soles reminded him that their grade of culture differed from his" (*D* 179) [155.126–31]. Cultural snobbery is an authoritarian tendency to marginalize others by making value-charged distinctions about difference.[9] Old ladies are worthless and not to be listened to (or old maids, as with Maria in "Clay" [Norris, "Narration"]). So also drunks, like Freddy Malins, who are to be cared after like infants but not to be taken seriously.

Interestingly, however, it is perhaps Freddy who seems to have some real aesthetic culture and appreciation.[1] While Gabriel, despite his intellectual pretensions, cannot appreciate Mary Jane's piano performance of academic pieces because they lacked melody (*D* 186) [161.354], it is Freddy who is able—perhaps with the clarity of vision shared by the dispossessed and marginalized—to see through (or ignore) Aunt Julia's old-maid exterior and to realize how wonderful her singing is tonight, for, as the narrator admits, "To follow the voice, [Julia's] *without looking at the singer's face,* was to feel and share the excitement of swift and secure flight" (*D* 193, my emphasis) [168.589–91]. And so Freddy congratulates her effusively if a little drunkenly. Similarly, he is able and willing to admit that one of the finest tenor voices he has ever heard was that of a black man, "a negro chieftain singing in the second part of the Gaiety pantomime who had one of the finest tenor voices he had ever heard" (*D* 198) [172.771–73], a comment everyone else chooses to ignore (after all, he is only a drunk): "—And why couldn't he have a voice too? asked Freddy Malins sharply. Is it because he's only a black?" (*D* 198; one recalls "without looking at the singer's face") [173.781–82; 168.589].

"And why couldn't he/she have a voice too?" is a Joycean question which, as we have seen, could be asked here about Gretta, Lily, Freddy, and Ireland herself, among others. And of course about Aunt

9. A comment by Terry Eagleton applies incisively in this context: "This bankrupt Irish Arnoldianism is particularly ironic when one considers that the title of Arnold's own major work, *Culture and Anarchy*, might well have been rewritten as *Britain and Ireland*. The liberal humanist notion of Culture was constituted, among other things, to marginalize such peoples as the Irish, so that it is particularly intriguing to find this sectarian gesture being rehearsed by a few of the Irish themselves" ("Nationalism," 33).

This sectarian gesture reflects Frantz Fanon's elaboration of the complicity in values between the colonialist intelligentsia and the colonizer: "The colonialist bourgeoisie, in its narcissistic dialogue, expounded by the members of its universities, had in fact deeply implanted in the minds of the colonized intellectual that the essential qualities remain eternal in spite of all the blunders men may make: the essential qualities of the [colonizing] West, of course" (*Wretched*, 36).

1. See also Norris ("Stifled" 500–1) on Freddy Malins.

Julia, who does have a real "voice," which she has exercised in a poignant performance of "Arrayed for the Bridal"—a very difficult soprano aria adapted from Bellini's *I Puritani*. Here I would refer you to Norris's compelling argument ("Stifled," 496–502) that Julia Morkan is repeatedly belittled, infantilized, and ignored in the story in spite of a brilliant performance that is likely the swan song to a frustrated career in subservience to a religious patriarchy which has, as Aunt Kate put it, "turn[ed] out the women out of the choirs that have slaved there all their lives and put little whippersnappers of boys over their heads" (*D* 194) [169.637–39]—for a papal edict in 1903 (*In Motu Proprio*, just months before the Morkans' Christmas party) had decreed that henceforward women were to be banished from church choirs. Julia's story is a painful and poignant one indeed; she is one of many voices, from the polylogic multivocality on the social and cultural margins of Dublin, which are suppressed and denied in *Dubliners*.

Even Gabriel's little jokes reveal unacknowledged cultural snobbery, as in: "—Now if anyone wants a little more of what vulgar people call stuffing let him or her speak" (*D* 198) [172.756–57]. Most revealing, however, is the funny anecdote he tells late in the party about "the late lamented Patrick Morkan, our grandfather" and his horse named Johnny: "One fine day the old gentleman thought he'd like to drive out with the quality to a military review in the park" (*D* 207) [180.1073–75]. These lines seem to suggest that, having made his money by owning and operating a starch mill, old Mr. Morkan developed pretensions to being "quality" and thus, co-opted by the economy of the empire, wished, like the "quality," to attend a "military review in the park," presumably a display of English military power. This buying-into the values of the oppressor is a trait of the grandfather which seems to have been inherited by both Gabriel's mother and by Gabriel himself.[2]

> —Out from the mansion of his forefathers, continued Gabriel, he drove with Johnny. And everything went on beautifully until Johnny came in sight of King Billy's statue: and whether he fell in love with the horse King Billy sits on or whether he thought he was back again in the mill, anyhow he began to walk around the statue.

2. This connection between horses and British economic collaboration and patriarchy will be extended in *Ulysses* to sexist Blazes Boylan, who—just as Gabriel is grandson to Patrick Morkan—is the son of a man who unpatriotically sold horses to the British during the Boer War. Boylan seems one extreme of Joyce's representation of the effects of the collusion between patriarchal imperial politics and patriarchal sexual politics.
   Owning horses was, through much of Irish history, itself a material and literal manifestation of British imperial/class politics and status. Under the Penal Laws, Catholics in Ireland were not only barred from Parliament, from the professions, and from public schools, but they were also forbidden to own a horse worth more than five pounds. See also chapter 9 of this study.

> Gabriel paced in a circle round the hall in his goloshes amid the laughter of the others.
>
> (D 208) [181.1086–93]

King Billy, of course, was William III, the Protestant prince of Orange, conqueror of Ireland at the Battle of the Boyne, and the scourge of Irish Catholics. This equestrian statue of King Billy on College Green was despised by Dubliners as a hated symbol of English domination and of the Irish defeat at the Boyne. As Adaline Glasheen points out (citing Gilbert's *History of Dublin*, III. 40–56): "In Dublin (before the Free State) the Ulstermen's brazen calf was a lead equestrian statue of King Billy on College Green which, on Williamite holy days, was painted white (a white horse in a fanlight is still a sign of Protestant sympathies) and decorated with orange lilies . . . and green and white ribbons 'symbolically placed beneath its uplifted foot.' Catholics retorted by vandalizing the statue, tarring, etc., and in 1836 succeeded in blowing the figure of the king off the horse" (*Third Census*, 309). So that Gabriel, notably clad in his "civilized" goloshes, circling round and round the hall in imitation of Johnny circling King Billy's white horse, is unknowingly reinscribing the marks of an Irish cycle of paralysis, of satellitic subservience to (and co-option by) the Empire.[3]

It is at this point in the story that Gabriel looks up the stairwell to see his wife in a striking and attentive posture:

> He stood still in the gloom of the hall, trying to catch the air that the voice was singing and gazing up at his wife. There was grace and mystery in her attitude as if she were a symbol of something. He asked himself what is a woman standing on the stairs in the shadow, listening to distant music, a symbol of. If he were a painter he would paint her in that attitude. Her blue felt hat would show off the bronze of her hair against the darkness and the dark panels of her skirt would show off the light ones. *Distant Music* he would call the picture if he were a painter.
>
> (D 210) [182.1149–58]

In his mind's eye he *is* a painter, for, as a number of commentators have noted, Gabriel engages here, as the Western patriarchal tradition has for centuries, in the aesthetic objectification of women as art and symbol, as object rather than subject.[4] As these critics have

---

3. It is interesting to note that, on the cab ride home, Miss O'Callaghan comments as they pass O'Connell Bridge, "—They say you never cross O'Connell Bridge without seeing a white horse"—to which Gabriel replies that "—I see a white man this time" (214). In the white horse and the "white man" (the snow-capped statue of Daniel O'Connell) we have here, emblematically represented, the opposing forces of the British Empire (King Billy's white horse) and the Irish-Catholic resistance ("The Liberator").

4. Most recently, for example, Norris writes ("Stifled," 482): "In this superb staging of the aestheticizing act, Joyce displays his acute awareness that in their genderized form, in the

noted (e.g., Norris in "Stifled," 486, 492), this moment should recall two previous intertextual references in the story to famous balcony scenes in literary history, *Romeo and Juliet* (D 186: "A picture of the balcony scene in *Romeo and Juliet* hung" over the piano) and "My Last Duchess" by Robert Browning (the poet who has been on Gabriel's mind and in his speech all evening). Recall that, in Browning's poem, the speaker (the Duke of Ferrara) is a domestic tyrant who domesticates (and presumably kills) his unacceptably high-spirited wife (too non-passive, too much a subject) by aestheticizing and literally objectifying her—that is, he turns her into a painting hanging above the stairwell—so that he may possess her as object and stifle her own emerging subjectivity. Browning's Duke is a ruthless patriarch engaging in an aggressively masculine colonization, aestheticization, and objectification of woman.

The song Gretta is listening to is a stunningly appropriate choice on Joyce's part, for "The Lass of Aughrim" is likewise a song about mastery, domination, and mistreatment (even rape) of a peasant woman by a patriarchal nobleman. "The Lass of Aughrim" is a version (among many, with many titles) of "Lord Gregory"; although the details differ from version to version, the version Joyce seems to have known[5] tells of Lord Gregory having forced himself sexually on the Lass ("Sorely against my will"), who then gets with child as a result; the song finds her standing in the rain outside the castle with her cold and dying child as she begs to be let in, only to be refused entrance and recognition by Lord Gregory (and in some versions also by his cruel mother).

Is Gretta Conroy a modern-day Lass of Aughrim? To begin with, Joyce's choice of this variant title/version ("The Lass of Aughrim") allies it with the West of Ireland, for the town of Aughrim is about thirty miles from Galway, the hometown of both Gretta and Nora Barnacle. Furthermore, as Ruth Bauerle points out, "The music's folk simplicity is at variance with the deliberately civilized, continental preferences of Gretta's husband Gabriel" (*Songbook,* 177). Note further parallels: like Michael Furey, Gretta (scorning goloshes) and the Lass both uninhibitedly stand in the rain; all three seem to suggest a primitive wildness as yet undomesticated. Gabriel, on the other hand, wears goloshes and retires to a nearby hotel to protect

---

male artist's representation of the female, the politics of representation are expressed in doubly brutal gestures of occlusion, oppression, and exploitation: doubly brutal, because these acts are masked as love. The very form of Gabriel's gesture toward woman—the rhetorical question ('He asked himself what is a woman . . . a symbol of') that proclaims its disinterest in what woman is in favor of parading its own profundity—masks artistic conceit as gyneolatry. The generality of the question implies an answer of indeterminacy and overdetermination, that woman is a symbol of anything and everything man wants her to represent—except her own sense of who or what she is."

5. See 124–25 of Bauerle ("Date Rape") for the words to this version of the song.

himself from rain and snow (just as Lord Gregory is sheltered from the rain in the warmth of his castle), and prefers the strictures of a "civilized" cultural code prescribed by Continental and English influences. Gabriel's mother had scorned Gretta's country-cuteness and low-bred backgrounds—just as Lord Gregory's mother scorns the abused Lass of Aughrim.

Furthermore, I would suggest that to Joyce and to his Irish readers the town of Aughrim should hold an even more potent symbolic value than has been heretofore noted in discussions of "The Dead"— for it is closely associated with the Battle of the Boyne and with the subjugation of Ireland by the English. The twelfth of July, known as "White Horse Day" (for "King Billy on White Horse"; McHugh, *Annotations*, 347) is celebrated by Ulster Protestants as the victory at the Boyne (in 1690) over the papists. But that date and that battle are also associated and frequently confused with another (and perhaps more historically significant) battle, the Battle of Aughrim. As the *Encyclopaedia Britannica* notes, although the Battle of the Boyne is celebrated on July 12, that date "is actually the old style date of the more decisive Battle of Aughrim in the following year," 1691. As R. F. Foster writes in *Modern Ireland 1600–1972*:

> [I]t is uncertain whether [the Boyne] was the decisive battle of the war, though Protestants celebrate it still. Jacobites saw it as an indecisive engagement, Aughrim a year later being 'the great disaster' . . . all hope went after Aughrim, where [the Irish forces] lost the day in a welter of heroics, confusion and alleged treachery: 'the most disastrous battle in Irish history' . . . The losses were enormous, in what was to be the last great pitched battle in Irish history.
>
> (148, 150)

It was the Irish defeat at Aughrim a year after the Boyne that finally and fully sealed English domination of Ireland. Aughrim, then, like Browning's murdered Duchess or the hapless Lass in the song, becomes itself a poignant symbol of domination and colonization by imperial patriarchs—that murdered Irish past, the dead, the bodies of, as Yeats wrote in his verse play *Purgatory*, "long ago / Men that had fought at Aughrim and the Boyne."

Thus, if we consider Gretta as a modern-day Lass of Aughrim, we find in Joyce's selection of this song heard on a stairwell a set of carefully designed parallels between conqueror and conquered, between imperial oppressor and colonized victim, in which Aughrim, its Lass, Gretta, and Michael Furey in the rain all merge into a composite image of the loss of the Irish soul and autonomy to the imperial masters: King Billy conquering the Irish at Aughrim and the Boyne; Protestant England dominating Catholic Ireland; Lord

Gregory raping the helpless Lass of Aughrim, then letting her perish
in the rain (as Michael Furey had perished) only to be eventually
aestheticized in folksong; Browning's Duke tyrannizing, then mur-
dering, and finally aestheticizing his last Duchess as a painting at the
top of the stairwell; and Gabriel Conroy's attempt to master Gretta by
infantilizing, then essentializing and objectifying her as art (as a stairwell painting titled *Distant Music*: "What is a woman standing on the
stairs in the shadow, listening to distant music, a symbol of"). As Spivak has written in reference to subaltern women: "Between patriarchy and imperialism, subject-constitution and object-formation, the
figure of the woman disappears" ("Subaltern," 296).

Even more sinister and disturbing is the fact that the subsequent
scene between Gabriel and Gretta in the Gresham Hotel *almost* pro-
vokes not just an intellectual and aesthetic domination, but physical
mastery and violation. For, as we have already seen in Gabriel's framing of *Distant Music*, it is the aestheticized *image* of Gretta, more
than Gretta herself, which (like an erotic Venus or a *Playboy* cen-
terfold) arouses Gabriel from his crisis of ego-confidence into brutal
lust: "She had no longer any grace of attitude but Gabriel's eyes were
still bright with happiness. The blood went bounding along his veins
and the thoughts went rioting through his brain, proud, joyful,
tender, valorous" (*D* 213) [185.1254–58]. Having been aroused by
an objectified fantasy of his wife, Gabriel now first reviews his erotic
memories of her, then fantasizes her undressing:

> Like distant music these words that he had written years
> before were borne towards him from the past. He longed to be
> alone with her. When the others had gone away, when he and
> she were in their room in the hotel, then they would be alone
> together. He would call her softly:
> —Gretta!
> Perhaps she would not hear at once: she would be undressing.
> Then something in his voice would strike her. She would turn
> and look at him . . .
>
> (*D* 214) [186.1290–98]

As they return to the hotel, Gabriel becomes more and more eroti-
cally aroused: "But now after the kindling again of so many memories, the first touch of her body, musical and strange and perfumed,
sent through him a keen pang of lust. Under cover of her silence he
pressed her arm closely to his side" (*D* 215) [187.1326–29]; "She
mounted the stairs behind the porter, her head bowed in the ascent,
her frail shoulders curved as with a burden, her skirt girt tightly about
her. He could have flung his arms about her hips and held her still
for his arms were trembling with desire to seize her and only the

stress of his nails against the palms of his hands held the wild impulse of his body in check" (*D* 215) [187.1336–42].

When Gretta does not respond to his caresses as Gabriel would wish, his mental reaction is one of smoldering sexual anger:

> He was trembling now with annoyance. Why did she seem so abstracted? He did not know how he could begin. Was she annoyed too about something? If she would only turn to him or come to him of her own accord! To take her as she was would be brutal. No, he must see some ardour in her eyes first. He longed to be master of her strange mood.
>
> (*D* 217) [189.1389–94]

These are startling lines, in which Gabriel rejects "taking her as she was" as "too brutal," since he needs to "see some ardour in her eyes first" and to be "master of her strange mood." A few lines later we learn that "He longed to cry to her from his soul, to crush her body against his, to overmaster her . . . He was in such a fever of rage and desire that he did not hear her come from the window" (*D* 217) [189.1397–1403].

As Ruth Bauerle has suggested in her provocative essay titled "Date Rape, Mate Rape: A Liturgical Interpretation of 'The Dead,' " Gabriel and Gretta almost literally re-enact the date rape at the source of the story of Lord Gregory and the Lass of Aughrim.[6]

Should we then despise Gabriel Conroy as a version of Lord Gregory or of Browning's Duke? We might consider that Gabriel's situation is not atypical of heterosexual men in our society, and that the basic situation in the Conroys' hotel room is a common scene that has been reenacted in bedrooms at some time or other by every sexually active couple in human history: one partner is sexually frustrated to discover that the other is not "in the mood," not as aroused as oneself. Too often, however, the result has been either physical violation or abuse, or, more frequently, passive acquiescence by the female ("taking her as she was"). The crucial difference here is that Gabriel is checked by his own highly developed self-awareness (which has earlier [179] [155.121–22, 134–35] already led him to question his own mastery and male-ness as a failure in both his conversation with Lily and in the speech he had prepared), so that when Gretta now reveals that all along she was not getting similarly aroused (as he had thought) but rather was thinking of the young, dead Michael Furey,

6. Bauerle writes: "Joyce would have felt little trouble calling the Lass of Aughrim's situation what feminists today call it: date rape . . . It seems very likely that [Gretta] now identifies with the Lass of Aughrim, a victim of date rape, and sees herself as having been, too often, a victim of unwanted and perhaps forced sexual attention—that is, of mate rape by her hypereducated, though shallow, husband" ("Date Rape," 115, 118).

Gabriel is assailed by "a shameful consciousness of his own person" (*D* 219–20) [191.1481], seeing himself now as "a ludicrous figure, acting as a pennyboy for his aunts, a nervous wellmeaning sentimentalist, orating to vulgarians and idealising his own clownish lusts" (*D* 220) [191.1482–84]. As his wife breaks into tears of passionate grief, Gabriel first "held her hand for a moment," and then, "shy of intruding on her grief, let it fall gently and walked quietly to the window" (*D* 222) [193.1546, 1547–48].

Gabriel's final epiphany, in this reading of the story, becomes, it seems to me, even more moving—for it is an act of emotional expansiveness, self-understanding, and generosity. The West and the snow in his final vision suggest all those repressed elements that Gabriel's ego has denied, sold out to, or been co-opted out of—including the uninhibited freedom of the Irish soul and of the marginalized others, in contrast to his patriarchal and imperialistic urge for mastery, dominion, colonization, and hierarchy. Gabriel's self-conscious willingness finally to grant Gretta a private space of her own, in which she can be her own emotional subject, inscribes a *possible* alternative by which to break free from the culturally-encoded male pattern prescribed by his mental framing of his wife as an aestheticized painting; and by the previous and parallel masculine matrixes suggested by the models of the British Empire over its far-flung colonies, King Billy at Aughrim and the Boyne, Lord Gregory over the Lass, and Browning's Duke over his late wife. Instead, Gabriel's final vision of the falling snow which "was general all over Ireland" [194.1605–06] attempts to break down the barriers of difference constructed by the patriarchal ego he is so deeply (if unconsciously) implicated in, into at least a recognition of generosity and sameness, all shades of equal color, whether these "shades . . . pass[ing] boldly into that other world" [194.1584–85] be Michael Furey, Aunt Julia, black opera singers, or himself: "One by one they were all becoming shades . . . Generous tears filled Gabriel's eyes" (*D* 223) [194.1584, 1590]. "Generosity"—a charged term in Joyce's personal vocabulary, suggesting a collective social conscience[7]—allows for the acceptance of

---

7. "Generous" as a key word in "The Dead" is given a much more ironic interpretation by Vincent P. Pecora in " 'The Dead' and the Generosity of the Word." In my own reading of "generosity" (as derived from *genus, generis* just as "kindness" is derived from "kind" and "kin") as a desirable, socialistic breaking-down of hierarchy and individualistic status-formation, I am conscious of the phrase Joyce himself had used (in his essay "A Portrait of the Artist") in describing socialism as "the generous idea," within a passage arguing for the leveling of hierarchies (see Manganiello, *Joyce's Politics,* 68–69):

> Already the messages of citizens were flashed along the wires of the world, already the generous idea had emerged from a thirty years' war in Germany and was directing the councils of the Latins. To those multitudes, not as yet in the wombs of humanity but surely engenderable there, he would give the word: Man and woman, out of you comes the nation that is to come, the lightening of your masses in travail; the competitive

others as subjects, breaking down the unified self into a consciousness of a shared or collective subjectivity, allowing the walls of the
ego to dissolve and for identities to mix in a vision, however momentary or melodramatic on Gabriel's part, of uncompartmentalized,
non-hierarchical sameness—as the snow falls faintly through the
universe and faintly falling, equally and non-preferentially, over
everyone, living and dead, usurper and usurped.

Works Cited

Anzaldúa, Gloria. *Borderlands/La Frontera: The New Mestiza*. San Francisco:
Spinsters/Aunt Lute, 1987.

Bauerle, Ruth. "Date Rape, Mate Rape: A Liturgical Interpretation of 'The
Dead.'" *New Alliances in Joyce Studies*. Ed. Bonnie Kime Scott. Newark:
University of Delaware Press, 1988. Pp. 113–25.

———. *The James Joyce Songbook*. New York: Garland, 1982.

The New Encyclopaedia Britannica, Fifteenth Edition, *Micropaedia*, Vol. 2
(p. 448: "Boyne, Battle of the"). Chicago: Encyclopaedia Britannica Inc.,
1992.

Cheng, Vincent J. "White Horse, Dark Horse: Joyce's Allhorse of Another
Color." *Joyce Studies Annual 1991*. Ed. Thomas F. Staley. Austin: University of Texas Press, 1992. Pp. 101–28.

Crenshaw, Kimberle. "A Black Feminist Critique of Antidiscrimination Law
and Politics." In *The Politics of Law: A Progressive Critique*. Revised Edition. Ed. David Kairys. New York: Pantheon, 1990.

Dahl, Robert. *Modern Political Analysis*. Englewood Cliffs, N.J.: Prentice-
Hall, 1970.

Deane, Seamus. *Celtic Revivals: Essays in Modern Irish Literature 1880–
1980*. London: Faber and Faber, 1985.

———. *Heroic Styles: The Tradition of an Idea*. Derry: Field Day pamphlet
no. 4, 1984.

———. "Introduction" to *Nationalism, Colonialism, and Literature*, by Terry
Eagleton, Fredric Jameson, and Edward W. Said. Minneapolis: University
of Minnesota Press, 1990. Pp. 3–19.

Eagleton, Terry. "Nationalism: Irony and Commitment." In *Nationalism,
Colonialism, and Literature* by Terry Eagleton, Fredric Jameson, and
Edward W. Said (intro. by Seamus Deane). A Field Day Company Book.
Minneapolis: University of Minnesota Press, 1990.

Ellmann, Richard. *The Consciousness of Joyce*. New York: Oxford University
Press, 1977.

Fanon, Frantz. *The Wretched of the Earth*. Trans. Constance Farrington.
New York: Grove Weidenfeld, 1968.

Foster, R. F. *Modern Ireland 1660–1972*. London: Penguin, 1988.

Gifford, Don. *Joyce Annotated: Notes for "Dubliners" and "A Portrait of the
Artist as a Young Man."* Berkeley: University of California Press, 1982.

---

order is employed against itself, the aristocracies are supplanted; and amid the general
paralysis of an insane society, the confederate will issues in action.

Gifford, Don, and Robert J. Seidman. *"Ulysses" Annotated: Notes for James Joyce's "Ulysses."* Revised Edition. Berkeley: University of California Press, 1988.

Glasheen, Adaline. *Third Census of "Finnegans Wake."* Berkeley: University of California Press, 1977.

Herr, Cheryl. *Joyce's Anatomy of Culture.* Urbana: University of Illinois Press, 1986.

Jameson, Fredric. "Modernism and Imperialism." In Eagleton et al., *Nationalism, Colonialism, and Literature.* Pp. 43–66.

JanMohamed, Abdul R., and David Lloyd. "Introduction: Toward a Theory of Minority Discourse: What Is to Be Done?" In *The Nature and Context of Minority Discourse.* Ed. Abdul R. JanMohamed and David Lloyd. Oxford: Oxford University Press, 1990. Pp. 1–16.

MacCabe, Colin. *James Joyce and the Revolution of the Word.* New York: Barnes & Noble, 1979.

Mahaffey, Vicki. *Reauthorizing Joyce.* Cambridge: Cambridge University Press, 1988.

Manganiello, Dominic. *Joyce's Politics.* London: Routledge & Kegan Paul, 1980.

McHugh, Roland. *Annotations to "Finnegans Wake."* Baltimore: Johns Hopkins University Press, 1980.

Norris, Margot. *Joyce's Web: The Social Unraveling of Modernism.* Austin: University of Texas Press, 1992.

———. "Narration under a Blindfold: Reading Joyce's 'Clay.' " *PMLA* 102.2 (March 1987): 206–15.

———. "Stifled Back Answers: The Gender Politics of Art in Joyce's 'The Dead.' " *Modern Fiction Studies* 35.3 (Autumn 1989): 479–506.

Pecora, Vincent P. " 'The Dead' and the Generosity of the Word." *PMLA* 101.2 (March 1986): 233–45.

Pratt, Mary Louise. "Arts of the Contact Zone." In *Profession 91.* Ed. Phyllis Franklin. New York: MLA, 1991. Pp. 33–40.

Said, Edward W. *Orientalism.* New York: Vintage, 1979.

———. "Yeats and Decolonization." In Eagleton et al., *Nationalism, Colonialism, and Literature.* Pp. 69–95. Scholes, Robert. "Joyce and Modernist Ideology." In *Coping with Joyce: Essays from the Copenhagen Symposium.* Eds. Morris Beja and Shari Benstock. Columbus: Ohio State University Press, 1989. Pp. 91–107.

Spivak, Gayatri Chakravorty. "Can the Subaltern Speak?" *Marxism and the Interpretation of Culture,* eds. Cary Nelson and Lawrence Grossberg. Champaign: University of Illinois Press, 1988. Pp. 271–313.

———. "The Rani of Sirmur." In *Europe and Its Others,* vol. 1, eds. Francis Barker et al. Colchester: University of Essex, 1985. Pp. 128–51.

Yeats, William Butler. *The Collected Plays of W. B. Yeats.* New York: Macmillan, 1935.

Young, Robert. *White Mythologies: Writing History and the West.* London: Routledge, 1990.

Abbreviations

CW   Joyce, James. *The Critical Writings of James Joyce*. Ed. Ellsworth
            Mason and Richard Ellmann. Ithaca, NY: Cornell University
            Press, 1989.

D   Joyce, James. *Dubliners*. New York: Viking, 1961.

Letters II Joyce, James. *Letters of James Joyce*. Vol. 2, ed. Richard Ellmann.
            New York: Viking, 1966.

U   Joyce, James. *Ulysses*. Eds. Hans Walter Gabler et al. New York:
            Vintage, 1986.

Selected Bibliography

• indicates a work included or excerpted in this Norton Critical Edition.

Adams, Robert M. "A Study in Weakness and Humiliation." *James Joyce's "Dubliners": A Critical Handbook*. Ed. James R. Baker and Thomas F. Staley. Belmont, CA: Wadsworth, 1969. 101–4.

Albert, Leonard. "Gnomonology: Joyce's 'The Sisters'." *James Joyce Quarterly* 27.2 (Winter 1990): 355–56.

Attridge, Derek. *Joyce Effects: On Language, Theory, and History*. Cambridge: Cambridge UP, 2000.

Baccolini, Raffaella. " 'She Had Become a Memory': Women as Memory in James Joyce's *Dubliners*." *ReJoycing: New Readings of "Dubliners."* Ed. Rosa M. Bollettieri Bosinelli and Harold F. Mosher, Jr. Lexington: UP of Kentucky, 1998. 146–64.

Baker, Joseph E. "The Trinity in Joyce's 'Grace.' " *James Joyce Quarterly* 2.4 (Summer 1965): 299–303.

Bašić, Sonia. "A Book of Many Uncertainties: Joyce's 'Dubliners.' " *ReJoycing: New Readings of "Dubliners."* Ed. Rosa M. Bollettieri Bosinelli and Harold F. Mosher, Jr. Lexington: UP of Kentucky, 1998. 14–40.

Bauerle, Ruth. "Date Rape, Mate Rape: A Liturgical Interpretation of 'The Dead.' " *New Alliances in Joyce Studies*. Ed. Bonnie Kime Scott. Newark: U of Delaware P, 1988. 113–25.

Beck, Warren. *Joyce's "Dubliners": Substance, Vision, and Art*. Durham, NC: Duke UP, 1969.

•Beja, Morris. "Farrington the Scrivener: A Story of Dame Street." *Coping with Joyce: Essays from the Copenhagen Symposium*. Ed. Morris Beja and Shari Benstock. Columbus: Ohio State UP, 1989.

———. "One Good Look at Themselves: Epiphanies in *Dubliners*." *Work in Progress: Joyce Centenary Essays*. Ed. Richard F. Peterson, Alan M. Cohn, and Edmund L. Epstein. Carbondale: Southern Illinois UP, 1983. 1–14.

Benstock, Bernard. *Narrative Con/Texts in "Dubliners."* Urbana: U of Illinois P, 1994.

Blotner, Joseph L. " 'Ivy Day in the Committee Room': Death without Resurrection." *James Joyce's "Dubliners": A Critical Handbook*. Ed. James R. Baker and Thomas F. Staley. Belmont, CA.: Wadsworth, 1969. 139–46.

Bonafous-Murat, Carle. "Disposition and Pre-disposition: The Art of Involuntary Memory in *Dubliners*." *Classic Joyce: Joyce Studies in Italy 6*. Ed. Franca Ruggieri. Roma: Bulzoni Editore, 1999. 361–71.

Bosinelli, Rosa M. Bollettieri, and Harold F. Mosher, Jr., eds. *ReJoycing: New Readings of "Dubliners."* Lexington: UP of Kentucky, 1998.

Boyle, Robert S.J. " 'Two Gallants' and 'Ivy Day in the Committee Room.' " *Twentieth Century Interpretations of "Dubliners."* Ed. Peter K. Garrett. Englewood Cliffs, NJ.: Prentice-Hall, 1968. 100–106.

———. "Swiftian Allegory and Dantean Parody in Joyce's 'Grace.' " *James Joyce Quarterly* 7.1 (Fall 1969): 11–19.

Brandabur, Edward. *A Scrupulous Meanness: A Study of Joyce's Early Work*. Urbana: U of Illinois P, 1971.

Bremen, Brian A. " 'He Was Too Scrupulous Always': A Re-examination of Joyce's 'The Sisters.' " *James Joyce Quarterly* 22.1 (Fall 1984): 55–66.

Brian, Michael. " 'A Very Fine Piece of Writing': An Etymological, Dantean, and Gnostic Reading of Joyce's 'Ivy Day in the Committee Room.' " *ReJoycing: New Readings of "Dubliners."* Ed. Rosa M. Bollettieri Bosinelli and Harold F. Mosher, Jr. Lexington: UP of Kentucky, 1998. 207–27.

Buzard, James. " 'Culture' and the Critics of *Dubliners*." *James Joyce Quarterly* 37.1/2 (Fall 1999/Winter 2000): 43–61.

•Cheng, Vincent J. *Joyce, Race, and Empire*. Cambridge: Cambridge UP, 1995.

Ciniglio, Ada V. " 'Two Gallants': Joyce's Wedding Guests." *James Joyce Quarterly* 10.2 (Winter 1973): 264.

Collins, Ben L. " 'Araby' and the 'Extended Simile.' " *Twentieth Century Interpretations of "Dubliners."* Ed. Peter K. Garrett. Englewood Cliffs, NJ: Prentice-Hall, 1968. 93–99.

Connolly, Thomas E. "A Painful Case." *James Joyce's "Dubliners": Critical Essays.* Ed. Clive Hart. New York: Viking Press, 1969. 107–21.

Corrington, John William. "Isolation as Motif in 'A Painful Case.' " *James Joyce's "Dubliners": A Critical Handbook.* Ed. James R. Baker and Thomas F. Staley. Belmont, CA.: Wadsworth, 1969. 130–39.

Culleton, Claire A. " 'Taking the Biscuit': Narrative Cheekiness in *Dubliners*." *ReJoycing: New Readings of "Dubliners."* Ed. Rosa M. Bollettieri Bosinelli and Harold F. Mosher Jr. Lexington: UP of Kentucky, 1998. 110–22.

Cunningham, Frank R. "Joyce's 'Grace': Gracelessness in a Lost Paradise." *James Joyce Quarterly* 6.3 (Spring 1969): 219–223.

Deane, Seamus. "Dead Ends: Joyce's Finest Moments." *Semicolonial Joyce.* Ed. Derek Attridge and Marjorie Howes. Cambridge: Cambridge UP, 2000. 21–36.

Doloff, Steven. "On the Road with Loyola: St. Ignatius' Pilgrimage as Model for James Joyce's 'Araby.' " *James Joyce Quarterly* 28.2 (Winter 1991): 515–17.

•Ehrlich, Heyward. " 'Araby' in Context: The 'Splendid Bazaar,' Irish Orientalism, and James Clarence Mangan." *James Joyce Quarterly* 35.2/3 (Winter/Spring 1998): 309–31.

•Fairhall, James. "Big-Power Politics and Colonial Economics: The Gordon Bennett Cup Race and 'After the Race.' " *James Joyce Quarterly* 28.2 (Winter 1991): 387–97.

———. "Colgan-Connolly: Another Look at the Politics of 'Ivy Day in the Committee Room.' " *James Joyce Quarterly* 25.3 (Spring 1988): 289–304.

———. *James Joyce and the Question of History.* Cambridge: Cambridge UP, 1993.

Feshbach, Sidney. " 'Fallen on His Feet in Buenos Ayres' (D 30): Frank in 'Eveline.' " *James Joyce Quarterly* 20.2 (Winter 1983): 223–26.

Finney, Michael. "Why Gretta Falls Asleep: A Postmodern Sugarplum." *Studies in Short Fiction: Special "Dubliners" Number* 32.3 (Summer 1995): 475–81.

Freely, John. "Joyce's 'The Dead' and the Browning Quotation." *James Joyce Quarterly* 20.1 (Fall 1982): 87–96.

Garnier, Marie-Dominique. "From Paralysis to Para-lire: Another Reading of 'A Mother.' " *European Joyce Studies 7: New Perspectives on "Dubliners."* Ed. Mary Power and Ulrich Schneider. Amsterdam: Rodopi, 1997. 231–46.

Gates, David A. "Tom Kernan and Job." *James Joyce Quarterly* 19.3 (Spring 1982): 275–87.

Ghiselin, Brewster. "The Unity of 'Dubliners.' " *Twentieth Century Interpretations of "Dubliners."* Ed. Peter K. Garrett. Englewood Cliffs, NJ: Prentice-Hall, 1968. 57–85.

Gibbons, Luke. " 'Have You No Homes to Go To?': James Joyce and the Politics of Paralysis." *Semicolonial Joyce.* Ed. Derek Attridge and Marjorie Howes. Cambridge: Cambridge UP, 2000. 150–71.

Gifford, Don. *Joyce Annotated: Notes for "Dubliners" and "A Portrait of the Artist as a Young Man."* Second Edition. Berkeley: U of California P, 1982.

Giles, Jana. "The Craft of 'A Painful Case': A Study of Revisions." *European Joyce Studies 7: New Perspectives on "Dubliners."* Ed. Mary Power and Ulrich Schneider. Amsterdam: Rodopi, 1997. Pp. 195–210.

Gordon, John. " 'A Little Cloud' as a Little Cloud." *European Joyce Studies 7: New Perspectives on "Dubliners."* Ed. Mary Power and Ulrich Schneider. Amsterdam: Rodopi, 1997. 167–80.

Grace, Sherill E. "Rediscovering Mrs. Kearney: An Other Reading of 'A Mother.' " *James Joyce: The Augmented Ninth.* Ed. Bernard Benstock. Syracuse: Syracuse UP, 1988.

Haughey, Jim. "Joyce and Trevor's Dubliners: The Legacy of Colonialism." *Studies in Short Fiction* 32.3(Summer 1995): 355–65.

Hayman, David. "A Mother." *James Joyce's "Dubliners": Critical Essays.* Ed. Clive Hart. New York: Viking, 1969. 122–33.

Henke, Suzette A. *James Joyce and the Politics of Desire.* New York: Routledge, 1990.

Herr, Cheryl. *Joyce's Anatomy of Culture.* Urbana: U of Illinois P, 1986.

Hodgkins, Hope Howell. " 'Just a little . . . spiritual matter': Joyce's 'Grace' and the Modern Protestant Gentleman." *Studies in Short Fiction: Special "Dubliners" Number* 32.3 (Summer 1995): 423–34.

Horowitz, Sylvia Huntley. "More Christian Allegory in 'Ivy Day in the Committee Room.' " *James Joyce Quarterly* 21.2 (Winter 1984): 145–54.

Howes, Marjorie. " 'Goodbye Ireland I'm Going to Gort': Geography, Scale, and Narrating the Nation." *Semicolonial Joyce.* Ed. Derek Attridge and Marjorie Howes. Cambridge: Cambridge UP, 2000. 58–77.

Ingersoll, Earl G. *Engendered Trope in Joyce's "Dubliners."* Carbondale: Southern Illinois UP, 1996.

• Jackson, Roberta. "The Open Closet in *Dubliners*: James Duffy's Painful Case." *James Joyce Quartery* 37.1/2 (Fall 1999/Winter 2000): 83–97.

Johnsen, William A. "Joyce's *Dubliners* and the Futility of Modernism." In *James Joyce and Modern Literature*. Ed. W. J. McCormack and Alistair Stead. London: Routledge and Kegan Paul, 1982. 5–21.

———. "Joyce's Many Sisters and the Demodernization of *Dubliners*." In *European Joyce Studies 7: New Perspectives on "Dubliners"*. Ed. Mary Power and Ulrich Schneider. Amsterdam: Rodopi, 1997. 69–90.

Kain, Richard M. "Grace." *James Joyce's "Dubliners": Critical Essays*. Ed. Clive Hart. New York: Viking, 1969. 134–52.

Karrer, Wolfgang. "Gnomon and Triangulation: The Stories of Childhood in *Dubliners*." *European Joyce Studies 7: New Perspectives on "Dubliners."* Ed. Mary Power and Ulrich Schneider. Amsterdam: Rodopi, 1997. 45–68.

Kelly, Joseph. "Joyce's Marriage Cycle." *Studies in Short Fiction* 32.3 (Summer 1995): 367–78.

Kenner, Hugh. "Molly's Masterstroke." *James Joyce Quarterly* 10.1 (Fall 1972): 19–28.

———. *Joyce's Voices*. Berkeley: U of California P, 1978.

Kershner, R. B. *Joyce, Bakhtin, and Popular Literature: Chronicles of Disorder*. Chapel Hill: U of North Carolina P, 1989.

Khanna, Ranjana. " 'Araby': Women's Time and the Time of the Nation." *European Joyce Studies 8: Joyce: Feminism/Post/Colonialism*. Ed. Ellen Carol Jones. Amsterdam: Rodopi, 1998. 81–101.

Klein, Scott W. "Strongarming 'Grace.' " *James Joyce Quarterly* 37.1/2 (Fall 1999/Winter 2000): 113–26.

Lamos, Colleen. "Duffy's Subjectivation: The Psychic Life of 'A Painful Case.' " *European Joyce Studies 10: Masculinities in Joyce/Postcolonial Constructions*. Ed. Christine van Boheemen-Saaf and Colleen Lamos. Amsterdam: Rodopi, 2001. 59–71.

LeBlanc, Jim. "All Work, No Play: The Refusal of Freedom in 'Araby.' " *James Joyce Quarterly* 37.1/2 (Fall 1999/Winter 2000). 229–33.

Leonard, Garry M. *Reading "Dubliners" Again: A Lacanian Perspective*. Syracuse: Syracuse UP, 1993.

Levenson, Michael. "Living History in 'The Dead.' " *James Joyce's "The Dead": Case Studies in Contemporary Criticism*. Ed. Daniel R. Schwarz. Boston: Bedford Books, 1994. 163–77.

Lin, Paul. "Standing the Empire: Drinking, Masculinity, and Modernity in 'Counterparts.' " *European Joyce Studies 10: Masculinities in Joyce/Postcolonial Constructions*. Ed. Christine van Boheemen-Saaf and Colleen Lamos. Amsterdam: Rodopi, 2001. 33–57.

Lloyd, David. "Counterparts: 'Dubliners,' Masculinity, and Temperance Nationalism." *Semicolonial Joyce*. Ed. Derek Attridge and Marjorie Howes. Cambridge: Cambridge UP, 2000. 128–49.

Lowe-Evans, Mary. "Who Killed Mrs Sinico?" *Studies in Short Fiction* 32.3 (Summer 1995): 395–402.

McCarthy, Patrick A. "Introduction." *ReJoycing: New Readings of "Dubliners."* Ed. Rosa M. Bollettieri Bosinelli and Harold F. Mosher Jr. Lexington: The UP of Kentucky, 1998. 1–9.

McLean, Barbara. " 'The (Boar)ding House': Mrs. Mooney as Circe and Sow." *James Joyce Quarterly* 28.2 (Winter 1991): 520–22.

Melzer. Sondra. "In the Beginning There Was 'Eveline.' " *James Joyce Quarterly* 16.4 (Summer 1979): 479–85.

Miami University Research Group Experiment (MURGE). "Analyzing 'Araby' as Story and Discourse: A Summary of the MURGE Project." *James Joyce Quarterly* 18.3 (Spring 1981): 237–54.

Miller, Jane. "O, 'She's a Nice Lady!': A Rereading of 'A Mother.' " *James Joyce Quarterly* 28.2 (Winter 1991): 407–26.

Morgan, Jack. "Queer Choirs: Sacred Music, Joyce's 'The Dead,' and the Sexual Politics of Victorian Aestheticism." *James Joyce Quarterly* 37.1/2 (Fall 1999/Winter 2000): 127–51.

Mosher, Harold F. Jr. "Clichés and Repetitions in *Dubliners*: The Example of 'A Little Cloud.' " *ReJoycing: New Readings of "Dubliners."* Ed. Rosa M. Bollettieri Bosinelli and Harold F. Mosher, Jr. Lexington: UP of Kentucky, 1998. 53–67.

———. "The Narrated and Its Negatives: the Nonnarrated and Disnarrated in Joyce's *Dubliners*." *Style* (Fall 1993): 407–28.

Mullin, Katherine. "Don't Cry for Me, Argentina: 'Eveline' and the Seductions of Emigration Propaganda." *Semicolonial Joyce*. Ed. Derek Attridge and Marjorie Howes. Cambridge: Cambridge UP, 2000. 172–200.

Munich, Adrienne Auslander. " 'Dear Dead Women,' or Why Gabriel Conroy Reviews

Browning." *New Alliances in Joyce Studies*. Ed. Bonnie Kime Scott. Newark: U of Delaware P, 1988. 126–34.

Newman, F. X. "The Land of Ooze: Joyce's 'Grace' and the Book of Job." *Studies in Short Fiction* 4 (Fall 1966): 70–79.

Niemeyer, Carl. " 'Grace' and Joyce's Method of Parody." *College English* 27 (December 1969): 196–201.

• Norris, Margot. *Suspicious Readings of Joyce's Dubliners*. Philadelphia: U of Pennsylvania P, 2003.

O'Connor, Frank. "Work in Progress." *Twentieth Century Interpretations of "Dubliners."* Ed. Peter K. Garrett. Englewood Cliffs, NJ: Prentice-Hall, 1968. 18–26.

O'Grady, Thomas B. "Little Chandler's Song of Experience." *James Joyce Quarterly* 28.2 (Winter 1991): 399–405.

Owens, Coílín. "Clay' [I]: Irish Folklore." *James Joyce Quarterly* 27.2 (Winter 1990): 337–52.

Paige, Linda Rohrer. "James Joyce's Darkly Colored Portraits of 'Mother' in *Dubliners*." *Studies in Short Fiction: Special "Dubliners" Number* 32.3 (Summer 1995): 329–40.

Pecora, Vincent P. "The 'Dead' and the Generosity of the Word." *PMLA* 101 (March 1986): 206–15.

Pound, Ezra. "Dubliners and Mr James Joyce." *Literary Essays of Ezra Pound*. Ed. by T. S. Eliot. New York: New Directions, 1968. 399–402.

Power, Mary. "The Stories of Public Life." *European Joyce Studies* 7: *New Perspectives on "Dubliners."* Ed. Mary Power and Ulrich Schneider. Amsterdam: Rodopi, 1997.

Power, Mary, and Ulrich Schneider, eds. *European Joyce Studies* 7: *New Perspectives on "Dubliners."* Amsterdam: Rodopi, 1997.

Rabaté, Jean-Michel. "Silence in *Dubliners*." *James Joyce: New Perspectives*. Ed. Colin MacCabe. Bloomington: Indiana UP, 1982. 45–72.

Rabinowitz, Peter J. "A Symbol of Something': Interpretive Vertigo in 'The Dead.' " *James Joyce's "The Dead": Case Studies in Contemporary Criticism*. Ed. Daniel R. Schwarz. Boston: Bedford Books, 1994. 137–49.

Scholes, Robert. " 'Counterparts' and the Method of *Dubliners*." James Joyce. *"Dubliners": Text, Criticism, and Notes*. Ed. Robert Scholes and A. Walton Litz. New York: Viking, 1969. 379–87.

———. "Semiotic Approaches to a Fictional Text: Joyce's 'Eveline.' " *James Joyce Quarterly* 16.1/2 (Fall 1978/Winter 1979): 65–80.

Schwarz, Daniel R. "Gabriel Conroy's Psyche: Character as Concept in Joyce's 'The Dead.' " *James Joyce's 'The Dead': Case Studies in Contemporary Criticism*. Ed. Daniel R. Schwarz. Boston: Bedford Books, 1994. 102–24.

Senn, Fritz. "*Dubliners*: 'Renewed Time after Time.' " *European Joyce Studies* 7: *New Perspectives on "Dubliners"*. Ed. Mary Power and Ulrich Schneider. Amsterdam: Rodopi, 1997. 19–43.

———. "Dynamic Adjustments in *Dubliners*." *European Joyce Studies* 7: *New Perspectives on "Dubliners."* Ed. Mary Power and Ulrich Schneider. Amsterdam: Rodopi, 1997. 1–18.

• ———. "The Boarding House' Seen as a Tale of Misdirection." *James Joyce Quarterly* 23.4 (Summer 1986): 405–13.

———. "A Rhetorical Analysis of James Joyce's 'Grace.' " *Moderna Sprak* 74 (1980): 121–28.

Shloss, Carol. "Money and Other Rates of Exchange: Commercial Relations and 'Counterparts.' " *European Joyce Studies* 7: *New Perspectives on "Dubliners."* Ed. Mary Power and Ulrich Schneider. Amsterdam: Rodopi, 1997. 180–94.

Sloan, Barbara L. "The D'Annunzian Narrator in 'A Painful Case': Silent, Exiled, and Cunning." *James Joyce Quarterly* 9.1 (Fall 1971): 26–36.

Spoo, Robert E. " 'Una Piccola Nuvoletta': Ferrero's *Young Europe* and Joyce's Mature *Dubliners* Stories." *James Joyce Quarterly* 24.4 (Summer 1987): 401–10.

Staley, Thomas F. "A Beginning: Signification, Story, and Discourse in Joyce's 'The Sisters.' " *Critical Essays on James Joyce*. Ed. Bernard Benstock. Boston: G. K. Hall, 1985. 176–90.

Stone, Harry. " 'Araby' and the Writings of James Joyce." *Dubliners: Text, Criticism, and Notes*. Ed. Robert Scholes and A. Walton Litz. New York: Penguin Books, 1996. 344–67.

Tadié, Benoît. "Memory and Narrative Deadlock in 'Dubliners.' " *Classic Joyce. Joyce Studies in Italy* 6. Ed. Franca Ruggieri. Roma: Bulzoni Editore, 1999. 373–80.

Torchiana, Donald T. *Backgrounds for Joyce's "Dubliners."* Boston: Allen & Unwin, 1986.

Valente, Joseph. "Joyce's Sexual Differend: An Example from *Dubliners*." *James Joyce Quarterly* 28.2 (Winter 1991): 427–43.

Vesala-Varttala, Tanja. *Sympathy and Joyce's "Dubliners": Ethical Probing of Reading, Narrative, and Textuality*. Tampere: Tampere UP, 1999.

Walzl, Florence L., *"Dubliners." A Companion to Joyce Studies.* Ed. Zack Bowen and James F. Carens. Westport, CT: Greenwood P, 1984. 158–228.

———. *"Dubliners*: Women in Irish Society." *Women in Joyce.* Ed. Suzette Henke and Elaine Unkeless. Urbana: U of Illinois P, 1982. 30–56.

———. "Joyce's 'The Sisters': A Development." *James Joyce Quarterly* 10.4 (Summer 1973): 375–421.

Wawrzycka, Jolanta W. "Text at the Crossroads: Multilingual Transformations in James Joyce's *Dubliners." ReJoycing: New Readings of "Dubliners."* Ed. Rosa M. Bollettieri Bosinelli and Harold F. Mosher, Jr. Lexington: UP of Kentucky, 1998. 68–84.

Weir, David. "Gnomon Is an Island: Euclid, and Bruno in Joyce's Narrative Practice." *James Joyce Quarterly* 28.2 (Winter 1991): 343–60.

Werner, Craig Hansen. *"Dubliners": A Pluralistic World.* Boston: Twayne Publishers, 1988.

Wicht, Wolfgang. " 'Eveline,' and/as 'A Painful Case': Paralysis, Desire, Signifiers." *European Joyce Studies 7: New Perspectives on "Dubliners."* Ed. Mary Power and Ulrich Schneider. Amsterdam: Rodopi, 1997. 115–42.

Williams, Trevor L. "No Cheer for 'the Gratefully Oppressed': Ideology in Joyce's *Dubliners." ReJoycing: New Readings of "Dubliners."* Ed. Rosa M. Bollettieri Bosinelli and Harold F. Mosher, Jr. Lexington: UP of Kentucky, 1998. 87–109.

Wohlpart, A. James. "Laughing in the Confession-Box: Vows of Silence in Joyce's 'The Sisters.' " *James Joyce Quarterly* 30.3 (Spring 1993): 409–17.

•Wright, David G. "Interactive Stories in *Dubliners." Studies in Short Fiction* 32 (1995): 285–93.

———. "The Secret Life of Leopold Bloom and Emily Sinico." *James Joyce Quarterly* 37. 1/2. (Fall 1999/Winter 2000): 99–112.